WILLIAM J. CAUNITZ

THREE COMPLETE NOVELS

WILLIAM J. CAUNITZ

THREE COMPLETE NOVELS

BLACK SAND

SUSPECTS

ONE POLICE PLAZA

WINGS BOOKS

New York   Avenel, New Jersey

This edition contains the complete and unabridged texts of the original editions. They have been completely reset for this volume. This omnibus was originally published in separate volumes under the titles:

Black Sand, copyright © 1989 by William J. Caunitz
Suspects, copyright © 1986 by William J. Caunitz
One Police Plaza, copyright © 1984 by William J. Caunitz

This 1994 edition is published by Wings Books,
distributed by Random House Value Publishing, Inc.,
40 Engelhard Avenue, Avenel, New Jersey 07001,
by arrangement with Crown Publishers, Inc.

Random House
New York • Toronto • London • Sydney • Auckland

Printed and bound in the United States of America

Library of Congress Cataloging-in-Publication Data

Caunitz, William J.
    [Novels. Selections]
    Three complete novels / William J. Caunitz.
        p.   cm.
    Contents: Black sand — Suspects — One
Police Plaza.
    ISBN 0-517-11844-0
    1. Detective and mystery stories, American.
    2. Police—New York (N.Y.)—Fiction. I. Title.
PS3553.A945A6 1994
813'.54—dc20   94-8401
                                                  CIP

8 7 6 5 4 3 2 1

Contents

BLACK SAND

In loving memory of a Greek mother,
ANNA INTZEKOSTA

Far-stretching, endless Time
Brings forth all hidden things,
All that buries that which once did shine
The firm resolve falters, the sacred oath
is shattered;
And let none say, "It cannot happen here."

Sophocles, Ajax

ACKNOWLEDGMENTS

Black Sand is the story of policemen solving an unusual case. It is not, nor does it pretend to be, an academic work. Any mistakes of a factual or scholarly nature are mine alone and not the responsibility of the many experts who gave their time so generously helping me with my research.

My preparation for *Black Sand* required extensive reading. Some of the essential books that informed many of the pages of *Black Sand* are: *Plutarch's Lives*, translated by John Dryden; *Alexander the Great*, by Robin Lane Fox; *A Rare Book Saga*, by H. P. Kraus; *The Iliad of Homer*, translated by Richmond Lattimore; *Scribes and Scholars—A Guide to the Transmission of Greek and Latin Literature*, by L. D. Reynolds and N. G. Wilson; *The Treasures of Time*, by Leo Deuel; *Gods, Graves, and Scholars: The Story of Archaeology*, by C. W. Ceram; *The Bull from the Sea* and *The King Must Die*, by Mary Renault; *The Harvest of Hellenism*, by Frank Peters.

I am deeply grateful to the following members of the Hellenic Police Department for their help and for reinforcing my belief that the "Job" is the same the world over: Brigadier General Stephanios Tsintziellis, Security Division; General Stefanos Tsetselia, Security Division, Greek Constabulary (Retired); Colonel Spyros Roikos, Antiquity Squad, Security Division; Major Theodore Charalampopoulos, Interpol, Ministry of Public Order.

I am also indebted to Mr. Yiortos Chouliaras and Mr. George Dardavillas of the Permanent Mission of Greece to the United Nations for helping guide my way through the government bureaucracy and opening so many doors for me; Mrs. JoAnn Tfoukos of the American Women's Organization of Athens, Greece, and my interpreter in Greece, Mr. Dentrios Mitsos.

Black Sand could not have been written without the generous help of scholars who gave me glimpses into their world of erudition. I am particularly grateful to Dr. Barbara Gail Rowes for pointing me in the right direction, and to Dr. Helen Evans of the Metropolitan Museum of Art for transporting me back in time to the days of Alexander the Great; to Joan Leibovitz of New York University's Institute of Fine Arts for her help with Ph.D. dissertations and for a tour of the Duke Mansion; to Dr. Marit Jentoft-Neilsen of the J. Paul Getty Museum for showing me how to unroll papyrus scrolls and teaching me the difference between Greek and Roman pottery; to Dr. William Voekle of the Medieval and Renaissance Collection of the Pierpont Morgan Library for his help with ancient texts.

To those experts at the Metropolitan Museum of Art and the Smithsonian Institution's Freer Gallery of Art who requested anonymity, thank you.

I want to thank Mr. John Ross, Director of Public Relations for the Metropolitan Museum of Art, for his help, and Dr. Warren Scherer, Director of Research, Department of Operative Dentistry, New York University's School of Dentistry, for showing me how to make forensic casts.

I am also grateful to Mr. Artur R. Katon of Issco, Westbury, New York, for teaching me how to use pinhole cameras, and to Mr. Allen Gore of Alert Management Systems for showing me how certain kinds of alarm systems function.

To my friend Mr. Albert Levi, who acted as my Greek translator in New York and who shared with me some of the rich tapestry of Greek life in New York City, I say, Giassou, Albert.

The following members of the New York City Police Department have been most helpful, and I thank them for their kind help and cooperation: Chief of Department Robert J. Johnston Jr., Captain Tom Fahey, Sergeant Donald O'Donnell, Sergeant Peter P. Sweeney, and Police Officer Peter Fokianos, President, Saint Paul's Society, NYPD.

I am deeply grateful to my agents, Knox Burger and Kitty Sprague, for always being there for me, for their tireless help in working on the manuscripts, their suggestions and many worthwhile criticisms. Thank you for helping the dream continue.

To my editor and good friend James O'Shea Wade, whose magical pencil continues to work wonders, I say, thank you, Jim. And to the members of the Crown Publishing family, whose ceaseless efforts make it all work, I say, thank you, thank you, thank you.

1

Takis Milaraki sat on his fourth-floor terrace, gazing at the islands, recalling those boyhood days when he and his friends used to row out to the two specks of land and spend hours pretending they were valiant members of Alexander's Shield Bearers, defending Greece against Darius's hordes.

A long time ago, he sighed, patting the roll of fat hanging over his belt. He missed those carefree days almost as much as he missed his friends, most of whom had left Greece to seek their fortunes in the United States or in other parts of Europe.

But not Takis. He had remained in Voúla. He could never bring himself to leave his village, or his two islands. They were the places that gave meaning and energy to his life; those places, and his family, were world enough. A lighthearted wind brushed across the terrace. Takis reached out and picked up the cup from the glass table. Sipping the syrupy liquid, he returned his gaze to the wine-dark sea.

After staring at the sea for several minutes, he reluctantly finished his coffee, returned the cup to its saucer, and got up. Moving into his apartment, he paused to identify the different smells coming from the kitchen. Lamb. Okra. Mary, his wife of twenty-three years, was already busy preparing for the midday meal. After doing that, she would clean her house, do the laundry, go shopping, have tea with her girlfriends, and then return home to her kitchen.

Walking up behind her, Takis realized that today was Tuesday, the twelfth of May. His name day was two days away; he wondered what surprises his wife had planned. Watching over her shoulder as she chopped fresh basil on a cutting board and brushed it into a pot, he slid his arms around her waist, pressing her close. "I'll try and come home after the midday rush."

"Make sure that our sons are not here."

"Our boys are already at the beach trying to screw tourists. Both of them will rush home at one, gulp down their food, and rush back to the beach." He kissed her neck. "Remember how we met?"

She smiled. "Go to work."

At exactly eight A.M., Takis Milaraki unlocked the doors of the Elite Café in the center of Voúla's main square and began to put out the tables and chairs. After he did that, he would make the espresso, arrange fresh pastries in the display cases, and await his first customer of the day.

In an apartment on Voúla's seafront, a couple lay entwined, each aware of their racing hearts. The bed was soaked with the tallowy smell of lovemaking; the sounds of the sea rushing into their second-floor bedroom.

"Eighteen years of marriage," Andreas said, gasping, "and I still can't get enough of you."

Breathing hard, Soula Vassos stroked her husband's damp hair. "I love you so."

"I wish that I were ten years younger so I could start right up again."

She bit his chin. "I'm patient."

Andreas Vassos pushed himself up so he might look down into her saffron eyes, drink in her beautiful face. She tightened her legs around her husband and rubbed her body against his. In a gesture of marital intimacy, she turned her head, showing him what she wanted him to do. Obligingly, he caressed her ear with his tongue, gliding it around the rim, sucking on the lobe. At the same time his hand roamed her body, causing her to moan with delight.

She relaxed her grip on his body and whispered, "Taste me."

He kissed her and slid down on her body until his face was between her legs. His finger went into her slowly and softly. She groaned and gently pressed his face to her. Suddenly the bedroom door burst open. Five-year-old Stephanos plunged into the room. "Mommy. Daddy. Let's hurry to the beach. All the *tendas* will be taken."

Andreas Vassos jackknifed into a sitting position.

Soula Vassos grabbed the sheet and covered her nakedness.

Stephanos hurled his little body on the bed, his all-seeing eyes fixed on his father. "Daddy, what were you doing to Mommy?"

"Well, I . . . I . . . was . . . looking for my ring. See?" He held up his hand so that his son might see the golden ring. "It came off during the night . . . and I was searching for it. See, I found it."

Soula Vassos yanked a pillow across her face and laughed.

A long line of buses stretched along the south side of Athens' National Gardens. People queued at the waiting stations. Fumes from the corn vendors' charcoal blended with the clean, sharp smell of wisteria. The sun rose higher in the sky. George Sanida walked from the dispatcher's shack and, shielding his eyes with his hand, looked up at the sky. It was going to be a perfect beach day. Carefully examining the line of female tourists waiting to board, Sanida thought: maybe I'll get lucky today.

He opened the door, climbed into the driver's seat, and turned to watch the boarding passengers file past him, making sure that each one deposited the thirty-drachma fare. He studied each of the foreign women as they passed, sneaking a look at their bouncing tits and cute asses.

A blond woman in her early twenties stopped in front of the box and opened the drawstring of her beach bag, searching for her fare. She was dressed in bikini bottoms and an oversized, lightweight white cotton shirt. A blue nylon rucksack was strapped to her back, pulling her shirt taut in front, accentuating her large, unhaltered breasts. Her nipples stuck out: big brown rings.

Sanida unbuttoned two more buttons on his shirt so that she might better see the hair on his manly chest. He smiled at her. She smiled back, dropping in her fare and moving to the back of the bus. He watched as she shrugged off her rucksack and set it down on the floor between her legs. She saw him watching her and smiled at him. Yes, today might be his lucky day, Sanida thought, closing the door and turning to check the side mirror for traffic.

Takis Milaraki was engaged in a heated political argument with his communist friend, Dinos, when the police car drove headlong into the space in front of the Elite Café. Two policemen got out and ambled over to the newsstand a few meters to the right of the café. Takis realized that it was time to roll down the awning. While he was unfurling the canopy, Takis noticed that the policemen were loafing around the newsstand. One was sucking on an ice cup while the other talked on the telephone, probably to his girlfriend, Takis thought as he secured the awning clamps.

Looking across the street, Takis saw a group of boys straddling their Japanese motorbikes. The Greek Rambos were trying hard to impress the admiring girls gathered around them. Takis smiled. He had seen them all grow up from babies; he enjoyed watching them play out their adolescent mating games under the stern eyes of Voúla's black-mantled gossips who spent their days cooking, praying, and leaning out windows. No matter how many tourists came, village life would never change completely.

Golden sand swept up from the rolling sea, melting into a lush savanna where people reclined on sun chairs. Boys played soccer; girls talked while lolling on the grass. Fifteen meters from shore swimmers dove off anchored platforms while several men cut through the blue-green sea on jet sleds.

Major Andreas Vassos, Security Division, Athens Station, lay on his back under the tenda's cloth roof. The past five months had been difficult ones for Vassos. His section had been conducting several major investigations into terrorist activities and narcotics networks operating in the Athens area. He had put in long hours and had not had a day off in six weeks. He loved his career and the excitement that went with being a policeman; he even enjoyed the meticulous attention to detail that his work demanded. But he did not enjoy being able to spend so little time with his family. He had seen too many of his colleagues give up their family life for the department. It was not going to happen to him; he was going to be there to watch his son grow into manhood.

Several days ago Vassos had slapped leave papers down on his boss's desk and announced, "I've rented an apartment in Voúla, near the beach. I am taking my family there on a ten-day holiday. I won't have a telephone—and you won't have my address."

Colonel Dimitri Pappas spread his hands in a pleading gesture. "Andreas? So many of our important cases are just coming together. Put off your holiday a little while. Till June. As a favor to your colonel."

"I'll see you in ten days, Colonel," Vassos said, backing out the door with a slight bow.

Vassos stretched his lean body under the dark green cloth of the sun shelter. It was wonderful to be doing nothing.

At forty years of age Andreas Vassos was a handsome man whose receding hairline complemented his olive complexion and majestic nose. He had a cleft chin and unusually dark blue eyes. Soula was fond of calling his eyes her Mediterranean pools because by day they appeared to be a deep blue, and by night, inky black.

I'm a lucky man, he reflected, watching his son build a mud fort at the water's edge. His gaze slid to Soula, who was sunning herself on a straw mat next to the tenda. She was wearing the brown-and-white bikini that he liked so much. Her arms were outstretched, her legs slightly apart as she lay on her back. He pushed himself out from under the shelter, resting his head on his wife's flat stomach.

"My other child is here to pester me," she said, opening her eyes.

"I didn't seem to be pestering you this morning," he said, tilting his head so that he could see down the front of her bikini bottom.

She playfully hit him. "Don't be fresh. And next time make sure the bedroom door is locked. Our son rushes into our room and discovers his father doing *that* to his mother."

"He has to learn sometime."

"Don't be disgusting."

Stephanos ran over to his parents, spraying sand over them. "Mommy, I'm hungry."

Soula sprang up off the mat. "Can't I ever relax?"

Stephanos jumped up and down. "Mommy, please, can't we go into Voúla. I want ice cream. And I want to ride in the spacecraft. Oh, please, Mommy, please."

"We can have ice cream here at the beach, it's less money," she said.

Andreas took his wife's arm. "Let's go into Voúla. It's a short walk— and the Elite Café has wonderful pastries."

She smiled sternly at her husband and his sneaking passion for sweets. "You're a big baby, you know that?"

Ten minutes later the Vassos family strolled into Voúla. Soula had wrapped her slender body in a beach sarong and her husband had slipped into an oversized brown T-shirt.

"Mommy. Daddy. The spacecraft," Stephanos shouted, breaking away and dashing for the mechanical ride in front of the Elite Café.

Andreas swung his son up into the cockpit. He dug a five-drachma piece out of his handbag, inserted it in the slot, and stepped back to watch as the toy sprang to life.

"Major Vassos," a voice called out.

Andreas Vassos looked up and groaned inwardly when he saw the policeman approaching them, a glow of recognition lighting up the officer's face. He immediately regretted the decision to come into town. Now the local cops would know he was in Voúla and would feel that a visiting dignitary had to be entertained. Just once, Vassos thought in desperation, I'd like to be a private citizen on vacation with his family.

It was a little after eleven o'clock when the No. 122 bus lumbered out of the winding streets onto Voúla's main plaza. About a dozen passengers remained aboard; the rest had gotten off at the beaches along the route. George Sanida drew the bus to a stop at the light.

Glancing up into the mirror, he saw the blond tourist sitting in the back. She was studying a map spread open across her lap. A black Ford Escort pulled alongside and stopped. Sanida looked down into the car and saw two men. The driver was sitting alone while another man sat in the back. They're not Greeks, Sanida thought. Greek men sit up front with the driver; to do otherwise is rude.

He could not see the driver clearly. The passenger was a fat man with bulging cheeks; he wore a watch with a heavy gold band. Americans or Germans, he thought, looking back at the traffic signal.

The light turned green.

The Ford bounded ahead.

Sanida maneuvered the motor coach around the maze of parking medians and into the bus terminal, which was on the edge of a vacant lot bordered by walnut and cypress trees. The last stop.

Passengers began to file from the bus. The blond tourist remained in her seat, studying her map.

Sanida slid out of his seat and, moving to the back of the bus, sat down beside her. *"Parlez-vous Français?"* he asked.

"No, I'm Canadian. From Vancouver."

Shit, he thought, knowing his English was bad. "I help you?" he said, pointing to the map.

"Would you, please? My girlfriend told me there was a wonderful pay beach here in Voúla that only costs fifteen drachmas to get in."

Shit, the only damn words he understood were beach and drachmas. He smiled, nodding understanding, moving in close to study the map, admiring the fine blond hair on her legs. She was blond all over, he thought, and felt his blood stir.

"Beach," he said, stabbing the map with his finger.

"Pay beach? Drachmas?" she said, brushing two fingers against her thumb to indicate money.

"Yes, yes, pay money."

"How . . . me . . . get . . . there?" she asked, walking two fingers in front of her.

He struggled to give directions in English. She shook her head, not understanding. Realizing he was not making himself understood, he took her hand and led her up to the front of the empty bus. He began to point the way to the pay beach. While he was doing this he saw the Ford Escort was double-parked alongside the police car in front of the Elite Café, just a block away from the terminal. The passenger in the back of the car picked something up from the floor and passed it over the top of the seat to the driver. George Sanida stopped talking, wide-eyed with disbelief. The driver of the Ford got out and stood by the open door looking around. The fat man rolled down the window and pointed the barrel of a machine gun at the outdoor café.

The driver stuck his head into the car and said something to the man in the backseat. The fat man lowered the weapon and sat back.

George Sanida shouted at the tourist.

"I don't speak Greek," she said, unnerved by his sudden change of tone.

"Look! Look! They have guns," he shouted, jabbing his finger against the windshield.

She shrugged her shoulders, smiled nervously.

Frustrated at not being understood, the bus driver grabbed the back of her head and forced her to look in the direction of the Ford Escort.

"I don't know what you want me to see," she said, noticing the man one block away who was standing by the open car door.

"Look!" he shouted in Greek.

Her face showed utter confusion. She saw the man standing by the open door reach inside and slide something off the front seat. A fat man got out of the backseat of the car. When she saw what both men were holding in their hands, she clutched her chest and gasped.

"Nai! Nai!" Yes, yes, he shouted, using both hands to mime the firing of a machine gun.

Takis Milaraki was wiping off a table when the sound of a blaring horn caused him to look up from his work. His eyes drifted to the bus depot. A blond woman was leaning out the front door, shouting, gesticulating. Someone had his hand pressed down on the bus's horn. Takis looked around. People were taking their late-morning coffee, eating pistachios. A waiter made his way among the tables, carrying a tray laden with desserts. Everything seemed normal. He looked back to the bus. What the hell was that crazy woman doing? The bus was backing out of the depot, but she was still leaning out the front door. She appeared to be stabbing her finger in the direction of the police car. His gaze darted to the police car and then he saw the two strangers moving up onto the sidewalk. "My god!"

He had heard him lecture on methods of interrogation at the Police College, the policeman told Vassos. The major smiled, thinking of how he was going to get rid of the pest. Then frightened screams startled Vassos; distracted, he stopped watching the policeman. Suddenly a curiously muffled sound of gunfire echoed across the square.

Andreas Vassos hurled himself at his wife, throwing her down on top of the toy spacecraft and protecting her and their son with his own body. The policeman to whom he had been talking had his revolver out when a chunk of lead plowed into his face, causing him to topple backward.

The officer by the newsstand dropped the phone and made a grab for his weapon as a spray of bullets stitched its way across his chest, hurling him back into the stand where he slumped awkwardly to the ground.

Panicked people ran screaming in all directions; others flattened themselves on the ground, playing dead, praying for deliverance. Vassos could hear his wife saying calming things to their son. He raised his head and saw the dead policeman. His eyes focused on the nearest officer's revolver. The two killers were heading for a double-parked car. Vassos reacted instinctively. "Stay down," he shouted. He slid off his wife and got on the ground; he crawled toward the revolver. Grabbing it, he got to his feet and, running crouched, put some distance between himself and his family before he threw himself behind an upturned table and fired two rounds at the departing killers.

The tall, thin man whirled around, enraged by the challenge. "You cocksucker!" he screamed, leveling his weapon at the prone crowd.

The slow-moving but curiously graceful fat gunman turned and shouted at his partner, "Frankie, don't! Let's get the fuck outta here."

Heeding him, the other man raised his weapon and turned to run for the car.

Vassos fired two more rounds double action. The thin man stumbled into a Citroën and slumped to the ground, blood staining the back of his shirt. The other, furious at the sight of his wounded friend, ran back, firing bursts of parabellum bullets into the helpless victims lying on the terrace of the café. Hysterical people leaped up off the ground and made desperate dashes for safety only to be cut down by the lethal spray of bullets.

The wounded gunman propped himself up against the Citroën's front wheel. The fat killer ran back to him and, clutching him under the shoulders, helped him up off the ground.

Vassos, crouched behind the table, opened the cylinder of the revolver to check on how many rounds he had fired; two live ones were left. He closed the cylinder.

The fat one held his partner in one arm as the two men backed away together toward their car, their weapons pointed in the direction of the carnage. Vassos popped out from behind the table and fired his last two rounds at the retreating killers. The wounded man sagged in the other man's embrace. The fat man, with his wounded friend in tow, continued to back up toward the car while responding with a deadly burst of fire.

Vassos picked the table up by its metal leg; using it as a shield, he charged the killers. The fat killer fired at him. Bullets impacted on the table, striking the metal base and hurling the shield up into Vassos's face, knocking him unconscious.

The still-untouched gunman pushed his badly wounded partner into the front seat of the Ford and ran around to the driver's side. He had just gotten behind the wheel when George Sanida rammed the car broadside with his bus, wrapping the Ford's frame around the rear of the police car. A burst of gunfire from inside the Ford hurled the blond tourist up out of the door well, splaying her body over the dirty floor.

"Murderers!" Sanida screamed as he ground the transmission into reverse and then roared back, aiming the shattered grill of his bus at the smoldering Ford. The bus shot forward, crashing into the Ford. Metal twisted. Glass shattered. The force of the impact pushed the scraping mass up onto the sidewalk. Bodies lay among the upturned tables and chairs. Bewildered people tottered from doorways. And a young woman in a beach sarong lay limp over a dead child inside a toy spacecraft while her unconscious husband lay in a pool of blood.

Sirens screamed in the distance.

George Sanida was sprawled across the steering wheel, listening to the steam billowing from the mangled grill. His body was soaked in sweat and a stream of hot urine coursed down his leg. He struggled up out of the jump seat and stumbled over to the dead tourist. He knelt beside her, crying silently. He brushed her hair from her face, mouthed the words "thank you," then bent and kissed her stilled lips. Her lifeless legs were spread in an unladylike way, so he reached out under the driver's seat, pulled out an oil-soaked blanket, and covered her. He became conscious of people outside the bus screaming curses. Pushing himself up off the floor, he looked out the window and saw an angry crowd hurling maledictions at the wreckage.

A thin man, covered in blood, was struggling out of the car's shattered window. A large flap of skin hung down over his jawbone.

The crowd watched. Waited.

Sanida found himself cheering the man's efforts. He watched as he wiggled his way on top of the wreckage and fell to the ground. The wounded man tried to get up, only to fall backward onto his haunches. He looked up, his hard eyes glaring at the crowd, a strange expression of contempt curling his lips. Sanida grabbed a wrench from the emergency tool chest under the driver's seat and leaped down off the bus. Plunging through the crowd, he pushed his way up to the killer and began beating him with the tool.

The crowd surged forward.

Takis Milaraki lay on his back, his hands feebly pressing a slimy mass back into his stomach. Dimly aware of the noise around him, he blinked several times in an effort to make out what it was that he saw in the sky. A vaguely familiar form was floating down toward him. He squeezed his lids tightly closed to clear his vision. Now he could see clearly. Drifting in the sky were his beloved islands. They were silhouetted against a blue canvas, beckoning him. "I'm coming," he moaned, and then he died.

2

Colonel Dimitri Pappas sat behind his spindle-legged desk on the fifth floor of 173 Leoforos Alexandras, studying field reports on the recent consolidation of the gendarmerie and the city police into one national department, the Hellenic Police. Each report stated that the unification was an unqualified success. Pappas knew better; it was cover-your-ass time in the department. The politicians wanted one national police force and the officer corps was not about to go against the politicians who had the power to approve or disapprove their promotions. It was incredible to Pappas that, under the new system, the mayor of Athens—or the mayor of any city or village—would no longer have any say in the running of their local police. A bad omen. It reminded Pappas of the days of the junta; the dark, bloody days of the colonels.

Dimitri Pappas commanded the Athens and Salonica Security Prefecture, which encompassed the plainclothes and intelligence forces of Athens, Voúla, and Glifádha. He had begun his career in the gendarmerie thirty-two years ago. At that time the city police force was responsible for Athens, Patras, and Corfu; the gendarmerie policed the rest of the country.

Pappas had broad shoulders, narrow hips, and a mane of silver hair. His chin had long ago merged with his neck, leaving his chin with no definition. He loved wearing jacketlike Greek shirts but, when forced to by the occasion, he would don his uniform. This morning he wore a light blue shirt with gray slacks and brown shoes.

Pappas had just reached for another report when his door burst open and his adjutant, Lieutenant Sokos, blurted, "There's been a massacre in Voúla."

The wop-wop-wop sound of the helicopter's main rotors became Voúla's death dirge as Pappas and his adjutant left the craft and ran through a whirlwind of dirt and paper toward the waiting police car. The sergeant who met Pappas delivered his report as they drove to the scene. The initial investigation showed eleven dead, eighteen wounded. Two of the dead had been policemen; they died with their guns drawn.

A cordon of police had sealed off the village from the rest of the world; all domestic and international flights out of Athens had been grounded; ferries and hydrofoils leaving Piraeus had been ordered to remain at their docks. Security Division investigators had been rushed to Voúla and a temporary headquarters had been established in the Ionian and Popular Bank of Greece across the street from the Elite Café.

Looking out the window of the car, Pappas could see policemen struggling to restrain grieving relatives and friends. The crime scene had been roped off, a frozen zone established. A shaken driver sat on the ground next to his bus answering investigators' questions, still unsure of exactly what had happened. Lieutenant Sokos rushed up to Pappas. Looking at his adjutant's ashen face, Pappas thought: he does not function well under pressure. "Well, are you going to tell me the result of the preliminary or do I have to drag it out of you?" Pappas growled.

Sokos's head made small nervous shakes. "Most of the witnesses confirm that the two killers stood on the curb and without warning fired into the crowd. They used Ingram model two submachine guns equipped with sound suppressors."

"What have we found out about these brave killers?" Pappas asked, staring grimly at the café's pockmarked facade.

"They're Americans."

"What did you say?"

"Americans," repeated the adjutant, handing the colonel two passports.

Pappas examined the photographs pasted inside the official documents. Frank Simmons, age 32, born New York City. George Cuttler, age 34, born New York City. Both passports had been stamped by Athens customs control. The killers had entered Greece five days ago. He noted that both passports had been recently issued and that they bore no other country's admittance stamp. They came here to kill, Pappas thought, looking over at the body bags awaiting transport. At that moment Pappas knew that the reason for the massacre would be found only in New York.

Sokos was talking. ". . . Simmons tried to escape. The people ran after him, there was a struggle, and Simmons was killed."

Pappas gave his adjutant a long, hard look. *He's learning how to lie, maybe there's some hope for him.* "And this George Cuttler?"

"He was rushed alive to the hospital in Glifádha."

"Where are the rest of the wounded?"

"Some are here in the hospital, and some went to Glifádha, and the rest to Vouliagméni."

The adjutant stopped and swallowed nervously. "We also found four thousand dollars U.S. and two first-class tickets on Olympic Flight 411 leaving Athens at twelve fifty-five today."

Tapping the passports against his palm, Pappas said, "I don't think our American friends are going to make their flight."

The lieutenant handed Pappas four grainy photographs. "These were taken from Simmons's body."

Pappas opened the evidence bag and took out the pictures. They showed two men relaxing in a taverna. "Who are they?"

"The one on the right is Tasos Lefas, and the one the left is Lakis Rekor. They're the two policemen who were killed here this morning."

Pappas looked at his adjutant. "What else?"

The lieutenant paled. His eyes fell to the roadway. "Sir, Major Vassos was on the scene when the shooting began. He picked up one of the dead policemen's guns and shot Frank Simmons. The major was hurt, but . . ."

"But what, Lieutenant?"

"Major Vassos's wife and son were killed, sir."

Pappas gasped, his face sagging in anguish. He sucked his lower lip into his mouth and dug his teeth into it.

The rotors were winding down when the door opened and a tall man rushed down the large helicopter's steps into Voúla's main square. Colonel Pappas waited outside the blades' arc. Antonis Vitos, the Minister of Public Order, walked over quickly to meet his old friend.

"It looks like we have a bad one on our hands," Vitos said, shaking the colonel's hand.

"Yes, it does," Pappas agreed, leading the minister away from the aircraft, noting the black pouches under his eyes and the disturbing raspiness in his voice. *Vitos had aged a lot since they joined the gendarmerie together so many years ago. But then, I guess I've changed too,* Pappas conceded.

"What facts can you give me, Dimitri?"

"I'm afraid that we don't have very much to go on, yet, Minister."

"I have to tell Papandreou something," Vitos said, walking beside the colonel.

"You can tell the prime minister that there were two of them, and that they were both Americans."

A mask of disbelief froze on the minister's face. "Are you sure?"

"Yes. We found their passports."

"Were they terrorists?"

"I don't believe so. The evidence so far suggests that they came here for the sole purpose of killing two policemen."

"Bastards," Vitos said, lighting up a cigarette. "What do we know about the policemen?"

"I've sent to Athens for their folders." The minister watched three policemen struggle to restrain a hysterical woman. His thoughts seemed to wander.

Pappas waited.

Suddenly Vitos was roused from his lethargy. "What have you told the press?"

"Only the barest of facts. And nothing about the Americans or the two dead policemen."

"Good. Don't tell them anything."

"I've taken it upon myself to have telephone service in and out of Voúla cut off, except for to and from the bank that we're using as our headquarters."

"A wise precaution, Dimitri."

"Do you want to inform the American embassy?"

"Not yet. Wait until we know more." Vitos softened. "What about the woman who was killed helping the bus driver?"

"Her name was Debra Wright. A schoolteacher from Vancouver. She was twenty-four years old."

Vitos threw his cigarette down and ground it out with his heel. "Bastards. Have you notified the Canadians?"

"Yes."

"See to it that her body is sent home as quickly as possible. Cut all the red tape. And Dimitri, I want an honor guard of *evzones* to accompany her body home."

"I'll see to it, sir."

They moved over to the crime scene and watched in silence as body bags were solemnly lifted into the back of an ambulance.

"It is unbelievable that such a thing could happen here," Vitos said.

Pappas sighed and said quietly, "With all the terrorist attacks and the assassination of ten PLO members in Athens over the past six years, our people are learning to live with violence."

"Every one of the incidents you've just mentioned was directed against foreign nationals. But this?" He swept his hand across the crime scene. "This was aimed at Greeks. Why, Dimitri? Why?"

"We don't know yet," Pappas answered, the cries of wailing women catching his attention. His fists clenched tightly. "But I promise you that we will know and that the people responsible will be made to pay dearly." His face clouded. "Major Vassos was here in Voúla with his family on vacation. The major's wife and son were killed."

Vitos grabbed his friend's arm and spoke in a low tone of warning: "Be careful how you handle this case, Dimitri. There are foreign nationals involved. We don't want any problems with the Americans."

"I understand."

"Good. Has anyone questioned the injured American?"

"I'm going to Glifádha now," Pappas said. "I've already sent a man ahead to ask the hospital to keep him conscious. I'm anxious to have a chat with our Mr. Cuttler."

Vitos placed a hand on his classmate's shoulder. "Dimitri, please remember what I told you; no problems with the Americans. Be discreet when you question Cuttler."

"I'm always discreet, Antonis."

Pappas sat in the passenger seat of the small, unmarked police car. His driver, a corporal, was a skinny man with a thick nose that had been broken in three places when a husband had unexpectedly returned home and the corporal found it necessary to dive out of an upstairs bedroom window. Pappas told his driver not to park on the hospital grounds. There was a lot of traffic inside; the colonel did not want to have his official car boxed in as a result of the Greek penchant for parking anywhere and then taking the keys with them. He might have to leave in a hurry.

The Asklipeion Hospital in Glifádha was on Miramare Street, just off the coastal road, on the same corner where the No. 122 bus made a left hand turn into the village of Voúla. The main building had two wings coming out at forty-five-degree angles from the central structure and was partially hidden behind a screen of cypress and eucalyptus trees.

Pappas got out of the car. Turning around, he stretched his arms out over the car's roof, gazing across the road at the sea. A cruise ship glided across the horizon; a barkentine followed in her wake, its sails billowing. The beach was crowded. Yachts tugged gently at their anchors and the masts of boats swayed to the lap of the waves. Sucking in a mouthful of sea air, he turned and hurried past the hospital gate onto the grounds.

A detail of one sergeant and five policemen had been rushed to the hospital to maintain order and to guard the prisoner, Cuttler. Much to his annoyance, Pappas discovered the sergeant, a fat, slovenly man about forty, standing outside the emergency room entrance smoking a cigarette.

The sergeant saw Pappas hurrying up the path and quickly tossed the butt away.

"Where is your prisoner, Sergeant?" Pappas asked, looking down at the burning cigarette.

"He's in examining room D, Colonel."

"And am I safe in assuming that someone is guarding him, or have your men also abandoned their posts?"

Flustered, the sergeant answered, "He's guarded, sir. I only stepped outside for a minute or two."

"A minute or two is all it takes, Sergeant. If anything has happened to the prisoner, I'll personally see to it that you end your career teaching the *Syrtaki* to Albanian tourists."

"It won't happen again, sir," the sergeant said, rushing to open the door.

Doctors rushed up and down the corridors examining charts, holding hurried consultations. Walking into the emergency room, Pappas told the sergeant that he wanted to speak to the doctor who had treated the American. The sergeant hurried off, returning within a matter of minutes with the doctor.

"I'm Dr. Christopoulos. As you can see, Colonel, I'm a bit busy this morning."

"I only need a few seconds of your time, Doctor," Pappas said, slipping his arm through the doctor's and leading him off to the side. "How is this Cuttler?"

"He has compound fractures of both arms and both legs. His right shoulder is crushed, as are most of his ribs. Several of his ribs have punctured his lungs and there is internal bleeding."

"Has he been operated on yet?"

"As you requested, we waited until you got here. And, he has been given only mild sedation."

"When do you expect to operate on him?"

"There are only four operating rooms in this hospital—they are all full of Greek citizens. There are many who are more seriously wounded than the American. But, he should be under the knife in about forty minutes or so."

Pappas leaned in close to the medical man and whispered, "There is no rush, my friend. Take care of our people first."

The doctor wiped his arm across his brow. "I agree," he said, and walked away.

Colonel Pappas pushed the curtain aside and motioned the policeman from the room.

"See that I'm not disturbed," Pappas commanded the departing officer.

George Cuttler lay naked on a gurney; a sheet neatly folded across his groin. A tube ran from his arm up to a bottle that hung from a steel pole. His head was propped on a small rubber pillow. Both his knees were skewed over the sides of the gurney; shards of bone protruded from scarlet fissures on his arms and legs. His shoulders were awkwardly positioned and his eyes were closed.

Pappas noticed that his ears were small and clove-shaped; he watched the waves of fat roll over Cuttler's hairless body every time he breathed. He looks more like a circus freak than a professional killer, Pappas thought, moving up to the hospital trolley. "How do you feel?"

Cuttler's eyes fluttered open, focusing on the stranger.

"How do you feel?" Pappas repeated in flawless English while his eyes surveyed the tiny, bare cubicle.

"They gave me a shot for the fucking pain, but it's wearin' off," Cuttler groaned.

Pappas moved up to the cream-colored medical cabinet that was against the wall. "I'd give you some more, George, but unfortunately, we're running somewhat short this morning."

"Where'd you learn your English?" Cuttler asked as his fat face grimaced in pain.

Studying the contents of the cabinet, Pappas said, "When I was a young man I worked as a waiter on cruise ships. I learned to speak English, French, and German." He opened the cabinet door and, reaching inside, removed two plastic bottles of peroxide. He put the bottles down and lightly touched Cuttler's leg.

Cuttler let out an anguished howl.

Pappas snatched his hand back. "Oh, I'm sorry, George. I didn't realize that you hurt there."

Wincing, Cuttler said, "Don't touch, okay? That painkiller is wearing off." His eyes widened with suspicion. "Who are you, anyway?"

Pappas picked up one of the bottles and unscrewed the cap. "I'm Colonel Dimitri Pappas, Security Division, Athens Station, Hellenic Police." Tossing the cap aside, he leaned over the American. "George, I've been a policeman for most of my adult life. And during that time I've seen a lot of people do a lot of stupid things. But what you and Frank Simmons did this morning is memorable in its imbecility." He shoved his face close. "Did you really think that you could slaughter our people and then calmly waltz your ass onto the next flight back to the States?"

Cuttler turned his head away. "I wanna see someone from the American embassy. I got my fucking rights."

Pappas smiled. "Ah, yes, your famous American rights. Well, I really don't have the time to discuss them with you. So, I'm going to ask you a few simple questions, and you will give me a few simple answers. Who paid you to kill the two policemen? Why did that person want them killed? Who was your contact in Greece? And anything else that you might want to tell me."

"Fuck you. I wanna see—"

Pappas calmly poured peroxide over the shard of bone protruding from Cuttler's left leg.

A piercing shriek exploded from the prisoner. Waves of fat heaved over his body as it levitated up off the gurney and cartwheeled onto the cold floor. Screaming, Cuttler rolled from side to side, shards of bone hitting against the floor, the wheels of the gurney.

Two policemen rushed into the room. Pappas calmly shooed them back outside. Grabbing the other bottle, Pappas knelt down beside the writhing prisoner and began to unscrew the cap. "Are you going to tell me, George?"

Pappas then appeared to have second thoughts; he reached under his shirt jacket and slid out his revolver. Gripping the weapon by its barrel, the colonel slammed the butt of the weapon against the bone jutting from the prisoner's left leg.

Thirty-seven minutes later, Pappas stuck his face out of the cubicle and motioned the policemen back. "See to our guest. He slipped off the trolley."

The green unmarked police car turned onto Cathedral Square. The five-kilometer trip along the coast road from Glifádha to Athens had taken a bit over a half hour, with the blue roof light on.

"Do you want me to go with you?" the corporal asked Pappas.

"I want you to stay with the car and radio Lieutenant Sokos to meet me here with those folders. I'm anxious to see what we can find out about our two dead heroes."

The corporal reached out for the handset. Pappas shoved open the door and squeezed out of the car. Walking across the tiled square, he came to the twelfth-century Byzantine Church of Aghios Eleutherios, which nestled in the shadow of the cathedral. He stopped and examined the old marble walls and the frieze of the Attic festal calendar, the bas-reliefs of symbolic beasts and heraldic designs, wondering as his eyes ran over them if life was any simpler then.

Walking across the plaza toward Plaka, the old city of Athens, which was tucked away on the northern and southern slopes of the Acropolis, he spied the huge red-and-white banner stretched across the street, proclaiming in English: WELCOME TO FLEA MARKET OF PANDROSSOU STREET. We've become the damn flea market of the tourist world, he thought, moving into the narrow streets lined with shops. The windows of jewelry stores sparkled with gold trinkets. Shills beckoned from doorways.

When he reached the corner of Kapnikareas Street, Pappas turned left and stopped in front of number Forty-three. The peeling gold letters on the glass door spelled: ORHAN ISKUR, OBJETS D'ART. A dirty shade covered the other side of the door. Pappas checked the time. 2:11. Siesta time throughout Greece. But not here in Plaka. Here the rhythm of life was determined by the ebb and flow of the tourists. Pappas tried the door and was surprised to find it was open. The overhead bells tinkled as he slipped inside. The store was empty; quiet save for the monotonous hum of three ceiling fans. Horseshoe-shaped display cases filled with copies of antiquities lined the walls of the shop. Rugs and kilims covered the wood floors.

There was a door behind the display case. Pappas went behind the counter, reached out, turned the doorknob, and pushed the door open. He stepped into a cluttered storage area. There were boxes of *calyx kraters* and wine jugs, racks of silver-plated bowls with handles in the form of human heads, and there were funeral *stelae*, ranks of *amphorae*, and rows of Euphronios kraters. It was a junkyard of obvious and rather crude imitations.

Two cats darted out from behind the amphorae and disappeared behind cartons overflowing with plumed helmets. Cats, used before refrigeration to protect the meat from rats, now overran Greece. There was a short hallway that led from the storage area to a door. Pappas moved cautiously along the passage, sliding his revolver out from under his shirt jacket. He reached the door and stopped; listening as he quietly worked the knob. Finding it unlocked, he hurled the door open and fell into a combat stance. "Shit!"

The body lay on its back with the feet protruding from behind an ornate desk. A high-backed chair lay on its side close to the head. A trickle of dried blood ran from the small hole in the dead man's eyebrow. The mouth was open, revealing many gold teeth; one eye was open, one closed. A shocked expression had congealed on the dead man's face. An armchair stood in front of the desk. The killer must have been sitting there when he shot him, Pappas reasoned.

Orhan Iskur knew his murderer, trusted him; Orhan Iskur did not trust many people.

Pappas knelt next to the body and placed his hand on the forehead.

It was cold, clammy. The beginning contractions of rigor mortis had stiffened the head and neck. You made one deal too many, Pappas thought, lifting up the right hand, examining the inch-long pinkie nail. A Turkish affectation, a man wore that nail long to demonstrate that he made his living by using his brain rather than his hands. He dropped the wrist.

Pappas's first contact with Orhan Iskur had been in October of '71. Rubens' *Christ on the Cross* had been stolen that past September in Liege, Belgium. Interpol had sent an all-stations flash to Athens advising that they had confidential information that Iskur was negotiating for the sale of the stolen Rubens with a German collector. Pappas did a fast check on Iskur and discovered that he was a man of Turkish origins who had acquired Greek citizenship and presently lived and worked in Athens. Iskur had been one of the many former Allied operatives who after World War II used their old boy intelligence network to deal in stolen and plundered art works.

When Pappas questioned the Turk, Iskur denied any knowledge of the stolen painting. He was a mere dealer in tourist trinkets, he had reassured Pappas. Iskur was put under tight surveillance for several months. No illegal activities were observed and the stakeout was terminated.

Pappas had concealed his surprise when George Cuttler told him that he and Frank Simmons had been met at the airport by a Turk named Orhan who had gold teeth and a long pinkie nail on his right hand.

It had been Orhan, Cuttler told Pappas, who supplied them with the weapons, and it had been Orhan who got them the rooms in the Orion Hotel in Athens; Orhan who gave them the photographs of the policemen and got them the black Ford and gave them the emergency telephone number that turned out to be the one at his own store. Iskur had also set up a very clever escape route for them.

Pappas removed his handkerchief and carefully put it over the billfold lying next to the body. It contained sixteen thousand drachmas and a great many credit cards. Jade worry beads strung on a gold strand lay next to the body. Pappas picked them up and fingered them. He liked the way they felt; he dropped them into his shirt pocket. The appointment book on top of the desk contained only blank pages; Iskur obviously carried his schedule in his head. The desk drawers were stuffed with invoices and worthless artifacts.

Pappas stood in the center of the room staring at the cartons of swords and helmets stacked on the leather sofa. A painting on silk of a fish hung on the wall. Pappas recognized Dvogvos's bold signature. He searched the closet and looked behind paintings and under rugs. He rummaged through cartons. Finding nothing, he stared down at the body. Gray nylon socks had collapsed around the corpse's marble white ankles. Damn, Dimitri, do this the right way. He covered the handset of the telephone with his handkerchief, lifted it, and dialed Athens headquarters.

Lieutenant Kanakis, a tall gangling cop with a boyish face, led the search team that screeched to a stop ten minutes later in front of 43 Kapnikareas Street. Orhan Iskur's store was methodically taken apart by the Security Division's special team. Electrical fixtures and plates were removed from walls and ceilings; moldings were pried from baseboards; floor coverings were taken up; rugs and furniture were vacuumed, the fibers carefully deposited into plastic evidence bags. All the papers were removed from drawers and cabinets and then indexed and cross-referenced. Photographs were taken; fingerprints were lifted.

Pappas moved about, supervising the operations, his hands behind his back, fingering his newly acquired worry beads. He watched as plastic bags were placed over the hands and tied around the wrists of the corpse in order to preserve any scrapings that might be wedged under the nails or in the crevices of the hand.

Outside, Security Division investigators moved up and down the street, canvassing for witnesses. Uniformed officers maintained a security zone in front of the shop, chasing away the curious. Shopkeepers grumbled; they were losing business. Lieutenant Sokos appeared in the doorway with two folders tucked under his arm. He looked a bit like a very worried accountant, an impression reinforced by his prematurely graying hair. "Here are the files on the dead officers," he said, handing them to Pappas.

Looking around the store for some quiet place and finding none, Pappas went out into the street, using the folders to shield his face from the sunlight, and crossed the street to his adjutant's official car. It was parked half up on the narrow sidewalk, blocking the front of a clothing store whose owner was locked in argument with a nearby policeman. Pappas slid into the rear of the car; Sokos got into the front. The lieutenant told his driver to go grab a smoke; draping one arm over the seat, he turned and watched the colonel study the files on the two murdered policemen.

Fifteen minutes later, Pappas looked up into his adjutant's blank face. "Have you studied these?"

"Yes, sir, on the way here."

"And your conclusion?"

Sokos hesitated. "Well, I'm not really sure. I . . . ."

"Damn it, Spiro," Pappas said, using the adjutant's first name in order to take some of the sting out of the admonition. "You must learn to make judgments on the given facts. You read their folders. Now tell me what you think."

"I think that both officers lived above their means. They both recently bought apartments in an expensive neighborhood, and—"

A knock on the car's roof interrupted them.

"Yes?" Pappas said to the sergeant who was staring into the car.

"Lieutenant Kanakis sent me to get you, sir. He's found something."

Pappas got out of the car and returned to the cool, dark interior of the shop. Kanakis's head and shoulders were visible above the amphora. He was kneeling before a row of the tall, two-handled storage jars, examining one.

"What have you found?" Pappas asked, edging carefully along the row. Kanakis looked past the colonel and nodded hello to Lieutenant Sokos. "I think this amphora might be real, Colonel."

Pappas looked at the storage vessel and made a dismissive grunt. "Junk, the same as the rest of them."

"I don't think so, sir," Kanakis insisted.

Pappas's face showed impatience. He knelt next to the lieutenant. There *was* a spirited freshness about this amphora. The oranges were bright; the blacks were the pitch-black of night, and the blues, the blue of a Greek morning. The scenes depicted were alive, real. Ancient times were reborn.

"I studied art history, Colonel," Kanakis said in a low voice. "I'm no expert, but I think that this piece might be the real thing."

There was a strangely regal quality about it, Pappas admitted to himself as he slid his hand over the side and up to the rim. Kneeling upright, he stretched his arm down into the vessel. His fingers encountered a cold, granulated substance. Scooping up a handful, he held his palm up to show the lieutenant.

"Black sand," Pappas said.

A priest chanted the litany of prayers for the dead. Women clustered in front of the grocery store making keening, howling cries, crossing themselves. The sounds were as ancient as the chorus from *Agamemnon*. The stairway was crowded with milling people; the elevator was stuck on the fifth floor.

Pappas shouldered his way up to the third floor. As he pushed his way into the dead policeman's apartment on Euphorinos Street, the air pressed in on him. He glanced at the time. Five P.M. Had it all begun a bare six hours ago? He thought of the fishing boats returning to their berths at Piraeus. He was going to miss the *Peripato*, the habitual evening stroll around the harbor. There would be no cold *demestica* to wash down the eels and crayfish. Not this evening; this evening Pappas would be looking for the truth.

A dazed woman was slumped into an armchair in the living room. Other women stood around her trying to comfort and console her.

Lakis Rekor's widow, he concluded, knowing that there was no way that he would be able to question the distraught woman, at least not for a while. He noticed the doilies on the backs and arms of the furniture and wondered why women loved to crochet them. He moved unnoticed through the crowded apartment to the open door that led out onto the terrace. Two men were sitting at a table, drinking, smoking, picking at the plates of snacks, seemingly oblivious to the commotion going on around them.

Stepping outside, Pappas lowered himself into a chair, saying, "I'm looking for Thanos and Kostas Koukoudeas."

"And who are you?" one man asked abruptly. His hair was black, and he had thick, dark eyebrows over deep-set, somber brown eyes.

Pappas introduced himself. "I've come to offer my condolences."

"I'm Thanos," the one with the brown eyes said. "This is my brother, Kostas."

Pappas figured Thanos to be the younger of the two brothers. Kostas, his heavily jowled face and gleaming, shaven head supported by a thick neck, was a man in his middle forties. The colonel poured ouzo into a glass and added water, watching as the clear liquid turned milky. "Your brother-in-law was Lakis Rekor?"

Both brothers wore open-collared shirts and were watching the policeman with troubled expressions.

"Yes. He was married to our sister," Kostas Koukoudeas said.

Pappas ripped off a piece of bread and swept it across the *taramosalata*.

"Your brother-in-law was a good policeman. A brave man," Pappas said, and tossed the bread into his mouth.

Kostas's worried eyes fixed on Pappas. "Lakis always wanted to be a policeman."

"Yes, most of us do," Pappas said, digging a chunk of bread into a bowl of *gigantes*, pushing the huge kidney-shaped beans onto the bread. "We know that we'll never be rich, but it's a way of getting out of the village and securing a steady job with a pension. And, of course" —he stopped and ate the gigantes—"there is always the chance of making some fast money."

The brothers shifted uneasily in their seats.

"I have to ask you a few questions," Pappas said.

"Of course, we'll do anything to help," Thanos said.

"I thought you might," Pappas replied, taking out his notepad and flipping it open. He read aloud the dead policemen's official biographies. Both of them had come from the island of Kos. They were appointed to the gendarmerie together on June 1, 1979. They went through recruit school together; they did their probation together on the island of Crete, after which they were assigned together to the duty station on the island of Thíra. On October 9, 1984, both officers submitted form E 6c Request For Transfer. When the police force was consolidated they were reassigned to the Athens patrol district. "From the record they appear to have been close friends," Pappas said, looking up from his notes.

"They grew up together," Kostas said. "Both were best men at the other's wedding."

Pappas scooped up some *mezedakia.* "Yes. I've noticed many similarities between them." He ate. "And their families."

The Koukoudeas brothers became guarded.

"How's that?" asked Thanos.

"Well," Pappas said, carefully wiping his fingers on a paper napkin, "it appears that there was a sudden infusion of money into the Koukoudeas and the Lefas families. And this sudden good fortune took place around the same time that Lakis and Tasos requested transfer off of Thíra. Both officers bought expensive apartments in Athens. And all on a salary of fifty drachmas a month. Their wives must be wonderful managers."

Thanos stole a look at his brother.

"We wouldn't know anything about their finances," Kostas said.

"Wouldn't you?" Pappas said, sipping ouzo, checking his notes. He read aloud. "Thanos Koukoudeas, worked as a waiter in Pappa Spiros until November of 'eighty-four. Kostas Koukoudeas, worked as a tour guide for Atlas Tours until December of 'eighty-four. Both brothers left good-paying jobs to open the Taverna Apollo on Tripodon Street in Plaka." He watched the brothers closely. "It takes considerable money to open a taverna in Plaka. I have to assume that you both had the good fortune to marry financial wizards."

"We saved our money," Thanos insisted, taking a long sip of ouzo. Drink your courage, my friend, Pappas thought, you're going to need it.

The dirge from inside the apartment grew more intense. The widow ran screaming out onto the terrace and threw herself across Thanos's lap.

"Lakis! They murdered my Lakis!" she wailed.

Both brothers comforted her, helping her up onto her feet and escorting her into the waiting arms of several women. The brothers walked back out onto the terrace. Kostas slid the glass door shut. "I don't know why you're standing on our balls, Colonel. Our sister's husband has been killed in the line of duty, and you're treating us like we're criminals."

"Criminals?" Pappas said with a mock amiability. "You're not criminals, you're businessmen who've had a sudden windfall; unfortunately you've neglected to pay any taxes on that windfall. I believe that you owe our government some money." He sipped his drink, his stare fixed on the two brothers. "And then, of course, there's the small matter of your brother-in-law's pension. I hope that your sister gets it." He drank some more ouzo.

"What do you mean by that?" demanded Kostas.

"Well, you see, police regulations prohibit policemen from engaging in outside occupations or from having a proprietary interest in any business." A frown, a slight shrug of the shoulders. "We know, of course, that many policemen do work on the side and have businesses in their wives' names, or in the name of a family member, such as a brother-in-law."

Beads of sweat suddenly popped out at Thanos's hairline.

"Most of the time," Pappas continued, "the department looks the other way, but when there is a problem, then we must investigate. I believe that Lakis Rekor and Tasos Lefas came into a lot of money while they were assigned to Thíra. And I also think that they used their families to invest that money in businesses. It was Lakis's money that opened the Taverna Apollo." Pappas reached out and pushed aside some of the bottles so that he could have an unrestricted view of the brothers. "We have evidence that shows us that the policemen were the intended victims of the Voúla massacre. And I think that you both know why and who is responsible."

"We don't," Thanos blurted. Even in the half-light, his nervous pallor was obvious.

"Withholding evidence and hindering a police investigation is a very serious matter. Compounded with your tax problems and the loss of your sister's pension, I'd say that you had a few problems that you had better resolve."

The Koukoudeas brothers exchanged nervous looks.

Kostas asked, "Have you spoken to anyone in the Lefas family?"

"Not yet," answered the colonel.

"And if we do tell you what we know?" Thanos asked, a deep flush reddening his ears.

"Then I think it would be safe to assume that some accommodation would be reached that would protect your sister's pension and save your business from the greedy tax collectors."

Kostas wiped his damp hands on his trousers. "It all began . . ."

The measured treads of the evzones echoed over the Tomb of the Unknown Soldier. Clusters of tourists kept a respectable distance, watching the tall soldiers, resplendent in their white tunics, white skirts, white stockings, and heavy, tassled shoes, stride with military precision across the marble pavement of the national monument.

Colonel Pappas had directed his driver to let him out at Syntagma Square so that he might watch the Sunday morning changing of the guard. The Minister of Public Order had called an emergency meeting for 10:00; he had a half hour to spare. The last five days had been hectic ones. The massacre continued to dominate the media. A brutal act of terrorism had been the official lie. Unconfirmed reports hinted that Turks or Cypriot nationals might have been behind the massacre. Disinformation goes a long way in helping to keep the lid on things so that the police can devote their energies to solving the case—or so Pappas had argued.

Damn cloud, Pappas thought, wiping his eyes as he glared at Athens' perpetual shroud of pollution. Making his way along one side of the National Gardens toward the Presidential Palace, Pappas checked his sleeve to make sure that the stain was gone. When Anna, his wife, had pressed his uniform that morning, she'd discovered the spot. "It won't do, Dimitri," she announced, wiping it with a wet rag. "You must look your best when you are with Vitos. Especially when the rest of the wolf pack is going to be there too."

The evzone guards presented arms as Pappas passed them. The colonel returned their salute and hurried into the cream-colored palace.

Pappas paused outside the first-floor conference room to tug down the front of his uniform blouse and smooth his thick white hair. He opened the double doors and entered a large room filled with the haze of cigarette smoke. Middle-aged men sat around a polished oval table; a manila folder was in front of each one, as was a silver tray with a glass and a bottle of mineral water. The crystal ashtrays were already filled.

Antonis Vitos, the chief of the Public Order Ministry, chaired the conference; he was at the head of the table. On his right sat Lieutenant General Constantinos Politopoulos, the commanding officer of the Hellenic Police. Politopoulos had a peasant's strong, squat frame and a warm, heavily lined, and intelligent face. His olive drab uniform was exquisitely tailored; the thick wrists and stubby hands sticking out of its sleeves seemed incongruous. The tall, thin older man who sat on the minister's left seemed to carry his own chill with him. His unblinking, reptilian eyes watched everything that was going on without betraying the slightest hint of emotion. This was the mysterious Major General Philippos Tsimas, the head of the Central Information Service, Greece's unpublicized but quite effective intelligence organization. The one man who seemed definitely the odd man out in this gathering was a frail, elderly, and distinguished-looking man with snow-white hair who rested his hands on the curved top of a cane and gave Pappas a single, dignified nod of greeting.

"Talk to me, General Politopoulos," beseeched Vitos. "Tell me what our excellent police have discovered. Prime Minister Papandreou is crawling over my ass for answers, and I'm about to climb over yours, General."

The general clasped his hands in front of him. "Minister, I would prefer to have Colonel Pappas of the Athens Security Prefecture make the report. The investigation is his direct responsibility." You socialist goat fucker, Pappas thought. You're always looking to crawl out from under.

Antonis Vitos looked down the table at his old classmate. "Dimitri, let's hear your report."

CIS smiled. Vito's use of Pappas's first name did not go unnoticed.

Pappas glanced surreptitiously at his sleeve and began his report, beginning with the when, where, who, what, how, and why of police work used the world over. Cuttler had confessed to participating in the massacre along with his dead accomplice, Frank Simmons. Both men had been approached in New York City by a man known to them as Denny McKay who frequented a bar in New York City called The Den. McKay had offered them fifty thousand dollars each to come to Greece and kill two policemen, then fly out the same day. They were each to be paid another fifty thousand dollars upon their return to New York.

Cuttler told Pappas that Orhan Iskur had met them at the airport, provided them with the weapons, and given them the photographs of their intended victims. Orhan also provided them with the policemen's addresses and work schedules. "When I asked Cuttler who wanted the policemen killed and why, he told me that he did not know. He and Simmons had never bothered to ask," Pappas said.

"And you believed him?" Vitos asked, an edge of disbelief in his voice.

"Yes, I did," Pappas answered. "Professional killers do not ask why, they only want to know who and how much."

"Do you think that this Denny McKay could have been the source of the money?" Vitos asked, lighting up another cigarette.

"I don't think so," Pappas answered. "I believe that McKay was the contact man. Cuttler told me that McKay, to the best of his knowledge, had never traveled outside the United States. I had our records checked and discovered that the two policemen had never been to the United States. In fact, Lakis Rekor had never left Greece."

"Why did they kill all those people?" Professor Pericles Levi asked softly.

Pappas focused his attention on the professor. "Cuttler told me that once Major Vassos fired at them, they couldn't stop. You see, Professor, there are some people who enjoy killing."

"Merciful God. All those poor people," groaned Pericles Levi, sinking further into his seat.

"Continue, Dimitri," Vitos said, ignoring Levi's distress.

Pappas went on to tell the group about his first meeting with the Turk, the theft of the Rubens, and the old boy intelligence network that Iskur used to move his stolen art. Pappas noted that when he mentioned the intelligence background, General Tsimas, the head of CIS, was suddenly busy studying the tabletop. Pappas wondered if CIS had used Iskur in some fashion. That could be trouble.

When Pappas finished giving his report, the minister asked, "What do we know of the three Americans, Cuttler, Simmons, and this Denny McKay?"

"Nothing," Pappas answered.

"What?" Vitos shouted. "You did not request a background check from the FBI? Why, Dimitri?"

"Because both Simmons and Cuttler are dead, and—"

"Cuttler died?" Vitos said in a surprised tone.

"Yes, several days ago," Pappas said, shuffling papers inside the folder. "An unfortunate accident. It appears that he fell off his bed and several ribs punctured his lungs. Internal bleeding, I'm afraid. I took it upon myself to have the Americans notified that Cuttler and Simmons were innocent tourists killed in the terrorist attack. I explained away the delay in notifying the American authorities by saying that they were unidentified; they did not have their means of identification on them. I've arranged for our government to extend condolences to the Americans."

"Why, Colonel?" General Tsimas asked slyly.

"Because I think it is safe to assume that both Cuttler and Simmons have extensive criminal records, as does their New York contact, Denny McKay. I do not believe knowing the details of those records would be of any help to us now. And since McKay is the only surviving link to the people responsible for the massacre, I think it wise that we do not let anyone outside this room know that we know about McKay. I'd like very much to keep Denny McKay alive."

"Why?" General Tsimas asked, looking at the colonel with open suspicion.

Pappas looked down the table to the professor and said, deadpan, "While we were searching Orhan Iskur's shop, one of my lieutenants discovered an amphora that was half-filled with black sand. It appeared to be genuine, not one of Iskur's fakes, so I had it delivered to Professor Levi at the museum."

Heads turned toward the elderly professor.

Pericles Levi stirred. With his right hand he reached into the folder, took out a glossy nine-by-ten color photograph of the amphora, and held it up so that all the men could see it. The others reached into their folders and removed their copies of the photograph. Colonel Pappas extracted a mechanical pencil from the breast pocket of his uniform blouse and began to sketch the mourning Athena on the cover of his folder.

"If you will look at the scene that is painted on the amphora," Levi began, "you will see that it depicts the struggle of Herakles and the centaur Nessos." Pointing, he continued, "You can also see that the three Gorgons and the Medusa have already been beheaded by Perseus." He sighed. "This amphora, gentlemen, is genuine. We know from original sources that two amphorae were made in Athens in 600 B.C. by the painter Demaratus. The sister of this amphora is on display in the museum. The one in the photograph had been considered lost. We know that a silk merchant from Luxor bought it for his mistress and brought it back to Egypt around 400 B.C." His lips trembled. "I suspect this amphora was used to store an irreplaceable part of our heritage, something that has now been stolen from us."

The sound of tires crunching over gravel outside broke the heavy silence.

Pappas drew pleats into the mourning Athena's chiton.

With a weary sigh, Minister of Public Order Vitos asked, "What has been stolen from us?"

Professor Levi studied his audience, his eyes going from man to man.

Pappas sketched the temple of Poseidon next to his other drawing.

Professor Levi slowly clasped his hands in front of him, and began to talk about Alexander the Great. He lectured on how Alexander's father, Philip, had sent to the island of Lesbos for Aristotle, son of Nicomachus, to teach his son. Aristotle taught the prince about the stars and about navigation. He also taught him many languages and explained the truths of justice, rhetoric, and philosophy.

Levi's frail body produced a surprisingly forceful voice as he told how Aristotle and his pupil spent hours reading the epic poems of Homer, poems called the *Iliad* and the *Odyssey*, poems that were at least three hundred years older than Alexander. Levi spoke about Alexander's belief that the blood of Achilles coursed through his own veins, and how Alexander had implored his teacher to make him a copy of the *Iliad*. And this Aristotle did for the young prince. Aristotle did not employ scribes; he wrote the text out himself and personally presented it to the prince on his birthday. This gift Alexander valued above all his other possessions. Years later, when Alexander had taken the field against his enemies, it was said that he used to sleep with his *Iliad* and a dagger under his pillow, calling the *Iliad* his journey-book of excellence in war.

During the second year of the Persian War, at the battle of Issus, the most precious of the great King Darius's treasure chests or caskets was captured and brought to Alexander. The king decided that he would store his precious *Iliad* in the chest, and from that moment Alexander's *Iliad* became known as the "casket-copy."

"We know this from the writings of Callisthenes, Aristotle's nephew, who was with Alexander in Persia. And from Eumenes and Ptolemy, who were also there and served as Alexander's chroniclers," Levi said, "and from other surviving sources. And secondary sources such as Plutarch."

Levi reached out and poured water into his glass. Using both his hands to steady it, he drank slowly. He put the glass down on the silver tray, looked up at his audience, and said, "On May twenty-ninth, 323 B.C., outside Babylon, Alexander gave a party for Medius, his friend from Thessaly. The king stood before twenty or so guests and recited extracts from Euripides' play *Andromeda*. He drank wine to his guests' health and fell to his knees, ill." It soon became clear that Alexander the Great was dying. Levi told them how Alexander had written his will, given his ring to his friend, Perdiccas, and designated him

Successor. In the throes of death Alexander placed the hand of his wife, Roxane, in Perdiccas's, and with a nod and a final smile, commended him to her.

The Great King was dead.

Pericles Levi sat forward, his elbows on the table, palms up. "Alexander lay in a golden coffin on a golden bed, covered with purple embroidery on which rested his armor and a Trojan shield."

Levi told how a weeping queen had placed Darius's treasure chest containing her husband's beloved *Iliad* at the foot of the coffin. He paused to wipe his eyes with a handkerchief.

Pappas thought, the old bastard is good. He has them hooked. Ptolemy, Alexander's boyhood friend and now pharoah, intercepted the funeral chariot on the road outside of Babylon, Levi recounted. "He secretly set off to Egypt with the chariot. Ptolemy had it put on display in Memphis and later had it moved to Alexandria."

"What happened to the chariot?" asked General Politopoulos, stroking his thick, busy peasant's mustache.

Levi's face crinkled in an expression that seemed to say: who knows? "We do know that Augustus saw the chariot when he visited Egypt three hundred years later. Most scholars assume that the chariot was destroyed in the city riots of the late third century."

"But not you," said General Tsimas, his cold eyes fixed on the professor. Levi ignored the interruption. "Apollonius of Rhodes was the chief librarian in Alexandria in A.D. 246. One of the few items to survive the fire that destroyed the library was one of Apollonius's records of library holdings wherein he described removing the casket-copy from Darius's treasure chest and storing it inside an amphora. He described the storage jar in great detail. There is no question in my mind that the amphora found in Orhan Iskur's shop is the same one that Apollonius of Rhodes used to store the casket-copy."

"And the *Iliad*, what happened to it?" asked General Tsimas.

"Nothing was heard of the funeral chariot and its contents for more than twenty-one hundred years," Levi responded, reaching out for a bottle of mineral water, pouring, and drinking a glass before going on. "Until the collapse of the Ottoman Empire. By the early twenties refugees were streaming out of Egypt and the rest of the empire. They came carrying family treasures on their backs. Treasures that had been in their families for centuries; treasures they hoped would buy them a new, secure life.

"And the vultures came too. Collectors and art dealers from around the world flocked to the Mediterranean ports with one purpose uppermost in their minds: to cheat these desperate people out of their possessions. Most of the antiquities proved to be of minor importance. But some were priceless. And many of the collectors made fortunes."

"And Alexander's funeral chariot reappeared?" General Politopoulos asked hopefully.

"Alas, no," Levi said. "I'm afraid it is still lost."

"Then what has been stolen from us?" asked Vitos.

"In June of 'thirty-nine, a collector named Paolo Matrazzo wired his partner from Thíra that he was on the verge of making a great acquisition. Matrazzo instructed his partner to wire him two million U.S. Matrazzo's partner wired back demanding to know the nature of the acquisition," Levi said.

"And?" demanded the minister.

"Matrazzo wired back: 'I have found the casket-copy.' "

"And then what happened?" asked General Tsimas, leaning forward.

"Matrazzo's partner wired him the money." Levi shrugged. "Word leaked out that Matrazzo was after the casket-copy, and some of the vultures started to circle over Thíra. Anyway, the draft arrived from Rome on a Thursday. It was never cashed. Paolo Matrazzo was found dead in his hotel on Saturday. An apparent heart attack."

"And the casket-copy?" asked General Politopoulos, the head of the Hellenic Police.

Levi shrugged.

"A swindle," announced General Tsimas.

"I think not, General," Levi retorted. "Matrazzo was then one of the world's foremost dealers, specializing in Greek antiquities from three hundred B.C. to four hundred A.D. It would have been almost impossible for him to have been deceived by a fake. And he would, without question, have had the artifact authenticated before he wired Rome for the money."

Pappas held up his pencil to ask a question. "Professor, is it your opinion that the casket-copy had been kept in the amphora that we found in Orhan Iskur's shop?"

"Yes," Levi answered.

"Then why not take the amphora? Why would Iskur's killer leave it behind?" Pappas asked.

"Amphorae are not rare. True, this one is worth a considerable sum, but it is not priceless. And it is big. Perhaps whoever killed Iskur did not know it was in the shop."

Playing with his pencil, Pappas asked, "Do you believe that the casket-copy was taken out of Greece and transported to the United States?"

"Circumstances force me to that conclusion, Colonel," Levi responded. "The killers of the two policemen, and of all those other poor souls, were from New York City. One must assume that the person who hired them was also from the United States."

A hush fell over the room.

General Tsimas slapped the table. "You and the professor expect us to send someone to the United States, don't you, Colonel Pappas?"

"I want to see the casket-copy back in Greece. And"—Pappas leaned forward in his seat, pointing his pencil at General Tsimas, his voice heavy with rancor—"Most of all, I want the people responsible for Voúla punished."

"Proof," General Tsimas shouted across the table, slapping his hand on it in anger. "Where is your proof? We cannot send someone off on a wild-goose chase. Tell us the connection between the two policemen and Iskur. Proof, Colonel."

Pappas pushed his chair back and stood up. He put his palms down flat on the glistening table and looked directly at Tsimas.

"Proof, General? When I questioned Kostas and Thanos Koukoudeas, the brothers-in-law of one of the murdered policemen, Lakis Rekor, they confessed that Rekor and his partner, Tasos Lefas, had discovered something of great value in the ruins of Akrotiri on Thíra. I had the logbooks checked. Akrotiri was within their patrol zone. Kostas Koukoudeas, the older of the brothers, told me that Rekor and his partner used to park their patrol car outside the ruins at night and roam about searching for undiscovered treasure. As I'm sure you are aware, excavations were begun at Akrotiri in May of 'sixty-seven, and they are still not complete. Well, one night in the fall of 1984, in the Temple of the Egyptians, Officer Rekor noticed a depression in the ground and began to dig. They dug for most of the night while the watchman slept in his shack. They found something of great value.

"Thanos Koukoudeas told me that they quickly contacted Orhan Iskur, and he arranged the sale of the object to an American collector."

"And did he also tell you what this precious object was, Colonel?" General Tsimas asked.

"No he did not," Pappas said, lowering himself back into his seat. "Lakis Rekor told his brothers-in-law that they were better off not knowing."

"I see," said General Tsimas. "And did you speak with the other dead officer's family?"

"Yes, I did," Pappas answered. "At first they denied any knowledge. But after I carefully explained their situation to them, they confessed. And their story was basically the same."

"Colonel, you still have not presented any proof. Hearsay is not proof," Tsimas said, a thin smile compressing his lips.

"Alexander's *Iliad* was in that amphora," Professor Levi said sternly, his face set in a stubborn look.

"And how do we know that?" General Politopoulos demanded.

"The black sand tells us," Levi answered with authority. "Sand keeps moisture out and helps protect ancient writings from rot and decay. The ancients used it as a preservative. They knew that water was the main destroyer of parchment and papyrus. That was why Apollonius of Rhodes removed the *Iliad* from the casket and stored it in the amphora, which, I am positive, was filled with sand from the desert. Whoever brought the casket-copy to Thíra put the island's volcanic sand into that amphora to preserve Alexander's *Iliad*."

"If what you say is true," Antonis Vitos, the Minister of Public Order, said, "are we then to assume that Alexander's *Iliad* would be intact?"

Professor Levi's lips fluttered. "I don't know. No one can know the answer to that question with any degree of certainty. Perhaps it is a fragment. A scroll or two. Perhaps more. But think of it, gentlemen, the *Iliad* written in Aristotle's own hand for Alexander."

"If your somewhat imaginative conjecture is correct, Professor, then please tell me why this elusive American would go to such extraordinary lengths to arrange the deaths of two Greek policemen and an antiquities dealer," asked Antonis Vitos, crushing out the stub of a cigarette in an ashtray.

Pappas answered: "Because the two dead policemen had overextended themselves in business and thought that they could go back to the well and draw out more water. But, unfortunately for them and the people of Voúla, whoever this person is did not want to pay again for what he had already paid for once."

General Tsimas furrowed his brow. "Then why kill Orhan Iskur?"

"To sever all connections with himself," Pappas answered.

"Why?" asked General Politopoulos. "This American had whatever he wanted. He was safely back in the States. Why not tell them to go to hell? What could they possibly have done to him?"

Professor Pericles Levi chuckled. "You are not a collector, General, or else you would understand. Collectors are paranoid when it comes to their collections. Their acquisitions are kept secret from the world. Why do they do this, you ask? Because they know that other collectors are as crazy as they are. They know that other collectors will commit murder to possess certain pieces; pieces that they have spent most of a lifetime aching to possess, only to have someone else acquire them. Have you, General Politopoulos, ever heard of the Treasure of Priam?"

"Of course," answered Politopoulos. "It was the treasure that

Schliemann unearthed at Troy. It was housed in the Berlin Museum and was destroyed during a bombing raid during World War Two."

"Correct, General," Pericles Levi said. "A treasure that caused Schliemann to send his famous telegram to the King of Greece: 'I have gazed on the face of Agamemnon.' Only the collection was not destroyed. It was stolen. Three of the museum's guards removed the collection during the raid. Later they sold it to a Canadian who now lives in dread that someone will steal his prized collection. He knows that there are those of us in the art world who *know* that the Treasure of Priam exists. And he knows that there are many who would kill to possess that treasure.

"And that, gentlemen, is exactly what your two dishonest policemen had to sell this elusive collector, their continued silence. Because if they, or Orhan Iskur, had revealed his name, then he, too, would have to spend his life in mortal fear."

NEW YORK CITY
JULY 1987

The furry head poked out from behind the tree trunk. Darting out onto a branch, the black squirrel reared up.

"Good morning, Ajax," Teddy Lucas said, standing near the kitchen window of his second-floor Stuyvesant Town apartment, located off Manhattan's First Avenue. He was spreading peanut butter over a cracker. "Sorry I'm late this morning." He broke the cracker and put the halves out on the sill. Stepping back, he picked up his coffee mug and watched the creature run out to the end of the branch and leap onto the windowsill.

Ajax reared, nostrils twitching, his bushy tail curling around his body. The squirrel scooped up a half and began to nibble away at the cracker. Dressed only in undershorts, Lucas sipped his coffee and talked to his friend. "So? How goes it, Ajax? You getting much?" Lucas wryly reflected on how surprised his men would be if they heard their tough boss talking to a squirrel.

Ajax's teeth champed into the peanut butter.

Teddy Lucas and Ajax had been friends for three years. Their friendship began the day Lucas moved into the one-bedroom apartment. He had been unpacking dishes in the kitchen when the squirrel appeared on the windowsill. When he noticed the squirrel watching him, Lucas leaned up against the kitchen counter and began to talk to the creature. It was someone to talk to, to confide in, maybe even be friends with. And for no special reason, he named the squirrel Ajax, after the hero of the Trojan War.

The next morning Ajax reappeared. Lucas put some peanut butter on a cracker and left it out on the sill. They'd been friends ever since. It was nice to have someone to talk to, another living creature to help break the loneliness of the morning.

At forty-seven, Teddy Lucas was trim and muscular, although he was beginning to notice some extra baggage around his middle. High black eyebrows added intensity to his dark eyes, and a forelock of black wavy hair fell down over his brow. Flat cheekbones, an olive complexion, and finely defined features combined to make him an unusually handsome man.

Ajax finished the crackers. He quickly brushed his mouth with his paw, looked up at Lucas as if to say thanks, and hopped back onto the branch. Lucas rinsed out the mug and balanced it on top of the pile in the dish rack. He walked through the living room into the bedroom and got dressed: tan slacks, brown loafers, a blue shirt with a white collar, no tie. He took a beige sports jacket from the closet and tossed it on the unmade bed. Going over to the oak dresser, he opened the middle drawer and, reaching under his socks, took out his holstered .38 Colt detective special and slipped it into his trousers, clipping it securely over his brown leather belt.

As he pushed the drawer closed, he spotted the small icon tucked away in the back. His mother used to pray to the damn thing every day. He remembered her giving it to him, telling him that it would protect him. He asked himself why the hell he was saving it; was it a part of his life that he wanted to hold on to? He reached into the drawer, took out the painting of Christ, and set it up on top of the dresser. He stepped back, studying the golden aureole that illuminated Christ's melancholy face. The sight of the icon brought back painful and embarrassing remembrances: fights with neighborhood kids who would make fun of his Greek-speaking parents; his mother having to clean other people's homes in order to make ends meet; his proud father's struggle to support his family in a foreign land.

Teddy Lucas was born Theodorous Loucopolous on September 2, 1940, in the northern village of Kilkis, close to the Yugoslavian border. He had picked a bad time and a bad place to make his entrance into the world. The Italians invaded Greece in 1939, then came the Germans, and then in 1943 the civil war broke out, pitting communist and royalist guerrillas against each other.

The civil war raged throughout the northern part of Greece. Of his childhood memories, fear ran through the most vivid ones. He could remember his mother clutching him tightly as she ran up the side of a hill with Melina and Thalassa, his two sisters, in tow; they were desperately trying to escape the shelling. He remembered the houses in his village aflame, and the explosions, and the dead, and the wounded begging for water. He remembered his mother and his two sisters cowering behind boulders, praying to the icon to spare the family. He had no recollection of his father during that period of his life. He was to learn years later that his dad had been in the hills fighting on the side of the ELAS, the communist guerrillas.

The Germans were driven out of Greece in 1945 and the civil war ended in 1949, a civil war that was to cost six hundred thousand Greek lives.

Teddy was nine years old when his parents gathered the family together in the living room of their whitewashed house and told them that they were moving to America. He could still vividly recall his father's weathered face and sad eyes as he explained that he wanted his children to grow up away from the ravages of war, safe and secure in a land of plenty: America. Although Teddy felt sad at the thought of leaving his beloved grandparents behind—they would continue to live in the family's house—he was glad to be leaving Greece. He had nothing but bitter memories; memories and the anxious fear that someday the bombs would begin to fall on them again.

The Loucopolous family settled in the Greek section of Astoria, Queens, in New York City. Their new home was in the basement of a three-family brick house. One room acted as their kitchen, bedroom, and living/dining room. At night a thick brown blanket separated his parents' bed from the one in which his two sisters slept. Teddy slept on a cot in the boiler room.

The beginning years in America were hard. His father worked double shifts in a factory that made cardboard boxes. Both his sisters helped their mother clean people's houses. Their new home had a small backyard; the landlord gave permission for the Loucopolous family to grow vegetables in it. The family garden became Teddy's responsibility. He enjoyed working the soil; he liked the smell of the earth and the feel of the cold dirt under his feet. Teddy felt safe in America. He had looked forward to shedding his Greek ways and becoming an American. He wanted to immerse himself in the culture of his new homeland. But that was not to be; the part of Astoria where the Loucopolous family had settled was predominantly Greek. Instead of experiencing a new culture, he found himself living smack in the center of a kind of transplanted Greece.

By the time he was eleven years old he could speak English haltingly. After school he would deliver orders from Mr. Skoulas's grocery store. Although he had trouble speaking the language, he was able to read and understand it quite well; he devoured mystery stories. He loved to play soccer with his friends and was quite good at the game. Playing soccer developed his powerful legs and gave him an accurate awareness of their strength and fluidity that most American boys his age lacked.

When he was fourteen years old his parents changed their last name to Lucas, took every cent that they had saved, and bought a "handyman's special" in Ridgewood, Queens. Teddy had never before heard the term handyman's special. He was to learn that in this case it meant a frame house that was attached on both sides and had an old, leaky roof, a wet basement, and a frayed electrical system along with a boiler held together largely by hope, faith, and patchy repairs.

Ridgewood was a vastly different neighborhood from Astoria. Mostly, the people were of Italian, German, and Irish stock. The few Greeks who did live there were completely assimilated into the culture and refused to speak Greek, except in private.

The neighborhood kids in Ridgewood used to make fun of the new Greek family who dressed differently and did not speak English well. Teddy in particular became the butt of their hazing. Many times the tough guys would lie in wait for him after school. They'd taunt him, making fun of his short pants and sandals. Sometimes they would circle him and shove him from one to the other. It was during these awful times that the memories of the war flooded back into his thoughts and he would feel helpless, a peasant fleeing for his life, not understanding why he was being punished. Their vicious insults made Teddy want to strike out with his powerful legs and hurt them.

But he could do nothing. He could not react to them because peasants do not strike their betters. Peasants learn early in their lives to be subservient, to cast their eyes downward, to bear the humiliation, to endure. Teddy was positive that if he ever did strike back and hurt any of the cowards, they would call the police. Then the police would come, and the foreigner would automatically be at fault, and the police would deport his whole family to Greece. Then all that his family had struggled so hard to achieve would be lost because he had not been strong enough to endure the taunts of cowards. During those times he would steel himself against his tormentors and vow that he would shed everything about himself that was Greek. He was going to become a true American—then he and his family would be safe.

He worked hard and his English gradually improved. He read everything in English that he could find. When the weather was nice he would work in the garden of their new home and whenever he had the time he would travel back to Astoria to play soccer with his Greek friends.

One spring day Teddy was working in the yard, hoeing his garden. He was barefoot and wearing gray short pants that his grandmother had sent him from Greece. He heard snickers behind him and tensed, resisting the temptation to turn. He continued working, but when the laughter grew louder he did turn around and saw six of the toughest neighborhood kids leaning over the fence in the rear of the yard watching him. They started yelling obscene insults at him. "Fucking foreigner, go back to your commie country."

Four of them leaped over the fence and rushed into the garden, trampling the vegetables, tearing them out of the earth and tossing them around the yard. Teddy stood by, doing nothing to stop them, tears of shame burning his eyes. Suddenly he heard Melina's frantic voice and he turned in time to see his sister running up out of the basement. She shouted at the tormentors to stop, yelling that they should be ashamed of themselves. The jeering kids circled Melina. They began to manhandle her. She fought back, slapping and kicking and cursing them in Greek. One of the youths made a grab at her breast. She kicked him. He punched her in the face, sending her spinning onto the ground.

Teddy saw his sister lying in the dirt. He screamed at the tormentors and threw his hoe at them. They hesitated, briefly taken aback by Teddy's unexpected bravery. Then they began to laugh at him, standing their ground with adolescent bravado.

Teddy rushed at them, targeting the biggest one, a tall burly boy with husky shoulders and big biceps. He could feel the power surging through his legs as he struck, arching his right foot up into the boy's face, knocking out teeth and toppling him onto his knees. Teddy wheeled and smashed his foot into the boy's stomach, splaying him backward onto the ground.

The other boys backed off, but Teddy's fury propelled him forward. He kicked another of them in the groin, and when he doubled over, he struck out with his foot, splattering the boy's nose like a crushed tomato. The ferocity of his attack caused the others to break and escape over the fence. Teddy helped his sister up off the ground and into the house, leaving the remaining two rolling in the dirt. His worst fear never came to pass: the police never came to his home; that was not how things were settled in Ridgewood.

That night when Teddy and his sister told their father what had happened, the father smiled, ruffled Teddy's hair, and said, "You did right."

Teddy was never again bothered, nor was any member of his family, after the incident in the backyard. As he grew older, Teddy became more attuned to his new way of life. He would refuse to speak his native tongue unless it was absolutely necessary to do so. At some point he decided that he wanted to be a policeman. Policemen were safe from the taunts of others and they helped other people, peasants, immigrants, and others in need of help. There were still times when he would get that anxious peasant feeling, and it was then that he re- membered the bombs and got scared.

Staring at the icon, he saw his mother and sister praying behind the rocks. He grabbed it off the dresser, tossed it back into the drawer, took his lieutenant's shield off the top, and left for the office.

Chief of Detectives Tim Edgeworth, a big man with a heavy, over- hanging brow, cold blue eyes, and thick lips, lit his pipe, unpinned the communication referral slip from the UF49, and tossed the pin into a glass ashtray. Another heavy, he sighed. The pink slips come down the chain direct from the police commissioner. He scanned the rows of endorsements; each one summarized the report and gave conclusions and recommendations. Some of them continued on the back of the official letterhead.

C of D Edgeworth removed the translation of the communication the NYPD had received from the Hellenic Police. One Major Andreas Vassos, Athens Security Prefecture, was being sent to New York City to investigate the murder of two Greek police officers.

"Fucking cop killers," Edgeworth muttered, thinking of the six cops who had recently been shot in El Bronxo. He studied the report from the State Department. State requested that the NYPD render all possi- ble assistance to the Greek police. He read it a third time and frowned. Tossing it on his desk, he leaned back in his chair and looked medita- tively at the ceiling. It didn't make any sense: why would the feds step aside on something this sensitive? Normally they would have insisted on assigning a small army of FBI and State Department people for liaison, rather than just the one man listed as a federal liaison contact. His name was Hayden. Instead here they were, handing the NYPD this one on a silver platter. Or was it on the end of a long, dirty stick?

Edgeworth picked it up gingerly and read it through again. The original Greek request had been filed with the U.S. embassy in Athens. It was approved and sent on to the Bureau of Diplomatic Security in Washington, D.C. Hayden's agency. Washington approved the request and forwarded it along with accompanying documents to the Diplo- matic Security field office in NYC.

The request had been hand delivered to the PC. The First Deputy Commissioner's recommendation: APPROVAL. Chief of the Depart- ment: APPROVAL. Deputy Commissioner, Administration: AP- PROVAL. Deputy Commissioner, Legal Matters: APPROVAL. Edge- worth read the PC's final endorsement:

Major Andreas Vassos, Hellenic Police Department, will be extended every courtesy by members of this department. He will be assigned to a subordinate command within the Detective Division. The CO of that command will be responsible for the major's supervision and control. Major Vassos should, if possible, be assigned to a command where one or more members are fluent in the Greek language.

Forwarded to the C of D for implementation and report. Recommend: APPROVAL.

C of D Edgeworth studied the printout listing Greek-speaking detectives and their present assignments. Thirty-seven members of the Detective Division had demonstrated some proficiency in the language. Lieutenant Teddy Lucas, the Whip of the Sixteenth Detective Squad, spoke Greek. Edgeworth leaned back and fondly recalled the eight years he had spent in the Sixteenth Squad. They were great years, the best. Was it possible, really possible, that that had been over twenty-five years ago?

He snapped forward in his seat and pressed one of the buttons in the row on the right side of his desk. Sergeant Jacobs, Edgeworth's lead clerical, came in with a stack of folders neatly tucked under his beefy arm. "Yes, Chief?"

"Did you look over the forty-nine on this Major Vassos?"

"Yes, I did," he replied, settling comfortably into the chair on the side of the desk with the relaxed air of a confidant.

"Will Vassos be cross-designated?" Edgeworth asked.

Jacobs stacked the folders on his lap. He pulled one from the pile and spread it open. Glancing at the contents, he said, "I checked with the Legal Bureau, Chief. Only U.S. law enforcement personnel can be cross-designated from one agency to another."

"Will Vassos have arrest powers?" asked the C of D.

"No, sir. Any collars will be taken by our people. The arrest will be made on the complaint of the Greek government. The perp will be arraigned in federal court and held pending extradition."

The C of D smiled. "I assume that we have an extradition treaty with the Greeks."

"We do. I checked."

"Will the major be permitted to carry firearms?"

"Technically, no. But since he'll be traveling under a diplomatic passport, he'll be able to carry a weapon, if he wants to."

"What about his living accommodations?"

"The Greek consul general is responsible for making those arrangements."

"Going on the assumption that they'll quarter him in Manhattan, I guess we ought to assign the major to a Manhattan command."

Sergeant Jacobs held his pencil at the ready. "Which one, Chief?"

Teddy Lucas read the report typed under "Details of the Case" on the bottom of the DD5 Supplementary Complaint Report, commonly called simply the five, the detective form used to report all phases of an investigation. He checked the crime classification code to insure that the fairy tale complied with department policy and procedures and, satisfied that it did, affixed his signature in the space provided on the bottom of the report.

I've become a goddamn fiction editor, he thought, reaching into the tray for another five.

The undersigned interviewed the complainant, who stated that she could add nothing further to aid the investigation. A recanvass of the place of occurrence met with negative results. Pending further developments, the undersigned requests that this case be marked: CLOSED, NO RESULTS.

The Squad's caseload last year had been 2,240 cases. These were divided among fifteen detectives, which meant that each detective had to spend a good part of each tour in front of a typewriter banging out fairy tales. But clearances must be maintained. The Palace Guard does not care how you do it; in fact, they don't want to *know* how you do it. Just be sure that your clearances are up and your paper is current.

Burglary complainants usually got a phone call, a fast PR job, and sympathy. Robbery complainants got to look at mug shots. If they were unable to pick out the perp, the case would be marked active for a few months, a few fives would be added to the case folder for color, and then the case would be marked: CLOSED, NO RESULTS.

precious street time had to be spent on the heavy ones: homicides, felonious assaults, maimings, rapes, and any incident involving a diplomat or a famous person. The Job was uptight when it came to publicity. Stroke 'em, gently, and make sure that they don't come in your face, Edgeworth constantly reminded his borough commanders.

As a boy growing up, Lucas used to fantasize about becoming a cop. He wanted to match wits with master criminals; become Astoria's Maigret or Holmes. He was going to destroy criminal cartels, protect the downtrodden. He had been on the Job eleven months before he realized that nobody really cared about the downtrodden. And he was in the Detective Division two years before he realized that there was no such thing as a master criminal. There were only mutts—and their wailing lib-blab lawyers who had learned to master an inane, archaic criminal justice system.

Lucas pushed back from his desk and got up. He walked over to the fan on top of the library cabinet and turned it to high. Another scorcher, he thought, ungluing his shirt. He glanced around his office, his home away from home. The rows of clipboards: DD64b Recapitulation of Detectives' Arrest Activity, DD60 Detective's Report on Lost or Stolen Property, DD52 Wanted File, Special Operating Procedures, department bulletins. The green leather divan flush against the wall, the splotches of dirt, the file boxes and trays. The maps: Sensitive Locations, Crime Prone Locations. It wasn't perfect, but it was where he wanted to be: the Whip of a detective squad. He still longed to make like Maigret or Holmes. At this point he'd even settle for making like Kojak.

He reached for another five.

Detective Ivan Ulanov stuck his big Slavic face into the office. "Your ex is on the phone."

"Tell her I'm patrolling the east coast of Tahiti."

Ulanov nodded and disappeared back into the squad room.

The red telephone on Lucas's desk rang. "Lieutenant Lucas."

"Lou, this is Sergeant Jacobs from the C of D's office," the voice said, using the diminutive of lieutenant that was routinely used throughout the Job. "The bossman wants to see you, forthwith."

Grabbing his sports jacket off the coatrack, Lucas grumbled, "Everything in this job is 'forthwith.' Why can't they once say 'Report at your leisure'?"

C of D Edgeworth was studying July's recapitulation of force figures when Lucas entered.

"Sit down, Lou," Edgeworth said. "I'll be with you in a second."

Lucas watched the C of D's frown at the column of numbers. The massive shoulders and strong hands gave a hint of the man's brute strength. He looked out of character sitting behind a desk.

"There just ain't enough bodies to plug all the gaps," Edgeworth said, tossing the printout into a file tray. He leaned back, a sly smile tugging at his lips. "So? How goes it with your squad, Teddy?"

The old fox knows damn well how I'm doing. But Lucas would stick to the approved ritual: always have an answer ready, make up any numbers to show that you're on top of things. More important, make the boss feel important. "Everything's pretty good, Chief. My robberies are down twenty-two percent this quarter. Homicides are down thirty percent. I've reduced overtime forty percent—overtime was a biggie—and Inspections gave the Squad an above average rating last time around. And I'm sitting here wondering what you got in store for me."

A sunburst grin broke across Edgeworth's face. "Right to the point, Teddy. That's one of the things I always liked about you, you're a no-bullshit guy." He flopped his hands on top of his desk, leaned forward, "How'd you like to get away from the paper and play detective for a while?"

Lucas gave the expected good-soldier reply: "I'll do whatever you want, boss."

"Washington just threw us a heavy, and I need a Greek-speaking detective to run with it."

"Who'll run the Squad while I'm out playing Kojak?"

"Your Second Whip. Roosevelt can look after things for you, like he does when you're out getting laid or on vacation."

"What's the case?"

Edgeworth told him about Major Vassos and the two murdered Greek policemen.

"What do I do if I need some detectives to hit a flat or kick some ass?" Teddy asked.

"Use your people. Take them off the chart if you have to. And if things get hectic, get on the horn to me and I'll fly some men in to cover your chart."

"What authority will this major have?"

Edgeworth explained the nuances of cross-designation and why Vassos would not be cross-designated or authorized to make arrests but would be permitted to carry a weapon. "You'll have to make out a ten card for him. The Greeks will want to know how many hours a week he worked. Carry him on your roll calls. And Teddy, you're responsible for his control and supervision."

"How far do you want me to go with this thing? Do you want me to go through the motions, or do you want me to be for real?"

"All the way. Do whatever is necessary to bring the case to a successful conclusion. The Greeks are going to be conducting a parallel investigation. You'll keep each other informed."

Lucas nodded curtly. "When is the major arriving?"

Edgeworth looked at his desk calendar. "Monday, July thirteenth. That's today. Olympic Flight 812, arriving Kennedy at four thirty-five. So you've got just about five hours to fill your Second Whip in on what's going down before you get out to Kennedy and pick up your new partner."

"If I'm coming off the chart, I certainly don't want to catch any borough duties. Are you going to send down a telephone message taking me out of the chart?"

"I don't want to go that route. I'll telephone your borough CO and tell him that you're on a special assignment for me and not to be looking for you for any other jobs."

"Who do I report to?"

"To me. I want a phone call every day."

"What about wheels and expenses?"

"You've been assigned a confiscated car with Jersey plates. A Buick. You can pick it up in the garage when you leave." He slid an envelope across to him. "The registration and the keys are in here along with two hundred dollars, compliments of Uncle Sam." He passed him two signature cards. "Sign these. You'll be getting credit cards in department mail. Keep receipts."

Lucas signed the cards and got up. As he was making for the door, Edgeworth called to him. "Whenever the feds ask me to conduct an investigation for them I get this tingling sensation in my balls, like I'm about to get fucked."

Reaching for the knob, Lucas answered, "I know the feeling, boss."

Portable steel barriers formed a funnel through which travelers had to pass when exiting the customs area of the International Arrivals Building. People jammed up against the barricade watching the trickle of passengers come out from behind the frosted glass doors, their anxious eyes scanning the crowd for a familiar face. Black-capped chauffeurs, holding up cardboard signs bearing the names of clients, clustered at the neck of the funnel.

Teddy Lucas edged his way through the waiting crowd into the isolation area. A customs inspector rushed over to him. "You're not allowed inside here, fella."

Lucas showed him his police credentials. "Inspector Cutrone is expecting me."

"You here to pick up the VIP from Greece?"

"Yes."

The customs man pushed open the heavy doors. "To your right, up two flights, and then go left."

The observation deck ran the entire length of the inspection area and was enclosed behind a wall of one-way glass. Agents perched on stools, scanning the deplaning passengers through binoculars. Four agents sat in front of a panel of TV monitors.

"Cutrone?" Lucas asked the first agent he came to.

"Through that door," said the agent.

Cutrone was a surprisingly small man with a southern drawl and oversized yellow-tinted aviator glasses. "How y'all doin'?" he said, pumping Lucas's hand while one eye remained fixed on the television monitor. "You're going to have to bear with me for a bit. We got something going down, down there." He folded his arms across his chest and intently watched the monitor. Lucas stood beside him.

Hidden cameras zoomed in on a couple moving up to the inspection stand. The bearded husband wore a fur cap and had long side curls. The woman's head was covered by a kerchief. Lucas's trained eyes spotted the male and female undercovers inching up to the unsuspecting couple.

"That little ol' gal down there got a diamond-filled prophylactic stuck up her pussy."

The husband tossed one suitcase up onto the counter. Suddenly they were surrounded by agents who hustled them off through a door on the side of the inspection area.

Cutrone turned his attention to his guest. "Now to your problem. Your friend landed six minutes ago. He'll be here shortly."

Eleven minutes later the door opened and a customs agent stuck his head inside. "Here's our guest."

A blue nylon bag was slung over Vassos's right shoulder, and another was in his hand.

"Welcome, Major," Lucas said, moving to greet him, noticing both the European cut of his clothes and his grief-stricken eyes. "I'm Lieutenant Teddy Lucas, NYPD."

Shaking hands, Vassos answered in Greek. "I'm pleased to meet you. I'm Andreas Vassos."

"I prefer not to speak in Greek. Do you speak English?"

Vassos's eyes grew chilly. "Yes, I do speak English."

"Let me help you, Andreas," Lucas said, taking the handgrip and waving a thank-you to Cutrone.

A jumbo jet lumbered up off a runway, its nose straining to gain altitude as they walked out of the terminal. Lucas's assigned car was double-parked at the curb. The Port Authority cop he had asked to look after it stood nearby.

"Thanks," Lucas said to the cop, pulling the back door open and tossing the suitcases onto the seat. He stepped off the curb and walked around to the driver's side. Vassos was already in the passenger seat when Lucas squeezed in behind the wheel.

"At last I can see for myself," Vassos said, watching the PA cop give directions to a group of women.

"See what?"

"On television and in the movies your police always carry so much equipment I do not know how they can move about."

Lucas looked out the windshield at the cop. "Revolver, holster, twelve-extra rounds, handcuffs, traffic whistle, mace, billy, flashlight, memo book, summons book—all normal equipment, Andreas," he said, sticking the key into the ignition. "What do your people carry on patrol?"

Vassos said, deadpan, "Their revolvers."

"Nothing else?"

"No, nothing."

"They're lucky." Driving out onto the roadway, Lucas asked, "Where to?"

Vassos handed him a slip of paper. "My address in Manhattan."

They drove in silence, Lucas paying attention to the traffic; Vassos was absorbed by the scenery. The car glided up the ramp leading off the Van Wyck Expressway onto the Long Island Expressway. Lucas braked and merged into the traffic. "Where did you learn your English?"

"At Police College. It is not possible to obtain promotion without fluency in another language."

"Good idea," Lucas said, inching the car into the middle lane.

"I was told that a Greek-speaking officer would be assigned to work with me."

"A foul-up. I haven't spoken Greek in years."

"But you are a Greek, yes?"

"Greek-American."

"Your name is not Greek," Vassos observed, watching the driver.

"I was born Theodorous Loucopolous. My father had it shortened to Lucas."

A grimace. "Here everyone has to be American, yes?"

Lucas eased the Buick into the curb in front of the Hotel Olympian's blue-and-white canopy on Eighth Avenue near Thirty-second Street. The digital clock on the dashboard read 7:26. The hotel was a second-rate affair pressed between an abandoned movie house and a glass office building. Lucas tossed the vehicle identification plate onto the padded dashboard and slid out of the car.

Standing on the curb, Vassos watched homeless men gathering under the marquee. Shopping carts crowded with paper bags and bedrolls were lined up against the boarded-up doors of the movie house.

Lucas opened the car's back door and yanked out the luggage. He tossed one to Vassos. "Catch."

Snagging it with both hands, Vassos inclined his head toward the homeless people. "Are there many such persons in New York?"

"Enough. And in Greece?"

"None."

The hotel's oval vestibule had a vaulted ceiling. Painted wall panels depicted fishermen casting nets under a cloudless sky. The lobby was long and narrow, and led to a desk cage made of brown marble and faded brass. Two settees were the only furniture; they were worn and shiny.

"Do you have a reservation?" the desk clerk asked, looking up from his racing form.

Lucas put down his bag. "Vassos."

The clerk ran his finger over the reservation tray. He slid out a card, read: "Andreas Vassos. Direct billing to the Greek Consulate, Press Information, 601 Fifth Avenue."

"That is correct," Vassos said.

The clerk handed him the necessary form to fill out and then passed him his plastic keycard. "Room ten-ten."

Plastic pie-shaped light fixtures lined the ceiling of the long hallway. Vassos slid the plastic keycard into the slot above the knob. The light on the right of the lock turned green and the door opened. They walked into an ice-cold room. Vassos rushed over to the window, threw the curtains aside, and pushed the window up as far as it would go. Manhattan's sounds and moist, hot July air rushed into the room. The major looked down at the strange city. "I hate air-conditioning. It is unnatural." He looked around, found the temperature control, and fiddled with it until the flow from the air-conditioning vent stopped.

Lucas tossed the bag onto the bed and looked around the small, rather drab room. A night table, writing desk and chair, and a pay television with two movie channels. The remote was on the night table. One wing chair by the window.

Lucas sat on the lumpy bed and leaned back to the wall. "What do you think of the city?"

Vassos turned. "It is big and noisy."

Lucas noticed the blue of his eyes. They were the eyes of a truly homeless man, forever sad.

"Thank you for meeting me, Teddy."

"My pleasure, one cop to another." Vassos removed his sports jacket and slung it over the back of the chair.

Lucas's attention was immediately drawn to the automatic that was stuck into the slide holster on Vassos's hip. "That's some piece of equipment you're carrying."

Vassos glanced down at the weapon. He slid it out of the holster, pressed the release button that dropped the clip into his hand, extracted the chambered round, and handed the gun to Lucas.

"Nice balance," Lucas observed. "A nine millimeter Beretta. You don't see too many of these in New York."

Vassos sat down next to him. "It has some unusual features. This is a 93R model. On the left side of the frame there is a fire selector switch that allows the weapon a three-round burst capability." Reaching under the barrel, he slid down front handgrips. "When the weapon is on full automatic, it is advisable to hold onto the grips."

"It's a little heavy," Lucas said, hefting it in his palm.

"One point twelve kilograms. That is about two pounds."

"How many rounds in the magazine?"

"Twenty."

"Not bad," Lucas said, looking down at the two extra magazines protruding from the leather slip pouch snapped around Vassos's belt. "You're lugging sixty rounds around with you. I think that it might be a good idea if you fill me in on this investigation of ours."

Vassos took the weapon back and laid it on top of the night table. He unzipped the smaller of the two nylon bags and took out a bottle of scotch. "Black Label, duty free," he said. "Will you join me?"

"Why not?" Lucas said, getting up and going into the bathroom and returning with two glasses.

Vassos poured. He lifted his glass to Lucas. "*Giassou*, Teddy."

"Cheers," Lucas replied.

"Why won't you speak Greek with me?" Vassos asked.

"Why don't you want to tell me about the case?"

Vassos smiled, watching Lucas over the rim of the water glass. "It began nine weeks ago in Voúla . . ."

When Vassos finished telling about the shooting and the casket-copy twenty-six minutes later, Lucas looked at him and asked, "Why did they send you?"

"Are you married, Teddy?"

"Divorced. My ex decided that marriage with me was not for her."

Shaking his head, Vassos said, "I heard American women were rather unpredictable." Moving over to his sports jacket, he reached inside the breast pocket and removed his passport. He flipped open the cover, reached inside the leather case, and removed a photograph. Stepping back across the room, he passed it to Lucas. A beautiful woman posed with a toddler clinging to her shoulder.

"My family. They were among the dead at Voúla." He looked out the window at the gathering summer twilight. "If only I had not acted as a policeman that day, they might still be alive." He turned back to Lucas. "What sort of a policeman are you?"

"The kind that believes in justice," Lucas said, sipping the scotch.

Vassos gave him a hard look. "Real justice?"

"Yeah, the real kind, where the bad guys get it put to them and the good guys are the heroes."

"We believe that the people responsible for killing my family are here in your city. Will you help me?"

"My orders were to render all possible assistance. And if that means helping to nail the people who killed your family and returning some book to Greece, you got it." He slapped his hands over his knees and pushed himself up off the bed. "We might even get to bend a few rules together."

"We bend rules in Greece too, every now and then."

"Get some rest. We'll start in the morning."

When Lucas had gone, Vassos locked and chained the door. He moved to the telephone, read the instructions under the night table's glass, pressed six, and hearing the tone, dialed.

The voice came on the line after the third ring. Vassos spoke in Greek. "Professor Pericles Levi asked me to telephone you."

At 10:45 the following morning, a Buick with New Jersey license plates turned left onto East Sixty-seventh Street from Third Avenue and parked in front of the Sixteenth Precinct station house. Lucas put the car in park as Vassos, carrying a briefcase, slid out of the passenger seat and stared across the street at a dirty building that had all its shades drawn. Police barricades lined the curb in front of the building, and a sergeant and six officers guarded the entrance.

"What is that building?" Vassos asked, pointing with his hand.

"The Soviet Mission to the United Nations," Lucas said.

"Ah, yes, we too must guard certain locations." He turned and looked over at the station house's facade. "Renaissance with some Romanesque details," he observed.

They hurried up the station house steps and crossed the threshold into the precinct's muster room. Vassos moved slowly about, watching, fascinated: the cop on telephone switchboard duty; policemen moving around; a screaming prisoner with a gauze turban around his head; the high, ornate desk; the radio rasping out police calls; a blackboard covered with hastily chalked notifications; a civilian cleaner polishing the brass railing in front of the desk.

The Desk sergeant called out to Lucas, "Hey, Lou, something came for you in department mail. You gotta sign for it."

Lucas introduced Vassos to the sergeant and the cop on the switchboard. The sergeant handed Lucas a white envelope that had three 49a's stapled to it. Lucas ripped off the receipts, signed two of them, and handed them back to the Desk officer. The third one he slid into his pocket.

The Desk sergeant stapled one of the receipts into the property receipt book. And, holding the second one in front of him, he made an entry in a long, thick ledgerlike book with a gray cloth cover. He noted the time and date of delivery, the name and rank of the member of the force to whom he delivered the envelope, the page number of the property receipt book wherein he had filed the other receipt, and the serial number of the communication.

"What is that book called?" Vassos asked.

"The blotter," Lucas said, tearing open the envelope and taking out two credit cards. "It's used to record the chronological assignments, activities, and developments affecting the command."

"We call ours the service book," Vassos said, following Lucas out from behind the desk.

"Hey, Major," the telephone switchboard cop yelled, "how much does a Greek cop make a month?"

"About three hundred U.S.," Vassos called over his shoulder.

They walked upstairs and stopped in front of the wooden railing leading into the second-floor detective squad room.

Lucas draped his hand over the gate, reached down, and pushed open the release latch. "Welcome," he said, sweeping his hand through the air to include the entire squad room and announcing to the detectives, "This is Major Andreas Vassos of the Hellenic Police Department."

"I'm Ivan Ulanov," the huge detective said as he got out of his chair. "Glad to meet you, Major."

Shaking the king-sized hand, Vassos said, "Ulanov is a Russian name."

"My parents came from Kiev."

"Welcome, Major. I'm Detective Frank Gregory."

Vassos measured the strong Serbian features, the flat cheekbones. "Where did your parents come from?"

Gregory grinned. "I was born in Dubrovnik on the Dalmatian Coast."

"Yugoslavia," Vassos commented, "but Gregory is not a Slav name."

"We shortened it from Goregorievitch."

Mildly confused, Vassos said, "For some reason I thought that your department was composed of Irishmen."

"We got plenty of them, Major." Ulanov laughed.

"Please call me Andreas." He looked to Lucas. "You are fortunate to have men who speak so many languages."

"I don't speak Russian," Ulanov said, going back to his desk.

"And I don't speak Serbo-Croatian," Gregory announced with an expression of mild annoyance.

"Did I say something out of place?" Vassos asked Lucas.

"Not at all," Lucas said, darting a warning glance at Gregory and Ulanov.

Sergeant Roosevelt Grimes came out of his office. Lucas made the introduction. "Roosevelt is my Second Whip."

Vassos's face showed confusion and then understanding. "Ah, yes. We would call Roosevelt the Second Terror. I am the First Terror."

"It's all the same J-O-B, Major," Grimes said, and walked over to Gregory to ask him about one of his fives.

Vassos moved up to the squad room's wall maps. "What are the pins for?"

Lucas said: "The greens are foreign missions, the whites are foreign consulates. There are over forty-five diplomatic missions within the confines of the Sixteenth."

"And the red pins?" Vassos asked.

"They're the Soviet Mission, the Yugoslavian Mission, and the PLO Mission. We maintain around-the-clock details at those locations."

Turning in his seat, Ulanov asked, "How is your department organized, Major?"

Gregory and the Second Whip stopped what they were doing to listen.

"Our department covers the entire country and is commanded by a four-star general who reports directly to the Minister of Public Order. The country is divided into fifty-three prefectures. Each one is commanded by a colonel, except for the Athens and Salonica Prefecture, where a two-star general commands."

"And where are your detectives assigned?" Gregory asked.

"We do not have detectives in the same sense as you do. Our department is divided into three branches: Uniform, Security, and Traffic. A two-star general commands each one. All of our investigations are conducted by the Security branch. This includes criminal, intelligence, and street crime patrol. The men assigned to the Security branch are rotated between the various units."

"I'm sorry to interrupt," Lucas said, stepping over to Vassos and taking his arm, "but Andreas and I have work to do." He led the major into his office.

The Whip's cubicle had a stale smell. Lucas pushed the one window up as high as it would go, turned the fan on high, and pushed the blackboard next to his desk away from the wall. "Correct me if I make a mistake," he said. Taking a piece of chalk, he began to outline the case on the blackboard.

Rolling the chalk in his palm, Lucas said, "Tell me about Iskur."

"Colonel Pappas discovered his body at around two P.M. on the day of the massacre. The pathologist placed the time of death between ten-thirty and eleven o'clock."

Lucas added, "And if I remember correctly, your Colonel Pappas was told by Cuttler that Iskur had visited them in their hotel room that morning."

"That is correct. As I told you last night, Iskur arrived at the hotel at around eight forty-five and remained about one half hour, then left."

"What killed Iskur?"

"One bullet from a 7.65 automatic."

"Is it possible that Cuttler or Simmons killed Iskur?"

"We do not believe that to be possible."

"Okay. Tell my why."

"Several reasons. Iskur was their only hope of escape if something went wrong. That is what Cuttler told Pappas. Therefore, we do not believe they would kill Iskur. There is also the fact that Iskur was killed in his office in Plaka. The old city. Narrow, winding streets. Both Cuttler and Simmons were strangers to Greece. How would they be able to murder someone in Plaka and then drive to Voúla? Impossible. And we suspect Iskur was killed perhaps a bit before the shooting started in Voúla. We know that Iskur provided them with detailed maps of the drive from Athens to Voúla. He even insisted that they make several rehearsal trips. Cuttler told this to Colonel Pappas." Vassos came over to the other side of Lucas's desk and opened his briefcase. "Our forensic investigators discovered fingerprints on Iskur's billfold that did not belong to the victim." He removed copies of the latents and passed them to Lucas. They showed an enlargement of three blurred fingerprint fragments. Individual characteristics were noted on the side of the blowup. A total of nine common characteristics had been discerned among the three fingers.

"We need twelve points for a positive I.D.," Lucas said.

"So do we." Vassos went on to tell him how Cuttler had told Colonel Pappas about the taxi driver who was to have been waiting for them three quarters of a kilometer outside of Voúla. The driver was to have taken them to the Athens airport. Upon hearing this from the prisoner, Colonel Pappas had rushed a detail of men to the location outside of Voúla.

Farmers in the area were questioned. Several of the locals remembered the taxi waiting on the side of the road with its blinkers flashing. A description of the taxi and its driver was obtained. A shepherd recalled a partial license plate number.

It took two days of canvassing every taxi driver who worked the Athens area before the correct one was found. His name was Leykam. Investigation showed that he was an innocent pawn who was hired to pick up a man named Aldridge Long at the Athens airport on the morning of the massacre, drive Long to Iskur's office in Plaka, and then drive to Voúla and pick up two men who would meet him outside of the village. He was to drive these men directly to the airport.

Leykam had worked with a police artist to develop a composite sketch of Aldridge Long. Vassos removed the sketch; it was slipcased in plastic. He handed it to Lucas. "Our men checked the immigration control cards. They quickly found Long's. His passport number was checked with Washington. His address was a convenience postal box that was closed out soon after the passport came. He arrived in Athens on Flight 605 and left the same day on Flight 793 for New York."

Lucas studied the pencil sketch of a middle-aged man with a receding hairline. His nose was thick; he had bushy eyebrows and a heavy chin. "Our Aldridge Long appears to be a careful man who knows how to enter and leave a country undetected." He looked up at Vassos. "I think such a man would take precautions against anyone recognizing him. He'd take steps to see that no one would remember his face."

Vassos dipped into his briefcase and pulled out an eight-by-ten color photograph of a man. "And here's what his passport photo looked like. Your State Department provided this copy." He handed it to Lucas, who studied it with a frown of puzzlement.

"Well, there's a big difference between the man in the composite and the man in this photo. Maybe the sketch shows him in some kind of disguise. Look at the different hairlines."

Vassos pounced on the point quickly. "And it is entirely possible that the man in this photograph is not Aldridge Long, but a substitute. It could be anyone. The man at your embassy in Athens who got this for me explained that in your country you can get a passport through the mail. The photograph on the passport merely has to match the bearer. But if the man who actually traveled on this passport sent in pictures of someone who looked vaguely like him and then used some makeup and whatever to match up exactly with the man in the photograph . . ."

Lucas looked thoughtfully at Vassos. "So we don't know exactly what this guy Long looks like—just that he is a little like the composite sketch and a little like the passport photo."

"And the fingerprints on Iskur's billfold?" Vassos asked. A wily smile came over Lucas's face. "Even dogs and cats gotta get lucky sometimes."

The telephone rang.

The Second Whip was calling from his next-door office. "Lou, this thing that you're doing for the C of D, you going to want a sixty-one number?"

Sergeant Roosevelt Grimes had just made the minimum height requirement for the Job: five feet eight inches. He was a thin man with a bony face, coal-colored skin. He wore his hair flat on his head, and his deep brown eyes seemed too large for their sockets. He was known as one of the best second whips in the Job, with a rare combination of street smarts and paper smarts. Many a detective had been jammed and dumped back into uniform for conducting unauthorized investigations; the only difference between authorized and unauthorized was a piece of paper. If a copy had a sixty-one number assigned to a case, it certified that the case was kosher and the cop's ass would be covered. "Make out a complaint report and give it a number," Lucas said into the mouthpiece.

"And the crime classification?"

"Confidential Investigation/FOA."

"For Other Authorities?"

"Yes. And Roosevelt, thanks."

"You got it, boss."

Lucas hung up and returned his attention to the blackboard. "Andreas, give me the story again, from the top."

When Vassos finished his account, Lucas said, "You really don't have much, do you? Some partial prints that are worthless, a composite that some Athens taxi driver made, a dubious passport photo, and Professor Levi's assumption that Alexander's *Iliad* was found and spirited out of Greece. Not a lot to go on."

Vassos turned solemn. "We also have the sudden, unexplained rise in the standard of living of two policemen and their families, and we have the statements of those families. We also have the amphora and the careful record that Apollonius of Rhodes made out when he stored the casket-copy inside the amphora."

"Ancient hearsay and wishful thinking is all you have, my friend." Lucas slid up onto the edge of his desk; he looked questioningly at Vassos. "Do you have any idea how difficult it is to extradite a person from this country to a demanding country, especially when that person was not in the demanding country at the time of commission of the crime?"

"Difficult, I would imagine," Vassos said quietly.

"Difficult? It's almost impossible."

"My family was taken from me, Teddy, and I want the people responsible purged."

"Punished," Lucas corrected, studying the board. He took in a deep breath, let it out slowly. "Maybe you're right, I don't know. What have your people come up with on Paolo Matrazzo?"

"An important art dealer who died after sending his telegram."

"But the bank draft that his partner sent him from Rome was not used, right?"

"Correct."

"Anything else on Matrazzo?"

"No, only that his body was shipped back to New York."

"Why here?"

"Although he had offices in Rome and London, he was an American and lived in New York City."

Thoughtfully rubbing his hands together, Lucas asked, "And Iskur?"

"Worked for Allied intelligence. Since the war he's roamed the art world buying and selling stolen works."

"Did your people contact the intelligence community about him?"

"Yes, we did. And we were told that they never heard of him."

Walking over to the two lockers that were up against the wall, Lucas said, "Bullshit, those guys wouldn't know the truth if it reared up and bit them on the ass. But I know someone who might be able to help." He worked the black-faced combination lock of the locker that had the word *Supplies* stenciled across the door. He lifted up the handle and opened the door. A small refrigerator was on the floor and two cases of Stolichnaya vodka were stacked on top. Lucas took out two cans of cold beer and passed one to Vassos.

The major peeked into the locker, a look of admiration lighting up his otherwise somber face. "Policemen always find ingenious places to hide their 'supplies.'"

"We drilled a hole in the back for the plug."

"I see that you have a good stock of Russian vodka."

Lucas pushed down the tab and drank. "We have a friend across the street," he said, brushing the back of his hand across his mouth. He leaned over the desk, opened a side drawer, and put the beer can inside the drawer.

Vassos did likewise and pushed the drawer closed. "We do the same thing," he said, smiling at Lucas, "in case a watch commander comes snooping around."

"Do your guys eat on the arm?" Lucas asked.

"I do not know that term."

"You know, a friendly restaurant owner, you work his sector . . ."

"Oh that, of course, they eat on the arm. It is only natural, yes."

"Of course," Lucas said, mimicking his partner's accent. "Did anyone think to ask Professor Levi what the casket-copy is supposed to look like?"

"Papyrus scrolls."

"More than one?"

"They think so, yes. The *Iliad* is composed of twenty-four books, and the experts think that there must have been more than one scroll."

"How many?"

"Nobody knows for sure. In the middle of the nineteenth century a scroll containing the twenty-fourth book was unearthed in Egypt. It was from about the same period. It had survived and was in excellent condition."

"I don't know anything about scrolls," Lucas said, rubbing his jaw, studying the black slate, "but it's my guess that you don't get them unrolled at your local stationery store. Which means that our boy has got to go to a specialist, someone trained to unroll them, and that means that he is going to have to come out into the open to get it done. That's one avenue we're most definitely going to have to look at."

"Any other recommendations?"

"I think that we should take another look at Iskur and Matrazzo. There is a chance that whoever stole your book was connected to one or both of them, somehow, somewhere in the past." He reached over the top of the desk, opened the drawer, and took out the two beer cans. He passed one to Vassos.

They drank beer, studied the blackboard.

"You are beginning to talk as though you believe the casket-copy exists," Vassos said.

Lucas responded quietly, "Dead bodies don't lie. You got yourself a homicide, that I don't question. I just doubt that some book could have survived down through all the centuries. But, it's your game; you threw the ball into play and I'll run with it."

"Will we also examine the criminal records of Cuttler, Simmons, and this Denny McKay?"

"Of course. There has got to be a link there. But you know, Andreas, one of our biggest problems is going to be getting hold of an expert on ancient writings. Someone who can keep his mouth shut."

Vassos brushed his mouth with the back of his hand. "I can help with that. Professor Levi gave me the name of a reliable scholar to contact, an expert on ancient writings. I telephoned last night after you left the hotel room. We have an appointment at three o'clock today."

"Who is this guy?"

"*She* is curator of Ancient and Medieval Manuscripts at the Pierpont Morgan Library."

"Good," Lucas said, and then called out, "Ivan."

Ivan Ulanov sauntered into the office. "Yeah, Lou?"

"See if our friend can meet us in ten minutes, the usual place," Lucas said.

Ulanov picked up the telephone on the Whip's desk and dialed an outside number. When someone answered, the big detective began to speak in flawless Russian. Ulanov spoke for about four minutes, interspersing his conversation with laughter.

Ulanov hung up. "Twenty minutes," he said to Lucas as he strolled from the office.

"I do not understand," Vassos said, making circles with his hands. "He does not speak Russian, then he speaks Russian. Gregory is born in Yugoslavia and he does not speak the language. You are Greek, you do not speak Greek. It is all very strange."

Lucas drained his can, bent it in half, put it into the wastebasket, and pushed it under the trash so that it was hidden from sight. "You have to understand the Job, Andreas. We have a problem when it comes to foreign languages. Most of our supposed linguists are assigned to the Intelligence Division. They get extra money, they have weekends off, they don't generally pull night duty; it's a sweet detail. Only problem is, they don't speak the languages that they're supposed to. They are the lovers and relatives of important people in and out of the Job. But when someone is needed to speak Russian, or Serbo-Croatian, or Greek, the department has to reach out into the trenches."

"And the people in the trenches conveniently forget to speak their mother tongue unless they are asked to by someone in the same trench," Vassos said. "That is sad."

Ranks of flowers bathed Park Avenue's center mall in a rainbow of summer colors. Taxis honked their familiar symphony; rushing people packed the sun-drenched streets; office workers ate their lunches, lounging around outside the fountains of glass office towers. To the south, the golden spire of the Helmsley Building looked down on the magnificent avenue.

Andreas Vassos stood in the lobby of the Chemical Bank Building in awe, trying to absorb the full impact of the lush, exotic greenery. "I have never seen so many plants inside one building," he said to no one in particular, moving over to where Lucas and Ulanov were standing, watching the passing parade. "Who do we wait for?" Vassos whispered to Lucas.

Before the Whip could answer, Ulanov said, "There he is," and quickly moved off, leaving the building.

"He's going to meet a Soviet cop," Lucas confided, standing in the lobby, watching the detective melt into the crowd.

"KGB?" Vassos whispered.

"A cop like us," Lucas said. "He's our liaison with the mission."

"Why do you have such an elaborate method to meet?"

Lucas shrugged. "They have their ways, and we have ours. We get along fine; occasionally we do each other small favors."

"Such as Russian vodka?" A sly twinkle brought his eyes to life, and he added, "On the arm."

Vassos smiled, proud of his correct use of NYPD slang.

"Something like that," Lucas added, smiling back at him.

Ulanov mixed in with the crowd waiting for the light to change. When it turned to green, he was immediately caught up in the surging mass of pedestrians.

Lucas followed his bobbing head across the avenue.

"Where is the Russian policeman?" Vassos asked.

"Mixed in with the crowd."

"What are you asking him to do for you?"

"Dig up whatever information he can on Matrazzo and Orhan Iskur."

Ulanov reached the other side of the avenue. He did an about-face and waited for the light to change. When it did, he crossed back across the avenue.

"Message delivered," Ulanov said, coming over to them. He shook out a cigarette and offered one to Vassos.

Vassos was about to take one when a memory burst into his consciousness. Soula and Stephanos had always been after him to stop smoking. "Greek men and their damn cigarettes," Soula would complain. Stephanos would leave him drawings of birds, each with the same note scrawled on it: *Daddy, birds don't smoke.* His eyes brimmed over. Pinching the lids together, he turned away and said, "No, thank you, Ivan. I do not smoke."

5

Management Information Systems Division was on the seventh floor of police headquarters at One Police Plaza, near Wall Street and City Hall. Rows of pentagon-shaped machines lined the glass-enclosed office. In the adjoining room technicians sat in front of consoles, typing in access codes, demanding information from the silent warehouses of data. Lucas signed the visitors log for both of them, and Vassos had a sticker pasted on the lapel of his jacket that read: VISITOR. The duty officer then assigned a thin, bookish fellow who wore a small yarmulka pinned to his thinning hair to assist them.

They stood behind the technician, watching him type in the necessary codes. Within seconds the printer to the right of the console started churning out reams of paper.

"Are all of your criminal records on tape?" Vassos asked.

"Practically everything in the Job is on tape. Even our roll calls are computerized."

The technician ripped off the printout and passed it to Lucas. "Here are the arrest records, Lou."

Lucas studied them. Frank Simmons and George Cuttler had extensive records. He passed them to Vassos.

The major looked them over and passed them back. "I'm not familiar with your terms."

Taking them back, Lucas said, "Simmons had eight previouses: robberies, burglaries, a couple of felonious assaults. He did three years on a seven-and-a-half-year sentence for armed robbery. Cuttler had six falls and did eight years inside for manslaughter. Both of them have falls for homicide and manslaughter."

"They do not appear to have been the arty type, do they?" Vassos observed.

"They certainly do not," Lucas agreed, turning to the technician. "Are the nineteens on tape?"

"Yes, Lou."

"Dig out their associates on each collar," Lucas said.

The computer man swung around and danced his fingers over the keyboard.

Watching the bright green screen, Vassos asked, "What's nineteen?"

"A Prisoner's Modus Operandi and Pedigree Sheet. Every time someone is arrested, the arresting officer prepares one. It lists how the perp committed the crime and any special characteristics of his MO, along with his physical description and his associates on that collar."

"That is our S six form," Vassos offered.

The printer chugged out paper.

"What is the difference between your UF and DD forms?"

"UF stands for Uniform Force, and DD for Detective Division. I suppose that your S forms are used by Security Division."

"That is correct."

The technician handed Lucas the printouts.

"Is there someplace where we can work?" Lucas asked the civilian.

Next to the console area was a bare, cheerless room, with one long table and several chairs, walls and ceilings muffled by acoustic tile, floored with black-and-white linoleum, and windowless save for a half-silvered window on one wall that afforded a view of the work area.

Lucas placed the spread sheets on the table. He took a lined pad out of the folder and started to write down the names of associates who had been arrested with Simmons, Cuttler, and Denny McKay. This done, he left the room and gave the list to the technician. "I'd like their records too."

The computer man adjusted his yarmulka. "And then you're going to want the associates of the associates."

"War is hell, kid," Lucas said, going back inside.

Each of the criminal records came with several sheets of grainy, black-and-white photographs of the prisoner. Lucas arranged the records alphabetically. He wrote the names on the pad, along with each date of arrest, the crime, and the names of associates listed on that arrest.

Vassos examined the list of names. "They appear to be mostly Irish names. Does that mean anything?"

A deathly pallor came over Lucas's face and his lips set in a hard line. "Denny McKay is the boss of the Purple Gang."

"Who are they?"

"Scum! The gang evolved from a mob founded in the twenties. Mostly Irish hoods who went in for strong-arm stuff. Our department intelligence people reported that sometime in the seventies they began to do contract killings. They were recently discovered by the newspapers, who dubbed them the "Westies" because they come from the West Side of Manhattan."

Vassos was standing, his palms flat on the table. "Do you think they would take an overseas job?"

"If the money was right and the right guy gave the order, yes."

"You seem to hate them."

"I do," Lucas said, shuffling through the sheets, pulling out Denny McKay's folder.

An unasked question formed on Vassos's lips.

Lucas said, "McKay is fifty-six years old; he's taken two collars. His first one when he was twenty-one, right after the Korean War." He pulled out McKay's nineteens. "On his first arrest he presented his army separation papers as identification." He read from the report, "U.S. Army, serial number, served active duty May nine, 1950, to January fourteen, 1953. First Cavalry Division.

"Strange. He gets out of the army and takes his first fall for a burglary when he stole quote 'a seventeenth-century medallion pendant studded with rubies and inlaid with cloisonné enamel.' Appears McKay acquired an interest in art soon after he got out of the army." Lucas wrote something on a piece of paper and turned his back to Vassos. He took out his roll of expense money, palmed two tens and a five, and left the room. He found the computer man having a private conversation with a female computer person near the water cooler. Interrupting, Lucas slid his arm around the computer man's shoulder and steered him away from the woman. "I'd like the sixty-ones on these arrests." He handed the man a sheet of paper listing the arrests of McKay, Simmons, Cuttler, and their associates.

"You want the Complaint Reports on all of these?" the technician asked with typical civil service reluctance to do any more work than the rules required. Lucas discreetly slipped the expense money into the waiting palm. "Here, let me buy you lunch."

Closing his fingers around the money, the technician said, "And then you'll be wanting the sixty-ones on the associates of the associates."

"Exactly. Send them to me through department mail." Lucas gave the clerk one of his cards and then stuck his head back in the room.

"Andreas, let's you and me go see our scroll expert, and after that, we'll pay Denny McKay a visit."

Her white linen suit had padded shoulders, a V neckline, and hidden buttons. Her honey-colored hair was pulled back to form a single braid that started near the crown of her head. She wore long black-and-white summer earrings. Her sleek hairstyle, high cheekbones, piercing green eyes, and exquisite mouth gave her face a classic look. She was quite tall and had a striking figure.

"Andreas Vassos?" she asked, extending her hand. She had been waiting for them near the coatroom of the Morgan Library.

"Yes," Vassos said, taking her extended hand and introducing his partner. "This is my colleague, Lieutenant Teddy Lucas."

"Hello to both of you," she said. "I'm Dr. Katina Wright, the Morgan's manuscript conservator."

"Nice to meet you," Lucas said, guessing that she was in her late thirties.

"Shall we go downstairs?" She made a sign to the security guard, who opened the door directly in front of the coatroom. Her basement office was a glass cubicle filled with books and rolling tray cabinets. Two small plants and a stuffed panda adorned her desk.

Lowering herself into her chair, she motioned them into seats and said, "Dr. Levi's telephone call and letter intrigued me. I gather you gentlemen are on the trail of the casket-copy."

"Yes," Vassos said, asking, "Didn't Dr. Levi explain everything to you?"

"He did, but I'd prefer to hear it again from you two. Professor Levi has a tendency to speak and write in rather oblique terms."

Vassos got up from his seat and closed her office door. He returned and told her the story of Voúla and about their search for Alexander's *Iliad*.

"Matrazzo's famous telegram was the last hint that the casket-copy might have been found," she said.

"Could it have survived all those centuries?" Lucas asked.

She looked at the New York City detective. "Of course it could have survived. The Dead Sea scrolls survived, and they were written between the first century B.C. and the first half of the first century A.D. An entire library of scrolls was unearthed in Herculaneum in 1754."

"How many scrolls made up the casket-copy?" Lucas asked.

"We have no way of knowing for sure. They only wrote on one side of the papyrus and the scrolls were not very long. Maybe fifteen scrolls, who knows? Maybe one for each book." She looked at Vassos. "Did you see the amphora that was found in Orhan Iskur's shop?"

"Yes, Professor Levi insisted that I examine it," Vassos said.

A slight smile crossed her face. "Yes, he would. Tell me about it, everything that you can remember."

Vassos described the tall storage jar in detail. "It was half-filled with black sand, and the inside was lined with some kind of thick materials."

"Cartonnage," she said to herself.

"What is that?" Lucas asked.

"Papyrus paper," she said, looking up at them. "It's made from layers of papyrus that have been stuck together, sort of a papier-mâché. The Egyptians used it as mummy casing. They would take it from the garbage dumps. Cartonnage is a wonderful preservative because it is airtight and therefore makes the contents immune to the effects of moisture. The ancients went to great lengths to preserve their scrolls. They were aware that papyrus was vulnerable to insects and moisture, so they used cylindrical containers of wood and ivory to store their scrolls. They treated papyrus with cedarwood oil as a preservative and insecticide." She again turned her attention to Vassos. "Did Professor Levi conduct tests on the black sand?"

"Yes. He told me that the sand definitely came from the island of Thíra," Vassos said.

Lucas sat forward with his hands clasped between his legs. "Katina, I'm a cop and I think like a cop, so please bear with me."

"I shall forbear, Teddy," she said with a pleasant smile.

"If we should get lucky and get our hands on the casket-copy, how can we be sure that it's not a forgery? I read where the Egyptians used to make phony trinkets to sell to the Greeks and Romans."

"There have always been dishonest antiques dealers. Tomb robbery is the world's second oldest profession, and forging antiquities is the third," she said, "but today we have many different techniques to establish provenance. Alexander's *Iliad* would almost certainly have a colophon, an inscription at the end that identified the scribe and the date and place where it was written. And, more than likely, it would also have a sentence or two stating that it was prepared for Alexander, son of Philip, King of Macedonia."

"Are there samples of Aristotle's handwriting that we can use for comparison?" Lucas asked.

"Unfortunately, none of the originals of his works are extant," she said.

"Then we still cannot be sure it is not a forgery, can we?" Lucas asked.

"The critical principle when establishing the provenance of a writing is to compare the rhythmical patterns of the meter to the corpus of the author's work."

"What about carbon dating?" Vassos asked.

"It is not precise enough," she answered. "Carbon dating can only place a thing within a few hundred years. There are more exact techniques."

Lucas glanced at his Greek partner. "If someone did come into possession of the scrolls, how would he go about getting them unrolled?"

"Any major museum or library. And there are private laboratories."

"But he would want to have the job done without anyone knowing about it, wouldn't he?" Lucas said. "If he went to a museum or a library, the word would be out that he had the casket-copy."

"You keep saying 'he,' Teddy. A woman might have them, did you ever think of that? And yes, I suppose that the person who did have the scrolls would want to be discreet."

"Is there some special machine that is used to unroll them?" Lucas asked.

She smiled. "Yes. Would you like to see what it looks like?"

"Very much," Vassos answered.

She led them from her office along the aisle that ran between the high workbenches. Four young women sat on stools peering through large magnifying glasses, laboriously restoring ancient parchments and codices. The policemen paused to watch them. One woman was gingerly brushing flaking vegetable pigments off a papyrus. Another was restoring the ink of an ancient script. Katina looked over the policemen's shoulders. "Martha is working on a manuscript by Poggio that was written in 1425."

Martha looked up from her work and smiled.

"Hello," Lucas said.

"Hello," Martha replied, looking back down through the glass at her work.

Katina led them to the end of the restoration area and stopped before a bench crammed with the tools of her trade. "Here is our scroll unroller," she announced, placing her hand on the machine.

"A humidifier?" Lucas said, unable to hide his surprise.

"A *super* humidifier," she corrected. "We added a hose so that we can direct the vapor into the scroll."

"How does it work?" Lucas asked.

She thought for a moment and answered. "When papyrus is kept dry it has remarkable powers of survival. But it becomes brittle when desiccated, and then it has to be moistened in order to regain its flexibility so that it may be safely handled, flattened, and mounted in permanent form.

"Since it is so brittle in the dry state, the first thing that we have to do is to relax it by moisture before any attempt is made to unroll it; otherwise the scroll would break into many pieces. We start the relaxing process by wrapping the roll loosely in several layers of damp blotting paper and then setting it aside for an hour or so on a sheet of glass. By that time the outside of the scroll has become sufficiently limp so that we can manipulate it without having it crack; then the unrolling can begin. We then put them on blotting paper to absorb excess moisture. There's a lot more to it, but those are the basics." She shrugged her shoulders and smiled. "This process is very, very slow and it must be done with the utmost care. But, after umpty-ump centuries, what's a little more time?"

"Wouldn't the water run the ink or get absorbed in the blotting paper?" Lucas asked, unable to conceal his fascination.

"Not at all," she said. "We immerse manuscripts completely without that happening. Carbon inks present no complications and even the fugitive iron inks leave a tracing of rust when they decompose that is unaffected by a slight degree of moisture." She studied the policemen. "Any more questions?"

Shaking his head no, Lucas thought: beautiful and smart.

She continued: "Once the papyrus is flat it must be dried without delay by changing the blotting paper several times in the course of a few hours. As a protection against molds we sterilize the papyrus by pressing it with thymol-impregnated blotting paper for several days. After that is done it may be mounted passe-partout between two sheets of glass."

"Does it have to be glass?" Lucas asked.

"Absolutely," she said. "Acrylic gives off static electricity. Papyrus is composed of cellulose and under magnification looks a little like shredded wheat. The electricity in acrylic compounds would pull the fibers apart and destroy the document."

"If I had the casket-copy," Lucas asked, "and I wanted to sell it secretly, how would I go about doing it?"

"Well, since you obviously would not have the necessary export papers, that would eliminate the auction houses, museums, and important libraries; you would be left with a handful of rare book dealers accustomed to dealing with pieces of such magnitude. And, of course, private collectors."

"How many dealers?" Lucas asked.

"In New York, five or six, and an equal number in London and Rome."

"Would you be able to provide us with their names?" Vassos asked.

"Of course," she said.

Lucas leaned against the workbench, watching the restorers peering through their portable glasses. "Katina? How much would the casket-copy be worth in dollars and cents?"

She shook her head in dismay, studying the policemen. "You both have no idea what it is that you're looking for, do you?" She turned and hurried back to her office.

The policemen looked at each other, turned abruptly, and followed her.

Her back was against a tray cabinet, her hands out at her sides tucked into the tray's thin handles. One leg was crossed over the other, the linen outlining her shapely legs, molding her ample breasts into the white material. "Please sit, gentlemen."

She reminded Lucas of a teacher about to lose her patience, but her calm voice reflected her easygoing logic. "Teddy. Andreas. Alexander's *Iliad* would be the greatest archaeological find ever unearthed. It would be worth more than all the treasures dug out of Egypt; worth more than all the property looted from Etruscan tombs; worth more than all the booty stolen from the Americas." Her hands came out of the handles.

"Why would it be so valuable?" Lucas asked quietly, taken aback by the force of her beauty.

"Several reasons," she said, sitting down. "Anything connected with Alexander and Aristotle would inflame people's imaginations and give the item great intrinsic value. But the main reason would be the ancients' tradition of oral history." She crossed one leg over the other.

"I don't understand," Lucas said.

"The concept of silent reading was unknown during classical times. Everyone read aloud."

"You're telling me that when Alexander read his *Iliad* to himself, he read aloud?"

"That is exactly what I'm telling you. Silent reading was an invention of Christian monasticism in the fifth century A.D. Homeric poems were handed down orally through several centuries. The first written text of the *Iliad* was made in Athens in the middle of the sixth century B.C. And copies were not duplicated or circulated, they were used only for references." The phone on her desk gave out a muted ring but she ignored it and continued.

"In ancient times there was little if any punctuation or word division. Texts were read aloud and often did not indicate a change of speaker. This meant that the reader had a difficult time and in many cases made up characters or changed lines as he went along. The first formal Greek grammar was prepared around 130 B.C., and Latin did not begin as a written language until the third century B.C. Formal grammar throughout the rest of Europe did not come about until the Middle Ages."

"Katina," Lucas pleaded, "what has grammar got to do with the value of the casket-copy?"

"Don't you see?" she asked impatiently. "We know that Aristotle tutored Alexander between 343 and 336 B.C. Which would mean that the casket-copy would have to have been copied down during those seven years."

"So?" Vassos asked.

"It is believed that the *Iliad* that has come down to us today is not the same one that Homer wrote, or even the same one that Aristotle copied for Alexander. What we have today is a corrupted version of Homer."

Lucas looked puzzled. "And why is that?"

"Texts copied by hand are prone to corruption. If four policemen were to copy your police regulations from memory, not one of them would be correct; each copy would be slightly different. It's the same with the *Iliad*. Storytellers would add their own words and thoughts, scribes who did not like a passage would make up their own; if an ancient reader found a passage difficult to understand, he'd change it. Every time the *Iliad* was told, it came out differently." She took in a deep breath. "All scholars consider the *Iliad* to be one of the most important works ever written. It is, without question, one of the essential underpinnings of our literary tradition. To have a copy, or even a portion of a copy, that dates from the fourth century B.C. would be a priceless find."

Vassos cast his eyes downward. "Katina, you understand we intend to return the casket-copy to Greece?"

"Yes, I know that," she said.

"Will you help us?" Lucas asked.

"Help you," she echoed. "That was decided before you arrived here. You see, gentlemen, Professor Levi is my father." She stood up, the look on her face saying no further glimpses into her private life would be allowed. "Would you like me to go with you when you visit the book dealers?"

"Yes," Lucas said, "you could be of help. Most of the dealers know you, don't they?"

"Yes, they do," she said, paging through her appointment book. "I have nothing I can't change scheduled for the remainder of this week. When would you like to start?"

"As soon as possible," Lucas said.

"I'll prepare a list of the dealers and telephone for appointments," she said.

"Will they see us?" Lucas asked.

She smiled. "It would be most unusual for any of them to decline to see the Curator of Ancient and Medieval Manuscripts of the Morgan Library."

The Den was located on the west side of Ninth Avenue, between Forty-eighth and Forty-ninth streets. It was on a dilapidated block of abandoned tenements and boarded-up storefronts. Lucas parked the Buick three blocks away on the east side of Ninth Avenue.

McKay's hangout was a dingy West Side saloon on the ground floor of an abandoned four-story tenement with boarded-up windows. A pizzeria was one door uptown from the bar. Two derelicts shared a pint of muscatel in a nearby doorway. Cars continuously pulled up in front of the bar and double-parked; men rushed into the bar, stayed some minutes, and rushed back out to their cars.

"A lot of activity," Lucas observed, slumped down behind the wheel. He slid his arm over the back of the velour-covered seat, observing the foreign cut of Vassos's suit. "How'd you like to take a look inside that bar, let me know what's happening. If any of them so much as got a whiff of me, they'd make me for a cop."

Vassos reached inside his jacket and unsnapped his holster and ammo pouch. He stuffed them under the passenger seat. "I'll see you soon, partner."

Lucas grabbed his arm. "Andreas, observe and report, nothing more, okay?"

"You have it, Lou."

"You got it, Lou," Lucas corrected him, smiling.

Vassos reflexively shuddered at the artificial cold of the air-conditioning as he entered the darkened bar. The smell of beer mixed with a thick fog of cigarette smoke. Music blared from a jukebox. To the left of the entrance was a long bar; on the right, six leatherette booths.

Vassos moved inside and over to an empty stool at the end of the bar near the entrance, ignoring the inquisitive looks coming his way. Several men stood at the bar drinking and talking in lowered tones. The bartender, a grungy man with a day's growth of beard, came over to Vassos. "What'll it be, pal?"

Putting on a heavy Greek accent, Vassos ordered a beer, the same brand he'd consumed earlier that day at the precinct. He leaned forward, resting his arms on the bar, looking straight ahead, minding his own business. An open door at the end of the bar led into a kitchen. Vassos could see black pans hanging on the wall and part of a large commercial stove. A wide aisle separated the bar from the tables.

The bartender put down a beer and moved off.

From the corner of his eye, Vassos recognized a face from the mug shots he'd seen at police headquarters. Denny McKay, the head of the Purple Gang, was sitting in the last booth. Four other men were crowded into the booth with him. Although McKay was sitting, he looked much bigger than he did in his police photographs. Half-glasses were perched on his nose and wisps of gray hair fell untidily over the collar of his shirt. The pocket of his short-sleeved shirt was stuffed with pens; he wore white socks and sandals.

Brawny men kept coming into the saloon, each of them stopping to pay respects to McKay. Some of these men walked past McKay into the back room, stayed several minutes, came out, and left.

Vassos saw the bartender make eye contact with McKay. The man behind the bar picked up a towel and began to wipe his way over to the policeman. "You from around here, pal?"

"I am from Greece," Vassos announced in an accent.

"You, er, live in Greece or over here, in the States?"

"I live in Kaloni, a small village on Kriti," he said, using the Greek word for the island of Crete.

"What brings you to the States?"

Vassos saw McKay watching, chewing on his cigarette's filter. "A woman. She was beautiful, the kind of woman you want to do it to the moment you see her. And she was a virgin."

"What happened?"

"What happened?" Vassos echoed with a philosophical shrug of shoulders. "I wanted to fuck her so I became engaged to marry her, and after I did it to her for a month, I got bored with her and broke the engagement. Her brothers are hunting me, and I must stay out of Greece until my family makes things right."

The bartender made the universal money sign with his fingers. "It's gonna cost you."

Vassos nodded.

The bartender moved off, looked over at McKay. Vassos saw the bartender's head tilt and McKay's facial expression relax.

Vassos slid off his stool and, making his way along the bar, asked the bartender, "The toilet?"

"Straight ahead," the man behind the stick said, drawing a draft beer.

Moving past the entrance to the kitchen with his nonthreatening eyes cast downward, Vassos entered the back room. There was a shuffleboard in the center of it and groups of men sitting in booths. Conversation stopped. Tough, hostile-looking men studied the policeman. There were two doors on his left. Vassos opened the first one and discovered a large closet with a skeletonized staircase leading upward. The banister, risers, and stringers were intact, but the treads, the steps one normally stood on, had been removed.

"What the fuck you looking at, pally?"

Vassos turned. Two ugly men were staring him down. "I need the toilet, please."

"Next door, pal," the uglier of the two barked.

The tiny, ill-lit bathroom reeked of urine. Vomit splattered the wall and sink, and soggy cigarette butts clogged the urinal. Vassos stepped up to the trough and urinated. He zipped up and meekly pushed past them out into the saloon. The dank bar was a welcome relief after the stench of the toilet.

He finished his beer standing up, left two dollars on the bar, and walked out into the sunlight. He turned left, passed a group of men and the open-front pizzeria, and walked three blocks north before turning east.

The Buick came to a stop alongside some parked cars. Lucas leaned across the seat and pushed open the door. "Well?" he asked as Vassos slid inside.

Vassos gave him a brief report and told him about the closet with the staircase without stairs.

"That's an old trick used by narcotics dealers," Lucas said. "They removed the treads so that any cops who visit them will have to grip the banister with both hands and climb up on the risers or the stringers that support the bannister. The bad guys wait on top." He glanced at the man in the passenger seat. "I'd say McKay's got something going on up there that he doesn't want the good guys to know about. Well, we're just going to have to make it our business to find out what."

Sergeant Roosevelt Grimes, the Second Whip of the Sixteenth Squad, had a steel plate in his head compliments of an overzealous white cop who had enjoyed cracking black heads with his nightstick during the Columbia riots. Before the black undercover officer could utter the code word that would have identified him as a member of the force, the uniformed cop beat him unconscious.

It ain't easy being a black undercover in *Nueva York.*

Grimes was sitting behind his cluttered desk massaging his forehead when Lucas came in and flopped into a chair.

"You got pain, Roosevelt?"

"It's the heat, Lou."

"And in the winter it's the cold. Why the hell don't you throw in your papers and sail off into the sunset? No more fives, no pressure."

"I got two more kids to put through college." He opened the side drawer, took out a bottle of orange pills, popped two into his mouth, swallowed, and asked, "What's up, Lou?"

Lucas, lifting up out of his seat, handed his Second Whip a slip of paper. "I want you to get me a copy of Denny McKay's army record and have a couple of our guys try and locate any relatives of a guy named Paolo Matrazzo. He went DOA on a Greek island that the Greeks call Thíra, but the rest of the world calls Santorini."

"When did this Matrazzo guy pack it in?"

"Nineteen thirty-nine."

Grimes looked at the paper and then up at the Whip. "This caper connected to the CI you're doing for the C of D?"

"Yes it is, but I can't fill you in on it yet."

"You want a list of McKay's duty stations too?"

"I want everything."

"You got it," Grimes said, sliding the paper into the border of his desk blotter.

Detective John Leone, a handsome man with black hair, dreamy eyes, and a bushy mustache he referred to as his carpet sweeper, had a partner named Jack Owens who stood a hair over six feet and whose chest and shoulders flowed smoothly into a broad expanse that resembled a minor league dam. Owens was a black man who the guys in the Squad called Big Jay. When Lucas came out into the squad room ten minutes later, he found Leone pontificating to Vassos, Ulanov, Gregory, and Big Jay.

"You guys ever wonder how women piss in them little cups?" Leone asked. "I mean, they got nothing to aim with. I've been thinking about that ever since I took my physical last week."

"How do you figure they do it?" asked Big Jay.

"Well," Leone began, "they must hold the cup under their pussy and sort of get the range, maybe spritz a few drops, and then, when they're on the target, they give it a good squirt."

Ulanov turned back to the typewriter. "This place is funner than *Mad* magazine."

Big Jay placed a gentle hand on Ulanov's shoulder. "Don't you find yourself always thinking about women? How you're going to score the next one, how she's going to open her legs for you?"

Ulanov looked up into the smiling black face. "Naw," he said seriously, "pussy makes me sneeze."

Lucas motioned Vassos into his office. The Whip flipped open the case folder and saw that Grimes had inserted a copy of the complaint report marked: Confidential Investigation/FOA. He thought about his

Second Whip and wondered what it must be like to have children to worry about, to work so hard to help them get a start in life. He decided that it must be wonderful. He jotted reminder notes on the inside flap: *1. Russian info re: M and I; 2. McKay's army record; 3. Old 61's on Purple Gang; 4. PM's relatives.*

When Vassos came into the office, Lucas said, "I want to do some research on the casket-copy. I'm going to the public library. Want to come with me?"

"I would like to, Teddy, but I must report to my embassy. They want to see me to make sure that I am alive and well." His finger traced the figure eight on the edge of the desk. "Would you like to have dinner with me tonight? The night clerk at my hotel is a Greek and he has told me of this restaurant in Astoria."

Lucas checked his watch. "What time would you want to go?"

"Late. Around ten."

"I'll pick you up at nine-thirty," Lucas said, moving out from behind his desk.

She slid out of the bed and padded into the bathroom. The warm golden glow of a summer evening slipped through the blinds and threw bars of light on her naked body. Lucas watched her lissome form move gracefully over the carpet. Long legs, well-developed figure, creamy skin, auburn hair. Her first name was Joan. Her last was Karsten. Six months ago Lucas had been in the supermarket reaching for a jar of peanut butter. She had been reaching for grape jelly. He did not want involvements; she wanted a weekly matinee. It had seemed like a perfect arrangement at the time.

He raised himself up on his elbows and watched her come back to the bed. He liked her goose pimply nipples and her delicate brown pubic hair. She stepped silently into her underpants and hooked on her bra. Her glum expression told him that something was on her mind. She lowered herself onto the edge of the bed and caressed his face.

"Teddy," she began, "you're a nice man, and you've been up front with me from the beginning, so please, please don't misunderstand what I'm going to say."

He fluffed the pillow up under his head, sat up higher, and waited.

Her eyes fell on the sheets. "I think that from now on we should use condoms. I have no way of knowing how many others you are seeing or who they are seeing, and, well, it just gets so complicated . . ."

Looking into her anxious eyes, Lucas thought: we've fucked up our criminal justice system; we've fucked up our ozone layer; we've fucked up our ecological balance; and now, we're fucking up sex. Only man could be such an asshole. He brushed a strand of hair from her brow. "Do you make your husband use a condom?"

She laughed. "Mr. Wonderful? No need to worry about him. Mr. Wonderful's interests, in descending order, are: making money, football, basketball, baseball, and expensive cigars. Once every month or so he'll roll on top of me, grunt, and roll off."

"Why don't you leave him?"

"Because I'm forty-seven years old and scared. And because all the Prince Charmings have been taken, except you." She reached out and gave his penis a playful squeeze. "You wouldn't by any chance be interested in a more meaningful relationship?"

"I hate that word."

"Which one, meaningful or relationship?"

"Both of them," he said, reaching over the side of the bed, groping for his underwear.

"Will I see you next week?" she asked, a concerned edge to her voice.

Sitting up and heaving his feet onto the floor, he answered, "Yes."

"Teddy, may I ask you a personal question?"

Unsure eyes darted to her. "What?"

"Why me? You're a handsome man. You're a gentleman. Why get yourself involved in a dead-end relationship? There are a lot of available women out there looking for a man like you."

Joan was not the first woman who had asked Teddy Lucas that question. His stock answer was that his wife had left him because she felt that marriage was stifling her. He didn't think he'd ever tell anyone the truth; it was still too painful. Before he could give her his standard reply, Joan fell on her knees between his legs and hugged him around his waist. "I look forward to our weekly rendezvous."

"Me too," he said, pressing her head to his stomach. "Are you pressed for time?"

She looked up at him and smiled knowingly. "I have a few minutes," she said, pushing him back down on the bed.

After Joan left, he spread the sheet out over the bed, went into the bathroom, and showered. He dried himself off and telephoned the Forty-second Street branch of the public library. It was open until 8:45 that evening. He picked up the phone and dialed the C of D's direct number at One Police Plaza.

Edgeworth's gruff voice came on the line. Lucas brought him up to date on the conduct of the investigation.

"What's your feel for the case?" Edgeworth asked.

"I'm still not sure if I'm investigating a flight of fancy or if there is a real case to be made. But I'll tell you this much, Chief, we're a long way off from handing anyone up for extradition to Greece."

"What kind of guy is Vassos?"

"He's a good guy. Seems to know his stuff."

"Well, be sure to keep me informed."

"Ten-four, boss," Lucas said, using the affirmative police code signal.

"Yes, sir," C of D Edgeworth said into the telephone. "That is correct. Lieutenant Lucas just reported in to me, and he was not very optimistic about the course of the investigation. . . . Yes, Mr. Hayden, I most certainly will keep you posted."

Edgeworth thoughtfully replaced the receiver. He stared at the instrument, then snapped it back to his ear and dialed the PC's centrex number. "This is the chief of detectives. Is the boss still in the building?"

Police Commissioner Franklin Vaughn's ruddy complexion brightened when his C of D entered his office. He waved Edgeworth into one of the chairs arranged in front of his desk. "Your people did an outstanding job on that Rabbi Goldstein homicide, Timmy."

"A hanger, boss. Four local Jew haters got their loads on and went hunting. They left enough physical evidence behind for us to track them to Mars and back."

Vaughn reached into the bottom drawer of his desk and came up with a bottle of scotch. "Want a taste?"

"No thanks," Edgeworth said, watching the PC pour some into his coffee mug. A tingling sensation stung his lips and mouth. Maybe just one? No! He hadn't picked up a drink in four years and he wasn't going to today. He quickly checked the time: six-thirty. Shit! He'd miss the 7:00 P.M. meeting at St. Claire's. Now he'd have to rush uptown.

Vaughn drank, clutched the mug to his stomach. "You still on the wagon, Timmy?"

"Yes. One day at a time."

Vaughn shook his head. "Ya gotta be able to control the hard stuff, Timmy. I can stop any time I want to stop. I only take a few short belts now and then to help me relax. I think better with a few under my belt."

"Right, boss." He watched the PC take another swig.

"What's on your mind?"

"It bothers me that we have to report to this guy Hayden at the State Department on the conduct of one of our cases."

"The Greek thing?"

"Yes."

Pouring more scotch, Vaughn said, "The white-shirt boys are interested in this one, Timmy. Big diplomatic hullabaloo."

"We could be jeopardizing the integrity of the case by reporting to them. They're whores. We have no way of knowing what they're doing with the information we're feeding them."

"It's their case, Tim ol' boy."

"That's my point. Why toss it to us when there are at least six federal agencies with jurisdiction? It doesn't make sense."

"Who knows? Who cares? Maybe they felt that we could handle it more expe . . . ex . . . faster." The word was out in the Job: the PC was on the sauce. The sharks smelled blood and were circling; the sniping had started. Vaughn had been dubbed the King of Nowhere.

The PC's head shot up. "Keep me informed."

"Right, boss."

Edgeworth started to stand. Vaughn said, "Wait a minute," and passed him a slip of paper that he had taken from under his desk blotter. It contained the name, shield number, tax registry number, and present command of a female detective.

"When you get the chance," Vaughn said, "move her into the Bond and Forgery Squad."

"B and F is three over their quota now."

"The lady is Congressman Berns's girlfriend."

Edgeworth frowned in an effort to keep his face from showing the disgust he felt. "I'll take care of it."

Major General Philippos Tsimas, the head of Greece's Central Information Service, had five agents-in-place in New York City. Their main duties were to gather economic and political information and to sow as much harmful disinformation about Turkey as was discreetly possible. The station chief in New York was a short, feisty, sixty-year-old woman with a throaty voice and an affinity for man-tailored clothes, gold bangle bracelets, and gaudy rings. Her name was Elisabeth Syros; she was Vassos's control. Her cover was that of a secretary in the consul general's office.

"How do you like working with the American police, Major?"

Vassos continued to stare down at the black statue in front of Rockefeller Center. "They are like us in many ways."

"Have you made any progress?"

Vassos turned from the window and moved to the couch against the wall. "The investigation is just beginning. The lieutenant who has been assigned to help is competent and we work well together."

She lowered herself down next to him. "Your primary purpose is to return the casket-copy. I hope you understand that."

"And the people responsible for murdering my family?"

"I think we have to be realistic about our chance of extraditing an American citizen back to Greece to stand trial for murder."

"You think it impossible?"

"I think that any expectation of success is, at most, unrealistic." She gently searched his face. "Andreas, why do you think you were chosen for this assignment?"

He met her scrutiny without flinching. "Because of what happened to my family, and because I am a policeman."

"Yes, those are reasons. But not *the* reason. You were sent because it was felt that you would have the proper motivation, and the courage, to do whatever was required to return the casket-copy to us." She shrugged. "As for the people responsible for the Voúla massacre, we have no objections if you consider that a *personal* matter."

He looked out the window at St. Patrick's Cathedral's north tower. "I would prefer to handle the matter on a personal basis."

Detectives Ivan Ulanov and Frank Gregory huddled in front of the Sixteenth Precinct's computer console located in the muster room, behind the Desk. The days when the dogged detective had to spend a good part of his tour knocking on doors and seeking out information had gone the way of the truncheon and the *Police Gazette*. Today, by keying identity codes and access codes into police computer banks, detectives were able to retrieve a broad spectrum of facts about anyone. "Gimme their name and social security number, and I'll own 'em for life," Ulanov said to Gregory as he keystroked the Matrazzo name into the automobile registration bank.

"What is it with this Matrazzo caper and the Greek major?" Gregory asked, looking over his partner's shoulder.

"Don't know," Ulanov said. "The word is that the boss is doing a confidential for the C of D."

A list of Matrazzos who owned cars registered in New York State appeared on the lime green screen. Ulanov pressed the PF 8 button. The printer on the side of the console came alive, pushing out computer paper.

Frank Gregory tore off the spread sheets and slipped them into a folder. Ulanov typed in the access code for the boat and aircraft bank, then entered the Matrazzo name.

The precinct roll call man, a skinny guy with thinning gray hair, walked behind the Desk and glanced over at the detectives. "Hey, Frank, how's your love life these days?"

Gregory looked at his old radio car partner. "It don't go up so often."

"Yeah, but it do last longer," the roll call man said, putting the roll call sheets for the third, first, and second platoons down on the desk.

Gregory tore off the sheets that had just been ejected from the printer and slipped them into the folder. The police radio on top of the Desk belched out a 10:30 in progress. He picked up the telephone and, looking up at the list of telephone numbers taped to the wall over the console, dialed New York Telephone security. An appointment was made for later that day. He made other appointments with Consolidated Edison security and the Burgerwade Credit Company, Ltd.

Ulanov typed in his tax registry number and signed off the machine.

"Where do you want to go first?" Gregory asked as they stepped out from behind the Desk.

Ulanov glanced up at the wall clock. "Why don't we call it a day? We can hit the Board of Elections tomorrow and see how many Matrazzos vote."

Anna Grantas bustled around the restaurant dimming lights while her husband Spiro played backgammon in the lounge with two of the waiters. The last of the American patrons had left five minutes ago. The Greeks would be arriving shortly. The night was winding down; the clock behind the bar read 10:24. The bartender slowly turned the pages of a newspaper.

Zorba's was located on Thirty-sixth Street, three blocks west of Steinway Street in Astoria, Queens. The trendy Manhattan crowd usually arrived there early in the evening. They'd cross the Triboro Bridge in their cars and drive into the Greek section of Astoria to eat exotic foods, listen to exotic music, watch waiters dance, and break plates on the floor, the cost of which was added to their bills at a markup of six hundred percent. Breaking plates was good business.

The dining room was to the left of the entrance, down four short steps. It was a large room decorated with garish gold wallpaper; a vaulted ceiling with golden rococo molding framed swirling white clouds against a blue sky. A huge crystal chandelier dangled over the parquet dance floor; spaced at regular intervals were glittering glass candelabras set in niches in the walls.

At 10:46 five men sauntered through the glass doors. Anna Grantas called to the waiters to turn up the lights as she and her husband rushed to greet their guests. The new arrivals shouted greetings in Greek to the waiters and bartenders. One of them rushed to reach across the bar and shake hands. The band climbed back onto the bandstand.

More men arrived, coming in groups. Each of the male guests made a peacock's stroll into the restaurant. Soon couples and families began to arrive. An unmarried daughter of the owner ambled over to the steps to look into the restaurant, her eyes evaluating the available men.

Lucas and Vassos pushed their way through the door. Spiro and his wife greeted them warmly. A waiter escorted them to a table on the edge of the dance floor.

"Do you want me to order?" Vassos asked, seeing that the late-night menu was in Greek.

"That'll be fine," Lucas said, glancing around the room. Nothing had changed since his father had brought him here on his sixteenth birthday. Mr. and Mrs. Grantas looked the same; the waiters still wore white shirts open at the collars and black flared trousers to hide their elevator shoes. The late-night patrons still spoke Greek and the men still wore clothes with a European cut. Many of the men still carried handbags tucked under their arms. The ashtrays were forever filled with the butts of strong Greek cigarettes.

Lucas felt strange being there after so many years. He had the uncomfortable feeling of not belonging. He wondered why Greeks clung so tenaciously to their culture, why they held on to the past so longingly. Then a waiter appeared and began to put down plates of appetizers. Another came and put down two water glasses and a pitcher of the house *retsina*.

Vassos poured the homemade wine. "Giassou," he toasted.

They raised their glasses to each other.

It had been many years since Lucas had tasted retsina. His grandfather used to make it out in a shed behind the house back in Greece. He hadn't thought of his grandfather in years. He pictured the old man's stern countenance, his upswept mustache, his warm embrace and loving heart. Suddenly he was enveloped in a wave of guilt because he so seldom thought of his grandfather, or his grandmother.

"Was your homework at the library a success?" Vassos asked.

Lucas cut off a slice of bread and scooped up cucumber salad. "Moderately. I didn't have much time but I learned that there is a lot to learn. I also learned that the plural of papyrus is papyri, that it comes from Egypt, and that when Alexander was a boy there was a shortage of the stuff because of the Persian occupation of Egypt." He sipped some of his wine. "Alexander's dad, the king, ordered a special supply of papyrus be sent to Aristotle so that he could copy the *Iliad* for his son."

"Yes, I know," Vassos said, trying to decide on an appetizer.

Lucas sipped retsina.

As heavy bouzouki music blared from the amplifiers the waiter brought more appetizers: rice-stuffed grape leaves, pies of cheese and spinach, fried squid, souvlaki. Lucas made wet circles with his glass, waiting for the waiter to leave. When he did, Lucas said, "The last time there was any mention of the casket-copy was on June tenth, 323 B.C., when Alexander went DOA." He ate a round of squid. "I don't believe that your people were killed over some papyrus fragments."

"What are you trying to say, Teddy?"

"I'm suggesting that there might be a different motive behind the massacre."

"Such as?"

"I don't know."

Vassos leaned across the table and said, "Teddy, you spent a little while at a library looking in a few books. Do you really think that you could have even begun to know such a subject in so short a time?"

"Of course not. And I certainly don't think that I'm any expert on Alexander. But I read enough to know that I've good reason for my skepticism." He watched as Vassos poured more of the amber wine into their glasses.

"Teddy, before you make up your mind concerning the existence of the casket-copy, I ask you to please wait until we speak to the book dealers."

Lucas picked up a grape leaf, studied the green blade dripping with lemon juice, popped it into his mouth, and said, "Fair enough."

The music grew in intensity.

A man leaped up onto the dance floor, his shuffling feet and flailing arms keeping time to the music. Another man ran up and danced, twirling his body over the parquet. The tambourine rattled louder. The steel guitar and the bouzoukis played in melody with the *Udte*. Three men linked arms around each other's waists and danced. The waiter came over to their table and put down plates of lamb heads.

"*Kefalaki*," Lucas said. "I haven't eaten lamb heads in years." He speared one onto his plate. Using his pinkie, he gouged out an eye and, impaling it upon his nail, sucked it into his mouth, savoring the cold membrane. He chomped down slowly until it squished, splattering inside his mouth.

Watching Lucas eviscerate the head with his knife and fork, Vassos commented, "And you tell me that you are not Greek. You eat *kefalaki* like a Greek." He laughed, a dry, mirthless hacking sound, then suddenly slammed his glass down on the table and leaped up onto the dance floor, slowly spinning around on one foot with his arms outstretched at his sides, his head thrown all the way back.

Lucas's hands and feet tapped to the beat of the music. He realized that he had eaten Kefalaki the Greek way, and he also realized that for the first time in many years he felt Greek.

Patrons began to toss plates. Waiters rushed to keep tabs on the wreckage.

Vassos twirled around the floor.

Lucas gulped down more retsina. He felt light-headed, full of fun. He tossed a plate out onto the dance floor. Vassos saw him do this and laughed as he twirled around. Spinning back into his seat, gasping for breath, he said, "I saw you throw that plate." Still fighting for breath, he smiled, shook a finger in his partner's face, and said, "We have a saying, my friend: a man cannot erase what is written on his blood."

Lucas drank wine. "And we have a saying too: A guy who goes through life with one foot in yesterday and another in tomorrow is bound to shit all over himself."

"Giassou, Teddy."

6

Sunlight streamed through the grated windows, casting a diamond netting of shadow over the detective squad room. A cleaner moved about emptying wastebaskets into a plastic trash bag. He scattered cleaning compound on the floor and swept up a night's worth of butts and dirt with a long-handled broom.

"Is he a policeman?" Vassos asked, standing in the doorway of Lucas's office.

"A civilian cleaner assigned to the precinct. The precinct CO is responsible for the building's housekeeping."

Floor fans hummed in the morning heat. Vassos turned and looked into the office, watching Lucas sitting on the edge of his desk, studying the blackboard. "You did not dance last night."

"It's not the custom here for men to dance by themselves or with other men."

"One day you will dance." Vassos moved into the office. "Thank you for paying the bill last night."

"The Job picked up the tab," Lucas said, turning to look at the sixty sheet, or the UF60 Chronological Record of Cases. He was relieved to see that nothing heavy had come in during the night. He might be off the chart, but it was still his squad, his cases, his clearances.

The metallic cadence of police calls droned through the squad room. Lucas looked at the wall clock: 9:32. He telephoned downstairs and asked the desk sergeant if the mail had arrived. It was being sorted, he was told. Moving into the squad room, he saw that Ulanov was typing a report. Gregory was interviewing a complainant over the telephone and Big Jay Owens was studying the case folder of an unsolved, seven-year-old homicide. John Leone had his feet up on the desk and was reading a newspaper.

"John," Lucas said, "do me a favor and go downstairs and get the mail."

"Right, Lou," Leone said, putting down the newspaper.

Leone returned in ten minutes with a wire basket brimming with mail. He moved to the pigeonhole lockers and began to sort the mail into slots.

"Anything for me?" Lucas asked.

Leone foraged through the basket searching for mail addressed: CO 16 Sqd. He handed the Whip a bunch of envelopes and went back to his newspaper.

Taking the handful of multiuse envelopes and folders back into his office, Lucas began to go through the pile, looking for anything from Central Records. He found what he was looking for in three double-packed folders. He untied the flap and slid out the contents: printouts of all the complaint reports that Denny McKay and his friends had collected over the years. He put them aside and opened the case folder and removed the arrest reports that he had brought back from Central Records. He took his time matching up the complaint and arrest reports. That done, he arranged the arrest reports alphabetically by name of prisoner. Most of the collars had been made for burglary, robbery, and felonious assaults. With the arrest reports arranged by names, he wrote down the names on a lined pad and beside each one listed the crime, as well as the details of the crime. Looking over the arrest report on a Bucky McMahon, Lucas noticed in the Property Information box: "one old book by Aristarchus. Value: $500,000. Property not recovered at scene." He jotted down the sixty-one number and the complainant's name and address.

Vassos was studying the blackboard.

"An old book was stolen during the course of a robbery by one of McKay's men. It happened eleven years ago, and the complainant was a Mr. Belmont E. Widener. The property was never recovered."

Vassos turned from the board. "Do you think there's a connection?"

"I don't know," Lucas said. "It's one more thing we're going to have to take a look at. In fact—"

"You fucking cunt!" a frantic voice screamed out in the squad room.

Lucas and Vassos rushed outside in time to see a man come sailing over the wooden railing.

A hatless policewoman, heavyset, with a head of thick black hair, threw open the gate and stormed inside. "Get in that cage, asshole."

The man leaped up, yanked down his fly, pulled out his penis, and screamed, "Suck my prick, you cunt."

Ulanov continued to type.

Gregory covered the telephone's mouthpiece with his hand.

Big Jay turned in his seat, draping his arm over the back of his chair.

The Second Whip closed the door to his office.

John Leone casually moved to the police radio and turned up the volume, then strolled back to his desk, shaking his head disdainfully at the man as he passed him. The insolent prisoner's well-defined muscles shaped his dirty T-shirt. He stood in the middle of the squad room snarling at the policewoman, casting unsure glances at the detectives.

The policewoman's partner, a sloppy man in his early forties with a ponderous gut and a small waxed mustache, calmly walked past the prisoner and opened the door to the detention cage. He waited for his partner to make her move.

"I'm not about to tell you again, asshole, get into that cage."

"Suck this, you Puerto Rican douchebag."

Rolling her eyes with bogus irritation, she walked over to the prisoner, suddenly pivoted to her right, hunching down, and whirled around, throwing a right directly into the man's genitals. He gasped and doubled over in pain. The policewoman struck again with a left hand that caught him flush on the temple. He crumpled onto the floor, rolling onto his stomach.

Big Jay sadly shook his head. "You should be ashamed of yourself, letting a woman beat the shit out of you." He turned back to his case folder.

The policewoman straddled her prisoner, reached down, grabbed him by his belt and, scissoring him up off the floor, dragged him across the room into the cage. Her partner slammed the detention cage door, slid the locking pin through the steel bar, and moved to a vacant typewriter to help with the paperwork.

Vassos's lips pursed in approbation. "Are all your women officers that efficient?"

"We have some that don't row with both oars in the water, but most of them are okay, and a few, like Josey, are damn good."

"What am I being arrested for?" the prisoner shouted, struggling up on shaky legs.

"Possession of a big mouth," Josey said, rolling an arrest report into the machine.

The man sitting across from Trevor Hughes in the Oak Room of the Plaza Hotel waited for his guest to butter his roll. Hughes's feigned cheerfulness had not deceived his host. "How goes it in Athens, Trevor?"

"Fine," Hughes said, his gaze sweeping the intimate, cozy restaurant, its dark oak walls and groined ceiling. "As you know, Greece can be quite civilized," Hughes added.

"Did Nancy come with you?"

"No. She stayed on Paros. We rented a house there for the summer. I manage to pop over some weekends and whenever I can sneak away from the embassy."

"How are the children?"

"Grown and scattered all over the place, doing their own things."

"Well, I guess that's the way of it all." The host raised his water glass. "What brings you to New York?"

Hughes placed his butter knife across his bread plate and looked across the table at his host's ring. "I've always loved that ring."

"Yes, it *is* special," he said, sliding it off his finger and passing it to Hughes. "Emperor Caracalla had the coin struck around 215 A.D. from the imperial mint at Ephesus. Alexander is on the obverse, and on the reverse is a scene showing him hunting boar with Meleager."

Rolling the heavy gold ring over his palm, Hughes observed, "It must be quite valuable."

"Not really. There are many coins and medallions around from that period."

Hughes brushed a crumb off the tablecloth. "There was a massacre in Greece. In Voúla, a village outside the capital." He watched the waiter roll the desert cart past their table.

"I read about it in the newspapers. Those damn terrorists are getting a bit out of hand, I'd say." The host forked some Caesar salad into his mouth.

"Terrorists were not responsible," Hughes said, dabbing his napkin at the corner of his lip.

"Really. Who was?"

"Two Americans. They were hired in New York City to murder two Greek policemen."

"Incredible. How do you know this?"

"I read the intelligence reports that are sent to the ambassador. And our FBI liaison has good sources within the Hellenic Police. The terrorist thing was a cover story that the government let out."

"I see."

"Cuttler and Simmons were their names."

"Whose names, Trevor?"

"The killers'."

A crash of dishes caused people to look up from their plates.

"Simmons was killed at the scene trying to escape." Hughes broke off a piece of roll and buttered it. "Cuttler was taken alive."

A muscle at the corner of the other man's jaw began to twitch. "I imagine that the Greek police must have some unique interrogative techniques." He lifted his wineglass to his mouth and drank.

"Actually not. They're concerned abut civil rights and that sort of stuff."

"I'm glad to hear that they're so enlightened."

"Cuttler died in the hospital." Hughes cut his pan-blackened sword-fish steak. "But not before he talked."

Maneuvering lettuce onto his fork, the host asked, "Did this Cuttler say who hired them?"

"He didn't live long enough."

"Pity."

"They're sending someone."

"Who is sending someone?"

"The Greek police. One of their men is coming here to try and find the people who hired Simmons and Cuttler and to find out why these people wanted the two policemen killed. He'll be working with some-one from the NYPD." Hughes's face set in a disapproving scowl.

"Why the look, Trevor?"

"Orhan Iskur was murdered the same day as the massacre."

"Orhan probably had his spoon stuck in somebody else's pudding."

"You're more than likely right," Hughes said, cutting more fish. "On the other hand, Simmons and Cuttler would have needed a contract in Greece, to help move things along."

"Yes, I suppose they would."

"Orhan would have made the perfect point man. Don't you agree?"

"Yes, I suppose he would have."

"But then, *our* Orhan would never have been persuaded to under-take such a task without explicit orders from you, would he?"

Both men sipped wine, their inquiring eyes peering over the rims. Silence grew between them.

Hughes lowered his glass. "I'm planning on retiring next year. I've bought a chalet outside of Bern."

The host smiled. "Sounds idyllic."

"I've enjoyed our occasional entrepreneurial adventures."

"Yes, they have been mutually rewarding."

Hughes blurted, "I'm leaving Nancy."

The man with the golden ring was surprised. "You're been married for over thirty years."

His guest looked somewhat sheepish as he explained, "I'm in love. For the first time in my life, I'm really in love." The host looked at his guest with a weary expression. Hughes added nervously, "She's younger, of course. She's twenty-four."

"Trevor! You're fifty-seven years old. What in the name of—"

Hughes angrily pointed his knife at his host. "I don't want to hear any of that. I'm trim and in excellent shape. She loves me and she excites me."

The man sitting on the other side of the table shrugged in indifference, raised his wineglass to salute his guest, and said, "I wish you the best of luck and happiness."

"Thank you. My new situation does, however, present me with certain problems. Problems that I had hoped you might help me solve." He relaxed, slowly twirling the stem of his wineglass.

A nasty undercurrent infiltrated the host's voice. "And what problem is that, Trevor?"

"As you well know, Nancy has all the money. Oil and railroads and real estate, mostly. I was always the charming poor boy from Harvard. I'll have my pension, of course, and I've managed to put the money from our private enterprises to work."

"Well then, you should be able to live in relative comfort."

"But you see, old friend, I've become accustomed to a certain lifestyle; without Nancy's wealth behind me, well, I'll be hard-pressed to live the way I want to. What I need is a cushion."

The host's eyes narrowed into a hard look. "Naturally."

"I've been thinking of starting a private newsletter."

The host stroked the back of his ring with his thumb. "A newsletter?"

"The Greek policeman will be working with the NYPD under the authority of the State Department's Bureau of Diplomatic Security. Reports will be required topside, the ambassador will have to be informed of the current standing of the case, prevent any embarrassment to Washington, that sort of thing. I'll have access to all of these reports."

The host smoothed down his end of the tablecloth. "How many subscribers do you envisage?"

"Oh, it would be a restricted membership. There'd be no annual or monthly dues. Only one lifetime subscription fee."

"You've become quite the businessman, Trevor."

"I've had some excellent teachers."

"Yes, I suppose you have." His eyes narrowed. "How much?"

"A half million U.S. should do nicely, I think."

The snow leopard basked in the afternoon sun while her cubs frolicked among the rocks. Peering through the thick glass, Denny

McKay watched the spotted cat, wondering if he'd be able to take it out in a one-on-one fight. He imagined himself making like Tarzan, armed only with a knife, and the cat, crouched up on a Ninth Avenue fire escape, baring its fangs, ready to pounce. I'd take her fucking eyes out, he thought, turning away from the viewing glass and pushing his way out of the crowded grotto.

Five minutes later Denny McKay tossed away his cigarette and entered the Bronx Zoo's World of Darkness. Day was suddenly night. This is a scary fucking place, he thought, watching hundreds of bats streaking around their glass cave. He took in the outlines of people moving about the display of nocturnal animals. He had picked a strange place to meet, he reflected while he looked for the rendezvous point. He made his way over to the display of sugar gliders. He felt queasy standing so close to them. He saw an owl eyeing him and looked away.

A low voice startled him. "Hello, Denny."

"Where are you?" McKay whispered, an edge of desperation in his voice.

"Behind you."

McKay turned and saw the outline of a man standing in the corner. "Why'd you pick this spooky place to meet?"

"Because it's safe."

"What's so important?" McKay asked, watching the kit foxes.

"Cuttler talked before he died." The man pushed away from the wall and moved along the darkened passage, examining the displays.

McKay moved with him, anxious to see the light of day. They exited from the World of Darkness and McKay lit up a cigarette. They moved along the path leading to the house of the giant panda.

"Cuttler told the Greek police why they were sent there," the man with the golden ring said. "Fortunately, he did not live long enough to tell them who had sent them."

"George Cuttler was a standup guy; he wouldn't talk."

The man walking next to McKay smiled. "The vernacular of the lower classes never ceases to amaze me. Standup, I believe, applies to a person who is willing to go to jail, even die, rather than betray his friends."

"Yeah, that's right."

"Well, Denny, let me enlighten you. *Your* Mr. Cuttler was not standup. Most people aren't."

McKay bit down hard on his cigarette's filter. "What did he tell them?"

The man recounted the high points of his lunch with Trevor Hughes.

Denny McKay was concerned. "A stranger showed up at The Den the other day. A Greek. He checked out okay, I'm sure it was a coincidence. Nothing to worry about."

"Then why mention it? If he returns, kill him."

"There ain't no way that they could be onto us. Cuttler and Simmons didn't know a thing."

"You're wrong, Denny. They knew that you hired them."

"But you just said that they didn't tell that to the cops."

"Correct. But then, the police might be keeping that bit of information to themselves, mightn't they?"

McKay shrugged and moved off to buy cotton candy. He returned with a stick of the puffy pink sugar. "Want some?"

The man with the ring looked disdainfully at the fibrous candy. "No, thank you." They walked along the path. "You're sublimely unconcerned over the possibility that the Greek police might know about you."

"I've been on the wrong side of the law most of my life. And I know that if they don't catch you with the gun in your hand, they don't got shit. As for a job going down in Greece? Forget about it. Ain't nothing to worry about." He took a big bite of the candy. "What about our next shipment? Do we send it?"

"Yes. Go ahead as though nothing had happened."

"What about Orhan's replacement? How we going to work it without him there?"

"I've already seen to that." He slid his ring down his linen lapel. "Denny, we're going to have to build a moat around ourselves and fill it with hungry piranha."

McKay's questioning eyes fell on the man with the golden ring. "You mean what I think you mean?"

"Exactly. Take out Trevor Hughes. Do you have any problems with that?"

"Of course not. Come on, let's go see the giraffes."

Lucas and Vassos pushed their way through the press of people engaged in conversation in the crowded bar area. The cuckoo sprang out of its tree house behind the bar and chirped seven times. Dirndl-clad waitresses rushed about inside the restaurant. Heidi's was decorated with Victorian bric-a-brac, antique clocks, and stained-glass windows.

The restaurant's location, on the northwest corner of Second Avenue and Fifty-third Street, made it a perfect watering hole for the detectives of the Sixteenth Squad. Far enough east to be away from the midtown limelight, yet close enough to the station house for a detective to rush back if any 10:2's—forthwiths—were telephoned to the cop phone Heidi had installed behind the bar.

"Over here, Lou," Big Jay shouted, his big hands waving over the heads of people at the bar.

John Leone, Ulanov, Gregory, and Big Jay pushed back to make room. Slipping in next to the detectives, Lucas gestured to the bartender for a round of drinks. The ferret-faced man working the stick began to set down six weiss beers on the bar.

Lucas saw that the Second Whip was among the missing. "Where's Roosevelt?"

Big Jay's eyes drifted down to the forest of tall tulip glasses with slices of lemon bobbing inside of them. "Sergeant Grimes had a moonlighting job to go to, a wedding, I think."

"You got watering holes in Greece, Major?" Leone asked.

Vassos's brows furrowed. "Watering holes?"

Sipping beer, Lucas explained.

"Ah, yes, we have them," Vassos said. "Some of the larger police districts have their own clubs."

A waitress squeezed past the detectives holding a tray of drinks out in front of her. Leone made an obscene squeal, looked at Gregory, and said, "I met this broad last week and still haven't been able to score her. She's harder to get into than Fort Knox."

Lucas wiped beer suds from his mouth with the back of his hand. "Maybe you're not making the right deposit."

Vassos shivered from the air-conditioning.

Ulanov inched up close to the Whip. "Gregory and I checked out the Matrazzo family this morning."

Lucas threw back his head, draining the glass. "And?"

"We came up with a cousin," Ulanov said, sticking a slip of paper into Lucas's shirt pocket.

"How do you know they're related?"

Ulanov shrugged. "I called and asked."

"Any word from your Russian friend across the street?" Lucas asked.

"Not yet," Ulanov said, watching a towering, square-faced woman push her way through the crowd. Her massive bosom rose and fell under an extra-large man's shirt.

She rushed up to the detectives and bear-hugged Lucas up off the floor. "Teddy, *mein Liebling*," she bellowed.

"Heidi, you're breaking my ribs," Lucas gasped.

"You are so handsome that you make me go wild," she said, kissing him repeatedly on his face. "One day we will do it, ja?"

"What about Hildegard?" Big Jay said, a big grin sparkling across his black face.

"We will not tell her," Heidi said, releasing Lucas. "I will cheat, like all *men* do." She brushed back her mannishly styled hair.

"Andreas, this is the famous Heidi. Heidi, this is Major Andreas Vassos. He's a Greek policeman," Lucas said.

She tipped her head back, looking directly at Vassos. "You are from Greece?"

"Yes, I am."

Heidi turned serious. "Is it true that Greek men all want to do it in the behind?"

Vassos smiled self-consciously. "Some do, yes. But it is the same here, no?"

"Once, many years ago when I still did it with men, I let a man do it to me there. I hurt!"

John Leone looked at her with his dreamy eyes, licked his mustache, slid his arm around her waist, pulled her close, and said, "I'd be gentle."

Breaking away from him, Heidi said, "Men don't know how." She caught the attention of the man behind the stick and shouted something in German.

The bartender came over and slipped six coasters onto the bar in front of the detectives. "Whenever you're ready, Heidi would like to buy you a round."

Big Jay toasted the owner. "A rare treat!"

Heidi quaffed her *Kirschwasser* and moved off to greet another group of regulars. The detectives spent the next forty minutes drinking beer, asking Vassos about the Job in Greece, and taking turns going to the bathroom. Skating his glass through a lagoon of spilled booze, Lucas said to Vassos, "Once we start interviewing the book dealers the investigation will be out in the open."

"I've thought of that," Vassos said. "Perhaps it's better that way. Let them know we're searching for them. Fear is a policeman's colleague."

"Did you know Katina was Greek?" Lucas asked.

"Katina is a Greek name, but I was surprised when she said she was Professor Levi's daughter."

"How's your hotel?"

Vassos shrugged indifference. "A place to sleep, and think." He looked at the American lieutenant's unsmiling face. "Hate and I have become friends these past months, Teddy. I know what it looks like, feels like. I saw it on your face when you told me about the Purple Gang and Denny McKay."

Lucas looked down into his tall glass and gave a single emphatic nod. "McKay killed a friend of mine."

* * *

A street lamp beam illuminated the deserted playground. Lucas looked out his living room window. The charcoal sky was full of bruised purple clouds. He turned abruptly and went into the bedroom, peeling off his clothes as he went, throwing himself onto the unmade bed. Linking his hands in back of his head, he stared up at the shadows, listening to the darkness. Vassos had made him think of Cormick McGovern and his hatred for McKay and his crew. He closed his eyes and let his thoughts slip back into the past.

Patrolman Cormick McGovern had rosy cheeks, a thick neck, and a Derry brogue. When Probationary Patrolman Lucas was in recruit school, department policy required rookies to be sent out into the field for one weekend a month in order to acquire practical experience alongside a seasoned cop.

Lucas's first tour in the street was in the Six-seven, a four to midnight. The rookies, in their starched gray uniforms, stood smartly at attention behind the outgoing shift, called a "platoon"; each one of them anxiously awaited assignment to a field training officer. They were eager to start their march to glory. A silver-haired Desk lieutenant called the roll, assigned each member to their posts. He gave them ringing times to call the station house, meal hours, and announced special post conditions.

After the roll had been called, the lieutenant assigned the rookies. "Probationary Patrolman Lucas."

"Here, sir," snapped the recruit, his enthusiasm evident on his spanking young face.

"Lucas, you're assigned with Patrolman McGovern."

A ripple of laughter swept through the platoon. "Knock it off," hissed the Desk lieutenant.

Assignments made, the lieutenant barked, "Sergeant, post the platoon."

"Yes, sir," the sergeant said, giving him a salute with his nightstick. He executed an about-face, called the platoon to attention, and marched it out of the station house. Once outside on the high stoop, the sergeant ordered, "Take your posts."

The platoon broke ranks. Members of the second platoon immediately appeared from doorways and rushed up the precinct steps to get at the sign-out book.

Seeing all the policemen suddenly appear from nowhere, not waiting on their post relieving points as required, Lucas realized for the first time that the Job wasn't the way they said it was in the Academy.

"Lucas? Lucas?"

He turned to face the humorless stare of Cormick McGovern. "Here, sir."

"Come with me, lad," McGovern said, a mellow smile suddenly lighting up his large face.

Lucas marched route step beside his field training officer. Up Snyder Avenue, left on Flatbush, past Albemarle Road, past Tilden Avenue, and directly into the grandiose lobby of the Loews Kings movie palace.

Cormick McGovern strutted past the ticket taker with the regal arrogance of a knight, his subservient squire in tow. Lucas followed his leader up the darkened back staircase to the last row of the balcony.

"Laddy, this is your post for the remainder of your tour. You're to stay here and do nothing. I'll be back to get you."

"Yes, sir," Lucas said, feeling his ardor sinking.

"Your first lesson in the street is to follow orders and don't get involved," McGovern said. "Do you know why you're spending your first tour here?"

"No, sir."

"It's so that you won't get into any kind of trouble that could jam you up while you're on probation and cause you to lose your job."

Lucas looked around the balcony and saw several classmates contentedly watching the movie.

During the next five months Lucas and the other recruits spent their field duties stashed away in movie houses, garages, and firehouses.

Graduation.

Chief Clerk Flynn read out the names off the assignment sheet. "Lucas, T."

"Here, sir."

"The Six-seven."

Lucas ran into McGovern on his second tour.

"Teddy, now that you're out of the Academy, how'd you like me to teach you the real Job?"

"I'd like it a lot."

Cormick McGovern commenced his in-service training course. He showed Lucas how to maintain two memo books, one for the bosses and a protector, a book that contained altered versions of each entry, designed to cover your ass. He demonstrated the correct way to search a prisoner, warning him not to be squeamish about searching women. "They can kill you just as dead."

McGovern gave him his trust/no trust list. Trust: Italians, wiseguys, Jews, Greeks, Irish, WASPs, Hispanics, except Puerto Ricans. No trust: hookers, junkies, dealers, FBI, newsmen, West Indians, all lawyers, girlfriends. Golden rule: never tell your wife, your girlfriend, neighbor, relative, friend *anything* about the Job, especially how much money you earn. He told Teddy about one of his friends who had died. When

the grieving widow went to the pension bureau to inquire about Patrolman Bill Murphy's pension, she was advised that no Patrolman Murphy had died. However, a Lieutenant Bill Murphy had recently expired. "Now there was a cop who knew how to keep his mouth shut,"
McGovern said.

Cormick McGovern's public relations tenet: send the following
cards to businessmen on your post—Christmas, Hanukkah, bar mitz-
vah, Holy Communion, confirmation, weddings, get well, and condolences.

Three years later Lucas was transferred into one of the department's
plainclothes gambling units. McGovern's final lesson was: "Teddy, my
lad, never go back."

Six years later Lucas found himself the Second Whip in Second
Homicide. The district took in the Ninth, Tenth, Thirteenth, and
Fourteenth Precincts. He and his old field training officer had kept in
touch through occasional telephone conversations, met at a local watering hole, had dinner together once or twice a year. Lucas was surprised one day when he read in the Personal Orders that Cormick
McGovern had been dumped out of the Six-seven and into the Fourteenth during one of the Job's mass corruption upheavals.

Lucas telephoned his friend. "What happened?"

"A lad with a year in the Job bragged to his girlfriend about the
Christmas list and then a month later stopped seeing her. I don't know
what they're taking into the Job these days."

"Are they taking care of you at the Fourteenth?"

" 'Tis a lovely house to work in, Teddy. The roll call man and I are
old friends. I'm out there meeting people and sending out my greeting
cards, making friends."

The following June, Second District Homicide found itself swamped
with Homicides coming off the docks in the Fourteenth and Eighteenth Precincts. Lucas looked up his old friend. They met in the back
of Roth's liquor store. Sipping Irish whiskey from a mug, McGovern
said, "It's Denny McKay and his bunch."

"What's going on?" Lucas asked.

"A leprechaun who drives a forklift on the dock whispered into my
ear that some young turks are trying to wrestle control from McKay."

"Will you nose around for me, see if you can dig up anything that
will stand in court?"

"Will do, Teddy. I'll give you a call in a day or two," McGovern said.

Three days later Cormick McGovern's body was found lying face up
at the end of Pier Thirty-eight. His features had been pounded into
gore; fourteen bullets had mutilated his body; someone had defecated

on his face. His shield had been torn from his uniform and was missing. The word that seeped through the pall of silence that fell over the docks was that Denny McKay had ordered McGovern killed because he had found out something about the killings that had been done on McKay's orders. But Teddy Lucas did not have to be told that. He knew that his friend had died because he had been poking around asking questions, speaking to the people to whom he had sent greeting cards.

Lucas did not get his chance to get at McKay. The district commander had the Second Whip transferred. The forty-nine read: "His personal friendship with the victim precludes objectivity."

Ten years and some months later, despite a maximum effort by the NYPD to nail McGovern's killers, the case folder was stored with the rest of the unsolved homicides in the old record room of the Second District Homicide Squad. And like the rest of the homicide folders, it was weighed down by the perfunctory addition of semiannual DD14 Resumé of Homicide Case forms.

Lucas would visit the old record room from time to time and sit in a musty corner with the McGovern folder. He would read through the file, looking for any additional facts; there never were any. He'd study the crime scene photos of his friend's battered body and recall the vibrant man who used to stash him in the Loews Kings. Time had distilled Lucas's rage into pure and abiding hatred for McKay and his people. C of D Edgeworth's assignment to work with Vassos had given Lucas another shot at McKay. The Job has a strange way of giving you another turn in the batter's box, he thought, turning onto his side and closing his eyes.

Tomorrow was a big day.

Trevor Hughes walked out of the lobby of the Plaza Hotel and stopped on top of the steps to admire the urban view laid out before him. Hansom cabs and taxis cluttered the street; a stream of people flowed along Fifth Avenue; stylish mannequins stood in Bergdorf's windows; a reggae band played in the plaza.

Hughes took a deep breath and let it out slowly. Everything was going as he had planned; he felt wonderful. With half a million dollars, plus his pension and investments, he could continue to live the good life without his wife. He adjusted his tie and moved down the steps, wondering why the man with the ring was so insistent on meeting him now, at eleven o'clock at night. Just like him, he thought. Secretive to a fault. "Wear a bright yellow tie and walk north along Central Park West," he had said when he telephoned an hour earlier. "Sit on the thirteenth bench along the park wall. I'll meet you there tonight at eleven, and we'll make arrangements for the delivery of the initiation fee."

"Why not come to my hotel?"

"Walls have ears, Trevor, or have you forgotten? I stretched a point by having lunch with you there."

He went west on Central Park South and then turned at Columbus Circle. Walking north along Central Park West, Hughes painstakingly counted park benches. When he reached the right one, he sat down. A bicyclist whooshed past, blowing his whistle, startling him. Eerie night sounds floated out of the park. More than a little spooked, he looked around. The park side of the street was dark. On the other side people strolled in much brighter light. On his side he could see people moving north a long way from him. A black man on a skateboard wove his way toward him.

Hughes felt terribly isolated and vulnerable. A chilling thought popped into his mind. He was alone; why couldn't they have met in the lobby or in some other public place? My God! I've allowed greed to overcome my common sense. He leaped to his feet. A rustle behind him caused him to whirl, his scared eyes searching the shadows in the bushes on the other side of the low stone wall. Seeing nothing, he turned to cross to safety on the other side of the street. He started to run. The skateboarder wove in front of him and pivoted to an abrupt stop, blocking his path.

Hughes saw only a mouthful of flashing white teeth. He heard a pop and felt himself backpedaling, his arms flailing out at his sides. He crumpled onto the bench. Clouds were forming over his eyes, but he was able to make out the smiling black face that looked down at him.

"You've killed me," Hughes said, and died.

The skater lifted his brightly colored shirt and tucked the nickeled .38 caliber S & W Chief into his waistband. He pulled a gravity knife from his back pocket and popped the blade out. He stripped off the dead man's wristwatch and wedding ring and added them to the collection.

He looked around. A lone taxi sped past. The skater pushed off on his board. At Seventy-second Street he jumped the curb into the roadway and whirled to stop on the driver's side of a double-parked automobile.

Denny McKay rolled down the window.

"A piece of cake," the skater said, passing McKay the bag.

He opened it and looked inside. "Is it all here?"

"Yeah, it's all there."

"You didn't get stupid and grab a souvenir, I hope."

"M'man," protested the skater, "I bees a motherfuckin' professional."

"See ya 'round." The window slipped up and the skater danced off into the night.

7

Colonel Dimitri Pappas braked for the red light on Amalias Street. Morning traffic was heavy; the cloudless sky seemed an infinity of blue. A broad grin pulled up Pappas's lips when his gaze fell on the graffito on the wall of St. Paul's Anglican Church. "Long live Rudolf Hess" was bracketed between two swastikas. The subtleties of Greek political life, he thought, are endless. Prime Minister Papandreou was a politician with a socialist kink; the graffiti artist had an obvious neo-fascist twist. The meaning of the urban art: Fuck you, Papandreou.

Driving along Vassilissis Sofias, Pappas passed the gardens and slowed the car so that he could look up at the huge flag billowing atop Lykavitos Hill. A sense of pride surged through him, as it always did whenever he looked up at Athens' highest hill and saw the emblem of Greek sovereignty.

Seventeen minutes later Colonel Pappas was walking up the steps of 173 Leoforos Alexandras, headquarters of the Hellenic Police Department. It was a square building constructed entirely of white marble, with a bank of doors made of silvery one-way mirrored glass. Pappas went inside through the only unlocked door and was fed into the security cordon that funneled him to the control desk manned by four officers, three males and one female. The sergeant in charge of the checkpoint recognized the colonel and entered Pappas's name, rank, and the time in the service book.

Pappas stopped at his office and read the night's situation reports. One shooting in Piraeus, four stabbings in Kolonaki, a rape in Athens, and one armed robbery in Glifádha. We're becoming like New York, he thought, ripping off the top page of his desk calendar. It was Monday, July 13.

He left his office and took the elevator to the thirteenth floor. Interpol, Minister of Public Order, was written in French across the glass doors. He pushed inside the suite of rooms. Eight A.M., the change of tours. Tired men and women gathered in offices to pass on information to the day team. The communications room, a large space crammed with sophisticated equipment, was on Pappas's right. The rancid smell of stale cigarettes seeped into the hallway. Pappas walked quickly down the corridor to the end and entered the suite occupied by Colonel Teddy Tritsis, the minister's representative to Interpol.

Tritsis nodded Pappas into a chair while he spoke on the telephone. There was a large painting of Christ baring his bleeding heart on the wall. Pappas absently stared at the other man's thick, bushy white hair; it had an almost startling band of black around it just over the top of his ears.

"Dimitri, how are you?" he asked, hanging up the telephone.

"Good, Teddy, and you?"

"Busy as hell. Everyone wants their information yesterday. Want some coffee?"

"That would be nice."

Tritsis pushed the intercom button and spoke into the machine. "So? How goes the Voúla investigation?"

"I need a name, Teddy. One name. Someone who was close to Orhan Iskur."

The head of Interpol leaned forward. "Was his murder tied in with Voúla?"

"We think so, yes. But that is confidential."

Tritsis raised his palms. "Of course." He signed regret. "I might not be able to help you on this one, old friend."

"Why the hell not?"

"This assignment puts me in an awkward position sometimes. I'm a Greek policeman, assigned by the minister to run Interpol's Greek station. The job guarantees me promotion, but it also guarantees me a lot of headaches. I've got to do a balancing act between our regulations, Interpol's, and my own loyalty to the department. I'm required by this assignment to operate within sets of rules set down by both organizations."

"So?"

"The damn problem is that Interpol is prohibited from getting involved in any investigation with a racial, religious, military, or political angle. Voúla, from everything I know, was the work of terrorists, which would make it political." He leaned back, drumming his fingertips on the top of his desk.

Pappas noticed how deeply Tritsis's cheeks had sunken over the years. Then a tall man entered the office carrying a Turkish *aski*, a tray, suspended on three chains, holding two small cups of coffee and two glasses of water. Raising the tray's chains, the man removed the coffee cups and set them down in front of each man. The water came next.

"How was the traffic this morning?" Tritsis asked, watching the man turn to leave.

"You need the eyes of Argus to drive in Athens," Pappas said as the door closed. Tritsis sipped his coffee.

"Voúla was murder, pure and simple," Pappas said. "The terrorist thing was a ploy we used so that we could conduct the real investigation without having the newspapers crawling up our asses."

"Who was the intended victim?" Tritsis asked, lowering his cup.

"Takis Milaraki, the café owner," Pappas lied. "We think that Iskur and Milaraki had narcotics deals going that turned sour."

Grinning broadly, Tritsis shook his finger at Pappas. "You old fox. That terrorist story sounded phony to me from the beginning." He got up and moved out from behind his desk. "I anticipated that someone would be around to ask about Orhan Iskur, so I telephoned Paris and asked them to send me whatever they had on him." He crossed the room to the row of locked file cabinets. He punched in the combination and the top drawer of the middle file opened. He took out a folder, opened it, and removed a sheet of paper. Walking back to his desk, Interpol's station chief said, "Iskur was always a very careful man."

Two kilometers outside of Vouliagméni, on the coastal road leading toward Voúla, a thin road branched off and seemed to go nowhere. The artery twisted and turned under an umbrella of cypress trees that at night created a tunnel of darkness. The landscape on either side of the road sloped up the sides of hills, and here and there a light sparkled in a distant farmhouse.

Suddenly, when you least expected it, the tunnel burst into a street of glitter and noise known as the Vari district. It was a long block of *hassapo* tavernas, meat restaurants, each one with a butcher shop attached to it where patrons could make a leisurely selection for their main course from the rows of lambs, goats, and pigs.

Each taverna was aglow in flashing lights and had its own man in the roadway, thrusting his body in front of moving cars, beckoning drivers into his taverna. Many of the tavernas had strands of cowbells hanging from posts and young boys to shake them in a further attempt to lure customers.

George's was the gaudiest of the tavernas and was famous for its wine room, a damp, earth-floored space in the rear where patrons wandered among the rows of casks, sampling the homemade wines, choosing the brew that most tempted their palates. George's was also famous for its deserts, especially the homemade *meli*, a platter of thick yogurt smothered with golden honey.

Yiannis Yiotas, a small, weasel-faced man with two brown moles on his nose, had just finished eating a platter of goat meat and french fries. He poured the last of the retsina from the pitcher and settled back to enjoy his cigarette and people watch before he ordered his meli.

Yiotas was a thief and a bigamist. A thief because the thought of working for a living made him sick to his stomach. A bigamist because he loved to screw fat women, and because there were so many of them and they were so easy to get into bed and they were so grateful and motherly, he just couldn't break their hearts by leaving them, so he ended up getting married to them. Having more than one wife added a pleasant dimension to Yiannis's life. He loved leading a life of lies, living on the edge.

He looked around the restaurant—a mixed bag of Greeks and tourists. Children ran up and down the aisles; cats crouched near tables, waiting for scraps; a butcher was chopping up a lamb. Yiannis finished his wine; the homemade brew had a heavy pine-resin taste that caused him to smack his lips. He yelled out to the rushing waiter, "*Pahrahkahlo.*"

The waiter paused long enough to look his way.

"Meli and retsina," Yiannis yelled.

The waiter nodded and rushed off.

He lighted and drew hard on a cigarette, pulling the relaxing smoke in deep, savoring its tranquil cloud. He thought about Niki, the fattest of his four wives. She lived in Filothei and thought her loving husband was a deckhand aboard a cruise ship. He thought of her pretty face and her big, wrinkled ass. And he thought of the sounds she made when he stuck his prick up her ass and played with her pussy at the same time. A warm flush spread through his groin, and he decided that he would visit Niki tomorrow. No! Tomorrow was Tuesday, bad luck for a Greek to plan anything. This had been so since that Tuesday in the fifteenth century when Constantinople fell to the Turks.

The waiter rushed over to his table, set down the meli and wine, and rushed off. Yiannis crushed his cigarette out in the tin ashtray, poured wine into his small glass, picked up the spoon off the platter, and began to stir the yogurt and honey into a pink mixture. The sound of bouzoukis and tambourines floated across the night.

Yiotas was enjoying his solitary pleasures when a feeling of dread came over him. He sensed a presence lurking behind him, watching him. He tensed, ready, if need be, to leap up and run. Continuing to stir the dessert, he began to cast his eyes from side to side without moving his head in an attempt to see who was standing there. He heard movement and saw the torso of a man come from behind him and go around to the front of the table. A chair scraped back. The stranger sat down. Yiannis continued to mix the meli. When he had steeled himself, Yiannis shyly raised his eyes up to look at the intruder. He blanched and suddenly felt sick to his stomach.

"Hello, Yiannis," Colonel Pappas said, pulling a spoon from the glass in the center of the table and scooping up Yiannis's meli. "I love this, it's my favorite." Licking the spoon, he added, "How have you been, Yiannis? I haven't seen you—let me see, it's been over ten years. I arrested you for a payroll robbery in Plaka."

Yiannis Yiotas had a sudden urge to go to the bathroom. "Hello, Major," he said, forcing courage into his voice.

"It's Colonel now. What a pleasant surprise, running into you at George's."

"I eat here a lot, Colonel."

A raw edge came into Pappas's voice. "I know." He picked up the pitcher and poured wine into one of the empty glasses on the table. He offered the copper wine pitcher to Yiannis, who held up his glass and uneasily watched the colonel pour retsina.

Pappas put down the pitcher and laughed. "I read in the newspaper this morning about a prison riot in New York City. A place called Rikers Island. The prisoners were upset because there were not enough telephones for them to use." He scooped up more meli. "Can you believe that? Telephones for prisoners. They even have televisions on this Rikers Island."

Yiannis laughed nervously. "I can't believe that, Colonel. It sounds more like a hotel."

Pappas drank wine. "It doesn't sound like a Greek prison, does it, Yiannis?"

"No," Yiannis snapped.

"Here we know how to treat prisoners. We make them pay for their clothes and food. We don't go out of our way to make their miserable lives easy. Isn't that true, Yiannis?"

"Yes, sir." Yiannis's legs were shaking.

"How old are you now?"

"Forty-six."

"Forty-six," Pappas echoed solemnly. "You're lucky that you have given up your old way of life. Prison would be difficult for you now, very difficult."

"Yes, sir, it would be," Yiannis said, sliding his hands under the table and grabbing his knees in an attempt to stop the shaking.

"It's too bad that your boss got himself murdered," Pappas said, licking the spoon's underside.

"Boss? What boss?"

"Orhan Iskur."

"I didn't work for him. I used to run errands for him sometimes, that's all. I know nothing about his business."

Pappas spread his hands in disappointment. "Yiannis, it's not nice to lie to a police colonel. It upsets me."

"I never worked with him, I swear."

Waving his spoon at the thief, Pappas said, "Let me tell you a story. Sixteen years ago in London, two men with Greek passports tried to sell a fake antiquity to an American. The American happened to be a dealer, and he recognized the statue as not being genuine. He called the police, and the two men were arrested. A few days later, for reasons we'll never know, this American decided to drop the charges against the two men. Constable Wade, who was the arresting officer, was a conscientious policeman, so he went back to his station and prepared an Interpol intelligence report. The duplicate copy remained at his station; the triplicate went into the central file, and the original made its way to Paris, where it remained until an inquiry was recently made by the Hellenic Police Department." He stabbed the spoon at the thief's sweating face. "Yiannis Yiotas and Orhan Iskur were the two men arrested."

"I forgot all about that," Yiannis blurted. "It was a mistake, I swear. We didn't know that it was a fake."

"Of course you didn't." Pappas drank some more retsina. He lowered the glass and made wet circles on the paper tablecloth. "Did Iskur have a mistress?"

The thief's eyes widened. "How did you know about her?"

Pappas smiled. "Men like him have either a mistress or a young boy."

Yiannis was so relieved at the shift in direction that he took a deep breath and went on to tell Pappas about Nina Pazza. A tall, strikingly handsome woman, Iskur had met her in Rome ten years ago, when she was sixteen. He fell in love with her and brought her back to Athens with him, installing her in a fashionable apartment on Aristodimou Street.

"What can you tell me about her?"

"Nothing, really. I used to chauffeur her on some of her shopping trips. But she never talked to me about anything. Just park here or there and wait for me."

Yiannis Yiotas's legs still would not stop shaking.

Pappas looked hard into the thief's eyes. "Why don't we talk about the Voúla massacre?"

Yiannis's mouth fell open; he began to tremble violently.

"We know it was you who got the car that was used by Cuttler and Simmons. We also know that it was you who followed officers Tasos Lefas and Lakis Rekor and learned their routines, and it was you who took the photographs of the officers to give to their killers," Pappas lied, following nothing more than an educated guess.

Panic filled Yiannis Yiotas's face, and Pappas knew that his dart had hit the bull's-eye. He had to keep up the pressure, not give the thief time to think, increase his panic, and then when there was no hope, to throw him a lifesaver. "You're going to spend the rest of your miserable life in prison." Then he smiled at the thief. Yiannis was shaking so much that Pappas thought he might faint. Now was the time to play nice guy. "Of course, if you cooperate, we might be able to work something out so that you don't have to go to jail, maybe not even be arrested."

Yiannis clutched the lifeline. "You won't arrest me?"

"I'm not interested in you. I want the people who planned Voúla. If you tell me everything you know, I'll see to it that you don't go to prison."

Yiannis Yiotas covered his face with his hands and wept. People at nearby tables turned and looked at him in open astonishment.

Pappas needed an admission of guilt. "You didn't know why Iskur wanted you to do those things, did you?"

"No. I swear, I didn't know. I didn't know."

"It was you who made the arrangements with the taxi driver to pick up Aldridge Long, the American, at the airport and drive him to Iskur's shop, wasn't it?"

Yiannis absently nodded his head. "Yes."

"Were you with Iskur when Long arrived at the shop?"

"No. He made me leave before he got there."

"Had you ever met Long?"

"No."

Pappas glanced around the taverna. This was not the place to conduct an interrogation. He had opened the door a little; he'd open it a lot more on the top floor of 173 Leoforos Alexandras. He motioned to the waiter. "My friend would like to pay the bill."

Watching the waiter add up the tab, Yiannis happened to notice that the wall clock inside the butcher shop read six minutes after midnight. It was now Tuesday, a bad luck day.

8

Teddy Lucas walked out of his building's lobby and stopped. The air was crisp and vibrant with the sounds of Manhattan. He looked up at the green canopy of trees and saw Ajax perched on a tree trunk. He moved jauntily down the steps. In a nearby playground, toddlers dashed under the shower's gentle spray while their mothers relaxed on benches next to it.

Lucas turned right, moving onto the wide concrete path that wound through Stuyvesant Town's carefully maintained shrubs, down the steps, and onto the sidewalk, which led to the city streets.

"Teddy," a familiar voice called out.

He stopped, aware of the immediate pounding of rage inside his head. He turned and saw her stepping out from behind a tree, a nervous smile on her lips.

He warned himself to stay calm.

"Hello, Teddy," she said quietly. "I didn't mean to ambush you, but you wouldn't answer any of my calls."

He glared at his ex-wife. Heavy brown leather sandals, loose-fitting Indian cotton dress, long hair swept up behind her head with a leather thong. No makeup, pallid skin, and dark circles under her otherwise pretty eyes. He tried in vain to recall some intimate detail of the life they had once shared. Only hurt and deceit came out of the grave of his memory.

"What do you want, Ellen?"

"Just to talk."

He heard a slight catch in her voice and found himself walking in silence beside her to a bench. Ellen sat, slapped the folds of her dress between her spread legs. Watching kids run under the spray, she said, "We wanted children once, remember?"

Stay cool, he thought. "Why don't you get to the point?" A memory floated into his head. The sad look of disappointment on his father's face when he announced his plans to marry Ellen. "But she's not Greek," his dad had said as his mother squeezed her husband's arm in a mute plea for silence.

"As you can see, I'm back in New York."

"I'm busy, Ellen. What's the problem?"

"Well, you see, I'm working in this boutique on Columbus Avenue and I've gone back to college. I'm majoring in psychology. I don't get home till eleven at night and I have to be up at six to make an eight o'clock class." She shifted uneasily on the bench, fanned her calves nervously with the hem of her dress, and slapped it back down between her legs. "I have a tiny apartment in Bensonhurst; it's the pits. My life would be so much easier if I could live in Manhattan, but I can't afford the rents. So, I was wondering"—she ran her finger over the design on her dress—"if you might let me come and stay with you. I'd sleep on the couch and pay my share of the rent. I'd cook and clean; it would just be until I got on my feet again." She seemed to run out of words and looked down at her lap, her ears bright pink from embarrassment.

He laughed and said, "You always did have a big pair of balls. You run off with another man and then reappear five years later asking to move back in because you can't afford Manhattan rents. Where's your boyfriend?"

"Gone. He left me for a nineteen-year-old."

He shrugged and looked away from her. "You're out of my life. I have no intention of letting you worm your way back into it."

"Teddy . . ."

"Listen to me, lady," he said, his angry eyes boring into hers. "I married you because I loved you. And I was a pretty good husband." He stopped and frowned. "I admit, I did spend more time at work than I did with you. So maybe I didn't think enough about what you needed."

She nodded in embarrassed agreement.

"You wanted to join the community school board, so I didn't object. And that was how you met the love of your life. . . ."

"Teddy, please . . ."

"Listen," he said, pressing his finger against her lips. "You left me for a forty-year-old creep with a beard who never worked a day in his life. He's mastered the art of stroking colleges and corporations out of grants so he could spend his worthless life studying some language that only two people in the world speak. Well, you made your choice—live with it." He got up to leave.

"Your damn male Greek ego won't let you forget that I left you for another man, will it?" she snarled.

"You're wrong, lady. I could have forgiven unfaithfulness. But what I won't forgive, what I can't forgive, is that you used to go to his apartment and wash his goddamn socks. That kind of a commitment I'll never forgive." He turned and moved off to the sounds of her sobs.

At ten minutes before ten o'clock that beautiful morning, the blue Buick slid into the curb in front of the Pierpont Morgan Library. Lucas tossed the vehicle I.D. onto the dashboard and he and Vassos got out of the car.

Katina was waiting for them inside the vestibule. She was wearing a pink linen suit, bone-colored sling-back shoes. Her long legs were bare. "Good morning," she said cheerfully, and turned to lead them down the gleaming mahogany staircase into the basement work area. Walking into her office, she picked up a sheet of paper from her desk and handed it to Lucas. "The book dealers that I've contacted."

Lucas studied the list. "Widener Books? Widener?" He looked at Vassos. "Where do we know that name from?"

Vassos leaned forward in his chair, suddenly intense. "Belmont E. Widener?"

Lucas's voice went up several notches as it came to him. "Hey, he was the complainant who had a book stolen by one of McKay's boys in 'seventy-seven."

"The book by Aristarchus," Vassos said.

"Aristarchus of Samothrace?" Katina said, crossing her legs.

"Dunno," Lucas said, and proceeded to tell her everything that he could remember about the 1977 robbery. "Have you heard of this guy, Aristarchus?"

Her smile bore a trace of impatience. "Yes, Teddy, I've heard of him."

"Fill us in, will you?" Lucas asked.

"Aristarchus lived between 217 and 145 B.C. He was one of Alexandria's great librarians," she began, going on to tell them how Ptolemy had ordered that a complete collection of Greek literature be gathered and stored in the great library. This had never been done before so the librarians had to develop catalogues of the texts to be copied, and then they had to rent or borrow the texts from other kings so that the scribes of Alexandria might copy them. In order to protect against forgeries, the librarians were forced to develop new principles of textual criticism. In order to properly copy Homer, for instance, the librarians had to first decide which text passages were accurate transcriptions of oral recitations and not merely the writings of some unknown actor or scribe. They would study Homer's work and then write commentaries indicating which verses they considered fraudulent or corrupted by scribal emendation. Aristarchus used marginal notes to point out what he considered irregularities or spurious verses."

"Where were these notes made?" Lucas asked.

"On the text itself," she said. "He developed an entire system of marginal scholia."

"Then Aristarchus, after he made his notations on the original text, would write up his report, which you call a commentary," Lucas said.

"Yes," she agreed.

"Were these commentaries made part of the original text?" Lucas asked.

"No, they weren't," she said. "Since they were meant to be read only by scholars, they were prepared in separate texts. The librarians would hold weekly meetings to discuss the commentaries and try to agree on what changes the scribes should make in the texts that were being copied."

"Then it's safe to assume that Aristarchus prepared commentaries on the *Iliad*?" Lucas asked.

"On the *Iliad* and the *Odyssey*. Aristarchus was fascinated by Homer and he became the library's resident Homeric scholar." She got up, smoothed her skirt. "Would either of you like a cup of coffee?"

"No, thank you," Lucas said, suddenly aware of a strong aroma of coffee.

Vassos shook his head.

She left the office and returned shortly holding a delicate cup and saucer.

Lucas waited until she was seated to ask, "Katina, if I remember correctly, the casket-copy was stored in the library during the time Aristarchus wrote his commentaries."

"Yes, that's true," she said, taking a sip from her cup.

Her lipstick left a thick impression around the rim.

"If I were Aristarchus and I was preparing a commentary on the *Iliad*, I would certainly use the casket-copy as an authoritative and established text."

"I do not see how he could have failed to do such a thing," Vassos said, awaiting her pronouncement.

She returned the cup to the saucer and placed them on her desk. She picked up a pencil and began tapping it over the green blotter. "Yes, I believe that he would have done that."

"And if he did," Lucas said, feeling the strong glow of excitement stirring in his chest, "then he would have made marginal notes on the casket-copy."

His comments stilled her hand. She let the pencil fall, regarding him with newfound respect. "I agree with your reasoning, Teddy."

Lucas continued: "Aristarchus's commentary, along with the marginal notes that he made on the casket-copy, would go a long way toward authenticating Alexander's *Iliad*."

Vassos leaned back in his chair, his eyes drifting over to a poster on the wall of a gondola gliding down a Venetian canal.

"There's a flaw in your reasoning," she said.

"What?" Lucas demanded.

Vassos kept his stare fixed on the shimmering black canal flowing under the stone bridge.

"Aristarchus prepared commentaries on other authors besides Homer. The commentary that was stolen from Belmont Widener in 1977 might have been on any number of texts, not necessarily the casket-copy," she said.

"Did many commentaries survive?" Lucas asked.

"Perhaps ten out of six hundred," she said, reaching for her cup.

A summer breeze swept across Manhattan, seasoning the air with the salty smell of two rivers. Widener Books was quartered in a slender, five-story building jammed between two glass skyscrapers on Seventeenth Street between Park Avenue South and Broadway. The building's cream-colored facade was brightened by window boxes overflowing with summer blooms. Muses and caryatids garnished the roof's balustrade.

Belmont E. Widener was waiting for them. A man of medium stature with pointy ears, he had sagging ivory bags under deep-set eyes and thick wavelets of brown hair swept back over a rather large head. The yellow silk bow tie that he wore was patterned with tiny pink butterflies.

He rushed forward to greet Katina. "Dr. Wright, what a great pleasure. I could hardly believe my ears when my secretary told me that you were coming to pay us a visit. And with the police, no less." He clasped his dainty hands to his chest and looked innocently at the policemen.

Katina made the introductions.

A salesman's grin spread across the book dealer's face. "Are you two gentlemen interested in purchasing rare books? If you are, I've recently come into possession of a Voloretti codex."

"We're here to ask you some questions concerning a robbery that took place in 1977," Lucas said.

"Eleven years ago? Really? That's yesterday's news." His bright, curious eyes examined Vassos. "You're not with the NYPD."

"I am a major in the Hellenic Police Department. Here on special assignment."

Lucas thought that he detected a fleeting expression of fear on the book dealer's face.

"I see," Widener said, and turned brusquely to Katina. "Dr. Wright, before we discuss whatever police business brought you here, I would love to show you my prized possessions."

"I'd be delighted," she said, asking for her companions to be patient by lifting an eyebrow.

Widener guided them up through three floors of books. Brass chandeliers illuminated dark parquet flooring covered with brightly colored oriental rugs. There were rows upon rows of rosewood bookcases, the contents of which were protected by fine black metal mesh. The musty scent of books and the comfortable smell of worn leather pervaded each floor. Widener was a joyous child showing off his treasures. He brought out ancient vellum manuscripts, maps, tomes of Barcherlo and Stair. He twirled a great Cussennelli globe signed and dated 1587. Finally he led them single file into the fourth-floor vault, a stainless steel monster with massive locking pins.

"My best stuff is here," he said, and proceeded to show them a tenth-century Bloomberg missal, a first edition *King Lear* dated 1608, a set of three Shakespeare folios. His last treasure was a first edition of de Reuyter's *Voyage to Foreign Lands*, dated 1579.

"May I?" Katina said, holding out her hands. "I love to listen to the music of the old paper."

"Oh, yes, so do I," Widener said, with an air of excitement bordering on sexual arousal. He placed the book into her waiting hands. She held it up close to her ear and gently flipped the pages, sounding each one with a sharp push of her fingers. Her head was tilted slightly into the book so that she might better hear the music, her eyes lifted in concentration.

Lucas watched her fingers caress each page, sending them past with a snap. They were exquisite hands, the beautifully cared for nails glowing with polish. His eyes drifted down to her bare legs, and he fantasized about the dark mysterious treasure at their apex.

Widener moved between her and the policemen. "Each page should give an authentic rag paper crackle," he explained.

She added, "If it's not a forgery." She snapped the last page and handed the dealer back his book. "A wonderful collection."

Widener beamed. "Thank you. Now. Shall we go to my office on the second floor and discuss this eleven-year-old crime?"

The office looked out at the colorful mixture of architecture in the area. A carved walnut desk with high-relief scenes of Hercules and the Sphinx dominated the richly furnished office. A golden tapestry depicting the Adoration of the Magi hung on one wall.

"Please sit," Widener said, moving behind the desk and lowering himself into a carved walnut armchair. His expression became serious. "Why are the police suddenly interested in this crime?"

Vassos took out and fingered his jade worry beads, the ones that Colonel Pappas had taken off of Iskur's body and then given to Vassos for good luck.

"Mr. Widener, we have some reason to believe that your stolen commentary might be connected to the theft of an antiquity from Greece," Lucas said.

A flush came to the dealer's cheeks. "What antiquity?"

"The casket-copy," Katina said dryly.

He looked at Vassos. "Your government has sent you here to try and recover it?"

"Yes," Vassos said.

"And you, Dr. Wright, have been enlisted to render whatever technical assistance that the police might require?"

"Yes," she said.

"I see." Widener slumped, his shoulders sagging under some invisible weight. "The casket-copy," he said reflectively. "The collector's ultimate dream."

"Was your Aristarchus commentary on the *Iliad?*" Katina asked, holding her breath.

"Yes," Widener answered.

"Would you tell us how you came to own it?" Lucas said.

Widener sighed. "The Duke of Siracusa was selling his private library back in September of 'seventy-five. The sale was to take place at the duke's castle in Lichtenstein." He sighed at the memory of it. "I went, of course, and bought some interesting things. Late one afternoon, I was browsing in the east wing of the library when I saw a scroll sticking out from behind a stack of books. I bent down and removed it. It was obviously quite old. I rushed to check the card index but there was nothing on it. So, I did the next best thing and asked the duke. He informed me that his great-grandfather was notorious for buying things and sticking them on library shelves without bothering to enter them in the index." A sly smile. "The duke and I engaged in some genteel haggling. He asked an outrageous sum, citing the scroll's antiquity. I pointed out that it might contain worthless business records, or even be blank, or illegible. I also told him that I'd have to spend a considerable sum on restoration and deciphering."

"But you did buy it?" Lucas said.

"Yes, and for not a lot of money," Widener said smugly.

"When did you realize what you had bought?" Lucas asked.

"Not for several months," the dealer said. "As soon as I returned home I entered into negotiations for a manorial land grant by William the Conqueror. That piece of business kept me occupied for the better part of three months. I stuck the scroll into the bottom drawer of this desk and forgot about it for a while. Five months later I had it unrolled and deciphered."

"What did you do when you discovered what you had bought?" Lucas asked the dealer.

"I did nothing," Widener said. "I knew that the scroll's value was not going to decrease."

"You didn't show it off to any of your friends or colleagues in the book business?" Lucas said, a disbelieving edge to his voice.

"In this business, Lieutenant, you wait before revealing your treasure. A smart dealer first makes sure that there is demand for his find." He tugged at his ear. "The greater the demand, the higher the price."

"And you create the demand," Lucas said.

"Exactly," Widener said, adjusting his tie.

"How do you do that?" Lucas asked.

"By going to dinner parties given by the right sort of people. Dropping tantalizing tidbits about Aristarchus of Samothrace and the great library at Alexandria."

"And after you've created demand?" Lucas wanted to know, catching Katina looking at him, a haze in her eyes. When he looked at her, her gaze dropped away.

"Then you let it be known at some cocktail party that you've located one of Aristarchus's commentaries, but that, unfortunately, the owner refuses to part with it," Widener said.

"And the word spreads," Lucas said.

"With the speed of light," Widener said. "Within days I had collectors and dealers calling me from all over the country. There was so much interest that I decided to hold an auction. So I announced the offering in my next catalogue."

"Was there any unusual interest?" Katina asked.

"There was a lot of interest, but nothing unusual," Widener said.

"Tell us about the robbery," Lucas said.

"A few days before the auction I received a telephone call from a Mr. Dwight Roget. He wanted an appointment for the next day so that he could examine the commentary. I told him to be here at eleven o'clock."

"Wasn't that unusual?" Lucas asked.

"Not at all," Widener said. "Most collectors want to see an item before bidding on it."

"Did you know this man?" Vassos asked, closely watching the rare book dealer.

"No, I didn't. But then, one does not know every dealer and collector, does one?" Widener said, adjusting his tie.

Vassos became agitated. "I think it very strange that you could show such a valuable thing to a person without making an identification of him first."

"The man with whom I spoke, Major, knew the rare book business. He knew the jargon, what was currently available. I had no reason to be suspicious," Widener said, a trace of anger in his shrill voice.

"You made the appointment, then what happened?" Lucas asked.

"The next day, at the appointed time, two well-dressed men appeared. One of them, a stocky fellow, introduced himself as Dwight Roget. The other one didn't say very much, as I recall. Just grunted hello. I escorted them upstairs and asked them to wait while I went into the vault to get the commentary. Suddenly, they were inside with me, the quiet one pointing a gun at my head." He clutched his chest in painful remembrance. Beads of sweat appeared on his nose. "They handcuffed me inside the vault and left with my commentary."

Vassos persisted: "I still find it very strange, sir, that you would see such persons without knowing them."

"Major, we in the art world are not accustomed to being confronted by gangsters with guns. It just doesn't happen."

Katina interceded in Greek. "He's right, Andreas."

"You're handcuffed inside the vault, then what?" Lucas asked.

"Luckily, they didn't close the door. So as soon as I saw them get into the elevator, I began to scream. It was early in the morning and no one else was on the floor. But fortunately, Mrs. Wooley, my assistant, was walking up from the next floor when she heard my screams. She ran up, saw me chained like a dog, and, thank God, had the presence of mind to press the alarm. One of your police cars was passing at the time. They caught one of the bandits, but regrettably, not the one with the commentary."

"Bucky McMahon was the man the officers arrested," Lucas said.

"Yes, that was his name. After eight months of interminable court postponements, he was permitted to plead guilty to robbery in the second degree," Widener said.

"Were you shown mug shots in an effort to identify the other one?" Lucas asked.

"Hundreds of them," Widener replied. "But I was unable to pick anyone out. They were all disgusting-looking people."

Katina slipped off her earring and laid it down on top of her pocketbook. She glanced at Lucas with a look that said: my turn.

"Mr. Widener, I must confess that I have always been fascinated by your two specialties."

Widener sparkled. "I have one of the world's greatest collections of incunabula and letters from nineteenth- and twentieth-century revolutionaries."

"I hear rumors," Katina confided, "that the Soviet government is negotiating for your collection of letters by Lenin and Trotsky."

Widener crimsoned. "That's a damn lie. I'll never break up my collection. Never! The Russians would love to get their grubby hands on those letters, but they never will."

A smile spread across Katina's lovely face. "See how adamant collectors are about their collections."

Lucas smiled back at her.

"Who unrolled and deciphered the scroll?" she asked.

"Edmonds at Columbia deciphered it and Goodman at the Met unrolled it," Widener replied.

"Mr. Widener, does the name Orhan Iskur mean anything to you?" Lucas asked.

"No, it doesn't. Should it?" asked the book dealer.

"No," Lucas said.

Vassos took out the composite sketch and the passport photo of Aldridge Long and handed them to Widener. "Do you know this man?"

The rare book dealer studied the photo and the drawing for a long time. Finally he said firmly, "No, I don't believe I do."

"Did you have much of a conversation with the men who robbed you?" Lucas asked.

"As I recall they didn't say too much," Widener said.

"Mr. Widener, can you tell me if either of them was the same man who telephoned you to make the appointment?" Lucas asked, watching the book dealer.

Widener's mouth dropped open; his eyes grew wide. "Good heavens, it was a long time ago." He sat pondering, his hands clutching the ornate arms of his chair. "It wasn't the same man," he announced with sudden vigor. "The man who telephoned was educated, articulate, and he knew the business."

"Then why did you let two men, neither of whom sounded or looked quite right, into your shop?" Vassos demanded.

"I . . . I didn't realize until just now. No one ever asked me," Widener explained.

Vassos's face betrayed open disbelief. He got up abruptly from his chair and said, with no pretense of courtesy, "I think we have heard quite enough. There are other people who can tell us what we need to know."

9

A roll of fat bulged around the fingerprint man's waist. Acne scarred his face and his flamboyant, greasy black mustache was grossly unkempt. He sat in front of the print scanner examining the latents from the Iskur crime scene. Lucas and Vassos stood behind him, studying the magnified impressions on the screen. Katina stood off to the left, her curious eyes taking in every detail of the Latent Unit's fifth-floor office.

They had left Widener's thirty minutes before. Lucas decided to stop off at One Police Plaza before continuing on to the rest of the dealers; he wanted the prints from Greece examined by an NYPD technician.

"What were those lifted off?" asked the technician, as he slid the latents around under the glass, obviously attempting to note all the characteristics.

"The victim's billfold," Vassos said.

"What can you tell us?" Lucas asked.

"Right up front I can say that there are not enough points to make a positive I.D. I can only make out nine points among the three fingers, and as you guys both know, we need twelve in each finger."

Katina drifted over to the machine. "What does that mean, enough points?"

Lucas said: "There must be twelve similar points of comparison before any two fingerprints can be positively identified as coming from the same person."

"What must be similar?" she asked.

"The ridges that form the fingerprint pattern," Lucas answered.

The technician picked up a pencil from the workbench. "This is a bifurcating ridge," he said, pointing. "See how it runs along and then forks into three branches?"

She leaned in between the two men to get a better look. As she did, she brushed against Lucas. He felt a charge of electricity course through his body. Embarrassed, he stepped back in order to make room for her.

". . . this ridge we call a divergence. Notice how the two ridges run parallel and then spread apart."

"Yes, I see them," Katina said.

"When we can point out twelve similar characteristics in another finger, we have a positive I.D.," the technician said.

Lucas found himself standing behind her, watching her as she bent toward the machine. The scanner's illuminated screen backlit her skirt, revealing the vague outline of her thighs. Vassos picked up on Lucas's hungry stare, and his face crinkled in a knowing smile. Katina backed away from the machine.

Lucas took her place, placing his hand on the man's shoulder, leaning forward as if to study the screen, whispering, "What can you tell me, unofficially?"

"Educated guesswork, Lou," he whispered back.

"I'm listening." Lucas became painfully aware of the man's rancid body odor.

"Well, for one thing, they're the prints of a man. Women have smaller, narrower ridges. And the array of the fingers show that they're from the middle, ring, and pinkie, most probably of the right hand," the technician said.

"Why the right hand?" Lucas asked.

Using the pencil as a tracer, the fingerprint man said, "The ridges of the pinkie enter on one side of the impression, recurve, and flow down the other side."

"I see that," Lucas said.

"We call that kind of an impression a loop. There are two kinds: ulnar loops, which flow out toward the ulnar bone, and radial loops, which flow out toward the radial bone. The overwhelming percentage of pinkie loops are ulnar, which would mean that the chances are pretty good that this pinkie came from the right hand."

"But not a certainty."

"That's right," he said. "The ring and middle finger appear to be tented arches, which would narrow down the search considerably, *if* we were going to search the files. Another thing, see how the ridges at the bottom of the ring finger appear to have been ripped apart, how they have a jagged white line running through them?"

"Yes," Lucas said.

"That's a permanent scar."

Lucas glanced around at Vassos and tossed him a "get lost" look. Vassos answered with a nod, took Katina's arm, and waltzed her over to the wall display of blown-up marked fingerprints made for jury presentation in notorious trials.

Lucas leaned in close to the seated man. One of his zits was oozing pus. "Would you check these latents out against a list of B numbers for me?" he whispered, referring to the permanent identification number prisoners receive when they are first arrested.

"No problem, Lou. But you gotta understand, there just ain't no way I can give you a positive. The best you can hope for is a maybe."

"I'll take it. What about checking out the criminal and civilian files for me?"

"Lou," the technician moaned. "we ain't allowed to search the civilian files on a criminal matter. You wouldn't want me to violate some taxi driver's constitutional rights, would you?"

"Hey, perish the thought," Lucas whispered, asking, "Where's the john?"

The technician jerked his thumb over his shoulder. "Behind me and to the right." He shut off the humming machine and got up.

Passing Vassos and Katina, Lucas gestured to the major to keep her busy and moved down the aisle between machine-laden desks. As he moved past one desk he spotted a book of matches and picked it up.

Entering the white-tiled bathroom, Lucas stepped into an empty stall and locked the door. He reached into his left trouser pocket and took out the expense money that the C of D had given him. He peeled a fifty from the wad, folded it in such a way that Grant's portrait showed, and slid it behind the red-tipped forest of matches in the open book. He closed the book's cover, securing the lid behind the flap, and left the bathroom.

This was the part of the Job he hated. Years ago it was a cop's job. You did for each other out of a common sense of loyalty, a common purpose. No more. Civilization had come to the NYPD. The department was awash in political patronage, a pork barrel full of boa constrictors, each one with its mouth open.

The technician was at the photocopy machine duplicating the Iskur latents. Lucas walked up to him and handed him the list of Denny McKay's men that he had taken from Vassos on his way back from the bathroom. He gave the list to the technician and asked him to make a dozen copies.

The fingerprint man said, "Sure, Lou. No problem. Everybody's out to lunch so I don't have to worry about tying up the machine," and lifted the machine's rubber mat cover, laid the paper on top of the glass, blanketed the mat back over the paper, and pushed a green button.

The machine sprang into life, spewing out sheets of white paper into the side tray.

Lucas leaned against the copier, watching the light glow each time the top slid back and forth. "Would you check those latents against the fingerprints of the men on that list?"

"Sure, Lou," the technician said, switching off the machine.

"If you come up dry, would you also check the criminal and civilian files for me?" He slipped the book of matches into the technician's shirt pocket. "Here are your matches back."

Tucking in his chin, the fingerprint man looked down into his pocket. He stuck two fingers inside the pocket and pried open the cover. Pushing the row of matches forward, he spotted Ulysses Grant's dour face and smiled. "Lou, them civilian rights? I fuck 'em where they breathe."

Shielding his eyes with his hands, Lucas scanned Police Plaza for an empty bench. He spied four women getting up from a stone square. "Andreas, why don't you and Katina grab that seat and I'll go get us lunch."

Lucas returned shortly, gingerly balancing three cardboard plates holding hero sandwiches overflowing with crimson onions. A cardboard holder for sodas was clutched in his other hand, straws protruding out of punch-in cans. He eased the sodas down on the bench between them and handed them both a plate.

"How much do I owe you?" Katina asked, reaching into her pocketbook.

"Nothing, you made a score," Lucas said.

"What does that mean?" she asked.

"It's on the NYPD," Lucas said.

"Thank you, NYPD," Katina answered, gracefully nibbling onions. She looked at Vassos. "Have you ever eaten a hero sandwich before?"

"In Greece such a thing would be called souvlaki, and we use pita bread." He smiled. "But Pericles Levi's daughter must surely know that." He chomped into the hero.

"What do you think of police work?" Lucas asked her.

"It's fun," she said, her eyes sparkling. "It can get a bit boring patching up ancient parchments. Do you think we've accomplished anything?" she asked, wrapping her lips around the straw.

"I hope we've started some people worrying," Lucas said, looking at her wet lips.

She looked around the sun-drenched plaza. "Do most of these people work for the police department?"

"Most of them," Lucas answered, putting his plate down on his knees and looking at Vassos. "What did you think of Widener?"

Vassos made a noncommittal shrug. Katina responded instead: "He's got a slightly murky reputation. I think he is definitely hiding something. Maybe he's no victim at all."

Paul Mastri was a handsome man in his sixties, 'tall and well built, with a sinewy body that moved with the graceful assurance of success. Mastri Associates was located in a triple suite of interconnecting rooms on Madison Avenue north of Fifty-sixth Street. A male secretary led the trio into Mastri's office. The large room's white marble floor and walls gleamed softly.

"Dr. Wright, what a pleasure," Mastri said smoothly, moving out from behind his desk to kiss Katina on both her cheeks.

Katina made the introductions.

Lucas noted that Mastri's handshake was firm, his clothes jaunty: he wore a tie of bold blue stripes against a blazing orange background, a blazer of white linen, a fluffy orange handkerchief in the pocket, blue trousers. "I must have gotten a dozen telephone calls so far this morning telling me about your visit to Widener Books," Mastri said, carefully spreading the folds of his jacket to avoid sitting on them and wrinkling it. He lowered himself into his carved and gilded throne of a chair, which was covered with scarlet velvet.

"That's some chair you've got," Lucas observed.

"Thank you," Mastri said. "It's Venetian, circa 1730." He turned his attention to Katina, wiggling a finger at her. "You've tantalized the industry, Dr. Wright, with your inquiries concerning the casket-copy."

"Word travels fast," Lucas said.

Mastri leaned forward, sliding his elbows onto the desk. "Has the casket-copy really been unearthed?"

"We think so," Katina said.

"Think? Only think?" Mastri relaxed back into his seat. "Hasn't anyone seen it? Established provenance?"

"No, not yet," Katina said. "The entire matter is a bit confused."

"Confused?" Mastri said. "What is the Morgan's interest in all this?"

"Absolutely none," Katina said. "The police requested our help and we agreed. The library is not involved in any other way."

"Not involved?" Mastri said, a disbelieving smile evident on his smooth face. "One of the greatest finds ever, and the Morgan is not involved. I find that a very difficult morsel to swallow, Dr. Wright."

"Nevertheless, it's the truth," she said.

"Mr. Mastri, if someone were to bring you the casket-copy, would you be able to sell it?" Lucas asked.

"I wouldn't touch it without the necessary export papers," Mastri said.

Lucas leaned forward on the low-slung white sofa, his hand making tiny circles. "Just suppose that everything was in order."

An insincere smile exposed Mastri's capped teeth. "The legendary casket-copy? I would be able to dispose of it within the day."

Vassos was subdued and thoughtful. "At what price?"

Mastri fixed his eyes on the ceiling. "Truthfully? I don't know. Prices in the art world have come unglued since Van Gogh's *Irises* went at auction for fifty million dollars. There is no limit anymore, no rationale. What price? I would make up some ridiculously absurd number. And I would get it." He looked at Katina. "Dr. Wright, I would just love to show you my latest acquisition." He got up and went over to the bookcase. Cabinets lined the bottom. He opened one of the doors and removed a book, its green cover heavily embossed with gold. He went over and handed it to her, then stepped back.

Katina placed the book on her lap and turned back the cover to reveal an ancient script written in silver ink on purple paper. Slowly turning each sheet, she took in each decorated page with muttered approval. Toward the end of the book she looked up at the policemen and explained, "This is a translation of the Bible into the Gothic. Sixth century, I think."

"Very good, Dr. Wright. You know your subject," Mastri said.

Carefully closing the cover, she handed the book back to the dealer and said, "Magnificent."

"Thank you," Mastri said, beaming proudly.

"Before today, had you heard of any interest in the casket-copy?" Lucas asked.

"No, I hadn't. The last I heard of it was when I heard of the famous Matrazzo telegram. And frankly, I just do not believe that it could have survived all those millennia. Fragments perhaps, but the complete *Iliad?* I can't believe that," Mastri said.

Lucas got up and moved aimlessly around the room. "You don't appear to have any alarm system in place, Mr. Mastri."

"We're well protected, Lieutenant," Mastri said. "There's all sorts of state-of-the-art gadgetry hidden about. Insurance regulations require it."

Vassos asked, "Do you know Orhan Iskur?"

"No, I don't. Is he in the trade?"

"Not really," Lucas said. "He deals in cheap imitations."

"I wouldn't know such a person," Mastri said dismissively.

"Mr. Mastri, did you know that Belmont Widener had come upon one of Aristarchus's commentaries on the *Iliad?*" Katina asked.

"My dear Dr. Wright, the entire trade knew once he announced it in his catalogue." He smoothed back his stone-colored hair, taking great care that all the strands were tucked neatly behind his ears. "I, of course, knew long before he announced."

When Lucas asked him how he knew, Mastri tossed him a patronizing look and said, "I've been in this business long enough to spot a dealer who is making the rounds drumming up demand."

Pompous ass, Lucas thought, smiling thinly at the dealer.

"Mr. Mastri, are you aware of any dealer or collector with a special interest in ancient material relating to the development of silent reading?" Katina asked.

"You are confusing scholarship with collecting, Dr. Wright. A collector desires to possess some great object from antiquity, but . . ."

Lucas saw the fire blazing in the dealer's eyes. He'd seen the same look on the faces of other men. He'd seen it on a gambler's as he waited for the last card to be turned; he'd seen it on an alcoholic's as he hurried up to the bar to get his first drink of the day; he'd seen it on Andreas Vassos's whenever he spoke of his murdered family. Driven men, consumed by emotions they did not fully understand, each with an unalterable passion, and an uncontrollable one.

". . . a scholar seeks answers to questions. How did civilization progress from point A to point B? And why? A collector does not concern himself with such matters."

Vassos dumped his worry beads into his shirt pocket and took out the composite sketch. "Do you know this person?" he asked, passing the sketch and photo to the dealer.

A minute passed. Mastri handed them back. "No, I have never seen this gentleman before."

"Would you let me know if you should hear anything about someone offering the casket-copy for sale?" Katina said.

"You can count on it, Dr. Wright," Mastri said, standing.

Katina moved up to the desk to admire a black lacquer box. A hunting scene in a medieval forest was painted on the lid. She noted that the painter had made the blood of the dying boar all too real.

The air-conditioning in C of D Edgeworth's unmarked Plymouth had not been repaired, despite assurances from the Wagon Board that a new condenser would be installed "forthwith." This had not particularly improved his humor during the long, very hot drive up to mid-town Manhattan from One Police Plaza. His driver stopped in front of the heavy stone facade of the Millennium Club, the iron bars over its windows and the heavy, dark-wood double doors of its entrance offering a rather forbidding welcome for the uninitiated guest.

Inside, the large marble-floored lobby afforded a cool refuge from the blazing afternoon heat. Edgeworth was met by a dignified black man in a gray uniform and courteously directed to an uncomfortable bench, very like a pew, that stood on one side of the lobby. "Mr. Borden hasn't arrived yet," he was told. Asked if he wanted to "freshen up," Edgeworth merely grunted a negative response and plumped himself down on the bench reserved for strangers. While he waited, with mounting impatience, he read a long and thoroughly puzzling article in the *Journal of the National Association of Chiefs of Police* written by a chief from a small western city, a prodigy who had a Harvard Ph.D. The article discussed ways of building department morale; Edgeworth found it as exotic and as irrelevant as a book by Margaret Mead on courtship in Samoa that he had read, under duress, while an undergraduate at Hofstra.

He was attempting to understand what his fellow cop meant by something called "male bonding" when a beautifully shined pair of handmade shoes appeared in the lower left quadrant of his vision. He looked up to see the bright blue eyes of Gerald Borden regarding him indulgently, his hectic red complexion set off by a waxed white mustache; a gray, pin-striped, unwrinkled summer suit, blue Brooks button-down, and a jaunty bow tie wrapping up the package.

"I'm grateful that you made time to see me, Tim. And that you came up my way. I have to catch a six-fifty train, and we need some time to catch up."

Edgeworth was wondering about what precisely they had to talk about as Borden led him up the wide staircase to the second floor, where they sat down in deep, leather-covered chairs. Large yellowing oil portraits decorated the walls; below them were bookshelves crammed with multicolored bindings. Edgeworth was making a cop's thorough mental inventory of the place when he saw Borden writing out an order for drinks while a waiter hovered deferentially nearby. "And you, Tim?"

"Just a soft drink, Gerry; whatever they got that's real cold."

Borden pushed back in his chair and looked over the low round table between them. He took an immaculate white handkerchief out of his breast pocket and blew his nose vigorously.

"I believe you have been in touch, er, more or less, with one of my former associates?"

Edgeworth regarded him sourly and said, "Is *that* what all this fuss is about? I thought Hayden was State Department, not one of your gang."

Borden took the bourbon old-fashioned that the silently reappearing waiter offered him on a silver tray, then picked up a tall glass of ginger ale and handed it to Edgeworth, who downed half of it in one gulp.

The waiter left and Borden continued in a lower tone of voice. "Strictly speaking, he isn't one of us. He was a contract employee, a paramilitary type. Police background, not too scrupulous about what sort of jobs he would take on. We put his talents to good use in Laos, back in the days of the great crusade."

Edgeworth sat forward, hands on his knees. "Just what sort of jobs did he do for you?"

Borden smiled benignly and said, "That comes under the great blanket of 'national security'—and I don't think you have a need to know." His eyes suddenly turned cold. "The Agency cut him off a long time ago. In fact, we helped him get a job with State because we wanted to get rid of him."

"And keep his mouth shut, too, I bet," the C of D said with a tiny smile.

"Ah, yes, we did ensure his . . . uh . . . discretion. Unfortunately he got used to working with some of my colleagues out there, some of my former friends who were a little too enthusiastic about helping the Hmong get their poppy crop to market."

Edgeworth had first met Borden when both men were on a joint Agency, DEA, and NYPD task force in the Golden Triangle engaged in antinarcotics operations with the less than enthusiastic authorities in Thailand. He knew Borden hated dope and anyone who made a profit out of the misery it caused. His son had gotten hooked on heroin while serving as a marine in Vietnam. Men like Hayden had helped to put the needle in the kid's arm. But Borden's son had kicked the habit the hard way. Six months after his return to the U.S., he shot himself in his bedroom in the Borden home in Virginia.

"These former friends of yours—are they still in the Company?"

Borden looked thoughtfully down at the polished oak floor. "No, the lure of private enterprise, as well as the suspicions of some of my DEA brethren, proved sufficient incentive to make them retire and go into other lines of work. Hayden is still their gundog, though. He'll clean up their messes, do the dirty jobs they won't touch." He reached over and put his hand on the sleeve of Edgeworth's rumpled tan suit. "Unfortunately Hayden is still on State's payroll. I hear that he finagled his way into a certain assignment so he could watch out for the interests of some of his old associates. And they have friends, very rich, very powerful friends. I expect I can find out more when I get back to Washington next week. I'll do a little nosing around, quietly. Don't want to alarm anyone unnecessarily, you know."

Edgeworth got out of his chair and looked at his friend without speaking for several moments. "I gotta go, Gerry. But you know my private number. My home phone is secure. I want to know a *lot* more. I got a bunch of damn good cops mixed up in something that's beginning to smell real bad. And I don't want any of the shit you guys deal in sticking to them."

As Edgeworth left the room, Borden was still wearily slumped down in his chair, looking at his feet. Edgeworth knew he had an ally. He just could not be sure how much Borden's pain and anger would overcome the ingrained tendency of any Agency person to protect the Company and its officers, even if they were rogue elephants.

The row house had brown curtains. It was in the middle of Markham Mews, an undistinguished block in the Red Hook section of Brooklyn. Adele Matrazzo was a registered Democrat and the sole occupant of the house with brown curtains.

Adele taught social studies at PS 181 until crippling arthritis forced her retirement. That was six years ago; now she passed her days confined to a shiny electric wheelchair. Her once-beautiful legs, which so many men had admired, were now motionless appendages hanging stiffly over the edge of her chair. And her graceful hands were now rigid, deformed claws with chestnut-sized knuckles straining the skin over them.

She had stationed herself by the parlor window after she received the telephone call from the police. A minor matter, the police lieutenant had said. Adele could feel the knot of anxiety in her throat as she thought about what the police really wanted to know. She had been preparing for such a visit for many years. She prayed that he was all right. Perhaps she should call him just to make sure that nothing had happened to him. She quickly decided against doing that. He had warned her many times never to call him unless it was some kind of emergency that she could not handle without getting him involved.

At a little before four o'clock a blue Buick stopped in front of her house. From behind the curtains, Adele could see two men and a woman get out of the car and stand on the sidewalk staring at her house. They made a handsome trio. She felt a strong desire to talk with them—and an equally powerful apprehension about the questions she feared they might ask.

"Number eleven," Lucas said, looking up at the house number as he lifted the metal bar. The gate hinge groaned, and almost as if on cue the front door opened.

"Yes?" asked the woman in the wheelchair.

Peering inside, studying the crippled woman, Lucas showed her his shield and made the introductions.

"Please come in," Adele said, reversing her wheelchair into the parlor.

"I hope we're not interrupting anything," Lucas said, following behind the wheelchair.

"As you can see, my dance card's hardly filled these days," Adele said, wheeling around to face them. She waved her crooked hand at the couch. "Please sit."

They sat, Katina in the middle.

"What is this all about?" Adele asked.

"We're trying to locate relatives of Paolo Matrazzo," Lucas said.

A surprised expression transformed Adele's heavily made-up face. "They're all dead, except me."

"How were you related to him?" Lucas asked.

"Uncle Paolo was my father's brother. Why in the world would the police be interested in any of the Matrazzos?" she asked, reaching into the candy box on her lap.

Lucas replied: "The Greek government has asked us to help them try and locate—"

"Alexander's *Iliad*," Adele interrupted, digging out a candy with a walnut on top.

"Yes," Vassos said, resting his hands on his knees.

Adele forced her hand up to her mouth and sucked the candy between her lips. After swallowing it, she said, "As a little girl I was forever hearing about Uncle Paolo's *Iliad*. No one in the family really believed it existed. I can tell you one thing for sure, if he ever did find it, no one in this family ever benefited. He died on Santorini, leaving his wife and two sons almost penniless."

"Paolo Matrazzo was a well-known collector," Katina said. "It's hard to believe that he did not leave a substantial estate."

"Believe it. He might have been a famous collector, but he was no businessman," Adele said sadly. "He squandered a small fortune running around the world searching for that wretched book. When he died, his partner told my aunt that there was almost nothing left in the business. Paolo's Folly, my aunt used to call Alexander's *Iliad*."

"Who was your uncle's partner?" Vassos asked.

"A man named Jean Laval. He bought out my aunt's interest in the business."

"Do you know what happened to him?" Lucas asked.

"He died in 1947," Katina said.

Lucas looked sharply at the beautiful woman sitting next to him. "How did you know that?"

Katina shrugged. "Art world trivia."

"I see," Lucas said, slowly turning his attention back to the woman in the wheelchair. "What happened to your uncle's family?"

"My aunt died in 1946. Anthony, the oldest son, was killed on Guadalcanal. Paolo Junior came out of the army a captain. He married, had two sons and a daughter. After he received his Ph.D. from New York University, he accepted a job teaching art history at NYU. He died of cancer in 1968."

"What happened to his wife and children?" Lucas asked.

Adele shook her head. "I don't know. We just sort of lost touch."

"Did you ever hear anyone in your family suggest that your uncle might have smuggled the *Iliad* out of Greece before he died, or that someone was with him on Santorini when he allegedly sent that telegram to his partner?" Lucas asked.

Adele laughed. "No, Lieutenant. My uncle's obsession was his alone." She looked suspiciously at Vassos. "Why after all these years is there interest in the casket-copy?"

"We consider it a national treasure and would like to see it returned to Greece. My government, of course, would be willing to make any *necessary payments* to secure its return."

Looking at the stuffing leaking out of the couch's arm, Adele said thoughtfully, "I could certainly use some *necessary payments*, but I'm afraid that there isn't much hope of that."

"Does the name Orhan Iskur mean anything to you?" Vassos asked, opening his briefcase.

"No, I can't say that it does," Adele said.

Vassos got up and slowly walked over to the wheelchair. He held up the composite sketch and photograph of Aldridge Long. "Do you know this person?"

Adele squinted, her eyes close to both sketch and photograph, looking from one to the other, taking her time. An expression of fright and disbelief pulled back her mouth, causing dimples to appear. "He looks an awful lot like my Uncle Paolo. But that's impossible, isn't it? He's been dead since 1939."

10

eddy Lucas walked into the Sixteenth's squad room and stopped
dead. The detention cage was filled with shouting prisoners,
many of whom wore silly-looking sailor hats. Detectives were busy
at their desks, helping officers in uniforms prepare arrest reports and
invoice property.

Lucas looked up at the wall clock: 5:20. The joint was jumping. He
looked behind him at Vassos and Katina. "We'll go into my office." He
reached over the gate and pressed the release latch. The prisoners spotted Katina; a chorus of hoots and whistles issued from the cage.

The two men convoyed Katina across the squad room into the
Whip's office. Vassos closed the door. "You're busy this evening," he
said, lowering himself down onto the department-issue green swivel
chair.

"Seasonal trade," Lucas explained, rolling the blackboard away from
the wall. "Rivergoing office parties that get out of hand. Happens every
summer."

"In Greece such persons would be taken directly to court," Vassos
said.

"Here too, normally," Lucas said, "but, according to our *Patrol
Guide*, prisoners arrested on the navigable waters who can not be arraigned in court immediately must be brought to the nearest station
house for search and detention. Those beauties outside won't be arraigned tonight; there's too much paperwork involved."

Vassos nodded in understanding.

Katina stood off from the men, looking around the Whip's office.

Lucas picked chalk up from the runner of the blackboard and wrote the names of the people they'd interviewed, including the other dealer they had visited after leaving Adele Matrazzo's house.

Lucas stepped back from the board, his gaze fixed on the black slate. Out in the street a truck squealed to a stop; a cacophony of horns bubbled up into the squad room.

"They all have one thing in common," Lucas observed, leaving the rest of his thought unspoken.

Katina focused on the blackboard.

Vassos fingered his jade worry beads.

"In addition to being dealers, each one of them is also a collector," Lucas said.

"Most dealers are," Katina said.

"My gut instinct tells me that whoever has the casket-copy has one powerful urge to show it off," Lucas said, moving around his desk and sitting.

"Before you get the wrong impression," Katina said, "most dealers are also collectors, and many of them are secretive about their private collections."

Lucas made a dismissive grunt.

A detective out in the squad room screamed for quiet. The ruckus continued. The familiar sound of a swivel chair crashing against the bars of the detention cage caused a knowing grin to pass between the two policemen.

Lucas leaned back, his legs stretched across the desk's side table, studying the slate. "If Iskur did have a coconspirator in the States, they'd have to communicate with each other, wouldn't they?" He looked around at Vassos. "Were Iskur's transatlantic telephone calls checked out?"

Vassos muttered a curse in Greek. "I don't know, but I can find out." He got up and went over to the squad commander's red telephone. He lifted the receiver, and dialed. He spoke for about one minute in Greek and hung up. "I must meet someone within the hour."

"How do you manage getting around the city?" Katina asked him.

"I have a book of maps in my briefcase," Vassos said, asking her, "What time does Bloomingdale's close?"

A benevolent smile crossed her face. She asked in Greek, "Have you ever been inside Bloomingdale's?"

"*Okhee.*" No, he said.

"I think they close at six-thirty tonight," she said.

Vassos turned the door knob. "Ten o'clock tomorrow, Lou?"

Lucas smiled. "Ten o'clock, First Terror."

After Vassos had gone, Katina said, "I hope that we accomplished something today."

"Time will tell," Lucas said, acutely conscious of her perfume. He looked into her beautiful face and wanted desperately to reach out and touch her, to ask her to have dinner with him. Don't be a putz all your life, Lucas. Ask her. All she can say is no, or I'm busy tonight, or I'm involved with someone. He slipped his feet off the desk and was about to ask her when he looked at the elegant, educated woman that fate had thrown in his path and imagined the unbridgeable gulf between them. So he merely smiled ruefully and said, "Come on, I'll drive you home."

Despite her sixty-two years and her infirmity, Adele Matrazzo's big black eyes were still capable of capturing a man's heart.

Adele enjoyed putting on her makeup every morning, pretending that today was the day he would visit her. She loved to paint her lips a glossy red and add a heavy streak of eyeliner, then brush mascara onto her long lashes. It was a painful struggle for her to do these things now, but she did them nonetheless. She relished her morning "get ready for the day" sessions; they gave her something to look forward to during the long nights. And, you never knew, today might be the day when he'd visit.

Adele's world consisted of the bottom floor of the two-story house: a parlor, bedroom, small kitchen, and a full bath with gripping bars on all the walls. She spent a good portion of her day watching the soaps on the twenty-five-inch television screen that he had gotten for her last Christmas. And there were her chocolates. Oh, how she loved chocolate. She loved the way the creamy pulpiness of the candy felt as it melted in her mouth, and the way it felt when she mushed it about with her tongue. There was always a golden box nearby.

Adele still received occasional telephone calls from old friends and colleagues. And there were her wonderful neighbors who would look in on her and even do her shopping. She was particularly grateful to Mrs. O'Rourke, who lived across the street. She would come by twice a week and have tea with Adele. They would watch "Search for Happiness," and Adele would smilingly endure the same worn litany of complaints against Mrs. O'Rourke's ungrateful daughter-in-law.

Sometimes when she was alone she'd make the radio music loud and play with her wheelchair's control box, spinning her cold metal throne about the room, pretending she was dancing with some remembered lover. She would close her eyes and dwell on the hardness rubbing up against her, and a shroud of lust would cover her loneliness.

But the high points of Adele's confined existence were his visits. She would never know when he would come by. There was always a telephone call first. "Adele, dear, are you alone?" She would say yes, and he would show up within the hour. She never dared question him about his other life; she knew better. He had always been withdrawn and secretive about himself, even as a child. She was thankful that they had been able to share a hedonistic life together. It had all begun when they were children. So long ago. A joyous shiver shook her shoulders as her mind replayed his last visit.

He had stood over her watching as she popped chocolates into her mouth. With her eyes locked on his, she put them in one at a time and rolled them about, turning them into delicious dark brown mud. He took out his beautiful thing and ran it over her wet lips, and when he told her to, she opened her mouth wide and took him into the chocolaty muck, ravenously sucking him until his hot juice spilled into her mouth.

Stepping back from her, his penis dripping with chocolate sludge, his arms suddenly went akimbo, his back arched, and he laughingly said, "Adele, dear, I've just made you a black and white soda. I do hope that you've enjoyed it."

"I did. I did."

Adele Matrazzo spun her wheelchair around to face her visitor. Her admiring eyes locked on him as he moved across the parlor and sat on her shabby sofa. He had come promptly in response to her phone call.

He leaned forward, watching her. "Adele, dear, do tell me all about your unexpected company."

She clawed a chocolate from the box and proceeded to tell him about Lucas, Vassos, and a woman named Katina Wright. When she finished, her visitor leaned back, his gaze fixed on a cobweb of ceiling cracks. Adele put another candy into her mouth.

"They know nothing about me?" he said.

"Nothing."

His lips pulled into a menacing scowl as his head came up off the back of the sofa. "Adele, did you ever mention me to any of your neighbors or friends?"

"I never mentioned you to a living soul. You've been my life's secret."

"Do you have any pictures of me, anything from the past that might tie us together?"

"There is nothing."

"Do you have me listed in your address book?"

"Of course not."

Her eyes widened with sudden realization; her deformed hands crushed the sides of the candy box. Her mouth quivered as she whispered, "You have it, don't you?"

A beam of sunlight pierced the dirty window and reflected off his golden ring. "Yes, I have it." He slid off the sofa and moved over to the wheelchair where he kneeled down next to her. He brushed a stray wisp of hair from her brow. "You've been a good, loyal friend all these years."

Her misshapen hand caressed his arm. "I've loved you since we were children."

"I know," he said softly. "Would you like me to relax you?"

She caught her breath, leaned her head against the back of her prison, and closed her eyes. "Yes."

He played with her breasts. She moaned.

Her thoughts drifted to other times, other places. Her young, healthy body was straddling his, lowering onto his straining cock. She felt the warmth of past ejaculations and her breath began to come in hard gulps. "Do my nipples."

He unbuttoned the front of her housedress and unhaltered her breasts. He took one into his hand, milking it. Bending forward, he sucked it into his mouth and gnawed the thick, brown crown.

"Harder," she demanded.

As he stimulated her, he looked up at her contorted face and saw that chunks of mascara had fallen on her cheeks. Her head lay still and she made mewing noises through her open mouth. She started to emit a hoarse, gagging sound, and her head began to rock back and forth. She stiffened. Her head came up sharply; she gagged several times and then screamed. She relaxed, slumping down into her seat.

Gripping the chair's arm, he pushed himself up onto his feet and, bending, buttoned the front of her dress.

"Would you like me to give you a blow job?"

"I have something else in mind," he said, taking a length of thin wire from his pocket; slipping behind the wheelchair, he held it over her head like a blessing.

"What is that?" she asked.

"The E string of a violin."

"What can we do with that?"

"The ultimate thrill, Adele, dear." He snapped the string around her neck, pulling tightly on both ends.

At first Adele Matrazzo did not scream or attempt to defend herself. She sat still, not understanding what was happening, not believing that it could happen. And then, as life-sustaining air fled her body, her alarm gave way to wide-eyed panic, and a terrifying, almost inaudible scream burst from her mouth. Her useless hands fought vainly against the E string. His powerful arm hoisted her up out of her seat, dark thick fluid drooling over her lips as her body convulsed in life's final dance.

Andreas Vassos walked into a wonderland of glass and black marble. Young, fashionably dressed women stood behind glistening counters, holding out perfumes in designer bottles. Weaving through the first-floor fragrance department at Bloomingdale's, Vassos became more and more conscious of the obscene display of luxury. Names shouted from the walls: Chanel, Saint Laurent, Givenchy. He thought of the modest and rather drab perfume stores in Greece, and as he watched an elegantly dressed woman pause to allow a saleswoman to dab a fragrance on her wrist, he thought also of how his mother and grandmother had labored in the fields picking tobacco, his grandmother until well into her sixties.

He stopped at a counter, looking confusedly at its contents.

"May I help you, sir?" She wore strange makeup: bluish eyebrows, purple eyeliner, and mauve lipstick. Her nails were painted blood red; she wore large pieces of jewelry around her wrists and neck so that she clanked every time she moved.

"I would like a bottle of Anaïs-Anaïs, please."

Her capped teeth gleamed. "You are Greek."

Bemused, he answered, "Yes I am."

The saleswoman clutched her chest. "I fell in love with your country. It's *sooo* charming, and the people are *sooo* friendly. My girlfriend and I go to Mykonos every year. In fact, we're going next month. We *always* go dancing at the Nine Muses; I mean, it's like a sacred thing with us."

His face a blank mask, Vassos thought, why are they always so dumb and so damn nasal? He made a few agreeable grunts, lingered a few seconds more, and said, "I must hurry, miss, I have an appointment."

"I'm sorry. I do run off at the mouth whenever I talk about Greece."

He watched her wrap his purchase. He paid; she returned his change. As he was leaving, she said good-bye. "*Ahndeeo.*"

He smiled at her and rushed out of the store, anxious to escape the cloying bouquet that fouled the air. He looked around for a cab.

Ficco's was crowded. A fully extended orange-and-green awning sloped down over the sidewalk café's rows of tables, and a waiter trundled a gaily decorated cart from table to table, serving drinks. Vassos stood in front of the restaurant. It was directly across the street from Lincoln Center. He looked around carefully for his control. He spotted her sitting at a table in the last row. She waved at him. He acknowledged her by raising his briefcase. Squeezing through the cramped space, he reached her table and sat down across from her.

Looking across Broadway at the gushing fountain, Elisabeth Syros said in throaty Greek, "How goes it with you, Andreas?"

He shrugged and frowned at the same time, a gesture that meant "I'm not sure," and then he proceeded to bring her up to date.

A waiter glided over and took his order: ouzo and a plate of cheese and crackers.

"I want you to do something," he said.

"What?"

He checked out the people sitting near them. Leaning in close, he spoke softly in Greek. "I want a list of Orhan Iskur's overseas telephone calls for the past year."

"Only those made to the States?" she asked, her espresso cup poised before her lips.

Fascinated by all the rings on her hand, he managed to reply, "Every call made to anywhere outside of Greece."

The waiter leaned in from the row in front of them and set down his order. Pouring water into his ouzo, Vassos said, "Overseas telephone records are kept for two years so there shouldn't be a problem." He stirred his drink. "How long will it take you to get the information?"

"A day, perhaps two. I'll transmit your request to Tsimas tonight. He'll have it on his desk in the morning."

He had forgotten about General Philippos Tsimas, the head of the Central Information Service, Elisabeth Syros's boss. He wondered how Colonel Pappas was doing with his parallel investigation. Sipping the licorice-flavored drink, his eyes drifted over the tables. "Just suppose I do happen to come up with the . . . merchandise? What do I do about delivering it?"

She reached behind her and lifted her pocketbook off the back of the chair. Snapping it open, she took out a pad, removed the ballpoint attached to the side, and wrote down several addresses and telephone numbers. "You can deliver it to any of these locations at any time of the day or night. And, if you should ever need any help, call any of these numbers and tell whoever answers that you're a friend of the lady from Thessalonika."

Vassos arrived back at the Hotel Olympian at seven-thirty. Harry, the night desk clerk, greeted him in Greek. Harry was a small man who had had the misfortune of being born without a chin, so that his face resembled that of a fully grown rat. The thin mustache that Harry affected looked like a rat's twitching whiskers. Harry didn't know that his newfound friend from Greece was a cop, nor did Harry know about the gun that Vassos wore clipped to his belt.

As Vassos approached, Harry leaned across the desk, his face shrinking into a conspiratorial grin. "I've made those arrangements for you. Let me know when you're ready."

"Tonight," Vassos said, heading for the elevator.

Vassos tossed his briefcase on the wing chair and went over to shut off the air conditioner, amazed that a chambermaid would waste energy cooling an empty room. He pushed the tall window open; a strong current of hot air rushed in, bringing with it the clamor of Manhattan.

He unhooked the holster and tucked it under the mattress. He undressed, showered, stepped into fresh underpants, turned off the light, and sprawled across the sagging bed, listening to the harsh sounds of the city.

"Soula, Stephanos," he groaned, and then fell into an easeful darkness.

A soft knocking caused him to swallow his sorrow and call out in his own language, "Who is it?" He had lost track of time. He must have drifted off. It took him a moment to remember where he was.

"Harry sent me," she answered in Greek.

He rolled off the bed and padded over to the door.

She quickly brushed past him into the room. Early thirties, black hair, pretty face with a bit too much makeup, and a shapely body that was starting to add pounds. Crossing to the window, she said in Greek, "Harry told me that you wanted a woman who spoke our language, and that you had certain *requests*."

"Nai." Yes, he said.

She turned abruptly, shrewd eyes evaluating him. "No animals, no pain, and no bondage."

"My needs are simple."

"Sixty dollars for a straight lay, anything else is extra." She moved over to him and slid her hand between his legs, rubbing him. "Okay?"

He moved over to the briefcase and took out the perfume. He placed the bottle into her hand and told her what he wanted. The hooker softened; she kissed him on the cheek, nodded, and slipped into the bathroom.

He sprawled back across the bed, listening to the shower's muted roar. The sound of the water carried his thoughts back to the day he met the woman who would become his wife. Soula had been showering at Vouliagméni's pay beach that day. He sprinted across the sand and ran under the next shower. Turning under the sprinkling water, he thrust his face up and bent down at the same time to wash sand from his feet. He lost his balance and stumbled into the next open stall, toppling both of them out onto the grass.

"What's the matter with you?" Soula demanded, trying to untangle their arms and legs.

"I'm sorry," he said, feeling like an awkward and clumsy fool. At first he did not see her face, he was too busy trying to pick himself up off the grass. At some point he found himself staring into her saffron eyes, and then he was at a loss for words. He wanted to know this woman. The next seconds were lost in a mist of embarrassment. He remember that he reached out to stop her from getting up so that he could ask her name. She turned abruptly; he reached over, intending to tap her on the shoulder, and somehow ended up with her bikini top dangling in his hand.

"You clown!" she screamed into his mortified face. Covering herself with her hands, she ran off into the ladies' locker room.

He jumped to his feet and pursued her through a gauntlet of laughter. Running into the women's locker room just behind her, he found his path blocked by the formidable body of the matron. "Cool your buns, young man, and wait outside," she said, grabbing the top out of his hand.

He slunk out of the brick building and waited just outside. A fig peddler passed. A peace reparation just might turn the tide in his favor, so he called out to the old man: "One kilo of figs." Realizing that he had no money, he ran around the other side of the building to the men's locker room, asked the attendant for his basket, took money out of his trousers, and ran back outside in time to pay the peddler four drachmas for the bag of figs.

A few minutes later Soula came out, her swim top repaired. When she saw him leaning up against the side of the building, she turned in a huff and hurried along the path leading down to the beach.

He ran after her. "I'm sorry. Please, wait one second and let me explain. Please." He stuck the bag in front of her face. "I've bought these figs for you."

Four meters away from them, some boys were playing soccer. One of them kicked the ball. It shot across the grass, passed people sunning on chaise longues, and caught Vassos between his ankles, causing him to go sprawling over the path in front of her, spewing figs all over the place.

Realizing all was lost, he picked up a fig and handed it to her. "I guess I'm not the suave type."

She took the fig out of his hand, peeled back the grainy skin, and said, "I think you're adorable."

*　　*　　*

The bathroom door opened. The naked woman switched off the light, made her way over to the bed, and lowered herself down next to him. She kissed his brow. "I love you, Andreas."

He pressed her close, intoxicated by the scent of Soula's favorite perfume. "Soula, I miss you so very much."

She stroked his hair. "I'm here, Andreas. I'll always be here for you, always, my darling."

Eddie Burke was what cops called a "predicate criminal." He was proud of the eighteen arrests on his yellow sheet; he was proud that he had never done an honest day's work in his life; proud that he didn't pay taxes, or have a social security number, or a credit rating. Eddie didn't exist, except in the criminal record files of the NYPD and the FBI.

He was a powerfully built man with wavy chestnut hair and a deeply lined face. He talked with a soft voice that sometimes bordered on a whisper. Burke liked to think of himself as a street guy with a heart of gold. He loved playing with children and watching the sunset. Eddie's buddies in the Purple Gang had a different opinion of him. Long ago they hung the moniker "Crazy Eyes" on Eddie because of the way his large tawny eyes popped out of his head whenever he got angry.

Whenever any of the Purple Gang got together their conversation would frequently make its way around to the time the late Frankie Airlake made a pass at Shirley Case, Eddie's live-in girlfriend. When Eddie heard about it, he threw an ax into a big shopping bag and went looking for Frankie Airlake. He found him in The Den, standing at the bar, talking to Louie D and Mush McCarthy. Eddie stormed over to the trio, shoved Louie D and Mush aside, buried the ax in Frankie Airlake's head.

As the dying man lay in a pool of blood, Eddie worked the ax free and began to chop open Airlake's chest. Placing one foot on the other side of the bloody trench, Eddie bent down and pried open the rib cage, reached into the warm gory mess, and ripped out Airlake's heart. Slapping the organ down on the bar, Eddie laughingly announced, "Ol' Frankie boy's done lost his heart to love."

Eddie Burke sat behind the wheel of the Plymouth Sundance watching a mounted cop slowly riding on his horse up Twelfth Avenue. He had rented the car earlier that day with some funny plastic. The motor was running; the air conditioner was on high, and the radio blared. Eddie's loose-fitting white shirt hid his muscular frame and his drawstring pants flared down over his stolen Bruno Magliloafers. He wore no socks; his only jewelry was a stolen Piaget watch.

Denny McKay had telephoned Eddie at his girlfriend's around eleven that morning and told him to get a car and meet him at nine-thirty that night at the northwest corner of Forty-fifth and Twelfth Avenue. Eddie wondered what was up. Probably a fast score to be made or some asshole who needed his legs broken. His eyes drifted to the dashboard's digital clock: 9:45. When he looked back out the windshield, he saw Denny McKay standing on the corner, fanning his open shirt against the oppressive heat, the familiar Marlboro cigarette clenched between his front teeth, his half-glasses perched on his nose, held there by a black cord stretched around his head. McKay's furtive eyes swept the scene, making sure no unwelcome parasites had attached themselves to him. A shower of sparks rained down from a wildcat construction job, causing McKay to jump back and scream curses up at the oblivious workmen.

Eddie Burke laughed.

McKay's gaze moved along the row of parked cars and locked on the Sundance. He gave a barely perceptible nod. Eddie Burke released the handbrake and let the Sundance glide to the corner, where he leaned across the seat and chucked open the door.

McKay lowered himself into the cramped space. "Couldn't you get a bigger fucking car?" he said, pressing his knees up against the glove compartment. He reached down and pushed the control lever back, sliding the seat to the rear. "That's better." He turned and looked at his friend. "How goes it with you, Eddie?"

"No complaints. Where to?"

"Pier Ninety," McKay said, crushing out his cigarette in the ashtray and lighting up another.

A few minutes later the Sundance's tires drummed over the pier's timbered entrance. The guard wasn't in his shack, so Eddie Burke drove out onto the wharf and parked the Sundance between two stacks of containers.

"Whadda we waitin' for?" Burke asked, watching two homosexuals holding hands at the end of the pier.

McKay cracked the window at the top and tossed out his butt. "I made a new coke connection."

"Colombian?"

"No. A Chink with a good source of supply. He'd tied in with the Wu cartel."

Eddie was impressed. "That's heavy-duty shit. How much can he deliver?"

"As much as we can buy."

"What's the price?"

"Thirty-five a key with a discount on anything over fifty keys."

"Sounds good."

McKay playfully punched his friend's arm. "Where you been hidin'?"

"I've been hustling a livin'. Made a good score in Jersey, a truckload of liquor."

"Hey, Eddie, remember how Sister Maria used to beat the shit out of us whenever she caught us fucking up?"

Burke laughed. "She was a tough old nun. She used to bang me around with that ruler she kept hidden up her sleeve. 'You two are no good!' she'd scream, remember?"

Nostalgia brightened McKay's face. "Yeah, I remember. Guess she's long dead, may her soul rest in peace."

"And remember Sister Rose?"

A lecherous grin perked McKay's mouth. "I always wanted to hit on her. I used to jerk off pretending I was fucking her."

"Me too." Burke laughed.

"Hey, Eddie, you remember a few years back you took off that book dealer for me?"

"That fucking queen squealed like a pig when I shoved the piece in his face." He looked at McKay. "I never could understand why you wanted that damn scroll."

"I got it for a friend of mine," McKay said, lighting up another Marlboro.

"Well, that favor cost Bucky McMahon eighteen months inside."

"You ever mention doing that job to anyone?"

"You said forget it, so I forgot it. Besides, it wasn't one of my more memorable scores. You only paid me two large for the job."

"I didn't make a dime on it myself. Like I told you, it was a favor."

Burke shrugged indifference. "No big deal."

"Bucky McMahon did the cop with you, didn't he?"

"McGovern? Yeah, he done it with me. I'll tell ya, that old cop was one tough Irishman. He went down fighting all the way. I carry his shield around with me for good luck." He looked at McKay. "Why you asking about the old jobs for anyway?"

"Aw, nothing. I was just—hey, here comes our man."

"Where?"

"On your left," McKay said, pointing.

Eddie Burke turned to look. He heard the explosion and dimly felt his head toppling onto the steering wheel. Blood gushed from his eyes, nose, and mouth. He didn't hear the second shot.

McKay tucked the .38 S & W Chief into his belt and tossed his cigarette out the window. He took out his handkerchief and wiped the seat lever. He placed the cloth over the door handle and got out of the car. He walked away, not looking back. The sight of dead friends depressed him.

Teddy Lucas had made his nightly report to the chief of detectives some time ago. He was still annoyed with himself for not being able to get up the courage to ask Katina to go out with him. He was going to have to shake that peasant out of his system and get on with his life. His tour had been over hours ago and here he was, hanging around the Squad drinking stale coffee and trying to decide what to do with the rest of the night. He could run over to Heidi's and have a few with the guys, but he wasn't in the mood to spend the rest of the night bullshitting about the Job and the way it used to be. Joan had said she would stop by his place the day after tomorrow for a quickie before her ten o'clock dentist appointment. He made a mental note to buy condoms. He hated those damn things; they made a woman taste lousy afterwards. Aw, the hell with it, he'd go home. He'd grab a bite at the new Polish joint on Eleventh Street, do his laundry, and sack out watching the late movie on the tube.

He started to get up out of his chair when Big Jay stuck his black face into the office and barked, "We just caught a homicide on Pier Ninety. A small-timer named Eddie Burke got himself blown away."

Lucas tensed. The name Burke rang a bell. He reached out and flipped open the case folder. Fishing through the thick file, he asked, "Who caught it?"

"Leone. He's making the notifications now." Big Jay stepped into the office and leaned against the side of the file cabinet, watching the Whip go through the folder. "You going to ride on this one?"

Lucas yanked a sheet of notes from the folder. He quickly read through it, put the pages back in the folder, and slapped the cover closed. "Yeah, I'm riding on this one."

Yellow CRIME SCENE signs swung from the orange tape that corralled the Sundance between the stacks of freight containers. Two RMPs, radio motor patrol cars, were parked on the edge of the pier, the strobe light on one of them hurling colored streaks over the murky water. No boats were berthed at the pier; no crush of people intent on sating morbid curiosities pressed against the police barricades. The Forensic Unit's blue-and-white station wagon had its back door open; black valises were stacked on the platform. Two attendants stood near the ambulance chatting quietly with the patrol sergeant. Big Jay and John Leone stood by the radio cars interviewing the first crew that had arrived on the scene.

Lucas stood just outside the frozen zone, gathering first impressions.

Technically he was off the chart and not required to be there. Both the *Patrol Guide* and the *Detective Guide* mandated an immediate notification to the Borough Command whenever a homicide occurred. If the Whip or the Second Whip wasn't aboard, then the detective supervisor covering the borough would respond to the scene and take charge of the preliminary investigation.

As soon as Lucas realized who had been offed, he telephoned the Borough Command and told the sergeant on the operations desk that he was present in the Squad and would respond to the scene. He had not forgotten Cormick McGovern or the casket-copy. He stepped over the tape and circled the Sundance, examining the outside of the car.

Big Jay and Leone came over to the barrier. "Lou, we got ourselves a virgin crime scene," Big Jay said. "The first cops to arrive on the scene roped off the area and prevented anyone from entering."

"What were they able to tell you?" Lucas asked, bending down to examine the small pile of cigarette butts under the passenger window.

Leone checked his steno pad. "They drove out onto the pier to have their coffee. They both spotted the DOA at the same time and got out of their car to investigate. Both of them recognized Burke as one of the Purple Gang crew. They secured the area and called us by land line."

"Good," Lucas said, pleased that the cops had used the public telephone at the end of the pier to make the notification, preventing the media from knowing that a homicide had gone down; it gave them time to do their jobs before the arrogant vultures descended on them.

". . . the guard wasn't in his shack when the RMP drove onto the pier," Leone said, a cynical grin curling one end of his mustache. "When he finally showed he told the cops that he was taking a dump in the portable toilet."

"A dump, huh," Lucas said, his voice full of scorn. "I think you two are going to have to give him an enema of the mouth."

"Be a pleasure, Lou," Big Jay said.

The patrol sergeant, a dumpy black woman with a puffy Afro, came up to the barrier accompanied by the two black ambulance attendants. "Lou," she began, "the stiff hasn't been pronounced."

Lucas glanced around at the body. Thick strands of blood hung down from the face; an exit wound had splattered blood and brain matter over what remained of the window on the driver's side.

Lucas looked at the two attendants. "Pronounce him at the morgue."

"Lou, we're required to pronounce at the scene," said the smaller of the two, a man of thirty with crooked teeth.

Lucas stepped back over the tape and slid his arms around the two attendants' shoulders and waltzed them back over to their ambulance.

"Look, guys, this is a mob hit and I have a personal interest in seeing that everything is done right, so you can see why I don't want anyone inside that car until we're done doing our thing."

"Lou," Crooked-teeth protested, "we're supposed to check for vital signs before we pronounce."

"M'man, his vital signs bees all over the window," Lucas said, affecting an inner city drawl.

The other man was fat and had long dreadlocks. "Lou, we'd like to do the right thing, but suppose we pronounce him without checking his vitals and the man don't be dead? Shit. They'd have our asses for breakfast, lunch, and dinner."

Lucas slid his arms from around their shoulders, turned his back to them, and took out his expense money. He shaved a Grant off the wad and slipped it into Dreadlocks' shirt pocket. "Lemme buy you guys lunch."

Crooked-teeth smiled. He looked back at the crime scene. "That motherfucker sure bees dead to me." Thus Eddie Burke was pronounced.

Lucas snapped on plastic gloves and stepped back into the frozen zone. Turning around, he said to the patrol sergeant, "Send your driver to the Hotel Olympian on Eighth Avenue and Thirty-second and pick up a Mr. Andreas Vassos and deliver him here."

"Right, Lou," she said, motioning to her driver.

Big Jay and Leone snapped on disposable latex gloves and followed the Whip into the frozen zone. Crime Scene Unit detectives waited patiently nearby. Their turn would come soon.

The Sixteenth Squad detectives moved cautiously around the Sundance, avoiding the pile of cigarettes. Leone had caught the case, so the collection and the preservation of the chain of evidence was his responsibility. He waved the photographer into the frozen zone. Big Jay maintained the crime scene log, listing the name, rank, and shield number, and the time each person entered the frozen zone.

Accompanied by Leone, the photographer snapped his pictures of the car's exterior; the pile of cigarettes was shot at several different angles to show its relationship to the passenger window. The outside of the car was divided into quadrants and searched, starting with the quadrant containing the driver's door and continuing clockwise until they had searched all quadrants of the car's exterior.

Leone crouched down next to the pile of cigarettes. Using a rubber-tipped tweezer, he picked one up, examining it. "Marlboro, with a chewed-up filter." He took out his pen and wrote his initials, shield number, and the date and time on the cigarette paper. He deposited the butt into a serial-numbered evidence bag. Big Jay noted the bag's number in the log.

The car door was open; the photographer snapped pictures of the body. Big Jay and Leone wrestled the corpse out from behind the wheel and laid it out on the ground. Burke's hands were immediately bagged; photographs were taken of the body.

Leone searched the body. Big Jay vouchered the contents of the clothes. Leone removed a shield case from Burke's trousers. Time had molded the contours of a patrolman's shield into the outside of the worn leather case. He looked down at it and then up into the Whip's grim face. He passed the case to Lucas. Taking it in his hand, Lucas heard Cormick McGovern's voice boom across time-worn memories. "Laddie, let me tell you how the Job works."

Bile rose in Lucas's throat. He snapped open the case. A silver patrolman's shield: NYPD 5593. He looked down at the corpse. "Burn in hell, you bastard." He slid the case into his pocket.

Big Jay asked softly, "Want me to record finding it, Lou?"

"Finding what?"

The interior of the Sundance was divided into eight search zones, starting with the driver's compartment floor. All areas under the seats were searched; the seats were removed and their undersides examined. All folds and creases in the upholstery were searched. The contents of the ashtray were photographed, invoiced, and initialed.

Their tasks completed, Leone motioned to the crime scene detectives. "It's all yours."

The fingerprint technician snapped open his valise.

Lucas, Big Jay, and Leone climbed out of the frozen zone and ambled over to the edge of the pier.

"Whaddaya think?" Big Jay asked the Whip.

"Hit up close by someone he trusted," Lucas said. "He wasn't carrying, so we have to assume that he didn't expect trouble."

Leone nodded his agreement. "The hitter smoked Marlboros and is in the habit of chewing the filters."

"No other brand of cigarette was found in or around the car and none were found on Burke, so we have to assume that the hitter was the smoker," Big Jay said.

Lucas said to Leone, "I want you to put a hold on the body. Get impressions of Burke's teeth and have the saliva extracted from the filters."

"I went that route once, Lou," Big Jay said. "The ME doesn't have any forensic dentists on staff. Whenever they have occasion to use one, they farm it out to a few that they have on call. But the kicker is that we have to pick up the tab, which means getting the borough commander's approval for the expenditure of department funds."

"I'll call the C of D at home," Lucas said. "He'll approve it for us." He looked directly at the two detectives. "You two are off the chart. Stay with this one."

"Can you tell us if this hit is tied in with what you and the major are working on?" Big Jay asked.

Lucas watched a beer can bobbing in the river. "No can do, not yet. Trust me, okay?"

"Ten-four, boss," Leone said.

Six minutes later Andreas Vassos leaped out of the front seat of the RMP and rushed over to the detectives. "What is it?" he asked excitedly.

Lucas led him away from the others and told him what had happened and explained to him the course that the preliminary investigation had taken.

"You think the casket-copy is involved in this murder?" Vassos asked.

"I think that someone is scared that we might be getting close and wants to make sure that all we find are dead ends."

"The dental impressions are important, then?" Vassos said.

"They'll exclude Burke as the smoker, leaving only the killer." Lucas looked out at the dark river and continued, almost as if he were talking to himself. "When we find the perp we'll get a court order to take his dental impressions. That, with the saliva which will give us blood grouping, will nail him to the crime scene."

Somewhere in the distance a ship's forlorn horn sounded.

11

Eddie Burke's body lay on a gurney surrounded by other cadaver-laden trolleys in the basement of the medical examiner's office. The steel ice boxes were filled; the dead were crowded in the hallways. Burke had been dead about twelve hours; the preliminary investigation had been completed. Lucas had telephoned C of D Edgeworth earlier. "I need a forensic dentist, now."

"Wait at the morgue; one'll meet you there," Edgeworth had promised.

Lucas and Vassos waited in a glass-enclosed office, drinking coffee and watching the double door with the black rubber piping, trying to ignore death's irritating odor. An attendant wheeled a body into the autopsy room; a radio blared Willie Nelson singing: "Won't you ride in my little red wagon."

A bronze-skinned blond woman pushed her way through the doors. Late thirties, dressed in tailored blue slacks, white blouse, carrying a medical bag. She had a distracted look on her face as she searched for the man she was supposed to meet. Lucas waved. She smiled, waved back, and made her way through the field of gurneys into the office. "Lieutenant Lucas?"

"Yes, and this is Andreas Vassos."

"Hi, I'm Dr. Helen Rodale. I apologize for taking so long. The ME caught me just as I was leaving to take my son to his tutor." Her eyes roamed over the still forms. "Which one is yours?"

Lucas pointed out Burke. The body hadn't been washed. The distorted face was caked with gore.

They walked out of the office. "I'll need some water," the dentist said. Lucas went over to an attendant and asked him for water. Shoving gurneys aside, Dr. Rodale made her way over to her subject. She put her medical bag down on Burke's knees, opened it, and, reaching inside, looked at Lucas and said, "You understand, Lieutenant, that your department is responsible for my fee?"

"Yes, I'm aware of that, Doctor. What is your fee?"

"Fifteen hundred."

Vassos rolled his eyes.

She removed a chamois from the bag and spread it across Burke's chest. She reached back in and took out a paper pad, two tubes that resembled toothpaste, a horseshoe-shaped instrument with a handle, a metal putty spatula, and three plastic cups.

The attendant came over with a liter of water in a plastic bottle. "Hiyadoin', Doc?" he asked, working the bottle down between the cadaver's legs.

"Fine, thank you, Igor," she said.

When the attendant had gone, Lucas whispered, "Igor?"

"Yes, isn't that a pity?" She reached back into her bag and came out with a rectangular block of hard rubber. She snapped on a pair of latex gloves and pressed open the dead man's mouth. "Say ahhhh," she muttered, inserting the bite block between the back row of teeth, propping open the mouth. She opened one of the tubes and squeezed out a two-inch strip of paste onto the pad. She did the same with the other tube. Using the spatula, she mixed the two strips together.

The detectives gathered close to watch.

She explained: "One of the compounds is a rubber-based polyester impression material; the other is a catalyst. We stir them together until we get a homogeneous mix." She worked the spatula. The paste took on a purple hue. "That should do it," she said, picking up the horseshoe-shaped instrument. "This is an impression tray," she said, loading the concoction into the tray's reservoir.

She inserted the tray into Burke's mouth and pressed the paste up into the top row of teeth, holding it firm with the pressure of her thumbs under the bottom of the tray while her fingers fanned out over the clay-cold face. "Do either of you have children?"

"Yes," Vassos said, then quickly correcting himself, "No, I don't."

"My older one is sixteen," she said. "We pay six thousand dollars a year to keep him in a fancy private school, and I still have to run around getting him tutored for the college boards." She removed her hands from the tray. The instrument remained motionless, cemented to the upper teeth, the handle protruding from the mouth.

She mixed more paste, troweled it into one of the cups she had taken from her kit, and asked, "Who has the cigarettes?"

Vassos removed the plastic evidence bag from his briefcase and handed it to her. She removed one of the butts and held it up to the flourescent light. Using both hands, she carefully straightened the cigarette and implanted the filter into the paste. Turning her attention back to the cadaver, she took hold of the tray's handle and wiggled it free of the teeth. She removed the cast from the reservoir and put it down on the paper pad. She poured water into the basin and cleaned out the tray. That done, she mixed more paste and repeated the procedure on the bottom row of teeth.

After she had done that, she reached into Burke's mouth and removed the bite block, wrapped it in a disinfectant-soaked cloth, put it in a plastic bag, and tossed it back into her medical bag.

She opened a jar of wax and, picking up one of the molds, began layering wax around the outside of the impression.

"Why you doing that?" Lucas asked.

"In order to raise the base of the mold," she said. "This way I'll create a dam for the dental stone."

"Stone?"

"Dental stone is similar to plaster, only faster drying," she said. "We mix it with water and pour the solution into the holes that the teeth made in the mold. When it dries we'll have a replica of Burke's teeth."

Lucas looked down at the butt sticking up out of the cup. "Same procedure for that?"

"Yes," she said.

"How long will it be before you can tell us if Burke smoked those cigarettes?" Lucas asked.

"I can tell you that now," she said. "Those impressions were not made by the dead man."

Detective Ivan Ulanov was talking into the telephone, attempting to placate the moonbeam lady, a telephone regular who was convinced her landlord was attempting to regain her rent-controlled apartment by trying to kill her with moonbeam. "Yes, Martha, I know that it's rent-controlled, but I really . . ." He rolled his eyes at the Whip.

Frank Gregory was typing the unusual occurrence report on the Burke homicide, a need-to-know report that circulated up the chain of command.

Lucas asked Gregory, "Where're Big Jay and Leone?"

The Slav pointed his cheerless face at the old record room.

Passing the bulletin board, Lucas focused on the new flyer, one of many that regularly arrive in department mail, written by one of the Job's many anonymous authors:

SIX PHASES OF A POLICE DEPARTMENT PROJECT

1. Enthusiasm   4. Search for the Guilty
2. Disillusionment 5. Punishment of the Innocent
3. Panic   6. Praise and Honors for the Nonparticipants

Someone had written "The Job Sucks" across the bottom.

Lucas and Vassos entered the old record room, a cramped place that smelled moldly and was lined with green erector-set shelves crammed with department cartons containing the files of long-forgotten cases. Homicides were tucked away on the left side of the room; the victims' names and the dates of occurrence listed on the sides in bold, black letters.

A frail alcoholic was slumped in a chair. He looked sixtyish but was probably in his forties; he had a blooming complexion and bloodshot eyes.

Vassos inched his way along the shelves.

Lucas watched Big Jay's face. The black detective remained stoical, save for a subtle lift of his right eyebrow.

"Now, Eddie," Leone said wearily, "tell us again why you left the shack."

"I hadda take a shit," the watchman said. "How many fuckin' times I gotta tell ya?"

Big Jay's mock fury unleashed itself on the nearest carton, his fist punching through the side. "You're a fucking liar. You left cause you knew a hit was going down."

The watchman turned defiant. "Prove it."

"Prove it!" Big Jay bellowed. "You miserable little scumbag, I'll prove it." He clasped the bottom of the watchman's chair and lifted it up off the floor, tossing it against the shelf. The tops of several cartons came undone; the guard sprawled onto the floor.

"Hey! None of that stuff!" Lucas shouted. "Help the man up."

"Yes, sir," Big Jay said meekly.

Leone motioned to Lucas. "This is Inspector McCann, and this is" —he pointed to Vassos—"Captain Lopez. They're from the Mendicant Squad."

"Nice to meet you, sir," Vassos said.

"A pleasure," Lucas added, turning to Vassos and saying, "Captain, go to the supply locker and get something to relax Mr. Walsh."

Vassos nodded and left the room.

"Mr. Walsh," Lucas said, "we believe that you left your shack at that particular time because you were told to."

The guard waved a protesting hand at Lucas. "Naw, dat ain't it. I told ya, I hadda take a dump."

Vassos slipped back into the room with a bottle of vodka and a stack of pleated paper cups. Lucas motioned Leone and Big Jay out of the room. Vassos handed the guard a cup and passed one to Lucas. Big Jay and Leone left, closing the door behind them.

Vassos poured the clear liquid into the guard's cup, making sure to fill it to the brim. Lucas watched the guard toss down the drink and hold up his cup for another. "Edward, that is your name?"

"I ain't been called that in years," the guard said.

"My father's name was Edward," Vassos lied.

The guard looked squint-eyed at Vassos. "Dat's a funny accent you got. You from New York?"

"Puerto Rico," Vassos said.

"You know, Edward, you're not a bad guy, but you got yourself caught up in something that could jam you up," Lucas said. "We might be forced to hold you as a material witness."

The guard held up his empty cup to the fictitious Captain Lopez. Vassos poured more vodka. Walsh gulped down the drink, pulled a sour face. "Ya know, McCann, I never had any real ambition. I just wanted to go through life with enough fuck-you money in my pockets so I didn't have to take no shit from anyone." He shrugged philosophically. "But, dat didn't work out either. I'm a drunk who everyone dumps on."

"Some people put you in a whole lot of shit, Edward," Lucas said.

"Fuckin'-A right they did," the guard said, picking at a scab on his face.

Vassos poured more vodka into the guard's sloshing cup. "Did they telephone you or tell you in person?"

"Telephoned me in the shack."

Vassos looked at Lucas. "What did they tell you?" he asked the guard.

"To take a hike between nine and ten, and to keep my trap shut."

"Do you know who telephoned you?" Lucas asked.

"Naw. Some guy. On the docks you don't ask too many questions."

Disappointment showed on the policemen's faces. Lucas swung open the door. "Big Jay, drive Mr. Walsh home."

"What do we do next?" Vassos asked, sitting in one of the swivel chairs.

"Burke took several falls with a guy named Bucky McMahon. He's the one who was arrested for the Widener robbery." Lucas ransacked the top of his desk. "I sent a request to the Probation Department to try and locate McMahon. Their answer should have arrived in the department mail. Here it is," he said, pulling a multiuse envelope out of the basket. He opened it and read the slip of paper. "Shit! Bucky McMahon died three years ago." He balled up the paper and tossed it into the wastebasket on the side of the desk.

Ulanov sauntered into the office. "We're calling it a day, Lou. Wanna pop over to Heidi's for a taste?"

"I'm not in the mood."

12

Sunlight filtered through the bedroom blinds; the air still held morning's freshness. Dressed in undershorts, with his arm around Joan's shoulder, Lucas steered her into the living room toward the door.

She kissed him. "Thank you."

"Thank you," he echoed, reaching for the doorknob, anxious to get on with his day. She reached out shyly, touched his hair which was still wet from the shower, and put her arms around him. Hugging him tight, she savored what she suspected were their last moments together. "I'll miss you."

"Me too," he said, surprised to find, even as he said it, that he felt a pang of regret.

"What do I mean to you, Teddy?"

"You're a nice woman, Joan. I like you."

"A nice woman?" Her hands slid off his shoulder. "I'm available, I make no demands, and I'm a nice woman too. You got yourself a real bargain."

"Get off it, Joan. You understood from the beginning . . ."

She smiled and tilted her head back to look into his eyes. "I know, lover. It's just that I'm a hopeless romantic. But when reality sets in, I can cope." She reached down and gently bounced his scrotum in her palm. "Don't take any wooden nickels." She threw open the door and stepped out into the empty hallway. "By the way, I don't know who you thought you were doing it to just now, but it certainly wasn't me."

*　　　*　　　*

"Kahleemehrah." Good morning, Vassos greeted Lucas thirty minutes later.

"Kahleemehrah," Lucas said, going into his office.

Biting into a doughnut, Leone observed, "Not in such a great mood, our boss."

The Second Whip was in the Whip's office pawing through the morning mail.

"Anything important?" Lucas asked, scanning the sixty sheet.

Grimes pulled out a thick, multiuse envelope from the pile and handed it to Lucas. "Identification Section, addressed to you."

Lucas unstrung the jacket and slid out a clump of fives. The blue forms were pinned together. He worked out the pin and tossed it into the coffee can that dressed up his desk. A gigantic lollipop stuck out of the can. It read: "Winning isn't everything, but losing sucks." The fingerprint technician had prepared a five on each known member of the Purple Gang, summing up the results of the comparison of their fingerprints with those of the latents that had been lifted at the scene of the Iskur homicide.

Each report ended with NR, negative results. The technician had tacked on a personal note: "Lou, none of them came close. Sorry."

Lucas opened the bottom drawer of his desk and shoved the fives into the case folder. He glanced over at the composite sketch tacked onto the blackboard. Looking at Grimes, he asked, "Anything else?"

"A few things," Grimes said, pulling a stack of folders out from under the basket. "I've heard from the army on Denny McKay. He was a printer, worked in an intelligence unit that operated out of Japan during the Korean War."

"What were you able to find out about his unit?"

"I made a few phone calls. Seems he worked in a 'disinformation unit.' They used to print phony enemy orders, pay records, transfers, that sort of stuff. McKay remained there for the duration."

"Was he a printer before he joined the army?"

"He didn't join. He was drafted. It seems that he graduated from George Westinghouse Vocational High School where he learned printing." He passed the folder to the Whip.

"What else?"

"I've prepared our Quarterly Case Management Study," Grimes said, passing another folder to the Whip.

Lucas took out the report, a review of all active cases designed to insure increased supervisory direction and control of investigations. Glancing through the several pages, he thought: more fodder for the Palace Guard, that bureaucracy of self-preservation that had raised busywork to a managerial art form. "I'll sign this. What else?"

"That's it," Grimes said, leaving the office.

Lucas spun around in his chair and checked the list of important telephone numbers taped to the wall. He picked up the telephone and dialed the Legal Bureau. A civilian attorney answered. Lucas told him about the dental impressions and the result of the saliva test. The person who had smoked the cigarettes had A-positive blood.

"And you want to secure a search warrant that will enable you to forcibly take the suspect's dental impressions—and draw blood," the lawyer said.

Here we go again, Lucas thought, picking up on the attorney's bored and patronizing tone. "Correct."

"I'm sure that you're aware, Lieutenant, that allegations of fact supporting a search warrant may be based upon an officer's personal knowledge, or upon information and belief, provided that the source of the information and the grounds for the belief are stated."

"I know that, Counselor. I'm acting on information and belief, an informer, one John Doe, a person whom I've used in the past, someone who has always proved reliable."

"Is this informer of yours registered with the department?"

"Come on, Counselor, you know as well as I do that most informers refuse to go into the register."

"Sure I know. But the courts are not interested in what you and I know. PD regulations require informers to be registered with the department. Now, if you try and play games with the court, you could end up having a mighty big problem."

"One of my detectives observed the suspect chewing on the same brand of cigarette as was found at the crime scene. And I know from the suspect's army record that he has the same blood type."

"Not enough, Lieutenant. You need something that tends to connect him to the scene."

"Thanks," Lucas said, slamming down the phone.

Vassos was in the doorway, watching him. Lucas told him what the department lawyer had said.

"You have strange rules, Teddy. In Greece we would drag McKay in and he would do what we told him to."

"Regrettably, we have different rules."

"Is there no way to get around these rules of yours?"

"There are several things we could do. But if we got caught doing them, there'd be a good chance that the case against McKay would go bye-bye. We'll wait. Good cops need a lot of patience. McKay is going to trip over his prick one day, and I'm going to be there when he does to make sure that he takes the fall."

Ulanov poked his head into the office. "Our friend from across the street just called. He wants to meet the both of us, now. Says he's got something for you."

Leaving the squad room with Vassos and Ulanov, Lucas asked Leone if they had come up with anything on the Burke homicide.

"Nothing," Leone said. "We traced Burke's movements back twenty-four hours before the hit but came up dry. His girlfriend, a debutante from Hoboken, told us that he had an appointment around nine, but she didn't know with whom. Claims he never talked business with her."

"Anyone on the pier see anything?" Lucas asked.

"Not even the seagulls," Big Jay replied.

"Let it slide then. Work on it when you have time," Lucas said, opening the gate.

Ulanov parked the unmarked police car on the west side of Park Avenue, in front of the Banco di Sicilia. Hands gripping the steering wheel, he people watched. Lucas, in the passenger seat, studied the golden statuary of Jupiter and Juno that adorned the golden clock of the Helmsley Building. Vassos sat in the rear of the car watching a bag lady scavenging for food in a refuse container.

The radio trumpeted police calls: 10:67, traffic condition, Madison and Five-six; 10:59, alarm of fire, Third and Four-seven.

"You're sure that he said he wanted to see both of us?" Lucas asked Ulanov.

"That's what the comrade said," Ulanov said, watching a long-legged woman with a very short skirt cross the avenue.

Leaning forward and draping his arms over the back of the front seat, Vassos asked Lucas, "Do you know this person well?"

"Colonel Sergei Nashin is the KGB's liaison with the NYPD," Lucas said. "Usually he only wants to meet with Ulanov. But I've met with him on several occasions. He's not a bad guy."

"There he is," Ulanov announced, "on the other side of the street, walking south."

"Wait in the car," Lucas told Vassos.

Nashin waited on the corner of Forty-sixth and Park until the two detectives had reached him and then crossed the street southward with the two policemen.

Nashin nodded to Ulanov. "Comrade."

"Colonel," Ulanov responded.

They strolled through Helmsley Walk East, an arcade that tunneled through the ground floor of the Helmsley Building. They exited onto Forty-fifth, crossed the street, and stood under the vaulted entrance to the Pan Am Building.

"I love this town," Nashin said in flawless English.

"Me too," Lucas said, admiring the KGB man's pressed, blue seersucker suit and open-collared blue shirt. Nashin's youthful face belied his forty-nine years, and his thick flaxen hair gave him a Germanic aspect.

"I hear the PC is getting out," Nashin said, his cagey eyes playing the afternoon crowd. He delighted in using NYPD slang when he was with cops.

"Rumors," Lucas said. "The police commissioner is always retiring, according to the grapevine."

Nashin smiled. "It's the same in my job. The latest rumor is that the Politburo is pissed off at the director because he was screwing an Olympic gymnast thirty years younger than he."

"Hey, that don't make him a bad person," Ulanov said.

Nashin laughingly agreed. "How's your son, Ivan?"

"Getting ready to go off to college," Ulanov said. "And your daughter?"

"She just finished her first year at Moscow University," Nashin said proudly. "She thinks she's smarter than her papa and her mama." He looked at Lucas. "You should visit the Soviet Union, really. I'd set the whole thing up for you. You'd have a ball, and I'd see to it that it was, ah . . . on the arm."

"Maybe someday," Lucas said.

A panhandler approached the trio. Nashin waved him off. "They always seem to have money for booze and cigarettes."

"You said that you had something for me," Lucas said.

"Let's walk," Nashin suggested.

They backtracked through Helmsley Walk East and strolled up Park Avenue, heading north. At Fiftieth Street they climbed the steps of Saint Bartholomew's Church and slowly walked through the plaza that ran between the church and its community center. Nashin peeled away from the other two and sat on the stone coping that ran above Fiftieth Street. He placed his hands behind him and leaned back, admiring the church's stone tracery and tiled dome. "I love church architecture. Either of you ever see the fan vaulting in King's College Chapel at Cambridge?"

The detectives said no.

"You ought to go see it; it's really incredible." Taking a small, elegant leather notebook out of his pocket, Nashin said, "Iskur worked for the Allies during the war. Mostly around the Mediterranean. During the Korean War he did some intelligence work in Japan. We don't know what he did, but we do know that he spent some time there." He looked at Lucas. "Why are you interested in Iskur?"

Lucas knew better than to lie to the Soviet policeman. "We have reason to believe that he was involved in smuggling antiquities into this country."

"From where?" Nashin asked.

"Greece," Lucas said.

Nashin turned serious. "Iskur has been murdered."

"How did you know that?" Lucas asked, trying to smooth the surprised edge of his voice.

"From the collators," Nashin said. "We have people in Moscow who spend their days cutting articles out of newspapers and magazines from all over the world. They translate them and then feed them into computers. Some of our people believe that it was no coincidence that Iskur was killed the same day as the Voúla massacre."

Lucas looked cautiously at Nashin. "Why do I get the feeling, Sergei, that you have a vested interest in what happened to Iskur?"

"We are extremely interested in Iskur and his associates," Nashin said.

"Why?" Lucas asked.

"We are a big country, Teddy, with thousands of churches and monasteries scattered through the most isolated regions. All of them are crammed with ancient art. A criminal network is looting our patrimony; we have reason to believe that Iskur was involved."

"How do you tie him into it?" Lucas asked.

"Last year our border guards stopped a truck trying to enter Turkey at Yerevan. According to the papers that the driver and his helper tried to pass, they were delivering potash to Yerevan. For whatever reasons, the guards became suspicious and searched the truck. Hidden inside a false gas tank they found a Cyrillic codex from the eleventh century and a tenth-century Byzantine diadem. Both had been stolen from the monastery at Orsk."

"I assume that your people had a talk with the driver and his helper," Lucas said.

"Oh, yes. They are both serving thirty-year sentences in a most disagreeable labor camp," Nashin said.

"I wish we could send some of our mutts to one of your labor camps," Lucas said wistfully.

"Thank you, but we have enough mutts of our own," Nashin said. "The comrades told our interrogators that they had been paid by a man in Orsk, who sent them to a dealer in Yerevan. There they were provided with forged travel documents and the necessary export papers."

"Printed documents?" Lucas asked.

"Very good quality forgeries. We believe that the counterfeits were made in the States and shipped to the Soviet Union."

"Don't you have enough of your own forgers?" Lucas asked.

"Yes, we do. But our crooks do not have the high-tech electronic copying machines that you have in the West, nor do they have access to special paper. Our experts tell us that the documents came from the West, probably the States."

"What happened to the dealer in Yerevan?" Lucas asked.

"Some of our people paid him a visit. Some money changed hands and he confided that the eventual destination of the stolen art was Athens."

Lucas looked at Nashin. "Orhan Iskur?"

"You got it, kiddo," Nashin said.

"A network of art thieves with Iskur running the operational end," Lucas said.

"That is what we believe," Nashin said. "Turkey, Italy, and Spain have a similar problem."

"What happened to the man who hired the driver and his helper?" Lucas asked.

"He disappeared before we could arrest him. We'll catch him, eventually." Nashin watched several people climb the church steps. "I've been authorized to offer you whatever help you might need."

"Thanks. I'll stay in touch, Sergei," Lucas said, making a move to leave.

"There is something else," Nashin said. "Eight years ago a Greek Scylites manuscript depicting Oleg's campaign against Constantinople was stolen from Saint Andrew's Church outside of Kiev." He looked at Ulanov. "Your hometown."

Ulanov screwed up his face. "A long time ago, Sergei Sergeyevich."

Nashin smiled. "The manuscript resurfaced last year in Rome. A respectable dealer was offering it for sale. We ransomed back what had been stolen from us."

"Why didn't you go into court and sue to get it back?" Lucas asked.

"It was a political decision. The *nomenklatura* who decide such matters felt that it would not do for my government to go into a court in Rome and have to admit that we were unable to protect our national treasures. It would have shown, I believe the word was 'vulnerability.'" He sucked in a deep breath. "We were bamboozled. The manuscript was a forgery."

"They steal the original, make copies, and peddle them around the world," Lucas said.

Nashin continued wearily. "Our agents went back to the dealer and told him that it was a fake. He returned our money along with his apologies."

"Do you think he was in on the scam?" Lucas asked.

Nashin said carefully, "There is no way of knowing for sure. He claims that he, too, was taken in. Would you care to guess from whom he acquired the manuscript?"

"Iskur," Lucas said firmly.

Nashin nodded. "Let's stay in touch?"

"Absolutely," Lucas said.

The policemen walked away from the plaza. Two fashionably dressed women passed as they were descending the steps. "Good afternoon, ladies," Nashin said, smiling at them.

"Gentlemen," the taller of the two women responded good-naturedly.

"I have to get back to the office," Nashin said, shaking Lucas's hand; then, with a mischievous grin on his face: "Say good-bye to Major Vassos for me."

Adele Matrazzo's body had become a swollen black mass. Larvae squirmed over her lifeless eyes; insect eggs lined the corners of her mouth and nostrils.

Lucas, Vassos, and Ivan Ulanov stood amid the bizarre activity that homicide engenders. The stench of decaying flesh infested the house. Every ground-floor window had been thrown open; plates sprinkled with disinfectant crystals were scattered about. The big-screen television was still on, the sound turned down.

Seven-two Squad detectives gathered around the body; another day, another case. The heavy noon heat didn't make it any easier. Lucas suggested closing the windows and turning on the big window air conditioner full blast.

"What the fuck is it?" asked one detective.

"Looks like a long piece of wire," observed another.

A third announced: "It's a string from a stringed instrument. Most likely from a violin."

"No shit?" said the first. "It sure cut the hell out of her neck."

Sandy White, the Seven-two Whip, a lean veteran with a craggy face, spotted Lucas and the others and came over to them.

"A friend of yours, Teddy?" White asked, pointing to the body on the floor.

"I interviewed her regarding a nothing case my squad is carrying," Lucas lied. "I left my card with her."

"I found it; that's why I called you," White said. "Why don't we get some fresh air?"

They abandoned the crime scene for the sunlit world of the living. Once outside, Lucas introduced the Seven-two lieutenant to Vassos and Ulanov.

"Greek, hmmm?" White said, eyeing the major.

"Yes. I am here on an exchange program," Vassos said.

"Exchange program?" White echoed disbelievingly. He turned to Lucas. "Why you interested in my murder victim?"

"We're looking for a cousin of hers in connection with a larceny," Lucas said.

"What's the hump's name?" White asked.

"Paolo Matrazzo," Lucas said.

White asked, "Is he connected?"

"An independent," Lucas said. "No tie-in with the wise-guys."

White silently ran the name through his memory, then said, "Paolo Matrazzo? Never heard of him."

Lucas asked White what his detectives had come up with on the initial canvass. White told him that the victim had been strangled, and that there was no sign of a forced entry into the house. "We figure she'd dead maybe twenty-four hours, no more than forty-eight. It's hard to tell in this heat, they melt fast. We interviewed the people living in the immediate vicinity. The neighbors did her shopping, but none of them knew shit about her. A Mrs. O'Rourke"—he pointed to the green house across the street—"she and the victim used to have tea together a few times a week. She's the one who discovered the body. She don't know anything about her either."

Lucas glanced at the O'Rourke house in time to see someone duck behind the curtains.

". . . a retired schoolteacher with no known relatives. I've sent one of my men to the Board of Ed to have a look at her records," White said.

"No one saw anyone enter or leave the house?" Lucas asked, glancing across the street in time to catch a glimpse of someone ducking back from the same window.

"No one saw nothing," White said.

Lucas turned his head slightly so that his peripheral vision could take in the O'Rourke house. He could see a woman peeking out, watching them.

"Ya'know, Teddy, if you want this case, I'll be more than happy to bang out a five and transfer it to your squad," White said. "My intuition tells me it ain't going nowhere."

"Thanks, pal. But I'm carrying enough open homicides. I don't need another one to drag down my clearances." Lucas dropped his voice. "Any objections if I have a talk with the O'Rourke woman?"

"Be my guest," White said.

"Wait here," Lucas told Vassos and Ulanov.

"Mrs. O'Rourke?" Lucas asked when she opened the door. He produced his shield and I.D. card.

She was a short woman with gray hair pulled back and held in place with a rubber band. Her face was alive with barely suppressed excitement. She wore a peach-colored housecoat, white anklets, and sandals. She studied Lucas's photo identification card, comparing it with the smiling face in front of her. "I told the other policeman everything that I know."

"A moment of your time, please?"

"Well, I guess it'll be all right. After all, Adele was a dear friend. God rest her soul." She stepped aside to admit him into her house.

He walked into a cheerless room filled with overstuffed furniture swaddled in plastic. He lowered himself down into a yellow armchair. "It's a lovely neighborhood," he began.

"It used to be a grand neighborhood," she complained, "but it's changing, for the worse, if you know what I mean?"

"I think I do," he said, and for the next several minutes smilingly endured her rambling monologue before he felt she had relaxed enough for him to ask, "Have you lived her a long time, Mrs. O'Rourke?"

"Himself and I raised six children in this house. My husband passed on twelve years ago, God rest his soul."

"I guess you must know everyone on the block."

"Yes, I do," she said proudly. "Mrs. Cohen—she lives three doors down—moved in three years ago." Leaning forward, lowering her voice to a conspiratorial whisper, she added, "She keeps kosher, if you know what I mean?"

"Yes, I do."

"Once a week," she continued in her conniving tone, "a man who has those funny strings that religious Jewish men wear around their waists visits Mrs. Cohen."

"Those fringes are called *tsitsis.*"

"Well, I can tell you, I wouldn't be a bit surprised if he played with Mrs. Cohen's *tsitsis,* if you know what I mean?"

"I think I do, yes." Leaning forward in his seat, he went on: "I understand that you and Adele had tea together a few times a week."

"Yes, but we never discussed anything about her private life. I'm not one to pry, you know."

"What did you two talk about?"

"Mostly she listened to my problems. Adele was a very good listener. One of my daughters-in-law doesn't believe in cooking, working, or cleaning. Humph! The modern woman. I tell you, my Johnny is forever buying that no-account wife of his presents. No one ever buys me presents. And I'll tell you something else, Adele agreed with me. No one ever bought her presents either, except that one at Christmas. And I'll tell you something else, too—"

"What one at Christmas?" he asked, on the edge of his seat.

"The television. The one with the big screen in the parlor. Adele told me that it was a gift from her wonderful cousin."

"What cousin?"

"I don't know. She just said in passing it was a gift from her cousin. And then she added 'my wonderful cousin.' "

"Did she ever mention any other member of her family?"

She thought; shook her head no.

"Did you ever see anyone visit her?"

"I play bingo and go to exercise classes most days at the senior citizen center, so I'm usually not home."

Lucas retreated into his own thoughts. Adele Matrazzo had told him that she had had two cousins: Anthony, who had been killed on Guadalcanal, and Paolo Jr., who had taught art history at NYU and had died in 1968, leaving behind a wife and two children. He hadn't checked out any of that information. It hadn't seemed relevant at the time. He got up from his seat and thanked Mrs. O'Rourke.

Walking out of the house into the bright sunlight, he saw the morgue attendants carrying Adele Matrazzo's body to the meat wagon. Her shroud was a dark green body bag, compliments of the City of New York.

Waiting the following morning in front of the stone mansion on the northeast corner of Fifth Avenue and Seventy-eighth Street, Teddy Lucas watched the passing parade. First came a file of roped-together nursery-school children who were shepherded by several teenage girls. Next came a dog walker struggling with ten leashed canines.

He checked the time and saw that he was twelve minutes too early for his nine-thirty appointment with Katina. He had telephoned her late yesterday afternoon after he returned to the Squad from the Matrazzo crime scene. "Is there some way that we can check on Paolo Matrazzo Junior's academic credentials to see if he really existed?" he had asked her. She had said yes and they arranged to meet the next day.

Lucas had shaven carefully this morning. He wore a paisley tie with a white button-down shirt, a brown sports jacket, and his beige slacks. He wanted to look his best for her. The imaginary insects in his stomach began to buzz when he saw her hurrying along Seventy-eighth

Street. He quickly admired her pale yellow dress and black leather pumps. Her large yellow earrings and the way her hair was pulled back in an arrangement that accentuated her beautiful, high-cheekboned face. He wanted to rush up to her and tell her how wonderful she looked, but instead he just jerked his thumb at the stately building and said, "Some shack."

"The Duke Mansion," she explained, looking at the facade. "The family left it to New York University's Institute of Fine Arts. If Matrazzo Junior received his Ph.D. from NYU, his doctoral dissertation will be on file here."

They climbed the steps and entered the vestibule. She signed for both of them in the visitors' log at the security desk.

He looked around at the enormous marble reception hall just beyond the vestibule and felt like a tourist. An elaborate curving marble staircase with a gilt-and-black wrought-iron bannister dominated the hall.

"Shall we walk up, or ride?" she asked.

"Walk. I want to see as much of this place as I can."

A quarter of the way up he stopped to admire a wall relief of putty, cupidlike children without wings. Climbing farther, he paused to look at a tapestry hanging on the stairwell's wall. When they reached the second-floor landing, he leaned over the railing to get a better look at it.

The library was at the end of a long hallway. They moved inside and went over to the blue-labeled card catalogue. "Do you have any idea when he was supposed to have written his dissertation?" she asked quietly.

"No."

"They're filed by year and then alphabetically, by author."

"Adele told us that his brother Anthony was killed in the war. So why don't we assume that the brothers were about the same age and begin with 1935."

She slid out a drawer and flicked index cards to the year. Some minutes later she had worked her way through to 1943. "He's not here."

"Adele might have lied to us."

"I did not have that feeling when she was talking to us," Katina said. "I thought that she was proud of Junior's accomplishments."

Lucas mulled over the problem. Researchers moved about the racks of books; others worked silently at long tables.

"Paolo Junior might have gone back to school on the GI bill after the war," he said.

"Makes sense," she said, flipping index cards up to the year 1949, her fingers dancing over the tops to the Ms. "Teddy, look."

The call numbers were typed on top of the card and were followed on the next line by the title of the dissertation: "In Defense of Alexander's *Iliad*." By Paolo Matrazzo, Jr.

Five minutes later they were alone inside a small reading room, sitting at a square table. Above them three stacked circular catwalks lined with books led upward to a skylight of opaque gray glass. A faded lavender binder lay on the table between them. He opened the cover. Brown age marks stained the edges of the pages. She inched her chair closer to his; they read together while she turned the pages. She went on to tell him how some scholars considered the casket-copy to be apocryphal, a fable made up to add to the legend of Alexander.

Matrazzo's thesis defended the existence of the casket-copy. Katina gave Lucas a detailed explanation of original and secondary sources and told him how Matrazzo had cited Callisthenes, Aristotle's nephew and Alexander's official historian in Asia, as the primary source for the world's knowledge of the existence of the casket-copy.

Lucas looked up. A woman was on the lowest catwalk, consulting her call slip as her finger slid over the spines of books. Very quietly he asked, "Could the casket-copy be forged?"

"On papyrus scrolls?"

"Yes."

"I would think that very unlikely. The aging of the papyrus. The ink. And the scrolls? A fake would never be able to withstand scientific scrutiny."

"Suppose a buyer accepted it as genuine without having its authenticity verified?"

She shrugged in disbelief. "I cannot believe anyone would be that stupid."

"Greed makes the smartest people foolish, Dr. Wright. It's the con man's staunchest ally." He shifted in his chair to face her. One of his knees got between hers accidentally. "There are many people in this world who are heavy with money but also short on brains."

"That's true," she agreed with a warm smile.

"Let me give you a scenario. An art dealer with an impeccable reputation, and a captivating foreign accent, offers a one-of-a-kind antiquity, one that has, regrettably, been stolen from another country. So it lacks the necessary export papers; thus the prospective buyer can't have provenance checked."

"And this wealthy buyer thought he, or she, was getting a bargain."

"You got it," he said, aware of the tiny ringlets of fine hair around her ears. "How does the art world stay informed about stolen objects?"

"Trade publications, insurance bulletins, word of mouth. And then there are the flyers from the FBI and Interpol."

Lucas looked up at the skylight and did not speak for a minute or so, his expression serious and thoughtful. "I wonder."

"What?"

"I get the feeling that there is someone out there laughing at me. And I'm also wondering if . . ."

"If what?"

"Nothing, it's too farfetched. Can we meet later today?"

"It will take me most of the day to research his writings. Why don't you and Andreas come to my apartment tonight around seven. I'll make us a light dinner and we can go over whatever I come up with on Dr. Matrazzo."

"Sounds good to me." Lucas watched her gathering up her notes. As they were leaving she asked, "Where is Andreas?"

"He had an urgent call from his embassy."

A gray cloud of pigeons landed around the fountain in Lincoln Center. Across the street in Ficco's, Elisabeth Syros sipped espresso while she sat in the front row. Her cowboy shirt had leather fringes running down the sleeve; her brown-and-white boots not only gave her an extra two inches in height, but also complemented her western-style jeans. Her wrists and fingers were gleaming with silver Navajo jewelry.

Sipping the strong coffee, her hungry eyes followed a long-legged beauty passing the restaurant. Caught up in a sudden erotic reverie, she licked her lips and unconsciously put her hand between her legs where a wonderful warmth began to spread out. Aroused, her nipples showed their points even through the thick denim of her shirt. Like her ancient ancestors, Elisabeth Syros loved both men and women, but she preferred the latter.

One hand gripping the railing, Vassos edged his way into the aisle and squeezed into the empty chair at her tiny table. Beckoning to the waiter on the other side of the railing, he ordered espresso. She slid a folded slip of paper over to him. "This arrived in the pouch. It's from Pappas. Iskur's telephone calls," she said in Greek.

Vassos unfolded the paper and studied the list of calls. They were printed out alphabetically by country, followed by the cities within the country, followed by the numbers called within each city. The listings covered calls made to England, Greece, Italy, Turkey, the Soviet Union, and the United States. The majority of the calls to the United States were to a 212 number in Manhattan. "Do we know whose telephone numbers these are?"

Elisabeth passed another slip of paper over to him. The waiter came and, stretching his arm over the railing, handed Vassos his espresso. When the waiter had gone, Vassos removed the hand that was covering the slip of paper, picked it up, and studied what was written on it. Each telephone number had the subscriber listed below the digits. The frequently called 212 number belonged to a Brandt Industries. It had the same address as The Den, Denny McKay's Ninth Avenue head-quarters. He folded both slips and put them in his shirt pocket. "Any-thing else?"

They continued to speak in Greek.

"Pappas has located the man who did Iskur's legwork," she confided. "His name is Yiannis Yiotas. He's in custody and has admitted making the arrangements, but he denies knowing what Iskur was planning."

Vassos ran a finger over one of her rings, a silver band with a tur-quoise stone. "Iskur took his orders from someone in the States."

"Pappas has come up with a name."

His face grew stern. "Who?"

"According to Interpol, seventeen years ago in London Yiotas and Iskur tried to sell a fake antique to a tourist who turned out to have been a dealer. He had both of them arrested. Then, without any expla-nation, the American refused to go forward with the court case and the charges were dropped."

"The dealer's name?" he demanded.

"Belmont E. Widener."

Chief of Detectives Tim Edgeworth was standing by the window of his office contemplating the panoramic view of the Manhattan skyline when Lucas entered. He waved the lieutenant into a chair. "Any pro-gress on the Greek caper?"

"Several things are beginning to take shape," Lucas said, sitting in one of the three chairs arranged in front of the desk. "I want to take four of my men off the chart to work with Major Vassos and me. That's going to mean telling them the nature of the investigation."

Edgeworth turned away from the window. He looked tired and drawn. He moved over to his desk and sat down behind it. Picking up his pipe, he lit it with slow deliberation. A swirl of white smoke partly concealed his expression. "Do you have any disciplinary problems in your squad, Teddy?"

"All my men are solid, Chief."

"Well, I hope so. But if you do have any problems, get rid of them. If you don't, you'll take the fall with them. Did you hear what hap-pened in the Five-three?"

"No."

"Two detectives are doing a night duty. They lock up a burglar and process him for central booking. But they have a problem. There's a precinct stag party in a local VFW hall that the two supersleuths want to attend. And they know that if they go to central booking with their prisoner, they'll be stuck there for at least three hours and will miss most of the festivities. So what do you think the two birdbrains do?"

Lucas swallowed a smile, forced himself to wear a grim expression. "They brought the burglar to the party."

"That's right! And it gets better," Edgeworth said, stabbing his pipe at the lieutenant's face. "They had *entertainment* at this soiree. The two birdbrains belted down a few balls and decided that they were going to be nice guys. So they chipped in and got their prisoner a blow job." He was banging his pipe on the desk; a few embers spilled out of the bowl onto the blotter. "We used to beat the shit out of prisoners. Now we're getting them blow jobs." He leaped up out of his seat and pointed his finger at Teddy. "That's the result of all that goddamn human interaction bullshit they teach at the Academy." He threw his pipe into the glass ashtray.

Lucas grabbed a folder from the desk and discreetly smothered the embers.

"Goddamn those men," Edgeworth shouted, slumping back down into his chair. "At the arraignment the next morning the legal aid lawyer asked the burglar how the cops treated him. 'Great,' the burglar said, and then blabbed about the party."

"What's going to happen?"

"Both detectives are being flopped back into the bag, along with the Whip, who wasn't even at the party. With authority—"

"—goes commensurate responsibility," Lucas chimed in.

Edgeworth pushed his chair back, bent down, and blew stray ashes off his blotter. "How many men did you say?"

"Four—Leone, Big Jay, Ulanov, and Gregory."

"Your squad working two-handed?"

"Generally, yes. Occasionally I'll have a three-man team covering a duty."

"Are these four guys partners or are you splitting teams?"

"Partners."

"How long do you think they'll be off the chart?"

"A month, maybe longer."

Edgeworth opened the top drawer of his desk and slid out the Force Figure Folder, a projected thirty-day analysis of the manpower pool available within the Detective Division. He studied the tear sheets. "With vacations and military leaves we're always short bodies in the summer. Let me see now, I'll fly in one detective from the Staten Island Robbery Squad and another from Queens Robbery." He flipped pages. "I don't want to pull any men away from the busy squads, but I don't want to send you any duds. Okay. Here are the other two, both of them from Manhattan North's Crimes Against Senior Citizens Squad."

"Thanks, Chief. I'll assign them to work with detectives from my squad until they familiarize themselves with the precinct."

"Can those guys of yours keep their traps shut?"

"I wouldn't have selected them if they couldn't."

"I hope so. We don't want the press getting wind of this investigation. Those bastards would turn it into a circus."

"I understand."

A veiled expression came over the C of D's face. "I have something that might interest you." He lifted up the desk blotter and slid out a report. He handed it to the lieutenant. It read:

From: Commanding Officer, Central Park Detective Squad

To: Police Commissioner

Subject: HOMICIDE OF U.S. DIPLOMAT WITHIN THE CONFINES OF THIS COMMAND.

1.   On July 15, 1987 at approximately 2300 hours on the east side of Central Park West, thirty feet from the northeast corner of West Sixty-fourth Street, a white male, identified as Trevor Hughes, the political officer of the U.S. embassy in Athens, Greece, was the subject of a homicide under the following circumstances . . .

Lucas looked up at the C of D with a frown of puzzlement and then read the rest of the report. When he finished, he put the report back on the desk. "Any leads?"

"The detective who caught the case thinks it was a hit that someone tried to make look like a mugging."

"What makes him think that?"

"The perp employed a mugger's MO of cutting out the pockets. But only pack muggers do that. Two mutts will grab the victim and a third mutt will cut out the pockets. Hughes was shot. A mutt with a gun don't cut out pockets. He just shoves his piece into his victim's face and tells him to fork over his possessions."

"What have they turned up on Hughes?"

"He took a vacation and flew to New York. Checked into the Plaza. That's it."

"Was he married?"

"He left his wife in Greece."

"Any girlfriends?"

"None that they were able to come up with."

"Boyfriends?"

Edgeworth shrugged.

"Any alarm bells go off in the State Department when they were notified one of their people had been murdered?"

"Not a tinkle."

"Strange. A diplomat gets whacked and nobody in D.C. raises an eyebrow."

Packing tobacco into his pipe, Edgeworth said, "You'd expect a political officer to be a savvy guy who'd know better than to go strolling around Central Park at night. Unless he was looking to get bungholed, or unless he had an appointment." Putting the stem into his mouth, he added, "We think like cops, don't we?"

"That's what we're paid to do, isn't it?"

"Yeah, that's what we're paid to do." Edgeworth looked down at his desk and said in a low voice, "I'm gonna give you a little bit of unofficial guidance, Teddy. For your ears only—not a word to anyone else, especially Vassos."

The C of D got up and walked over to the window. "I can tell you now that we will be getting somebody to 'liaise' with us." Edgeworth spat out the phrase like he was getting rid of something foul tasting on his tongue. "You don't need to know anything more than that for the moment. Whatever shithead shows up, I don't care if his credentials have been signed by God Almighty, you give him nothin'. Don't trust him. Give him a hand job, blow smoke up his ass, and report back to me on everything he says, everything he does."

Lucas stared at the broad back of the C of D. "You make it sound like he isn't exactly on our side."

Edgeworth whirled around. "You said it, Teddy. We got to find out damn fast just *what* side he's on. So from now on, anybody who comes at you from Washington should be handled like a fucking cobra— because that's what they're sending us."

Forty-seven minutes later Teddy Lucas gathered his detectives inside his office. Leone, Big Jay, Ulanov, Gregory. The Second Whip stood in the doorway, his shoulder leaning against the jamb, a can of diet soda in his hand.

The rim of the blackboard was covered by crime scene photographs: Iskur, Burke, Matrazzo, Trevor Hughes; homicides linked to an ancient book. Lucas untacked one of the Voúla crime scene pictures. Sitting on the edge of his desk, he held the grim photograph up and said, "This is the kind of a case you dream of. It surfaced last year in Voúla, Greece. But it really began after the battle of Issus in 333 B.C. . . ."

The men listened as Lucas unfolded the complexities of the case. When he had completed the briefing he asked if there were any questions. At first no one spoke. Each detective seemed to be absorbed in his own thoughts. Finally, Big Jay said, "Why was Major Vassos assigned to the case?"

Lucas held up the photograph of the Voúla crime scene. "The woman and child in the spacecraft were Major Vassos's wife and son."

Lucas watched the faces of his men; he could see they were thinking of their own wives and children. "It's no secret in the Job that Cormick McGovern and I were close. It's also no secret that Denny McKay ordered the hit on Cormick. As I just got through explaining, McKay and his people are involved in Voúla. That means we got another turn in the batter's box." His angry eyes rested on each detective in turn. "I don't intend to strike out again." He removed the case folder from the bottom drawer and slapped it down on the desk. "Familiarize yourselves with the fives."

The detectives got up and gathered around the desk.

"I've got news from Greece," Vassos said, rushing into the office, shrinking back when he saw the detectives collected around the case folder.

"It's okay, Andreas," Lucas said. "From now on, they're going to be working with us."

"That is good," Vassos said, and went on to tell Lucas about his meeting with Elisabeth Syros. He gave the Whip the list of telephone calls. Lucas read the list. He moved to his desk and copied down several numbers and their subscribers. He passed the new list to Ulanov. "See that Nashin gets this."

Ulanov looked over the list of Soviet telephone numbers. "I'll see to it."

Vassos sat in the chair next to Lucas's desk and announced, "I want to bring in Belmont Widener for questioning." A flush of anger darkened his complexion.

Lucas tensed. "Why?"

Vassos related what his control had told him about Widener. "I never believed his story about how the Aristarchus commentary was stolen."

"Pappas got his information about Widener from Interpol?" Lucas asked Vassos.

"Yes. And despite my experience with Interpol, I would consider the information reliable for once. We should bring Widener in here right away and force him to tell us what his connection is with Iskur and Yiotas."

"Now is not the time," Lucas said gently, hoping to defuse Vassos's anger.

"Not the time. Why not! Iskur made telephone calls to Brandt Industries, McKay's headquarters. We now have a direct link between them. I cannot believe that you do not want to question Widener."

Becoming aware of the stares of the detectives, Lucas turned to them and said, "Will you men excuse us? The major and I have something to discuss."

They left the room; Grimes closed the door behind him.

Vassos was standing by the blackboard, clenching his fist.

"Andreas, I want to talk to Widener as badly as you do. But he's not the one behind this. He doesn't have the balls, and McKay doesn't have the brains."

Vassos's face rankled with discontent. "So we wait. Question more people while you build your endless chain of evidence."

"It's the smart move, Andreas."

"If it had been your family, would you say it was the smart move? I think not. You'd drag Widener in here and break his kneecaps if you had to." Driven by frustration, Vassos whirled and ripped a photograph of Voúla from the blackboard. "Look! That's my family. And you say to be patient?"

"Andreas, you told me that getting the people responsible and returning the casket-copy to Greece were the reasons you came to the States. If we rush out and scoop up Widener we'll blow the case. It's a different ball game over here, with different rules."

"You're a Greek who is ashamed to be a Greek. You could never understand how I feel."

His words stung. "I'm a cop, just like you are. So don't feed me that bullshit about not feeling Greek. We belong to the same fellowship, don't you forget that, my Greek friend."

Vassos looked at Lucas with cold resolve. He spoke in Greek. "If your way does not work, then we will do it my way?"

"Nai."

13

"Didn't Andreas come with you?" Katina asked Lucas as he stepped into her eleventh-floor apartment which overlooked Gracie Square.

"He was unable to come and asked me to give you his regrets," he said, walking through the small marble foyer.

They moved into a tastefully decorated living room filled with American and English antiques and adorned with two large Victorian-era sofas. Teddy thought about the contrast it made with the Salvation Army decor of his own apartment.

Katina was dressed in white Bermuda shorts, a cotton tank top, and white espadrilles. "May I offer you something to drink?"

"No thank you," he said, noticing the sliding glass doors leading out onto the terrace. Moving over to them, he said, "Great view." He stepped out and looked down at the promenade and the East River.

"I was lucky," she said, coming out and standing close to him. "I moved in here six years ago when it was a rental. The building went co-op four years later, and I was able to buy it at the insiders' price. I could never afford to buy it today."

The darkened silhouette of the Queensboro Bridge loomed off in the distance; across the river in Long Island City, the Pepsi Cola billboard cast a crimson glow over the lightly wind-ruffled water.

He felt her presence beside him and turned. He caught her looking at him. He had the urge to reach out and touch her, to bring her into his arms, kiss her wet lips. But instead he led the way back inside to the cluttered coffee table that stood between the two sofas. Long yellow legal pads and pencils were lying on photocopies of articles from academic journals. "I see you've been working."

"Yes, yes, I have," she said, summoned back from her own private thoughts. "I've made copies of some of Dr. Matrazzo's academic writings. I also telephoned NYU, where Adele told us he had taught. An old classmate of mine is chairwoman of the fine arts department. She looked up Matrazzo's employment record for me. It turns out that he only taught there for one semester. He left and that was the last they ever heard of him. On his employment application, he listed his marital status as single and Adele as the person to be notified in case of an emergency."

"She told us that he was married with two children."

"She sure did."

Bending forward, Katina began to gather up papers. As she did her breasts pushed against her tank top. Desire flowed through Lucas's body, causing him to want to reach out and caress her.

When she had gathered up the copies and put them on her lap, she leaned back and said, "Dr. Matrazzo was an intelligent man with varied academic interests. Most academics confine their inquiries to a narrow field of research. Matrazzo's writings show a much broader range—Greek history and literature, a keen interest in the technical aspects of the restoration of ancient materials." She broke off and smiled apologetically at him. "I'm sorry, Teddy, you must be hungry. I've prepared a salad and I've got a bottle of wine cooling in the refrigerator. Would you like to eat now or wait until we're done working?"

"I'd just as soon wait."

"Me too," she said quickly, a glow lighting up her face. "Back to work." She pulled out another article. "This is one he wrote on paleography, which is the study of writings on papyrus, wax, parchment, and paper. And this one is on the use of X-ray crystallography and ultraviolet spectrometry in the detection of spurious materials."

Lucas leaned forward, studying the glass top of the coffee table. "Do you think that he'd have the ability to unroll ancient scrolls?"

"I would certainly think so."

"In your opinion, would he possess the technical knowledge to forge antiquities?"

"Yes, I believe he would."

Lucas pushed himself up off the sofa and moved over to the sliding doors. "I'm just wondering what the odds are that Matrazzo is alive and well—and involved in this case."

Her hands rose and fell onto her lap. "I don't know."

He turned and faced her; their eyes held steady. She broke the spell. "Shall we eat inside or out on the terrace?" she asked.

*   *   *

A flickering candle illuminated their faces as they sat across from each other. Reaching across the table, he poured wine into her glass, then his.

"To Big Al," he toasted.

She tilted her glass at his. "To Alexander."

He picked at his salad, wondering how to get her to talk about herself. He wanted to know all there was to know; he felt the need to know. Something was happening between them; he wasn't exactly sure what it was.

They continued to eat in silence. Finally, he said, "Andreas and I were surprised when you told us that Pericles Levi was your father."

She turned her head and cast brooding eyes across the river. "We've been estranged for several years. When he telephoned me from Athens and asked me to help you, I was, well, frankly, I was overjoyed." She looked back at him. "I saw it as an opportunity for us to reconcile. I love my father." She hurriedly picked up her wineglass and sipped, watching him over the rim. She put down the glass. "My mother was born in New York. She met my father when he was teaching at Columbia. They fell in love, married, and had me. She died when I was fifteen. I'd lived all my life in the States, except for the summers we spent in Greece. When we lost Mother, my father and I decided that there were too many memories here, so we moved to Greece." She took a deep breath. "I came back to the States when I was seventeen to attend college." She sipped her wine, gathering the will to continue. "Papa could never forgive me for marrying a twice-divorced man who was twenty-six years my senior."

"I guess many fathers would have a similar problem."

"I suppose," she said, playing with her glass. "I met Kenneth on a dig in Vergina. They were excavating the Macedonian Royal Tombs. I had just finished my doctoral dissertation and had decided to spend that summer in Greece, trying to sort out what it was that I wanted to do with the rest of my life. I had dual citizenship so I had to decide where I wanted to live and work."

"What year was that?"

"June of 'seventy-nine. I had just turned twenty-five. I'd been home for about three weeks and had visited all my relatives and friends, and I was bored to tears. My father suggested that I go on the dig. Kenneth Wright, a colleague of his from Columbia, was in charge of the excavations. Have you ever been to Vergina?"

"No I haven't," he said, noticing the glimmer in her green eyes.

She lapsed into Greek. "Vergina is located in the shadows of the Piéria Mountains. The Aliákmon River flows nearby, and at night it's very romantic. The first time I saw Kenneth he was up on a scaffold studying the frieze of the Royal Tomb. He was gorgeous," she said, looking down at the shimmering wine. "He was wearing shorts and sandals and he had on a floppy sun hat. In the next few weeks Ken and I worked closely together cataloging the contents of the tomb. At night we'd all walk into Vergina and spend the evening in one of the tavernas. Later we'd stroll back to camp. One by one the lovers would peel away from the rest of us, making their way down to the river." She stared at the flame, remembering. "One night Kenneth took my hand and led me off toward the river. He didn't say anything. He really didn't have to." She sighed. "We got married five weeks later. It was a civil ceremony. My father refused to attend. He called my marriage to Kenneth an act of immaturity, said that it could never work. I tried reasoning with him, but he refused to speak to me. Anyway, Kenneth and I moved back to New York. And then I accepted my position at the Morgan. We moved into one of Columbia's subsidized apartments on the Upper West Side."

"You never heard from your father?"

"He wouldn't answer my letters or take any of my phone calls. I was distraught over it, but there was nothing that I could do to get him to accept the marriage."

"And then what happened?"

Again her brooding eyes looked out across the river. "The first three years were wonderful. Then? I wanted a baby. Whenever I brought up the subject, Kenneth would say he was too old for parenting and we'd end up in a fight. I did a foolish thing. I stopped taking the pill without telling him. When I became pregnant, he was furious with me. He demanded that I have an abortion. I couldn't. I just couldn't.

"Overnight I became Kenneth's enemy. He accused me of ruining his life: all of a sudden I'd become a pariah. I couldn't believe it was happening to me.

"Then, when I was in my third month and miserable, I dragged myself home from the obstetrician one Saturday and found Kenneth in the living room with one of his graduate students." She brushed tears from her face. "He was screwing her, right there in *our* living room, on *our* sofa. I ran away from the house and never returned. I went to my aunt's in Astoria. Kenneth and I were divorced shortly after that."

"And the baby?"

"I don't want to discuss that, not now." A desperate cheerfulness perked up her face. "What's your story, Lieutenant?"

A faint smile turned up the corners of his mouth. "Your everyday American love saga: married and divorced."

"Children?"

"Regrettably, no." He checked the time. "It's almost eleven. I'd better get going."

They pushed away from the table. She walked with him to the door. "Thank you for dinner, and for the conversation." He went to shake her hand good night.

She stepped into his arms and kissed his cheek. "Good night, Teddy."

14

Belmont Widener looked down Seventeenth Street for a car with the familiar triple-X sign in the windshield. He had telephoned the car service at six and told them that he wanted to be picked up at eight. It was now 8:10. The heavy beat of rock music from a nearby club irritated him. Gramercy used to be a quiet and even genteel neighborhood, he thought. Now, with Yuppie restaurants opening on every other corner and condos blooming everywhere, its charm and atmosphere had been ruined.

Looking across the street at Union Square Park, Belmont thought that at least the real estate boom had gotten rid of the junkies. He checked his wristwatch again. His dinner date was for 8:30 and he did not want to be late. He had been surprised and delighted to receive an invitation from his dear friend to have dinner at Maison Blanche.

Belmont patted his hair, checking to see that his ringlets were still all in place. He had taken extra care dressing for this dinner. He wore his white silk suit, complemented by a blue shirt with bold stripes and an oversized blue bow tie.

As he waited Belmont remembered how they had met. In retrospect, he realized that their meeting eighteen years ago had not been a chance encounter. His friend's motive had obviously been to get him to drop the criminal charges against Iskur and that disgusting man, Yiotas. But that was all in the past now; the important thing was that they had met.

Belmont had been sitting at the bar in London's Imperial Hotel, sipping a whiskey and soda, when he glanced to his left and saw him standing nearby. Belmont was immediately taken with the man's almost excessive handsomeness—then he saw the magnificent gold ring on his hand.

The stranger became aware of Belmont's interest and, taking his drink with him, came over and stood next to him. He put down his drink and slid off his ring, placing it down on the bar in front of Belmont, and said in a pleasant, mellow voice, "Emperor Caracalla had the coin struck around 215 A.D."

Belmont, his pulse accelerating, picked up the ring.

"The scene on the reverse shows Meleager and Alexander hunting boar."

Belmont was brought rudely back to the present when an Oldsmobile sedan stopped in front of him. "You're late," he said coldly, sliding into the backseat. The car drove off toward Broadway. A rented Ford sedan with Connecticut license plates backed out of a parallel parking space on the side of Union Square Park. Leone was driving; Big Jay sat in the passenger seat; perched in the rear, with his arms crossed over the top of the front seat and his burning eyes fixed on the departing taillights, was Andreas Vassos.

15

Frustration gnawed at Colonel Dimitri Pappas. His investigation of Voúla had stalled at Yiannis Yiotas. No matter what avenue he went up, he kept dead-ending at Yiotas. There must be something he had overlooked, some witness he had failed to locate, something he had neglected to do.

He left home an hour early that morning to do what he always did whenever he felt discouraged by a lack of progress in a case: wander around ancient Athens, allowing his mind to sift the facts, searching for a new beginning.

Driving his unmarked car along Amalias Street in the center of Athens, he reached the part where the street opened into a large busy triangle and saw to his right the imposing columns of the Arch of Hadrian, the monument erected in 132 A.D. to mark the boundary of the ancient city and the start of "New Athens."

He steered the car through the heavy traffic, maneuvering it toward the curb. The traffic policeman, on duty in the middle of the avenue, saw him and watched with an expression of mixed incredulity and anger. When Pappas parked in the forbidden zone, the policeman snatched the white pith helmet off his head and ran screaming over to Pappas. "Are you out of your fucking mind? Move that car. Now!"

Pappas dug into the pocket of his trousers and came out with his credentials. "I won't be long."

"Yes, sir," the traffic man said, returning the helmet to his head and retreating back to his post.

Shoulders hunched, hands plunged deep into his pockets, Pappas strolled the relic's external boundary, pausing occasionally to kick a stone. One side of the arch bore the inscription in classical Greek: THIS IS ATHENS, ANCIENT CITY OF THESEUS; the other side was inscribed: THIS IS THE CITY OF HADRIAN AND NOT OF THESEUS.

Why had the case stalled? Pappas asked himself over and over again. Iskur's calls outside the country suggested the involvement of many more people in this confederacy of thieves. Why hadn't he been able to come up with any in Greece? He believed Yiotas had told him everything that he knew about Iskur. He also believed that Iskur was too smart to have confided in a person like Yiotas. Still . . . There had to be some unpicked morsels inside Yiotas's mind, something he knew without realizing its importance.

Pappas angrily kicked the dirt in the circle around the arch. He suddenly realized that the only person connected to Iskur who he hadn't interviewed was Nina Pazza, Iskur's mistress. He hadn't bothered with her because he'd assumed that she was just another one of Iskur's objects, to be used and displayed in public. Damn! She should have been questioned. How did he know what their relationship was? Policemen did not have the luxury of assuming anything. In all the years he'd been in the department, he still hadn't been able to overcome that damn chauvinistic Greek attitude toward women. That was a serious flaw in someone in his line of work. He'd telephone her this morning and go see her. But first he thought he'd go see Yiotas and replow some old ground, Pappas decided, wondering how Yiotas was enjoying his isolation cell in the basement of police headquarters.

Two hours later, after leaving an exhausted and frightened Yiotas in his cell, Pappas stopped at an open-front stand and ate three souvlakis and then drove to Nina Pazza's section of town.

Siesta was just ending and tourists were lining up for the funicular, which would take them to the top of Lykavitos Hill. Pappas parked his unmarked car two blocks away from the Aristodimou Street apartment and walked. It would not be smart to give a witness the opportunity to connect him to the small car that he drove.

He was anxious to meet Iskur's mistress, to see for himself if she was worth an apartment in one of Athens' more exclusive areas. She was. He had expected to see a beautiful woman in expensive clothes, but was not prepared for the sight of the Eurasian beauty who opened the door. "Nina Pazza?" he asked, unaware of the slightly stunned expression on his face.

She smiled. "Colonel Pappas, how nice to meet you."

Long black hair cascaded down her back. She had perfectly defined cheeks and almond skin; a white caftan flowed over her tall, ripe body, increasing her radiant sensuality.

He walked past her into a large room splendidly decorated in white wicker; carefully placed antique pieces—a late Roman head, a broken torso in gleaming black stone—were artfully placed around the room on small, low tables. "You were Orhan Iskur's mistress?" he asked, noticing the silk damask walls of the dining area and the Tabriz rugs.

"Yes, I was," she answered forthrightly, sitting in a wide-armed chair.

"You're an Italian citizen?" he asked, unable to stop staring at her exotic beauty.

"Yes, I am."

"Your passport, please."

An arched eyebrow, a sneering smile. "Of course." She shifted in her seat and reached into the pocket of her caftan, pulling out her official documents. "I thought that you might want to see it, so I had it ready for you. Policemen seem to enjoy examining passports. As you can see my other papers are there too, my visa and my resident card."

This one doesn't scare, he thought, checking her travel history. "Your Greek is excellent."

"I've had a lot of practice."

He managed a little smile. "I see that you don't have a work permit."

"I don't work, Colonel. Orhan was an exceedingly generous man."

"You've done a lot of traveling."

"We both enjoyed visiting other countries; Orhan did not like to travel alone."

"How long had you been with him?"

"Ten years. We met in Rome when I was sixteen."

"Didn't your parents object to you going off with a man so much older than you were?"

"They had no say in the matter, Colonel. My mother was a Japanese graduate student doing research on Castiglione when she met my father in Rome. He is an Italian philanderer and one of the most hateful men in the world. He never married my mother. She died shortly after I was born, and he consigned his mistake to a convent orphanage."

He handed her back her documents. "What can you tell me about Iskur's business dealings?"

"Nothing. I can only tell you that he was a kind, gentle man who trusted no one. Orhan confided in very few people."

"Evidently he trusted you."

"To an extent he did, yes. I guess I was the closest thing he had to a friend. But the only thing he ever told me about his business was that he made and sold souvenirs."

"What were his interests?"

"Classical art and literature. He was an extremely well-read man."

"And business associates?"

She shrugged.

"His family?"

"He had an ex-wife and three grown sons. He'd go to visit his children from time to time, but he never took me on such trips, of course."

Looking around the apartment, Pappas asked, "He lived here with you?"

"Yes, but I suspect he had another place somewhere."

"Why do you believe that?"

"Because sometimes he'd be gone for days and when he returned he would be wearing different clothes, ones I'd never seen before."

"Another woman?"

She answered with swift assurance. "I saw to it that he had nothing left for another woman."

I'm sure you did, he said to himself, then spoke aloud: "What did he tell you about his army days?"

"Sometimes when he had a little too much wine he'd reminisce about those days, his friends, and what it was like to do intelligence work, but never anything of earth-shattering importance. As I'm sure you *do* know, he was born in Turkey. His family moved here when he was a boy and settled in Macedonia, around Kavalla."

"I know. They came with the Turkish influx of the twenties."

"He served with the Greek forces in Korea. I don't know what he did during World War Two."

"Did he ever mention the names of any of the men he served with?"

"No, he didn't."

Pappas got up and wandered idly around the room. He stopped at a bust of a woman, a life-sized, elongated face with wide, seductive eyes.

"The Queen of Sheba," she said, coming over to him. "She ruled one of the five kingdoms that flourished in the thirteenth century B.C. in Arabia. It's said that she traveled to Jerusalem and gave Solomon a hundred and twenty talents of gold and spices."

Running his hand over the head, he asked, "Is it real?"

"A copy. Orhan was the king of the fakes."

Pappas moved back to his seat and took the sketch and photograph out of his briefcase. "Do you know this man?"

"No. Who is he?"

"Someone who took a taxi from the airport to Iskur's office the day he was murdered."

She restudied both. "I don't know him. I'm sure."

He reached back into the briefcase, took out the photograph that had arrived last night from New York, and showed it to her.

"No, I don't recognize him either."

"He's an American named Trevor Hughes. I thought you might have had some contact with him."

"I'm afraid not, Colonel. I've never met the man and I don't know anyone by that name."

"Do you know who killed Iskur or why he was killed?"

She remained quite composed under his steady gaze. "No, I don't." She got up and walked out to the terrace. Gossiping women talked from balcony to balcony. Their buzzing increased when Nina stepped outside.

Pappas followed her.

"I loved him, you know," she said, looking down at the narrow street.

"I'm sure that you did." He paused, and asked casually, "You didn't know any of his associates, but you did know Yiannis Yiotas."

"He's a chauffeur, an errand boy."

"I want to search your apartment."

"And if I refuse?"

"Then I would give you five days to settle your affairs and leave Greece."

A shadow of alarm passed over her face. "You can't do that."

"I can, and I would."

Her color deepened with anger. She tossed back her hair, smoothing it at the sides with her palms. "I'd be happy to let you search my home, Colonel."

For the next two hours he looked through closets, drawers, bookcases, vanities, and tables. He looked under the rugs and inside the appliances. He emptied closets, piling clothes on the bed, searching each article, including the shoes. Finding nothing, he pushed the pile aside and sat on the edge of the bed, absentmindedly opening the drawer of the end table. He took out the Athens-Piraeus telephone directory and the Blue Book, the business-tourist directory. Holding them, he looked around the bedroom. "You lived with a phantom."

Wearing a satisfied smile, she said, "That is exactly what I've been trying to tell you, Colonel."

He put the book down on the bed, got up, and slowly walked out into the living room, around the dining area, out on the terrace, and back into the bedroom. She's a cool one, he thought. No man, no matter how secretive he is, lives without personal articles in his home. She must have gotten rid of everything. Which means that there is something that she is trying to hide. I'm going to have to take a close look at this Nina Pazza, he thought, looking down at the book. He saw a white border showing between the blue pages of the Blue Book. He opened the book to the page and removed a black-and-white photograph. Three young men posed in front of a Shinto shrine. The lens had captured Japanese couples in the background strolling in a park at cherry blossom time. He showed her the picture. Her surprise was genuine. "I've never seen this before."

"That's Orhan on the right, but who are the other two?"

"I don't know."

And Pappas knew that neither of the other two men looked like the composite sketch or the passport photo. So how on earth would he be able to identify them?

Piraeus was a city of three harbors and four police stations. It took Pappas the better part of an hour to make the drive from Nina Pazza's apartment to the station on Vassilissis Georgious 1. He could have telephoned in his instructions, but he had learned early on that if you wanted to make sure things were done the way you wanted them to be done, you had better make the arrangements in person.

Entering the station house, Pappas walked behind the watch desk and signed himself present in the service book. Lieutenant Kanakis's gangly body stiffened to attention when he spotted the colonel entering the third-floor office.

"You did a good job at the Iskur crime scene, Lieutenant," Pappas said, moving across the room to the double windows.

"Finding that amphora with the black sand pointed us in the right direction." He looked across the wide boulevard at the passengers boarding the ferries for Aegina and Póros. "I have another job for you. I want you to use your best people, only those capable of instant amnesia."

"All my men suffer from that ailment when necessary, Colonel."

"Good. This is going to be a surveillance. I want you to make sure that your people can blend into any crowd."

Kanakis moved up behind the colonel. The sound of the busy port filled the airy room. "This harbor used to house the triremes of the ancient Athenian fleet; now it harbors the yachts of the rich."

They stared out at the luxurious boats, each man momentarily lost in his own thoughts. "Does this job have anything to do with the Voúla massacre?" the lieutenant asked.

"It's directly related, Lieutenant."

* * *

A humming, throbbing mass of people pressed through Plaka's narrow arteries. At the end of Ifestou Street a stone stairway wound upward to the slopes of the Acropolis. Along the way an intricate network of narrow byways branched off to form shop-lined streets.

Sitting under a pepper tree in one of the tavernas, Major General Philippos Tsimas sipped ouzo as he tried to pick out the passing women who were not wearing underpants. Dressed in brown slacks and a white pullover, he looked more like a tourist than the head of the Greek intelligence service. Fingering worry beads, he focused on the folds of a lanky blonde's skirt, on how it creased into her marvelous young ass. Sipping his drink, he spotted Pappas climbing the steps right behind the woman.

"Dimitri, good to see you," Tsimas said, inviting Pappas to sit next to him, watching as the policeman came into the café's garden. Bright, colorful flowers in borders surrounded the tables occupied by people having early evening aperitifs.

Without any preliminaries, Pappas poured himself a drink and added the water. "I received a request from Vassos for information on Trevor Hughes, an American diplomat stationed here."

"I know about Hughes. What information does Vassos want?"

"Whatever you can give him. Andreas sent me a photo of Hughes."

Tsimas picked up a slice of feta. Gnawing the edges, he asked, "How are things going in New York?"

"Your head of station is running Vassos, so you probably know more about that than I do."

Tsimas's face remained expressionless. He scraped his chair closer to the table. "Dimitri, I'm worried. No matter how much I want to, I can't bring myself to believe that the Americans will ever allow Alexander's *Iliad* to leave the country. The big museums would never permit it. They'd steal it outright if they could, or make up some false claim to get their greedy hands on it."

Pappas was startled by his colleague's outburst. "The investigation being conducted here, and the one in the States, are both covert. The American museums have no way of knowing about this case. We've been careful, very careful."

Tsimas added more ouzo to their glasses. "For a seasoned policeman, you're terribly naïve. Tell me, my friend, how was the New York end of the investigation arranged?"

"Through the American State Department."

"And the State Department is run by tight-assed American aristocrats, the same sort of people who run the museums. Do you really believe that word of the casket-copy hasn't been leaked to important curators?"

Pappas clenched his jaw. "I don't know."

"Those fucking people have stolen most of our national treasures." He slammed his glass down; ouzo splashed over the sides. "The people of this country would never tolerate it if they knew the truth about Voúla and the casket-copy. Their outrage would be such that I'm sure the government would be shaken." He leaned close and whispered, "If the casket-copy cannot be returned, it should be destroyed."

Pappas's mouth fell open. "You're serious?"

"No matter what the politicians of this country say in public, they know, as I do, that Greece's future is irrevocably tied to the United States." He took an orange from the bowl on the table and rolled it between his hands. "See how easy it is for me to do this?" Suddenly he slapped the orange and watched as it flew off the table.

Cats pounced on the fruit.

"I just knocked it into a different orbit. It is the same way with countries, Dimitri. All you need is the right pretext to tilt a country's policy. The casket-copy could be the vehicle to knock Greece into a much more Eastern alignment."

The whitewashed church set on the top of Lykavitos Hill glowed in the bright morning sunlight. Tour buses discharged their passengers in front of the funicular. Taxis cruised Aristodimou Street. At a little past seven that morning a gray van had parked at the end of the block; at nine o'clock plain-clothes policemen began their apparently aimless promenade around the area. Inside the van Lieutenant Kanakis waited by the communications monitor, arms folded, listening to negative field reports.

Meanwhile, three kilometers away at 173 Leoforos Alexandras, Colonel Dimitri Pappas worked at his desk, waiting for Kanakis to inform him that Nina Pazza had left her apartment.

Reading the report on Trevor Hughes, Pappas grudgingly gave Tsimas an A-plus for efficiency. The folder not only contained photographs and biographical data on the dead American, it also detailed every time he had left Greece, giving the date and time of departure, his destination, and the date and time of his return.

Pappas noticed that all of his trips were within Europe and of short duration; most of them had been made on weekends. A courier with a diplomatic passport would have been an asset to any smuggler. Pappas put the file down and telephoned his wife to tell her that he would not be coming home for Saturday lunch. She reminded him, in an unyielding tone of voice, that his name day was next week and that his daugh-

ters were planning a surprise for him. He was ordered to be home that
night, no matter what. "I'll be there," he said, replacing the receiver
just as the green phone on the confidential line began to ring.

Many fashionable cafés were located within walking distance of
Syntagma Square. All of them were places where a person could inex-
pensively pass a day or evening watching the cosmopolitan life of Athens passing by; places where Greek men, wearing the latest American
and Italian casuals, could stalk female tourists. The Everyday Café,
located at 15 Standious Street, had shiny tube chairs with brown calf-
skin seats. Outside the tables formed an arch around the café's curved
front.

At 1:10 Nina Pazza stepped from a taxi and passed the first two
outside rows, choosing a table in front of the café's gleaming window.
Driving away in his taxi, the "cab driver" reached under the seat and
slid out a walkie-talkie. A gray van pulled up at the curb across the
street from the Everyday Café. Policemen inside it aimed movie and
still cameras through the one-way glass set in the side panel. Using the
van's cellular telephone, Lieutenant Kanakis communicated their location to Colonel Pappas.

Twenty-three minutes later Pappas parked his unmarked car at the
other end of Standious Street, far enough away so that the subject
would not see him or the car. He quickly blended into the mass of
people flowing along the busy shopping street, stopped by the side
door of the van, and knocked. It slid open and Pappas climbed inside.
"What's she doing?"

"Sitting and drinking tea," Kanakis said. "She might be waiting for
someone."

"Why don't we arrange to eavesdrop," Pappas said.

Kanakis opened the supply drawer above the communication console and took out a magnetized M5A microtransmitter. "Paper-thin,"
he said, showing it to Pappas. He called over one of the six policemen
squatting on the portable bench that folded down from the wall. The
officer took the transmitter and left the van. Pappas and the lieutenant
watched the policeman cross the wide street and saunter into the café.

George Dangas, a member of Kanakis's elite unit for the past seven
years, moved across the Everyday Café's marble floor to the cashier,
who was sitting behind her machine adding up checks and putting the
register's tapes on the waiters' trays. Dangas told her that he wanted to
see the owner. "Over there," she said, pointing with her head.

Dangas walked up to a short, bowlegged man and showed him his
shield. "I need to talk with you a moment."

Five minutes later George Dangas, wearing a white waiter's jacket and carrying a tray, reappeared outside; he worked his way along the rows, bussing the sidewalk tables. He cleaned the tin tops and emptied and wiped ashtrays. When he came to Nina Pazza's she gave him an indifferent glance and returned her attention to the people passing by.

When her attention was elsewhere, Dangas fastened the microtransmitter to the underside. He continued working along the row until he came to the end, where he turned and worked his way back to the café's entrance.

Inside the surveillance van the policewoman manning the console's sophisticated communications equipment flicked on the receiver switch and began monitoring instruments on the front of it. Loud fragments of conversations and laughter burst forth from the speakers. She painstakingly worked the controls until the clink of Nina Pazza's teacup was clearly discernible, at which point she looked up at Kanakis and said, "We're zeroed in, Lieutenant."

Leaning against the van's wall with his arms folded across his chest, Pappas asked the lieutenant, "Is the entire area covered?"

Kanakis nodded and picked up the hand mike.

A young man on a motorbike stopped in front of the café and called out to a passing woman. She hesitated, looking in the direction of the voice. "John," she called out, and rushed over to the bike, throwing her arms around him. As she did this, the policewoman said into the transmitter fastened inside her blouse, "Orange three on station."

Two women sat at a table in the row directly in front of Nina Pazza. They immediately leaned across the small space and began to gossip about a friend who was having an affair with a married man. As they talked, the redhead pulled a tissue from her shoulder bag and wiped a fleck of dirt from her eye. While doing so, she whispered, "Orange five on station."

Lieutenant Kanakis looked at the colonel. "I've got my people scattered throughout the café. I've also got some nearby motorbikes ready to go after her if she bolts on us."

They waited; fifteen minutes passed.

Kanakis was the first to spot the woman heading between the tables toward Nina Pazza. She was well dressed and had a designer scarf around her neck. She looked to be in her mid-thirties and had short auburn hair. An attractive woman, she moved with the grace and sureness of a professional dancer. Coming up to Nina Pazza's table she sat, speaking in English with a decided British accent, "I could not get rid of a silly customer."

"I hope you made the sale."

"Of course I did. How are you, Nina? You look wonderful. Widowhood appears to agree with you."

"It does." She leaned close and whispered, "Ann, a policeman visited me yesterday, a Colonel Pappas. He questioned me about Orhan's murder."

"What did you tell him?"

"What do you think I told him? The truth, of course."

"Of course."

"He searched my apartment and found a photograph of Orhan and two other men. One of them was his friend from New York, Denny McKay. I don't know who the other one was," she lied easily.

"Why on earth didn't you destroy it with the rest of his things? You should have anticipated a visit from the police."

"I didn't destroy it because I didn't know it was there. The old fool hid it in a telephone book." Nina sipped her tea. "I don't think we have any reason for concern. There is just no way that they can connect us to New York."

"Don't be too sure of that, Nina. Yiotas has been arrested and Trevor has been killed. I don't like it. Everything ran smoothly for years, but now unpleasantness is cropping up all around us."

"We have nothing to worry about. Yiotas knows nothing. Besides, he was always getting himself arrested for one thing or the other. And people are always getting murdered in New York."

"And Orhan?" Ann asked, beckoning to a waiter. "That was no accident?"

"He more than likely had his hand in someone's pockets. You know how he was."

A waiter came up to them. Ann ordered tea with lemon. "Will you share a baklava with me?"

"I'll nibble," Nina said.

The waiter walked off.

"You don't think the police know anything about the business?" Ann asked anxiously.

"Absolutely not."

Ann sucked in a deep breath. "I can't help wondering if Orhan's death had anything to do with what happened in Voúla. It was the same day, Nina. Coincidences like that just don't happen."

"Of course they do. Don't let your imagination play tricks with you. Use your common sense."

"I suppose you're right."

The waiter came with Ann's order. He put it down and left. Picking at the honey-soaked pastry, Ann asked, "What are we going to do without Orhan?"

"They asked me to come to New York to discuss taking his place."

"Oh, Nina, that's wonderful," Ann said, leaning up out of her seat to kiss her friend's cheek. "I'm so happy for you. You're going, of course."

"I'm trying to book a flight sometime this week."

Ann squeezed lemon into her tea. "Do you miss him?"

"I guess so, yes. I miss his brains and the way he made me laugh. But I don't miss the other part, the pretending. Ugh. I hated it."

Ann inched her hand across the table until their fingers touched. "Do you enjoy it with me?"

"How can you ask that?" she said, brushing fingers over Ann's. "Would you like to come home with me?"

"Very much."

The surveillance on Aristodimou Street resumed at 2:31.

At 4:32 Ann walked out of the lobby of Nina Pazza's apartment and hailed a passing taxi. Standing on the curb, she turned and waved up at Nina, who was standing on her terrace dressed in her white caftan. Ann's lips puckered into a silent kiss. She turned and slid demurely into the taxi.

Eighteen minutes later Ann got out on crowded Othonos Street in front of the Pan Am ticket office. A few doors away two policemen, with machine guns strapped across their chests, guarded the entrance of the El Al ticket office. Walking west, Ann passed the Albert Café, the Boutique Regina, and entered an exclusive-looking shop with a marble facade and the name *Delos Antiques* written in gold script in both Greek and English above the entrance.

A gray van parked across the street from the Albert Café. "Get someone inside that store and find out who this Ann is," Pappas said to Kanakis.

The lieutenant called a policewoman off the bench. "Areta, be careful," Kanakis said to the officer.

Areta opened the supply drawer and took out a microtransmitter. Turning away from the others she unbuttoned the front of her blouse and clipped the transmitter to her brassiere. She buttoned up, smoothed down the front of her blouse, and climbed down out of the van. Bustling city sounds echoed inside the surveillance van as Pappas and the lieutenant watched Areta enter Delos Antiques.

A door opening, a tinkling bell, the woman called Ann speaking Greek: "May I help you?"

"I'm just browsing, thank you," Areta said.

Silence.

Inside the surveillance van, Pappas leaned up against the communication console, his ears close to the speakers.

Ann, speaking Greek, said, "It's beautiful, isn't it?"

"Yes it is. My husband and I have been searching for a table for our entrance hall. This looks as though it would be perfect," Areta said.

"It's French, early eighteenth century. It's made of tulipwood and kingwood veneer and has ormolu mounts."

"How late are you open?"

"Until seven."

"I'll come back with my husband. Are you the owner?"

"Yes, here is my card."

"Ann Bryce," Areta read. "Your Greek is excellent."

"That's because I am Greek."

"Really?"

"My parents emigrated to the U.K. when I was three. I married an Englishman, but that didn't work out, so after the divorce I decided to come home to Greece."

"How interesting. We must talk more when I return with my husband."

Athens was quiet, the night clear, the cafés almost deserted. Two revelers walked unsteadily into the lobby of the George I Hotel. A garbage truck drove slowly along Syntagma Square, its crew gathering and emptying refuse cans. On Othonos Street two policemen lurked in the shadows of the El Al ticket office.

A gray van rolled up onto the sidewalk in front of Delos Antiques. Two police cars appeared from nowhere and blocked both ends of Othonos Street. A fire truck skirted around the car blocking the east end of the street and drove up on the sidewalk, stopping behind the gray van. Firemen jumped down and began lugging hose out of the truck's bay. A man came out of the van and knelt down in front of the gate protecting the antique store's windows. He removed a set of manufacturer's keys from a black pouch and went to work on the padlock. Firemen tugged hose into the lobby of the office building that housed the antique store.

Inside the van Pappas and the lieutenant reviewed the plan. Working with a detailed diagram of the store that the policewoman, Areta, had made, it was decided that the antique store would be searched using the "wheel" method.

The search would be conducted outward from the center of the store, in straight lines out along the spokes of an imaginary wheel. Teams were assigned to each of the spokes.

"It's open," radioed the key man.

Pappas and the lieutenant entered the darkened store at 3:24 A.M. A team quickly followed them and installed a black cloth over the window.

The lights were switched on. The interior was long and narrow and crammed with furniture, clocks, stelae, and pedestal busts of gods and warriors. In the rear six steps led up to a balcony that served as an office.

Search teams entered and went about their tasks. One team climbed up to the office and began to empty the desk and file cabinets. A woman member of the team put a self-stick label identifying what had been removed in the exact spot where the item had stood. This was done so that the object could be put back in exactly the same spot. An aluminum table was set up and each item was removed, then photographed. Teams moved gingerly out along the radii, searching everything within the confines of the spokes. Pappas and Kanakis remained in the front of the store, observing the Special Operations policemen do what they had been trained to do.

One of the teams removed all the electrical fixtures; some members of the unit probed walls, ceilings, and floors with a magnetic box that registered hollow spaces. In the building's lobby the firemen relaxed, waiting for the word to return to quarters; their part of the charade was over.

A policewoman dressed in jeans and a UCLA sweatshirt and sneakers crawled between a chest and a commode, over to a long case clock topped by an allegorical bronze figure representing Time. She ran her hand over the front and around to the sides. Squeezing into the cramped space between the clock and the commode, she lay on her right side and stretched her arm between the wall and the back of the clock. Running her hand over the smooth wood she felt an almost imperceptible crack. A ridge? A joining? "Someone give me a flashlight," she requested. A policeman twisted his way through the furniture over to her and passed down a light. She aimed the beam behind the clock and made out the outline of a panel fitted into its base. Looking for a latch of some kind and finding none, she transferred the light to her left hand and, throwing the light over the back of the clock, tried to dig out the panel with her nails. "Shit, I broke a nail." She studied the panel, trying to determine how to get it open. "A nail file," she called out.

The policeman who had given her his flashlight repeated her request, and a policewoman came over to him and gave him a nail file, which he passed down to the policewoman lying on the floor. She worked the blade into the crack and began prying out the panel. After loosening it, she pulled it free and leaned it up against the wall. Maneuvering her hand inside the clock, she felt the stiff binding of buckram-covered ledgers. Contorting her body, she worked out three books. A big smile on her pretty face, she passed them up to Lieutenant Kanakis. The rapid clicking sounds of high-speed camera shutters soon shattered the eerie stillness that had fallen on the antiques store.

With the pages of the ledgers photographed and everything returned to its proper place, Kanakis ordered his men out. The blackout curtain was taken down and folded; the grill pulled across the front of the store, and the padlock returned to its rightful place.

Othonos Street was reopened to traffic at 4:45 A.M.

Colonel Pappas returned to his office to await the development of the film, and to try to get some sleep. He left instructions with the night duty officer to awaken him as soon as the film was ready, then collapsed on the leather couch and fell into a deep sleep.

A harsh sound roused him, causing him to spring up and dash barefooted for the phone. "They're ready, sir," a woman's soft voice said.

"Thank you." He fell heavily into the chair. "I'm too damn old for this kind of life," he muttered to his wiggling feet on the cold floor. He was uncomfortably aware that he had forgotten to bring fresh socks and underwear from home.

"I thought you might need some coffee," the duty officer said, coming in with a tray. She had pretty eyes and full lips. A sergeant at thirty. The new breed, he thought, watching her put down the coffee. I bet she has extra underpants and stockings in her locker. "Thank you."

She smiled and left the office, returning shortly with a clump of folders. She put them down on his desk, asked if there would be anything else, and left.

Pappas dumped the contents of the folders onto his desk, separating the business records from the photographs. He propped one of the surveillance photos of Nina Pazza and Ann Bryce against the desk lamp. Next to it he added one of Trevor Hughes and another of the three men posing in front of a Shinto shrine. The cast of characters was getting bigger, he mused, draining the bitter sediment from the bottom of his cup. For the next hour he studied copies of the ledgers. The entries in the first column appeared to be abbreviated names of artwork and countries. The next column listed the dates the items were shipped to the United States. He looked up from the page, wondering why they sent art to the States and then had it shipped back. The third column showed the date that the item was returned to Greece followed by a circled number, usually a 3, 4, or 5. He noted that in every instance the merchandise was sent from Greece to Brandt Industries in NYC. What did the circled numbers stand for? Fishing through the invoices, he found many recorded shipments of souvenirs and toys from Brandt Industries to Delos Antiques.

Trying to decipher unfamiliar business records with an exhausted mind just doesn't work, he thought. His tongue, sour from too much coffee, pushed grounds out of his teeth. His eyelids started to fall shut. Placing his head down on folded arms, he gave in to his fatigue. After a while he felt a soft warmth envelop him and he dreamed of the first time he made love to his wife. Pappas felt his prick stretching into a hard shaft. He asked himself if ancient policemen got as horny on night duties, wondered if he was awake or sleeping. Then he felt firm, relaxing hands caressing his shoulders. He was sure that he was not dreaming so he opened his eyes and saw the photos of records scattered all over his desk. He sat up slowly, conscious of the light summer blanket over his shoulders.

"I didn't mean to awaken you, Colonel," she said, "but I worried that you might catch a cold."

"Thank you," he said to the duty officer, gathering the blanket at his neck.

"I'll be outside," she said, leaving the room, her maternal instincts satisfied.

His improvised cape secured around his shoulders, Pappas reached out and pressed the start button of the tape recorder. Nina Pazza's latest telephone conversations flowed from the machine. Ann Bryce had telephoned to thank her for a wonderful afternoon. "It was marvelous," Nina agreed. "We must do it again, *soon.*"

"Please, please."

They laughed.

The next call was from a travel agent. Nina was booked first class tomorrow on Olympic Flight 641, leaving Athens at 12:55, arriving Kennedy 4:15 New York time. The agent informed her that she had an open-return ticket and that her reservation had been confirmed by the Plaza Hotel.

Pappas listened to the clicks as she made a transatlantic call. Outside he could hear people on the morning shift coming down the hall and passing his closed door. A man answered in English. "Hello."

"Belmont, it's Nina."

"Everything okay?"

"Yes," she answered, and went on to tell when her flight would arrive and where she would be staying.

"I'll meet you," he said, and hung up.

Just a curt conversation between friends. He'd been a policeman long enough to recognize the special intimacy of thieves. Scooping up the photographs that leaned against the desk lamp, he shut off the recorder and hurried from his office, dropping the blanket to the floor.

Yiannis Yiotas, his trousers gathered at his ankles, was sitting on the stainless steel toilet contemplating his laceless shoes when the cell door swung open and Pappas marched in.

In an embarrassed flurry Yiotas made a hasty effort to pull up his trousers.

"You needn't stand," Pappas said, lowering himself to the bunk. "We're pretty informal around here." Sniffing the air, he added, "I see you're using a new after-shave." He held out a photograph taken at the Everyday Café. "Who are these women?"

"The one with her back to the window is Nina Pazza, and the other one is the lady from the antiques store." Yiotas crossed his palms over his groin.

"What antiques store?"

"Delos on Othonos Street. On Wednesdays whenever Nina and Orhan were together I'd drive them there. I could see them talking to her through the window."

"What's her name?"

"I don't know."

"Did they ever meet anyone else in the store?"

"Sometimes the three of them would leave and meet a man in the Albert Café and have lunch."

"Who was the man?"

"I don't know. He wasn't a Greek. Maybe English or American."

Pappas showed him a photo of Trevor Hughes.

"That's him."

Pappas sprang up from the bunk and left the cell. Moving down the corridor toward the elevator, he heard the clank of the steel door closing and thought: One down.

Back in his office, he picked up the blanket and draped it around his shoulders, then sat behind his desk. He picked up the telephone receiver and dialed the international access code, the country code, the city code, and the number Andreas Vassos had sent him. After a series of metallic clanging sounds and a tidal wave of rushing air, he heard a ring and gruff voice answer, "Lieutenant Lucas, Sixteenth Squad."

So, Pappas thought gleefully, they have to work on Sundays, too.

16

People with American passports move to your left, all others go to your right," two immigration agents instructed the deplaning passengers from Olympic Flight 641. Coming off the moving stairs, the travelers flowed along a short passage that fed into the immigration checkpoint, an auditorium-sized room with manned booths.

A very short, slight man dressed in civilian clothes and wearing oversized aviator glasses with yellow tinted lenses moved among the foreign travelers. "Have your passports, visas, and landing cards ready," Inspector Cutrone said, sweeping his eyes over the line, searching for a Eurasian beauty named Nina Pazza.

Waiting just beyond the booths, uniformed as a customs inspector, Teddy Lucas waited along with the real inspector. He spotted Nina Pazza moving into the room and taking her place in line. Sexy, he thought, watching her. She was dressed in a raw silk suit with epaulets and beige open-toed, open-heeled shoes. She carried an overnight bag and had a large pocketbook slung over her shoulder.

Cutrone moved along the line checking documents. When he reached her, he slid the visa that she had obtained with some difficulty on short notice out of her passport, gave it a cursory examination, and handed it back to her. He continued along the line for a bit and turned, motioning Lucas and the other agent into the empty booth at the end of the row.

Lucas and the real inspector squeezed into the booth. Cutrone moved back along Nina Pazza's queue, arbitrarily broke it off four passengers in front of her, directing them to line up at the newly opened checkpoint.

"What is the purpose of your visit to the United States?" Lucas asked Nina Pazza, taking her documents.

"Holiday," she said.

Looking up from her passport and landing card, he examined her face casually and said in a bored tone of voice, "You're staying at the Plaza Hotel?"

"Yes."

Handing her back her papers, he gave her a worn smile. "Enjoy your visit."

When Pazza had exited the inspection area, Lucas hurried from the booth into the ground-floor supervisor's office in the front of the inspection area. Vassos was waiting for him. Lucas changed back into his street clothes.

Nina joined the other anxious passengers gathering around the baggage carousels. To her pleasant surprise she immediately saw her one piece of Hermès luggage sliding down the chute onto the shiny plates. Quickly passing through customs, she walked into the crowded lobby and brightened when she saw Belmont Widener waving to her.

A few feet away from the reunited couple, Detective Ivan Ulanov spoke into the transmitter clipped to his shirt pocket. "They're leaving, get ready."

Nina Pazza and the rare book dealer left the terminal and crossed the street to the parking meridian on the other side and a waiting sedan.

"We got 'em," Big Jay said into the radio.

John Leone, sitting in the rear of a taxi, rapped on the protective grill. "Don't lose them."

"Fuck you. I don't lose people."

Inspector Cutrone led Lucas and Vassos through a labyrinth of security doors. Exiting at the rear of the building, they were met by a wall of heat and the roar of engines. "There's your helicopter," Cutrone said, pointing to the blue-and-white police department craft.

C of D Edgeworth rose from his chair to greet his visitors. "Major Vassos, nice to meet you at last."

"Nice to meet you, sir," Vassos said, looking around the plaque-filled office.

Returning to his desk, Edgeworth asked, "Is Lieutenant Lucas looking after you, Major?"

"Yes, sir, very nicely."

"Good, good," Edgeworth said, filling his pipe with tobacco. He looked across the expanse of his desk at Lucas. "What's so important?"

"Yesterday we received a call from Andreas's boss, a Colonel Pappas."

"Yes, yes, I know all about that, you already told me," Edgeworth said.

"Today we received records and other material from the colonel. We've spent all our spare time going over it. We now believe that the case can be brought to a successful conclusion."

Drawing on his pipe, Edgeworth said, "Then you know who has the casket-copy."

"No, not yet, but I believe we're getting close."

A cynical smile showed through the swirl of smoke. "Am I then correct in assuming that you need just a little more help before you're able to drop the net?"

"Surveillance vehicles, electronic equipment, and men for tail work, preferably experienced guys from Narcotics or Safe and Loft."

Edgeworth frowned. "Equipment, okay; more men, impossible."

"Chief, the case is starting to go, I can feel it," Lucas said. "I need some people watched around the clock and I don't have enough detectives to do it. One of them is Denny McKay, the hump who ordered the hit on Cormick McGovern."

Edgeworth bit down on his pipe, flipping it up and down between his teeth, regarding the lieutenant with stern eyes. He removed the pipe from his mouth and thoughtfully placed it in the glass ashtray. "Teddy, I judge leadership by what a commander does with his resources at hand. Every squad boss in the Detective Division is yapping for extra manpower. There ain't none; I'd be guilty of malfeasance if I stole more men and gave them to you." He looked at Vassos. "I hope you understand, Major."

"I do, sir. We have the same problem in Greece."

"I'm sure that you do, Major," Edgeworth said, returning his attention to the lieutenant. "There is another reason why I can't give you more people. Security. The more detectives I fly into your squad, the greater becomes the risk of a leak to the press."

Vassos asked matter-of-factly if the C of D was keeping Washington informed of the progress of the investigation.

"I brief a Mr. Hayden. He's with State's Bureau of Diplomatic Security. At the moment he's here in New York."

Vassos's placid face hid his concern. He recalled Pappas's admonition to destroy the casket-copy if it should prove impossible to get it back to Greece. He knew that he could never bring himself to do that.

Alexander's *Iliad* was going to be his memorial to Soula and Stephanos.

"The equipment?" Lucas asked.

"I'll make the arrangements," Edgeworth said, buzzing for his lead clerical.

A clap of thunder heralded the downpour. Within minutes the city's catch basins overflowed into the streets; traffic slowed to a crawl on all the major parkways. And then, as suddenly as it had come, the rain was gone, leaving a deep purple sky behind. Lucas stood on Katina Wright's terrace sucking in the cool, crisp air. The past days had been exhausting ones for the team. His detectives had been tailing Widener and Denny McKay, and each five on the surveillance ended with "nothing to report." Tonight his men had followed them to the Plaza Hotel, then waited outside and in the lobby until Widener left and returned to his home. Big Jay and Leone had stayed on Widener.

Every night since Monday, Vassos, Lucas, and Elisabeth Syros had been meeting in Katina's apartment to study and restudy the material from Greece. Lucas's expense money and credit cards bought the dinners. Vassos had never eaten Mexican food, so tonight Lucas had ordered camaróns, enchiladas, mole poblano, and nachos. Katina provided the soda.

Lucas had come to look forward to spending these evenings with Katina. He felt that being around her on a regular basis might give him the courage to say the things that he wanted to say to her. Once or twice he thought that he saw her looking at him and even imagined that he saw a certain receptivity in her glances. But he knew that that was only his wishful thinking. A woman like Katina does not let herself fall for a cop with only a high school diploma. On Friday night Lucas stole a look at Katina and clumsily tipped over a container of beef teriyaki, causing Vassos to look upward in an exaggerated gesture of prayer.

Tonight was to be their final meeting, the one where they were to sum up their findings before starting the operation that could lead them to the casket-copy.

Lucas stepped back inside. Paperboard cartons of food and dirty paper plates littered the table between the two sofas. One of the couches was covered with records and photographs; Vassos, Katina, and Elisabeth sat on the other one. The two women had gotten along well since Vassos first introduced them the previous Friday evening.

Katina, dressed in her usual off-duty outfit of Bermuda shorts, a tank top, and espadrilles, studied the photo of Ann Bryce leaving Nina's apartment. "Colonel Pappas said they're lovers?"

"Yes." Vassos replayed the tape of Nina's conversation with Ann.

While the recorder was on, Lucas picked up the photo of the men standing in front of the Shinto shrine. "Iskur and McKay, but who the hell is the other guy?"

The tape played out and Vassos shut off the machine.

"I'm sure that the first column in those ledgers is a record of stolen artwork," Katina said.

"That we all agree on," Lucas said, "but that doesn't help us find the casket-copy."

Katina shook her head at the records. "I assumed all of this was going to lead us to Alexander's *Iliad*."

"It will," Lucas said. "I would be surprised if McKay didn't know something about the casket-copy."

Elisabeth tugged at her cowboy boots. "I can't believe that Iskur would knowingly allow himself to become involved in something like Voúla."

"He didn't," Vassos said, his face a tortured mask. "I caused the massacre. Cuttler and Simmons were sent to Greece for the purpose of killing two policemen. If I hadn't taken action that day, they would have done what they had come to do and left, leaving all the others alive, my wife and son included."

Lucas jumped to his feet. "That's the craziest thing you've ever said. You're a cop, for chrissake. You think you're supposed to stand by and do nothing while two other cops are getting killed? What happened to you could have happened to any policeman in the world. Don't give yourself a guilt trip, Andreas."

They fell silent.

Katina was the first to speak: "Why would anyone want to kill Adele Matrazzo?"

"It was her uncle who rediscovered the casket-copy," Lucas said, closing one of the food cartons.

"But that was in 1939," Katina said. "He's long dead."

"Is he?" Lucas said, picking up another half-empty carton.

Everyone looked at Lucas.

"You're not saying he's alive?" Katina questioned.

"What I'm saying is that the only connection Adele Matrazzo had with the case is through her family. And the only reason I can come up with for killing her was to prevent her from talking to us, to prevent her from identifying some member of the family."

"You can't be serious," Elisabeth Syros said. "Paolo Matrazzo would be too old to commit murder."

"Yes, he would be ninety-seven," Lucas said, "but he had two sons." He picked up a yellow pad and read: "Corporal Anthony Matrazzo, B

Company, 1st Battalion, 7th Marines, killed on the night of October 24, 1942, during the battle of Bloody Ridge on Guadalcanal.

"Paolo Junior, the other son, the one Adele told us had died? Well, I can't find any record of his death. And army records show that he served in Japan during the Korean War. He was there the same time exactly as McKay and Iskur."

"Did the army send you a copy of his fingerprints?" Elisabeth asked.

"Yes," Lucas said. "So I had our fingerprint man compare them, and the best he could do was a possible maybe. There were not enough points of comparison in the latents lifted at the Iskur scene to make a positive I.D."

"What about a photo of Paolo Junior?" Katina asked.

"The army didn't have one and I can't find any," Lucas said. "We traced the guy all the way back to high school. He didn't pose for the yearbook, nor did he pose for anything during his college days. Seems to me that Paolo Junior was a very shy type." Lucas rummaged through the material on the sofa and came up with an artist's sketch. He compared it to the unknown member of the trio posing in front of the Shinto shrine. "Just doesn't look like the same man," he observed.

Elisabeth took them from Lucas and compared them. "They might be the same person."

"How?" Lucas questioned.

"Plastic surgery," Elisabeth suggested.

Katina added, "If I wanted to disappear and still remain in New York, that would certainly be an option I'd consider."

"Widener knows who our third man is," Vassos said. "Give him to me for a few minutes and we'll know too."

"That's not the way to go, Andreas, not yet, anyway," Lucas said.

"I still do not understand why your detectives prevented me from following Widener into that restaurant," Vassos complained.

"They did it because Maison Blanche is one of the more fashionable joints in this town. You can't get in without a reservation and you can't get a reservation unless your name is known," Lucas explained. "If you had tried to push your way inside, some blow-dried headwaiter would have tried to stop you and we would have had a commotion that could have alerted Widener to the fact that he had a shadow."

Vassos made a disagreeable face.

"We're going to be tailing a lot of people during the next few days," Lucas said. "It's too bad we don't have enough troops to cover the clock."

Vassos picked up his pad. "I've been worried about that so I've worked out a plan."

Lucas squeezed in next to Katina. "I'm listening."

"The best way to cover Pazza, Widener, and McKay is with a fluid surveillance. With your four detectives and the two of us, we have six officers. I'll be able to supply six additional men," Vassos said, watching the Whip.

"And from where will you get these six bodies?" Lucas asked.

"From me," Elisabeth said, "so, counting me, it will be seven additional bodies."

Lucas looked at Vassos's control, heaved a sigh, and thought: do what ya' gotta do, but do it right. "Are your people reliable?"

Vassos grinned. "I would think so."

They spent the next hour arranging schedules. When they had completed that, Vassos said, "There will still be a hole after two A.M."

"I'll take care of that," Lucas said, adding, "You understand, Andreas, that your people are to observe and report, nothing else."

"Of course," Vassos said, gathering up his notes.

"Andreas, nothing else," Lucas said.

"I understand," Vassos said, checking his watch. "It's after midnight."

"I'll drive you back to your hotel," Lucas said, starting to get up.

A gleam of humorous wisdom showed in Vassos's eyes. "Elisabeth can take me. Why don't you stay and help Katina clean up?"

Katina accompanied them to the door. She touched her lips to Elisabeth's cheek and said in Greek, "Thank you for all your help."

Elisabeth smiled and said good night.

Katina closed the door behind them to find Lucas carrying cartons and dirty plates into the kitchen.

She followed after him.

"Where's the garbage?" he asked.

"Under the sink," she said, bending to open the cabinet, and taking out a plastic bag. She held it open in front of her and watched as he dumped the refuse inside. "Why don't you like to speak Greek?"

Without replying, he stepped around her and moved back into the living room. She hurriedly placed the plastic garbage bag in the sink and followed him. She found him sitting on the sofa sorting through papers. "I didn't mean to pry. I'm sorry," she said, sitting beside him.

He looked at her and then went on stacking the papers in a neat pile, all the time brooding over the maddening inhibition he felt when he was close to her. "I'd better get going."

"Please stay."

Her warm hand came to rest on his arm and he felt a sudden thump in his heart. He returned her gaze and slowly, haltingly, moved to meet her lips with his.

*   *   *

..s sat up in the bed, gazing out the window at the orange sun pasted high in the sky. Recalling their night of unreserved lovemaking, he looked down at her naked beauty. For the first time in many years he felt really wanted and secure. He kissed her head, whispered, "You're wonderful."

"So are you," she mumbled, stretching. Suddenly her eyes went wide with disbelief, and she quickly gathered the sheet over her body. "I can't believe what I did last night. I . . . I actually asked a man to, to stay."

"I'm very happy that you did."

She tenderly brushed the side of his head. He took her into his arms and they made love again.

Afterward, as they were locked together on the rumpled sheets, she said, "I've been waiting a long time for you, Theodorous Loucopolous."

"Not as long as I have for you. How, may I inquire, did you know my Greek name?"

"I asked Andreas." She kissed his neck. "The last time we were together you asked me to tell you about my baby."

"I remember."

She shivered with a painful remembrance. "I miscarried in my fourth month. Kenneth didn't bother to visit me in the hospital."

He pressed her closer to him, pulling her leg across his stomach, and then, to his surprise, his own painful litany burst forth: his childhood, his self-image, his failed marriage.

When he finished he felt as though he had worked free of some awful curse. He kissed her and she kissed him back. "I'd better get going," he said softly.

She clutched him to her, "Just a few minutes more, please."

Andreas Vassos sat up, looking at his travel alarm clock for the time. His eye fell on the empty wine bottle on the writing desk. He looked down at the sleeping hooker next to him and came to the painful realization that his nocturnal fantasy could not stand up to the light of day. Her mascara had run and her hair was spread out over her puffy face. He didn't even know her real name, nor did he want to know it. His self-disgust rose. The driving force of his life now should be vengeance, not self-pity. He closed his hands over his face and spoke to Soula and Stephanos, telling them that he missed them and promising them their memorial.

He felt a warm hand on his back. "I love you, Andreas," she said in Greek.

"I have to get to work," he said, playing out his macabre part.

"Make love to me, please."

"You know I can't do that."

"No one has ever loved me the way you love Soula. Just once I want to be made love to that way, just once, even if it is make-believe."

"I can't do that," he said, pushing up off the bed and going into the shower.

Businessmen entered the atrium on the Fifty-sixth Street side and walked through into the lobby of the IBM Building. Homeless men and women had already gathered around the atrium's windows to eat their inadequate breakfasts and watch Madison Avenue's human traffic. Colonel Sergei Nashin, dressed in jeans, penny loafers, and a Konstantin chamois shirt, lounged at one of the tiny wire tables, his keen interest obviously on a woman passing by in an orange sundress.

"Good morning, Sergei," Lucas said, sitting across from the KGB man. "Thanks for coming."

"I assumed it was important. Where is Comrade Ulanov?"

"On an assignment."

"We've never before met alone. Are you planning to defect?"

Lucas laughed. "Not today, comrade." He shoved a roll of photocopied papers across the table. "Here are copies of some ledgers the Greek P.D. came up with. They record the theft of art from various countries in Europe, including yours."

Picking up the roll, Nashin said, "Thanks."

"Now I need a favor."

Nashin's eyes grew wary. "If I can."

"I'd like to borrow some of your people for a surveillance job."

Disbelief was plainly evident in the Russian's face. "Your brains must have turned to borscht, my friend."

"The bad guys are the same ones who've been helping themselves to your heritage. I just thought that you'd want to be in on it in case we recover any of your goodies, including, maybe, the painting of St. Sava that's listed on one of the sheets in that roll."

Pointing the roll at Lucas, Nashin said, "Policemen stationed in foreign countries—i.e., your FBI and me—are not, repeat *not*, to engage in criminal investigations within the host country. Their function is to act as liaison in the expeditious flow of criminal information and to report on developments in investigative and forensic methods and techniques." He made a self-satisfied nod, smiled, and asked, "Why not use your own policemen?"

"My allotment's been used up. I can't trust the feds so I've got to improvise. All you'd have to do is observe and report, nothing else."

"Observe and report?"

"Correct."

"And if I see you or any of your men in a difficult situation I'm to walk away."

"Correct."

"*Хербьина,* which translated means *bullshit.*"

17

Darkness had spread over the city, sending a swarm of transvestites out onto the street, where they dominated their Ninth Avenue turf. A tractor-trailer turned into the avenue. A hooker hailed the driver, stepping out into the roadway, gesturing to him by sucking on her lip and reaching into her open blouse and squeezing her breasts together. The driver steered the semi to the curb and parked. The hooker ambled over. A brief conversation ensued; the hooker removed her spiked heels and climbed up into the cab.

"Love is wonderful," Lucas observed, maintaining his grim vigil at The Den. They had parked the surveillance van in front of the pizza parlor that was one door uptown from the bar.

Lucas and Vassos had been planted there for almost an hour, watching people going in and out of McKay's headquarters and the gaudily-clad hookers turning tricks. They had spent the day cooped up inside the van listening to field reports. Nina Pazza had left her hotel at eleven in the morning, spent her day shopping, and returned to the Plaza a little after six. Denny McKay passed his day closeted inside the bar. He left around seven and drove to his Christopher Street bachelor apartment, arriving there at seven-twenty. Belmont Widener worked all day in his rare book store and retired upstairs to his living quarters a little after eight o'clock.

It was eleven P.M. when Lucas decided it was time to have a look inside McKay's headquarters. He slid off the stool and opened the equipment chest on the floor next to the communications console. He took out a pair of night surveillance binoculars, two ten-inch tubes that electro-optically amplified ambient light and used it to make green-phosphor images. It had a pistol-grip attachment, with a round, glass-fronted cylinder in front that gave out a powerful beam of infra-red light and acted as a kind of invisible spotlight.

He rested the rubber eyepiece against his face and scanned the area. The building that housed the bar and the two adjoining buildings were in the same state of dilapidation. With the exception of the pizza parlor and the bar, all the windows and doors had been cinder-blocked.

Carefully scanning the area with the glasses, he saw the transvestite raise her head off the driver's lap, adjust her wig, spit a wad into a tissue, and toss the paper out the window. She climbed down out of the cab, put on her shoes, and joined her sisters on the stroll.

Lowering the glasses, Lucas turned to Vassos and said, "Those hookers make good watchdogs. I can't imagine McKay allowing them to work his turf without some kind of payback."

"McKay's Praetorians," Vassos said, watching out the other window, studying the sleazy scene. "How are we going to get in?"

"It's time to break a few rules," Lucas answered, taking an army knapsack out of the equipment locker, selecting items he thought he might need, and shoving them inside the sack. Then he moved over to the radio locker on the wall and removed two walkie-talkies, handing one to Vassos. "I'm going to need you here to protect my back. We'll communicate with these. Set the channel selector switch to three. I'm going to keep my volume control low in case there's anyone inside the building. If you have to communicate, press the transmit button three times." Lucas did that and both radios squawked each time he pressed.

Lucas returned his attention to the street. "I'll wait until all the 'ladies' are working and then make a dash for the pizza parlor."

"Why not go directly for the bar?"

"McKay is the type of guy to have some extra insurance, like a couple of hungry pit bulls. I'll go in through the pizza store, make my way up onto the roof, cross over, and go down the roof stairwell into the bar."

"How will you make it from the store up onto the roof?"

"That type of tenement generally has a door leading from the street level store into the building's vestibule."

Fifteen minutes passed.

The street had become a runway for cars and vans, for hookers getting in and out of vehicles.

"Aren't there any female hookers in this area?" Vassos asked, sitting on the stool, watching out his side of the van.

"We've got plenty of them, too," Lucas told him, "but this is a transvestite stroll. The women are around the corner."

Vassos looked out both windows. "They're all busy, go now."

Lucas remained seated. "I learned a long time ago that when you're all set to go, wait." As if to confirm his instincts, a hooker pranced out from behind a stoop and strutted over to a car that had just double-parked.

Lucas slid open the side door, turned to Vassos. "If you get anyone snooping around, press that button." He pointed to a black disk on the control monitor and slipped outside, dashing into the deeply recessed doorway.

Pressing back into the shadows, he fell to his knees and slid the knapsack off his shoulder. He took out a penlight and stuck it between his teeth, aiming the beam at the lock on the door to the pizza parlor in the ground floor of the building that stood next to The Den. He inserted a pick and began raking open the cylinder, smiling when he heard a hooker shout, "Don't hold my ears. I know my job."

The latch sprung open. He slipped inside, closing the door behind him. Reaching down to his belt, he pressed the transmit button twice.

His radio gurgled twice in response.

The dry smell of flour and rotten tomatoes filled the air. Moving cautiously, the beam roving ahead of him, he searched for the door that would lead out into the building's common stairway. Unable to find it, he knelt and threw the beam under a rack of ovens; there he saw the door. Realizing there was not enough space between the wall and the back of the ovens to squeeze through, he got down on his stomach and, pushing the knapsack ahead of him, crawled under the oven to the door. The scurrying sounds of rats made him silently swear never to eat pizza again.

There was not enough space between the back of the oven and door for him to reach up and try the doorknob. He pushed against the bottom of the door trying to get it open, but the paint of countless years had sealed it into the jamb. He opened the knapsack and, directing the penlight's beam inside, fished around until he found the fiberscope. He took it out and snaked the quarter-inch braided steel cable under the door. He fitted the eyepiece to his face and pressed the trigger.

The optical glass fibers inside the cable transmitted images from the other side. Taking hold of the bottom of the cable, he twisted the scope's optical tip. The illuminated images he saw were those of a deserted staircase cluttered with debris. He became aware of the dryness in his mouth, the annoying tickle of flour invading his nostrils, and the distracting beads of sweat rolling down from his hairline. He wiped his face against the canvas knapsack.

The pine door had a panel seven inches up from the bottom. He took out a serrated hunting knife and scored a line until he pushed the blade through the wood. He took out a battery-powered jigsaw, inserted the blade through the hole, and cut out the panel.

After dropping the satchel through to the other side, he wriggled through the hole and stood in the tomblike cold of the building's central stairway, breathing in the alkaline odor of cinder block. He punched his arm through the knapsack's harness, shouldered the load, and projecting the circle of light ahead of him, climbed the squeaking staircase to the roof.

He crossed over the parapet to the roof of the adjoining building. After checking the roof door for alarm wires and finding none, he took out the fiberscope, pushed it under the door, and cursed when he saw the cutouts in the walls and ceiling of the immaculately clean staircase. They were about the size of two packages of cigarettes, and they ringed the stairs in an infrared alarm system that sent out sensory feelers that measured movement and heat changes. No wonder the stairs are so clean, he thought. Mice could set off the alarm. Rummaging through the knapsack and not finding what he needed, he slipped the radio off his belt and pressed the transmit button three times.

Vassos answered in Greek, "Nai?" Yes.

To his surprise, Lucas found himself whispering Greek into the mouthpiece.

Leaving his equipment behind, he made his way back over and down to the pizza parlor and waited. Soon a shadow appeared, dropped something in the doorway, and was gone. Lucas reached out, grabbed the package, closed the door, and made his way back up to the roof.

He undressed down to his shorts and stepped into the neoprene wet suit, pulling the hood securely over his head and face. Neoprene, a synthetic rubber derived from acetylene and hydrochloric acid, was one of the few available ways to circumvent an infrared system, permitting a person to pass through the system undetected.

He stuck the penlight up his sleeve. He knew that he wouldn't be able to use it because the heat from its tiny bulb would set off the alarm, but he decided to bring it anyway. He wouldn't be able to take the radio or his revolver because there was not room in the tight-fitting wet suit. Removing the hunting knife from the knapsack, he slid it up his other sleeve.

Working with the picklock and rake, he carefully unlocked the roof door leading to the staircase that went down to McKay's bar, but did not open it because he was afraid the ambient night light might be enough to set off the alarm system. Deciding he'd have to chance it, he opened the door just enough for him to slide inside. Holding his breath, he guardedly closed the door behind him. He remained perfectly still, forcing himself to adapt to his new environment. Soon he was able to make out the wall and the banister. He groped for the next step, and then the next, and the next.

He came first to the fifth-floor landing and discovered a steel fire door bolted shut. He continued down to the next level only to discover the same thing. He moved on to the third floor and was disappointed again. Groping in the dark toward the second floor, he became aware of the unmistakable odor of beer; he remembered Andreas's description of the closet in the rear of the bar that contained the staircase without stairs. Probing the space in front of him, he encountered some kind of soft material at the bottom of the flight of steps that led to the second floor. He stopped, gingerly patted the invisible material, and decided it was a curtain.

Sliding his hand over its softness until he reached the seam, he parted the material slightly, moved his hooded face to peek around to the other side, and saw that he was about to step down onto the second level above the street. It contained a landing with a bolted fire door and the stairwell of the skeletonized staircase leading down to the ground floor.

He stepped out from behind the curtain and saw that there was no alarm system. He squatted down and peered down into the light coming up from the back room of the bar. He could make out faint street sounds. The downstairs door to the closet concealing the skeletonized staircase was obviously partly open. He slipped out the penlight and cast its beam down into the stairwell, searching for an alarm system. Finding none, he got to his feet and, gripping the banister with both hands, slid his foot out onto the first riser's edge, starting down cautiously.

Reaching the bottom, he knelt, quickly assessing his surroundings. He slipped into a prone position and crawled out into the back room and then the front bar. Three transvestites were talking in the doorway just outside. There was enough light so that he did not have to use the penlight. Looking around, he could see no way of getting up to the sealed-off upper floors and decided to leave. He turned to crawl back to the staircase when he saw a dumbwaiter hatch on the wall at the end of the bar. He wiggled over to it. Lucas was about to reach up for the latch when he caught sight of something out of the corner of his eye and froze. A sudden urge to urinate caused him to stifle a moan. He lay in the unyielding stench of stale alcohol, his mouth open, his eyes wide in shock and disbelief. There, asleep on the bar's slatted floor, were the folded muscular coils of a huge boa constrictor. McKay's backup system. That crazy bastard, he screamed inwardly, recalling the street talk awhile back that some Colombian drug barons were flying in constrictors with their shipments to sell to other dealers who used them as persuaders.

Motionless, he watched the big snake, desperately trying to remember everything he knew about them. They kill their prey by crushing and suffocating them and then swallow them whole. They don't hunt often, maybe once a week or so, and most importantly, they don't move fast.

Lucas got up off the floor slowly and lifted the latch, opening the hatch and hunkering backward into the dumbwaiter.

The creature's eyes flicked open; its serpentine head coming up off its thick coil.

"Nice doggie," Lucas whispered, closing the hatch. Grabbing hold of the pulley ropes, he hoisted the cart upward.

"I gotta piss," he moaned quietly, working the ropes, positive that his bladder was about to burst.

Reaching the second-story hatch, he slid out the knife and worked the blade between the door and the jamb, pushing it upward until he caught the latch and kicked it up out of the gate. He opened the door and, peering out, saw no alarm system, so he slid out onto the floor. Working the rubberized zipper down his neoprene armor, he reached into the suit, hauled out his penis, and, emitting a long sigh, pissed into the dumbwaiter shaft.

Done, he zippered up and looked around. He was in a long narrow room that had been divided into several different work areas. Moving around the room, he saw a separate place for woodworking, another one for printing with the latest high-tech equipment, a painting section, and an area where marble was being worked on.

Brandt Industries, he thought, they steal it there and copy it here. Suddenly realizing that he had not signaled Andreas in a while, he reached for his radio but then remembered that he had been forced to leave it on the roof along with the other stuff.

His penlight beam hit a glass-enclosed office. Before entering it, he checked for wires. The big spenders wouldn't go for the money to protect every room, he thought, going inside. A rolltop desk, a filing cabinet, an illustrator's board, a photocopier, and an old-style telephone. He moved to the desk, lifted the receiver, and dialed Communications. When the police operator answered he asked to be connected to Citywide, the elite unit within the Communications Division that routes undercover and Detective Division transmissions.

"Citywide, Dolan," a gruff voice answered.

"This is Lieutenant Lucas, Sixteenth Squad. Pipe me through to surveillance van one-two-four."

"Hello?" Vassos's uncertain voice came on the line.

"How are things going?"

"Why are you telephoning instead of using the radio?"

"It's a long story. I'm inside the plant where they forge the art. They have enough equipment here to reproduce the Sphinx. How is everything on the street?"

"Busy. The prostitutes must be running a sale."

"I'm going to leave this line open while I look around," Lucas said.

Vassos spotted a pimp doing a sly sashay over to the van. He wore black leather trousers and a green shirt with the top five buttons open revealing a chest and neck bejeweled in a glittering array of nugget necklaces. The pimp tried the rear door. He opened the blade of a gravity knife and stuck it into the lock.

Vassos pushed the alarm button on the control monitor. The threatening growls of Doberman pinschers leaped from a speaker within the van; the pimp leaped back onto the sidewalk and rushed away.

Lucas had found nothing of interest in the rolltop desk. The top three drawers of the file cabinet were empty; the bottom one contained a swing-hinge binder with Brandt Industries shipping invoices for the years 1986 and 1987. He unfastened the joints and removed the invoices. Placing four of them at a time on the duplicating machine, he spent the next forty minutes making copies. He rolled them up and stuck them into his wet suit, returned the originals to the binder, and, picking up the telephone, told Vassos that he was on his way back.

After checking out the other floors and finding nothing, he got back into the dumbwaiter and lowered himself back down to the ground floor. He opened the hatch and peeked out. "Baby" was resting behind the bar. Dozens of transvestites strolled the street; three of them were holding a conference in the bar's doorway. He knew that he'd never make it to the van without being seen. He looked at the dormant snake and thought: why not?

He slipped out of the dumbwaiter and skulked on all fours over to the door. He quietly slipped the bolt and, leaving the door slightly ajar, crawled to the back of the bar. He remembered that a shuffleboard was in the back room. He crawled into the back room and picked up four of the disks. Rolling one of them into the barroom, he crooned, "Meow, meow, meow." The metal disk thudded into the bar stool and toppled over onto its side. He rolled another one.

Without warning the serpentine head popped up over the bar, swaying in the dark, seeking out its prey.

Lucas rolled another one. The snake's homing system zeroed in on the disk and its long, thick body flowed over the bar to the floor, slithering toward the sound.

"That mother wanted me to take it in the ass for twenty dollars. 'Honey,' I said, 'my ass is worth fifty,' " a hooker with orange hair was telling her sisters.

One with a rhinestone-studded blouse and short shorts confessed, "I did my golden shower trick tonight. That man just loves it when I pass my pissin' dick over his face. And he told me . . . what's that on the ground? Oho-l-ooo-ooooo!"

"Nooooooooo!"

"Uuummmmmmmmm aaaaahhhhhhhnnnnnn."

Their ghastly, panic-stricken screams reverberated across the avenue, setting off a wave of hysteria that sent the hookers fleeing, littering the street with an assortment of shoes, wigs, pocketbooks, and broken pint bottles of booze. The boa constrictor slithered out into the bar's doorway and arranged its muscular coils, its green diamond-backed eyes watching.

Steam misted the tiles. Lucas drew a line through the condensation and slipped deeper into the water, relaxing his head against the rim.

He laughed when he thought about the snake caper; it was the kind of tale that added to the Job's folklore.

After making his way back to the van, they had had to wait ten minutes for Emergency Service to come and gather up Baby in a snake bag for delivery to the animal shelter. Lucas was sure that McKay would blame one of his people for leaving the door open. Then they went back to the office so that Lucas could read the fives on the day's surveillances. All negative reports. But that didn't discourage him. Every cop bone in his body told Lucas that Nina Pazza was taking her time sanitizing herself; she'd come to New York for a meet and wanted to make sure she didn't have any guardian angels hovering nearby.

After going over the fives, Lucas and Vassos gave the surveillance units a "see." They were all on station. Elisabeth Syros and the Greek contingent were covering Belmont Widener. At 1:15 A.M. two Soviet policemen relieved Ulanov and Gregory at the Plaza Hotel.

At one-thirty in the morning, after parking the van in the Sixteenth Precinct's garage, Lucas and Vassos stopped off at Heidi's for a quick taste. They found the owner, Ulanov, Gregory, and Sergei Nashin together in a back booth doing a number on a bottle of Russian vodka.

A fast reading of the scene told Lucas that the impromptu party had all the makings of an all-night session. He had promised Katina that he would come to her place as soon as he was finished and fill her in on what happened. He had one fast drink and said good night, leaving

Vassos and Sergei corkscrewing on the dance floor, whooping what he assumed were Cossack war cries. Making for the door, Lucas heard Vassos call out, "One day you will dance, my friend."

Katina had greeted him in a pale pink nightgown and panties. She rushed into his arms, her tongue searching his mouth. He pulled up her nightgown and they made love on the floor, and then they got up and went into the bedroom and loved again.

Afterward, locked in a lovers' embrace, he told her about his day and how he had bent the rules.

"I don't want to lose you, Theodorous," she said.

"You're not going to." Reluctantly, he got off her bed and went into the bathroom.

Lucas reached out and picked up a plastic bottle: ESSENCE OF LILAC BATH GEL. He unscrewed the cap and poured the contents into the tub, stirring the water to make bubbles and causing waves of water to splash over the rim of the tub and make puddles on the floor.

Reaching up, he yanked down two towels from the rack. He leaned over the rim, soaked up the water, and left the towels in a sodden heap on the floor.

A soft knock came to the bathroom door. "Theodorous, may I come in, I need my makeup remover."

"Of course."

"Theodorous!" she said, stepping inside. "You've made a flood."

He made a weak-hearted shrug and sank below the water. When he surfaced he found her on her knees mopping up the floor with towels. "You don't look like the Morgan's Curator of Ancient and Medieval Manuscripts."

"Lieutenant, we have to have a talk."

"I'm sorry," he said, grabbing down the remaining towel and, standing, drying himself. He stepped out of the tub and, kneeling down beside her, mopped. "Is this what they mean by a meaningful relationship?"

She hurled a look of feigned anger his way and said, "I think so."

He worked his way behind her and lifted her bathrobe and nightgown.

She stopped wiping, remained on her knees.

"You're beautiful," he said, guiding his finger over the crescent opening between her legs.

"You make me feel alive again," she moaned, resting her face on the toilet lid, undulating against him and gasping when he opened her body and mounted her.

18

Belmont Widener daintily spread his fingers and admired his fresh manicure while Claude, the owner of the exclusive and ridiculously expensive Madison Avenue salon, styled his hair. Widener paid no attention to the woman who slipped into the adjacent chair. Elisabeth Syros hitched up her jeans and crossed her legs, revealing the Mayan design carved into the sides of her cowboy boots. She threw up her arms, letting her many bracelets slide down to her elbows, and said to her stylist, "Just a trim, please."

Denny McKay crashed his fist on the table and shouted, "I lost my fucking snake because one of you dumb cocksuckers left the door open."

The two men sitting in the same booth with McKay looked at each other uneasily.

Three other men were sitting on bar stools nearby. One gazed vacantly into the faded mirror, the second hunched silently over the copper-topped bar, and the third, a man called Patty Guts, sat with his back to the bar, his arms folded across his stomach, watching McKay's every gesture.

"I'll get you another snake, Denny, a bigger one," the man known as Bubblebelly promised, wiping beads of sweat from his upper lip.

"Yeah, Denny, a bigger one," the other man in the booth said. His name was Pussy Lyne.

"Make sure that the door is locked from now on, understand?" McKay growled.

"Yeah, Denny, I'll see to it," Pussy Lyne said meekly.

McKay studied the two men. "The take from the docks is off this week. You guys wouldn't be playing games, would you?"

"No. Denny, I swear," Bubblebelly said. "A few of the longshoremen came up short with their vig."

"One of them is three weeks behind," Pussy Lyne added.

"Three weeks," McKay repeated, thoughtfully pursing his lips and nodding slowly. "I want you two to employ some modern collection techniques with the hump who is three weeks late. Chop off his leg below the knee."

"Below the knee?" Bubblebelly questioned.

"Yeah," McKay said. "That way they can stick a peg leg on and send him back to work so he can play catch-up with the vig."

"Good advertising too, Denny," Pussy Lyne said with real enthusiasm. "They'll think twice before they miss a payment."

McKay lit a cigarette and bit down on the filter. "I want you to ask around. I'm looking for a decorative painter who can do gold leaf, French lacquer, marbleizing, and graining."

Bubblebelly started to say something when the front door flew open. Beams of sunlight outlined the silhouetted figure of a policeman standing in the opening, his hat cocked rakishly to the side, his hand menacingly close to the grip of his service revolver. Conversation inside the bar ceased; only Julio Iglesias continued to sing "Ron y Coca-Cola" from the old-style jukebox. Obviously and regally drunk, the policeman walked into the bar, his head high and his steps carefully measured.

"He's drunk outta his fuckin' gourd," Bubblebelly hissed.

McKay said nothing. He sat chewing his cigarette, his suspicious eyes locked on the approaching policeman.

"I gotta take a leak," the policeman mumbled with a booze-thickened tongue and then stumbled, falling across McKay's table.

Pussy Lyne jumped out of his seat and helped the officer off the table and onto his feet. The policeman shook a wrathful finger at the bartender. "Your floor is dirty. I oughta give you one for maintaining a licensed premises in an unsanitary condition." He staggered into the toilet and slammed the door.

Standing before the urinal, the policeman pulled an evidence envelope from inside his summer shirt and deposited the cigarette butts he had palmed when he staged his fall. He remained inside the stinking room for another moment and then left, weaving slightly as he crossed the sawdust-covered floor. Outside a patrol car and a bored-looking driver waited for him. "Let's go," the policeman said to the other cop, sliding into the recorder's seat in front of the radio set. The cop behind the wheel eased the transmission into drive and the police car slid away from the curb.

The recorder picked up the handset. "Sixteen Adam to Central, K."

"Go, Adam."

"Time check Central."

"Twelve forty-six Adam."

"Ten-four." The recorder wrote the certified time in the space provided on the evidence envelope and radioed: "Central, Sixteen Adam has left the licensed premises. We're still ten sixty-one, precinct assignment. We should be back in service in about five minutes."

"Ten-four, Adam."

The blue-and-white cruised down Ninth Avenue, turning west on Forty-fifth, continuing until Tenth Avenue, where it pulled over to the curb where Teddy Lucas was waiting.

"How'd it go?" the Whip asked the recorder.

"I'm ready for the big time, Lou," the raw-boned cop said, giving the evidence envelope to the lieutenant.

"I'll give you a receipt," Lucas said.

The recorder pulled his black, leather-bound memo book off the dashboard, wrote out a receipt under the last entry, radioed Central for the certified time, and made it a part of his entry along with their current location. He wrote down the names and shield numbers of those present and passed the official log out to the lieutenant.

Lucas signed his name on the consecutively numbered page below the officer's signature, handing the log back to him and asking, "What about the transmitter?"

The raw-boned cop casually tossed his log back on the dashboard. "When I fell I slipped it under the table."

"Thanks, guys," Lucas said.

"All part of the J-O-B, Lou," the recorder said, grabbing the handset and transmitting, "Sixteen Adam is now ten ninety-eight Central, resuming patrol."

"They're gonna chop off some guy's leg," Ulanov said, his big frame crouched on a stool in front of the surveillance van's communication center.

McKay's voice had come through the speakers with a slight scratch of static.

"Like the man said," Gregory intoned, "ye reap what ye fuckin' sow, bro."

The van was parked on Ninth and Fiftieth. Lucas drove back from his meet with the two policemen in one of the department's latest unmarked cars, a Jeep Cherokee. He parked on Fifty-first Street off

Ninth and walked over to the surveillance unit. Entering the van by the side entrance, he stopped once he was inside. Glancing at Vassos's tired face, he asked, "How late did you guys hang out last night?"

"Too late," Vassos moaned. "That Russian loves to dance."

Threading a telescopic lens onto a camera, Gregory complained, "My head feels like there are a lot of strange things dancing around inside."

Lucas sat down on the bench that ran along one side of the van. "You guys pick up on the assault they're planning?"

"Yeah, we heard," Ulanov said. "Some guy's gonna lose a part of his leg because he didn't pay his weekly vig."

"Phone in a sixty-one on McKay, conspiracy to commit assault one. Maybe Sergeant Grimes will be able to turn one of them," Lucas said, not really believing it. He looked at the detectives. "Can you guys handle it from here on?"

"No problem, Lou," Gregory said.

"I want you to stay in radio contact with me. Andreas and I are going to be jumping back and forth between units. Do you have the list of call numbers?"

Ulanov consulted the pad in front of him. "You're Mobile One. Leone and Elisabeth are Mobile Two and they're covering Widener. Big Jay's Mobile Three and he's on Pazza. We're Mobile Four and we're on McKay. The comrades are Mobile Five and they're late-tour reliefs."

"Correct. Remember that Sergei and his crew do not come out until tonight," Lucas said.

"Do the Russians have radios?" Gregory asked.

"Yes," Lucas said, "I gave Sergei two sets last night." He leaned forward in his seat, resting his elbows on his knees. "Listen up. I split the other teams, assigning a Greek with Big Jay and Leone, but I kept you together because you're going to be on McKay. You're to observe and report, nothing more. No hero stuff. Understand?"

"We understand, Lou," Ulanov said.

"Do you have heavy weapons?" Lucas asked.

"Shotguns and Uzis," Gregory said, pointing to the weapons locker bolted to the wall.

"McKay and his friends are bad people. Don't take any chances," Lucas said firmly.

"We won't," Gregory assured him.

Ten minutes later Lucas and Vassos slid into the blue Jeep with the smoked windows.

"Where did you get this?" Vassos asked.

"Motor Transport. It comes equipped with all sorts of high-tech goodies."

"Thank you for going out on a limb and planting that transmitter in the bar. I know you could be making trouble for yourself, not having a search warrant."

" 'S'all right, we didn't need a warrant." He started the engine, checked traffic.

Vassos was confused. "I thought . . ."

"We can turn a public place into a Hollywood sound stage if we have to," Lucas said, driving out of the parking space. "Nina Pazza has a right to privacy in her hotel room, but The Den is a public place. The courts have held there's no expectation of privacy in a public place."

"All your laws aren't so stupid, are they?"

"Not all of them," Lucas agreed, turning up the volume control on the police band radio under the dashboard.

Belmont Widener bought a pair of loafers at Gucci. He left the Fifth Avenue store and walked north. At Fifty-sixth Street he entered Trump Tower's marble lobby and strolled through the gleaming center hall, idly glancing at the expensive things for sale in the gold-plated display cases on either side. He paused to admire the cascading waterfall, occasionally glancing sideways at the crisscrossing escalators.

Elisabeth Syros, who had changed into a white spaghetti-strapped sundress in the back of a Mykonos Fruit Store delivery truck, was examining a gold necklace in the Blantree and Company jewelry store to the right of the waterfall. Detective John Leone, riding the up escalator, had one eye on Widener and the other on the shapely ass of the woman standing in front of him.

Nina Pazza stepped off the elevator inside the Plaza Hotel's lobby and paused to look at a diamond necklace in the display window of Black, Starr and Frost, Ltd. She stared at the glittering gems for a minute or so before she made her way through the lobby to the entrance of the Palm Court, the hotel's unenclosed restaurant separated from the lobby by a low wall made up of flowers and palms set in large Chinese vases. She had a brief conversation with the maître d' and was escorted to a table.

A string quartet played Brahms against the background noises of tinkling silver and glassware and the polite hum of muted conversation.

Big Jay, sitting in one of the lobby's armchairs, turned to Christos, his newly assigned partner, and said, "Looks like the lady is going to have lunch."

Christos, a fat little man squeezed into an ill-fitting, European-cut suit, leaned close to confide, "I'd love to feel her warm lips around me."

"Broads like that only suck cocks attached to wallets," Big Jay said, adjusting the tiny receiver in his ear. He inclined his head slightly and spoke into the microphone concealed by his jacket. "The lady is having lunch."

Lucas's voice came over the surveillance network: "Mobile Two, location of your subject, K?"

Leone, who had just followed Belmont Widener out into the street, radioed, "Leaving Trump Tower, walking north on Fifth, K."

Lucas: "All units, it's going down. Mobile Three, K."

Big Jay: "Mobile Three standing by, K."

Lucas: "Mobile Three, do you have a magnetic transmitter, K?"

Big Jay: "Negative, K."

Lucas: "Mobile Three, have your partner ten eighty-five this unit in three minutes at CPS entrance."

Big Jay: "Ten-four Mobile One."

Christos was standing on the hotel's steps when the Jeep Cherokee jerked to a stop behind a double-parked Rolls Royce. Lucas honked the horn. Christos rushed over to the Jeep, held a short conversation in Greek with Vassos, took the disk from Lucas, and hurried back up the steps, disappearing inside the hotel.

Big Jay surveyed the scene. The maître d' was busy checking the reservation book while a line of five people patiently waited to be seated. Nina Pazza was seated near the quartet, at a square marble-topped table.

"Wait here," Big Jay told his partner, and moved toward the restaurant. He passed the headwaiter, pretending to wave to a friend. Nina Pazza, elegantly turned out in a pink dress with matching accessories and a short-brimmed straw hat, was too busy watching the violinist to notice the man who stopped next to her table and tied his shoelace.

Big Jay: "Mobile One, K."

Lucas: "Mobile One standing by, K."

Big Jay: "Down and dirty, K."

Lucas: "Ten-four."

Lucas turned to reach into the supply box; he removed a receiver. He set it down on the console between the front seats and adjusted the sensitivity selector switch to screen out all low-level noises. He reached back into the supply box again and took out a maxi-powered mini tape recorder and plugged the attachment cord into the receiver.

"I have never seen one that small," Vassos commented.

Resting his head against the seat's headrest while he listened to the incoming transmission, Lucas said, "It weighs three and a half ounces."

"Nina, darling, you look absolutely stunning," Widener said, brushing her cheek with his lips.

"So do you, Belmont."

"Have you ordered?"

"I'm having the salmon."

"I think I'll have the grilled swordfish," he said, after studying the menu.

"Belmont, will you please tell me what is going on?"

"Whatever do you mean?"

"Orhan and Trevor. That is what I mean," she said angrily.

"I honestly don't know, Nina."

The waiter came to take their orders.

Elisabeth Syros walked into the hotel's main entrance. Leone entered on the Central Park South side.

Widener took his handkerchief out of his breast pocket and dabbed at his face with it. "The American and Greek police are interested in Alexander's *Iliad*."

Her eyes grew cold. "Are you sure?"

"They paid me a visit. A lieutenant from New York, a major from Athens, and a woman from the Morgan Library. They were checking out the major dealers to see if we'd heard anything about the casket-copy coming onto the market."

"And had you?"

"No. I was also questioned about my Aristarchus commentary. It was taken from me during a robbery a long time ago." Sipping water from his glass, he added, "One of the robbers was caught. Did you know that?"

"I'd heard."

"His name was Bucky McMahon. At his arraignment the DA informed me McMahon and Denny McKay were, er, friends."

She looked down at her place setting, perplexed.

"It would be a real coup for some collector to possess both the commentary and the casket-copy."

"Yes, I imagine it would be."

"I love your hat."

"Thank you."

"Would you know anyone who might be interested in both of them?"

"No one that I can think of," she said, reaching for her water glass.

He unfolded his napkin and carefully spread it out over his lap. "He wants to see you, tonight."

"How does he look?" she asked quietly.

"Don't be so gloomy, Nina. He looks wonderful, and he's anxious to be with you again."

"Where and when?"

"Your room, around nine. Ah, here comes our lunch."

19

M obile Two, your location, K?" Lucas radioed.
Leone, who had tailed Belmont Widener to the Plaza, radioed back: "In lobby with Mobile Three, K."

Lucas: "Mobile Three, your subject's room number, K?"

Big Jay: "Four-oh-two, K."

Lucas: "Mobile Two and Three, buy me twenty minutes, K."

Big Jay looked into the Palm Court, saw Widener and Nina Pazza deep in conversation, and radioed: "You got it, K."

Lucas opened the Jeep's door. Vassos grabbed his arm, stopping him. "I'll go with you."

"I need you here to monitor transmissions and to see that the tape recorder is working," Lucas said.

"You're going to break some more rules," Vassos said with a knowing grin.

"One or two little ones."

"Then I will go with you."

"Stay here, *pahrahkahlo*." Please.

Vassos looked down at the slow-moving reel and said, reluctantly, "Nai."

Lucas got off the elevator at the fourth floor and walked quickly down the carpeted corridor checking room numbers. This was going to be one of those times when expediency dictated police action. Approaching Pazza's room, he saw the chambermaid's supply cart and brightened at the thought of not having to use the set of picklocks that he had brought along with him. The door to room 402 was open; the maid was busy vacuuming the bedroom, her back to the entrance.

Lucas slipped inside the room and ducked into the hall closet. Listening to the drone of the vacuum, he smelled a woman's perfume all around him. His hand groped in the darkness and encountered a light cotton raincoat that gave off a strong aroma of evergreen. He thought of Katina and realized how much he wanted to be with her.

The droning stopped. He heard movements outside, a rustling sound, a door closing, and then silence. He stepped outside and found himself in a small entry foyer that opened into an attractive suite of rooms. The pale pink bedroom was off to the right of the living room. He moved around, studying the layout, resisting the temptation to search. Walking into the bedroom, he thought: she's neat. Frilly undergarments hung drying above the tub.

Seeing what he had come to see, he left, rode the elevator down to the lobby, and, stepping out, walked straight over to the reservation desk.

"May I help you, sir?" asked the clerk at the desk.

"Yes, my wife and I are in town for a few days, and we wondered if room 400 was available for tonight. You see, we spent our wedding night there and, well, you understand," Lucas said.

"Of course, sir," the clerk said, looking down and punching keys on the desk computer keyboard. Watching the screen, he smiled and said cheerfully, "I can let you have room 400 for one night, but you'll have to be out tomorrow."

"That will be fine," Lucas said, sliding the department credit card across the counter.

"Exigent circumstances" meant conditions requiring secrecy because there was a reasonable likelihood that a continuing investigation would be compromised if any of the persons under surveillance became aware of it. Lucas had looked it up in his manual on criminal procedure law.

After he left the hotel, Lucas went back to the Jeep and radioed all mobile units to stay on their subjects. He told Andreas to remain with the monitoring equipment and caught a taxi back to the Squad.

In the squad room he spent several minutes going over reports with the Second Whip. He then closeted himself in his office with copies of the *Code of Criminal Procedure*, the *Detective Guide*, and the *Investigators' Eavesdropping Handbook*. He did not intend to allow anyone in the Legal Bureau to tell him he didn't have sufficient probable cause for a wire, not this time.

He decided that he could claim "exigent circumstances," and went on to read the CPL's definition of probable cause. He read that an eavesdropping warrant could be issued only when one of the crimes designated in section 700.05 was being, had been, or would be committed by a particularly described individual. He read the long list of crimes, picking out several in his mind that applied to the case.

Lucas got up and went over to the form cabinet. He ran his finger over the dog-eared index thumbtacked to the inside of the door. Reaching into pigeonhole eleven, he pulled out Form 26:1—Eavesdropping Warrant.

He rolled the typewriter stand over to his desk, inserted the warrant application into the machine, spread out the case folder and the reference books on his desk, and, with a pencil firmly gripped between his teeth, started typing, saying aloud: "Once upon a time . . ."

At five-forty that evening a black van with a dish antenna on its shiny roof was parked on Central Park South, across the street from the Plaza.

"There they are," Lucas said, pointing to the van and pushing the Jeep's door open. He slipped around the end of a slow-moving, horse-drawn hansom cab and hurried over to the black van. When he got inside the department's special project mobile unit Lucas was met by two detectives dressed in dungarees.

"Lieutenant Lucas?" inquired the shorter of the two.

"Yes."

"I'm Covington, and this is Schwartz. Can I see your warrant, Lou?"

Lucas handed him the search warrant.

"Looks in order," Covington said, taking down a number four ledger from the shelf and making a long entry that included the date the warrant was issued, the name of the authorizing magistrate, and any time limitations specified in the warrant. "You understand, Lou, that you cannot record privileged communications. If the subject's lawyer or clergyman shows up, you must terminate."

"I understand."

"Sign here," Covington said, handing him a Receipt for Equipment form.

Schwartz picked up a suitcase from the floor and handed it to Lucas. "You know how to do the installation, Lou?"

"I know how," Lucas said.

Room 400 was the twin of 402. The detectives entered quickly. Lucas tossed the suitcase on the sofa. Vassos closed the shades and switched on the lights. Lucas opened the suitcase and removed a high-speed drill.

He inserted a bit into the chuck and looked around the suite, getting his bearings. The bedroom wall of room 400 was the living room wall of 402. He went into the bedroom, removed the lamp from the night table, and climbed up on it, turning to Vassos and saying, "Find out where she is."

Vassos: "Mobile One to Mobile Three, K."

Big Jay: "Standing by, K."

Vassos: "Subject's location, K?"

Big Jay: "Beauty parlor, K."

Standing on the night table, Lucas drilled a hole high up in the wall, pressing on the bit until he broke through the plaster on the other side. Vassos handed him the pinhole lens, and instrument about five inches long with an eighth of an inch lens at one end and telephone wires on the other. He took the jar of lubricant jelly from Vassos, greased the sides of the lens, and worked the instrument into the hole until it was about a sixteenth of an inch from the pinhole opening on the other side of the wall.

Vassos handed him a black box, a metal container about the size of a package of one hundred-length cigarettes that contained the camera's omnidirectional antenna. After he attached the lens wires to the box, Lucas got down off the table and went back into the living room.

He removed the microwave-receiving video recorder from the suitcase and set it down on the coffee table in front of the sofa. He switched on the machine and watched as the interior of suite 402 appeared on the screen.

Bubblebelly and Pussy Lyne strolled out of The Den, followed almost immediately by McKay and Patty Guts. It was after seven and the remaining sun gave no hint of the twilight soon to fall. McKay looked up and down Ninth Avenue, the others waiting silently and making a loose circle around him.

His instincts told him that something was wrong. His eyes narrowed as he scanned the street; McKay couldn't quite put his finger on what was out of place. Then he saw the van parked diagonally across the street, WARSHOW ELECTRIC COMPANY stenciled on its side panel. He lit a cigarette, and stared at the dark glass set in the van's side. "Wait here," he told the others and strolled off by himself, looking across at the stationary vehicle.

"He's made the van," Ulanov announced.

"Looks that way," Gregory said, calmly taking two mini Uzis from the gun locker and handing one to his partner. The detectives clicked thirty-two-round magazines into the guns' housings, unfolded the metal stocks, and slid the selector switches to full automatic. "Keep your eyes peeled," Ulanov said, spinning around on the stool and transmitting, "Mobile Four to Mobile One, K."

Lucas and Vassos were relaxing on the sofa when Ulanov's transmission came over the network.

Lucas sprang forward, grabbing up the walkie-talkie from the table. "Mobile One. Go, Mobile Four, K."

"They made us, K."

"You sure, K?"

"Pretty sure, K. Wait. Our boy is walking away, K."

McKay strolled back past his men, stopping at the open-front pizza parlor. "Hey, Giuseppi, or whatever the fuck your name is, how long's that van been parked there?"

The pie maker stuck his head out, looking. He studied the van and made an open-palmed gesture: How should I know?

"Terrific," McKay growled. "I got a blind pizza maker protecting my rear. That's terrific." He ambled back to his men. "Bubblebelly, I want you and Pussy to get a few of the boys and make swiss cheese out of that van."

Bubblebelly and Pussy Lyne walked back inside the bar.

Watching through the one-way glass, Gregory said, "I believe they're planning a surprise for us."

Lucas: "Mobile Four, what is your condition, K?"

Before Ulanov could radio his answer, Sergei Nashin's voice burst upon the network speaking in Russian. "Comrade Ulanov, two of my associates and I are on the way, K."

"No unauthorized transmission," Central radioed. "This is a restricted frequency. Stay off this frequency."

"*Пососи Мой хуй!*" Nashin transmitted.

"Such language," Ulanov radioed in Russian.

"No unauthorized transmissions," Central blared.

"Mobile One to Mobile Four, hightail it out of there, K."

"Ten-four, Mobile One."

Bubblebelly, Pussy Lyne, and three other men rushed out of the bar carrying shotguns hastily concealed in brown wrapping paper only to see the van driving off down Ninth Avenue.

"You want we should get our cars and go after them, Denny?" Pussy Lyne asked.

"Naw. Let 'em go. Me and Patty got something to do. You guys hang out until we get back."

Nashin: "Mobile Five to Mobile One, K."

Lucas: "Go Mobile Five, K."

Nashin: "We have McKay in view. Do you want us to stay with him, K?"

Lucas: "Affirmative, K. You're early."

Nashin: "We were bored, K."

Lucas: "Remember, Mobile Five, observe and report, nothing more, K."

Nashin: "Ten-four, y'all."

Denny McKay and Patty Guts waited in the West Fiftieth Street station for the E train.

Hearing the thundering rumble coming from the tunnel, they stepped back from the edge of the platform and watched the train come to a squealing stop. The doors opened; passengers pushing their way out of the train collided with the hordes shoving into the train. Patty Guts made a hole in the crowd for McKay and himself.

The door struggled closed; the train pulled out of the station. Twenty-one minutes later the E train stopped at the World Trade Center, and the two men joined in with the crowd flowing into the vast underground complex leading to the PATH trains and the twin towers.

They entered one of the arcade's open cafés and sat down, Patty Guts ordering cappuccino for both of them. McKay scanned the crowd, looking for a familiar face or a pair of eyes that wouldn't meet his.

McKay gulped down his cappuccino and said to Patty Guts, "Wait here." Leaving his bodyguard, McKay walked into the massive lobby of One World Trade Center and took the elevator up to the 107th floor. Stepping out into the Cellar in the Sky restaurant, he moved down the steps into the cocktail lounge and sat at the bar. He ordered a scotch on the rocks.

Clinking ice cubes, he turned on his stool and examined the faces of people in the bar, pausing only once to look out through the glass wall at the panorama of the city far below. Satisfied that he had not been followed, he paid the tab and rode the elevator down to the first floor.

Working his way to the front of the car so that he would be among the first to exit, McKay rushed out on the ground floor, turning to watch the faces of the other departing riders. He waited near the elevator bank for five more minutes before he walked over to Two World Trade Center, darted into the oversized elevator car, and rode up to the 107th floor, where he stepped out onto the open-air viewing platform.

He moved slowly, momentarily absorbed by the breathtaking view. Then he spied a solitary man who was leaning forward on an ivory-handled cane. He was well dressed and wore a golden ring.

McKay slowly approached and stood next to him. "The cops were watching my place in a surveillance van," he whispered, gazing off into the distance.

"Is that unusual? I would think that they would always be keeping an eye on people like you."

"Yeah, that's true, but now, with all that's going on, and in a van, I thought it might be something to be concerned about."

"Anything else out of the ordinary?"

"A few minor things," McKay said. "Someone left the door of my place open and my snake got out. The counter on the copying machine was unexplainably high. I figure one of my guys used it for something personal."

"We've been careful, Denny. I don't think we have a problem. Still, it's wise to look over your shoulder now and then."

Two men moved up and stood next to them. McKay and his friend stopped talking. One of the newcomers took out a cigarette and lighted it with a gold-trimmed butane lighter that concealed a modified Minox 16mm camera. The other newcomer pointed to something off in the distance and said something in Russian. The one with the butane lighter nodded his head in acknowledgment and said, "Da, da."

Moving out of earshot of the two strangers, McKay said, "Whaddaya gonna do about our lady friend?"

"I'm going to debrief her about what is happening in Greece and then I'm going to offer her Orhan's job."

"Do you think she can handle it?"

"Yes, I believe she can."

"You're the boss."

He looked at McKay. "Yes, I am."

20

Nina Pazza had returned to her room a few minutes past six. She undressed and padded into the bathroom and took a bath. Then she put her bathrobe on and moved into the bedroom. She set the clock for seven-thirty and fell asleep. When the alarm went off she got up and slipped out of her robe, dropping it on the foot of the bed. She admired her naked, gleaming body in the full-length mirror, turning sideways to look at her buttocks and deriving satisfaction from the firmness of her thighs. She spread her legs and pinched her inner thigh. "Disgusting," she said with an ironic grin. She went into the bathroom to wash her face and put on her makeup.

"That lady has a great body," Lucas observed, watching the video screen.

"She certainly has," Vassos agreed.

Nina went back into the bedroom and stepped into fresh panties. She took a bra from the dresser and was hooking the front together when she had second thoughts. She removed her brassiere and returned it to the drawer. Standing erect in front of the mirror, she caressed her firm breasts, gently kneading her nipples. Moving to the closet, she reached inside and took out a white cotton jumpsuit.

Lucas: "Mobile Three, your location, K?"
Big Jay: "In the lobby, covering exits, K."
Lucas: "Mobile Four, your location, K?"

Ulanov: "Parked across street, covering front entrance, K."

Lucas: "Mobile Two, your location, K?"

Leone: "We followed subject back to bookstore, K."

Lucas: "Mobile Two, leave that location and respond back here. Cover CPS entrance of hotel, K."

Leone: "Ten-four."

Lucas: "Mobile Five, your location, K?"

No response.

Lucas: "Mobile Five, do you read this unit, K?"

Static.

"Perhaps they're not in a position to transmit," Vassos said.

"I hope it's nothing more than that," Lucas said, watching Nina get up out of her seat to answer a knock at the door.

"How have you been, Nina?" he asked, giving her a perfunctory kiss on her cheek as he moved past her into the room. It was 9:03. He was always punctual.

She made no response other than to throw herself on the sofa and sulk. She drew her arms tightly across her stomach and glared at the tall, sinewy man as he moved around checking the room out with almost excessive caution.

"Damn!" Lucas exclaimed, watching Paul Mastri, the rare book dealer, lean his cane up against the side of the sofa and hand a gift-wrapped package to Nina.

"A present," Mastri said in a quiet, pleasant voice.

She looked away, avoiding his eyes. "No, thank you."

He gently turned her face toward him. "Please."

She unceremoniously snatched the gift from his hand and ripped off the wrapping to discover a small oil painting.

She sat down next to her. "A landscape by Il Grechetto. Signed and dated 1650." He leaned close to her, scratching his upper lip with his finger. "You do know who Il Grechetto was, don't you?"

She slapped his face. "You bastard!"

He grabbed her hand. "I thought you would like it, after all, Giovanni Castiglione was your mother's favorite."

She threw the painting down on the cushion. "I hate you." The tears came, and then the sobs, and she fell crying against her father's chest, remaining there while he gently stroked her hair.

Suddenly she recoiled from his caresses and ran crying into the bathroom. A few minutes passed before she returned, her makeup reapplied, hair combed. She lowered herself back down into her seat. "Why did you kill Orhan?" she demanded angrily.

He sighed and dismissed her question with a wave of his hand.

"Orhan suffered from a life-threatening malady: greed. He wanted me to sell our birthright and share the money with him."

"And the Aristarchus commentary? I thought Belmont was your friend; but you told your goons to steal it from him."

"Friend? That is a middle-class word that does not apply to people like us. The commentary helps authenticate Alexander's *Iliad*. I've been collecting everything that has to do with the casket-copy since my father died. I had no intention of letting Belmont know I was interested in it. His big mouth would have blabbed it all over the art world."

"You trust him enough to do business with him."

"Business is one thing, our heritage is another."

"I want none of it."

He grabbed her shoulders, forcing her to face him. "Your grandfather spent his life and his fortune searching for the casket-copy. The world laughed at him. Well, I took up his search. I gave up my name, my own face, everything so that I could reclaim our birthright—and you dare to sit there and tell me you want none of it? I brought you into the family business because I thought you were intelligent enough to comprehend how important the casket-copy is to us. To me! Damn it, it's mine. I earned it!"

"Please," she said, removing one of his hands.

He opened his mouth to say something when he noticed a few whitish flakes on the floor. Mastri reached for his cane and rose slowly. Moving over to the wall, he knelt, examining the small mound of plaster on the dark red carpet. He stood, backing away from the wall. Using the tip of his cane as a pointer, he prodded the wall suspiciously.

"What is it?" Nina asked, concern growing in her voice.

Mastri's features clouded with anger. "I think the Plaza has mice, my dear." Suddenly he stuck the pinhole viciously with his cane.

"He might try to escape through the connecting door. You take that, I'll take the door to his room," Lucas said, transmitting as he ran, "Mobile Two, Three, Four—ten eighty-five, forthwith."

"Three on the way," Big Jay radioed as he and Christos made for the elevator.

"Mobile Two," Leone shouted into the mouthpiece, making for the stairs with Elisabeth.

"Mobile Four coming," Ulanov radioed as Gregory swerved the surveillance van across Fifth Avenue, down Fifty-eighth Street, and made a sharp right turn into Grand Army Plaza, followed by a hard left that made the van go partway up the hotel's steps. As shocked guests watched, Gregory leaped down from the van and ran into the lobby, followed almost immediately by Ulanov, who had lingered only long enough to lock up the van.

Lucas ran out into the corridor, his revolver drawn. With his back to the wall, he reached out and tried the doorknob of Nina Pazza's room. It was locked. "Open up, Mastri. Police!" Lucas backed away and smashed his foot just above the knob. It did not give, so he kicked it again.

At the same moment, Vassos threw open the connecting door of his room and tried Nina Pazza's. It was locked. Drawing his automatic, he ran back into the room to gain momentum and hurled himself at the closed door. His body struck just as the door was jerked open from the inside, catapulting the policeman into the room. The cane sword smashed its way into his mouth, then went clean through to the brain. Both his eyes filled with blood; gasping, he blew a spray of blood through his nostrils and out his mouth. Through a crimson haze he saw Soula and Stephanos waving to him. He called out their names and ran to meet them.

Paul Mastri rushed into the policemen's room. Ignoring the video setup, he stood by the door, listening, waiting.

Lucas finally crashed into Pazza's room, his weapon at the ready. An unexpected, numbing dread seized him; then a piercing howl exploded from his mouth when he saw Vassos. He stumbled over to his fallen friend, automatically feeling for a pulse; there was none.

He stared in mute agony at Andreas's body, at the head propped on the sword handle, the smeared blade sticking out of the back of his head, the blood pouring onto the carpet and pooling in a dark circle. He should have taken the connecting door, sent Andreas through the front. Slowly the cloud began to clear and he became aware of sounds behind him. He turned and saw Nina curled up on the sofa in a fetal position, wrenching sobs coming from her distorted mouth.

In a state of shock, he automatically slipped his handcuffs from his belt and, leaning toward her, cuffed her right hand to her left leg. Only then did he kneel next to Andreas and begin to weep.

Paul Mastri had waited until he heard a crash against his hotel room's main door; he ran out into the corridor, headed for the fire exit. Rushing down the stairs, he heard the commotion of people coming up so he darted out of the stairwell onto the third floor. He pressed for the elevator and serenely stepped into it when it arrived. He got off in the lobby to find it a sea of shouting confusion and calmly walked from the hotel, using the Central Park South exit.

*　　　*　　　*

Big Jay and Christos rushed into the room. "Oh, my God!" Big Jay exclaimed, falling to his knees next to Lucas. "Lou, you okay?"

The Whip ignored him.

"Lou! You okay?" Big Jay repeated, shaking the Whip's shoulder.

Leone ran into the room, followed by Elisabeth Syros. She screamed and ran over to the body. Kneeling, Elisabeth rhythmically nodded her head and made signs of the cross, chanting the prayer for the dead in a near-choking voice.

Gregory and Ulanov sprinted inside, stopped, their stares frozen on the macabre scene. "Shit!" Ulanov shouted.

Lucas leaped to his feet and ran into the next room. The VCR was still running; it had recorded the entire ghastly murder. He rushed back into the crime scene, picked up the radio from the floor, and broadcast, "All units on citywide patrol, wanted for the homicide of a police officer, three minutes in the past, Paolo Matrazzo, alias Paul Mastri, description as follows . . ."

His control regained, Lucas finished his radio message and picked up Andreas's 9mm Beretta from the floor. He stuck it into his belt and, reaching down, unclipped the magazine pouches from Vassos's belt. He held back his jacket and fastened them on his own belt. Moving to the sofa, he grabbed Nina Pazza by the handcuffs and dragged her contorted body into the next room. He tossed her to the floor. "Where did he go?"

She fearfully shook her head.

"Where?" he shouted.

"I don't know," she screamed.

Elisabeth Syros ran in and started to kick the prisoner in the face. Lucas stepped between them, shaking his head.

Syros knelt down next to Pazza and said with threatening calmness, "You're going to spend the rest of your life in a Greek prison—and I'm going to be there to see that your life is a hell. Now! Where is he?"

"Ask McKay," she shouted. "He'll know."

Denny McKay took his time aiming the disk. He let it go, watching it slide the length of the shuffleboard, knocking Patty Guts's and Bubblebelly's off the board into the alley.

The muffled sound of a ringing telephone caught McKay's attention, causing him to look back into the barroom. His rule had always been no telephones in The Den, except for one locked in a drawer behind the stick. It was never used and it never rang. He went behind the bar and unlocked the drawer. Putting the handset up to his ear, he said, "Yeah," and listened.

*　　*　　*

"Park a couple of blocks away," Lucas told Gregory as the surveillance van turned into Ninth Avenue heading downtown.

Gregory drove to Fifty-first and parked the police department vehicle at a bus stop. Lucas took out the Beretta, slid out the magazine to check if it was full, and stuck the weapon back under his belt.

Big Jay, sitting on a stool, slid rounds into the chamber of a Remington Bushmaster pump shotgun. Ulanov handed Gregory an Uzi from the gun locker as he stepped into the back of the van. Lucas asked Ulanov if there had been any word from Nashin.

"Mobile Five is among the missing," Ulanov said. "Maybe his radio is dead."

"He could call us on the cellular phone," Lucas said in a worried tone.

"Maybe he can't get to a phone, Lou?" Gregory suggested.

Lucas nodded and removed six pairs of handcuffs from the supply locker, handing each of his detectives two sets. He unlocked the explosives box and tossed Gregory two stun grenades.

Before leaving the Plaza, Lucas had ordered Leone to take Nina Pazza to the station house and process her arrest reports. There was a lot of work to be done back in the squad room and he wanted Leone to take care of it. The video tape had to be invoiced as evidence, the "unusual" had to be prepared, notifications had to be made.

Elisabeth Syros had been unyielding in her demand to come with Lucas and his men until Lucas told her that he wanted her to tell her people throughout the city to be on the lookout for him. He was going after the casket-copy.

"You all know what to do?" Lucas asked.

The detectives looked around at each other. "Yeah, we know," Big Jay replied.

"Then let's do the sucker," Lucas said, shoving open the side door.

Denny McKay pensively returned the telephone to the drawer and looked up at the anxious faces gathered around him. "We might be having company. Pussy, clear out this place and tell whoever is hanging around outside to make themselves scarce. We're going upstairs to clean out some stuff, and then we're goin' to take a vacation."

Lucas got inside the pizza parlor, saw no customers, and closed the door. The pie maker's protests were cut short by the sight of the Beretta pointing at his stomach. "Don't hurt me! I'll give you my money."

"Close up this hole," Lucas ordered, reaching behind and locking the door.

The pie maker reached up and pulled down the accordion shutters. Going behind the counter, Lucas motioned the nervous man over to the oven rack and handcuffed both his hands to a stainless steel handle on the oven door. "Cry out and I'll come back and put a hole in your head."

The pie maker shook his head violently. "I won't. Only please, don't hurt me."

Lucas crawled under the oven, pushed out the door panel, squeezed through into the hallway, and made his way up to the roof.

Pussy Lyne and Bubblebelly stationed themselves on the landing of the second floor at the top of the stairway without stairs, each man cradling an automatic shotgun in his arms.

Patty Guts, his back to the other two and his shotgun held loosely in his hand, peered through the plastic cutout in the curtains, looking up into the staircase leading to upper floors and the roof.

Denny McKay hurried through the second-floor workshop into his office. Stretching his arm behind the rolltop desk, he pulled off a remote control module and rushed over to the file cabinet, shoving it aside. Getting down on one knee, McKay aimed the remote at a space on the wall, pushed the "on" button, and proceeded to punch in a code. A panel slid up into the wall, revealing a black dial safe.

Ulanov looked up from his wristwatch. "Now."

Gregory picked up the cellular phone and dialed 911.

"Police operator forty-two, may I help you?"

"Der guy who murdered the Greek cop in the Plaza Hotel is hangin' around right now in a bar called The Den, at Ninth and Forty-ninth," Gregory said into the mouthpiece, and hung up.

Big Jay wiggled a cigar out of its cellophane and stuck the unlit stogie in his mouth, clasping his hands behind his head, waiting.

"All units on patrol in the Sixteenth and adjoining precincts," Central broadcasted. "Central has just received an anonymous call that the suspect wanted in connection with the homicide of a police officer, this date, in the Plaza Hotel, is at a bar within the confines of the Sixteenth, located at . . ."

Ulanov waited until Central had radioed the bar's location and a description of the suspect before he transmitted, "Sixteen detectives to Central, K."

"Go Sixteen detectives."

"This unit is a block away from that location, Central. We're in surveillance van one-two-four. Request backup units, K."

"Sixteen Eddie on the way."

"Sergeant going."

"Adam-Boy going."

"Anticrime going."

Big Jay tapped Ulanov's shoulder and pointed to the cigar.

Ulanov nodded, and radioed, "Sixteen detectives to Central, K."

"Go Sixteen detectives."

"Advise responding units that there is a black member of the service with this unit. He's in civilian clothes; he's big, as ugly as sin, and he'll have an unlit cigar stuck in his mouth."

Responding units let go with a chorus of ten-fours.

Big Jay stood and locked the gates that sealed off the van's interior. Moving out front, he knelt between the seats and said, "All secure. Let's do it."

Surveillance van 124 screeched to a stop on the sidewalk, blocking the bar's entrance. Detectives leaped out and took up firing positions on both sides of the entrance.

Gregory tried the door; it was locked.

Standing off to the side, Big Jay fired a shotgun blast into the wood, sending the door flying open.

Gregory stepped into the doorway, aiming his Uzi into the deserted bar; Big Jay and Ulanov darted inside.

The detectives paused briefly to check out the area. A bar to the left of the entrance, a kitchen at the other end of the bar. Booths to their right. A sawdust-covered walkway separating the bar and booths, leading to a large back room with more booths and a shuffleboard. In this back room, Vassos had told them, was a closet that contained a stairway without steps.

The wail of approaching sirens filled the air.

The three-man fire team leapfrogged their way to the back of the bar, two covering while the third ran to take up a new firing position.

Bubblebelly and Pussy Lyne trained their weapons down into the stairwell.

Patty Guts tightened his grip on the shotgun's cold steel, his eyes fixed straight up in the direction of the roof door.

Denny McKay removed the .38 Colt from his belt and placed it on the floor beside him while he continued to sort through the safe, shoving money and records into a shopping bag.

Lucas flattened his back against the roof hutch that contained the top of the staircase that led down through the tenement to the bar.

His eyes were fixed on the second hand of his watch as it swept around the dial.

Ulanov, standing with the others outside the tiny chamber downstairs that housed the stairless staircase, saw his second hand hit thirty and shouted, "Now!"

Gregory threw open the door.

Bubblebelly and Pussy Lyne fired down into the stairwell, splintering the door between the back room and the stairs off its hinges. The alarm system went off, emitting the sounds of klaxons. Gregory, standing outside the tiny room, stuck his Uzi inside and emptied the magazine up into the stairwell.

Big Jay pulled the pin on the grenade, holding the spoon down.

Ulanov stepped into the doorway, firing up the stairwell in the general direction of the second-floor landing.

Big Jay moved across the threshold and tossed the grenade up onto the second-floor landing. It exploded in a smoky roar, sending all three men reeling.

Lucas threw open the roof door, ran to the third floor, and fired three bursts down the stairwell. Patty Guts lurched forward, ripping the curtain from its rod, shrouding himself in black cotton as he fell dead. Rushing down the steps toward the second-floor landing, Lucas emptied his magazine, crouching down to reload.

Pussy Lyne, retaining the cover of the wall, stuck his shotgun around the wall and fired two blasts up the stairwell at Lucas, forcing him to dive prone on the steps. Pussy Lyne darted out from safety to fire at the lieutenant. Lucas, lying on the steps, fired first, exploding Pussy's face in a geyser of gray jelly and blood. The dead man remained standing, his finger frozen against the trigger, the shotgun discharging automatic rounds up into the ceiling of the stairwell. Lucas fired another burst; it sent the corpse and weapon to the ground.

Big Jay, with covering fire from Ulanov and Gregory, climbed up the risers, his hands clutching the banister, his shotgun thrust in front under his belt.

Bubblebelly extended his arm and fired four rounds blindly down the stairwell. Taking careful aim so as not to hit Big Jay, Ulanov and Gregory fired alternate bursts, watching as their partner continued his perilous climb up the treadless staircase.

Lucas, his back to the stairwell's wall, automatic thrust downward, stealthily placed his foot on the next step down to the second floor.

Reloading, Bubblebelly shouted, "Denny, they're creepin' all around me."

"I need another minute," McKay shouted back, hurriedly sorting through records.

Guns drawn, uniformed policemen rushed into the bar and charged into the back room. Firing a short burst, Gregory shouted for the new arrivals to stay back and do nothing. An overzealous rookie pushed his way through the crowd of policemen and recklessly fired two rounds up at the unseen criminals. Ulanov's ingrained response was to swing his Uzi at the rookie, striking him across his forehead and sending him staggering backward, blood streaming down his face.

"You fucking asshole," Ulanov shouted at the stunned policeman, "we've got our own people up there!"

Lucas was three steps away from the second-floor landing. Big Jay climbed to within a foot of the top. The alarm system continued to scream its head off at a deafening level; the acid-sharp reek of potassium nitrates fouled the air.

Lucas hunkered down, his sweaty hands tight around the grips. Bubblebelly saw the shadow fall over the floor. He leaned his shoulder into the stock, aiming at the hidden source of the shadow in the stairwell.

Big Jay stopped just below the top, balancing carefully on the risers, and slid the shotgun out of his belt, waiting to make his move.

Ulanov fired a burst.

Lucas raised his walkie-talkie above his head, silently counted to three, and heaved it out onto the second-floor landing.

Instinctively Bubblebelly pointed his shotgun in the direction of the sound of the radio hitting the landing, saw what it was, and swiveled the weapon back to aim at the staircase.

Big Jay popped up and fired a blast into Bubblebelly's stomach, sending the fat man crashing back against the wall. He slumped against the shot-pocked wall, gaping with bewilderment at the bloody hole in his dying body.

Lucas dashed out from the staircase. Bubblebelly's body had collapsed against the wall. Approaching cautiously, Lucas picked up the shotgun and tossed it away. Sticking his foot behind Bubblebelly's, he yanked the dead man's legs out from under him, sending the corpse crashing to the floor. Lucas moved to the stairwell, extended his hand, and pulled Big Jay up onto the landing.

The detectives fanned out in the workshop, moving warily, their weapons at the ready.

"Give it up, Denny," Lucas shouted. "You and I can make a deal. I want Matrazzo, not you."

McKay, clutching two bulging shopping bags and his revolver, crawled behind the printing press to take cover and consider his options. The blocked windows offered him no escape. Cops were all over the place. He'd never make it to the roof alive and staying alive was what it's all about. There would have to be a trial. That meant lawyers, and bail, and appeals. "I'm coming out. Don't shoot," he shouted, and stood up, hands above his head, his revolver dangling from his forefinger.

Ulanov rushed over and took the weapon from him. Big Jay frisked the prisoner.

Lucas, his face a mask of icy contempt, grabbed McKay's arm and led him away. "Denny, we don't have much time, so listen. You give me Matrazzo and the casket-copy, and you walk."

"I wanna call my lawyer," McKay snarled.

"You're going to be arrested and charged with murder in Greece. Your boy George Cuttler made a dying declaration before he checked out, naming you as the one who sent him and Simmons over to hit the two cops."

"I don't know what you're talking about. I've never been to Greece."

"After that, you'll be extradited to the Soviet Union and charged with the theft of government property. I don't think you're going to like it there, Denny. And after all that, if they don't kill you, I'm going to arrest you for homicide."

A shadow of concern crossed McKay's face. "What homicide?"

"Eddie Burke."

"Wheredja hear that shit? Eddie was my friend."

"You whacked him, Denny, and I can prove it. You left your cigarettes in the ashtray and outside the car. A forensic dentist will testify that it was your teeth that left the marks on all the filters. And the saliva we extracted from the cotton has your blood grouping."

"Circumstantial evidence," McKay said uneasily.

Lucas nodded in agreement. "But it's powerful evidence, Denny. Anyway, we got this new gadget in the lab. It takes bioforensic 'fingerprints.' That means it analyzes DNA, that's the stuff we all have in our genes. This machine measures several millionths of a gram of any body fluid. It's a positive I.D. just like prints. Your saliva is going to buy you twenty-five to life." He pulled him close and said grimly, "If the Greeks or Russians don't get you, I will."

McKay pulled away. Nodding his head at the two shopping bags on the floor. "There's two hundred K. Take it."

"Denny? When I came on the Job the theme song was 'The Best Things in Life are Free.' Today it's the *Ave Maria*."

McKay shoved his hands into his pockets, regarded his shoes. "I walk?"

"You walk."

"I'm not sure where he is. He telephoned and told me to get out. I know he got a house someplace in Queens and another one out in East Hampton. It should be easy for you to find out where. My guess is that he's making for one of them."

"And Alexander's *Iliad?*"

"I don't know nothing about that. He had me send a couple of boys to take care of the Greek cops. Orhan did all the background work on the job. That's all I know."

Lucas turned to his detectives. "Read him his rights. Then book him for everything we got on him."

"You promised!" McKay shouted.

"I lied," Lucas said, walking away.

21

C of D Edgeworth was huddled in the back of the bar with the detectives, conducting a hurried rehearsal of the who, what, when, where, how, and why of the eventual official version of what had transpired. "Where did you get your reasonable cause for busting in here without a warrant?" Edgeworth asked.

"We were on patrol looking for the suspect wanted in connection with the Vassos homicide when we responded to a radio message that the perp might be here," Lucas said, casting a warning look at his men. "We entered, saw armed men running to the back, identified ourselves as police officers, at which point one of them turned and aimed a shotgun at us, necessitating the use of deadly physical force."

"Okay," Edgeworth said, nodding satisfaction. "Evidence?"

"We discovered two shopping bags filled with records," Lucas said. "We haven't had a chance to go through it all, but a cursory examination reveals records recording the theft, counterfeiting, and resale of art."

"No money?" Edgeworth asked.

"None," Lucas lied smoothly.

"Was this evidence obtained as the result of an illegal search?" Edgeworth asked as he walked into the closet with the stairless staircase.

Lucas and his men followed. "No, sir," Lucas answered. "It was in plain view when we arrested McKay."

"Did McKay make any statements?" the chief asked.

"Before we had a chance to read him his rights, he pleaded for us not to kill him and claimed that he sent Cuttler and Simmons to Greece only on Matrazzo's orders."

"Good. Good," Edgeworth said. "A *res gestae* confession, spontaneous and extemporaneous." He looked at Lucas. "The Greek ambassador telephoned me. They want no mention of Major Vassos in any of this. As far as anyone is concerned he was the victim of a robbery attempt."

Lucas said, "I understand."

"Anything else I should be made cognizant of?" the chief asked.

"No, sir," Lucas said, turning to look at Ulanov. "Ivan, the van is still blocking the entrance. One of our radios is still missing. Will you see if you can locate it?"

"Sure, Lou," Ulanov said, and quickly walked away.

Emergency Service trucks cordoned off Ninth Avenue between Forty-eighth and Fiftieth streets. The department's searchlight truck illuminated the building. Scruffy people leaned out of windows, watching the free show. Ulanov climbed up into the surveillance van and, bending, made his way inside, lowering himself to the stool in front of the communication console. "Mobile One to Mobile Five, K." Only static cracked in response from the speakers.

"Sergi Sergeyevich, where the hell are you?" Ulanov radioed in Russian.

Police Commissioner Franklin Vaughn arrived at the scene at 2:47 A.M. accompanied by two men. One of them was a big mean-looking man around fifty dressed in a single-breasted seersucker suit with pleated trousers; he casually twirled a Panama hat on one finger. The other one was tall and thin, midforties, dressed in a dark blue suit; he had busy eyes that missed nothing and blow-dried brown hair streaked with gray at the sides.

"You and your men did a good job, Lieutenant," the PC said, nodding his approval at Big Jay and Gregory. "I'm going to see that all the detectives who worked on this case get grade money." Motioning the two civilians over, Vaughn made the introductions. "This is Mr. Warren Cribb of the National Institute for the Fine Arts. And this is Mr. August Hayden of the State Department's Bureau of Diplomatic Security," the PC said, pointing to the man in the Panama hat.

Oozing forced affability, Hayden said, "You did a good piece of police work, Lou."

Hayden talked with the gruff sureness of a cop. Lucas studied him for a long moment and said, "You sound like you might have been on the Job."

"Georgia State Police for ten years. I left there for a stint with the U.S. Marshal Service. And now I'm with State."

Looking Hayden in the eye, Lucas said, "I've heard of Diplomatic Security."

Hayden gave him a thoroughly unpleasant smile.

Warren Cribb, the man from the National Institute for the Fine Arts, stepped forward to pump Lucas's hand. "Your country and your department can be proud of you, Lieutenant. You and your men have enriched our cultural heritage."

Lucas hurled a quizzical look at the C of D, who shrugged ignorance.

"I don't understand. Enriched what cultural heritage?" Lucas said, his mistrust growing.

"Alexander's *Iliad*, Lieutenant," Cribb said. "You've rediscovered a lost national treasure."

Lucas forced himself to remain calm. "I thought it belonged to Greece."

"That's a matter for the courts, Lou," Hayden said, "not a couple of cops like us. Besides, the Greeks think that they have a claim on everything ever dug up in their country."

"I see," Lucas said, stealing a look at his detectives.

Big Jay spit out the unlit cigar.

"Actually, my understanding is that Paolo Matrazzo legally purchased it in 1939 and surreptitiously shipped it into this country," Hayden said, twirling his hat.

Cribb burst out angrily: "We have legal justification for taking Alexander's *Iliad* into our possession. I can assure you, Lieutenant, that the National Institute for the Fine Arts is above reproach."

Bullshit, Lucas thought. Aloud: "I'm sure it is, Mr. Cribb, but you see, we don't have it."

"You don't have it?" barked the PC. "I was told that the case had been broken. What the hell is going on here?"

C of D Edgeworth stepped forward. "A communication foul-up. We got the perps but the big cheese got away. We'll have him before the day is out."

"Does he have the casket-copy with him?" Hayden asked.

Thinking fast, Lucas said, "I don't think so. He didn't have time to come back here to get it."

"Then you believe it's hidden somewhere in this building?" Cribb asked, rubbing his hands in anticipation.

"Yes, sir, I do," Lucas said. "Secreted upstairs, someplace."

"Didn't you search for it?" Hayden asked, watching the lieutenant's eyes.

"You should know better than to ask that, Hayden. We didn't have a search warrant. We put too much work into this caper to have it go out the window because we didn't take the time to get a warrant," Lucas said, meeting Hayden's searching stare.

"But your police commissioner told us that you retrieved a lot of evidence," Cribb said.

"We only seized what we saw out in the open," Lucas said, going on to explain, "Whenever a police officer makes an arrest he may take possession of any evidence that is in plain view but is required to get a warrant to search further."

"Well, we're not police officers," Hayden said. "How do we get upstairs?"

Lucas pointed to the staircase. "Put your feet on the risers, grab hold of the banister, and climb."

Hayden put on his Panama and began to climb the staircase without stairs. His face soon turned red and sweat began dripping off him. Lucas turned and moved out into the bar, followed by his two detectives.

"Two untrustworthy types," Gregory observed to Big Jay.

"Uptown we'd call them a couple of hoodoo cunts," Big Jay said, spitting out a snippet of tobacco. Lucas headed for the van.

"Mobile Five, do you read this unit, K?" Ulanov radioed, tapping his knuckles over the control board.

"Mobile One, pick up your land line, K," Central ordered.

"Ten-four." Ulanov looked around for the cellular telephone and, not seeing it, remembered that they had secured it in the locker before the raid. He got off the stool and retrieved the instrument from the locker. As soon as he switched it on it began ringing.

"Detective Ulanov."

The frazzled rush of air that came over the line was punctuated by clanging electronic sounds, then came an accented voice speaking in careful English: "Lieutenant Lucas, please."

"He's not here. Can I help you?"

"I am Lieutenant Suslov, and I am telephoning from Moscow. I have an urgent message from Colonel Sergei Nashin for Lieutenant Teddy Lucas."

Ulanov took out his pen and, reaching for the notepad, said in Russian, "You did say, Moscow?"

"*Da. Moskva.*"

22

Manhattan's jagged profile shimmered under the rising morning sun as surveillance van 124 sped east on the Long Island Expressway. Ulanov steered it off the parkway at Woodhaven Boulevard and headed south at high speed. Lucas grinned nervously as Ulanov twisted the wheel, dodging around a taxi and a bus, arousing a host of angry horns as he fought his way through traffic. "You sure of the location?" Lucas asked.

"Yep."

"From Moscow?"

"Yep."

Lucas raised the radio to his mouth. "Big Jay?"

"Yeah?"

"They miss us yet?"

"Negative."

Lucas lowered the radio to his lap.

Ulanov made a sharp left turn on Myrtle Avenue and drove through Forest Park, exiting onto Park Lane South, continuing around the circle to Park Lane where he made a left up the driveway leading to the parking lot of the park's administrative offices. He made a sharp turn in the lot and stopped the van alongside a black Chevy Monte Carlo with diplomatic license plates. Lucas pushed open the door and got out, leaving Ulanov monitoring transmissions.

The parking lot was on a hill overlooking a section of Kew Gardens Hills, an exclusive enclave of well-manicured lawns and gardens and large expensive houses ranging in style from 1930s Tudor to ersatz Palladian. All was quiet in the clear light of the new day.

Sliding into the Monte Carlo's passenger seat, Lucas said, "Good morning, Sergei."

Nashin angrily shook the police department radio at Lucas's tired face. "Your radio stinks. I can receive, but I can't send."

"Happens, even in the Soviet Union."

Nashin's weary face betrayed his deep sadness. "I'm sorry about Andreas. He was a good policeman."

Lucas closed his eyes and sucked in a mouthful of cool morning air. "Yes, he was a good policeman. And a good man." He shifted in the seat, struggling to control his emotions. "What happened to you?"

"We followed McKay to a meeting at the top of the World Trade Center. I got pictures of him with Matrazzo. When they left the building, I decided to follow the new man, not knowing who he was at the time. We tailed him to the Plaza and watched him go inside. I assumed that you would be there for the meet with Nina Pazza, so I stationed myself on Central Park South, across the street in the taxi stand where I could watch both exits. When I heard you pull Leone off of Widener, I dispatched my two men to take his place."

"Good move," Lucas interjected.

"When I heard your emergency transmission and then saw Matrazzo leave the hotel and jump into a taxi, I did what any policeman would do; I followed him."

"Where is he now?"

Nashin pointed to a large stone house with leaded windows, rich ornamental details, and a slate-covered roof. The house was near the corner, at the top of a lawn that sloped down to the street.

Lucas reached inside his jacket and took out the Beretta. He ejected the magazine and checked the number of rounds in the clip. Satisfied, he shoved the magazine back into the housing and, leaning forward in his seat, reached behind his back and stuck the automatic into his belt, to the right of his spine. Reaching down in front, he drew his .38 detective special from its in-trouser holster, checked to see it was fully loaded, and replaced it. "What was with that call from Moscow?"

"I couldn't leave this location and there are no public phones around, so . . ." He reached under his seat and pulled out an instrument that was shaped like and about the size of a hardcover book, with a recessed computer keyboard and a four-inch-long liquid crystal display on the top. "A burst transmitter radio, direct to Moscow. I had to wait until four o'clock when our relay satellite comes into orbit. Moscow Center relayed my message to you."

Lucas looked at him, a sardonic smile on his lips. "Standard equipment for the cop on the beat. Our job's changing, my friend." He pushed open the door and turned when he heard footsteps approaching.

Ulanov, who had come over from the van, thrust a radio transceiver at him. "They're calling you."

"Big Jay?" Lucas queried.

"You've been missed. They're sending out the hounds."

"Ten-four." Lucas passed the set back to Ulanov. "Wait here with Sergei."

"I wanna come with you, Lou," Ulanov said.

"It's my endgame, Ivan," Lucas said.

Folding his big frame into the passenger seat, Ulanov said, "Good morning, comrade."

Lucas drove the van out of the lot and across the street, straight into the winding driveway of the house. Tires crunching on the gravel in the parking area, the van lurched to a stop. Lucas leaped out, heading toward the vine-covered entrance portico.

The heavy door was open, the sound of a Mozart divertimento coming from somewhere inside the house. He cautiously went inside and found himself in a ground-floor foyer that had a black-and-gray marble floor. He walked quietly over the carpet of the long hallway that led off the foyer, past heavy wood doors, and into a huge oblong room with a wall of French doors opening onto an emerald lawn with a towering weeping willow. A large tapestry, depicting a lush savanna and tropical birds, hung over a stone fireplace on the wall opposite the French doors.

Following the sound of the music, he moved through a formal dining room with two crystal chandeliers and found himself standing in front of a closed door. The Mozart was clearly coming from the room on the other side of the door.

Uncomfortably aware of the smell of his own unwashed body and the sweat pouring down his sides as well as the foul, "late-tour" taste in his mouth, Lucas drew his .38, threw open the door, and crouched inside in a firing stance.

On guard, he trained his revolver around the room. He had never been in such a strange place; the cavernous chamber had four granite pillars which reached up to support a vaulted ceiling. Sitting on a wooden folding chair next to one of the pillars, a tape deck played Mozart.

Display cases were arranged in a circle inside what was obviously some sort of shrine. All the tops were open; a dolly was on the floor inside the circle and strapped onto it were twenty-six unfurled papyrus scrolls encased between thick sheets of glass. His heart pounding, Lucas moved inside the ring, continuing to move his pointing gun around the room. Seeing that he was alone, Lucas knelt down beside the dolly.

Eyes wide with wonderment, he looked down at the ancient Greek words. He started to touch one, but jerked his hand back as though afraid of committing sacrilege. And then, slowly, reverently, he placed his palm on one and was immediately overcome by feelings that he could not have described.

The music stopped abruptly.

Lucas knelt in the sudden and ominous silence, apprehension freezing on his face. He turned to assume a prone firing position.

Matrazzo stepped out from behind a column in back of the policeman, a .45 automatic pointing at the back of Lucas's head.

"You might try and get a round off before I blow your head apart, Lieutenant, but you'll be dead before you turn around. Now! Put your weapon down and slide it back to me."

Lucas looked across the room at the silent tape deck.

"I pulled the plug," Matrazzo said. "Extension cords are so helpful, don't you think?"

Lucas hesitated, and then reluctantly put his revolver on the floor and pushed it behind him. Matrazzo picked it up and stuck it in his belt. "You may now get up, but keep your hands clasped behind your head."

Standing, Lucas said, "You know you're playing with half a deck, don't you?"

Matrazzo's hand holding the gun was shaking from the man's barely controlled rage; his eyes were icy. "Don't you dare call me crazy, you pathetic civil servant. My father was a great man. I devoted my life to reclaiming what was his and is now mine. Now! Push the dolly through that door." He motioned to a solid wood door between two leaded windows. "My treasure is going with me."

"You're going to forge the casket-copy and sell the fake," Lucas said, not moving. "And you're betting that a certain museum is so anxious to have it that they'll never even notice they're buying a fake."

"Very astute of you. It will take me about twenty months to do a good job. I'll make my own ink. I intend to sell both the casket-copy and the commentary. Thanks to your meddling, certain people in the art world are foaming at the mouth to get their greedy hands on the scrolls. I've already been in touch with some Japanese who fancy themselves collectors. They're willing to pay up to sixty million. And I'll get to keep the real ones. Now move the cart."

Bending, Lucas pushed the wheeled cart into a breezeway connecting the house and a stone garage.

"Inside the garage," Matrazzo ordered, treading softly behind the lieutenant.

A station wagon was sticking halfway out of the front of the garage. It was set back from the main house, at the end of a parterre, with an asphalt lane winding down into the main driveway. It was too far back and off to the side for Ulanov and Sergei to see his deadly predicament. Easy does it, kiddo, easy does it. Wait for the right moment, Lucas counseled himself, looking around the garage. Gardening tools and an aluminum ladder hung from the wall, and there was a lawn mower on the floor next to two red gasoline cans with yellow bands around their centers.

"Start loading them into the back," Matrazzo ordered.

Lucas held back. Matrazzo waved the .45. "I'll splatter you all over the floor and walls. Move!"

Lucas unbuckled the belt securing the plates on the dolly. He slid his hands under three of them and picked them up, commenting, "They're in a remarkable state of preservation."

"The ancients knew how to reserve their heritage. Now, stop stalling and load."

Lucas lugged the plates over to the back of the station wagon. Bracing his knee under the plates, he tried to open the rear door. "It's locked," he lied, struggling to get his load back to the dolly.

Matrazzo looked at the policeman. "Sit on the floor facing the wall with your hands behind your head."

Lucas carefully set the glass plates on the dolly and lowered himself down, his back to the dolly, the gasoline cans a few feet beyond his reach. Keeping his automatic trained on Lucas's back, Matrazzo slowly moved backward toward the driver's side. Lucas inched his torso back, winding it up for a forward leap, waiting for that instant when his enemy would be off balance. He tilted his head slightly to the right so that his peripheral vision included Matrazzo.

Reaching behind with one hand, Matrazzo felt for the handle. He opened the door. With his eyes riveted on Lucas, he transferred the automatic to his left hand and, bending at the knees, groped under the dashboard for the tailgate latch release.

Now! Lucas sprang forward, grabbing a gasoline can and hurling it at Matrazzo; then he dived for cover behind the dolly.

Matrazzo got off one round with an unsteady hand; it missed. The can struck his chest, knocking off the spout and dousing his front; he staggered back across the driver's seat. Lucas grabbed the Beretta and fired a shot under the dolly that struck Matrazzo's foot.

Screaming obscenities, Matrazzo grabbed the automatic with his right hand and pulled himself up into a sitting position. "Get out from behind my *Iliad*. Get away, you son of a bitch! Leave my *Iliad*," Matrazzo screamed, aiming for a clean shot.

Lucas popped out from around the side of the loaded cart, firing a round at the killer. The driver's seat exploded in a reddish blue fireball that engulfed Matrazzo and turned him into a flailing, thrashing gargoyle with blue and yellow streamers fluttering out his eyes and mouth. Lucas leaped up off the ground and hauled the dolly past the roaring fire out onto the driveway. He ran bent over, trying to put distance between himself and the garage.

The force of a violent explosion hurled Lucas across the dolly, toppling him and the cart over the lawn, spilling the plates onto the grass. Slowly regaining his senses, Lucas straightened up and looked back at the inferno. A deformed hand was sticking out of the hungry flames, a gold ring reflecting the savage light of the blaze. Then the hand disappeared in the fire.

The Monte Carlo came racing over the lawn and jerked to a stop. Ulanov and Sergei leaped out and ran over to him.

"Are you all right?" Nashin shouted.

"I'm okay," Lucas said, uprighting the dolly. "Help me pick up these sheets."

"Matrazzo?" Ulanov asked, picking up some scrolls.

"In there," Lucas said, jerking his thumb at the now blazing garage. Ulanov smiled grimly. "That's a conviction that won't be overturned."

"Where is he?" August Hayden, the man from Diplomatic Security, demanded. They were standing outside The Den, a cluster of police officials that included the PC, the C of D, Warren Cribb, the man from the National Institute of the Fine Arts, the Duty Captain, and two detectives from the Sixteenth Squad.

"I don't know where he is," Big Jay answered.

"Me neither," Gregory followed.

Repeatedly digging his forefinger into Big Jay's chest, Hayden warned, "You'd better tell me, Officer, or it'll be your ass."

Big Jay scowled down at the offending finger. "If you stick that thing at me one more time, we is gonna be rushed to the hospital. They's gonna be extracting my foot from your asshole." Since all of them had spent a sleepless night, tempers were ragged. The coolness of a new day did little to ease the tension.

Angrily snatching off his Panama hat, Hayden said to the PC, "You oughta instill respect for civilians in your men, Commissioner."

Police Commissioner Vaughn met Hayden's glare. "Fuck you," he said, turning away and walking over to his car.

Hayden glared at the C of D, who looked away from him.

"Let's get out of here," Hayden said to Cribb, and the two of them ran to their car.

Edgeworth looked at the two detectives and said, "You'd better get on the horn to your boss and tell him some uptight people are going to be looking for him."

23

Before noon August Hayden had set up a temporary command post in the garage on the Forty-fifth Street side of the United States Mission to the United Nations.

"This was to have been uncomplicated," Cribb complained.

"We can't always control events," Hayden said, pacing back and forth in front of the open garage door. "Obviously Lieutenant Lucas has his own plans for Alexander's *Iliad*."

"Then you do think he has it?"

"He has it all right. But the question is, what is he going to do with it?"

"What do you mean?"

"He might want to sell it to the highest bidder, or he might want to turn it over at a full-blown press conference, get some publicity for himself and his men. Or . . . ?" He let the word drop, glancing at this men lounging around the double-parked sedans on the street outside.

"Or what?"

"The lieutenant and Major Vassos were partners. I wouldn't expect you to appreciate the significance of that, but take my word, among policemen it means a lot." Hayden thoughtfully tapped his fist against his chin. "I think he's going to return it to the Greeks."

Cribb's mouth dropped open. "You must not allow that to happen. Kill him if you have to, but that *Iliad* must remain in this country."

"Kill an American cop?" Hayden said, his voice full of contempt. "I get paid to pull dirty tricks on people but I don't murder Americans, not for any price."

"But . . . but . . ."

"There are no buts, Cribb." Hayden called one of his men over and told him to go inside the mission and get a Manhattan telephone directory. When the man returned, Hayden put the thick book on the hood of the town car parked inside the garage and copied several addresses onto a page of his notepad.

"What are you doing?" Cribb asked.

"If I were Lucas, I'd go get the casket-copy and make for a Greek government facility in New York."

"Why? Why not some fish store in Astoria?"

"Because it's not extraterritorial, outside the territorial and judicial limits of the United States," Hayden said, reaching for the walkie-talkie atop the town car's hood. "And the Greek UN mission and consular office are."

Northbound traffic crawled along York Avenue from Fifty-third to the entrances of the Franklin D. Roosevelt Drive at Sixty-first and Sixty-third streets. Lucas thought: my luck is holding.

They had just finished loading the plates into the back of the Monte Carlo when the fire engines arrived at the scene. Traffic had moved briskly on the way back into Manhattan. Big Jay's transmission had alerted Lucas that the bad guys were looking for him. Figuring that Hayden wouldn't be able to gather enough people on short notice, he drove all the way east, hoping to slip through any cordon placed to intercept him. He looked out into the sideview mirror and saw the surveillance van behind him. Ulanov was driving; Nashin, copiloting. He prayed that Elisabeth had alerted her people.

Traffic agents worked cars into the northbound entrance at Sixty-first Street. Lucas cut the car out into the far left lane, skirting around the packed mass of cars trying to get on the drive.

The light turned red; he gunned the engine and sped north, with the van staying close behind him. At Seventy-ninth Street, Lucas made a left turn off of York Avenue and double-parked. He got out and ran back to the van. Ulanov rolled down the window. Lucas told him that he was headed for the Greek consulate between Park and Madison avenues.

"Right behind you, Lou," Ulanov said.

Lucas looked at Nashin. "Sergei, why don't you grab a taxi back to your mission and report the car stolen? Stay out of it, you've done more than your share."

Nashin let go with a litany of Russian obscenities.

"What did he say?" Lucas asked Ulanov.

"You don't wanna know, Lou. But the bottom line is, he's coming with us."

The Greek consulate was located in a town house on the north side of Seventy-ninth Street. Three low steps led up to two arched doorways with ornamental ironwork, separated by a large window. Approaching Park Avenue, Lucas saw the blue-and-white Greek flag hanging over one of the doorways. He also spotted the crescent-shaped barricade of black sedans blocking the entrances and the men standing alertly behind the cars.

Hayden's read my mind, Lucas thought, hurriedly stopping at the curb and parking. He got out and stood between cars, looking into the next block, desperately pondering his next move. He knew that he had to get the casket-copy to a safe place where Hayden and his crew couldn't get their thieving hands on it. The only really safe place would be a diplomatic mission. If Hayden had thought to cover this location, he'd have the Greek mission and other places covered too. I don't want Andreas to have died for nothing, he thought. No! I'm not going to let that happen. He could see Hayden and Cribb having a curbside discussion with three men. They're probably telling the Greeks that they are there to protect them against an imminent terrorist attack, he thought; then the surveillance van whooshed past him with Nashin leaning out the window signaling him to wait where he was.

"Tighten your seat belt, comrade," Ulanov shouted, shooting the van across Park Avenue against a red light.

"This is almost as much fun as getting laid," Nashin said, pulling the belt tight across his lap. Ulanov drove to the middle of the block and spun the wheel, forcing the van up on the sidewalk and plowing into the improvised barricade of cars in front of 69 East Seventy-ninth Street, bulldozing the front ends of two automobiles aside and making a hole. Frightened men scurried for safety. Pedestrians stopped short, unsure what to do.

"My neck," Ulanov shouted in pain. "I hurt my neck."

Nashin unbuckled himself and helped the detective out of the driver's seat. He jumped behind the wheel and, grinding the transmission into reverse, recklessly backed the van across Seventy-ninth Street. "Here goes my promotion," he said, ramming his foot down on the gas pedal and slamming into low gear, aiming for the disarranged sedans. The police department vehicle smashed through the barricade and crashed into the doorway, unhinging the grillwork and the door.

Once again throwing the van into reverse, its broken tail pipe gouging the sidewalk and throwing sparks, Nashin attempted, unsuccessfully, to shift gears but was unable to, so he drove off in reverse, heading west. He got about fifty feet away from the consulate before being boxed in by cars full of angry men aiming an assortment of firepower his way.

Nashin rolled down the window and calmly announced, "We are Soviet diplomats."

Lucas waited for the light to turn green. He stamped his foot down on the gas pedal, propelling the Monte Carlo west-bound on Seventy-ninth Street. He reached out and tightened the passenger seat belt around the stacked sheets of plate glass.

Reaching the smoking barricade, he spun the wheel and drove the car up onto the sidewalk, plowing into the doorway, wedging the vehicle into the threshold and sending chunks of concrete and mortar crashing down. He tried to get out but couldn't; the front doors were crushed shut against the building's doorjambs. He forced the window partway down on the driver's side and, placing his face in the gap, shouted to the people milling about inside the consulate that he had the casket-copy.

A man stepped out of the group of stunned and frightened people and asked, "You're from Elisabeth?"

"Yes. Yes," Lucas shouted back, turning to see Hayden and several men running his way.

Two men with fire axes rushed up onto the hood of the car and began chopping out the windshield. Lucas covered his face with his hands to protect himself from the flying glass. When the windshield was gone, the Greeks formed a human chain; Lucas passed the glass plates out to them.

"Open the fucking door," Hayden shouted, pulling on the handles of the back door. Lucas ignored him; he went on passing plates out to the two men standing on the hood.

Hayden grabbed a rifle from one of his men and smashed in the rear window. Reaching inside, he opened the door and jumped on Lucas's back, putting a headlock on the policeman.

Lucas dropped a plate on the front seat and hurled himself backward, smashing Hayden into the doorpost. The two men lashed about, Hayden maintaining his stranglehold, Lucas pounding his elbows into his assailant's ribs. Meanwhile one of the Greeks climbed through the windshield and resumed passing out Alexander's *Iliad.* Hayden was screaming curses into the policeman's ear. Lucas felt his oxygen-starved body going limp, a cloud of blackness sweeping over him. He thrust his hand behind him and grabbed hold of Hayden's testicles, digging in his fingers and crushing them.

Hayden yowled and, releasing his grip, lunged for the policeman's hand.

"We have them all," one of the Greeks said from the hood of the car. "Thank you."

Lucas collapsed on top of Hayden. "It's over," he gasped.

Retching as he held his hand over his aching balls, Hayden muttered, "How will I ever be able to explain all of this?"

Breathing deeply, Lucas answered, "You just begin your report with, 'Once upon a time . . .'"

24

The forklift's claws held the flag-draped coffin. An honor guard had formed just inside Olympic Airlines' freight hangar at Kennedy airport. C of D Edgeworth, Lucas, Sergeant Grimes, Big Jay, Ulanov, Gregory, and Sergei Nashin tendered a breast salute as the lift rolled past them on its way out to the waiting cargo jet. Katina and Elisabeth Syros stood together off to the side, both with tears in their eyes.

Elisabeth came over to the file of policemen and, working her way from man to man, thanked each one of them for all that they had done. When she reached Lucas she pressed a gold strand of jade worry beads into his hand. "Andreas would have wanted you to have these. And his Beretta."

"Thank you," he said, adding, "I'm glad you're taking him home along with the casket-copy." He reached into his pocket and took out Cormick McGovern's shield. Handing it to her, he asked, "Will you see that they're together?"

"I'll tell Colonel Pappas," she said, putting the shield in her pocketbook.

Lucas reached down and picked up Denny McKay's shopping bag. "This is for the people of Voúla."

She looked down into the bagful of money. "Thank you," she said, and kissed him.

Lucas turned to watch the forklift darting out onto the apron. He thought about the first time he met Andreas in the customs office at Kennedy. It all seemed so long ago. He laughed bitterly to himself as he thought of the newspaper headlines of two days ago: NYPD THWARTS TERRORIST ATTACK ON GREEKS. Andreas would have approved of that tale; there was a certain Greek panache to the lie.

Watching the coffin being lifted up into the aircraft, he brushed tears from his face and whispered, "Good-bye, my friend."

"Lou, we're going back to the Squad," the Second Whip said. "I've got a desk full of fives waiting on me."

Lucas turned and looked at the sergeant. "I'll see you in seven days. I hooked some vacation time onto my swing."

"I'll hold it down," Grimes said, walking off with the rest of the detectives.

Nashin came over to Lucas and asked, "How's your vodka supply?"

"Getting low."

"I'll take care of it."

"Did you have any problems with the car?"

"None at all. My superiors were delighted with the material you gave us. Our labor camp population is about to increase."

"See ya 'round, comrade."

"Ten-four, Lou." Nashin snapped back briskly and walked away.

Long after the Olympic 747 had taxied out and moved off to the runway, Lucas stood by himself, looking out at the busy airport but seeing, in his mind's eye, the faces of Andreas and his wife and son. He actually jumped, startled, when he felt a hand grip his arm. It was C of D Tim Edgeworth, looking unusually subdued and thoughtful. The two of them stood without saying anything for several minutes. Then Edgeworth cleared his throat with a cough and said quietly, "I don't think Hayden is going to be collecting a pension from State." He rubbed his eyes wearily and continued: "I wouldn't be surprised if he ends up needing a good lawyer. A friend of mine called from Washington this morning. Apparently Hayden is facing an administrative review hearing. And I sent a memorandum of information to the U.S. attorney's office."

Lucas turned and stared directly at his superior officer. A thousand possible questions ran through his head—and the vision of a murdered Greek family stayed with him like some awful retinal afterimage. His hand unconsciously felt for Andreas's worry beads in the pocket of his dark suit.

"Tim," he asked in a hoarse, strained voice, "who were those two clowns working for?"

Edgeworth returned his stare without any change of expression. "In a strictly technical sense Hayden did represent the State Department." He paused, looking off into the distance. "But Teddy, they, I mean the

guys at State, the feds in the Bureau, the spooks at the Agency—
they're a lot like the department, like us. I get the same kind of paycheck you get. And so do those assholes in our Intelligence Division.
That doesn't mean that we are all one big happy family. You got Hay-
dens everywhere. His paycheck came from State, sure, but that don't
mean his loyalty got paid back. This guy, Cribb . . ."

"Yeah," Lucas interrupted. "I never heard of his outfit, this fine arts
setup. Katina says it was founded only a year or so ago."

Edgeworth waved his hand impatiently. "Listen, OK, Teddy? Just
shut up for a minute." The chief looked like a man expending considerable effort to control his temper. "Cribb is a curator—I mean he *was*
a curator for a museum on the West Coast. A fairly new one, with a
hell of a big endowment but not a hell of a great collection. Anyway,
he got promoted sideways when this foundation was set up. The old,
established museums didn't want it, didn't need it. Seems that a
bunch of people in the government thought it was a great idea. The
foundation would represent the interests of the new, smaller or poorer
museums. The ones ready to cut a few corners. The ones with patrons
and donors who own things that they got through . . . well, ways that
weren't strictly kosher."

A jet howling its way out to the runway momentarily drowned out
what Edgeworth was trying to say. He waited impatiently and went on
after the noise of the plane receded. "I don't know all of the fine
details, but Mastri, I mean Matrazzo, and Iskur, and even that poor
bastard, that diplomat who got offed—well, they were all part of an old
boy network. From what I understand, it all got started when people
who chased around Europe after the war looking for art and stuff the
Germans had stolen, guys in CIC and OSS and whatever, learned how
much money could be made selling stolen art. So they went on working for all kinds of different parts of the federal government—damn it,
they got paid, they got diplomatic passports—look at that guy in Athens."

"You mean that late Trevor Hughes," Lucas said bitterly.

"Yeah, him. He was a courier. Even put stolen stuff in the goddamn
diplomatic pouch."

Lucas held the worn worry beads out in the sun. "And Andreas
Vassos screwed up a nice thing for them, right?"

Edgeworth gave Lucas a hard look, one that told him to stop and
not push any further. "Yeah, they killed a cop. A damn good cop. They
are going to regret it—and not just the people who aided Matrazzo.
Denny McKay got recruited back when he was stationed in Japan. He
was a good printer and engraver. They picked him when he was working at a CIA base in Atsugi, creating stuff to help our pilots who got

knocked down over North Korea use escape and evasion routes. There are a lot of McKays out there."

Lucas began to walk away, then stopped and turned to look at Edgeworth. "So who puts them away, *sir?*" The last word came out with irrepressible bitterness.

Edgeworth clasped his hands behind his back and, rocking slightly back on his heels, evaded Teddy's eye. "I remember an old scrap of Latin that every police supervisor should worry about." Edgeworth frowned and pronounced the words carefully: "*Quis custodiet ipso custodes?* It means: Who will police the police? Teddy, it stops here. We got the guys that pulled the trigger. On a good day, that's the best we can hope to do."

Spiro and Anna Grantas greeted their guests in their restaurant's gaudy lobby. It was a little after eight at night and the band was holding back, husbanding their energy for later, when the Greeks arrived. Lucas stood on top of the steps looking into the crowded restaurant.

Katina watched him walk down and go to the center of the dance floor.

"Music for a Greek," he shouted in Greek, jolting the musicians out of their lethargy. The men on the bandstand looked down at the stranger and, seeing his red, swollen eyes, understood his needs. The tambourine man raised his shallow drum, shaking the metallic disks as he beat the drum with his fingers. The bouzouki came alive, as did the steel guitar and the *udte.*

Lucas, one leg crossed over the other, his arms outstretched at his sides, swayed to the rising and falling sounds of the music. Katina, watching him from the lobby, felt tears come to her eyes.

Lucas slowly began turning his body, swaying to the music, shouting in Greek, "Andreas, look, I'm dancing. I'm dancing."

SUSPECTS

*"But if the while I think of thee, dear friend
All losses are restored and sorrows end."*
Shakespeare, Sonnet 30, line 13

William E. Farrell, journalist, *The New York Times*
Joseph I. Grossman, sergeant, NYPD

Acknowledgments

I wish to thank the following people for their help and encouragement in the writing of this book: Theodor Saretsky, Ph.D.; Irene Gellman, Ph.D.; and Carlo and Eugent De Marco of the Orthopedic Studio, Brooklyn, New York.

Detectives George Simmons, Frank Nicolosi, Anthony Tota, Robert Cotter, and Mike Albanese of the NYPD's Ballistics Squad.

Knox Burger and Kitty Sprague for always being there. Detective Milagro Markman, the NYPD's hypnotist, for showing me how it is done.

A very large thank you to Giampaolo Panarotto for translating my prose into Italian.

I acknowledge a special debt of gratitude to Capt. Edward Mamet, NYPD, who took the time to teach me about stump-sock maintenance, edema, and the true meaning of the word courage.

The old man walked unnoticed into the park. His face was badly wrinkled and shaggy gray hair covered the tops of his ears. His clothes were old, his shoulders stooped; in his right hand was a large shopping bag brimming with rags and newspapers.

It was Thursday, a slow June day. The summer was not yet in full bloom; the heavy wet heat of July and August lay ahead. Mothers had gathered their children inside the play areas while teenagers hung out, listening to boxes playing hard rock at full volume. Several joggers slapped around the park's block-wide perimeter; a lone skater boogied along a pathway with his cassette earplugs affixed and his cosmic antennae bobbing. People with Slavic features sat on benches speaking Polish.

At the end of the parkway the old man came to the monument that had been erected to the heroes of the Great War. He paused and looked up at the statue with the human body and the birdlike face. Turning away, he moved to a nearby bench and sat, his wary eyes taking in the indifference around him. A woman sitting nearby hefted a baby playfully. She glanced at him and smiled. He scowled back. She quickly looked away.

The newcomer pulled the shopping bag onto his lap and reached inside. The peanuts were on the bottom, wedged under the cold barrel of a shotgun. He worked out the bag of nuts, put the shopping bag on the ground, and locked it between his legs. Leaning forward, he began tossing nuts into the quickly swelling flock of pigeons. There was nothing for him to do now but wait.

McGoldrick Park, a wide expanse of trees and forgotten monuments, was sandwiched between Driggs and Nassau avenues in the Greenpoint section of Brooklyn. It had once been named Winthrop Park but that name had been changed in order to honor the eighteenth-century cleric who had built St. Cecilia's Church on Herbert and Henry streets.

Across from the park, on Russell Street, the Lutheran Church of the Messiah was squeezed between two renovated town houses. Some of the row houses and the brownstones on that block had small patches of tended grass in front, and some had blue-and-white Madonnas.

The peanuts were gone. Most of the birds had strutted away. Some lingered. The pigeon feeder looked at his wristwatch, reached down and took hold of the shopping bag, and got up. Directly in front of him were two one-story buildings that were connected by a colonnade of Ionic columns. He examined the decaying facade of the most grandiose public toilet in the Borough of Brooklyn. The structure was enclosed within a high wire fence that was topped by loops of vicious concertina wire. Its cornices were festooned with signs: Danger—Under Repair.

Passing the lavatory on the women's side, the old man wandered over to the Antonio di Felippo statue, a bronze man hauling on a rope around a capstan. As he strolled around the monument he glanced beyond the park to the A&P supermarket on Driggs Avenue. His friend was not there. Had something gone wrong? His stomach churned.

Gazing up at the massive bronze figure, he noticed the cupid heart that someone had painted on the right buttock: KB loves KS.

The old man turned his head and looked again in the direction of the supermarket. This time he saw his friend standing there, a wan smile fixed on his face. The hairs on the old man's neck bristled. His hands were suddenly clammy, and a sense of isolation engulfed him. He began a slow walk toward Driggs Avenue, his shopping bag firmly in hand.

One block away from McGoldrick Park, Joe Gallagher was backing his dented '71 Ford Fairlane into a space on Pope John Paul II Square directly across the street from St. Stanislaus Kostka Church.

Leaning forward in his seat, Gallagher looked out at the traffic signs. No Standing 8 A.M. to 7 P.M. He took the vehicle identification plate from behind the visor and tossed it onto the dashboard. NYPD Official Business.

He got out of the car, leaned back inside, and slid a cake box off the front seat. With palms firmly planted under the box he crossed Driggs Avenue, heading for the open telephone booth on the corner. He was dressed in tan slacks over which hung the tails of a gaudy Hawaiian shirt that covered his potbelly and the holstered gun tucked inside his trousers.

He slid his parcel onto the skinny ledge, holding it in place with his stomach, and lifted the receiver off the hook. Dialing, he noticed a woman leading a Chihuahua, and watched her bend to place a sheet of paper under the squatting dog's behind.

Yetta Zimmerman's candy store was on Driggs Avenue, one block west of McGoldrick Park and across the street from St. Stanislaus Kostka Church. It was six stores in from where Joe Gallagher was making his telephone call. The shop was a long, narrow place that blossomed in the rear into a good-size storage area where Yetta stacked cases of soda and where two video games stood. A row of bare light bulbs hung from grimy chains fastened to a tin ceiling. An old-fashioned soda fountain was to the right of the entrance, and next to it was a rotating rack of paperbacks. Behind the soda fountain there was a large wooden display cabinet with sliding glass doors, crammed with cheap games and toys.

Yetta was a hulking woman with sad gray eyes and a thick jaw that sprouted scattered gray whiskers. Pussy jaw, some of the neighborhood boys would tease.

Yetta's was a local landmark. She had been operating her candy store for more than twenty-five years. It was where the neighborhood women held their morning coffee klatch to gossip about the neighborhood men. And it was where the neighborhood men came to borrow a five till payday.

Most of the people in this section of Greenpoint were of Polish ancestry. They enjoyed their daily visits to Yetta's, where they could argue in Polish over events in their native country and discuss the pros and cons of gentrification. On this Thursday afternoon Yetta was wearing a faded housecoat buttoned down the front and white socks and sneakers. Her newsprint-stained right ring finger bore only a plain, worn gold band.

She had just slid out change to a customer when she remembered that the fountain was nearly out of soda. She shambled out from behind the counter and went to the rear of the store, where she picked up the top case of soda. Lugging it past the video games, she glanced at the three boys playing the machines and thought that they should be saving their money instead of squandering it on such nonsense.

She had just about finished replenishing her stock when Joe Gallagher appeared in the doorway. "Here's your birthday cake." He beamed.

Yetta bustled out to greet him. She pulled him into a bear hug, forcing him to hold the box out to his side to avoid having it crushed.

"You're a good boy, Joe. Ol' Yetta appreciates you going out of your way for her."

A harsh voice barked from the doorway. "Hey you!"

Turning to look, they slowly backed out of their embrace.

The three boys looked away from the video games to see who had called out.

The pigeon feeder was framed in the doorway, his right hand deep inside his shopping bag.

Gallagher slowly measured the stranger, instantly sensing the presence of danger. There was something about that voice. Something in those eyes. The irises were white and had little specks of gray and the pupils were a deep . . . No! That was not possible. He knew those eyes. He took several steps toward the door, looking, making sure.

The shopping bag slid to the floor. Bottles and rags and newspapers scattered about. A Coke can rattled across the bleached wood floor and hit against the soda fountain, making an eerie clatter in the still, cool, dim interior of the shop.

Gallagher saw the shotgun coming up at him and blanched with fear. He lunged to one side and frantically reached under his shirt with his right hand, grappling for his gun. He was too late. The blast severed his right arm, spinning him around. The second explosion turned his face into a grotesque, bloody mask and hurled him backward, a look of horrible disbelief forever frozen in his one remaining eye.

"No! Not like this. Not after all that I've been through," Yetta Zimmerman shrieked. She tried to scream but the sounds would not come out. They were clogged somewhere in her throat so that only a frenzied gurgle came forth.

She wanted to run, to flee to safety, but her feet would not move. And then, when she saw the barrel being swung toward her, she closed her eyes and threw up her hands to cover her face.

2

Tony Scanlon sat at the end of Monte's long bar playing liar's poker with Davy Goldstein and Frankie Fats, the bartender. The Mets game was on the tube. It was a little after two P.M. Most of the lunch crowd had departed, so the waiters had begun to set up for the evening rush. A few of the neighborhood regulars were scattered along the bar.

Scanlon sipped Hennessy as he studied the palmed bill. He was holding four sevens. His long, narrow face was complemented by black eyes and jet-black hair graying at the temples. He was a handsome, well-built man of medium height, who at forty-three had a still-youthful face, a quick mischievous smile, and a cleft in his chin that formed the inverted apex of a ragged triangle. If El Greco had painted a cop, Scanlon would have been a perfect model.

Davy Goldstein was an owl-faced man in his mid-fifties who had a fondness for Havanas. He liked to smoke them from a cheap amber plastic holder. Nodding his head in concentration, Goldstein bid four threes.

The other players reexamined their hands.

A customer at the other end ordered a Martell.

Frankie Fats slid off the bar stool and waddled down the length of the bar. He was wearing a white-on-white shirt with the collar opened and his tie wrapped but unknotted, the broad half rolled over the top.

Monte's was on Wither Street, a small side street one block from the elevated highway of the Brooklyn-Queens Expressway, which separated the Polish section of Greenpoint from the Italian section. The houses in the Italian part were mostly one- and two-story dwellings of wood and clapboard. The streets in both parts were clean, and the buildings, unlike those in other parts of the city, were graffiti-free. On every Monday, Wednesday, and Friday an array of neatly tied green refuse bags lined the curbs of Greenpoint awaiting the garbage pickup.

Frankie Fats returned and draped his considerable rump over the top of the bar stool. He glanced at his hand and bid six fours.

Scanlon bid seven sevens.

Davy Goldstein called him.

They showed their bills. Scanlon's sevens had won it. He raked in the other players' bills. They were all folding new bills when the private line under the bar rang. Frankie Fats reached under, pulled out the receiver, and grunted into the mouthpiece. When Scanlon saw the bartender's tiny, piglike eyes dart to him, he knew that the plans he had made for the remainder of his day had just been changed for him.

That Thursday had begun for Tony Scanlon when he opened his eyes and reached out to shut off the buzzing alarm. Turning back onto his side, he inched his bulk across the queen-size bed to the other form. He began to rub his body against hers. She made a small catlike sound and moved with him. When it was time, she turned onto her stomach, snatched a pillow down, stuffed it under her, and spread her legs.

He mounted her, doggie-style.

Sally De Nesto could always tell when a man was ready to finish. She thrashed her head over the bed, miming sleepy ecstasy. "Come, Tony. Come with me," she moaned moments before his orgasm.

Scanlon lay on top of her, catching his breath, permitting himself the pleasure of leaving her body naturally. Her backside felt warm and nice, and he rubbed himself into the wetness of her.

Sally De Nesto reached her hand up and ran it through his damp hair. "You're one of the best, Tony."

He rolled off her onto the bed. "Sure I am," he said with sudden annoyance. He moved to the edge of the bed and sat up, reaching out for the prosthesis on the nearby chair. He pulled it over and rested it across his lap. He rolled the stump shrinker off the stump of his left leg, folded it, and put it down on the bed beside him. With both hands he kneaded his stump. The edema wasn't so bad this morning. He took the stump sock out of the socket of his prosthesis and rolled it up over his stump. He tilted back on the bed, elevated his stump, and slid the socket of the prosthesis over it. He stood, pressing his weight down on both legs, ensuring that the patellar tendon rested firmly on the patella bar of his artificial leg.

He moved into the bathroom and sat on the lip of the tub. He removed the prosthesis and the stump sock, put the sock inside the socket, leaned the leg against the wall, and slid around into the tub.

A few minutes later Sally De Nesto sat up in bed with a sheet across her chest, watching him get dressed. She wondered why she was so hung up on this one-legged man. Why the hell did she feel so much compassion for this one? After all, there were worse handicaps. And he certainly did handle his affliction well. He walked without a limp, had a good job, a cute cleft in his chin, and a subtle animal aura about him that made women pay attention to him. As he sat on the bed and slid into his trousers, she asked herself what it was about him that made her want to know more about him, and she decided that it was the simple fact that he didn't seem to give a rat's shit about her. There were other reasons too: the way his lips pulled back to form the cutest dimples, and there were those magnificent eyes that were so full of sadness. Many times she wondered about the woman who must have put the sadness there. Hookers are real connoisseurs of sadness.

At ten o'clock that Thursday morning Detective Lt. Tony Scanlon parked his car on Freeman Street, in the space in front of the Nine-three Precinct that was reserved for the squad commander. He walked to the candy store on the corner and bought three packets of De Nobili cigars. He left the store and went half a block on Freeman Street until he came to the end, the western tip of the Borough of Brooklyn. His gaze went across the East River to the shimmering towers of Manhattan. South, to the Twin Towers, they were in the First. North, to the Citicorp, that was in the Seventeenth. To the Empire State Building, that was in Midtown South. That's how a cop remembers prominent locations, by the precincts within which they are located. His forlorn stare fixed on the distant skyline. Manhattan. The same job, a different job. The Tenderloin. He used to work there. But then, that was ancient history.

Six minutes later Scanlon walked into the Nine-three Precinct and asked the desk officer what was doing. The gray-haired lieutenant with the half-glasses and heavy brogue lowered the *Wall Street Journal*, peered down at Scanlon from behind the high desk, and said, "And what could be doing here, Anthony?"

Scanlon walked behind the desk. He moved to the long green clerical cabinet and picked up the teletype message book. He paged through, scanning the latest messages. He turned his attention next to the Arrest Record. No arrests had been made in the Nine-three for three days. Going through the Unusual Occurrence Folder, he saw that the last Unusual had been prepared eight days ago when a car had exploded on the Brooklyn-Queens Expressway, killing the five occupants.

He saved the Personnel Orders for last. They would give him the pulse of the Job. Tell him who was transferred where. An inspector transferred out of the big building, as the cops called police headquarters, to Manhattan South was tracked for promotion. The same inspector transferred to Brooklyn North was being given a message to put his papers in.

As he looked over the latest orders he sighed in disgust when he saw that Inspector Sean O'Brien had been promoted to deputy chief and transferred from Support Service Bureau on the tenth floor of the big building to Management Analysis on the twelfth floor. They never go far from the breast, he thought, walking out from behind the desk. He crossed the muster room, heading for the curving staircase.

The Nine-three was considered one of the best houses in the city to work in. There were few crimes, plenty of available women, and many good restaurants where the man on post was always welcome.

The caseload of the Detective Squad did not warrant a lieutenant assigned as the Whip. But Scanlon had been put out to pasture after he lost his leg in the Adler Hotel payroll heist. "Take it easy, Tony. Go over to the Nine-three and enjoy the good life. You've paid your dues," retired Deputy Chief Kimmins had told him after his year-long recuperative leave was up. That was four years ago. And today Tony Scanlon was a man bored out of his tits.

Sipping coffee from a mug with the words "Slave Driver" painted across it, Scanlon crossed the squad room and entered the cubicle that was his office. Moving behind his desk, he glanced down at the Sixty sheet, the chronological record of all the cases that the Squad had caught for the year, and was pleased to see that the night team had closed out two more cases. Although he was out of the trenches, he still had a Detective Squad to run. And he, and every other detective commander in the city, knew that clearances were the only real standard by which they would be judged.

Stuck into the corner of his desk blotter was a slip of paper with the present whereabouts of two of his detectives. Detective Hector Colon was at his Polish girlfriend's apartment undergoing horizontal therapy, and Detective Howard Christopher was at the Y, swimming laps. Detectives Maggie Higgins and Lew Brodie were out in the squad room, holding it down.

After he read the *New York Times* and worked the crossword puzzle, Scanlon signed the few reports that were in the basket and then leaned back in his ancient, squeaky swivel chair to plan out the remainder of his tour. Looking out of his office he could see Maggie Higgins fast at work typing her term paper on human infanticide. Maggie was a senior at John Jay College and hoped someday to go to law school. She was a big woman with short brown hair and a willing smile. She favored loose-fitting tops that concealed her heavy bosom and offered her some protection against the endless stream of snide remarks from male detectives.

Maggie Higgins was a lesbian. Three years ago she had come out of the closet in order to testify before the City Council on the gay-rights bill. The bill was shelved for the ninth time and Higgins was flopped from the prestigious Bond and Forgery Squad to Greenpoint. The Nine-three Detective Squad had become a dumping ground for fallen angels.

Whatever reservations Scanlon had had about Higgins soon disappeared. She had turned out to be one of his best detectives when there was work to be done, which wasn't often. The other members of the Squad liked her too. Cops like an underdog. Especially one who has guts. It *had* taken guts to do what she had done, to come out. But the way the other members of the Squad felt about her did not prevent them from exercising their male egos at her expense. A cop's machismo knows no bounds.

It was a little after twelve forty-five in the afternoon when Scanlon strolled from his office and dragged a chair over to where Higgins sat. Lowering himself, he glanced over at Lew Brodie, who was at the next desk with his feet up, reading an old issue of *Soldier of Fortune* magazine. "I'm going on patrol, Maggie," Scanlon said, leaning forward, reading the page in the typewriter. In the lexicon of the Job, "going on patrol" meant that the Whip of the Nine-three Squad was off to his favorite watering hole, Monte's.

Higgins looked up at him and smiled. "I've got the number, Lou," she said, addressing him with the diminutive of "lieutenant" that was regularly used in the Job.

It had been Maggie Higgins's hurried telephone calls that had sent Tony Scanlon running from Monte's to the double-parked department auto in front, and had sent Hector Colon fleeing from his girlfriend's apartment, and had caused Howard Christopher to rush from the Y without showering.

When Scanlon arrived at the crime scene he found Driggs Avenue clogged with police cars, many with their turret lights still whirling and splashing red and white light on the faces of bystanders. The wail of sirens continued to fill the air. Units were responding from adjoining precincts. 10-13, Assist Patrolman; Report of an Officer Shot.

A sergeant stood by the open door of his radio car shouting into the radio, "Call it off! No further. No further."

Two lengths of cord had been hastily stretched from the entrance of Yetta Zimmerman's candy store to the handles of two radio cars. Police officers stood behind the barrier holding back gawkers. The forensics station wagon was parked on the sidewalk. Technicians were sliding out black valises, preparing for their grim but essential tasks.

Traffic for a five-block radius around the candy store was at a standstill. Scanlon had to double-park three blocks away and run the rest of the way. When he arrived at the scene, he straddled the cord barrier with his right leg, pushed the rope down with his hand, hefted the artificial leg over, and ran into the candy store.

Maggie Higgins rushed over to meet him. Her face was drawn and shocked. "It's Joe Gallagher," she shouted, as though unable to believe her own words.

Scanlon was stunned. Not Joe Gallagher! Not the Joe Gallagher who was the past president of the Holy Name Society. Not the Joe Gallagher who was the chairman of the Emerald Society. Not the same Joe Gallagher who acted as the unofficial master of ceremonies at department promotion and retirement rackets. Not Lt. Joseph P. Gallagher, NYPD. Not *that* Joe Gallagher. That one was immortal; everyone in the Job knew that.

He brushed past her and rushed into the store, recoiling from the carnage. Shards of bone and gray globs of brain were splattered about. An eye was attached to a bloody optic nerve. Chunks of body parts plastered the walls and the tin ceiling. A severed arm lay in a pile of whipped cream. Fragments of cake and raspberry filling had settled into the gore.

Yetta Zimmerman's body was sprawled over the top of the soda fountain, her arms stretched unnaturally over her head. In the rear of the store, detectives had corralled the three boys who had been playing the video games. The detectives were trying to calm them down and get statements.

Scanlon bent down next to the corpse on the floor. The face was gone. The body was the same size as Joe Gallagher; it had the same strong frame. He looked around the scene. Higgins came over to him and bent and began to search the body. Scanlon looked at her and said, "Whaddawe got?"—automatically lapsing into the dialect of the Job.

She looked up from her grisly task. "Two DOA by shotgun." She passed him the leather shield case she had just removed from the body. He snapped it open. Stared at the photograph on the laminated identification card. That familiar face. That familiar grin. The man standing before the red backdrop wore a blue uniform shirt and a black tie. His commanding presence could be felt even in the photograph. Scanlon visualized him walking into the monthly LBA meeting. Tall, proud, his brother lieutenants rushing to shake his hand.

Lt. Joseph P. Gallagher, NYPD . . . Postman, Return Postage Guaranteed.

Higgins raised the dead man's shirt to reveal a .38 Colt Cobra secured in an in-trouser holster. "He never had a chance to get it out," she said.

"What do we have on the woman?" Scanlon asked Higgins, looking over at the corpse.

"Yetta Zimmerman, age sixty-three, according to neighbors. Been operating this store for about twenty-five years."

"Physical evidence?"

"Three shell casings were found near the entrance. We also found a shopping bag that we think was used to conceal the shotgun," Higgins said.

Scanlon looked to the store's entrance and saw the evidence technician putting a shopping bag into a plastic evidence sheath. Standing a few feet away from the technician was a familiar face from the Ballistics Squad, Frank Abruzzi.

Scanlon went over to the ballistics detective, who was wearing plastic gloves and examining the base of a shotgun shell through a magnifying glass.

"Hello, Frank, whaddaya got for me?" Scanlon said.

Abruzzi looked up from the glass. "Howya doin', Lou? Long time no see. For starters, your perp used an automatic shotgun and sixteen-gauge shells." He held the glass over the base of the shell. "Take a look."

Scanlon bent and looked through the round glass.

"That mark that you see at three o'clock is from the firing pin. And the one at one o'clock is from the ejector. The mark at twelve o'clock is from the extractor."

"Which all means?" Scanlon said, looking up from the glass.

"I can't be positive," Abruzzi said, "but there is a good shot that your perp used a Browning automatic, Sweet Sixteen model. The Sweet Sixteen makes an unusual configuration like that. In most shotguns the firing-pin mark is closer to the center, and the extractor and the ejector marks are more dispersed."

"Could it have been concealed in a shopping bag?"

"Yes. The Sweet Sixteen breaks down. You turn a screw and push the barrel down. It takes seconds to break the weapon down."

Yetta Zimmerman's housecoat was shredded; her right breast was gone, in its place a scarlet patchwork of puffy black holes. "What notifications have been made?" Scanlon asked Higgins, who was standing a few feet away.

"Command and Control and the borough have both been notified," she said, moving up to him and handing him the wallet she had just finished tugging from Gallagher's back pocket. "Temporary headquarters has been established across the street, in the rectory."

Scanlon rummaged through the compartments in the wallet. The driver's license and the car registration were tucked in behind a wedding picture. Scanlon moved to the door and stood in the entrance. The crowd had grown. Reporters shouted questions at him from behind the rope barrier. Ignoring their racket, he carefully examined the streets for Gallagher's car. A homicide victim's car was important physical evidence. People keep things in their cars, important things, telling things. He spied a car fitting the description on Gallagher's registration parked on Pope John Paul II Square.

Stepping into the street, Scanlon took a sergeant by the arm and led him aside. He described the car and its location. "If the plate checks out, call department tow and have it brought into the house. Store it in the garage and have it safeguarded for prints," Scanlon told the sergeant.

Lew Brodie was a tough-minded detective with a poorly repaired harelip, broad shoulders, hooded eyes, and a drinking problem. He had been flopped out of the Manhattan North Homicide Task Force eighteen months ago because of what the department perceived to be his persistent and unnecessary use of force on minority citizens. Lew Brodie had been classified as Violent Prone. The department shrink had recommended a less demanding assignment. There were no blacks living in Greenpoint. And Lew Brodie had quite a different idea on the whole subject: he was a good cop who was conducting his own urban renewal program.

Brodie came up to Scanlon, looking down at his steno pad. "According to the three kids, Gallagher walked in and Zimmerman rushed out from behind the counter to greet him. Shortly thereafter the perp appeared in the doorway and shouted, 'Hey you,' and then proceeds to produce a shotgun from inside the shopping bag and starts blasting. The kids take a dive onto the floor. Job done, perp flees. We came up with two housewives who were on their merry way to the A&P and were passing the candy store as the perp ran from the store to a waiting blue van. License number eight eight Henry Victor Robert."

"Description of shooter," Scanlon demanded.

Brodie read: "Male. White, between five-five and five-nine. Wearing old black pants with paint stains on both legs, a white pullover under an army fatigue jacket. He had long gray hair, a wrinkled face, and a scruffy beard." He checked his notes. "That's it, so far."

"Age?" Scanlon asked.

Brodie shrugged. "There we got a problem. None of the witnesses can agree on this guy's age. The three boys say he was old, maybe in his sixties. One of the women says in his forties, and the other late thirties."

Detective Hector Colon came up to Scanlon and Brodie, who were standing over Gallagher's body, and without prelude read from his steno pad. "Lieutenant Gallagher had twenty-two years in the Job. Married with two kids. Lived in Greenpoint, 32 Anthony Street. He was assigned to the Seventeenth Narcotics District. He ran one of the buy-and-bust operations and worked out of the One-fourteen. He worked a ten hundred to eighteen hundred yesterday and swung out. His next scheduled tour was Saturday, an eighteen hundred to oh two hundred." Colon lowered his pad. "The PC and the borough commander have been both notified. The CO Labor Policy and the Catholic chaplain are on their way to notify Gallagher's wife."

Scanlon sighed. "And the Zimmerman family?"

"She was widowed with two grown kids," Colon said. "The son, a doctor, lives on East Seventy-ninth Street in the big city. The Nineteenth is going to make the notification."

Scanlon asked Brodie if they had come up with anything on the van.

"The driver was a male, white," Brodie said. "We ran the plate through NCIC and it came back not stolen. Then we checked for the registered owner and discovered that the owner ain't on file. We figure that it's probably a new registration. It takes Motor Vehicles about ninety days to get the new ones into the system. Biafra Baby is across the street in temporary headquarters calling Motor Vehicles in Albany on the department tieline. They should be able to tell us something."

Scanlon took out a De Nobili and lit it, carefully inserting the dead match between the back cover and the bottom file of matches and putting the matchbook back into his pocket. He shifted the cigar to the other side of his mouth. "Anything on the murder weapon?"

"Among the missing," Higgins said, working the wedding band off Yetta Zimmerman's lifeless finger.

Sucking on the cigar, Scanlon surveyed the crime scene. First impressions were important; some overlooked point could later prove vital. Too many bad guys walked because some detective failed to do what he was trained to do during the preliminary investigation. He recalled the DOA that had been discovered last month on Crown Street in the Seven-one. The radio car team first on the scene reported back that the DOA appeared natural. The detective who responded to the scene found nothing suspicious. The ME in his not unusually casual fashion endorsed natural causes. The undertaker had the gall to report that he had discovered a tiny hole behind the left ear that later proved to have been made by a .22 short. There were a lot of red faces and a lot of excuses in Brooklyn North over that one. It pissed Scanlon off when a case went bye-bye because of police ineptitude. So he moved all around the crime scene, satisfying himself that what was supposed to be done was done.

He examined the glass fractures that the stray shotgun pellets had made in the doors of the display cabinet. The radial and concentric fractures formed cobwebs with holes the shape of volcano craters. Looking inside the opened door he noticed numerous flakes of glass in the guiding tracks. Some of the shot had embedded itself in the wall of the cabinet. He motioned to one of the forensics technicians. Moving out from behind the soda fountain, Scanlon went up to Hector Colon and told him that he was going across the street to the rectory.

According to the *Patrol Guide*, a temporary headquarters will be used to coordinate police resources at the scene of an emergency when the circumstances of the occurrence indicate that the police operation will continue for a period of time and when direct telephone communications and record keeping will improve efficiency. The green police standard and lantern were on station outside the rectory to indicate to members of the force that temporary headquarters was located inside that building. Scanlon took the rectory steps two at a time.

The NYPD had commandeered the waiting room to the left of the large foyer. The walls were done in mahogany paneling, and there was a heavy oak desk with ornate scrollwork edging its borders. A large crucifix hung on the wall behind the desk, and long lace curtains covered all the windows. Two elderly priests were sitting on a carved wooden bench watching with muted amazement as their serene residence was converted into a message center for a murder investigation. A sergeant with dirty-blond hair sat behind the desk manning the Headquarters Log, entering a chronological record of personnel and equipment at the scene, listing specific assignments.

Linemen from the Communications Division were busy installing additional lines, the numbers of which had already been telephoned to Command and Control, Patrol Borough Brooklyn North, and the Nine-three Desk.

Scanlon signed himself present in the Log. He went over the list of assignments with the sergeant. From the corner of his eye, he spotted

Detective Simon Jones elbowing his way through the crowd. Scanlon shouted to Jones, "What's with the van?"

Simon Jones had a long thin frame and a tiny potbelly, and a head of untamed kinky hair that looked like a beehive undergoing constant electric-shock treatment. His long bony arms appeared to reach down to his knees. His skin was coal-black and he had a voice laced with a heavy Mississippi drawl. Ten years ago a detective in the Fifth Squad had commented that Jones looked like one of the starving Biafra babies. The nickname stuck.

Jones came over to Scanlon. "Just got off the phone with the owner of the van," he said, patting down his hair. "The man done told me that he bought the van one month ago off a lot off Ocean Parkway in Brooklyn. He parked it last night three blocks from his home and when he went to get it this afternoon, the mother was gone. He was on his way to his local precinct to report it when I telephoned. The owner's name is Frank Lucas. He resides at 6890 South View Lane in Bath Beach."

Scanlon cursed under his breath; he had been hoping that the van had been stolen from someplace in Greenpoint. He had markers out in Greenpoint. He turned to the sergeant manning the Log and told him to telephone the precinct concerned in Bath Beach and have detectives dispatched to do an immediate canvass of the area where the van had been stolen. He picked up the receiver of one of the recently installed telephones and dialed the One-fourteen. He spoke briefly to the desk officer. He signed out in the Log, and he and Biafra Baby returned to the crime scene.

Higgins met them just inside the entrance. "Their property," she said, holding the victims' personal property in two separate evidence bags.

Scanlon turned to Biafra Baby. "I want you to transport the witnesses into the house. Make sure they're kept separated. I don't want them talking to one another about what they saw, changing their minds."

Biafra Baby nodded and made his way to the rear of the candy store. A short time later he reappeared leading three frightened boys. They came in single file, the witnesses looking away from the bodies, their feet attempting to avoid stepping on pieces of the two bodies.

Lew Brodie brought up the rear of the staggered column. Scanlon called to Brodie. "The witnesses agree—the perp yelled 'Hey you' and fired?"

"That's how it went down," Brodie said over his shoulder.

Parallel shafts of sunlight speared through the candy store's open facade, reflecting on the dead woman's matted hair and diffusing a shimmering hue of yellow through the pools of blood.

Higgins looked down at Gallagher's body. "Then it wasn't a robbery."

Scanlon's voice took on an edge. "It was a hit, Maggie. But on which one?"

3

Tony Scanlon stood back and watched the sergeant slip the steel jaws around the shackle of the black-faced combination lock. The sergeant's intense face was a sunburst of broken blood vessels. A cigarette that was one quarter gray ash dangled between his thin lips. Gripping the handles, he pressed the arms of the bolt cutter together and the lock fell apart.

Scanlon had wanted to be present when Gallagher's locker was broken into. A cop's locker was a secret place; it was a place to hide things. He had told Higgins where he was going and why, and then had left the crime scene. He knew that he wouldn't be missed for a while, not with all the commotion connected with a cop killing.

The drive from Greenpoint to the One-fourteen in Astoria, Queens, had taken Scanlon twenty minutes. The precinct was located on Astoria Boulevard, directly across from the sunken highway that leads onto the Triboro Bridge.

Many of the city's seventy-two patrol precincts provide space for "overhead" units, units whose responsibilities encompass entire borough commands, unlike patrol precincts that must operate within set boundaries. Queens Internal Affairs, Public Morals, and Narcotics were quartered in the One-fourteen.

When Scanlon arrived he had found the flag at half-staff and policemen standing on ladders hand-draping the mourning purple over the entrance. A group of grim cops stood bunched on the steps, talking in angry tones. Walking into the station house, Scanlon had overheard snatches of their conversation. It had been a robbery attempt, one said. Joe Gallagher had taken police action, another maintained. Cock-suckers, groused a third.

The foul smell of old sweat permeated the cramped space of the locker. Uniforms were pinched together; a gunbelt hung from a rear hook; several nightsticks were clumped together. The blouses and jackets had gold bars on the shoulders. The sergeant complained that the overhead units should have their own locker rooms instead of being grouped in with the precinct's. This was the fourth locker that he had had to break into during his twenty-two years on the Job. The sergeant pushed uniforms aside, looking around, searching.

Scanlon focused his attention inside the locker. If there was anything there to be found he wanted to find it before word leaked out that Lt. Joe Gallagher might not have died a hero. Things have a mysterious way of disappearing whenever a cop is jammed up. It had happened recently in the Three-six. IAD was set to arrest the sergeant in charge of the precinct's gambling car. The complaint alleged that the sergeant had a pad going with the numbers men along Lenox Avenue. Word was leaked to the Three-six's PBA delegate by a cop who used to work in the Three-six. The precinct's Residence Known Gamblers File, and the Arrest Record, and three years' worth of roll calls vanished. Overnight. IAD called it a concerted conspiracy to obstruct justice. The cops in the Three-six called it an obvious act of God.

The sergeant began his disagreeable task. As each article of uniform was taken out it was searched to ensure that there was nothing in the pockets that might prove embarrassing to the family. SOP. Scanlon watched everything the other cop did. A rosary was draped over the locker's face mirror, and stuck into the frame were the photographs of three smiling women. Scanlon pushed the sergeant aside, removed the pictures, and put them into his pocket. The sergeant saw him do this but said nothing.

Gallagher's helmet was on the floor inside its carrying case. Scanlon bent and felt with his hand around the inside of the case. It turned out to be the repository for several flashlights and packets of used memo books that were bound together by rubber bands.

On the top shelf there were winter and summer uniform hats stacked one inside the other, two boxes of ammunition, a slapper, three blackjacks, and an assortment of knives, razors, and ice picks. A Chuka stick was lying next to Gallagher's shaving things.

The sergeant thrust his hand into the inside pocket of Gallagher's cloak raincoat. "Look at what we got here," he said, removing a Turkish Kirikkals 7.55 pistol.

"Is it on his Ten Card?" Scanlon asked, knowing that it wouldn't be.

The sergeant picked up Gallagher's UF 10, Force Record Card, from the bench that ran along the aisle between the row of lockers. He turned the department pedigree form over, to the section at the bottom that listed the description and serial numbers of all the weapons that Lt. Joseph P. Gallagher, NYPD, was authorized to possess. The sergeant glanced over the card. "It's a throwaway," he said, tucking the unauthorized pistol into his waistband.

They were beginning to find things.

While the sergeant was busy searching the pockets of a winter blouse, Scanlon reached up into the locker and pushed the hats aside. A shoe box lay on top of a multi-use envelope. He took them both out and stepped away from the locker, sitting astride the narrow wooden bench. He lifted the lid of the shoe box. His eyebrows arched with surprise when he saw the double-headed dildo lying on a stack of amateurish pornographic pictures. He shuffled the contents about, searching. One of the photographs showed a woman on a bed laughing as she inserted a dildo into her body. In another, a woman's hand was guiding a penis into her vagina. He replaced the lid on the shoe box. Picking up the multi-use envelope, he unwound the red string on the flap.

"Whaddya find?" asked the sergeant, searching a summer blouse, not bothering to look.

"Just some papers," Scanlon said, studying the rent receipts and utility bills for an apartment in Jackson Heights. He reached behind and picked up the Ten Card. Gallagher's official residence was 32 Anthony Street, in Greenpoint.

The NYPD's Catholic Man of the Year for 1978 was fast becoming an interesting person.

A short time later Scanlon helped carry the uniforms and equipment downstairs to the Desk, where a blotter entry would be made of the forced entry into a member of the force's locker and the property that had been removed would be invoiced.

The uniforms were folded into a neat pile on a desk in the clerical office to await a member of the immediate family, whose unpleasant duty it would be to select Gallagher's burying clothes. It was then customary for the family member to donate the remaining uniforms to the precinct, where they would be stored in the "saver" locker. Whenever a cop needed to replace a torn or worn article of uniform he would go to the locker and search for a "saver" his size. Uniforms were expensive.

No record was made of the throwaway that had been found in Gallagher's raincoat. That too would be "saved," awaiting the proper police emergency.

Watching the desk officer make the entries in the blotter, Scanlon lit up a De Nobili, picked up the desk phone, and dialed temporary headquarters.

Higgins answered.

"How's it going?" he asked, passing the cigar under his nose.

"This place is a madhouse. The PC and his entourage have arrived."

"Are the witnesses in the house?"

"Yes. Brodie just called. They're being interviewed and are pretty much sticking to their stories."

"Anything back on the van?"

"Jacob from the Six-two Squad called. They did a canvass and came up dry. I transmitted a fifteen-state alarm."

Scanlon turned his back to the desk officer and said in a low voice, "Anybody looking for me?"

"Naw. All the brass are running around preening for the television cameras and trying to think up a synonym for 'perpetrator.' We have things organized and the worker ants are all out knocking on doors."

"Maggie," he whispered, "get to the PC and tell him not to go out on a limb on this one. There's a *problem*."

"What did you find?"

"We'll talk when I get back."

Eight minutes later Tony Scanlon left the station house and made his way along the side of the gray stone building to the walled-in motor pool. He wound his way around parked department vehicles to his own, which was near the gas pumps. He slid in on the driver's side, tossing the shoe box and the multi-use envelope onto the seat. He started the car. Remembering the photographs that he had taken from the rim of the face mirror in Gallagher's locker, he glanced down at the shoe box. He flipped off the lid and removed several of the pornographic pictures, spreading them out over the seat, separating them by actresses. He slid the pictures from the face mirror out of his pocket and began to compare faces. They matched.

"Lt. Joe Gallagher exemplified all that was good and decent within the police department. He was a hero who died as he lived, serving the people of this great city." Roberto Gomez's voice cracked. He turned away from the microphones, covering his face with his hands, slowly counting to twenty. A hush fell over the reporters as they waited for the police commissioner to regain his composure, to continue his impromptu news conference.

Bob Gomez was the first member of a minority group to become PC. He was himself a hero to the city's Hispanic community. To them it did not matter how the press and the public at large anglicized Gomez's name. He was their Roberto, their Bobby.

Gomez had started out in the police department as a real street cop, walking a beat in the Eight-one. He had worked steady six to two on a gambling post so that he might attend Brooklyn College during the day and later St. John's Law School. He was the first member of the Hispanic community to be promoted to the rank of captain. He had retired from the police department several years ago to head the city's Department of Social Services. When the present mayor had been accused three years ago by the city's black community of insensitivity to the needs of minorities, the mayor squelched the rising controversy with the appointment of Bob Gomez as PC. The blacks weren't happy about getting a Hispanic consolation prize, but they shut up. A master political stroke, the appointment was called in the press. The mayor was delighted. But there were many of the mayor's advisers who had counseled him against the Gomez appointment. It was an open secret within the city administration and particularly within the police department that Bob Gomez had developed several bad habits over the years. Habits that could hurt an ambitious mayor.

Bob Gomez dropped his hands and sighed deeply. He faced the reporters, ready to continue his performance. He immediately lapsed into his favorite homily on the need for more police, on the need for a judicial system that did not mollycoddle criminals, on the right of every citizen to be secure in his person and property, on the need for the abolition of concurrent sentencing.

With his arms stretched out at his side, Bob Gomez once again proclaimed that Lt. Joe Gallagher had died a hero.

When Scanlon arrived back at the crime scene he saw the PC answering reporters' questions. Gathered around the commissioner was the top echelon of the Job, grim men all in their late fifties. Conspicuously absent from the group was Chief of Detectives Alfred Goldberg. Scanlon spotted the CofD standing about twenty feet away from the PC surrounded by a loyal coterie of subordinates from within the Detective Division. Goldberg was glaring at the PC. It was no secret inside the Job that the two men hated each other. Goldberg had expected to be named PC, and when the job went to Gomez, Goldberg flew into one of his famous temper tantrums and proceeded to wreck his tenth-floor office, sending subordinates fleeing from his wrath.

Gomez had inherited Goldberg and would have replaced him with his own man if he could have. But he couldn't. The CofD was the darling of the Jewish real estate interests, the garment district, and the city's shadowy diamond industry. Neither the mayor nor the PC had the political clout to dump Goldberg. The CofD was entrenched and he damn well knew it.

As Scanlon paused on the rectory steps to take in the gathering of police brass, he noticed detectives scurrying through the crowd of onlookers canvassing for witnesses. What a way to run a job, he thought, entering the temporary headquarters. Scanlon moved directly up to the Log. A fifteen-block area around the crime scene had been divided into quadrants. A sergeant and ten detectives had been assigned to each quadrant. The occupants of every house and of every business would be questioned. People on the street would be stopped and questioned. Mailmen and bus drivers would be questioned. Emergency service units had been dispatched to search sewers and refuse cans for discarded physical evidence. Every assignment was listed in the Log; every assignment required a detailed report on a Five—a DD 5 Supplementary Complaint Report.

Scanlon found Higgins leaning over the rectory's ornate desk collating Fives and stuffing them into the Gallagher/Zimmerman case folder. "I just saw the PC making with a press conference," he said, coming up to her. "Didn't you give him the word?"

She looked up at him. "I most certainly did. But in his infinite wisdom Bobby Boy chose to ignore your advice. So up his." She went back to her task.

"Did you tell him yourself?"

"Detectives do not personally tell the PC anything. I relayed your message through the first deputy commissioner and he passed it on to Bobby."

Scanlon looked around at the crowd of policemen gathered inside the temporary headquarters. He turned back and asked her what she was doing. "I'm fastening Fives inside the homicide folder so that they coincide with each quadrant."

"Leave that for now," he said. "I want you to bang out the Unusual."

Howard Christopher was a tall, lean man who was always impeccably dressed in the latest Sears, Roebuck fashions for men. He had a pasty white face with an overlarge forehead. He was a gentle man with a warm smile and an addiction to soap operas and health food. As a major in the National Guard and a staunch believer in military courtesy, Christopher would never have thought of debasing the rank of lieutenant with the diminutive. He came up to Scanlon with his steno pad held out in front of him and began his report. "Lieutenant, it looks as though we're beginning to develop an outline of how this caper went down." Christopher went on to report that the killer's movements prior to the murders had been backtracked. There was a butcher in the Danzig meat market on Driggs Avenue who stated that he had seen a man who answered to the killer's description walk past the store a few minutes before the time of occurrence. And there was this A&P stock clerk on a coffee break. He had been leaning against one of the loading bays having a smoke when he noticed an old man with a shriveled face walk out of McGoldrick Park clutching a shopping bag. And there was a mother who had been sitting on a bench in the park playing with her baby. A creepy old man with an unfriendly glare had sat down on the next bench, she had told detectives.

Christopher reached into the pocket of his brass-buttoned light brown sport jacket and removed a glassine evidence bag containing peanut shells. He dangled it before Scanlon. "Lieutenant, I'm sending these to the lab. You never know, we just might get lucky."

Deputy Chief MacAdoo McKenzie, the CO of Brooklyn North Detectives, was an oversize fireplug of a man, a nervous type who wore ill-fitting clothes that never matched. Every time Scanlon saw him he was reminded of a bin full of used parts.

McKenzie pushed his way through the crowd inside temporary head-quarters and came up to Scanlon. In his customary caustic tone, he said, "Whaddaya got on this one, Scanlon?"

Scanlon led the chief away from the others and calmly confided the results of the preliminary investigation. "A hit!" growled MacAdoo McKenzie. He began to sweat. He yanked a dirty, snot-encrusted hand-kerchief from his pocket and wiped his hands. "Joe Gallagher murdered? I can't believe that. Not him. It just don't seem possible. I can't believe that he's gone."

"That's the trouble with death, Chief. Everybody wants to go to heaven but nobody wants to die."

McKenzie gave him a dirty look. "Gallagher must have been into something he shouldn't've been into. Nobody ups and whacks a police lieutenant for nothing. Maybe Joe went into the junk business for himself?" He wiped the back of his neck. "If the press gets hold of this they'll have a field day with it."

"It doesn't always have to be the cop who's the bad one, Chief. Zimmerman might have been the mark."

McKenzie's face flushed. "That's bullshit and you know it. It's al-ways the fucking cops, sergeants, and lieutenants who are forever get-ting jammed up. I'll tell you this much—this Job can't afford too many more scandals. Six cops and a sergeant were just arrested in the Tenth for riding shotgun for coke dealers. And another five in the One-ten went down the tubes for wheelin' and dealin' with Colombian juice joints. If we're not careful, we're going to get ourselves another Knapp Commission. And this time when the politicians are through with us we'll find ourselves with total civilian control over the Job." McKenzie looked uncomfortable. He was shuffling his weight from one foot to the other.

"Chief, I'm a team player. You know that. But you tell me how we're gonna play it didn't happen."

"Dunno. But I do know that you're going to sit on this one until we do know what happened inside that candy store. And as far as the rest of the world is concerned Joe Gallagher died a hero interrupting a holdup."

Watching MacAdoo McKenzie lumber away, Scanlon thought, How quick they are to always brand the cop the bad guy. Typical Palace Guard mentality. It's always the guys below them that screw up.

Scanlon moved around temporary headquarters making sure that everything was being done correctly. He noticed Howard Christopher pondering the bag of peanut shells and went up to him and asked him if there was a problem. Christopher looked at him with questioning eyes and said that he wasn't sure if a Letter of Transmittal was needed with the Request for Laboratory Analysis. Scanlon told him that it was and went on to remind him that the Letter of Transmittal preserved the chain of evidence. He patted Christopher on the shoulder and moved off. Higgins was busy folding copies of the Unusual into white department envelopes. Scanlon went up to her and read a copy of it. When he finished reading the report he folded it in the prescribed manner, in three equal folds parallel with the writing with the top fold folded toward the back of the letter, so that the entire heading could be seen without unfolding the communication, and handed it to her.

After she had addressed the last of the envelopes he told her to grab her pocketbook. They were going to take a little trip over to Jackson Heights. A cop's splash pad was a most secret place, and Scanlon was sure that he would find things there.

Scanlon pocketed the keys that Higgins had removed from Gallagher's body and pulled the door closed behind them. They were in a dark, musty place, apartment 3C. A narrow hall connected the front room and a kitchen. Higgins turned on her small pocket flashlight, found the wall switch, and flipped it on. A cheap redwood veneer covered the walls; five spotlights shone down from recessed fixtures. As they stepped into the apartment they saw a bathroom directly in front of them. Higgins went into it and switched on the three-bulb fixture over the sink. Cockroaches scattered into cracks.

Scanlon moved into the front room, went over to the gold-and-white drapes, and reached behind them. Finding the cord, he pulled. Late-afternoon sunlight came through the filthy windows. He looked around the room. Cobwebs were on the ceiling around the steam pipe. Carpet remnants covered the floor in a quilt of colors. A tweed convertible sofa was up against the far wall, and next to it was a three-legged serving table on which sat a telephone and an address book. He went over and picked up the address book and began to flip alphabetized tabs. The name Harris was listed under H. It had a 516 telephone number that had been crossed out and replaced by a 718 number. In parentheses next to it was "Luise" and a 212 number. The book also contained police department numbers, direct unlisted numbers. He found the telephone numbers of police benevolent organizations and police fraternal organizations. When he had gone through the entire book he discovered four additional names: Donna, Valerie, Mary, and Rena. The remainder of the numbers were all connected in some way to the Job.

The address book in a cop's splash pad would only contain a few numbers that were all connected to his secret life. And police department numbers; the Job was the bridge that connected both lives. The people in Joe Gallagher's other life would all have to be interviewed. He heard a noise and turned. Higgins was framed in the doorway. "What a dump."

"I'm sure that it served its purpose," he said, placing the address book on the sofa. "Find anything in the bathroom?"

"A few rusting blades and a rolled-up tube of toothpaste. No woman ever called this place home."

"What made you reach that conclusion?"

"Because a woman would keep certain things in any apartment that she was using as a rendezvous—cleansing lotions, a hair dryer, napkins, extra panties."

He rose effortlessly from the sofa and caught her watching him with the same astonished look that he had seen on so many other faces, a look that said: He moves and acts as though both his legs were real.

A pair of sliding doors enclosed the closet built into the wall directly to the right of the tweed convertible. He slid the right side open. A few articles of men's clothing hung from wire hangers. There was a movie screen leaning up against the wall, and on the floor next to it was an 8mm projector. The closet contained three shelves on brackets. The first one acted as the bar, and the second contained a stereo tape deck, record player, and AM/FM receiver. The top shelf was crammed with movie tins. He took out a handful and read titles aloud: "*Annie Can You Come? Big Cock Harry. Andy Hardy and the Nuns. Come Again Sweet Lips.*"

"Do you think the precinct CO might like to show a few of them at the next Community Council meeting?" she asked.

He burst out laughing. "Some of those biddies would drop their store-bought teeth." As he said this, his gaze fell to the bottom of the closet, to the department storage carton. He dragged it out and over to the sofa, where he sat and flipped off the cover. He spilled the contents onto the floor. Nipple creams and prolong creams, and joy jellies, and emotion lotions, and edible panties in many different flavors, piled up in a bizarre heap. He sat rummaging in the pile. Ben Wah balls, anal love beads, dildos, vibrators.

He glanced over at Higgins. She clasped her hands to her chest and with fluttering lids said, "What is this world coming to?"

He picked up one of the vibrators and read aloud: " 'A clitoral vibrator. This unique machine may be worn during intercourse. It is excellent for masturbation and for facilitating orgasm during intercourse. Luv-Joy Manufacturing Company, Brooklyn, New York.' " He dropped it back into the pile and picked up a set of Ben Wah balls. Turning them over in his hands, he glanced up at Higgins, a silly expression curling the ends of his lips, showing his teeth.

"Don't look at me," she protested. "I don't use them."

Before entering the apartment, they had canvassed the tenants in the four-story walk-up and found that none of them knew the occupant in 3C. A retired postal worker in apartment 1A had stated that he used to see the man in 3C entering and leaving from time to time in the company of different women. "It looked mighty suspicious to me," the toothless old man had confided.

During the drive into Manhattan, Scanlon noticed Higgins looking at her watch and saw the concern seeping into her face. "You pressed for time?" he asked.

"Gloria and I moved in together. She's making our first homemade dinner tonight." Gloria Lufnitz was a twenty-nine-year-old music teacher at Music and Art High School and Detective Maggie Higgins's lover.

"What made you decide to move in with her? I thought you were happy the way things were."

"She wanted to. I was perfectly content. We'd spend weekends together and a few nights a week and everything was great. But Gloria wanted to play house, so I went along."

"Good luck."

She smiled her thanks.

Higgins parked the department auto at the bus stop on Worth Street and went to telephone Gloria to tell her that she was going to be late. At five-thirty Scanlon hurried into the huge, empty lobby of the telephone building.

Two massive steel doors confronted him when he stepped off the elevator on the thirty-seventh floor. One of the four armed security guards stationed there asked to see his police credentials. After he handed them to the guard, and the credentials were scrutinized, he was permitted to sign in the Visitors Log. Then he was required to stand before a Polaroid camera that was mounted on a desk and have his picture taken. This done, a button was pressed and the steel doors opened, and he was permitted to enter Ma Bell's secret security service headquarters.

When Scanlon emerged from the building thirty minutes later he was in possession of the names and addresses of the subscribers whose telephone numbers had appeared in Joe Gallagher's most private address book. Sliding into the passenger seat, he said, "Did you make your call?"

Higgins drove out of the bus stop. "She was pissed off. Said that she cooked a roast and that it'll be dried out by the time I get home."

"Your girlfriend is going to have to get used to your being on the Job."

She smiled bitterly. "That's easy for you to say." She glanced at the list of names he was holding. "Are we going to pay the ladies a visit?"

"We'll let them stew awhile."

They lugged the carton of sexual paraphernalia and the address book into Scanlon's office and put it on top of one of the file cabinets.

Christopher walked into the Whip's office nibbling sunflower seeds. He brought Scanlon up to date on what was happening at temporary headquarters. He began his report with "Lieutenant" and went on to say that forensics technicians were still at the crime scene conducting tests, and that some of the detectives who had been "flown in" from other commands to assist with the preliminary investigation had been sent back to their own commands. Some of the buildings around the scene were still being canvassed.

Lew Brodie came into the office and handed Scanlon a long sheet of four-ply paper. "Thought you might wanna take a look at the Incident Log," Brodie said.

Scanlon took the paper from him and detected the faint odor of alcohol. He gave Brodie an annoyed look and then scanned the computerized printout of all the radio transmissions connected with the double homicide. He let his eyes sweep over the neatly arranged columns of computer symbols and abridgments. After one fast read-through, he went back to the beginning and started over, this time taking his time translating the symbols.

The initial call had been received at 911 by operator 42 at 1404 hours. The anonymous caller had reported that a police lieutenant had been shot at 311 Driggs Avenue. Operator 42 had typed the address into her queue and a display peeled onto the lime-green screen that had shown 311 Driggs Avenue to be within the confines of the Nine-three Precinct, sector Boy. RMP 1704 was assigned to that sector this tour, and the display showed that that radio motor patrol car was currently not on assignment. Operator 42 transmitted code signal 10-13, Assist Patrolman, Officer Shot.

Scanlon read the verbatim transmissions of the responding radio cars: "Boy, on the way. Sergeant going. George going. Frank going. Crime, responding from the other end."

Whoever had made that call to 911 had *known* that Gallagher was a police lieutenant. How? Gallagher had not been in uniform. Scanlon looked up at Christopher. "Where are the witnesses?"

"The women are upstairs in the Community Relations office with the department artist," Christopher said.

"Who interviewed the first team on the scene?" Scanlon asked.

"Colon," Brodie said.

"Where is that team now?"

"They're waiting downstairs in the sitting room," Brodie replied.

"I'm going upstairs," Scanlon said to Brodie. "When I come back I want to see those cops waiting for me."

"You got it, Lou," Brodie said.

The walls of the third-floor Community Relations office were covered with posters that were designed to address public fears: Be a Block Watcher; Vertical Patrol, the Answer to Residential Burglaries; The Auxiliary Police—Our Eyes and Ears.

A PR hand job, Scanlon thought, glancing at the posters as he plunged into the office. The department artist was a bald middle-aged detective who wore thick horn-rimmed glasses. The artist glanced up from his drawing board and nodded recognition to Scanlon. They had worked together on the Rothstein homicide, six years ago. Cops remember their unsolved cases. Two women sat on either side of the artist. The one on the right was Mary Cilicia, a woman of thirty-six or so who had a round plump face. She wore what appeared at first glance to be a bathing cap covered with blue plumes. Many women in Greenpoint wear such hats. She wore a blue polyester pantsuit with a diamond design. The other woman, Mary Adler, was twenty-eight; she had a tiny mole on the right side of her nose with two long hairs sprouting from it, and she had a potbelly and sagging breasts.

Scanlon walked up behind the artist and looked over his shoulder. "How's it going?" he asked, studying the charcoal drawing of a killer's face. A face with wrinkled skin and hair that covered the tips of ears.

"Okay, Lou," the artist said, making an erasure and blowing the residue away. "The ladies have been a big help."

Scanlon smiled at the women. They smiled back. He noticed that they both wore dentures, a not uncommon sight in his area. Poor people can't afford good dental care. "Do either of you ladies know who telephoned nine-eleven to report that a policeman had been shot?" He stared into their innocent faces.

Mary Cilicia didn't know who had made the call; the first they knew that a cop had been killed was when they were being driven to the station house. One of the detectives had told them.

There were two policemen waiting when Scanlon swept back into his office fifteen minutes later. He went up to his desk and wrote himself a note on the department-issued tear-off calendar: "Get tapes and do round robin on G." He turned his attention to the two policemen who were lounging on green department swivel chairs. Lew Brodie was leaning with his back against the wall, his left foot braced on it and his left arm draped over the top of a filing cabinet. Brodie introduced the cops to Scanlon. Stone and Trumwell.

Scanlon nodded at the cops and said, "Where were you two when the initial thirteen came over?"

Trumwell had a badly pockmarked face and red hair. "Apollo and Bridgewater streets," he said, stretching his legs out in front and examining the tips of his scuffed shoes.

"When you arrived at the scene, what did you see?" Scanlon asked, lowering himself onto the edge of his desk, wondering what Trumwell found so interesting about his shoes.

Stone had a bulbous nose and a receding hairline. It was he who answered the question. "A large crowd had developed. We got out of the RMP and pushed our way into the store. We found a woman sprawled over the soda fountain and Gallagher on the floor. There were three kids screaming in the rear of the store."

Trumwell continued, "I frisked the man and came up with a gun and shield. I got on my portable and told Central to have the Squad and the duty captain respond forthwith."

"Didn't you make an attempt to rush them to the hospital?"

"Lou?" Stone protested, spreading his arms. "There wasn't any doubt. They were both DOA. The ambulance arrived shortly after us. The attendant took one look and pronounced them both."

"Boy your regular sector?"

"Yeah," Trumwell said, still engrossed with his shoes.

"Did you both know Gallagher?"

"We knew 'im," Stone answered. "We used to see him hanging around Yetta's. He'd park his car in the restricted zone in front of the funeral home and put a PBA card, an LBA card, or his vehicle ID plate on the dashboard. One day we decided to check him out to make sure he wasn't some cop's relative using a hand-me-down card. He tinned us and then we both recognized him. We'd both seen him MC a couple of retirement rackets."

Staring past the two cops, Scanlon asked casually, "Yetta take any action in that candy store?"

The two cops exchanged nervous looks. Scanlon understood why. The NYPD had a strict policy of covert omission in its war on crime. The enforcement of narcotics and gambling laws was forbidden to the cop on post or in the sector car. The smoldering embers of Knapp and Serpico had made the Palace Guard paranoid about the corrupting influences of these crimes on the patrol force. The result was a proliferation of narcotics bazaars, juice joints, and gambling dens about which the cop on post could do nothing but submit a report which did nothing. Corruption Prone Locations were off-limits to the patrol force. But! Every cop in the Job knew that if any serious problem ever developed concerning one of these locations, it would be the cop on post or in the sector car who would have to take the weight. The Palace Guard would deny any policy of nonenforcement.

Trumwell sat upright in his chair and folded his arms across his chest, chin down. "I don't know anything about no gambling violations."

"Me either," Stone said.

A flicker of disgust creased Scanlon's face. "Hey, you two. A police lieutenant has been murdered. I'm on your side, remember? Anything that you say to me stays with me. You got my word."

Stone looked at his partner, shrugged shoulders, and said, "I guess he's a right guy." He looked at Scanlon and said defensively, "We ain't allowed to take gambling collars. We can't do dick about them."

"I know that," Scanlon said.

"Yetta'd book the ponies, numbers, and some sports action," Trumwell said with some reluctance.

"Who'd she lay off her action with?"

"Walter Ticornelli was her man," Stone said.

"Did you happen to notice him when you first arrived on the scene?"

Trumwell responded, "Not when we first arrived. But when I left to use the telephone on the corner to call the desk officer, I saw Walter across the street leaning against the church fence."

A cagey little smile. A remembrance. He'd had both his legs then. "I know Walter."

*　　*　　*

Inspector Herman the German Schmidt was a big man with a strong angular face and puffy discolored eyelids. He had powerful hands with wide thick nails. For the past forty-six months Herman the German had been in command of the Queens Narcotics District. He had recently been promised by the powers that be that he was next in line to be promoted to deputy chief. Everything had been going real good for him. His unit's arrests were up; the Inspection Division had recently issued an above-average evaluation of his stewardship; his youngest daughter was scheduled to graduate from Brooklyn Law School. Gallagher's death had suddenly changed all that. There was a chance now that he could end his glorious career by being demoted back to captain and losing his command. He'd end his thirty-two years as a fly captain who'd spend late tours responding to barroom brawls involving off-duty cops. Probably in Manhattan North, the dumping ground for defrocked inspectors.

Herman the German was a very worried man. The grapevine had whispered that Gallagher's death might not have been clean. And if that was the case, there would be an IAD investigation into Gallagher's background to determine why he was killed, to see if his death was in some way connected to his official life. If any hint of corruption was discovered, it would reflect on his leadership. The favorable Inspection Division evaluation would be forgotten. He had seen many fallen stars in the Job. Men who had been shunned by former friends and peers as though they had AIDS.

Herman the German had left the crime scene at about 1800 hours and driven directly to the One-fourteen. He wanted to comb through Gallagher's records for any clue to irregularities that might shed some light on why he was killed. He found none. It was a little after eight that night when he telephoned Scanlon at temporary headquarters and asked if he could meet him in Gallagher's office. He hoped that the Whip of the Nine-three Squad might be able to tell him what had really happened in that candy store.

The Seventeenth Narcotics District was quartered in a suite of six interconnecting offices on the third floor of the One-fourteen Precinct's station house. Scanlon arrived a little before nine and found Herman the German in Gallagher's office, partially hidden behind a cloud of cigar smoke. "Hello, Inspector," Scanlon said, making for the old wooden swivel chair.

Herman the German was not a man to mince his words. "I hear that you left the crime scene to personally break into Gallagher's locker."

"SOP whenever a cop is killed. You know that."

"It's not SOP for the squad commander to leave the scene of a double homicide in order to break into a goddamn locker. You could have directed a subordinate to do it."

"Joe Gallagher and I were brother lieutenants. I wanted to make sure that things were handled discreetly, that there wasn't anything mixed up with his personal property that might prove embarrassing to his family."

Herman the German frowned, leaned forward, resting his thick chin on a steeple of fingers. "If I want a hand job, Lou, I'll jerk my own prick. I don't need you to do it for me."

There was a strained silence. Scanlon was outside Herman the German's chain of command and was tempted to get up and leave. He decided to wait, to see what was on the inspector's mind. He watched Schmidt staring at him, chewing the tip of his cigar. A dark brown sediment coated the inspector's teeth. "You find anything in his locker?" His tone was low, inquisitive, and casual.

"Nothing interesting. A throwaway and some old memo books."

"A bird whispered in my ear that Gallagher was hit." He fixed Scanlon with a hard stare. "Any truth to that?"

Scanlon's stump hurt. "At this point we don't know for sure what went down inside that candy store. It might have been a holdup or it could have been a hit. But on who? Gallagher? Zimmerman? We just don't know."

"I have a personal interest in this case, Lou."

"I can understand that, Inspector."

"I don't want to end my days on the garbage heap. Joe Gallagher was one of my lieutenants, and I want his killer caught. So don't misunderstand what I'm about to say. But if he was into anything he shouldn't have been into it'll be my ass. Failure to supervise, they'll say in the big building."

Scanlon nodded his appreciation of Herman the German's position. "I had planned on stopping by to see you tomorrow to ask you some questions about Gallagher. Mind answering them now?"

Herman the German removed the cigar from his mouth, purposefully knocked the thick ash into a clean ashtray, and began tamping it with the glowing end of the cigar.

"I'll answer your questions," Herman the German said. "Most everyone in the Job knew Joe Gallagher. The *public* side of him."

"I need to know what he was really like," Scanlon said.

Herman the German thought a moment, rolling the tip of his cigar over the crushed ash. He let the cigar fall into the ashtray and heaved himself up onto his feet and started pacing restlessly. "What kind of a guy was he? He was the kind of a guy that they name streets after— one way, and dead end."

Scanlon's gaze followed him around the office. Large pin maps covered the walls. Narcotics Prone Locations were designated in green; buy locations, red; wiretap locations, white; surveillance locations, blue. A large map of the Borough of Queens had the five precincts that composed the Seventeenth Narcotics District outlined in black. Herman the German paused in front of the Queens map and let his hand move over it as though searching for a specific location. His back was to Scanlon. "What do you know about the Narcotics Division, Lou?"

"Not very much, Inspector. Most of my time in the Job has been in the Bureau."

"Each borough command is divided into narcotics districts, which are made up of a certain number of patrol precincts." His hand stopped. He turned abruptly to face Scanlon. "Each district gets buy money to run their operations. In our buy-and-bust units it's SOP for each undercover to have a backup whenever he or she makes a buy. Each district also runs operations that attempt to penetrate the top of narcotics networks. Those kinds of operations deal in kilo weight and take time, patience, and a lot of money. Joe Gallagher's assignment was to run this district's buy-and-bust unit, mainly nickel and dime bags. The men and women of this unit were his people. But they seldom saw him. Gallagher was a big star, the Job's unofficial master of ceremonies. The big man in the Holy Name. Joe Gallagher, superstar. But I'll tell you what he wasn't. And that was a leader. Whenever I or another boss paid this office an unannounced visit, Gallagher was among the missing. On patrol, they'd say, covering for him. He never went into the street with his people, never supervised any of his operations. He let the fucking office run itself. He couldn't tell you what operations his units were running. I tried on several occasions to get rid of him. But he had too much weight. I gave him bad evaluations. Recommended reassignment to less demanding work. I got telephone calls from the chief of Organized Crime Control suggesting that I reevaluate my evaluation of Gallagher. I raised his rating from below standards to above standards." His face flushed and the veins in his neck grew pronounced. He leaned his back against the map of Queens, waiting for the next question.

"Who ran the shop?"

"Nobody. His paper was a shambles. There was no record of the disbursement of his buy money. No documentation of overtime. His Eleven Cards were barely touched. There was no supervision of buy operations. The place was a goddamn mess." He punched his leg in anger. "Around two years ago Gallagher asked me to give him a Second Whip. He wanted to pick up Sgt. George Harris, who at the time was the Second Whip of the Two-eight Squad. They'd come on the

Job together and had worked together in the Manhattan South Rob-bery Task Force and a few other assignments. I put in a Forty-nine requesting Harris, and a week later we picked him up in orders. In a week! Can you imagine that? It usually takes a request for transfer three months before it's acted upon. Gallagher made one phone call. That was the kind of weight he had in the Job."

A Harris was in Gallagher's address book. His original number, with a 516 area code, had been crossed out and replaced by one with a 718 code. The name Luise had been written beside it in parentheses. She had a 212 number. "What's Harris like?"

"A bit of a maverick. But the guy knows how to run a shop. He wasn't here three weeks and the paper was all up to snuff and the office running the way a narcotics district should."

"And Gallagher?"

"He continued to be the darling of the Job. He was doing talk shows on the radio and television. Big narcotics expert. The silly shit couldn't find a junkie in Needle Park. Gallagher was more than content to let Harris run his shop for him."

"Where does Harris live?" Scanlon asked, taking out a De Nobili.

"Huguenot, on Staten Island. He recently moved back into the city from Port Jefferson. Taxes and commuting got too much for him."

"Do you know his wife's name?"

"Ann, I think. Why?"

"I knew a Harris on the Job. His wife's name was Geraldine."

Herman the German began to shake his head. "It might sound funny, but for all of Gallagher's faults there was something about the guy I liked. He was alive, never down. No matter how pissed off he made you, he'd always leave you with a smile on your face."

"He was that kind of a guy, Inspector." Scanlon lit his De Nobili. "Has Harris been notified about his boss?"

"He's with the family now. They were pretty close. Used to socialize together."

"If you have no objections, Inspector, I'd like to take Gallagher's personnel record with me. There might be something there that could help me with the investigation."

A suspicious expression came over Herman the German's face. "De-partment records may not be removed from a command except by due process or with the permission of the PC, a deputy commissioner, or a ranking officer above the rank of captain."

Examining the tip of his De Nobili, Scanlon said, "Inspector is above the rank of captain."

"True," Herman the German said. "But why don't you tell me why I should give that permission? After all, if there should be anything in his record that's important to the investigation and it should disappear from his folder and IAD or some other hump unit looks and can't find it, I'm the one who'd have to take the fall. So you tell me, Lou, why should I play Mister Nice Guy?"

Scanlon brushed lint from his knee. "Because one of your people got himself killed. And because if during the course of the investigation I should come up with anything that might reflect negatively on your stewardship of Queens Narcotics, I'll personally send a little bird to whisper in your ear."

By ten-fifteen that night Scanlon arrived back at the Nine-three Squad carrying Gallagher's personnel record in several folders wrapped in twine. Hector Colon was sitting in front of a yellow makeup mirror trimming the thick black mustache that he liked to lick every time Maggie Higgins looked his way. Colon was a trendy dresser with a handsome Latin face, an Irish wife, and two sons in Massapequa Park —and an unmarried Polish girlfriend who had her own pad in Greenpoint.

Scanlon put the package on top of the cabinet next to the carton that he and Higgins had removed from Gallagher's Jackson Heights splash pad. Colon came in and told Scanlon that he had just been notified that temporary headquarters had been secured. The Log, flag, and lantern were back in the property room. Higgins, Christopher, and Brodie had signed out for the day and would be back on deck early in the morning. Colon motioned to the carton atop the cabinet. "You goin' mention that stuff in any of the reports?"

Scanlon hung his jacket on the department-issued coat rack that was next to the barred window. "No," he said, moving back to his desk.

"*Señor Teniente*, the Palace Guard is gonna be highly pissed off if they find out that you held out on them."

Scanlon knew that every DD 5, Supplementary Complaint Report, that was used to report additional phases of an investigation was supposed to be confidential.

"Every Five that we send down to Crime Coding ends up in some reporter's hip pocket. Every civilian clerk there is some newshound's stool, for a price. And I have no intention of seeing Gallagher's reputation smeared so that those parasites can sell more newspapers. He had a family, and it's our job to protect them."

"Ten-four, *Teniente*," Colon said, turning to leave the Whip's office. "See you in the ayem. I'm spending the night with my lady friend, if you should need me."

When Colon had gone and Scanlon was alone, he turned and looked wonderingly at the carton. Joe, he thought, what kind of shit did you get yourself into this time? I owe you, Joe, so I'll do whatever I can to save your miserable reputation for you. You crazy son of a bitch.

Scanlon pulled over the homicide case folder and began to separate the reports into two piles. He put the forensics reports in one and the canvass results and the witness statements in the other. From the squad room outside he could hear the scratchy cadence of the radio calls mixed with the hunt-and-peck sound of a typewriter. He leaned back in his seat and stared up at the decaying ceiling. He had been on a high since he first received Higgins's urgent telephone call at Monte's. Now he felt drained. His day had been one that was filled with sadness and a strange feeling of personal satisfaction. During the time he had been the Whip of the Nine-three Squad the office had caught the usual assortment of residential burglaries, payroll robberies, a few muggings, about a half-dozen vehicular homicides, and a dozen or so husband-wife or boyfriend-girlfriend assaults. Nothing that a detective could dig his teeth into. And now the Squad had a mystery on its hands. Person or persons unknown had done a double murder, and in so doing had released Scanlon's dormant predatory instincts. He was a predator stalking urban prey. He was back in the only game that really mattered; his time in purgatory was over.

He leaned forward in his seat and pushed the start button on the cassette tape recorder next to the tear-off calendar. Earlier in the tour he had dispatched the Biafra Baby to the Communications Unit to sign out the original tape of the call to 911 that reported the double homicide. All calls coming into and out of 911 are recorded and held for ninety days before the tapes are erased and reused. "You'd better get someone over to 311 Driggs Avenue. A police lieutenant has just been killed." It was a man's halting voice with a deep, throaty resonance. The operator's calm, professional voice followed. "Is there a callback number where you may be reached, sir?"

"Cut the bullshit, lady. Have someone get over here right quick. I told you, a cop has been shot."

When the recording ended, Scanlon arched a finger down onto the stop button. He had wanted to hear it one more time, to be sure. He knew that voice. It belonged to Walter Ticornelli.

It was after midnight when Tony Scanlon walked into Monte's. The dining-room crowd had thinned out, but serious drinkers were still three deep at the bar. Carmine, the maître d', came up to him. "Would you like to eat, Lieutenant?"

"I didn't come to play boccie," Scanlon said, flashing a warm smile. Carmine led him into the dining room and offered him a choice of tables on either side of the room. He selected a small table under the hanging plants and had begun to slide into the banquette when the maître d' bent forward and pulled out the table for him. A tuxedoed waiter appeared, placed a menu down, and then backed reverently away to await his pleasure. Scanlon looked over the fare and gave his order. A busboy came over and deposited a basket of warm bread and filled his water glass. "That was something about them murders. You gonna break the case, Lieutenant?"

Scanlon looked into the grinning Latin face and winked. "We break 'em all, Julio." The busboy left with a big smile on his face.

Angelo Esposito, the barber from Hess Street, came over and sat down, uninvited. "Goodta seeya, Lieutenant," the barber said. "Who would have thought such a thing could happen in this neighborhood?" He leaned across the table to confide, "It was probably some nigger or spic from Flushing Avenue."

Scanlon answered the barber with friendly banality. "We have a few leads, Angelo. But nothing that I can discuss. You understand." He tossed the barber his best confidential wink, and was greatly relieved to see Julio approaching with his salad.

The barber saw Julio coming and got up.

Later, lingering over the dregs of his espresso and the last of his wine, Scanlon stared ahead at the grouping of plaques commemorating the Monte family's civic achievements. Sitting across from him was a distinguished-looking man who appeared to be a well-preserved sixty. Clinging to his arm, listening attentively to each pronouncement, was an attractive woman with glistening pink lips and long black hair, who appeared to be in her middle thirties. You never see them with poor old men, Scanlon thought.

He leaned back and lit a De Nobili, enjoying its rich taste and aroma. He reached into his breast pocket and pulled out the round robin that Biafra Baby had brought back with him from police headquarters. He reread the internal record check on Joe Gallagher. The units of the department responsible for internal security reported that they had no disciplinary record on Lt. Joseph P. Gallagher.

Fifteen minutes later when he walked from the dining room out into the bar area, Joe Bite, the night bartender, called him over and asked him if he'd like a nightcap. "Hennessy," he said, sliding his real leg onto the rail.

Joe Bite slapped down a cocktail napkin and set down the pony glass.

Swirling the brandy around, Scanlon spotted his waiter at the end of the bar, caught his attention, and with his free hand scribbled on air to indicate that he wanted his bill. The waiter came over to him and discreetly whispered that Angelo Esposito, the barber from Hess Street, had done the right thing. Scanlon nodded, took out a roll of money, palmed a twenty, and shook the waiter's hand, a cop's way of saying thanks.

Joe Bite came over. "One for the road, Lieutenant?"

What a Job! Christmas every day of the year, he thought, reaching for the half-filled pony glass.

Distant traffic sounds rumbled across the night. An airplane skimmed low on the horizon. Scanlon drove his car into Mill Street between Herkimer and the Newtown Creek. There were no buildings on the north side of the street, only a vacant lot filled with rubbish and ugly construction scars. Polker's Bar and Grill was on the south side of the street. Attached to the bar's southern extremity was a stucco-and-timbered house with a mansard roof. Flush against the house on its other side was a one-story, flat-roofed factory building.

Gretta Polchinski owned all the land on Mill Street between Herkimer and the Newtown Creek. The people in that part of Greenpoint could never seem to agree on the exact date that Gretta first appeared on the scene and opened her establishment. But everyone in the neighborhood did agree that Gretta's brothel was run very discreetly.

It was one-forty in the morning when Scanlon drove up into the curb cut, honked the car horn twice, and waited for an eye to peer out of the elongated peephole that had been cut into the steel door. A metallic click, surprisingly loud in the quietness of the street, was immediately followed by the churning of the heavy door upward.

Once the door was fully open, Scanlon was directed inside by a pop-eyed black man. He parked his car between two foundation columns and got out. He became conscious of garage smells as he looked around the building, searching for a particular car. Spotting the one he was looking for, he walked over to the attendant, slipped him a five-dollar tip, and made for the four steps that led into the cinder-block passage that emptied into the basement of the house. He inserted his plastic key into the slot in the metal-sheathed door and waited a few seconds until the door clicked open.

The dominant motif was knotty pine. A carved bald eagle was over the bar, and above it two crossed flags. The Stars and Stripes and the Polish Imperial Banner. An old-fashioned jukebox outlined by a rainbow of moving lights stood against the wood-and-glass partition that separated the bar from the small dance floor.

Scanlon moved slowly, looking for Gretta in the crowd. He did not see her. He went up to the outer edge of the dance floor and looked into the darkness beyond. He saw her sitting alone at one of the small tables that ringed the dance floor, her face dimly visible in the faint light from the bar. She was dunking a silver tea egg into a porcelain cup.

"Looking for a good time, handsome?" she said as he approached her.

"How's business, Gretta?" he said, pulling out a scroll-back chair.

Gretta Polchinski was a short, squat woman with a high, flat forehead, a sagging chin, and a wild head of platinum hair that resembled brittle straw. She was fond of wearing low-cut dresses that displayed her wrinkled cleavage and the rows upon rows of gold chains around her neck.

She laid her bejeweled hand on the top of his and confided, "Tony, I have just taken on the most magnificent creature you have ever seen in your life. A Vietnamese. With a body that is not to be believed. And because I like you so much, you can have her for the night, on the arm."

"I'm here on business, Gretta."

She pulled her hand quickly off of his and leaned back into the shadows, causing a veil of darkness to descend over her face. She picked up her cup with both hands and sipped tea the oriental way. "Oh?" she said, watching him warily over the brim.

"I have to talk with Walter Ticornelli."

"Walter's not here."

"His Ford is parked in your garage."

"I let a lot of people store their cars in my garage when they go on trips."

He exhaled a sigh of disappointment. "Gretta, my love, did I ever tell you about my rule?"

"No, love, you didn't."

"When I ask a question of someone who operates in the gray area of life, they have to answer me, or else I get mad at them."

Her face jutted out of the shadows to challenge him. "Walter ain't here."

Scanlon assumed the benign expression of a disappointed teacher. "Gretta, I just can't tell you how shocked I am to discover a house of ill repute in this most Catholic of neighborhoods. And so shockingly close to the church."

"The monsignor is a regular, and he don't pay either."

"Be that as it may, my child, I'm afraid that it's my duty to hand you a collar for Promoting Prostitution as a D Felony in that you did manage, supervise, control, and own a prostitution enterprise involving the activity of two or more prostitutes."

She slammed her cup down, and tea splattered on the table. She half rose from her seat. "You peglegged, shit-on-a-shingle fuck! Just where the fuck do you think you're coming from? You sashay your ass in here whenever the mood strikes you, take your pick of the litter, and sashay out without it costing you a nickel. And now you got the balls to bust in here like fuckin' J. Edgar Hoover and lean on me. Well, fuck you!"

"Gretta?" he said in a hurt tone. "Is that any way to talk to your neighborhood good guy? Mr. Nice. I'm really surprised at you."

A babble of shouting came from the bar, causing her to look momentarily away, watching the crowd of longshoremen at the end of the bar. When the angry voices were replaced by slurred laughter she lowered herself back into her seat and glared at him.

An uncertain silence separated them.

At length he flashed a smile and blurted, "C'mon, Gretta. I only have to ask Walter a few nothing questions. Be a friend."

"Damn you, Scanlon," she said, breaking into a reluctant grin. "Walter's on the third floor."

He leaned up and kissed her nose. "Thanks, lover."

"Up yours."

Scanlon lit a De Nobili and blew the smoke into the surrounding darkness. "What do you know about the sexual paraphernalia business?"

She threw him a sharp look. "You thinking of changing occupations?"

"A friend of mine asked me to pick her up a vibrator. Seems her husband has lost interest."

She guffawed. "Most do. A few years ago women used to have Stanley and Tupperware parties in their homes. Today they're into Fuckerware parties where the hostess shows off her wares and the ladies fill out order forms and then seal them so that nobody knows what their pleasure is."

"Is it a big business?"

"Sex is always a big business."

"Are the wise guys into it?"

"Do a hobby horse have a hickory dick? Of *course* they're into it. They're into everything."

"You said the third floor," Scanlon said, standing.

"Let me go with you. I don't want you walking into the wrong room."

She led him through the lounge to the two-person elevator that she had had installed four years before to accommodate clients who had had bypass operations and did not want to trudge up stairs.

A mincing transvestite in a long yellow robe trimmed in marabou greeted them as they stepped off the elevator. The prostitute daintily kissed Gretta on both cheeks, whispering, "Is he for me, darling?"

"He's not your type," Gretta said, then asked, "What room is Walter in?"

"The Teak Room, darling," the transvestite said, staring at Scanlon and sucking on his bottom lip.

Scanlon threw open the door and entered the room.

"Can't a guy get any privacy around here?" Walter Ticornelli shouted. He was sitting up in a king-size bed with a brass headboard, his arm draped over the shoulders of a black transvestite.

"I need a word with you, Walter," Scanlon said, motioning for the prostitute to leave.

Ticornelli patted his lover's leg. "I'll catch you later."

The transvestite slid ladylike from the bed and snatched a thin white robe from a nearby chair. His female features, silicone breasts, and exaggerated female movements contrasted sharply with his limp penis and flouncing balls.

He slid on the robe, bunched it at the throat, and huffed past Scanlon on his way out of the room.

"Your friend is kinda cute," Scanlon said, sitting on the edge of the bed, glancing up at the mirror set into the bed's gold canopy.

Ticornelli folded his hands across his chest. "She's going into the hospital next week to get her plumbing altered."

Scanlon winced at the thought of castration. He noticed the five-carat diamond ring on Ticornelli's right pinky. Street talk said that it had been a gift from Joey "the Nose" Napoli when Ticornelli went through his candle-and-blood initiation into the Genovese crime family.

Ticornelli fixed his hooded eyes on Scanlon. "What's on your mind, Anthony?"

"I see that you still got the hots for black transvestites. Do the wife and kids that you got stashed out in Munsey Park know about your peculiar life-style?"

"What's a guy going to do, Anthony? We all got our hang-ups, right? Take you, for instance. You smoke them guinea stinkers of yours as a protest. You want the world to know that you're Italian even though you got an Irish name." He leaned forward, black ringlets falling over his forehead. He spoke in Italian. "You and me, we go way back. To the old days on Pleasant Avenue when you were a wild neighborhood kid with a drunken Irish cop for a father and an Italian mother who only talked to you in Italian. Tell me, Anthony, how many of your cop friends know that you speak Italian? How many of them know how much you hate their Irish guts? Not many, right? You're still a little bit ashamed of being Italian, aren't you?"

Scanlon rammed his hand into Ticornelli's groin, squeezing. He said, "*Come ti piacerebbe diventare uno castrato?*"

Color drained from Ticornelli's face as it furrowed with pain. "Let go," he said in Italian.

"What's the magic word?" Scanlon said in English.

"Please," he gasped.

Scanlon released his grip. He noticed the beads of sweat at Ticornelli's hairline. "I don't like to be talked to like that, Walter. It shows disrespect. You wouldn't open a mouth like that to one of your capos, so don't try it out on me." He playfully slapped Ticornelli's cheek. "Okay, paisan? Now, taking care of your padrone's gambling and usury interests in Greenpoint, you get to meet a lot of people, see and hear a lot of things. You have your hand on the pulse of the community, so to speak."

"Why don't you get to the point?"

"I heard your voice on a tape today, Walter," Scanlon said, smoothing down the edge of the sheet.

"What tape?"

"All calls coming into nine-eleven are recorded."

Ticornelli beamed. "So? That just goes to show what a public-spirited person I am."

Scanlon nodded in agreement. "This is so, Walter. What I would like you, as a public-spirited-type person, to do for me is to tell me exactly what you saw go down inside that candy store."

Ticornelli licked the sweat from his lips and reached for the pack of Camels on top of the night table. He shook one out, lit it, sent a stream of smoke through his nostrils, and leaned back and relaxed.

According to Ticornelli, he had been standing across the street from the candy store talking with Father Rudnicki about the problems in Poland when he heard three explosions in rapid succession. He heard squealing tires, looked in the direction of the blasts, and saw a blue van blocking his view of the candy store. Walking slowly away from the priest, he started to cross the street. He saw that the driver of the van was a white man who had on sunglasses and a brown hat pulled down over his head. He saw the driver reach across the seat as if to open the door on the passenger side. Someone rushed into the van on the passenger side, and the van sped off. He rushed across the street into the candy store, saw the bodies, and called the police. He knocked the ash of his cigarette into his palm. "That's it. The whole story."

"Did you know Gallagher?"

"From the neighborhood."

"Did you see him enter the candy store?"

"Like I told you, I was bullshitting with the priest."

Scanlon got up off the bed and went over to the chair that was next to the window. Ticornelli had carefully laid out his clothes on the chair. Scanlon picked them up and threw them on the bed. "Putcha clothes on, Walter. We're going into the station for a little chat."

Ticornelli began to gather up his clothes, a look of bewilderment plastered across his face. "Why are you doing this to me, Anthony? You got no call to lean on me this way."

"Gallagher's own mother would not have recognized him. His face was gone. But you knew who he was. Howdya do that, paisan? You clairvoyant?"

The gambler sat with his clothes bunched between his legs, pondering his situation.

Scanlon continued to press him. "Because you're a big money maker your puritanical friends on Mulberry Street overlook your sexual idiosyncrasy, as long as you're discreet. I wonder what they're going to say when I drag you in in cuffs? How are they going to react when they read the headlines in the *Post*? 'Genovese soldier discovered in homosexual tryst.' " He snapped his fingers miming error. "I'm sorry—'alleged Genovese soldier.' "

Ticornelli flushed with anger. "You're a first-class Irish scumbag, Scanlon."

"This is true, Walter." He leaned over the bed, bracing his palms on the mattress. "Walter, my old friend from Pleasant Avenue. Why don't you make it easy on the both of us? Tell me what I want to know, now, here."

Ticornelli punched the mattress in frustration. "Gallagher was into me for five large," he blurted. "He was supposed to meet me at Yetta's to make a payment."

A tremor of disbelief shook Scanlon's head. "You lent a police lieutenant five thousand dollars?"

"Whatsamatta, their money ain't the same color as everyone else's?"

"What was the vig?"

"Three points. And that was only because he was a cop. It shoulda been five points. But you know that I'm a soft touch when it comes to you guys."

"A hundred and fifty dollars a week interest on a lieutenant's salary? Ain't no way, Walter."

"Gallagher'd been into me before and he always anted up."

"Was he behind in his payments?"

"A little. The bread that he was supposed to give me today woulda brung him up to date."

"How much, paisan?"

"A week's vig and two large off the principal. He telephoned me last night at the club and asked me to meet him at Yetta's."

Scanlon tried to recall what was listed on the property voucher that recorded the personal property that had been removed from Gallagher's body. If he remembered correctly, item one had been sixteen dollars and something in U.S. currency. If Ticornelli had just told him the truth, where was the money? Trumwell and Stone were the first cops on the scene. If a score was to be made, that was when it would have had to be done. He dismissed the idea. Cops don't score other cops, particularly dead ones. "What was Yetta Zimmerman into?"

"The old broad wasn't into nothin' except her lousy candy store and bookin' a little action on the side. She didn't have an enemy in the world, and for that matter, neither did your Irish friend Joe Gallagher."

Scanlon wanted to say that one of them sure as hell did. But he said nothing. Smart cops know when to keep their mouths shut.

4

Tony Scanlon walked into the squad room a little before 0800 the next morning and found it in disarray from the night's activities. A half-eaten pastrami sandwich had attracted flies; three slices of curled-up pizza lay in a white box; empty beer cans threatened to overflow the waste barrel. The television blared: on the screen a woman with oversize glasses was recapping the morning news: the President had warned a Miami audience of the dangers inherent in the Soviet-Cuban-Nicaraguan axis. Here we go again, Scanlon thought, snapping off the set. It was much cooler inside the station house than outside, where the morning air was already promising a really hot day.

Settled in behind his desk, he reached for the first folder. As he did he glanced at the early-bird edition of the *Daily News* that had been left on his desk. The headlines told of Joe Gallagher's death. A hero, killed in the line of duty. There was another story inside the paper that told of a man who had murdered six people because he liked the way it felt. One of the victims had been shot dead because the killer had been full of the Christmas spirit. Scanlon read the stories, rolled up the newspaper, and threw it into the basket at the side of his desk. He wondered if the criminal justice system in this country was workable. How can Anglo-Saxon law be applied to savages? Might not Islamic law be the answer, an eye for an eye? There were entrepreneurs in the city who had already recognized that as a profitable truth. Grieving relatives now flocked to the gangs of Chinatown and Ninth Avenue seeking retribution against those who had murdered, raped, and maimed their loved ones, knowing that justice would not be forthcoming from the courts of this state. And who the hell can blame them? he thought, flipping open the folder.

The ballistics report detailed the gauge of the shells and the size and weight of the shot. Numerous latent prints had been found at the scene. They would be useless unless a suspect was found to match them up against. The place of occurrence was a public place; all that the fingerprints could do was connect a suspect to a scene, not tell when he was there. Fingerprints had been discovered in the tombs of the pharaohs. There is no way to tell when a fingerprint was left.

The crime-scene sketch had been done by the polar coordinate method. Triangulation had shown that the perp was between five feet five and five feet seven and that he had fired from a distance of sixty-two inches. The autopsy protocols were done on gray onionskins. They stated, in the impersonal language of the forensics pathologist, the causes of death. Cross projections of the human body were printed in the margins. Dotted lines traced each entry wound; narratives detailed the destruction each intrusion made. Shotgun wadding had been found in the wounds. Both victims had suffered cadaveric spasms at the times of their death. Scanlon recalled from one of his police promotion courses that cadaveric spasm was the immediate stiffening of a body after death. It was caused by great fear at the time of death or by severe damage to the central nervous system.

When he finished the forensic reports he turned to the investigative reports. The narratives typed under the details of the case were done in familiar police prose: At T/P/O, the time and place of occurrence, the undersigned personally interviewed Mary Hollinder F/W/22 of 1746a Nostrand Avenue, Brooklyn, who stated that she is employed as a waitress at the Warsaw Restaurant located at 411 Driggs Avenue, Brooklyn. Witness stated that at T/O she observed a male, white, who answered to the description of the perp walk east on Driggs Avenue moments before the crime occurred. Hollinder further stated that when the perp passed her he had a shopping bag clutched in his left hand. Hollinder stated that she was engaged in conversation with a friend whose identity is known to this department (statement 60# 897-86). Hollinder stated that she heard three loud reports and turned to see the above-mentioned perp running from the place of occurrence carrying what appeared to be a rifle. She stated that she saw the perp get into a blue van. Witness told the undersigned that she would recognize the perp if she saw him again and that she would make herself available to view a lineup.

He read the statements of storekeepers and pedestrians, reports of the emergency service crews who searched for physical evidence, reports of the detectives who had conducted the canvasses. All of them ended with the same capitalized letters, NR—negative results.

When he came to the Five on the three boys who had been present in the candy store at the time of occurrence he noticed that they had been identified only by their pedigrees. That was because department regulations forbid the identification of children who have been the victims of or the witnesses to crime. The report reiterated what Lew Brodie had told him at the crime scene. It was the last sentence that caused his lips to pull together into a thin, frustrated line: Witnesses state that they would not be able to identify perp if they saw him again. The parents of the foregoing witnesses state that they refuse to allow them to view photos or to attend lineup. Scanlon knew he had just lost his only eyewitnesses to the killings.

A noise in the squad room caused him to look up from the reports. He saw Christopher putting the filter into the top of the Dial-a-Brew machine. After he poured in the water, Christopher reached down and measured in the coffee. He ripped open the bag of bagels and bialys he had brought in with him. Since he was catching the first three hours of the tour, it was his responsibility to make the morning coffee and pick up the bag of goodies that was waiting at Wysniewski's Bakery. Tradition.

Soon the air was filled with the aroma of freshly made coffee. The day team began to arrive. To a man they shambled over to the coffee pot. Eric Crawford, an overweight detective with sagging shoulders, shuffled out of the four-double-decker-bed dormitory in his underwear, yawning and scratching his behind. He glanced at Maggie Higgins, who was standing in front of the urn buttering a bagel. "Hey, Maggie," he called out, hefting the front of his underpants into the palm of his hand. "Take a look at what I got for you."

Higgins glared her disdain at him. "Whaddaya hear from your head these days, Crawford? Nothing, I bet. You just get a steady dial tone."

Shaking his organ, Crawford said, "I bet this'd make you whistle 'Dixie.' "

She sauntered over to him. "Break it out, numb nuts. Let's see what you got."

He took her dare, spreading the fly of his underpants, revealing himself.

She took a few steps backward, looking in at the shriveled organ, shaking her head in pitying disbelief. "There's not enough there to fill a thimble. Thank God I'm gay." She went back to the urn. The other detectives laughed at the chunky detective in his oversize checkered boxer shorts.

Scanlon got up from his desk and went over and kicked the door closed, a signal that he did not want to be disturbed. His stump throbbed and his phantom leg was receiving messages. That happened whenever he did not get enough sleep. He took a pad from the bottom drawer of his desk and made notes. He recounted his conversation with Gretta Polchinski and Walter Ticornelli. He reread a Five that he had gone over last night. Something about it bothered him.

At T/P/O the undersigned personally interviewed Sigrid Thorsen F/W/27 of 2347 Avenue Z, Brooklyn, who stated that at T/O she was sitting on a bench in McGoldrick Park playing with her eight-month-old daughter when a man who answered to the description of the perp sat down on the adjoining bench. Witness states that the man fed pigeons peanuts. She stated that she looked over at him and he gave her a nasty look and she turned away. Witness further states that there was something peculiar about this man, but when pressed by the undersigned to state what, was unable to do so.

He pushed the Thorsen statement aside and after a brief search through the case folder came up with the statement of another witness, Thomas Tibbs. A M/W/32 of 1 Pinkflower Drive, Scarsdale, New York, who stated that he was the manager of the Gotham Federal Savings Bank located at 311 Wall Street, New York City. Witness stated that at T/O he was walking east on Driggs Avenue when he heard three loud reports that sounded like gunfire. He looked in the direction of the reports and saw a man running from a candy store toward a blue van that was parked at the curb. This man, stated the witness, was carrying a single-barrel shotgun in his right hand. Tibbs stated that he would make himself available to view photos and that he would recognize the perp if he saw him again.

"Why Tibbs on Driggs Avenue at that time of day?" Scanlon wrote.

After filling seven pages with notes he turned to the department envelope containing the photographs of the crime scene. He untied the string and removed colored 8x10s. He studied each one, searching for some telling piece of overlooked evidence. In the end, he thought, raw meat always looks like raw meat. He slid the photographs back into the envelope and turned his attention to the composite sketch of the perp. Studying it, he thought, Who are you, pally? What was your motive? He had become painfully aware of the scarcity of physical evidence and hoped that the lab boys would come up with something that he could hang his hat on.

As he restudied his notes, he mentally reviewed his conversation with Walter Ticornelli. A week's vig and two large off the principal, the shylock had said. He reached back into the pile of department forms and pulled out the property clerk voucher. As he had thought, Higgins had invoiced sixteen dollars and thirty-two cents in U.S. currency. If Ticornelli had told him the truth, and if his calculations were correct, Gallagher should have had twenty-one hundred and fifty dollars on him at the time of his death. So, he asked himself, where was that money? After thinking about that for a minute or so, he heaved himself out of his chair and left the Squad.

Police Officer Kiley O'Reilly had never read Interim Order 11 dated March 4, 1983—Early Identification and Referral of Employees with Alcohol Problems.

O'Reilly had been on the Job sixteen years, and as close as his peers could figure, he had been drunk for the last eleven. Despite all the publicity about its modern management techniques, the NYPD protects its drunks.

O'Reilly had become part of the Job's folklore. At one time he was the scourge of the bars of Manhattan North. His frequent toots often ended with him using the terraced bottles of booze behind the bar for target practice. Miraculously, no one had ever been hurt during one of O'Reilly's toots, and he became a legend. But, alas, the day came when the borough commander of Manhattan North lost his sense of humor with Kiley O'Reilly. It all happened on a November evening, a payday, on or about 1800 hours. Police Officer O'Reilly found himself swaying in front of the rectory of the Church of the Redemption, stewed to the mickey. In his stupor, he associated the clouded second-floor window with instructions that he had received during his firearms training in Recruit School—aim for the gray area. And that was exactly what Kiley O'Reilly did. He put six standard-velocity lead bullets through the second-floor bathroom window. When the first of his bullets thundered through the window, Msgr. Terence X. Woods was seated upon the throne enjoying his nightly bowel movement and paging through the latest issue of *Playboy*. The right reverend monsignor leaped howling from the toilet seat, with his trousers gathered at the ankles, and made a desperate hop for the door in an attempt to escape the fusillade. He had made one good hop before he stumbled upon the cold floor, unable to control his bowel movement.

Within the hour, Kiley O'Reilly had his guns removed, and was transferred into the bow-and-arrow squad, and banished to the Nine-three, where he was assigned as the Broom, which meant it was his responsibility to keep the station house clean. He was most diligent in performing his daily chores, meticulously ensuring that the green Second World War–vintage window shades on every window were pulled down to exactly thirty-two inches from each sill. Duties finished, O'Reilly would retire to the garage and hide inside one of the two morgue boxes that were stored in every patrol precinct so that bodies found in a public place and offending public decency could be removed to the station house without having to wait for the meat wagon. Squirreled inside the morgue box was O'Reilly's "flute," a Pepsi bottle filled with whiskey.

Scanlon hurried out of the station house, passed under the two huge green globes that were affixed to the entrance of the fortresslike stone building, turned right, and made for the garage.

He pushed in the walk-through door and stepped into the garage. The interior was military-clean, with everything in its assigned place. Red buckets filled with sand were next to the two gas pumps; the portable generator was oiled and ready for the next blackout. The snow blower was next to the generator; the emergency string lights were strung over the brick wall.

Joe Gallagher's Ford was parked inside a rope barrier that had a single crime scene sign attached. The surface of the car was smudged with white fingerprint powder. Scanlon lifted the rope and ducked under. He peered inside the car and was relieved to see that the glove compartment was closed and that no personal property was strewn about. The precinct scavengers had not been at the car.

He climbed back out over the rope and went over to one of the morgue boxes. He flipped down the top lid. Kiley O'Reilly was stretched out with his feet crossed at the ankles and a Pepsi bottle at rest on his stomach. "Howya doin', Lou?" O'Reilly singsonged.

"You see anyone messing with this car?"

O'Reilly swung his legs out over the side and sat up, legs dangling over the edge. "That car belonged to the dead, Lou. Ain't nobody going to mess with it."

Scanlon took in the half-filled Pepsi bottle and went back to the car.

Scanlon entered the car on the passenger side and stretched his hand under the seat, searching. NR. Then he stuffed his hand between the front cushion and the back of the seat and inched along, slowly making his way across to the driver side. NR. Kneeling on the front cushion, he reached into the back of the car and yanked out the rear cushion. NR. Fascinated, Kiley O'Reilly watched him, taking short pulls from his bottle.

By now the seats were askew and all four doors open. Scanlon stood with his foot on the rear bumper, trying to guess where the money could be. After a few contemplative moments, he slapped his foot down and left the garage.

He returned within a few minutes twirling a key ring that he had just removed from the property clerk folder that contained Joe Gallagher's personal property.

Kiley O'Reilly took a long pull, anticipating.

Scanlon opened the car's trunk, leaned inside, and began poking around, moving tools and other things. When he didn't find what he was looking for, he unthreaded the wing nut that secured the spare tire in the well. Nut off, he hefted the tire out and set it down on the rim of the well. He spotted the department multi-use envelope on the bottom of the well. He reached in, removed it, opened the flap, and fanned twenty-one hundred-dollar bills and a brand-new fifty into the palm of his hand. Ticornelli told me the truth, he thought, looking down at the spread of money. But why had Gallagher been so cautious? Why hide money in his car? The gun and shield that cops carry usually give them a sense of invincibility.

The Gotham Federal Savings Bank had a glass facade. Bank executives could be seen at desks earnestly discussing things with customers. Higgins parked the department auto in the crosswalk and tossed the vehicle identification plate onto the dashboard. Scanlon started to slide out on the passenger side, hesitated, and reached back into the car and removed the radio handset from the black rubber cradle and laid it across the dashboard. "Now let one of the meter maids say she didn't know it was a department car that she hung one on."

"We should carry M&M candy wrappers with us and put them on the dash. That's how the parking enforcement people identify their private cars to each other," Higgins said, locking the door. They walked over to the bank and asked to see Mr. Tibbs.

"I told my story a dozen times to the other detectives." Thomas Tibbs was a man of medium height who wore his thinning black hair plastered down and parted on the side. He wore a three-piece gray business suit and had the obligatory college ring on his right hand.

"I'm afraid that you are going to have to tell it one more time," Scanlon said.

The banker came out from behind his desk and motioned the detectives over to a grouping of chrome-and-canvas chairs that had been arranged around a chrome-and-glass table. It was a large airy office with its own bathroom. As Scanlon lowered himself into the chair, he took in the precisely arranged photographs of bank executives that lined the nearby wall. They were all stern men with the look of acute constipation etched into their scowls. He looked away in time to catch the banker's gaze caressing Higgins's body. She had perched sideways on her chair, the fall of her blouse accentuating her healthy bosom. She too had noticed the banker's interest and had shifted in her seat and crossed her legs, ensuring that the hem of her skirt rode up above her knee, revealing some thigh. The witness stole a quick look and returned his full attention to Scanlon.

Higgins said, "We appreciate your seeing us, Mr. Tibbs." She used her best saccharine tone.

Tibbs looked at her and smiled. "It's my pleasure, Detective Higgins."

Scanlon leaned back and relaxed. This was going to be Maggie's show.

"Mr. Tibbs," she began, "you stated that the man whom you saw running from the candy store was carrying a single-barrel shotgun in his right hand."

Tibbs began to rub the stone of his college ring across his lips. "That is correct," he said, trying to make eye contact with her.

"The time sequence was in seconds," Higgins stated flatly. "How can you be so positive it was a shotgun that you saw and not a rifle or a stick, or a piece of pipe?"

Tibbs lowered his hand from his lips and responded smugly, "What I saw, Detective Higgins, had a ventilated-rib barrel and a plated breechblock. Only shotguns possess those characteristics."

Cocky bastard, thought Scanlon.

"There might come a time, Mr. Tibbs, when you will be asked to testify in court. If that time should come you are going to be asked what qualifies you to make such technical observations concerning firearms."

A confident smile caught the edges of Tibbs's lips. He sneaked another look at Maggie's thigh and said, "I'm an avid hunter, Detective Higgins. And when I was in the army I was trained as an armorer."

She started to ask the next question but he interrupted her and said, "Please make it Tom," so she continued, "Tom, did you notice if the stock or the barrel was cut down?"

"The stock was cut way down."

"In your previous statements you mentioned that you noticed something odd about the killer as he ran for the van. At the time, you were unable to say what it was. Now that you have had time to think about it, can you tell us?"

"I've racked my brains and I just don't know what it was about him that bothered me. But I do know that it had something to do with the way he ran. It was unnatural."

"Could you be more specific?"

"I'm afraid not."

"Would you recognize the killer again if you saw him?"

"Absolutely."

Before they'd left the squad room Scanlon had taken several composite sketches that were connected to other cases and the one that the artist had prepared in the Gallagher/Zimmerman case and had laid them out on a desk. He'd taken the Squad's Polaroid one-on-one camera and photographed the layout. He now picked up the envelope from his lap and opened it, hoping that the witness would pick out the correct one. Leaning up out of his seat, he passed the layout to Tibbs. "Would you please take a look and see if you recognize anyone?" Scanlon said.

Tibbs scrutinized the layout. "This is the man I saw running from the candy store," he said, tapping the fourth sketch.

Tibbs had selected the correct one.

Higgins looked at Scanlon with an expression that said, He's going to make one helluva witness.

Juries tend to believe bankers and priests; it's the veracity of cops, lawyers, and doctors that they hold in disrepute. Scanlon was bothered. At one time cops didn't concern themselves with the credibility of witnesses. That was the DA's job. That was no longer the case. And Scanlon had learned that the hard way. Several blown cases had taught Scanlon to learn everything there was to learn about potential witnesses.

Higgins broke his private reverie. "Got any questions, Lou?"

Scanlon cupped palms over kneecaps. Arched his back. "You're married, live in Scarsdale, and work in Manhattan. Correct?"

A kernel of apprehension crept into the witness's bland expression. "Yes."

"How do you get to work, Mr. Tibbs?"

"The seven-sixteen from Scarsdale. It gets me into the office . . ." The witness stopped in midsentence, his eyes dilated with sudden concern. Scanlon nodded knowingly at him. He knew his secret and he wanted him to know that he knew. Scanlon would not press the issue, at least not yet. Scanlon pried himself up off the chair. "Thanks for your cooperation," he said, shaking the banker's limp hand, staring into his worried eyes.

Sigrid Thorsen lived on the southern edge of Brooklyn, in Bath Beach, the Six-two. When she answered her door she was holding a baby and her hair was turbaned in a white towel. While Scanlon displayed police credentials and explained the purpose of their unannounced visit, Higgins reached past him into the two-bedroom apartment and playfully grasped the baby's tiny fist.

The witness opened the door for the detectives. Higgins walked at the witness's side, admiring the baby and cooing at her. Thorsen led the detectives into a large comfortable living room with a black folding room divider that separated the room from the dining area. There was a terrace that overlooked other apartment houses and terraces.

Sigrid Thorsen was a Nordic beauty: tall and thin with clear white skin that emphasized her wide umber eyes. Thin crescent lines were visible around her lips. She was wearing fawn-colored shorts and a white short-sleeved cotton top. Her nipples were evident through the soft cotton. She offered them seats and excused herself; it was time for her baby's nap, she explained. As she moved toward the bedroom Scanlon took in her long legs, tight calves, and round behind. Higgins, who had sat next to him on the long white couch, leaned close. "Nice," she whispered.

"Competition I don't need," he said, watching the legs disappear into a distant room.

When the witness returned some time later, Scanlon noticed that she had applied makeup and had brushed her hair out. It was long and had a soft yellow hue and flowed smoothly past her shoulders.

She sat in a low leather chair. "How may I help you?"

Scanlon led her through the statement she had given the other detectives. She listened attentively. At appropriate places during the narrative she would nod or say yes. She stared down at the shaggy carpet as he talked. "You told the other detectives that there was something strange about the man who sat on the next bench, that he frightened you. Can you tell me exactly what it was about him that made you feel that way?"

Sigrid Thorsen looked up at him. "There was something odd about him, but I can't put my finger on it."

"Anything else?"

She shook her head.

Watching her closely, he asked, "Would you be willing to submit to hypnosis, Mrs. Thorsen?"

"Hypnosis? Why?"

"Because you're the one person who got a good look at the killer. Under hypnosis you might be able to recall some bit of information that could prove important." He leaned forward to emphasize the importance of what he was going to say next. "I assure you, it's perfectly safe, and we'd provide you with transportation and a policewoman to baby-sit."

"I would have to discuss that with my husband. I'll let you know." Scanlon picked up the envelope containing the sketches. He removed the layout and handed it to her. "Would you mind looking at this and seeing if you recognize anyone?"

She took it and laid it down on her lap, studying the grouping of composite sketches. After a while she looked up and said, "It's number four. That's the man in the park, the one who sat on the next bench and fed the pigeons."

She had identified the same composite as Thomas Tibbs. Scanlon let his hands fall between his legs, rubbing his palms together. "Mrs. Thorsen, there is a question that I must ask you."

She tensed.

"What were you doing in McGoldrick Park?"

"I thought that was obvious, Lieutenant. I was sitting on a bench with my child, enjoying a beautiful June day."

"I see," Scanlon said, looking into her beautiful eyes. "Mrs. Thorsen, what is your relationship with Thomas Tibbs?" He watched her fight to keep her composure.

"Who?" she said.

"Thomas Tibbs," he repeated. "I believe that you drove into Manhattan and picked him up, and then drove to Greenpoint to spend some stolen moments together. You couldn't find a parking space, so you and your baby got out while he searched for a spot."

She said nothing; her gaze was unflinchingly fixed on him; her hands squeezed the cushion of the chair.

He continued. "You and Tibbs have stumbled into a homicide investigation, and until it's put to bed your lives are in the public domain. The only reason I bring up Tibbs is to advise you that at some point in time someone else might ask you about your relationship with Tibbs. And if that time should come, I'd like you both to be prepared."

"Thank you for your concern, Lieutenant." She got up. The interview was over.

"Will you discuss the possibility of being hypnotized with your husband?" he asked, walking with her to the door. "I'd really appreciate it if you would."

"I will discuss it with my husband," she said, reaching for the doorknob. "My husband and I discuss everything together—we have no secrets."

"I'm glad," Scanlon said. "That's how it should be."

Watching oncoming traffic for an opening, Higgins said, "How'd you know?"

"Their statements," Scanlon said. "She lives in Bath Beach at the ass end of Brooklyn and turns up in Greenpoint with her baby. He works in Manhattan, takes the seven-sixteen from Scarsdale, and then he shows up in Greenpoint in the middle of a business day. You don't have to be Holmes to figure that one out."

A bus passed, enveloping their car in a cloud of carbon monoxide and other noxious fumes. "Will we be able to use them in court?" Higgins said, driving from the space with a scrunch of tires.

"By the time this caper gets into court, if it ever does, they'll have their act together."

5

All the ladies had one thing in common: they'd all committed adultery with Lt. Joseph P. Gallagher.

Scanlon had Higgins telephone them at their homes and ask them to come into the Squad for a chat. Each of them sounded nervous about being associated publicly with the dead police hero. Higgins had assured each of them that they wouldn't be embarrassed. One of the best ways to secure the help of hostile witnesses is to instill a sense of security, eliminate the fear of exposure. Policemen lie a lot. After about forty minutes of not so gentle coaxing, Maggie Higgins had gotten each of the ladies to agree to come into the Squad and be interviewed. She had scheduled their appointments so that none of the ladies would meet.

Donna Hunt was a diminutive woman in her early forties. She brought to mind the phrase "pocket Venus." Her figure was beautifully proportioned and her green eyes perfectly made up. But her clothes and jewelry were just a bit too loud and emphatic. She was obviously nervous and wore a paper-thin smile when she appeared at the squad-room gate and asked to see Detective Higgins. She stood behind the carved gate wringing a lace handkerchief while Christopher went to get Higgins out of the property room.

After a quick introduction, Higgins led the witness across the squad room and into Scanlon's office. As soon as the door to the Whip's office closed behind her, Donna Hunt threw herself into a chair and cried hysterically. Without being asked a question, she blurted out her story.

Donna Hunt had been married for twenty-six years to Harold, who was an accountant, a good provider, a loving father, and the only man she had ever gone to bed with. At fifty-two, Harold had lost interest in sex. Whenever she initiated lovemaking Harold would inevitably demur on the grounds that he was too tired or not in the mood. She stopped trying. With her two children away at college, Donna Hunt found herself alone more and more. Harold worked late most nights. Clients, he said. But she was beginning to have her doubts.

One day while she was driving through Astoria on her way to meet her sister for lunch a police car pulled alongside and the driver motioned her to the curb. It was on Steinway Street, she remembered, across from the new Pathmark shopping center. Through her sideview mirror she saw a policeman get out of the car and swagger up to her. He had been polite. She had run a stop sign, he said. She protested that she hadn't. At some point during the exchange a man in civilian clothes got out of the police car and came over and told the policeman he was in a hurry. The man in the civilian clothes asked her her name and smiled. "I'm Joe Gallagher," he said, smiling again, and walked back to the police car.

Around noontime the next day her telephone rang at home and she was surprised when the voice at the other end announced that he was Joe Gallagher. He was a police lieutenant and had gotten her home number by running a make on her license plate, he told her. He was conducting an investigation into a payroll robbery that had occurred around the time she had driven past the Pathmark. Would it be possible for him to interview her concerning this crime? Perhaps they could meet and have a cup of coffee?

Six days after that first meeting, Donna Hunt went to bed with Joe Gallagher. It was the sort of experience she had fantasized about many times. She remembered lying beside him exulting in herself. A man had wanted her; had pursued her; had enjoyed her. She was a woman again. The affair gave her empty life meaning. She had been surprised at how guiltless she had felt. She had loved every moment of it—at first.

During one of their noontime rendezvous in Jackson Heights he had gotten out of bed and returned with a vibrator and a pair of anal love beads. Do you like to experiment? he had asked, gently pushing her legs apart. She had been shocked by the ferocity of her newly discovered passion.

Three days later Gallagher telephoned her at home. Never call before ten A.M., she had warned. Would she be interested in a threesome? he asked. He had a friend who had a friend.

Donna Hunt looked pleadingly up at Scanlon, who was perched on the edge of the desk staring down at her. Her eyes were swollen, her cheeks streaked black with mascara. Her sobs had turned to heaves, and she was fighting for breath. Higgins, who had been standing against the wall, came over and handed the witness some sheets of Kleenex. The witness smiled weakly and took them.

Hector Colon, who had slipped into the office while Donna Hunt was talking, left the office and returned with a glass of water.

After drinking the water, she began to make glass rings on the desk. "I did it," she whispered.

"Did what?" Scanlon asked gently.

"I participated in the threesome. It was with Joe and another woman. I'd never been with another woman that way. I realized that I was out of control. Like being in quicksand, being dragged deeper and deeper. When he called again I told him that it was over. That I'd never see him again. He telephoned several times but I held firm. Finally he stopped calling."

"When was the last time you heard from him?" Scanlon asked.

"Seven months ago." She looked up at Scanlon. "Harold is an unforgiving man. He'd leave me if he ever found out."

Scanlon felt sorry for her. A woman puts a lot on the line every time she spreads her legs, he thought. "Your husband will never know anything from us, Mrs. Hunt. Whatever you tell us will remain confidential." He didn't tell her that someday she might have to testify in court. Policemen have to lie a lot. She gripped his hands. "Thank you."

He picked up a photograph from the desk, one that he had found in Gallagher's locker. He held it up to her. "Is this you, Mrs. Hunt?"

"Oh, God!" She looked away. "He asked me to pose, and I did."

"Mrs. Hunt, what was the name of the other woman who participated with you in the threesome?"

"Luise Bardwell."

Scanlon looked at Higgins. The name Luise had been written in Gallagher's address book in parentheses next to that of George Harris, the sergeant friend of Joe Gallagher who had been brought into the Seventeenth Narcotics District to run Gallagher's unit for him.

"Was Gallagher an active participant in the threesome?" Scanlon asked.

Donna Hunt looked down at her hands. "Joe knelt on the bed watching and masturbating. He, he ejaculated over my breasts." She craned her head and looked at Higgins. "Is there a ladies' room?"

Higgins banged on the bathroom door and hearing no response pushed the door open and stuck her head inside.

Donna Hunt stopped just inside the doorway and took in the urinals. There was one doorless stall with a lot of crushed cigarettes and newspapers, and girlie magazines strewn around the base of the bowl. A large cardboard sign was on the wall: Female POs are to throw their sanitary napkins in the waste barrels and not in the toilet. Auth. C.O. 93 Pct.

Higgins saw her aversion. "Pretty disgusting, isn't it?"

"Don't you have a ladies' room?"

"The newer station houses have. We have to put up with unisex johns."

"But aren't they ever cleaned?"

"Every morning. But they don't stay clean long."

She looked around in disgust. "Men are such pigs."

"You've noticed," Higgins said, leaning her back into the door, preventing anyone from intruding.

"We wondered why we didn't find any personal things of yours in his apartment," Higgins asked her while she was still in the toilet stall.

"Joe wouldn't permit it," she responded. "He said that he didn't want me to leave anything incriminating. Not even in his medicine cabinet." The toilet flushed and the witness walked out of the stall, heading for the sink on the other side of the bathroom.

"Did he ever mention his wife?"

"No," Mrs. Hunt said, taking a handful of brown paper towels from the shelf above the sink and cleaning off the sink and the soap-splattered mirror. "I asked Joe if he was seeing any other woman and he assured me he wasn't. I was concerned with catching something." She balled up the towels and tossed them into the cardboard waste barrel next to the sink. Then she washed her face and hands.

Higgins remained on guard duty. "Did Joe ever mention any of his business dealings?"

Donna Hunt applied lipstick. "Nooooo."

"What ever possessed you to pose for those photographs?"

Donna Hunt lowered the stick from her lips, studying her reflection in the mirror, pondering the question. "I really don't know. He asked me to do it and I did. I never thought of the consequences."

Mary Posner was the next witness. She arrived thirty minutes after Donna Hunt had left. Posner was elegantly dressed in a white linen suit and heavy summer jewelry. She had short chestnut hair and a mature face that had retained much of its former beauty. Scanlon put her in her early fifties.

"Why the hassle?" Mary Posner said, crossing her legs and tucking her skirt under.

"No hassle," Scanlon said. "We'd just like to ask you a few questions concerning your relationship with Joe Gallagher."

Mary Posner reached into her leather pocketbook and removed a box of foreign cigarettes and lit one. "I don't like men very much. I wonder sometimes why I keep going to bed with them."

"It has something to do with the genes."

Mary Posner chortled. "You're cute for a cop." A look of concern came over her. "Before I answer your *fercockta* questions I want to know if you found a photograph of me in Gallagher's home-away-from-home."

"We did."

"I want it back."

"That can be arranged."

"Arranged my ass. No pitchee, no talkee." She flipped ash off to the side.

He watched her, not talking.

She took another drag on her cigarette and coughed. "I take it back, you're not cute."

He waited.

She tapped her foot, annoyed. At length she said, "Look, Lieutenant. I got a problem and I can use your help."

"We all have problems, Mary. A police lieutenant and a candy store lady have been murdered. That's a problem."

"I sure as hell didn't kill them."

"No one said you did."

She leaned out of her seat and reached for the brown department-issue ashtray on his desk. Thoughtfully stubbing out the cigarette, she said, "Sy Posner is my husband. He's one of the biggest factors in the garment district. Sy finances a lot of the rags that are made there. He's my last shot in life. I've been married three times before Sy and have been knocking around since before the Boer War. Sy and I have only been married three years. His first wife died five years ago. They'd been married for thirty-seven years and in all that time Sy had never been unfaithful." A disbelieving smile parted her lips. "Sy was probably the only faithful Jew on Fashion Avenue. Sy never had a big sex drive, and now that he's older. . . ."

"I understand," Scanlon said. "Tell me about you and Joe Gallagher."

Mary Posner sighed in resignation and began to recount her first meeting with the dead police lieutenant. Gallagher had used the same old traffic-stop ploy to meet her, the one that many cops use to meet women. But unlike Donna Hunt, this witness was no novice at infidelity. She had played the game from both sides of the street, as the wife and as the girlfriend. Her relationship with Gallagher had been brief. "I don't like kinky men."

"What do you mean by that?"

She told Scanlon of Gallagher getting up out of the bed and returning with the vibrator and anal love beads, and asking her if she liked to experiment. "I looked him right in the eye and said, 'Listen, kiddo, I've done all the experimenting I intend to do. The only thing that gets into my behind is suppositories.' I told him that if he was so hot on anal love he could string the goddamn beads up his own ass."

"What was his reaction?"

"He laughed and claimed he was only kidding. But I saw that tense look he was wearing. Your dead lieutenant was a sicky, a weirdo in blue. He proved that later."

"What happened later?"

She looked at her hands, examining brown spots. "We made love and then he dozed off. After a while he awoke and we went at it again. But this time when he was ready he withdrew and dirtied my stomach. Then he went down between my legs and licked up his own mess. I've been with a lot of men and none of them ever went in for anything like that. Your dead hero was a fag."

Scanlon exhaled. He looked over at Higgins and Colon, who both shrugged.

"Can you tell me anything else?" Scanlon asked.

The witness told how Gallagher had slid from the bed and gone to the closet and taken out a Polaroid camera and snapped her picture. She told of leaping naked from the bed trying to get the camera away from him. He was too strong for her. She never saw him again after that. She half expected him to try to blackmail her, sell the photograph back to her. But she never heard from him again.

"How long ago was that?" Scanlon asked, watching her face for the lie.

"Seven, eight months ago."

"Did you always go to his Jackson Heights apartment?"

She scoffed. "Some dump."

"Did he ever ask you for money?"

"I don't give men money. It usually works the other way around, presents and stuff."

Scanlon opened the top drawer of his desk and took out one of the Polaroids that he'd found in Gallagher's locker. He held it up to her. "You?"

"Me," she said in a disgusted tone. "Look at those thighs and that flab. I'm going on a diet."

"I can't let you have this back now. But I promise you that as soon as the case is over, I'll get it back to you."

"Are you going to have to use that photo in court?" she asked with a worried tone.

He held out a calming hand. "No way. I promise you that." He saw her relax and wondered why Donna Hunt had not asked him to return her photograph.

C. Aubrey White was one of the legal carnivores who show up each morning before the start of court to prey on the distressed relatives and friends of prisoners who were arrested the night before and were scheduled for morning arraignment. The arresting officer was the usual shill. He'd introduce the relative or friend to the lawyer and then discreetly leave to draw up the complaint, giving the lawyer time to discuss his fee. After being retained and extracting as much money up front as he could, the eminent member of the bar would then be most punctilious in his adherence to the most sacred of judicial ethics: bleed 'em and plead 'em. During one of the numerous defense-requested adjournments the arresting officer would be slipped his fifteen percent finder's fee, in cash, of course.

Scanlon was taken aback when he saw the silver-haired lawyer, accompanied by a woman in her early twenties, enter the squad room. He did not like C. Aubrey White or the rest of the legal carnivores, or the cops who did business with them, but like so many cops Scanlon realized there was nothing that he could do about it. The practice of "steering" had been going on for years, a practice that every judge and every district attorney in criminal justice was aware of and deplored, a practice that enhanced the contempt that honest cops felt for the system.

C. Aubrey White gripped his silver-topped cane and shifted his considerable weight forward, resting on it. "Tony, ol' friend, comrade in arms, this child is my dear sister's daughter, Rena Bedford. She asked her uncle Aubrey to accompany her to the Bastille in the hope of straightening out whatever minor unpleasantness might exist concerning her relationship with the departed hero, Joe Gallagher."

Rena Bedford was a pretty young thing with long hair the color of almonds. She had brown eyes and the bemused look of eternal virginity. Scanlon found it hard to imagine her getting it on with Joe Gallagher.

The lawyer was talking. "What's it about, Tony?"

"A few ends need tidying, Counselor."

A thoughtful smile set on the lawyer's lips. "Is my niece the subject of a criminal investigation?"

Scanlon's answer was forthright. "No."

"Might my niece be the subject of an accusatory instrument?"

"I cannot envision such a possibility." Scanlon noted that there was a faint smile on Rena Bedford's lips.

The lawyer waved his hand in front of him, making circles. He had the look of a man ready to expound life's mysteries. "Permit me, if you will, the opportunity to paraphrase a few recent decisions. . . ." Scanlon raised his hand in an effort to stop the legal harangue but instead dropped it in defeat, resigned to listening. Cops learn early not to interrupt lawyers when they are giving a performance for their client; it makes the lawyer uppity and hostile.

C. Aubrey White droned on. ". . . during a criminal investigation, a subject who has an attorney may not be interrogated about the case even though he has not been arrested and is not in custody, after the subject's attorney tells the police not to question his client in his absence, *People* versus *Skinner*."

Scanlon's nerves were sending strong signals to his phantom leg. Lew Brodie was sitting on a chair with the back turned front, listening and punching his palm with his fist. His eyes were bloodshot, his shirt-tail on the left side was hanging out, and the veins in his temples were throbbing.

Howard Christopher, who considered all lawyers to be communist, with the sole exception of Roy Cohn, was standing by the wall, glaring at the lawyer and munching julienne carrot sticks. A bad sign.

". . . when a defendant is represented by an attorney in a criminal matter, the policeman may not question him about any unrelated matter without the defendant's lawyer being present, *People* versus *Rogers*."

Scanlon wondered why it was necessary for lawyers to always put their legal prowess on display. He glanced up at the department clock, which had the day divided by civilian and military time, and decided the time had come to end the performance. Other witnesses were scheduled after Rena Bedford, and he didn't like the look on Brodie's and Christopher's faces. A shouting match between his detectives and the lawyer was most definitely not needed, so he let the lawyer say a few more things and then held up a pleading hand. "Counselor, spare us, please. We all read the legal bulletins. If your niece would prefer not to talk to us, that's okay. I'll just subpoena her before the grand jury. You of course realize that in that case, I'll not be able to guarantee confidentiality. You're aware of the tendency of grand juries to leak testimony to the press." He sketched a gesture in the air. " 'Coed in love nest with hero cop.' The mothers'll sell an extra fifty thousand copies at your niece's expense."

C. Aubrey White gripped the cane with both hands, pouting. "No big megillah, Tony." He glanced sideways at his niece. "You don't mind talking to these gentlemen, do you, dear?"

"Of course not, Uncle Aubrey," she said, casting her modest eyes downward.

Rena Bedford was a graduate student in Social Work and Human Development at the New School. A year ago she had taken a course in Urban Art. One of the requisites of the course was a visit to a subway train yard on Pennsylvania Avenue in East New York to study how urban Rembrandts profane public property with graffiti. It had been an elective course.

While driving her blue Porsche 944 along Linden Boulevard on the way to the train park, she had been stopped by policemen in an unmarked car. They had placed a flashing red light on their dashboard and motioned her to pull over. Two policemen in old clothes got out of the police car and came up to her. They told her that her car matched the description of a car that had just been used in a bank robbery. She protested and showed them her license and registration. An older man got out of the police car and came up to them. He was tall and had a commanding presence. He told her his name was Joe Gallagher, and they began to talk. He was an interesting man, and before she realized it they were discussing city planning. The other two policemen drifted back to their car. She liked the sound of Gallagher's voice, and thought he was cute, and since she was into getting it on with older men, she gave him her telephone number. From that point on, Rena Bedford's story paralleled those of the other witnesses. Only she was more graphic in her details of their sexual encounters.

Watching her sparkling face, Scanlon realized that she didn't wear makeup and had the kind of look that advertising people called country-fresh.

Rena Bedford had not shied away from Gallagher when he approached her with the vibrator and anal love beads; nor did she hesitate to pose for him, or join in the threesome. "A woman should experience all that there is to experience before she settles down," she said calmly, staring at Scanlon with her wide, modest eyes.

When she had finished her tale, Scanlon asked casually for the name of the other female participant in the threesome. "Luise Bardwell."

"Did Gallagher ever discuss money with you or tell you anything about his job, or his personal life?"

"No. The only thing we ever discussed was doing it. He was really into that." She tilted her head, as though trying to recall a faint memory. "Once he told me that one of his buddies had come into some money and that they were thinking of going into business together."

"Did he tell you the name of his buddy, or mention the kind of business?"

"No, he didn't."

* * *

Valerie Clarkson was the fourth witness scheduled to appear. She never showed. Repeated telephone calls to her home went unanswered. Scanlon sent a Telephone Message to her resident precinct, the Ninth, requesting them to dispatch an RMP to her home. The notification that the Nine-three Squad received back ended with the initials NR. Valerie Clarkson was not in her residence. A neighbor on the first floor of her six-story Manhattan walk-up stated that he had seen her leaving her apartment about midday. She was carrying an overnight case. She seemed to be in a hurry, the witness had stated.

At 1500 that afternoon the detectives gathered about a desk in the Nine-three squad room to eat lunch; three large pizzas, two six-packs of Miller Light, and a diet 7-Up for Higgins. Christopher was off in a corner watching his favorite soap, "The Guiding Light," and eating plain yogurt mixed with raw cashews. Biafra Baby was leaning against a desk arguing with his wife over the telephone. Higgins waved a crust at the detectives gathered around the desk. "Joe Gallagher was a perv."

"Women and the ponies are expensive vices on a married lieutenant's salary," Christopher joined in, intensely watching the screen. (John was about to confess his infidelity with his sister-in-law.)

Lew Brodie nibbled a strand of melted cheese. "Maybe Gallagher had a main squeeze who was picking up his tabs?"

Colon joined in: "And maybe this main squeeze didn't cotton to him two-timin' her and when she found out she got pissed off and had him whacked." He began to slowly lick the end of his crust, staring pointedly at Higgins's breasts.

"She'd know," Higgins riposted, looking away from Colon and folding her arms across her chest.

Biafra Baby slammed down the receiver and stalked over to them, mumbling curses. He threw himself into a chair, grabbed up a slice, and sat shaking his head.

"Wassa matter?" Brodie asked.

"That damn woman!" Biafra Baby said. "She spends half my salary givin' my kids lessons tryin' to turn them into bionic black people. I pay for piano lessons, and ballet lessons, and elocution lessons so they can learn to speak like white folk. But this time she has gone too far. She's givin' my son basketball lessons! He's the only black kid in the whole country who pays to learn how to play basketball."

Lew Brodie nodded thoughtfully. "That's what happens when you take 'em out of the ghet-to."

A contemplative silence was broken by Brodie peeling off the top of a beer can and tossing the tab into the wastebasket. "I still think one of his lady friends had him whacked," Brodie said, reaching down the front of his trousers to scratch his testicles.

Higgins looked away.

Biafra Baby reached in for another slice. As he did he lifted one buttock up to one side and passed wind.

Higgins heaved out of her seat. "You're disgusting!" she said, leaving the squad room.

"Where you going, *señorita?*" Colon called to her back.

"To a restaurant, to eat with normal people," she said over her shoulder.

They watched her storm out of the squad room and slam the door behind her.

Folding a slice, Biafra Baby said, "They never shoulda let women in the Job."

Scanlon pondered talking to them about their deportment in front of Higgins. The personnel and management texts said he should, but his instincts told him not to. It was something they were going to have to work out among themselves.

Higgins walked back into the squad room twenty minutes later. The other detectives were cleaning up the lunch mess. She hurried over to the ringing telephone and pushed down the flashing button.

"Nine-three Squad, Suckieluski." The fictitious Detective Suckieluski was a cop's equivalent of an answering machine. There was one such phantom in every squad. Higgins listened. Covering the mouthpiece, she signaled Scanlon with a glance and mouthed, "It's Dr. Zimmerman, the son."

Scanlon took the receiver and said, "Hello."

A deep voice at the other end demanded to know what progress had been made on his mother's murder. Scanlon was told that many family members were distressed that no police official had taken the time to come and inform them of the details of his mother's death.

"We thought it appropriate to wait a day or two before contacting you," Scanlon said.

"We are sitting shivah at my home. I'd appreciate it if you would come by tomorrow."

Saturday was his regular day off. Scanlon had nothing planned except to do his laundry and some vague inclination to spend some part of the evening with his hooker friend, Sally De Nesto. He plucked a pencil from the empty coffee can and wrote down the address and told the doctor that he would be there tomorrow afternoon, about one.

When he hung up, Colon gave him a bewildered look. "Tomorrow's your RDO."

"*Noblesse oblige*," Scanlon said, walking into his office.

"What's this *noblesse oblige?*" Colon said.

"It means that you don't gotta be a fucking putz all your life," Brodie said, arching a dead soldier into the wastebasket.

Sgt. George Harris had applied for and was granted four successive tours of emergency leave with pay. He was going to stand by the coffin in his dress uniform, with white gloves, and a mourning band stretched around his gold sergeant's shield.

All the members of Gallagher's buy-and-bust unit would be in attendance. They were authorized by the *Patrol Guide* to wear mourning bands on their shields when they were in uniform from the day of death until 2400 hours on the tenth day after death. Other members of the force were permitted to display their grief from the time of death until 2400 hours on the day of the funeral. As the dead lieutenant's friend and close colleague, Harris had incurred traditional responsibilities. It would be he who would greet the grieving members of the department as they lined up to pay respects at the closed coffin; it would be he who would be responsible for seeing that the gold lieutenant's shield was removed from the top of the coffin when it was removed from the funeral home and would return the badge to the chief clerk's office; it would be he who would be assigned to see to the needs of the bereaved family.

When Harris walked into the Nine-three squad room shortly before 1500 he was wearing jeans and a blue work shirt. "The grapevine says that Joe was hit," Harris said to Scanlon after introducing himself.

Scanlon stared at Harris's manicured nails and black cowboy boots, and noticed the way the man tilted his lithe body to the right. His thumbs were tucked into the side pockets of his jeans.

"Where did you latch on to that information?" Scanlon said.

"That's the word that's going around the One-fourteen."

Scanlon was solemn. "Well, we don't want the word to leak out, especially to the press."

"So it is true."

"We're not sure. It might be."

Harris casually stretched out his boot and hooked the tip around the leg of a chair and dragged his seat over. He sat. "Not to worry, Lou. I'll see to it personally that every cop assigned to the One-fourteen puts a zipper on his mouth."

Leaning back in his seat, Scanlon locked his hands behind his head and said, "Answer a few questions?"

"You kiddin' or somethin'? Joe Gallagher wasn't only my boss, he was my friend. We were partners, worked the adjoining posts in the old

Seven-seven. He brought me into the junk squad. You better believe I'll do anything to get the cocksuckers who wasted Joe."

"Did Joe ever discuss his gambling or his love life with you?"

Harris was annoyed. "Chasing pussy and gambling are a national pastime. Don't look to paint Joe bad just because he was human."

"I've spoken to a few of his lady friends. They tell me that his bedroom tastes ran the gamut from strange to kinky."

"Come on, Lou! What the hell is kinky today? Especially in this town. The damn city is being run by a clique of goddamn faggots. The Thirteenth just arrested two morgue attendants for screwing corpses. You got ten- and eleven-year-old boys peddling their asses along the Great White Way, and the movies' leading lady is into fucking German shepherds." Harris was agitated, shaking his fist. "And you talk to me about kinky sex? Joe Gallagher never forced any woman into bed. They went because they wanted to, and they did whatever they did because they wanted to."

A nod of the head, a flash of teeth. Scanlon recognized a good argument when he heard one. "Did his wife know that he was stepping out on her?"

"I don't know. But I don't think it would have mattered. Joe once told me Mary Ann was frigid."

"How is she taking it?"

"Pretty bad."

"I'm going to have to interview her, I'm afraid."

Harris thought it over in silence and then said, "I know. But can't it wait till after the funeral?"

"I guess so. When is it?"

"Monday morning."

"Did Joe ever talk to you about his gambling?"

Harris examined his boots. He buffed the right one on the back of his jeans. "He never discussed it with me, because he knew how I felt about it."

"And how did you feel about it, Sarge?"

"It's strictly for assholes. Only the bookmakers and the shys come away winners."

Scanlon changed the subject. "How do you like living on Staten Island?"

Harris shrugged and said, "It's okay. It beats driving in from the Island. But it's no bargain having to drive over the guinea gangplank every day, and it's expensive."

Scanlon felt his adrenaline rise at the sneering reference to the Verrazano Narrows Bridge. The complete urban cop, he thought bitterly.

Jeans, cowboy boots, and a big mouth. "Did Joe change much after he became a boss?"

"Hah. Joe was always the public relations type. I remember when we worked in the Seven-seven, old Captain McCloskey called us into his office because our summonses were off. In those days the quota was ten parkers and five movers a month. We hadn't given out any in three months. McCloskey was really pissed off. He called us the worst cops in the precinct. Named us Useless and Lukewarm. Joe was Useless. McCloskey yelled at us, demanding to know why no summonses. Joe got his Irish up and yelled back. He told McCloskey that he didn't believe in hanging paper on working stiffs' cars, costing them a day's pay, while across the river the rich bastards are allowed to double- and triple-park all over the place and nobody does shit about it. He asked McCloskey if he'd ever driven through the theater district, or past the Waldorf, or down Fifth or Park Avenue, and seen the mounted cops who'd been assigned to help the rich triple-park their limousines. McCloskey had a shit fit and threw us out of his office. We were lucky he was transferred the following week, because he was getting ready to come down hard on us."

Summonses were a familiar sore spot for policemen. That was why precinct commanders were forced to have summons men. For doing this onerous duty summons men were taken out of the patrol chart and worked days, with weekends off. Statistics must be maintained.

"What was Joe like as a boss?" Scanlon asked.

Harris gave him a half-smile. "He was different, I'll say that much for him. And he'd gotten over the ambivalence of being a boss. He made it damn clear to everyone in the unit that he was the boss man. 'Don't do as I do, do as I say,' he'd tell them."

Scanlon leaned forward. "Herman the German told me that Joe wasn't much of a leader."

"Lou, you know as well as I do that there are a lot of ways to supervise people. Joe really hated the paper connected with the job. Herman the German is a paper pusher. That was the main reason why Joe had me brought into the unit, to take care of the paper while he played cops and robbers and partied. He was one of the greatest PR men I've ever known. But he was a tough cop when it came to things that he took seriously. And junk was number one on Joe's hit parade. Our unit led the entire Narcotics Division in buy-and-bust collars. There was no bullshit about him when it came to the Job. Every person in the unit was personally picked by Joe. And if a guy produced for him and needed a day, and had no time on the books, Joe'd give him the day and swallow the Twenty-eight."

"Where do you think he got his gambling money from?"

"I don't know. I never asked him."

"I've never been assigned to the junk squad, so I'm not too clear on how the buy money works. Tell me, will you?"

A hostile edge crept into Harris's voice. "Forget it. Every nickel has to be accounted for."

"I understand that, Sarge. But tell me anyway, please."

Harris shook his head. "We always have a few grand on hand to make buys. Our undercovers sign out the money, usually a few hundred at a time. They have to sign vouchers, and each time a buy goes down it has to be observed by a supervisor, or at least it's supposed to be. But naturally, sometimes a supervisor can't see what's going down because they're in a basement or on a roof. But anyway, buying junk is the same as buying chop meat at the supermarket. A pound of eye round cost so much and a bag of junk cost so much. An undercover can't say he paid forty dollars for nose candy when the going rate on the street is thirty. The humps in IAD who monitor our funds know what the price is as well as we do."

"Does your unit ever deal in kilo weight?"

"Depends on how many keys. We can deal up to thirty grand—after that we have to ask permission from the division to play. If it's a real heavy deal, we turn it over to the boys in Special Investigations. And sometimes the deal can be so big that we turn it over to the federal boys."

"How often is the fund audited?"

"Every quarter. And there are unannounced spot audits, too. There ain't no way anybody can play around with that money."

"There's always a way, Sarge. Some enterprising cop just has to think of it." Scanlon picked up a cigar packet, saw that it was empty, and rummaged around in the top drawer of his desk for his reserve supply. While doing this, he asked in a low voice, "Luise Bardwell your girlfriend?"

Harris's expression turned ugly. "Stay out of my private life, Scanlon."

"Lieutenant Scanlon, Sergeant. And by the way, my mother's name was Vitale." He found the green-and-white box behind an old *Rules and Procedures* manual.

"My private life is none of the department's business." A declarative statement that every cop knew to be false.

Scanlon took his time lighting up, studying the man in front of him. He got up and went over to the low metal library cabinet against the wall, pushed one of the sliding glass doors aside, and removed the *Patrol Guide* from the top shelf. He balanced the thick blue book on his palm, holding it in front of him. "Sergeant, I give you the Job's holy bible. In particular, I'd like to call your attention to procedure one-oh-four slash one, six pages of prohibited conduct printed single-space. Everything from engaging in unnecessary conversation while on patrol to incurring liabilities which cannot be paid as they become due. Now, I can't quote you chapter and verse, but I *can* guarantee that somewhere in these six pages is a phrase that goes something like this: 'If married, thou shall not lie with another.' " He returned the book to its place in the cabinet. He had enjoyed his little performance, particularly when he had addressed Harris as Sergeant. *Lieutenant* Scanlon, Sergeant. Perhaps lawyers did have the right idea; a little drama is good for the soul.

Harris caved in reluctantly. "The lady is married."

"Aren't they all, George." The plastic button on the telephone flashed. He slapped it down and brought the receiver up.

Deputy Chief MacAdoo McKenzie's strained voice informed him that the PC wanted to see both of them, together. Forthwith, he added ominously.

"Right," Scanlon said, hanging up. He stared intensely at Harris. "I know that Gallagher participated in a threesome with your girlfriend."

Harris made a dismissive gesture. "Luise is a strange lady. The threesome was her idea. She's into that kind of stuff. She never wanted any kids because they leave stretch marks."

"She goes both ways?"

"Yes. She's open about it, too."

"How did Joe get involved with her?"

"Luise first brought up the subject to me. Said she wanted to get it on with me and a woman who she had been having an affair with. I told her that that wasn't my bag and suggested Joe. She liked the idea a whole lot."

"Didn't it ever bother you that Joe and your lady friend were going to hop into the feathers together, not to mention the fact that she went both ways?"

Harris made a weary little gesture. "That thing she's got between her legs don't have an odometer on it, and it don't wear out. As long as the lady is available when I want to see her, I don't give a good shit what she does or with whom."

True love is wonderful, Scanlon thought. "What's the story with the lady's husband?"

"They have an open marriage. He's a psychoanalyst with a fancy Manhattan practice. Luise told me that he ain't above taking a little tap in the ass every now and then. She told me that they sit around the dinner table discussing their adventures with each other."

"Then the husband knew all about you and Joe and the threesome."

"I got to assume that he did."

"I'm going to have to talk to both of them," Scanlon said.

"Lou, do what you gotta do. I'm on your side." He began to run his nails over the blue denim, studying the white strain in the fabric. "I've asked the borough commander to assign me to the case. Any objections?"

"No. But if you really want to help, I'd prefer you to stay where you are. Mix with the people in your unit, with the cops in the precinct. I need some ears over there. I have to find out where Joe got his gambling money."

"I'll do what I can, but it won't be easy. Cops clam up whenever they think there might be a problem."

6

The anteroom of the PC's fourteenth-floor office at police headquarters was surrounded by a glass wall. Blue sofas, low white tables made of plastic, and chrome tubular sand-filled receptacles for cigarette butts filled the area. People waiting their turn to see the PC talked in hushed voices, or kept their faces buried in magazines, while they silently rehearsed the arguments that they would use on the police commissioner.

On the other side of the glass wall, to the left of the double door, sat the PC's aide. He was a tall, lean man with short hair and spit-shined shoes whose tailored uniform bore the gilt oak leaf of a deputy inspector. Occasionally he would glance up from the stack of Unusual Occurrence reports to check the lights over the door; the red one was still on.

Deputy Chief MacAdoo McKenzie was also watching the red light. He thought that the damn thing had been on for an interminable length of time when in fact it had only been three minutes. Scanlon was sitting next to him, browsing through the latest issue of *Police Magazine*. An article entitled "The Keys to K-9 Success" had caught his attention. He wondered if a canine corps might not be the answer that everyone was searching for. Enough properly trained dogs let loose in high-crime areas at night might reduce the two-legged-animal population who stalked the streets and subway stations. He liked that idea. He liked it a lot. When those doggies made a pinch, they *really* made a pinch!

The silver-haired pastor of the Harlem Tabernacle Baptist Church was there to ask the PC if he would be disposed to transfer the pastor's nephew, a God-fearing boy, from an active patrol precinct in the South Bronx to the Detective Division. The lad had confided to his uncle that he would really enjoy an assignment in the Pickpocket and Confidence Squad. The pastor intended to remind the commissioner of the help that he had given the department in defeating the move by some Harlem liberals to civilianize the Civilian Complaint Review Board.

The president and the recording secretary of the Gravesend Planning Board were huddled on one of the sofas rehearsing the argument they would use to persuade the PC to assign additional police to the Six-one.

E. Thornton Gray, the executive director of the American Civil Rights Union, was one of the people waiting. He passed the time reading the *Wall Street Journal.* He was a content man. And with good reason. Alza had closed yesterday at twenty-eight a share. He had bought five thousand shares at five in January of '81.

Gray was privy to a lot of inside information concerning future business trends and mergers. Captains of industry wanted him for their friend. They knew how to discreetly nurture a friendship: a chance remark over cocktails, a slip of the tongue after an apéritif. And a quick call to one's broker.

Gray wanted to see the PC because he had heard disquieting rumors that the department was testing a new heavyweight bullet. Gray had led the fight several years ago to force the police department to adopt a lighter load of ammunition, thereby reducing the bullet's stopping power. The police hierarchy had caved in under the political pressure. This abject surrender resulted in policemen being maimed and killed. When Abou 37X and a detective locked arms on a Harlem street corner and began shooting at each other, they were inches apart. Yet the detective's new bullets bounced harmlessly off 37X's field jacket. An FBI agent's bullet had brought the fugitive down, but not before the detective had been wounded. As police casualties mounted, the evidence grew overwhelming: the bullets that the police were using were not as effective as they should be in today's hostile environment. Police line organizations had waged an uphill fight for a new bullet. The department, stung by the increase in police injuries, had reluctantly agreed to start tests on a heavier cartridge. E. Thornton Gray intended to do everything in his power to prevent that from coming to pass.

Scanlon tossed the magazine onto the table and let his eyes roam around the room. They came to rest on a vaguely familiar face at the other end. The face had a dour expression and belonged to a broad-chested man with brownish-gray hair. He tried to remember where he knew that face from. A glimmer of remembrance. He nudged Deputy Chief MacAdoo McKenzie. "Isn't that Inspector Loyd?"

MacAdoo McKenzie whispered, "He's been assigned by the mayor to baby-sit the PC."

"Has it gotten that bad?"

"It has. Hardly a week goes by that Bobby Boy isn't stopped for driving his private car on one of the city's streets in an intoxicated condition. Up to now all the cops who have pulled him over have done the right thing. But it only takes one incident to be page one."

"That's too bad," Scanlon said, stealing a look at Inspector Loyd. He didn't care about the PC's little drinking problem but he felt sorry that Loyd was stuck with such a miserable job.

"That's only the half of it. He used to be in the closet with his lady friends, but lately he's taken to waltzing them around town. A few weeks ago he showed up in Part 3B of Criminal Court with one of his Carmelitas. Both of them had a load on. He started to throw his weight around the courtroom, disrupting the proceedings, and the judge came within inches of tossing him into the slammer for contempt. He was lucky that a lot of cops were there to hustle his ass out before the judge came down on him. So poor Loyd's been assigned to keep him out of trouble."

Bob Gomez paced the handsomely furnished office in front of the great desk that had once belonged to another police commissioner, Teddy Roosevelt. Sunlight filled the office. Gomez made a dashing figure: tall, erect, with a caramel-colored face that belied its fifty-three years. An extremely well-built man for his age, he was, as always, immaculately attired in a tailor-made sport jacket and slacks. His brown loafers had wide tassels.

Today's hangover was a particularly bad one. The belt of pain was like a vise on his forehead. They were getting progressively worse. He was just going to have to stop drinking. If he didn't, it was only a question of time until the mayor got rid of him. And he liked having cognizance and control over the largest police department in the country. But he knew the Job could only protect him so far. That was it, he resolved. No more booze.

Gomez was also annoyed at himself for having made a fool of himself in front of those goddamn television cameras at the scene of the Gallagher/Zimmerman homicide. He should have listened to the first dep's whispered message that there might be a problem, and his advice that Gomez play down the hero angle. If there was a scandal brewing over Gallagher's death he didn't want to be dragged into it. He'd been lucky so far in his relationship with the press and the rest of the power brokers. He had gone out of his way to maintain open lines of communications with the news media and the rest of them. And it had paid off. He did their favors for them, promoted their damn friends and relatives, spoke at their goddamn dinners, assigned motorcycle escorts to them whenever their inflated egos required it. And, in return, they praised him as the best police commissioner that the city had ever had.

He had been able, by manipulating crime statistics, to give the impression that crime had actually been reduced under his administration. We're winning the war; we've turned the corner. Bullshit. He had been surprised that no other PC had thought of the idea.

At his first Precinct Commanders' Conference he had told them, obliquely, to handle their Sixty-one forms "with discretion." Wise and wary men, tutored by years of experience in the subtle nuances of cop talk, understood. Soon grand larcenies were being classified petit larcenies; robberies were downgraded to simple assaults; burglaries were turned into malicious mischiefs. An outstanding PC, Gomez reflected sardonically and walked back to his desk. One of his major concerns now was the damn cops. They were forever pulling off outlandish stunts that ended up in the press. Yesterday he had read a report from IAD about a radio car team in the Tenth who not only abandoned their assigned sector, but abandoned the entire city. They drove out to Suffolk County to attend a lawn party the recorder's girlfriend was giving. In a police car, no less. He was going to have to start handing down stiffer penalties in the Trial Room. No more Mister Nice Guy. But right now his main concern was this Gallagher mess. He was terrified by the possibility that it might not sink into serene oblivion fast enough.

He stood in front of the large picture window peering out through the white vertical blinds. The rays of a dying sun felt strong as his eyes moved along the tops of the buildings of lower Manhattan. Far below he noticed a mounted cop checking the parked cars along Worth Street. A group of tourists were being shepherded through the vaulted underpass of the Municipal Building. A five-member band was playing ragtime for the tourists in Police Plaza Park. He thought about the next day. He was scheduled to pay a visit to Gallagher's widow and present her with five thousand dollars from the Police Welfare Fund. The press was sure to be in heavy attendance. He'd wear a dark suit and a grieved expression and pose with the widow and her fatherless child, or was it children? He couldn't remember, and what did it matter, anyway? What was important was that it would be good PR. Moving away from the window, he stepped up to the row of buttons on his desk.

Deputy Chief MacAdoo McKenzie shot upright in his seat and nudged Scanlon when he saw the green light flick on.

As the doors to his office began to open, Bob Gomez quickly

grabbed the top report from the Urgent/In basket and began to read it. The report proved to be the translation of the Mexican police report on the arrest of José Torres, the escaped FALN terrorist who was known throughout the Job as No Hands because he had lost both his hands when he accidentally blew up his East Village bomb factory. "Damn Ricans could never handle that high-tech stuff," a Bomb Squad member had commented at the time.

Gomez read slowly and did not look up as his aide led the two police officials inside and quietly left the room.

They waited in front of the great desk, watching as the PC initialed the last page of the report and tossed it into the Urgent/Out basket.

With a sweep of his hand, Gomez motioned them to sit in the cushioned chairs arranged in front of his desk. "I'm glad that you both could manage to tear yourself away from your other pressing duties and come have a little chat with me," Gomez said.

Scanlon looked past the PC out the window to the glass-and-stone side of Pace University. Eager, wide-eyed students were in that building learning all there was to learn about the function of government in contemporary society. How little they'll learn, he thought, relaxing, ready for the civics lesson that he knew was about to begin.

Gomez said ominously, "I would like to know why I was not thoroughly briefed at the Gallagher crime scene." His glare fell on McKenzie, placing blame.

The deputy chief cleared his throat and squirmed. "It was my understanding that the first dep had been informed that there might be a problem."

"The first dep is *not* the PC. I am. And I should have been personally advised that Gallagher might be dirty."

Scanlon was looking down at his prosthesis; he had crossed the fake one over the real one. He looked up, his black eyes boring into the PC's angry face. "You were told," he said calmly.

Gomez sat ramrod-straight, his hostile stare fixed on Scanlon, his fingertips drumming on his desk. "Nobody told me *anything*, Lieutenant." His twisted face betrayed his lie. "But I do expect you to tell me now. I want to know exactly where the department stands on the Gallagher/Zimmerman homicide. And I want it all."

Unruffled, with professional nonchalance, Scanlon told the PC about the splash pad in Jackson Heights, the sexual aids to happiness, the girlfriends, the threesome, the gambling, the indebtedness to Walter Ticornelli, the shylock. When he'd finished, he leaned back in his seat and waited.

Gomez leaned his head back against the cushioned headrest of the high-backed chair and closed his eyes, sorting it all out.

A minute passed.

Gomez opened his eyes and spoke. "Yesterday in Federal Court, Detective Alfred Martin was convicted of kidnapping and robbing diamond dealers here and in PR. The *Daily News* ran five lines on page sixty-three, right next to an ad for Kal Kan dog food. The *Times* gave it ten lines on the obituary page. When Martin was arrested a year ago it was page one for three days and then died a natural death. But this Gallagher thing is different. It's the kind of story the press gets off on. It has page-one ingredients. Staying power. 'Sixty Minutes' would probably want to do a piece on the sex lives of American police." He was stern. "Gentlemen, this department, and *this* commissioner, does not want, or need, that kind of publicity." He shook his index finger at them. "No more rotten apples. What we want and need are heroes. John Waynes in blue. And I would be very appreciative if you two saw to it that Lt. Joseph P. Gallagher remained a hero, one of our honored dead." He raised his left eyebrow, sliding his gaze from one to the other. "Is my meaning perfectly clear, gentlemen?"

MacAdoo McKenzie pulled a filthy handkerchief from his rear pocket and wiped the sweat from his neck. "We understand, Commissioner. Whatever you want."

A smile appeared on Scanlon's lips. Every cop in the Job knows that every boss in the Job above the rank of captain has feet of clay. But when it goes up to their balls, it's hard to watch. "And what exactly do we do if the facts of the case do not warrant Gallagher's canonization?" Scanlon asked.

The PC checked the time. "Thank you for stopping by, gentlemen." Gomez pushed up out of his chair and went to the door. McKenzie followed. Scanlon remained seated. "Aren't you leaving, Lieutenant?" Gomez said.

"I'd like an answer to my question, Commissioner," Scanlon said, staring out the window at the distant clouds.

Gomez walked up behind him and whispered in his ear, "You do whatever you have to do, Lieutenant. But don't get me involved or it will be your ass."

Scanlon nodded his understanding and got up.

"I want a tight span of control on this," Gomez said. "You, Chief, will report directly to me. Lieutenant, you report to Chief McKenzie and to *no one else.*"

"And exactly what do I say to the chief of detectives when he calls and wants to know the status of the case?"

"You may tell that runty, Napoleonic psychopath to call me personally."

I guess they don't like each other very much, Scanlon thought, leaving the office.

It was after six that Friday when Scanlon arrived at Luise Bardwell's Battery Park penthouse. She was waiting as he stepped off the elevator. Five seven or so, he reckoned, trim body, capped teeth and a broad smile. She was barefooted and had on tight shorts and a white tank top that showed it all.

"Hi," she said cheerily.

"Luise Bardwell?" Scanlon asked, reaching for his shield.

"Yes."

He held up his identification for her inspection. "I'm Lieutenant Scanlon. I telephoned."

"Please come in, Lieutenant."

They were standing in a good-size entry hall of white marble. She led him into a glass-walled living room with a stone fireplace and Art Deco sculpture. "What a view," he said.

"Yes, it's quite nice." She moved ahead and slid open a glass door that led out onto a conservatory overlooking the Hudson River. The moist smell of heat and dirt came at Scanlon as he stepped into the rooftop greenhouse. It was warmer in there than it was outside. Tall plants stood between tables covered with potted greenery. In the corner, set against the glass wall, were two long pieces of furniture made of bleached planks. Patchwork pillows and cushions contrasted with the stark wood.

Luise Bardwell lowered herself onto the plank sofa and patted the space next to her. As Scanlon sat, she fluffed a cushion and pressed it to her chest. "Do you mind sitting out here?"

"Not at all. It's not often that I have the chance to take in such scenery," he said, looking out over the river.

"I find it very peaceful to sit here, with the smell of nature and the great view. Now. How may I be of assistance?"

"I would like you to tell me about your relationship with Joe Gallagher, George Harris, Valerie Clarkson, and Donna Hunt." He waved his hand and added, "And the rest of them."

She made a tut-tut sound, gave him a perplexed look, pressed the cushion close, and said, "My relationship with those people is not the concern of the police department."

"I'm investigating a homicide, Mrs. Bardwell. Not some college prank. I'd appreciate it if you'd answer my questions."

"Do I have to?"

"No, you don't. In that case, I'd have to get a subpoena and usher you in front of the grand jury. If you cooperate now I can guarantee you that there will be no mention of you or your husband to the press, no nasty publicity."

"My husband and I live in an open marriage."

"Hey? Whatever it takes, go with it."

She had a pretty face, a small nose, and a smile that was always there. She wore her yellowish-brown hair short, with bangs.

"I'm bisexual, and so is my husband. We both believe in enjoying the maximum pleasure that life has to offer."

"Will you talk to me about Gallagher and the other people you were involved with?"

"Yes, I will, if you promise that there will be no publicity about it."

"I promise."

"My husband is in his study—would you like to talk to him too?"

"I'd prefer to just speak to you, for now."

"Who shall I tell you about first?"

"Why not start with Harris?"

She ducked her head in a mock gesture of shyness, smiled, and for the next fifty minutes casually discussed her various and sundry relationships. When she'd finished, she rested her chin on the cushion and said, "Actually, I've got the best of both worlds."

"You have no children?"

"No. Max has three from a previous marriage. We have none together. I'm wise enough to know that I'd make a god-awful mother. Besides, I really believe that in this life, I was put on earth to give pleasure to men and to women. Do you believe in reincarnation, Lieutenant?"

"I never really gave it much thought."

"In one of my previous lives I was an Egyptian princess. My name was Isis and I had a son, Horus. I know that just as sure as the two of us are sitting here."

Scanlon was aware of the ache in his stump. He rubbed his missing ankle. "Tell what kind of a person George Harris is."

"Self-centered, ambitious, with a need to be the man in charge."

"And Joe Gallagher?"

"A sweet man who needed to be in the spotlight. He was always on stage, even in bed."

"How's that?"

"Joe was always looking to do something kinky, or what he thought was kinky. But he didn't really enjoy sex. He had the need to perform."

"And on what basis did you reach that conclusion?"

"I majored in psychology and my husband is a psychiatrist, a rather good one, I might add."

"Did Harris or Gallagher ever discuss their work with you?"

"Not really. Now and then George would feel like letting off steam and talk about their unit. Especially whenever Joe would cancel some decision that George had made."

"Did that happen often?"

"No. But it did occur every now and then, and whenever it did, George got furious."

"How did they get along together otherwise, George and Joe?"

"Pretty good, I think." She raised her foot up off the floor and rested it on the seat of the couch, and began to slowly move her knee back and forth. Her tight shorts embraced the contours of her body, as if teasing Scanlon.

He struggled to keep his eyes topside. "Did Joe ever discuss money with you?"

"Money wasn't his thing."

"What about Harris—was it his thing?"

"Most definitely. Shortly after his divorce I remember George boasting about how he had concealed assets from his wife."

Scanlon hadn't known about Harris's divorce. But that was not unusual in today's Job. The divorce rate was so high that the subject of equitable distribution had long since become a bore to most cops. Still, Harris had not mentioned it. "How long has Harris been divorced?"

"I'm not sure. I guess about two years."

"Did he ever tell you what the assets were that he concealed from his wife?"

"He didn't, and I didn't ask. I deliberately avoid asking lovers questions about their personal lives."

What a sweetheart, he thought. "When you and Harris got together, did you use Gallagher's pad in Jackson Heights or did you use a motel?"

She looked at him queerly. "George would take me to his own apartment."

"On Staten Island?"

"No. He has an apartment on Ocean Parkway, in Brooklyn."

"Did you ever go to Gallagher's apartment in Jackson Heights?"

"Yes, when I went with him and the ladies to have our little threesomes."

"I understand that the threesome was your idea."

"Yes, it was. I don't usually go with blue-collar types, and I thought it might be interesting to see what they were like."

"Is that why you went out with Harris and Gallagher?"

"Yes."

Suddenly two of the biggest cats that Scanlon had ever seen slunk out from behind one of the plants and leaped up on his lap.

"Oh, my babies are here," she said. "I was wondering where you were hiding. This is Puss," she said, petting one of the purring cats. "And my other baby is Fellatio. Aren't they adorable?"

She's a fucking banana, Scanlon thought, taking one of the cats and putting it down. He then picked up the other cat and put it on the floor too.

"Don't you like my babies?"

"I love them, only not on me." He watched the two cats move off behind a plant. "What can you tell me about the women who participated in the threesome?"

"Rena Bedford is a young thing who is into just about anything that will give her a thrill. She was an active participant."

"And Donna Hunt?"

"A middle-aged housewife wanting to savor a bit of life before it's over. Bored with her marriage and her husband."

"Was she an active or passive participant in the threesome?"

She smiled, pressed the cushion close to her chest. "She was very active. I think that she was quite surprised to discover that she was bisexual. And more than a little afraid."

The door to the conservatory opened and a paunchy man with an elfin face and a pepper-and-salt beard appeared. He was wearing black cotton slacks and a wide-collared shirt that was open. A heavy gold chain with a gold figurine of Buddha was around his neck. "Hi, I'm Max Bardwell," he said. "You must be the policeman my wife told me was coming."

Scanlon got up, and the two men shook hands. "Would you like some coffee or a drink?" Max Bardwell asked.

"Coffee might be nice," Scanlon said.

"In that case, why don't we go into the kitchen and I'll make some," Luise Bardwell said, getting up.

Scanlon followed them into a gleaming white kitchen. The wife made coffee. The two men sat at a long white table that had white canvas chairs. "Continue with your questions, Lieutenant," Luise Bardwell said, pouring water into the pot.

"Max, did you know of your wife's involvement with Gallagher and Harris and these women?"

"Yes, I did," the husband said. "Luise and I have no secrets with each other. Most people, including yourself, I guess, would consider our marriage unorthodox. And in the ordinary sense, it is. But it works for us, and that's what counts."

"It doesn't bother you that your wife goes with other people?" Scanlon said, watching the wife lay out cups and saucers.

"No, it doesn't," the wife answered. "My husband knows that I love him and him alone."

"Luise is correct, Lieutenant. Our love for each other is the important thing."

"You're both lucky to have found each other," Scanlon said, looking at the wife. "Tell me about Valerie Clarkson."

She poured coffee and sat down next to her husband. "I brought Valerie out. She's gay. I think that she is much happier now that she knows who she is."

Max patted his wife's hand. "You're a regular little therapist, that's what you are."

Another banana heard from, Scanlon thought. "Do you still see George Harris?"

"No. I stopped seeing him and the rest of them about a month ago."

"Any reason you stopped seeing them?"

"I thought that it was time to move on. Broaden my horizons, so to speak."

"You're telling me, Mrs. Bardwell, that you do not see Harris or any of the women anymore?"

"Yes."

"Lieutenant, according to the newspapers and the radio reports, Gallagher and Mrs. Zimmerman died during an attempted robbery. I can't understand why you are checking into Gallagher's relationship with my wife, or Harris, or the rest of them."

"Whenever we have a double homicide we have to delve deeper into the case to make sure there is no connection that we've overlooked."

"What you are saying is that you are not convinced that it was a holdup murder," the doctor said.

"No, that is *not* what I'm saying," Scanlon said. "The facts of the case bear out that it was a robbery that went sour. But I still have to go through the motions and ask my questions, just to make sure that there is not something there that should be brought out into the light. The department likes everything tidy." He measured the husband. "Tell me, Doctor, by any chance do you know Dr. Stanley Zimmerman? He's the son of the woman who was killed."

An undercurrent of hostility seeped into Max Bardwell's answer. "No, I don't."

Scanlon got up. "May I use your telephone? I have to call my office."

"Of course," Luise Bardwell said. "There's one on the wall here, but why don't you use the one in the living room. You'll have privacy."

Scanlon stood looking into the fireplace, waiting for someone in the Squad to answer the damn phone, and wondering if people who lived in the fifteenth and sixteenth centuries were as screwed-up as people were today. An Egyptian princess, my ass.

He heard a quiet click on the line. Someone had picked up an extension.

"Nine-three Squad, Suckieluski."

Scanlon recognized Hector Colon's voice. "Suckieluski, anything doing?"

"*Nada*. Most of the team have called it a day."

"I'm going home from here," Scanlon said. "Sign me out."

"Right, Lou."

When Scanlon came back into the kitchen he was taken aback to see Luise Bardwell sitting at the kitchen table next to her husband reading the latest edition of *Screw* magazine.

"Would you like some candy?" she asked Scanlon. "They're quite good; solid milk chocolate."

He took a look at the box she held out to him and recoiled at the explicit shapes of the goodies. That one was a vagina. The others he wasn't so sure about. "I'm on a diet. But thanks anyway. Where does one buy such delights?" Scanlon asked, watching her select a piece for herself and stuff it into her greedy little mouth.

"Joe Gallagher gave me a box of them," she said.

"May I see it?" Scanlon asked.

She placed it on the table in front of Scanlon.

The lieutenant looked at the candies and shuddered slightly. He replaced the top and turned the box over. In the right-hand corner on the back there was a label: Luv-Joy Manufacturing Company, Brooklyn, New York.

7

Great Jones Street is a continuation of East Third that runs for two short blocks between Bowery and Broadway. There is a wide stretch of undeveloped land on the west side of Engine Company 33's firehouse that is used as a commercial parking lot during the day and is empty at night, except for a few cars.

Tony Scanlon's second-floor loft could be reached by walking through the lot and using the fire escape zigzagging down the rear of the building. He enjoyed jogging up the metal steps. It helped him stay in shape. He also sometimes enjoyed shooting the bull with some of the firemen who hung out in front of the firehouse.

He parked his car in the rear of the near vacant lot and checked the time. Eight-sixteen P.M. He was tired of people and wanted to be alone. As he locked the car door he noticed a group of firemen ogling coeds rushing to a late Friday class at the nearby NYU campus. One of the firemen, a guy named Fred who lived out in Commack and had a large beer belly, spotted him and waved him over.

Approaching the group of firemen, Scanlon saw one of them make an obscene gesture at two passing coeds. "Did you catch the tits on them two?" the fireman said to Scanlon.

Scanlon wondered why firemen were always horny. "No, I didn't. What's up?"

"Whaddaya hear on the new contract? Think the mayor is goin' to go for eight and eight?" Fred asked.

"We'll probably end up with the same percentage increase spread over two years," Scanlon said, wanting to get away from the firemen, to walk. No matter how tired he was, a stroll through the streets of Greenwich Village always seemed to rejuvenate him. His phantom leg never hurt then; he was able to unwind and think.

The basketball games in the vest-pocket park on the Avenue of the Americas and West Third had attracted the usual throng of spectators and bettors. Sidewalk peddlers were selling batteries, pocket books, and gold jewelry along the curb. Artists were selling their horrible paintings.

Scanlon strolled, people-watched. Suddenly he saw an approaching couple. A big-boned black woman, outfitted in a black cowboy hat tilted rakishly to the side and tight red slacks and a tight red sweater into which she had poured two mammoth, unhaltered breasts, walked arm in arm with a white Greenwich Village Sikh with a beard down to his chest, a white turban rolled around his head, a white homespun that flowed down to his thonged sandals, and a ten-foot walking pole.

On Bleecker Street he passed a restaurant that had a hand-painted sign in the window that offered Szechuan and Thai food. He thought of the new wave of Asian immigrants that had taken over the city's produce industry and remembered how cops had had to learn to distinguish among these newcomers to our shores. The skinny black-haired killer extortionist from Hong Kong, the Korean stickup teams, and the Cambodian drug runners had all seen to that.

When he turned into West Fourth Street he noticed a group of giggling girls hurrying down the steps of the Pink Pussycat Erotic Boutique. He looked down into the display window and saw a collection of phalluses and edible panties. A big business, Gretta Polchinski had told him. He turned abruptly. There was homework to be done.

Tony Scanlon's loft had high ceilings and floor-to-ceiling windows. A teak polyurethaned floor had been laid diagonally. The galley kitchen had polished granite counters. The walls were natural brick, and there were two rows of iron structural pillars running through the middle of the loft. Rugs were scattered about, and there were groupings of natural wood furniture. In front of the kitchen was a dining area that consisted of four butcher blocks supporting a thick piece of glass. Nail barrels were used as seats. Off in the distance there was a sleeping area that consisted of a king-size platform bed with a heavy brass headboard. On the wall above the bed was a batik that depicted a sea god riding a dolphin through the depths.

Scanlon had bought the loft with money borrowed from his pension and a loan from the Municipal Credit Union. Jack Fineberg, who had owned the building and had converted it into co-op lofts, knew Scanlon and had offered him an insider's price. Fineberg was a retired bookmaker from Brooklyn who had invested his money in real estate.

Fifteen years ago Fineberg's daughter had been raped while on her way home from Brooklyn College. Detective Tony Scanlon had caught the case. Three days after the date of occurrence Scanlon and another detective named Hawkins went to Bainbridge Street in the Seven-seven to arrest one Leslie Brown for the attack on Fineberg's daughter. Brown, a shaven-headed giant, resisted arrest. During the melee Detective Hawkins sustained a broken nose and a deep gash along his hairline. The Unusual Occurrence report stated how in his attempt to escape Brown had fled the apartment and gone out on the fire escape, where he had lost his footing and fallen three stories, impaling himself on the spiked fence in front of the brownstone.

Mr. Brown had been rushed to Brookdale Hospital, where a team of doctors had removed his testicles. Brown was later to claim before the Civilian Complaint Review Board and the American Civil Rights Union that Detective Scanlon, upon seeing his partner lying unconscious on the floor, had gone crazy and beaten him about the head and body with a blackjack. When Brown was semiconscious, he claimed, Scanlon had picked him up bodily and had thrown him off the fire escape.

Detective Scanlon had vehemently denied the accusation. The result of it all was that Leslie Brown now sang soprano and Tony Scanlon owned a loft.

Scanlon entered by the fire escape entrance and immediately went around the spacious loft rolling down the wooden matchstick blinds. When this was done he made sure that the doors were locked and then double-checked the blinds. Prying eyes were one of the annoyances of Manhattan living. Although Great Jones Street was a cheerless street of machine shops and factories, Scanlon still was on guard against the omnipresent danger of some creep with binoculars. What he was about to do was his secret, and he intended to keep it that way.

He walked into the sleeping area and undressed. Naked, he went over to the eighteen-drawer clothes chest, opened one of the middle drawers on the right side, and took out a fresh pair of heavy support pantyhose. Sitting on the edge of the bed, he worked the pantyhose up his legs, taking care not to run the fabric as he moved it up over his prosthesis. He stood and, with his legs apart, pulled the undergarment snug in the crotch. He then went back into the clothes chest and took out a gray sweatsuit and stepped into it. He bent at the waist and ran both hands over the prosthesis, ensuring that it was snug inside the pantyhose, which acted like an athletic supporter for his artificial leg.

He went over to the music system on the third shelf of the bookcase and switched on a Richard Simmons aerobics tape. For the next thirty minutes Tony Scanlon danced aerobics. No pilgrimage to Lourdes had rid him of his limp. His own personalized form of physical therapy had: solitary aerobics and long, hard walks around the city, pacing the borders of his loft thousands and thousands of times, but most of all, his tenacious determination to stay a cop.

After showering, he toweled himself, put the prosthesis back on, donned a blue terry-cloth bathrobe, settled in at the table with the glass top, and began to read Joe Gallagher's personnel records. The latest semiannual evaluation stated that Gallagher was an above-average supervisor who instilled a spirit of participation in his subordinates. Bullshit. That was not what Herman the German had told him. There were many letters of commendation from various religious and philanthropic organizations praising Gallagher for his good works. The UF 10a, Foreign Language and Special Qualification Card, showed that Gallagher had none. The UF 11, Time Record Card, stated that Gallagher was entitled to both July 4 and Memorial Day.

He began to read Gallagher's old memo books. A cop's memo book is like a ship's log. Police regulations require that members of the force on patrol below the rank of captain maintain one. Before the beginning of each tour the date, tour, and assignment will be entered, and during the tour a full and accurate record of all duty performed and all police occurrences, including post changes and absences from post. If no police action was taken during a tour, "nothing to report" will be written and the entry signed. Gallagher's memo books were filled with nothing to reports. That did not surprise Scanlon. Streetwise cops put as little as possible in the serially numbered books. They know that once an entry is made it is etched in stone and subject to subpoena by the courts, the grand jury, the Trial Room, and the Civilian Complaint Review Board. No cop ever went to jail for an "I can't recall" answer under oath.

Time passed, and he became aware of the ache behind his right eyeball. He let the pencil fall from his hand and stretched in place. He pushed back from the table and got up. He walked into the kitchen, took down a bottle of scotch, and poured whiskey over ice. Clinking the cubes, he walked over the glossy floor to the bookcase, where he selected an Edith Piaf record and put it on the turntable. He went into the sleeping area, removed his robe and the prosthesis, and stretched out naked on the bed. There was a red halo around the tip of his stump. He put the glass down on the treasure chest that he had bought in a secondhand shop on Second Avenue and, leaning forward, massaged the stump with both his hands. It reminded him of a giant sausage. When the pain had subsided, he picked up the glass and lay back with his head resting against the brass rods. He strained the nerves in his stump, trying to wiggle his missing toes. He hated the way the stump looked next to his whole leg. A useless appendage. He looked down at his body. It was hard, lean, the stomach muscles clearly outlined. The tangled mass of black hair on his chest tapered into a line that led to his penis. His gaze followed the trail. He tweaked the organ and watched it jerk to life and fall back to rest on his body. In a sudden fit of anger he grabbed it, squeezing the head until it was blood-red. Man's lifelong fascination, his curse, his cross, he thought, pushing it aside.

He sipped scotch. Edith Piaf was singing "Mon Dieu." The haughty mournfulness of her voice and the relaxing effect of the scotch put him in a contemplative mood. That combination always did. Somewhere in the night a cat yowled. There was the sudden din of klaxon and horn. The men of Engine 33 were responding to a fire. He looked up at the skylight, peering out into the night, to some distant galaxy, permitting his thoughts to retreat into the past, to that awful day that had so inexorably changed his life.

It was the second week in February, a gloomy, dispiriting month. The pewter sky had dispensed three days of snow. The city was congealed in an eerie stillness. Plows had entombed cars, and only the foolhardy made unnecessary journeys. It was six P.M. and the detectives were responding to a location in an unmarked department auto. The wind howled, and Tony Scanlon had both his legs. Tire chains clanked; the window wipers appeared to be giving up the struggle. Detective Waldron had been driving. Keegan and Capucci relaxed in the rear. Detective Sgt. Tony Scanlon was in the passenger seat, gazing out at the falling flakes.

The Two-four Squad detectives had been on their way into Midtown Precinct North to arrest a suspect for an A&R that had gone down in their precinct. A female bird had dropped a dime. The son of a bitch was screwing her girlfriend, so sang the bird. Love's old sweet song.

Their destination had been a tenement on West Forty-seventh between Ninth and Tenth avenues. Driving was difficult. They had just passed Fifty-eighth and Eighth when the call came over the radio: "In Midtown North a report of a ten-thirty. Two male whites armed with guns. The Adler Hotel. 1438 Four-one Street. Units responding, K?"

The radio fell silent.

Central rebroadcast the alarm.

No response from the patrol force. The detectives were ten blocks away from the hotel. The *Patrol Guide* proscribed outside units from responding to crimes in progress that were more than five blocks away from their locations. Scanlon knew from experience that more than half of the patrol force scheduled for that tour had telephoned their commands and requested emergency excusals. They were snowbound in suburbia.

Central broadcast the alarm a third time.

The first response came: "David Edward George going."

"Any unit on a backup, K?"

Waldron glanced at Scanlon. The detective sergeant snatched up the radio handset from its cradle. "Two-four Squad detectives are five blocks away, Central. We'll back up."

"Ten-four, Two-four Squad."

The detectives were the first unit to arrive. They leaped from their car, leaving doors ajar and the roof light whirling flashes. They spread out, trudging through the packed snow, attempting to navigate their way up onto the sidewalk. The crust crunched under their feet. Scanlon and Capucci were the first to make it to the sidewalk. They arrived in time to confront two men fleeing the luxury hotel. Both suspects wore blue pea jackets and had ski masks over their faces. One of them carried a black valise. Capucci called out: "Stop! Police!" The two men stopped and whirled to face the policemen. Each of them was holding a Walther MP-K, a small machine pistol with a thirty-two-round magazine. Scanlon saw the weapons, and at first thought they were toys. His gaze was transfixed by the guns, each with its retractable tubular stock lashed to the side of the breech. He remembered that a small bird had lit on the hotel's gold awning. He crouched in a combat stance and fired. Explosions went off all around him. They hurt his ears. He was not wearing his goggles or his ear protectors. This was not the range; it was the street, and it was for real. He fired double-action. Snowflakes stuck to his nose. His gun was suddenly empty. Still crouching, he turned to one side and started to combat-reload. He had just closed the cylinder when he felt a sharp pain in his left leg. Suddenly he was upside down and the buildings were spinning all around him. He was on the ground, with his face in the snow. He struggled to raise himself up off the ground. Bracing himself on one hand, he leaned up and fired. Gunfire was all around him. He heard screams and wondered if it was he who had cried out. He managed to get off four rounds before he collapsed. His face was on fire. A warm sticky wetness gushed over his lower torso, and then blackness came.

He awoke scared and disoriented. He was in a bed with green sheets, and there was a gray curtain that hung from ceiling tracks. He heard muted gongs and a woman's voice over a loudspeaker, and a rattling trolley. Wires and tubes ran from his body to a monitor panel. His tongue was pasted to the roof of his mouth, and there was the sour taste of medicine. A blurred figure in a white winged cap hovered over him, saying incomprehensible things. Men in green tunics tended him.

One of the men had bulging eyes and wore a stethoscope. A leaden numbness weighed down his left leg. He attempted to move it and couldn't. A dread made him suddenly feel cold all over. He moved his hand under the sheet and probed a mound of gauze, inching beyond, straining to get at the source of his discomfort. There was nothing beyond! His leg was not there. He screamed and sprang up from the bed, throwing off the covers. He had to see, to prove to himself that it was only a vivid nightmare.

Doctors gently forced him back down, trying to calm him. One of them told him he was lucky to be alive. A burst of machine-gun fire had partially severed the distal shaft below the knee. The surgical team had had no option. They had been forced to amputate. He would be as good as new, the doctor with the stethoscope told him with an uneasy grin. He had been measured for a prosthesis while he was still on the table. The new artificial legs were technological miracles, they told him; he would even be able to disco.

"But I can feel my leg," he insisted. "It's still there. See, I'm wiggling my toes." His desperate tone conveyed fading hope. One of the doctors explained to him that all sensation comes from the brain. And that his brain did not know that his left leg was no longer there. His brain was still sending nerve impulses to his missing leg and would continue to do so for the rest of his life. "Your missing limb will always be with you, a sort of phantom leg. It'll itch, fall asleep. There will be times when you will forget that it's not there and try to step on it."

Scanlon turned his face so that they might not see his tears. It was unseemly for a detective sergeant to cry.

No visitors were allowed until the next day.

It was late in the afternoon when Inspector Albert Buckholz, the CO of the Tenth Detective District, burst into his room full of false cheer. Buckholz was a grotesquely fat man with a small head, dainty hands, and a cheap black toupée that looked like a Cracker Jack prize. He was known throughout the Job as Fat Albert.

Buckholz went to great lengths to assure him that he was going to be okay. The PC wanted him to know that the Job was behind him 110 percent, and that if he wanted to he could remain on the Job, and that his place on the lieutenant promotion list was secure. There were other handicapped men on the Job. Buckholz moved in close to confide, "The Job don't forget, Tony. We take care of our own."

Edith Piaf stopped singing. Scanlon abandoned his worn reverie and got up off the bed. He hopped one-legged over to the turntable and reversed the record.

Piaf returned. "C'est à Hambourg."

He hopped back into bed. Resting his glass on his stomach, he leaned his head back and again retreated into the past.

"Tell me what happened," Scanlon said to Fat Albert.

The right side of Fat Albert's face began to twitch. Capucci had been killed, Fat Albert related.

Scanlon looked away, watching the yellow beeps weave their way across the monitor screen.

". . . two perps were DOA at the scene," Fat Albert said with macabre glee as if their deaths evened the score for Capucci, for his leg. And then, in a sudden burst of exuberance, Fat Albert announced that there was an anxious lady waiting outside to see him.

Jane Stomer entered the hospital room with uncharacteristic timidity. She paused, her large black eyes darting between beds. When she saw him, she ran over and hurled herself across his chest in a relieved embrace. Her long brown hair fell in natural ringlets over his face. He breathed in her fragrance, relished her softness against his skin. His arms moved out from under the sheets and pressed her close to him.

At thirty-two, Jane Stomer was many things to many different people. To her male colleagues in the district attorney's office of New York County, she was the frighteningly intelligent, self-assured assistant DA who never walked into the courtroom unprepared; she was the lady who wore classic suits and sensible blouses that concealed an extraordinarily beautiful body. To her female colleagues she was the consummate professional. She was the girlfriend who warned against office romances with married men, but never chastised those women who did become involved. She was the acid-tongued feminist who championed women's rights within the male-dominated criminal justice system.

To Detective Sgt. Tony Scanlon she had been both lover and friend. They had met twenty-one months before he lost his leg. Scanlon and his detectives had arrested four men for the brazen daylight robbery of the U.S. Steel payroll. Jane Stomer had been assigned to prosecute. A week before the case was to be presented to the grand jury she summoned him to her office. They sat around her desk critiquing the original felony complaint and the supporting depositions, searching for legal flaws that might invalidate the accusatory instruments.

After the grand jury handed down the indictments, she scheduled more meetings with him to prepare for pretrial. During these meetings she quizzed him closely on the quality of the evidence supporting the state's case, and on the availability and reliability of the witnesses. Together they developed the People's strategy to defeat the inevitable defense challenges to the admissibility of the physical evidence.

He had known her by reputation and had expected her to be an antimale feminist. Instead, he discovered a pleasant, hardworking ADA who was skilled in the law and had an exceptional grasp of the real workings of the criminal justice system. He liked her crisp, businesslike manner and was impressed by her determination to win. Once during a brief lull he asked her if she had ever considered going into private practice. "You'd make a hell of an adversary."

She looked straight at him and said, "Someone has to get the licks in for the crime victims. Every one we put inside means one less to roam our streets murdering and stealing."

A week before the trial she summoned him to her office for a final conference. They began to work at exactly nine A.M. There were times during that final meeting that he found himself staring into her eyes searching for a message. He never found one. They broke for lunch at twelve-thirty and went their separate ways.

He walked out of the fortresslike Criminal Court building on Centre Street and sauntered down the wide steps, unsure where to eat. He passed the massive steel doors of the court's detention facility and crossed the street, heading toward Worth Street in search of a restaurant. He passed several, glanced inside, decided that they were greasy spoons, and moved on. Reaching Broadway, he moved north until he came to Duane Street, where he glanced to his right and saw a bright orange-and-yellow awning: Los Dos Rancheros. He didn't particularly care for Mexican food, but when he walked over to the window and looked inside and saw ADA Jane Stomer sitting alone at a table, he developed an overwhelming desire for guacamole and beans. He pretended to be surprised when he entered the crowded restaurant and saw her look up at him. She motioned him over to her table.

Conversation came easily, each agreeing on the screwed-up state of the criminal justice system and on the need for mandatory sentences. He liked her; they spoke the same language.

It was she who noticed the time. "We'd better get back. The distinguished district attorney does not countenance extended lunch hours for women," she said. They each paid their share of the bill and split the tip between them. During their hurried walk back he reached out and took hold of her arm. "Will you have dinner with me?" he asked. People passed them, intent on getting to other places. Some turned and stared at the two of them standing motionless, and unaware of what was happening around them.

She slowly freed her arm from his grip and pushed off ahead of him, saying over her shoulder, "I'd like that, Scanlon."

They decided that it would be wise to wait until after the trial before they went out together. Eight days later when the jury came in with a guilty verdict, they made a date for Saturday, two days off.

On their first date they went to Texas Roundup in Soho, where they ate barbecued ribs and chicken and rib-eye steak and homemade chili and bourbon baked beans. She had discarded her usual conservative clothes in favor of an oversize silk blouse and tailored jeans that were cinched with a narrow snakeskin belt. After dinner they went to Las Cuevas, where they discoed until dawn. The sun was up when he escorted her into the Art Deco lobby of her West End Avenue apartment and rode up with her to the fourth floor. She stopped in front of her door. "Thank you, Scanlon. I enjoyed myself."

He leaned forward and kissed her on the side of her lips. She smiled at him and turned to open her door. As she was inserting her key into the lock, he asked her if she was busy later that day. They could drive out to the Island, eat lobster. She stepped into her apartment. "That would be nice. Why not make it around three."

It was a beautiful Sunday afternoon with thin motionless clouds bordering the horizon. The cool summer breezes were laced with ocean smells. Seagulls stalked the beach, glided aloft. Holding hands, they made their way along the rugged headlands of Montauk Point watching the whitecaps roll up onto the sand and rocks, each aware that they were on the threshold of intimacy.

Eventually they got around to talking about their jobs. "Sometimes I think our society is on self-destruct," he said, guiding her around a group of boulders.

Scuffing seaweed aside with her sneakers, she said, "But can you imagine what life would be like without our court system? We'd be at the mercy of revolutionary guards meting out their own system of justice."

"Sometimes I think we'd be better off."

She moved close, put her arm around his. "But you don't really believe that, do you, Scanlon?"

"I guess not," he admitted, conscious of her breasts pressing against his arm. Watching the retreating surf, he asked her to tell him how she had become involved with criminal law. She withdrew her arm and walked away from him. Going over to a cluster of boulders, she climbed up and sat, staring out at the ocean. He climbed up after her. Lowering himself next to her, he asked, "Did I say something to upset you?"

She looked at him, her expression clouded. She seemed unsure how much of herself she wanted to reveal. She touched his cheek, looked into his softening eyes. After long hesitation, she tugged her knees up to her chest and wrapped them in her arms. A breaker pounded their boulder, lightly spraying them.

"I've always been an overachiever, Tony. In law school I was the one who could always be counted on by the professors to rattle off the case law. Both my parents are lawyers. Dad's specialty is admiralty law, Mom's is blue-sky corporate stuff. My father went to Princeton. I went to Princeton. We have a house in Princeton. It has all the comforts: gardens, pool, pool house, tennis court. I'm the only child, and I guess I was fated to be my parents' legacy to corporate law." She frowned. Her eyes moistened. "You see, Tony, I never knew my parents when I was growing up. I hardly know them now. They were too busy with their careers and their social obligations to spend time with a rambunctious little girl who peed in bed. I can hardly remember being hugged by my parents, or being kissed by them, or told that they loved me. At Christmas I would get toys from F.A.O. Schwarz and a firm hug. That was as much as they could manage.

"I was raised by a nanny. We lived in the south wing of the house, alone. Just the two of us, and Jasper, my cat. They're both gone now. Nanny's name was Helen McGovern. She was a warm, sweet old maid who showered me with her love and treated me as though I were her own child. I used to pretend that she *was* my mother, and that my parents were my cruel stepparents. She died last year, and I still miss her terribly." She unzipped the side flap of her white windbreaker and took out a package of tissues. She pulled one out and dabbed her eyes. "I was in my middle twenties before I realized that my parents probably loved me, but were undemonstrative, incapable of giving much of themselves." Jane looked at him, trying to decide whether to continue. She made a small dismissive shrug of her shoulders and leaned forward, resting her chin on her kneecaps. "I was a virgin until my senior year at Princeton. His name was David and he was the captain of the fencing team. We went together for seven months before David dropped me for a cutesy math major. I was devastated." She laughed self-mockingly. "Young girls are such romantic saps. They think love is forever. But I got over David. I'm a survivor, Scanlon. Anyway, after law school, Dad wangled me a position with one of the city's top firms. A very proper firm that accepts only top students from the best schools, people who have the proper family connections. And even then you needed what cops call a 'contract' to get a job with this firm."

He smiled. "Someone still has to make that old telephone call for you."

"Yes. It was while I was working there that I made the mistake of falling in love with one of the married partners. That little romance lasted a little over a year. And then one evening he announced that he could never leave his wife. And then he had the gall to add that I deserved more than a shabby little affair." She dabbed her eyes again with a tissue. "That bastard. He never did realize that I had never intended for him to leave his precious wife."

She took a deep breath, exhaled slowly. "I really hated working there. It was a dead, boring place full of assholes dressed in dark three-piece suits and fusty dresses and sensible shoes and high-collared blouses. I used to go home every night with a headache. It was only after eighteen months of paying a small fortune to a shrink that I realized I was living my life for the sole purpose of trying to gain my parents' love and approval. I decided it was time for me to grow up and start living my life for myself. My parents were disappointed, to say the least, when I informed them that I found corporate law a bore and had accepted a position on the DA's staff. 'But Jane, dear,' Mother said, 'criminal law is so *undignified.*'"

They both laughed.

"I don't know, Scanlon, perhaps I'm still trying to earn their approval. But I do know that I love my work and that I am damn good at it. And that, sir, is a very nice feeling."

He picked up a pebble, ran his thumb over its smoothness, and skimmed it out across the surf. "Are you seeing anyone now?"

"I haven't *seen* anyone in a long time. I need a strong man, Tony. A man who is not searching for a mother replacement. And, unfortunately, there just aren't too many of them around." She turned and looked at him. "Okay, Scanlon, it's your turn. What secrets are there in your life?"

Policemen find it difficult to talk about themselves, to let others peek into their world. The Job makes cops xenophobic. But slowly he overcame his reluctance and began to tell her of his life. He described the wise guys on Pleasant Avenue with their wide-brimmed pearl-gray hats, and pegged pants and pointy shoes, and how they used to hang out on corners with their hands clasped behind them, ready to drop the day's gambling action should any plainclothes cops appear. He described the rich, exotic smells inside Mr. DeVito's cheese store, and explained how they used to make pizza with pure olive oil.

They lived in a four-room apartment over a barbershop. He was the only child, and he had his own room next to his parents' bedroom. His father was a barrel-chested Irish drunk who also happened to be a sergeant in the NYPD. Haltingly he tried to tell her about his father's drunken tirades, and of the physical abuse that he and his mother suffered at his father's hands. His face expressionless, he recounted how he used to lie awake at night listening as his father staggered in after a four-to-twelve tour, of hearing his mother's whispered pleas, of trying to ignore the sounds of his parents' squawking bed, his father's hoarse grunts. He told about the times his father would pass out on top of his mother and of how he would have to get up and go and help his mother push the half-naked drunk off her slight body. He told of pretending to be asleep when his father would come home drunk and beat his mother. He spoke with bitterness of his father's hatred of Italians. "And my mother is Italian," he added balefully.

His mother had grown up on Center Market Place in Little Italy. She was short and had a strong peasant's face, olive skin, thick black hair, and luminous dark eyes. She was kind and generous and had a totally miserable life with his father. But still she maintained the pathetic and desperate illusions of a loyal wife: she told Tony not to judge his father too harshly.

He paused to light a De Nobili, his face flushed by emotions that he normally kept in the deepest part of himself.

Holidays spent with his father's side of the family were joyless. His Irish aunts and uncles shared his father's hostility toward Italians; in fact, he added with some dismay, they hated everyone who wasn't Irish Catholic. They were, as far as he was concerned, loathsome, miserable people. Days before a holiday, his mother would prepare. She cleaned the house, shopped for food, liquor, beer, spent hours in the kitchen making delicacies, baking. He could almost smell the big pots of simmering sauces, the strong aromas. When the relatives arrived in midafternoon they would trudge, many already drunk, into his home, ignoring his mother. They would treat her as though she were their servant. His mother's name was Mary. They'd address her as Maria. They would talk disparagingly of Eye-talians, in front of his mother, and tell awful ethnic jokes. With painful clarity he described the mounds of dirty holiday dishes in the sink, and him and his mother washing them while his aunts stayed in the parlor drinking cans of beer and smoking cigarettes. He told her about his childish fascination with the way his aunt's false teeth slid up and down when they talked. "Every one of them had store-bought choppers."

Jane Stomer stretched out her legs, crossing them at the ankles. She had a perplexed look on her face. "If your father felt that strongly about Italians, why in heaven's name did he marry your mother?"

A series of breakers rolled into their boulders. The spray felt good. He tasted salt on his lips. "I had trouble with that one too," he said, "until I took a few moments to compare my DOB with my parents' anniversary. It was off by four months."

Windsurfers offshore with brilliant orange and blue sails flew over the waves, while the people on them struggled to stay upright. His eyes followed them. "I grew up speaking Italian with my mother and her relatives. That was all we talked whenever my father wasn't around. The Italian side of my family was warm and wonderful. Kind, gentle people who went out of their way to make you feel at home in their houses. As a kid I dreamed of coming on the Job and of someday being my father's boss, and of making his life a living hell." He flicked ash into the ocean. "But he disappointed me in that too. Fourteen months after I came on the Job, he threw in his papers and ran off with his Irish girlfriend, another drunk."

"Where is he now?" she asked.

"Rotting in hell for all I know." He held up the De Nobili. "I began to smoke these when I came on the Job. I wanted the Irish Mafia to know that although my name is Scanlon, I'm a guinea through and through. It's my own personal affirmative action program."

"And what about Tony Scanlon's private life?" she said, staring out at the windsurfers.

That warm smile, that baring of teeth. "It's interesting."

"Come on, Scanlon, out with it. Don't try to palm off any of that laconic cop talk on me. I want specifics. Is there anyone important in your life?"

He became serious. "Not at the moment."

"Was there?"

"Sort of," he said with a sheepish grin.

"What do you mean, sort of?"

"Well, I was seeing two women at the same time." He added quickly, "But I liked both of them very much."

"And they, of course, did not know each other."

He became uncomfortable. "Well, not exactly."

His little-boy discomfort caused her to suppress a smile. "Out with it, Scanlon."

"As luck would have it they both went to the same place on the East Side to get their legs waxed. Anyway, they met there accidentally, and as women inevitably do, they got around to telling each other about their boyfriends. And it just so happened that they both were seeing a police lieutenant named Tony. You can guess the rest of it."

She pushed herself up and stood over him. Placing a friendly hand on his shoulder, she said, "Scanlon, you are a typical, lying, two-faced cop. You're the kind of man that women discuss in the powder room. Any woman who even considered becoming involved with you is a fool."

He made a weary gesture. "Guess I can't argue with that logic, Counselor."

*   *   *

The next night they went to Allen Street in the East Village to eat Indonesian food. They ate rijsttafel served by waiters wearing colorful headdresses, and folk garb over washed-out jeans. They had finished their dinner and their table was covered with many small dishes and rice crumbs. He caught her watching him and took note of her haunted expression. She lowered her eyes, brought her napkin to her lips. There was an awkward silence. She toyed with a skewer, avoiding his eyes. He became conscious of his own heartbeat. Reaching across the table, he took her hand in his. "Will you come home with me?" he said, an edge of uncertainty in his voice.

She squeezed his hand, scraped her chair back from the table, and got up.

They stood before his bed locked in a lingering kiss. His hand moved under her dress, and she stepped back, out of reach.

"Get undressed," she said, in a tone of mounting urgency. As he struggled out of his clothes, she came up to him, slid her arms around his neck, and kissed him.

Naked, he pressed into her, and again she pulled back from him, ordering, "Sit on the bed, Scanlon. I want you to watch me take my clothes off."

Standing a few feet away from him, her eyes locked on his, she removed her clothes, a garment at a time, carelessly letting each fall to the floor. Her slow, deliberate unveiling increased his desire for her. He sat motionless, breathing hard, his stare caressing her body.

She was now clad only in bra and panties.

He delighted in her long, smooth legs, her flat stomach, her breasts straining against her bra. His eyes swiveled down to the black mound that showed through her panties. They lingered there. His mouth dropped open, and he made a movement to go to her.

She thrust out a palm. "Patience, Scanlon. This is how I like it. Slow. Hard."

Her face was glowing with desire. She reached up to the front of her bra, paused, looked down at her cleavage, then to him, and unhooked her bra. Large breasts with protruding nipples rose and fell with each breath. She slipped her hand inside her panties and slid them down, stepping out of them.

"I want you," he gasped.

"Soon," she said, coming to him, lifting her leg over his, straddling him.

A searing sensation shot through his body as she lowered herself onto his penis, drawing him inside her body. She did not take him deep, but instead kept him at the entrance, slowly, methodically undulating her body over the head of his penis.

"Slow, Scanlon. Slow," she moaned.

Her exquisite torment caused him to catch his breath. His mouth was agape, dry. He made low grunts. He lunged his body up into her. She retreated. "Not yet, Scanlon. Soon."

Long deep guttural sounds came from her open mouth. Her eyes were closed in tight concentration. Beads of sweat dotted her brow. She was moving faster, faster, taking him deeper and deeper. He pulled her close, his mouth eagerly sucking on her nipple. She gasped. "Yes, Scanlon. Yes. Do it hard. Hard. Now. Now!" She plummeted onto his penis, wrapping her legs around his waist.

They lay in a naked embrace, gasping, their bodies exuding the sweaty scent of lovemaking. Time passed, and they dozed. He awoke first, his passion renewed. His lips moved along her neck, savoring the smell of her body. He pressed her close. His caresses stirred her out of her sleep. She began to respond. She pressed her body against his, and opened her mouth to his kisses. He slid down between her legs and sucked her up into his mouth, his tongue delicately caressing, and his finger probing deeper.

Her body was immersed in passion. Every touch, every tongue movement caused her to wrench, smear his face with her body. She was pulling her hair as her head thrashed on the pillows. She was making rough, grating sounds. Her body rose up off the bed at the waist, and she began to pound the mattress. Her nails clawed the sheets. "Yes! Yes!" she shouted. And then as orgasm ripped through her body, she grabbed a pillow to her face and screamed.

He moved up the bed on his knees, kissing her body as he went. When he was kneeling alongside her shoulder, he stopped and took her head into his hands and gently guided it toward his glistening penis.

Her face showed a momentary hesitation. She pulled back, vacillating, then looked up at him. "Please don't . . ."

"I won't," he interrupted softly, and then gasped and called out her name as her moist lips closed around him.

The needle scratched with annoying regularity. He came out of his reverie and put the glass down on the treasure chest. Pushing his hulk up off the bed, Scanlon hopped over to the turntable and changed the record. Then he hopped back, while Piaf sang "L'Accordéoniste."

A sip of scotch accompanied him on his now compulsive journey back into the past.

* * *

She appeared on his third day in the hospital: a tall, gangly woman in a hospital coat with an artificial leg under one arm and a shoe and several plastic envelopes in her hand. "Hi. I'm Alice Crowell. Are you ready to walk?"

He looked at her, and then down at his stump. "I wish the hell I could."

"I'm going to have you on your feet and walking in about five minutes. But first I'd like you to swing your legs over the side of the bed."

As he complied with her directions, she laid the prosthesis and the shoe on the bed. She stood in front of him and rolled the stump shrinker, which looked like an Ace bandage made into a sock, off his stump, and began to gently knead his stump. "There is a lot of swelling and edema, but that is to be expected."

Watching her hands work, he asked, "What's edema?"

"Body fluids that collect in the soft tissues. With your leg gone the normal body fluids that pass through your body can't make the return journey. Some of them collect in your stump and cause it to swell. Stump wrapping and elastic shrinker socks help reduce the edema." She lifted up his stump, examining it. "The surgeon did a great job beveling the bone into a cylindrical mass."

She carefully placed the stump down on the bed and picked up the plastic envelopes. She slid one envelope behind the other until she found the one she wanted and ripped it open. She put the remainder back down on the bed. "This is a stump sock, Tony." She dangled it in front of him. "From now on a good deal of your daily routine is going to be devoted to stump sock management."

He noticed that her teeth were slightly bucked.

"In the morning there is not much edema, so you might start off the day with a four- or five-ply stump sock. But as the day progresses and body fluids accumulate and swell your stump, you might have to change to a one-ply sock. You must wear a sock—otherwise there will be friction, which will cause abrasions, blisters, and denuded skin surfaces. And if you don't control the edema your stump might swell so much that it won't fit into the socket, and conversely, if it shrinks too much, the socket could become too loose." She smiled. "Got it?"

"Got it," he said, looking into the socket of the artificial leg.

She handed him the stump sock. "You put this on, and I'll put on your shoe."

She put a regular sock on his real foot, and then slipped a shoe on his foot. "You've probably noticed that the shoes and sock are yours. We got them from your mother." She tied the lace, then stood up. She picked up the prosthesis. Hefted it in front of him. The leg had the other shoe on.

"This is a temporary leg, Tony. The socket and the foot are adjustable. It'll take months until your stump has shrunk to its permanent size. At that time you'll be fitted for a prosthesis that will be made for the angulation changes for your best gait pattern."

He nodded at the prosthesis. "What's it made of?"

"Laminated polyester resin and fiberglass." She held the prosthesis up in front of him. "This is a PTB prosthesis. Which stands for 'patellar bearing tendon.' I want you to take both your hands and feel the little space under your right kneecap."

He cupped both hands over his right kneecap and pressed forefingers into the space.

"That is your patellar tendon," she said. "Your femur rests on top of it and the tibia below it. There are no pain receptors in that area, and the patella is therefore impervious to pain. It can bear somewhere in the neighborhood of fifteen hundred pounds of pressure per square inch. It's the patellar tendon that will bear the weight of your body."

"There are no straps. How does it stay on?"

She turned the prosthesis so that he might look inside the socket. "See this bar molded across the top of the socket?"

He looked inside to where her finger pointed. "Yes, I see it."

"That's the patella bar. Your tendon rests on that bar, supporting your body. It's as though your left leg were kneeling on top of the prosthesis."

"But what secures the stump inside the prosthesis?"

"Feel above the right kneecap. Feel that ridge on top?"

"Yes."

"Now raise and lower your leg. See how that ridge expands and then contracts?"

"Yeah. The ridge is there, and then when I lower my leg it's gone."

"That area of your leg is called the supracondylar. When you put your prosthesis on, you'll raise up your stump and slide the lip of the socket over the supracondylar. The lips of the prosthesis will cover the supracondylar, and when you lower your leg the bone will contract, locking the stump inside the socket." She lowered the prosthesis and held the socket a few inches away from his stump. "You ready to walk?"

"Alice Crowell, I'm good and ready."

She put the prosthesis onto his stump. "Slide off the bed, putting all your weight onto your right leg," she ordered, ready to catch him should he fall.

Gripping the mattress, he struggled off the bed onto his feet. He cried out from the pain and fell backward against the bed, gripping the frame.

She grabbed his shoulders. "I know. Your stump is swollen and very painful. But we have to get you walking today. So let's try again."

He took a deep breath and righted himself. His body felt as though it were balanced on an unsteady toothpick. Sweat rolled down his armpits. His stump felt raw and throbbed with pain. He watched her, waiting for her instructions.

"Just walk," she instructed him. "Right leg first. Heel, sole, heel, sole. Then bring your left leg through."

He had gone but a few steps when he lost his balance and crumpled to the floor. She hurried over to him and helped him up. Frustration gnawed at him. He was a cripple. On his feet once more, he pushed her away. He wanted to go it alone, to conquer this affliction. With his arms out at his side, he managed six exhausting steps before tumbling to the floor.

"That's enough for today," she said, bending to heft him up once more. Supporting him with her shoulders, she helped him back into the bed. He lay on his back, gasping for air.

She looked down at him with an expression of compassion and determination. "Listen, Sergeant, you're not the first guy to lose a leg, and you're certainly not going to be the last one. In fact, you are now a member of a very distinguished alumni association." She smiled at her stack of envelopes down on the bottom of his bed. "You'd be surprised who's in the club. We've got a federal judge who let his diabetes get out of control, a pilot who didn't exactly walk away from a bad landing. A lot of people who have one thing in common—and they call themselves the One Missing Club. When you feel ready, one of the volunteers is going to stop by and start working with you."

Scanlon looked up at her and asked bitterly, "And have you got any cops in your little club?"

For a moment she looked off balance, but she recovered very fast. "Well, we had a sergeant from your Bomb Squad a few years ago . . ." She blushed in confusion and came to a sudden halt.

"You mean Frank Lally?"

"I think that's the name. How did you know?"

"Because he didn't make it. He swallowed his gun."

Alice Crowell realized that she had a loner on her hands.

She pulled up his hospital gown and went to remove the prosthesis.

"No! Leave it. I'm going to wear it until it becomes a part of my body."

He was discharged from the hospital on Friday of the eighth week. Jane Stomer put in for a vacation day in order to drive him home. "I appreciate your visiting me every night, and, well, just being there."

She looked at him. Smiled. "You're a sweet man, Scanlon. But please don't go sentimental on me."

He reached across the passenger seat and touched her cheek. "I won't."

They entered his loft by the front entrance on East Fourth Street. There was an unwelcoming stillness about the loft that made him uneasy. It suddenly appeared to be too large, too dark, filled with too many inhibiting shadows. He limped over to the closest sofa and started to lower himself, then lost his balance and fell onto the cushions. She rushed to his aid.

"I'm a klutz," he said.

"You are not." She took him into her arms, comforting him. He pressed her close, needing the reassurance of her body. "Stay the night," he whispered.

She cupped his face in her hands, kissed him tenderly on the lips. "I thought you'd never ask."

She helped him off the sofa and over to the bed. She helped him undress. For the first time in his adult life he was dependent on someone else. He did not like the feeling; it scared him. Sitting on the edge of his great bed, he took off the prosthesis and handed it up to her. She took it and walked over to the clothes chest, examining it. She put it down on the chest and came back to him. Watching her, he felt a twinge of concern over the lack of sexual spontaneity.

Standing a few feet away from him, she began to undress, starting their foreplay. He gaped at her, anxious to see her step from her panties. When she was naked she came to him and slid onto the bed next to him. As she did, she took in his once-proud body, but looked quickly away lest her gaze linger on his stump. She began to kiss him. She saw that he was limp and ran her hand over his loins and took hold of him, stroking him gently. As he grew, she stroked harder. She had become the aggressor, he the passive partner. She was all over him, kissing, licking, saying arousing things.

Their foreplay proved arduous. His ungainly lopsidedness precluded the fluid, urgent movements of lovemaking. He could see her trying to avoid his stump's caress, because each time it brushed against her, gooseflesh came and she recoiled. She attempted to hide her revulsion behind a smokescreen of feigned passion.

When she had him hard she lay on her back and watched as he struggled to position his awkward body between her legs. She took hold of his frail erection and guided it into her dry body, rubbing it on the inside, hoping to lubricate. With his right knee bearing his weight, and with his torso balanced upright by the brace of his left hand on the mattress, and with his stump dangling weightily, he looked down and watched her efforts.

He felt himself going soft and thrust forward into her. She gasped from his tearing intrusion, and turned her face sideways so that he might not see her pained expression. Biting her lower lip, hoping that it would soon end, she moved her body to his thrusts. But it was no use. He became aware of her perfunctory movements, saw her expression, sensed her lack of passion. He lost his erection and withdrew from her body, falling dejectedly onto his back.

"I'm sorry if I hurt you."

"It wasn't your fault. I couldn't lubricate. It's been a long time since we made love."

"I guess I lost more than my leg."

She took hold of him and shook him violently. "Don't you dare do this to yourself. You've just undergone a great trauma. You can't expect to just pick up your life where you left off. It takes time for your body to adjust to the new situation. For us to adjust to each other."

A flash of teeth, a laugh laden with mocking sarcasm. "Sergeant pegleg limp dick at your service."

"Don't do this, Tony," she cried, suddenly overwhelmed with compassion for him. She felt a need to mother him, to make love to him, to make him a whole man again, to restore his self-confidence. She started to kiss his body, desperately wanting to reassure the man she loved. Her caressing palm massaged his genitals. Her tongue moved over his neck, down his body. He whimpered, closed his eyes, but did not grow hard. She shifted her body between his legs, pausing to gather the courage to finish the distasteful task that she had set herself. A task that she had done several times with her married lover; a task that when done to completion caused her to become sick.

He placed his hands on her head and nudged her down.

She felt his hot member on her cheek. She flicked the tip with her tongue, making wet little circles over the head. She leaned forward and ran her flattened tongue over the silky undershaft, glancing up at him, seeing that his eyes were half closed, his head writhing on the pillows. She moved her head up and closed her lips around him.

His body moved to the bobbing motion of her head. His cries encouraged her, and she drew him deeper into her mouth. Harsh sounds came from his throat, his grip on her head tightened, and he came in forceful spurts.

She froze, impaled upon his organ. And then, with one quick jerk of her head, she was free of him. A sour expression twisted her face. Her lips were pursed tightly together, and her eyes brimmed. She looked about, searching for some nearby place to unburden her load. She gagged and swallowed involuntarily. Slapping her hands across her mouth, she leaped from the bed and ran into the bathroom. With her hands gripping the cold rim, she leaned over the sink, her body racked by violent heaving. With her mouth wide, her tongue strained by dry retches, she lowered her face into the sink and vomited.

Scanlon lay on his back, listening to her. He wanted to rush from the bed to comfort her. But he could not. For in one frightful moment of insight he saw that he was now disgusting to women, and he knew that he never again would be able to make love to a normal woman. He buried his face in the mattress and cried.

They spent the night in his great bed with their backs to each other, staring out at the retreating darkness, falling in and out of restless periods of sleep.

The sense of emasculation affected his entire body, causing him to lie hunched over with his right leg blanketing his stump and his genitals tucked between his thighs, subconsciously trying to hide his shame. His manhood was gone, and Jane Stomer knew it. He would never be able to forget that look on her face every time his stump brushed against her. How could he forget her getting sick after doing that to him? He was a goddamn impotent freak. And worst of all, she knew. It could never be just his dark secret.

Several times during that night he shivered, and she moved close to him, placing her warm back against his. And each time he inched away from her.

A disquieting silence separated them in the morning. They sat at the table with the glass top and ate a light breakfast of juice, coffee, and warm croissants.

The uneasy silence lengthened.

Suddenly she announced that she was leaving to buy the Sunday *Times*. She was gone a long time, and when she returned she had the heavy newspaper tucked under her right arm and was holding a book in her left. She was late, she explained, because she had taken a taxi to her home in order to get a book she wanted him to look at. She put the newspaper down on one of the nail barrels. Facing him, she opened the book to a page that had a sliver of paper protruding from it and began to read aloud. Erectile dysfunction was the most common sexual problem for men. Its most common cause was psychological, a common way for men to express anxiety. There was no need for embarrassment, she read.

He was sitting a few feet away from her, his hostile gaze riveted to the book in her hands. With astonishing agility, he lunged up and grabbed the book from her, throwing it across the loft. He lost his balance and stumbled backward onto the sofa.

"Scanlon!" she cried, rushing over to help him.

"Get away," he said, shoving away her helping hands, struggling by himself to sit upright in the seat. He squared his shoulders, brushed down his ruffled hair with his hands. His face was impassive. "Don't you worry yourself about me. I'm going to be just fine. And I really don't want to hear any more of that goddamn shrink bullshit."

She lowered herself onto the sofa next to him. "Yes, Scanlon. Whatever you say."

They spent the rest of that Sunday morning listening to Tchaikovsky's *Swan Lake* and reading the newspaper. They seldom talked. The one-o'clock movie was *Casablanca*. Jane cried at the end; she always did. When the movie was over she looked at him as though she were about to say something, but changed her mind, and instead leaned close and kissed him.

He was cold and unresponsive.

"Would you like to make love?" she asked softly.

An orange-juice commercial had his attention. He did not respond to her overture. She rested her head on his shoulder and in a reassuring voice assured him that his impotence was a temporary problem. If he was that concerned, he might want to get some professional help. He quickly became hostile.

"You should talk about it, Tony."

"There is nothing to discuss."

"But there is," she pressed.

"Don't you understand the English language? I said that there was nothing to talk about."

"Men! They can never talk about what's bothering them."

He got up and changed the channel.

The following week he did not return any of her many telephone calls. On the following Friday she called again. Listening to her talk, he realized how very much he missed her. But instead of telling her that, instead of asking to see her, he told her he had been too preoccupied with teaching himself how to walk to return her calls. He promised her he would call her in the morning. He didn't.

The specter of his impotence haunted him, filling his lonely nights with fitful periods of sleep. The nightmare was the same, night after night. He and Jane were in the great bed. He was unable to get it up. He knelt on one knee, balancing himself with his left arm while he masturbated with the right, desperately trying to become erect. She watched, said nothing. A strange man stood off in the shadows, watching. A funny smile would come to Jane's mouth. He'd remain limp, sweating. She would suddenly burst out laughing just as his father stepped out of the shadows.

He'd awake with a start, drenched in sweat and trembling.

A week later, on Saturday, there was a knock at his door. He opened it and found Jane Stomer standing there with both hands planted firmly on her hips, her beautiful mouth quivering with anger. She glared at him briefly and then pushed past him into the loft. He closed the door and leaned against it, waiting for the expected outburst.

She faced him. Her voice cracked. "I have a right to know just exactly what your plans are concerning our relationship. If it's over, Scanlon, then damn it, be man enough to tell me so that I can get on with my own life."

Finding himself at a loss for the proper words, he looked at her pleading eyes and said nothing. How does a man tell the woman he loves that he will never see her again? How does a man sever from his life the only woman he has ever been completely happy with? "I'm sorry," he said feebly, his eyes falling to the floor.

She rushed at him, pushed him aside, threw open the door. "You're a fool, Tony Scanlon. A goddamn fool." She slammed the door and was gone.

The empty weeks soon became empty months. He became reclusive, spending his days in the solitary regimen of mastering his new leg. He'd jog in place, do aerobics, pace endless circles. Days sped by, nights lingered with loneliness.

He took to going to Roseland, always timing his arrival to coincide with the end of the evening's ballroom dancing and the beginning of the disco program. He would walk into the lobby and go up to the showcase and pretend to be looking at the collection of shoes worn by famous dancers, and look in the glass's reflection to see if there was anyone he knew. It would have been unseemly for a detective sergeant to be seen going dancing alone.

Once inside the ballroom he would walk onto the mammoth dance floor and lose himself among the twirling shadows, whirling himself under the glittering lights, clapping his hands to the booming beat. He had become a Roseland regular, one of the lonesome people harboring their own fears and their own secrets.

After eleven months on sick report Scanlon yearned to be returned to full duty. On his weekly visit to his district police surgeon he would ask the doctor to send him back to work. The doctor, a benign-looking man with a slight Scottish accent, would look askance at him and leave his request unanswered. On Monday of the first week of the twelfth month of sick report, Scanlon visited his district surgeon. When Scanlon entered the doctor's sixth-floor office in the Police Academy, the surgeon was writing in Scanlon's medical folder. "I'm sending you before the board, Sergeant. You're being surveyed."

"I don't want to go before the Medical Board. I want to stay in the Job," he protested. "I've been promised."

"I'm afraid you don't have any choice. The chief surgeon and I have decided that you're unfit for full duty." The doctor removed his glasses, assumed the expression of a maternal uncle. "Three-quarters tax-free isn't a bad pension, Sergeant."

"I don't want a goddamn pension."

"I'm sorry, you're out." He put his glasses back on and continued to write in the medical folder.

Scanlon rushed from the doctor's office. He telephoned Jim Gebler, the president of the Sergeants' Benevolent Association. He told the feisty SBA president what had happened, of Fat Albert's promise that he could stay on the Job and be promoted to lieutenant. "Can you get a contract in with the chief surgeon?"

"You get your ass over here now, I'll start making some calls."

When Scanlon arrived at the SBA office in lower Manhattan he went directly into Gebler's corner office. The SBA president's thickset face was flushed. "We got a problem, Tony," he said, going to shake Scanlon's hand. "I just got off the phone with the chief surgeon. He told me that the first deputy wants as many bosses as possible put off the Job during this fiscal year."

"But why?"

"They want your budget line so that they can promote friends. Things are getting rough. There ain't much money around for promotions. They gotta make vacancies."

"So I have to reach out to the first dep or the PC."

"Looks that way. And the first dep and I don't get along. I'll give the PC a shot for you." Gebler's face brightened. He snapped his fingers. "That's the way to go."

Scanlon quickened. "What? Tell me."

"Joe Gallagher. He and the first dep are asshole buddies. They go drinking and screwing together. If there is anyone in the Job who can put a contract in with the first dep it's Gallagher. Do you know Gallagher?"

"I was in the class behind him in the Academy. We still bump into each other in the Job."

Gebler went over to his cluttered desk. "The LBA is having their monthly meeting at Ricardo's this afternoon. Gallagher is sure to be there. You hustle your ass over to Astoria and I'll get on the phone and tell Gallagher to be expecting you."

The drive from Manhattan to Astoria, Queens, took Scanlon the better part of ninety minutes. He double-parked in front of the restaurant and hurried inside. The noontime meeting was long over, and most of the delegates and members were crowded into the large circular bar. Scanlon's eyes slid along the bar searching for Joe Gallagher. He picked out the largest group of men and pushed his way through, knowing that Gallagher would be in the center, holding court. "Joe," Scanlon called out, breaking through to the center.

"Tony Scanlon, luv. How the fuck are you?" Gallagher pushed away from the bar, draped his big arm around Scanlon's shoulders, and led him over to one of the cocktail tables on the raised part of the floor that circled the bar.

"Did Jim Gebler call you?"

"I spoke to him, luv. And you don't have a problem anymore." Gallagher's eyes held a gleeful glint.

"I don't have a problem?"

"Not anymore, luv. I got on the horn to the first dep. I told the lad of your difficulty, that you were one of the Job's true heroes, and that you were a personal friend of mine." Gallagher paused to sip the drink that he had brought with him from the bar. Good politicians always stop before they drive home their good deeds—it gives the supplicant time to ponder the magnitude of the favor that was just done him. "The first dep called the chief surgeon. He made an appointment for you to see your district surgeon in the morning. Nine o'clock. Okay, luv? Does Joe Gallagher do the right thing or doesn't he?"

Scanlon sagged with relief. "I owe you a big one, Joe," he said, taking Gallagher's hand, shaking it with enthusiasm.

"Nothing to it, luv. Maybe someday you'll be in a position to do the right thing for me. Right?"

That night Scanlon went to Roseland to celebrate. He'd never forget what Joe Gallagher had done for him, never. He thought that since he'd been returned to full duty, everything else might also have changed for the better, and perhaps now might be the time to try and make it with a woman. Perhaps being away from the Job had something to do with his problem. But how should he approach a woman, now? Every time he thought about it he was filled with anxiety and a tense ache gripped his chest. How does he tell a woman that he's an amputee? When does he tell her? What does he say to her? What if he does tell her and she rejects him, walks away? What does he do then? And worst of all, what if a woman does go with him and he can't perform, can't get it up? Hi. My name is Tony. I'm an amputee and I have erectile dysfunction. Why me? What did I do to deserve this cross?

He finally reasoned that he would be better off to try to make it with a hooker. He reasoned that they considered their bodies to be income-producing property, so there'd be no emotional involvement, no worry on his part about being able to perform, no embarrassment if he couldn't. It had to be different with hookers. They were used to servicing cripples. Hookers performed one of society's more useful functions.

He left Roseland around two in the morning and walked the four blocks to the Hotel Arnold. He stood at the green-cushioned bar studying the five ladies of the night who had staked out their territory with empty bar stools. The one on his far left looked hard and unsympathetic. The other one on his left, maybe. His hands were wet and he could feel the nervous twitch in his neck. The one closest on his right looked nice. She had short brown hair and hazel eyes and a lissome body. But most of all she reminded him of Jane. Perhaps it was her smile, or perhaps he just wanted her to be Jane. He really didn't know. But when she glanced in his direction, he smiled at her and she smiled back at him. Going over to her, one question plagued him: What will I do if she rejects me? He slid onto the stool next to her. "Hi. May I buy you a drink?"

"I only drink club soda," she said, hefting her glass at him.

"Oh, I see." He hesitated, aware of his heartbeat. Urging himself forward, he blurted, "My name is Tony Scanlon. I'm an amputee."

She put her glass down and put a cigarette to her lips. He picked up the white throwaway lighter from the bar and lit it. She held his shaking hands in hers and moved her head toward the flame. "I'm Sally De Nesto."

Scanlon put the empty glass down on the treasure chest and thought, No one ever promised you it would be easy. He picked up the receiver and dialed Sally De Nesto's number. When her machine answered he waited for the beep, and then told the machine to tell its mistress that he would like to see her tomorrow night. He knew that she liked him and that she would reschedule her appointments so that he would be her last date. He wondered how many tricks she turned in one day. But then, what did that matter? She was there for him whenever he wanted her. He still wished he could make it with a straight woman. If he could only get up the courage to keep trying. He turned on his side and beat his head into the pillow. Tomorrow he had an appointment to meet the Zimmerman family.

8

The streets were full of interesting people out for a Saturday-afternoon stroll. Scanlon decided to park his car several blocks from the Zimmermans' East Side town house and walk, people-watch.

He took the vehicle identification plate from behind the visor and tossed it onto the dashboard. It was one thing to work on your own time and quite another to feed a parking meter with your own money, especially at today's rates, twenty-five cents for twenty minutes. He slid out the ashtray and flipped the hidden toggle switch that cut off his car's ignition system, reached under the front seat and pulled out the Chatman mechanical brake-wheel lock, and secured it around the brake pedal and the steering column. Sliding from his car, he hoped that it would still be there when he returned.

Most of the houses on East Seventy-ninth Street had shield-shaped stickers glued in their windows—This House's Alarm System Is Connected Directly to the Police. There were other posted warnings: This Block Is Patrolled by the East Side Observer Corp. Arabesque grilles covered most of the first- and second-floor windows, designer bars to keep the burglars out.

Scanlon's concentration was fixed on house numbers when a woman jogger brushed past him. Her shorts were so brief that the cheeks of her behind jutted out like naked half-moons. He was reminded of the witness Thomas Tibbs: there had been something odd about the way the perp had fled the crime scene, the witness had stated. His thoughts about Tibbs ended when he noticed the chic woman with the blue rinse in her hair waiting patiently at the curb for her little fag dog with pink bows in both ears to finish its bowel movement. Secured in her hand was a yellow-and-brown pooper-scooper. Scanlon wondered if that was one of those designed by Mr. Henri of Paris, France. Shit shovels for the rich. Only in the Big Apple, he thought, pausing before a house to check the address written on the back of a matchbook.

Four strips of black Thermopane streaked vertically down the front of the antique orange brick facade. A brass nameplate by the door read: Stanley Zimmerman, M.D.

He rang the chimes and stepped back, glancing up at the scudding clouds. He breathed deep. Summer scents were in the air. No answer. He leaned forward and rang again. Peering through the square of glass in the center of the heavy door, he saw a narrow passage to the right of a mahogany staircase. Up against the left wall, next to the tall sliding doors that led into a room, was a table of carved, gilded wood with a top that was inlaid in ebony and pewter. He pressed the button again.

A man's voice came from the intercom set into the doorframe. "Who is it?"

He placed his mouth in front of the metal box. "Lieutenant Scanlon."

Zimmerman led the policeman into the room with the tall doors. Scanlon took in the delicate chairs with the bouffant cushions, the Queen Anne sofas. It was a stuffy room with a green-and-gold antique desk, a buffet, and a crowded bookshelf.

As Scanlon lowered himself onto one of the dainty chairs he noticed Stanley Zimmerman's hands. They were long and graceful, as though they had been sculpted.

"When we talked yesterday, I told you that our family would be sitting shivah today. I forgot that today was Saturday. We don't sit shivah on the Sabbath."

"I knew that," Scanlon said, hoping that the chair was sturdy enough to support him and his fake leg.

Zimmerman expressed surprise at Scanlon's knowledge of Jewish law. The policeman explained that as a rookie he had worked in the Six-four in Borough Park, a compressed Brooklyn neighborhood of over two hundred synagogues. Thirteenth Avenue had been his beat. It was there that he had learned to distinguish among the Lubavitcher and the Satmar sects, and it was there that he had learned the difference between kosher and glatt kosher, and it was there that he had learned about shivah, the seven days of mourning.

"I guess policemen learn a lot about other people's customs," Zimmerman said lamely.

"That we do."

Zimmerman's gaze fixed on some point behind Scanlon. "I miss her terribly."

Scanlon nodded sympathetically. He saw the anguish in the eyes, heard the sadness in the voice, and felt uncomfortable being there, as though he were an intruder among the bereaved.

"Tell me how my mother died," he said, looking down at the floor.

An attempted robbery that had gone awry, he told the doctor. He added that the entire resources of the department had been thrown into the hunt for his mother's killers, and that teams of detectives had been pulled off other cases to work exclusively on this one. Scanlon watched him closely as he talked. Everyone is a suspect, a truism among police adages. The doctor's face remained tense. Sunlight made a filigree design on the walls of the room. Scanlon finished his dismal narrative, leaned forward, waiting for the son's response.

"Why, Lieutenant?"

Thinking that he was referring to the heinous double homicide, Scanlon shook his head as though unable to comprehend the sense-lessness of the crime.

"Why would anyone, with an accomplice standing by, and with a van for a getaway, want to hold up a candy store? For what end? To steal some jelly beans and some small change?" Scanlon fell under his questioning gaze. "And why my mother's store?" The demand had sudden vigor.

Scanlon's phantom leg was distracting him. "Perhaps it was a target of opportunity for a couple of cokeheads."

"Really?" A mocking tone. "Has your investigation so far led you to any other conclusion?"

Scanlon shrugged. "There is, I guess, the possibility that it was a paid-for killing. Like the CBS murders, a contract on the life of one of the victims, the other unfortunate just happening to be in the wrong place at the wrong time."

"I suppose someone like Gallagher would make mortal enemies. Narcotics work must be a nasty business."

"That is true. And, of course, your mother might have been the intended victim."

Zimmerman leaped to his feet, his face ablaze with anger. "How dare you insinuate such a thing?"

Scanlon held up his palms in a gesture of appeasement. "I said a possibility, Doctor. That doesn't make it gospel."

"I don't want to hear any more of that talk. Do you understand that, Officer?"

"It's my job to examine every possible contingency, no matter how unpleasant or implausible it might seem to the victim's family."

"Not in my home, you won't. And for your information, my mother was a wonderful woman who didn't have an enemy in the world. She was a woman who did good for other people. She . . ." He began to sob.

Scanlon waited for him to regain his composure.

Wiping his eyes with a handkerchief, Zimmerman said, "I just don't know what we'll do without her. She was the rock that supported the entire family."

Scanlon thought of his own mother. "I understand that."

An air of uncertainty came between the two men.

Scanlon watched him twisting the handkerchief. "Do you know that your mother worked for organized crime?"

Zimmerman's eyes flashed at him. "You're crazy."

"She took gambling action for the local bookmaker. His name is Walter Ticornelli. Have you ever heard your mother mention that name?"

"No, I haven't. And I don't believe a word of what you've just said. Mother working for a bookmaker! It's ridiculous."

"No it isn't, Doctor. It goes with the franchise in that neighborhood. People didn't just flock to her store to see her, or to buy things. They came because they could lay ten cents or a quarter on a number, or bet the flats or the trotters. Your mother took that action. She might have accidentally stumbled onto something connected with the bookmakers' other business. Narcotics? A hit on someone? Something that made your mother a liability."

The air was heavy with unspoken anger. "I think you had better leave my home, Lieutenant."

"Our investigation to date leads us to believe that it was a holdup, but, as I told you before, I have to look into every angle. If you don't want to help, there is nothing that I can do to force you. She was your mother, not mine." He started to rise up from his seat.

"Of course I want to help."

Scanlon lowered himself back down. The interview had become stressful; most cops agree that such interviews are counterproductive. "Do you live here alone, Doctor?"

"With my wife and daughter."

"Are they home?"

"My sister and my wife are shopping for shoes for my daughter. I persuaded them to go."

Scanlon saw the wrenching sense of loss in his eyes and felt sorry for him.

Examining his hands, Zimmerman said, "Andrea, my daughter, was nine years old yesterday. We were to have a birthday party. Mother bought a cake. Instead we sat shivah." His eyes filled again.

Scanlon recalled the crime scene: chunks of cake and whipped cream and raspberry filling mixed with body parts and gore. Walter Ticornelli had stated that he had observed Gallagher carrying a cake box into the store. "Tell me about your mother, Stanley."

Zimmerman's face molded into a disturbed expression. Slowly it turned contemplative and he began to scour memories. "Mother was born in Warsaw into an upper-middle-class family. When the war came she had a husband, and three small children, two girls and a boy. The Nazis rounded them up and shipped them to Auschwitz, where her family was killed in the crematoriums." Tears were streaming down his face as he talked. "Mother was spared because those savages needed people to translate the camp bulletins into several languages. Mother was fluent in German, Polish, Russian, and Hungarian. She met our father in Auschwitz. He too had lost his entire family. He survived because he was an accountant and they needed inventory writers to keep track of all the property they stole from the living and the dead. My parents worked in the same barracks. They were two human, breathing skeletons, working next to each other, day after day, who somehow sustained each other and fell in love.

"They were married shortly after they were liberated and came to this country as displaced persons. They had two children. My sister, Linda, is three years older than I." A painful remembrance made him look away. "Dad was killed by a drunk driver, crossing Bensonhurst Street. The driver was convicted and given a suspended sentence. Mother opened the candy store to support us. She worked long hours, seven days a week. Linda had to come home directly from school to do the housework, the laundry, prepare dinner. On weekends my sister and I would help out in the store so Mother could get some sleep in the back."

He glared at Scanlon. "My mother work for organized crime? What nonsense. I'll tell you the kind of a woman my mother was. Look at me, Lieutenant. I'm not what you would call a handsome man. I'm short, I have a face like an owl, and my hair's like a monk's, but my mother made me feel nine feet tall and more handsome than Gregory Peck and Clark Gable. She was constantly telling me how wonderful I was, that I was going to grow up and be a great surgeon. That I was the one who was going to make up for our family that had been killed in the camps."

He held up his hands. "These hands held the power, Mother told me. It was my hands that made me handsome. My specialty is plastics, Lieutenant. My mother would send me neighborhood children who needed my special skills but could never afford to pay for them. Recently I did a cranial-facial reconstruction on a little girl who had a congenital birth defect. My mother sent her to me. And I should do it without a fee, Mother said. Because we have to give to those less fortunate than we are. To repay this great country for the good that it has done for us. And you tell me that my mother was a criminal. Does that sound like a criminal mind to you?"

Scanlon was determined not to become embroiled. His voice soft, he said, "How do you and Linda get along?"

"My sister and I are close. Growing up as we did made us protective of each other."

"How did your sister get along with your mother?"

"They were very close. Linda adored Mother."

There were sounds of people, the sudden babble of female voices. Scanlon craned his head in the direction of the door. Two women appeared. A girl followed behind them. A tentative silence filled the room. The doctor went to greet them. Moving a hand from one to the other, he introduced them. "This is my sister, Linda."

She smiled politely and moved over to one of the dainty chairs and sat in ladylike fashion.

Zimmerman introduced his wife. Rachel Zimmerman was an attractive woman with a curtain of banged brunette hair that fell to just above the eyebrows. She looked to be in her early thirties. She had on a plain cotton dress, Roman-style sandals, no hose, and was holding two shoe boxes. Standing beside her was a girl with chestnut hair, inquisitive brown eyes, and a shy little smile. She had on jeans and a baggy top with a big red-nosed Snoopy emblazoned on the front, and white sneakers with big blue tassels.

Rachel Zimmerman came over and shook Scanlon's hand. "Thank you for coming."

Andrea Zimmerman ran to her father, throwing her arms around his waist, hugging tight. "Mommy bought me a pair of penny loafers and Aunt Linda bought me sneakers."

"You really made out," said the father, hugging her close.

The girl turned and looked at Scanlon. "Are you a real policeman?"

"Yes."

"Are you as mean as Dirty Harry is in the movies?"

Scanlon grinned at her. "Meaner."

"Come on, young lady," the mother said. "Let's you and me go upstairs and try on those new shoes of yours. I'm sure that the lieutenant and your father have things they want to discuss."

Andrea Zimmerman looked up at her father. "Daddy, I miss Granny."

"So do I," Stanley Zimmerman said and cried. The room became silent.

"Why don't you go upstairs with them, Stanley? I'll talk to the lieutenant," Linda Zimmerman said.

Stanley Zimmerman took hold of his daughter's hand. "If you need me, I'll be upstairs," he told Scanlon, moving toward the door. When he came up to where his sister sat he stopped and whispered in her ear.

Scanlon could not hear what was said, but he did see Linda Zimmerman's eyes dart in his direction.

Linda Zimmerman pulled off her big-brimmed black straw hat and placed it on the walnut table next to her. She carefully tugged off one of her black lacy crochet gloves that matched her linen dress. She began to rake out her hair. Hair that flowed down to her shoulders and had a deep black sheen. She took her time removing the last glove, her face set in thought. She tugged it off and slapped it down on the hat's wide rim.

"Stanley tells me that you think there is a possibility that Mother's death was premeditated. He also said that you think that Mother was part of some criminal activity."

He made a dismissive gesture with his hands. "What I said was that I have to examine every possibility." He noticed that she wore no rings and wondered if she was married. He told her of her mother's gambling activities. Added, "All the evidence gathered so far indicates that it was a holdup."

"I see." She clasped her hands on her lap. "Would you mind telling me the details of the case?"

Scanlon related the official version of the case, taking care not to mention the Jackson Heights splash pad or Joe Gallagher's secret life.

"Those animals," she said, speaking with visible anger. "To snuff out two lives. Scum like that should not be permitted to live."

"It happens every day of the week. And most times it doesn't even rate two lines on the evening news."

An ugly expression of agreement came over her face. "Don't misunderstand what I'm going to say, Lieutenant. My brother and I want them caught and punished. What we don't want is unnecessary publicity."

"I can understand that, Miss Zimmerman."

"I don't think that you can, Lieutenant." She shifted slightly in her seat, tucked her dress under her thigh. "I am thirty-nine years old and I'm a vice-president of the trust department of Morgan Fidelity. My responsibilities at the bank include the maintenance of private investment portfolios for some of the wealthiest people in this country."

"I fail to see what that has to do with your mother's death."

"Banking, Lieutenant, is a stodgy world dominated by stodgy men who look down their stodgy noses at women. Scandal, no matter how far removed from me personally, could, and in fact would, hurt my career."

"Your mother's death could hardly be called scandal."

"In banking, it is indecorous to have one's name appear anywhere in a newspaper, except on the social page, the financial page, or the obituary page. It is one thing to have a close member of your family the unfortunate victim of a random killing, and quite another thing to have a member the victim of premeditated murder, or connected in any way to any illicit activities."

Scanlon went to answer her. "Miss Zimmerman . . ."

"Please, hear me out, Lieutenant. My family does not want to read any of your ridiculously absurd surmises about my mother being the victim of a contract killing or part of any crime family. Such stories would have an adverse affect on my and my brother's careers. If you want to look for reasons for the killings I suggest that you delve into your dead lieutenant's background, because there are no motives in my mother's. I hope you understand what I'm telling you."

He caught himself watching her with an intensity that surprised him. He looked down at his hands, politely hesitant to say what was on his mind. He leaned forward slightly and looked at her. "Miss Zimmerman, it is my job to arrest people who commit crimes. We are not talking here about a case of malicious mischief or Assault Three; we're talking about a double homicide in which a member of the force was one of the victims. We are going to break this case. And you and your family can be assured that the press will get nothing out of me or any of my men. You see, Miss Zimmerman, in the world of cops and robbers, newspeople rank several notches below whores and pimps. Do I make myself clear, Miss Zimmerman?"

A beginning smile caught her lips. "Perfectly. And my name is Linda, Lieutenant."

"And mine is Tony."

She put her fingertips to her lips and gave him a slow warming glance. "I'm glad that we understand each other, Tony."

He became aware of her fragrance. Evergreen and orange. She was more beautiful than he had first realized. "Did you and your mother speak often?"

"On the telephone, at least twice a day."

"Did she mention where she was getting your niece's birthday cake?"

"A cop friend of hers, she said. He was getting it for her wholesale."

Wholesale, a cop's way of doing business. "Was your mother a wealthy woman?"

Slight annoyance. "She was comfortable. And, before you ask, her estate will be divided between her children, equally."

"You and your brother appear to be successful people. Why was it necessary for your mother to work at her age?"

"It was necessary because she wanted to. My brother and I urged her to give up the store. She refused. Said that she would never become a burden to her children. You see, Lieu—Tony, my mother was a survivor of the Holocaust. Their minds never really recover. Mother would squirrel her money away, every cent that she didn't need to live on, preparing for the day when she would have to flee, to buy her freedom, her children's and grandchildren's freedom. It was only during the last few years that Stanley and I were able to persuade her to put her money in the bank and make prudent investments."

"Did you know that she took gambling action?"

"That was done as an accommodation for her friends in the neighborhood. I don't think she made fifty dollars a week taking those bets."

"How come your brother didn't know about the gambling?"

"Because mothers and daughters talk in more detail than sons and mothers. Women do generally."

"Did your mother ever mention Joe Gallagher to you?"

"She did mention the name once or twice. He was a friend from the neighborhood. That's all I know."

"What about Walter Ticornelli?"

"No, never."

"Gretta Polchinski?"

A frigid smile. "You mean the madam. Yes, Mother would talk about her. We would laugh over Gretta and her whorehouse. The women used to come into the store in the mornings and tell Mother they were glad that their husbands bothered Gretta's girls and left them alone."

"Did your mother have any business dealings with Gretta?"

"Hardly. Gretta Polchinski was not the kind of woman my mother would associate with. In Poland my mother had women like that to clean her house, not to have dealings with."

He got up and walked over to the display of African shields and spears on the far wall. He felt a spear point and carefully examined the shields. She was next to him, explaining, "Stanley collects them. He has done a lot of work in Africa for the United Nations."

He loved her fragrance and was aware of a desire to sweep her into his arms, caress her body, consume her. He wondered if women ever had sudden urges like that, had blunt erotic images. Even if he made a move and she responded favorably, then what? He could never get it up with a straight woman. He felt antsy.

"Linda, can you think of anyone who might want to cause your mother harm?"

She fixed him with a penetrating look. "No, I can't."

"Thank you for your cooperation, and please accept my condolences."

She moved to where her hat and pocketbook were and took out a dark-colored card holder from her bag. She removed a card and handed him one. "I can be reached at that number during business hours."

"And if it should become necessary to contact you after business hours?"

Her cynical look became a small smile. She went back to her pocketbook and removed a silver pencil and wrote a number on the back of the card. "I can be reached at this number at night. But only if necessary, and never after eleven."

It was late afternoon when Scanlon walked into the Nine-three station house. A lone policeman manned the telephone switchboard, whiling away his tour by flipping through worn copies of *Screw* and *Hustler* magazines. The muster room was empty, save for the coffee containers and the waxed paper that was scattered over tables and sills. Nobody sat behind the raised desk. The sergeant had left his post and gone into the one-twenty-four room to aid a new female typist with an inviting smile. The old rules and procedures of the NYPD, rule 124, delineated the duties and responsibilities of the clerical patrolman assigned to each of the three platoons. Hence the cop assigned to clerical duties would forever be known as the one-twenty-four man and his workplace as the one-twenty-four room.

Scanlon was struck by the pervasive quiet inside the station house. It was the weekend, and the Palace Guard does not work weekends. The highway safety man, the summons men, the youth officer, the Community Relations people, the lead clerical man, his assistants, and the entire civilian clerical staff, save the few who work the clock, were all at home making like nine-to-fivers. A strange stillness becalms station houses on the weekends.

The TS operator looked up from his magazine and nodded to Scanlon, then returned his attention to the centerfold's delights.

After Scanlon had left the Zimmerman town house he had decided to pay an unannounced visit to the Squad to see if there had been any new developments on the case. Police management texts state that unannounced visits are a meaningful supervisory tool. Scanlon knew better. He knew that the moment he climbed the staircase out of sight, the cop on TS was going to dial upstairs to the Squad. "Your boss is on his way up," he would say, and turn to the next color photograph.

That was the problem with management texts: they never take into account the realities of the real world. Whenever the borough shoofly is spotted within a precinct, that precinct's emergency code is immediately transmitted over the radio. "Apache. Apache." Beware, a Judas is among us.

A realistic man, Scanlon knew that his unannounced supervisory visit was nothing more than a way of killing time before he went to pay his respects at Joe Gallagher's wake and keep his late-night appointment with Sally De Nesto. He had already cleaned his apartment and danced his aerobics, washed and hung out his pantyhose, and now there was nothing for him to do but play cops and robbers.

When he walked into the squad room he found one industrious detective at his typewriter. "Anything doing?" he said, moving to the line of clipboards that were hooked on the wall to the right of the detention cage.

The gray-haired detective, Steigman, who had a stomach that spilled over his wide western belt buckle, looked up from the machine. "They found the van. It was torched."

"Where did they find it?" Scanlon asked, unhooking the roll call.

"Laurel Hill Boulevard, right next to Calvary Cemetery."

Scanlon knew the area. It was a deserted section of real estate located under the Long Island Expressway and the Brooklyn-Queens Expressway. An artery that led into the major highways and avenues of both Brooklyn and Queens. A perfect place to abandon a getaway vehicle and torch it. "Was forensics called to the scene?"

"Yeah, they were there. The van was a charred hulk. There was nothing there to be found, but they went through the motions. The fire marshal said that the fire was started from inside the body of the van. The Five is on your desk," Steigman said.

Looking over the roll call, Scanlon asked, "Where is the rest of the team?"

"Biafra Baby and Colon are out doing a canvass where the van was found. There are a few factories around there. Somebody might have seen something. And Florio is available," Steigman said with a sly glance at the lieutenant.

"Available" in NYPD argot meant that Detective Angelo Florio's whereabouts were known to his partner, and that he could be reached quickly, if needed, and that there was a blank Twenty-eight with his signature affixed if something should go wrong. If that should happen, the UF 28, Request for Leave of Absence, would be filled out and filed, and Florio's name scratched off the duty roster for that tour. Double homicide or not, life within the NYPD goes on.

Scanlon moved over to the waist-high tray cabinet near the Dial-a-Brew machine and moved his finger over the index annotations on the front of each tray: Resident Known Criminal File, Known Gamblers File, Precinct Directory File, Parolee/Released Prisoner File, Vulva File. He pulled out the last tray. Detective Florio's "available" telephone number was listed along with the name and address of his girlfriend. In the back of the tray was a stack of blank Twenty-eights, all signed. It was each detective's responsibility to see that the Vulva File was kept current.

Walking into his office, Scanlon unhooked the remote from his belt. He sat on his desk and dialed his home number. The first voice that played back was that of his mother inviting him to Sunday dinner. She was going to have a few of her friends from the neighborhood, she said. He broke into a big smile, for he knew from long experience the meaning behind his mother's guileless tone. For sure, included among her friends would be a single woman who his mother and her cronies had decided would make him a perfect wife. The last one that she tried to fix him up with played the piano and spoke French, his mother had confided in the kitchen of her rent-controlled apartment. Her one great desire in life was to get him married.

Sally De Nesto's voice was next. She confirmed their date for later that night and asked that he not arrive at her place before ten. She offered no explanation; none was needed.

He read through the Gallagher/Zimmerman case folder, jotting reminders to himself. Had Maggie Higgins located the missing witness, Valerie Clarkson, the only one of Gallagher's girlfriends to pull a Mandrake? Call Thorsen woman to ascertain if she'll consent to being hypnotized. Interview Gallagher's wife. He wondered what it must have been like to be married to a living legend. He'd have to wait until after the funeral to find out. He had started to jot down something else when he caught a whiff of Linda Zimmerman's fragrance. He wondered what it would be like to hold her in his arms. At one time when he used to fantasize about women he'd feel a stirring in his stomach, sometimes a sudden hardness. And now . . . He tweaked his genitals. They felt useless. He snapped the pencil in half, threw the pieces down on his desk, got up, and hurried from his office.

The exercise room in the basement of the station house was empty. The heavy bag hung still; the speed bag glistened. Weights and barbells were neatly lined up in their cases. He stripped off his shirt, took his gun out of his holster, put it on the shelf, and began doing bench presses with ninety pounds of bells.

Limp dick, with the pegleg, he kept repeating to himself, as the sweat appeared on his body.

The E. G. McGuinness Funeral Home had a porte cochere of four stately white columns. Tara of Greenpoint. It was on Austin Boulevard between Baker and Furbish streets. Scanlon arrived a little before seven. Police cars were lined up on both sides of Austin and on the side streets. Policemen's private cars also clogged the streets. A detail of one sergeant and ten cops had been assigned by the borough command to ensure the free flow of vehicular and pedestrian traffic. Wakes of hero cops were public affairs. The precinct designations on the radio cars attested to the solidarity of the patrol force. Every precinct command in the city was represented.

Inside, the funeral home was thronged with mourners. Every cop wore his dress uniform; no savers here. Every shield bore a mourning band. The portable walls on the first floor of the home had been opened to form one enormous room to accommodate the overflow crowd. There were hundreds of floral pieces. Many stands were filled with mass cards. There were dozens of chasubles and chalices that would be donated to churches and priests. An honor guard of six lieutenants was formed around the closed, flag-draped coffin.

Mourners queued up to the prie-dieu to pay their respects. A grim-faced George Harris was there to greet each one, to lead them over to the cushioned prayer stand, and wait as they silently prayed. As each mourner stood, Harris would escort him over to the widow, who sat grieving in the first row. Harris would wait as condolences were mumbled and then usher the mourner away.

The widow's chair distinguished her as the primary mourner. It was a wing chair with walnut cabriole legs and was covered with floral needlework on a black background. The other mourners sat on metal folding chairs that had thin black cushions tied onto their seats.

Scanlon's eyes played over the crowd as he shouldered his way into the viewing room. He spied the familiar group of retired cops clustered together talking about the old days. There were no cops on the Job then with names like Abdul Illah Baihat or Kim Lee Song. In those days the Job was lily-white, Christian. Scanlon recognized a few of the old chiefs. Some of them had been powers in the Job when he was a rookie. Now they were shriveled old men with nothing to do but attend cop retirement parties and wakes in the vain hope that someone would recognize them and acknowledge their past glories with a "Howyadoin', Chief?"

Across the vast room, standing by themselves, was the PC, and the first dep and Deputy Chief MacAdoo McKenzie. Scanlon thought that the first dep had put on a few pounds. He grimaced inwardly when he saw what MacAdoo McKenzie was wearing: trousers with a purple-and-white tartan design, a maroon shirt with a black tie, and a black double-knit sport jacket with white saddle stitching over the lapels and pockets. A motley assortment of used parts indeed.

McKenzie looked in Scanlon's direction and quickly turned to the PC and said something.

Scanlon stepped into the crowd and began to edge his way forward toward the coffin. He reached the front of the room in time to see Harris lead an elderly woman over to the prayer stand. Scanlon thought that Harris's expression was a perfect blend of graciousness and solemnity. Perhaps a wee bit too perfect.

When Harris turned to lead the woman over to the widow, he saw Scanlon and motioned to a nearby cop to take over for him.

"Thanks for coming, Lou," Harris said, shaking his hand. "Come on, I'll introduce you to Joe's widow."

Mary Ann Gallagher had dark shadows under her eyes. Her long, light brown hair hung limp around her pallid face. She wore an unflattering rusty black dress and no jewelry, save her wedding band. She had a rosary clutched in her right hand, and she slowly beat her chest in dazed prayer.

Scanlon bent to express his condolences. Her lips were lined with a white pastelike substance. Despite her disheveled appearance, Scanlon could see an attractive woman in her late thirties, a woman who had exquisite blue eyes.

Mary Ann Gallagher gazed blankly into Scanlon's face as he whispered his sorrow at her loss. Duty done, he turned to leave, but Harris held him by the elbow and bent to say something in the widow's ear. Suddenly a cold clammy hand gripped Scanlon's wrist. He looked down and saw that her face had come alive in some strange frightening way. Her nostrils flared as though to breathe flames; her lips were curled into an ugly snarl.

Anchoring herself on his wrist, she hoisted herself up out of her seat. Her face was inches away from Scanlon's, her breath stale. "Get them!" she shrieked. "Those animals who took my husband from me. Those savages who destroyed our lives. Kill them!" She went limp and collapsed into the chair. Women rushed from their seats to console her.

For the first time Scanlon took note of the two frightened children sitting on either side of the widow. The girl was about ten and obviously suffered from Down's syndrome. She wore Mary Janes, white lace socks, and a blue dress.

The boy was about twelve or so and had brown hair. His thin black tie was askew and his serge suit too large.

"Let's go outside and grab a smoke," Harris said.

They made their way out to the veranda. A purple twilight filled the horizon. The outline of the Malcolm X Housing Project was stark against the backdrop. Scanlon glanced at the compact mass of azaleas in front of the home.

They made their way through the lingering policemen and down the wooden steps. The grass was freshly cut and had a clean smell to it. They made their way over to the weeping willow in the center of the manicured lawn. Scanlon noticed that Harris was wearing black cowboy boots with his uniform. The *Patrol Guide* mandated that uniform and equipment conform to Equipment Section samples: shoes—black, plain, smooth leather, lace-type with flat soles and raised rubber heels.

Sergeant George Harris liked to break the rules.

They leaned against the tree trunk; Harris took out a package of cigarettes and shook out a half-smoked butt. Scanlon watched him light it. "Are things that bad, Sarge?"

"Cigarettes are expensive. I don't toss nothing away. Waste not, want not."

Reaching up, Scanlon pulled down a branch and smelled the tassel-like spike of flowers.

"A couple of your detectives were around looking for you."

Scanlon let go of the branch. It rustled upward. "Where are they?"

Harris nodded across Austin Boulevard to McJackoo's Bar and Grill. "They said that they were going to stop for a taste."

Scanlon looked over at the line of policemen leaving the funeral home and making tracks to McJackoo's. "Were you able to find out anything at the One-fourteen?"

"With the wake and all I haven't had much time to nose around. You gotta remember that Joe was a boss and didn't exactly socialize with too many cops. The few that I did rap with didn't know nothing about his private life."

Harris took a deep drag and then field-stripped the butt.

"You come up with anything?" he asked, with a side glance at the lieutenant.

"I interviewed the Zimmerman family. They're intelligent, affluent, and decent people. When I hinted that their mother might have been hit they were furious. Impossible, they said. The daughter said that if I don't believe it was a robbery then I should delve in Joe's life, because her mother's was as pure as the driven snow."

"Ain't we all," Harris said. "What makes you so sure that it was a hit and not a robbery?"

"Because we got witnesses that tell us that the perp just walked into that candy store, called out, 'Hey you,' and started blasting. We also know that the perp had a getaway van and an accomplice. There was no 'give me your money, get your hands up, open the till.' The guy who stepped through that door came to do murder."

"And you think that Joe was the mark?"

"He's the logical target. He was Mister Perfect in public, but we know what his private life was like. He wasn't exactly pure."

"Who the hell is?"

"I can't argue with that," Scanlon said. "Somewhere there is a motive, and I'm going to keep digging until I find it. And when I do, it'll be a blazing signpost that will point me in the direction of the perps."

"You got any ideas who or why?"

"All I got so far is suspects." Scanlon looked at him. "Joe ever talk to you about a woman named Valerie Clarkson?"

Harris's face hardened in concentration. "Not that I recall. Who is she?"

"One of his girlfriends. We asked her to come in for a chat and she agreed. Then she copped a mope. She was the only one of his lady friends to do that."

"You got people out on the streets looking for her?"

"Higgins," Scanlon said. "I didn't know that Joe had a child with Down's syndrome."

"Both them kids are adopted. Him and his wife made a home for two unadoptables. Gave them love, a family. The boy is slightly retarded. That's the kind of guy Joe Gallagher was. The fuck had a heart of gold. Never mind all that shit about his weaknesses. Look at those two kids. That will tell you the kind of man he was."

"How did you and Joe get along?"

"We were friends. On the job Joe was my boss. What he said went."

"You never had any disagreements over how to do things?"

"Of course we did," Harris said. "And Joe would listen to my side of the argument and then decide. Sometimes he saw it my way, and sometimes he didn't."

"I also interviewed Luise Bardwell and her husband." He watched for Harris's reaction at the mention of his girlfriend's name.

"What did you think of her?"

"A strange lady. And her husband certainly doesn't operate on all his cylinders either."

"Takes all kinds, Lou."

"Amen to that. You still seeing her?"

"Naw. I haven't seen her in a while. I'll tell you, with this AIDS thing I don't feature going with bisexual women. It's one thing if you don't know, but when you know it, and you still go with them, then you ain't operating with a full deck either."

"You going out with anyone else involved in the case?"

"No." Harris pushed away from the tree. "I gotta get back inside, Lou. I'll call you if I come up with anything."

A group of policemen left the funeral home and went down the stone path and across Austin Boulevard, heading for McJackoo's Bar and Grill.

More mourners arrived. Among them, dressed completely in black with a lace mantilla draped over her peroxide head, was Gretta Polchinski.

Scanlon caught up with her as she was about to go up the steps. He took hold of her shoulder, stopping her. Her face was heavily made up. "Black suits you, Gretta."

"I'm here to pay my respects to the dead. Not to get my balls busted by you."

He moved up close to her, said conspiratorially, "Got anything to tell me?"

She laughed and turned to leave. He stopped her. "I assumed that a community leader like yourself would be able to pick up some tidbits for your friendly policeman on the beat."

She jerked her arm free of him. "I heard that your dead lieutenant and his sergeant were as close as a quarter to nine. Harris ran the show for Gallagher. And Gallagher never said thank you. But then, that's just like a cop."

"Anything else?"

"Don't you ever stop working? You oughta get yourself a wife. That way you'd have other things to fill your time with than just breaking my chops."

Scanlon's right eyebrow arched. "I have a friend who's been married three times. He always looks depressed." He watched her march up the stairs.

Denny McJackoo was a paunchy man with a round, thick-jowled face, a perpetual twinkle in his clever gray eyes, and the bogs of Ireland fogging his booming voice. As the proud owner of six bars, all of which were located within a three-block radius of the local funeral home, Denny McJackoo knew from experience that the wakes of cops and firemen were sudden bonanzas. "Aye, reposing the dead is a thirsty business, for the dear lads do truly love their whiskey," Denny McJackoo had confided on more than one occasion to his seven sons. When he found out that the Gallagher wake was to be held at E. G. McGuinness's he prudently gave his regular bartenders off and replaced them with his sons, with the following admonitions: buy back every fourth round, work from an open cash drawer, and ring up every sixth sale. "Aye, lads, there'll be undeclared cash that'll need burying."

A squeamish feeling made Tony Scanlon hesitate in front of the entrance to McJackoo's. Many sad experiences had taught every boss in the Job about the dangers inherent in St. Patrick's Day and cops' wakes. These were the occasions when drunken policemen shot other cops. Scanlon took a deep breath and reluctantly pushed his way inside. His apprehension grew as he took in the scene around him. Raucous policemen reeled through the crowd to greet friends. A heavy cloud of smoke hung under the ceiling. From somewhere a jukebox blared "Old Fenian Gun." A large dice game was in progress in the rear of the bar. The camp followers who go to all cop functions to gamble were out in force, from all parts of the city. The shuffleboard had been converted into a twenty-one table. Policemen crowded in around the long board, watching the dealer, a tall cop wearing the jodhpurs of a mounted cop and with a corncob pipe gripped between his teeth, toss out hole cards to the many players. As usual in such large games four decks of cards were being used simultaneously by the banker.

Uniform blouses, minus their shields, were stacked high atop the jukebox. The coatracks that extended upward from the green leatherette booths were bundled high with uniforms. Every cop had his shield clipped onto his gunbelt or tucked securely into his pocket. Drunk or sober, cops are a wary lot.

Scanlon stood among the crush searching for his men. "Howthefuckarya, Lou?" an unfamiliar voice shouted. Scanlon nodded in the direction of the voice. Taking in the scene around him, Scanlon decided that it was time to haul his ass out of there. Too many cops in too small an area, too many loaded guns mixing with too much booze. He had just started to go for the exit when he heard a familiar voice shout his name. He turned and saw two pairs of arms waving wildly over the tops of heads. "Shit," he mumbled, elbowing his way over to the arms.

Hector Colon and Simon Jones were squeezed in at the end of the bar. Lew Brodie sat on a stool, hunched over a shot of rye, glaring down into the whiskey glass. His harelip was pronounced and red, the result of the alcohol in his system.

"You wanted to see me," Scanlon said, pushing his way up to them.

Colon jerked a thumb at Simon Jones. "Me and Biafra Baby have come up with something."

"I'm listening."

Colon put down his glass of beer, wiped froth from his mustache. "We finished a canvass of where the van was found and came up with nothing, so we went into the house to bang out the Five. As we were coming out we ran into Stone and Trumwell coming in on a personal. They were the two cops first on the scene."

"I know who they are," Scanlon said, irritated because of where he was.

Colon continued, "Stone stopped us. He said that he remembered a case that went down five, six years ago that might have some connection to the Gallagher/Zimmerman caper." He took a gulp of beer. "An attempted homicide on a dude named Eddie Hamill. It seems that Hamill was a certified nut job, a burglar, and a heavy-duty-type gambler. According to Stone, Hamill was into Walter Ticornelli for some real bread. Around twelve large, Stone said. The story goes that Hamill unilaterally decided to cancel out his debt with Ticornelli. And when the shy demanded the vig from Hamill, Ticornelli done got knocked on his delicate ass." Colon drank more beer.

Lew Brodie threw down the shot, grimaced, and chased the whiskey down with beer.

The tumult had grown louder. A shouting and shoving match between two cops at the twenty-one table was quickly broken up.

Colon drained his glass, licked his mustache clean.

Scanlon grew more impatient. His phantom leg itched. He leaned sideways and scratched it. "Continue."

"Ticornelli was supposed to have sent three gorillas around to change Hamill's attitude toward paying his just debts," Colon said. "The word is that Hamill sent the three of them to the hospital with various parts of their anatomy in splints. People in the neighborhood started to say that Ticornelli didn't have the muscle to back up the money that he had out on the street. And that, *Teniente*, is bad advertisement for a shylock. Ticornelli was supposed to have made a pilgrimage to Mulberry Street to seek permission from the head goombah to have Hamill hit. Permission granted."

Colon caught the bartender's attention and swept his hand around the group to indicate that he was ordering another round of drinks. "One gray March evening our boy Eddie Hamill is about to enter his six-story walk-up when two Italo-American types reeking of Sicilian olive oil step from the shadows and proceed to peg nine-millimeters at ol' Eddie Boy. The story goes that Eddie, being the athletic type, does a header off the stoop and lands on top of some garbage cans and proceeds to take off like an Olympic sprinter. But he ain't fast enough, because he wakes up in intensive care minus one kneecap, a spleen, part of a lung, and three toes off his right foot.

"When Hamill gets out of the hospital, the first thing he does is to telephone Ticornelli and tell him that he intends to return the fucking favor in spades."

A fight broke out in the dice game. Two cops were rolling on the floor, trying to punch each other. Several policemen attempted to pry them apart. Scanlon was reminded of the cop who shot his best friend while they were driving home after three days of St. Patrick's Day partying.

The fight was broken up, the game resumed.

Scanlon was determined to cut it short and get the hell out of there. He had no desire to be dragged before the grand jury or the Firearms Review Board as a witness to one cop shooting another. "So where the hell is the connection with Gallagher?" Scanlon asked, glancing in the direction of the dice game.

Biafra Baby took up the story. "Stone told us that Ticornelli was in the habit of showing up at Yetta's candy store around the same time every day to pick up the day's action. Fourteen hundred. Gallagher and Ticornelli are the same size and have the same build. And they both drive Fords. It could have been a case of mistaken identity. Hamill, or someone he hired to waste Ticornelli, might have mistaken Gallagher for Ticornelli. And they hit the old lady because she was a witness."

"So were the kids in the back of the store witnesses," Scanlon said.

"Yeah, but they were in the back of the store. And it's one thing to take out adults and another to take out a couple of kids," Colon said.

Scanlon was skeptical. "Why would Hamill wait so long to take Ticornelli out?"

"That's just it," Biafra Baby said. "Hamill didn't wait to get his revenge. The word is that there have been several botched attempts on Ticornelli's life over the past five years. And the word is that Eddie Hamill was behind every one."

"Stone also told us that Ticornelli has people scouring Greenpoint for Hamill and can't find him. Eddie Boy has become the Phantom of Greenpoint," Colon said.

Scanlon shook his head. "I'm conversant with every open case that the Squad is carrying. And I can't recall any attempted murder on Walter Ticornelli."

"Stone said that the first attempt came shortly after Hamill was released from the hospital. Stone and his partner responded to the ten-ten—Shots Fired. Trumwell took the original Sixty-one. And this all happened before any of us were assigned to the Nine-three Squad," Biafra Baby said. "And as for the other attempts on Ticornelli, he ain't exactly the type to file complaint reports with the police."

Scanlon leaned his back against the bar, digesting what he had just been told. Like it or not, he had just been tossed another suspect.

A heavy-set detective named Jerry Allowman from the Eight-three Squad tottered over and flopped an arm around Lew Brodie's shoulder. "You guys got a hump of a homicide on your hands."

Brodie scowled up at him. "No shit, Dick Tracy." He shoved Allowman away.

The Eight-three detective started to complain about the gross indignity that he had just suffered at the hands of a brother detective, then saw the ferocious look in Brodie's eyes, thought better of it, and stumbled backward into the crowd.

"Did you go back and check the Sixty sheets and the Sixty-ones for the original complaint on Ticornelli's life?" Scanlon asked Biafra Baby.

"We checked back three years," Biafra Baby said. "We couldn't go beyond that period because those files are locked up in the old record room."

"So? Why didn't you get the key from the desk officer and check them out?" Scanlon said, annoyed.

Lew Brodie's head shot up. "We couldn't get the key because the desk officer didn't have the key. The only people in the Nine-three who do have the key to the old record room are the lead clerical man and his gofer. And neither of them scumbags work weekends." He gulped down his whiskey and slammed the glass on the zinc bar counter.

Scanlon sighed frustration. "First thing Monday, dig out those files."

9

Sally De Nesto raised her head off the pillow and kissed the cleft in his chin, then sank comfortably into the crook of his arm. She liked Tony Scanlon; she liked him a lot. With the regular ones it was just business, but not with the sad ones. It was different with them. Her passion was real. She counted among her sad ones a paraplegic, two blind ones, and a cute nineteen-year-old who had been born without arms. Sally De Nesto considered herself to be a sort of social worker. A Sister Theresa of the hookers. And why not? Didn't she help emotional and physical cripples? Without women like her, where would those poor souls go? Most people never think about things like that. What does a man without arms and legs do for sex? She had a feeling of drowsy contentment. She moved in close to him and closed her eyes.

Scanlon half-turned his head and planted a light kiss on her cheek, content to let himself drift into a peaceful sleep. He had that warm exhausted feeling of a man who has just gotten laid, and he was damned if he was going to permit himself to wallow in self-pity by spending half the night staring into the darkness wondering why he could only get it up with hookers, and realizing how very much he missed Jane Stomer. Not tonight. Tonight he felt whole, and whole men sleep after they make love.

Not too far from Sally De Nesto's one-bedroom Yorkville apartment, Stanley Zimmerman lounged on a comfortable couch in his fifth-floor sitting room, his outstretched legs supported on an ottoman, a brandy snifter held loosely in his hand. He glanced at his wife, Rachel, sitting next to him with her knees tucked under her supple body, her head at rest on his shoulder.

It had been a long three days since Thursday. First the appearance of those two somber policemen in his office to tell him that there had been an accident. Then the shock of being told the truth, and the horrible experience of having to identify his mother's body at Kings County Morgue. And then notifying the relatives, the insincere platitudes, the cremation. What was he going to do with all those baskets of fruit that people had sent? He'd more than likely end up donating them to the hospital. He was going to miss his mother. There'd be no one to make him kasha varnishkas or give him chocolate-covered matzoh every Passover, as his mother had done. A practice which he automatically continued with his daughter. Funny, his mother was very Jewish, yet she wasn't a bit religious. He'd been surprised when the rabbi asked him to say the Kaddish. There are just some things that you never forget. They're in your subconscious, ready, waiting for recall.

He felt his wife's body pressing close to him. He kissed the top of her head. "Bed?"

She smiled. "Sounds good to me."

Holding hands, they walked down the corridor until they reached their daughter's bedroom. They tiptoed inside. A large room decorated with pink ruffles and frills. Rachel walked over to the bed and kissed the sleeping child. Tucking the soft summer blanket into the mattress, she beamed at her husband. "She's so precious."

He nodded his smiling assent.

He lay in bed patiently awaiting his wife, who was in the bathroom. No matter how difficult the loss, he and the rest of the family had to get on with their lives. He'd been impressed with the policeman. There was something strong about him that he liked.

Rachel came out of the bathroom in a black nightgown. As was her habit, she went over to the window and opened it a few inches from the bottom. She turned back in time to see her husband struggling out of his underpants. Walking to the bed, she felt a familiar tingling come to her stomach.

She stood next to the bed and slipped the lace straps of her gown off her shoulder. She pulled it off and dropped it at her feet. She remained motionless, permitting her husband's gaze to take in her body.

He tossed the covers back and she slid into bed next to him.

The Kingsley Arms, a six-story building with an Art Deco facade, had gone co-op three years ago. It was directly across the street from the Zimmerman town house.

It was after midnight, and a few scattered lights were on in the Kingsley Arms. The door leading onto the roof was ajar, the hasp hanging precariously by one screw. More screws lay on the stairwell along with long slivers of wood and chips of green paint.

A figure moved cautiously among the shadows. It was the outline of a man, bending low, taking his time, making sure of his footing. He made his way over to the ledge and knelt, carefully placing the case down beside him. Crouching, he snapped open the case slowly so that the clicking of the clamps was not carried in the quiet night.

He removed the rifle stock from its padded recess inside the case and unscrewed the indented screws in the butt of the stock. Removing the covering plate, he shook out an eighteen-inch barrel. He raised himself up and peered out over the ledge, his gaze going to the open bedroom window. Ducking down, he inserted the barrel into the opening at the front of the stock and turned clockwise until the barrel locked in place. Next he removed the trigger housing and slid it into place, sliding the side latch, securing the mechanism. He removed a piece of black felt and unwrapped a magazine containing six hollow-tip 5.56 caliber bullets. He slid the magazine into the housing. The night scope was removed from its protective cover and its flanges inserted into the grooves atop the barrel. He tightened the screws with a small screwdriver, fixing the scope in place.

A long bulbous sound suppressor was removed from the case and screwed onto the end of the barrel. With his right hand he slid back the bolt and guided it forward, sliding the first round into the chamber.

Kneeling with the heel of his right foot secured under his buttocks and his shoulder leaning firmly into the stock, he firmed the weapon on the roof's ledge and aimed downward. Peering through the scope, adjusting the magnification knob, he saw Stanley Zimmerman's head come into the gray-white light of the cross hairs. A head full of sweet dreams and good deeds.

He took a breath, held it, and began his squeeze.

When the bullet plowed into Stanley Zimmerman's head his body stiffened, jerked up, and sank back onto the bed.

Rachel Zimmerman awoke with a start, conscious that something was wrong. The hand that was between her legs was unnaturally limp. "Stanley?" She could feel something oozing over her shoulders and into her hair. There was the strange smell of oxidized iron in the air. She reached her hand behind her, into a pool of blood, and sprang up, causing the bullet that was meant for her head to plow into the headboard.

In horror, she gaped at her dripping hand. She screamed. Paralyzed with fear, she gnawed on the knuckle of her hand.

The third bullet exploded into her face just below her left eye, tearing a passage through the head and leaving in its wake a bloody path of torn muscles and ruptured tissues.

"Mommy, Mommy," cried the little girl, expecting her mother to come rushing into her room to comfort her. In the past her mother had always come. Andrea would be reassured that everything was all right and kissed affectionately, and then tucked back into bed with a loving hug. The hug was the best part. She had been dreaming of wearing her new sneakers to her best friend's birthday party when a shriek scared her out of her dream. Her head shot up from the pillow; her eyes darted around the darkened room. She began to cry.

Where was Mommy? She cried louder. Her throat was getting hoarse. Gradually her sobs subsided. Her feet slid off the bed and she padded her way out of the bedroom. A nightlight was on in the hallway. Strange black shapes dived out of the shadows at her, trying to capture her, to eat her. She panicked and ran for the safety of her parents' room. She rushed inside and froze.

At 0115 that night the team of a cruising radio car spotted a dazed little girl wandering down Lexington Avenue in a pink nightshirt with a giant lollipop on the front.

10

The bloodstained bodies lay cold and waxen. Several hours had passed since they ceased to live. It was early Sunday morning, the city's after-hours joints were closing. Throughout the city priests were preparing to offer mass. On East Seventy-ninth Street grim detectives stalked over a new crime scene with the impersonal demeanor of men used to working in the disquieting presence of death.

Detectives from the Nineteenth's night watch had made the connection with the Nine-three's double homicide. A police lieutenant and a candy store lady named Zimmerman had been murdered.

A telephone message had been transmitted to the Nine-three Squad. When Scanlon did not answer his phone at home, the Vulva File was consulted and Sally De Nesto's number dialed.

Scanlon leaped up in the bed, listening to the terse notification: Nineteenth Squad detectives report that Dr. Stanley Zimmerman and his wife, Rachel, were the subjects of a homicide at their residence on or about 0100 hours this date.

"Call everyone in," Scanlon had said, slamming down the phone and throwing off the sheet, wondering what it was that he had overlooked.

Detectives clustered in small groups inside the bedroom, comparing notes. A photographer took pictures.

The ME had come and gone; he had issued a preliminary finding of death by gunshot.

Scanlon stood at the foot of the bed staring down at the bodies; his face was a mask of unbearable sadness. An awful sense of guilt welled up inside him, his head ached, his stump throbbed. Were they dead because of some failure on his part, some omission? Had his personal problems made him neglect his duty as a cop?

Higgins and Colon came up behind him. Glancing at the bodies, Higgins read from her steno pad: the who, what, when, how, and why of death.

Scanlon listened, unable to take his eyes away from the bodies. Higgins finished her report, said softly, "That's it, Lou. It's not very much."

"Where's the daughter?" Scanlon asked in a whisper.

"In Doctors Hospital being treated for shock. Her aunt is with her," Colon said.

Scanlon nodded. He would have to face Linda Zimmerman. What could he say to her? "I'm sorry"? That just didn't seem to cut it, not now. He turned from the bed and saw Frank Abruzzi, the ballistics detective, looking through a surveyor's transit. "There seems to be a big black cloud over your head when you work, Frank."

"Ain't that the truth, Lou."

"What can you tell me?" Scanlon asked the ballistics man.

Abruzzi led Scanlon over to the window. "Let's start with the glass fractures," Abruzzi said, pointing to the three holes in the window. "You'll notice that the radial lines are longer on the bottom of the cones. That means that there was downward pressure, which means that the perp fired from some point above this window." He took a pencil from his breast pocket and pointed to the center bullet hole. "This one was the first shot. See how the radial lines go all the way to the bottom of the glass, and see this small fracture that comes out of the other two's concentric fractures and connects to this hole's concentric fractures. That shows us that this one was the first shot." A thin stick had been stuck through one of the holes and pulled up against the outside of the window. A string was wound around the stick and ran through the hole and across the bedroom, and was fastened to the bullet hole in the headboard. Abruzzi pointed along the line of the string. "Your perp missed one, and it lodged in the headboard. With two impact points we can fix the trajectory of the bullets. Using the surveyor's transit we set one end on one impact point and the other end on the other and we have the trajectory."

Scanlon peered into the surveyor's transit. One end was aligned with the roof of the Kingsley Arms. He saw men huddled on the roof, pointing to the bedroom. He looked at the detective. "Thanks, Frank."

"Anytime, Lou."

Scanlon's eyes wandered the room. Most of the detectives were from the Nineteenth of Manhattan South Detective Area. The Nine-three

Squad had been brought in as a courtesy, to compare notes. This one was a Manhattan caper.

Scanlon turned abruptly and left the bedroom.

Higgins and Colon followed close behind.

Hurrying down the staircase, Scanlon reached the second level, where he heard a burst of raucous laughter that had come from one of the rooms off the hall. He followed the sounds into a large room that had a bizarre display of scythes and antique pistols on the wall and, next to the French window, a maple bar with four wicker stools. Three unfamiliar detectives with their shields pinned to their jackets were at the bar. One, a big black man with thick glasses, was acting as the bartender. Another, a younger man with brown forelocks, was slouched in a chair with his right leg draped over the arm, talking into the telephone. His silly expression told Scanlon that the call wasn't official business. The third detective was older, heavyset. He was perched atop a stool. Rémy Martin and Chivas Regal bottles were on the bar. Scanlon glared at the three glasses in the three hands and couldn't keep the image of the two gory bodies in a single upstairs bed from overwhelming his mind. Police texts talk of unity of command: one man in command of each situation and only one man in direct command of each officer. Outside supervisors aren't supposed to order around cops who are not under their personal supervision unless there is an emergency situation that demands it. According to the books, Scanlon was supposed to report these three beauties to their own boss. "What the hell is going on here?" Scanlon demanded.

Higgins and Colon hurried down the staircase to the first level.

The three outside detectives took in the lieutenant's shield pinned to Scanlon's sport jacket.

"We stopped for a taste, Lou," said the bartender.

"A taste?" Scanlon said, glaring at the detective with the telephone glued to his ear. "And I guess that's official business."

The detective said quickly into the mouthpiece, "I'll get back to you," and hung up.

The detective who was on the stool put down his glass and slid off.

"Unless you three super-sleuths have an overwhelming desire to be flopped back into the bag, I'd strongly suggest that you haul ass out of here and do whatever it was you were supposed to be doing."

"Right, Lou," said the bartender, leading the other two detectives from the room.

Scanlon took in the open liquor bottles. Who the hell wrote those damn supervision texts? he thought. They were never on the Job, that was for sure.

*　　*　　*

"A crowbar was used to pry this door open," explained the forensics man to the group of detectives atop the co-op's roof. He pointed his bony finger at the gouges in the doorframe. "The claws made characteristic impressions in the molding. We're going to remove the molding and make casts of the striations." He looked slyly at the detectives. "If any of you aces come up with the right crowbar I'll be able to make a positive ID for you." He moved away and walked up to the first of a file of upturned garbage cans that ran from the door to the edge of the roof. He righted the can and squatted next to a cluster of plaster of Paris that was set into the tar roof. "The warm weather softened up the tar. So when the perp knelt to fire, his toe and part of his sole pressed into the tar." He pointed. "Here is the heel of his left foot. We added salt to hasten hardening."

The detectives gathered in close around the forensics man.

"This moulage is going to give us the perp's approximate size and weight. From the position of his foot when he knelt to fire, I can already tell you that the guy you're looking for is probably right-handed." He stood, carefully replaced the can over the impression, moved to the next can in line, righted it, bent. "More footprints. We're going to develop a 'walking picture' of this guy."

A fat detective who was busy sucking on a toothpick said, "Exactly what is that?"

The forensics man waved his hand in front of him as he explained. "A lotta things make up the walking picture. The direction line tells us the angle at which this guy put his foot down. The step line, which is the centers of two successive heelprints, is gonna tell us his size and whether he limps." A hint of humor came into his beady eyes. "All you aces gotta do is bring the hump and his shoes to me and I'll cement them both onto this roof."

"I was wondering why all that garbage was dumped in front of the building," commented the fat detective with the toothpick, looking down the line of upturned cans that had been brought up to the roof.

Scanlon stood at the edge of the roof listening to the forensics detective and looking down at the green, windowless ambulance: Department of Hospitals, Mortuary Division. Police vehicles were parked helter-skelter. A line of unmarked vehicles stretched to the corner. Two TV camera trucks were on the scene. Reporters pressed against the cordon, shouting questions at detectives.

Scanlon strained his calf muscles in an attempt to shoo away the gray numbness that had taken hold of his body. The painful, nagging feeling that he had missed something or had overlooked something he shouldn't have, that he could have prevented the murders, just would not leave him. A soul-wrenching thought kept going over and over in his mind: he'd fucked-up because his thoughts were concentrated on his personal problems, his limp dick.

A policeman came out of the town house and fastened open the door. Morgue attendants appeared wheeling collapsible gurneys that had black body bags buckled to them. Policemen helped the attendants get the gurneys down the steps. There was a sudden surge of people against the police lines. Death seems to fascinate civilians; but then they can deal with it from afar.

The bags were unbuckled and hefted off. The remains of Stanley and Rachel Zimmerman were slid into the body of the ambulance.

The meat wagon drove off, its siren wailing.

What's with the siren? Scanlon thought. There's no rush, not now.

"Don't lay a guilt trip on yourself, Lou," Biafra Baby said, attempting to flatten inky spikes of hair. "Ain't no way we could have prevented this."

"We missed something," Scanlon said.

"That's a crock of shit," Lew Brodie responded.

"We're only human, Lou," Higgins said.

Scanlon walked away, heading for the group of Nineteenth Squad detectives standing around the air vents in the middle of the roof.

Lieutenant Jack Fable, the Whip of the Nineteenth Squad, saw him coming and went to greet him. "Howya doin', guy?"

Scanlon cringed inwardly at Fable's salutation. "Guy" was the common greeting in the Job when the speaker knew the face but not the name. "Scanlon, Jack. Tony Scanlon, Nine-three Squad."

Belated recognition brightened Fable's face. "Oh, yeah. How are ya?"

Jack Fable wasn't the lanky, baby-faced kid Scanlon remembered as the class standard bearer. The years of drinking and eating on the arm in the city's top-drawer hotels and restaurants had taken their toll. A pelican chin sagged beneath Fable's heavy jaw, and his beefy neck overhung his collar.

"We were in the Academy at the same time," Fable said, patting Scanlon's shoulder. "Too bad you got so old-looking."

Scanlon wasn't in the mood for jokes. "Got anything on this caper?"

"We don't have shit," Fable said, rubbing his chin. "A radio car team discovered the daughter wandering the streets. They managed to get her name and address out of her. The rest is history. All the preliminary canvasses have proved negative so far. Nobody saw or heard nothing. The goddamn doorman was inside the package room making Zs. The perp pranced in and out without anyone seeing him."

The lieutenants strolled to the rear of the roof and looked out over a jumble of fire terraces and grilled windows.

"There's gotta be a connection someplace with your Brooklyn caper," Fable said tonelessly.

Scanlon shrugged, holding out his hands palms upward. "But where?" He glanced around the roof. "Where's all the brass?"

"It's a little early for them. But they'll all get here eventually. All except the PC. Command and Control can't locate him. His wife told the sergeant on the Situations Desk that she didn't know her husband's whereabouts."

Scanlon grimaced. "One of these days he's going to trip over his own cock." Scanlon watched a woman in a far-off apartment cupping her breasts and running in place.

Fable looked at Scanlon. "Wanna tell me what went down in Brooklyn?"

Scanlon gave a rundown on the Gallagher/Zimmerman case to Fable. When Scanlon was finished, Fable said, "I can't figure which end is up with this caper."

"Welcome to the club. When it first went down I thought that Joe Gallagher was probably the mark. Now? I just don't know."

"What about this Eddie Hamill guy?"

"Who knows? I guess it could have been a case of mistaken identity. Hamill or someone he hired to hit Ticornelli mistaking Gallagher for the shylock. It's certainly something that we're going to have to take a close look at."

Fable's eyes narrowed. "What's your gut reaction?"

Scanlon exhaled. "Gallagher."

"Tell me why."

"Shortly before the time of occurrence we put the perp inside Mc-Goldrick Park. We have him leaving the park about the same time as Gallagher is parking his car."

"And you figure that an accomplice signaled the perp that Gallagher had arrived on the scene."

"Something like that."

"The same accomplice who drove the getaway van," Fable said.

"Probably. But who knows? There could have been a third person involved," Scanlon said, making a mental note of how many times the woman in the apartment had run in place.

"Why not Yetta Zimmerman as the mark?"

"Then why wait for Gallagher to come upon the scene? She could have been taken out anytime."

"Maybe because someone wanted them taken out together?" Fable said. "An object lesson to others."

"I thought of that," Scanlon said. "And I have to admit that that theory does hold water."

Fable scratched his chin. "If Gallagher is the mark, why take out the doctor and his wife?"

"It doesn't make sense," Scanlon said. "Unless . . ."

"Unless what?"

"Unless we can tie Gallagher and Yetta Zimmerman into some heavy-duty money transactions that somehow spilled over into her family."

Reaching down the front of his trousers to scratch his scrotum, Fable nodded and said, "We got a real fucking mystery on our hands here."

"It do appear that way," Scanlon said, wondering where he was going to get the manpower to search for Eddie Hamill, do the other things that needed doing, and still have detectives available to cover the chart. He was going to have to get a couple of precinct anticrime cops on a "steal" for a day or two, he decided.

"We might get lucky," Fable said, leading Scanlon away from the edge of the roof, over to the upended garbage cans. He righted one, and the two lieutenants squatted around the rough piece of drying plaster.

Higgins came over and hunkered down beside Scanlon.

"When the lab boys lift this impression and clean it off, we're going to have a pretty good *portrait parlé* of the perp," Fable said.

Hector Colon wandered over to the three squatting figures. His eyes fell to Higgins's opened knees, and his lustful gaze darted under her dress.

"There's something funny about this footprint," Higgins noted, suddenly conscious of an intrusive presence. Her eyes flicked up and she brought her legs together and replaced the garbage can over the plaster.

Colon came up to her. "Señorita Higgins, you are indeed a very beautiful woman."

"Why thank you, Hector. Did you like what you saw?"

He moved in close to confide, "Very much. Latin men are turned on by hairy women." He looked around to make sure no one was listening, and said, "If you ever have the urge to change your luck, call me. I'd love to come inside you."

She patted his cheek. "How thoughtful of you, Hector. But to tell you the truth, I don't think you could come if I called you."

The lieutenants moved off by themselves. "Do you think we should form a task force to work both cases?" Fable asked.

Taking in the chiseled outline of Manhattan, Scanlon replied, "Off the top of my head, no. Task forces are cumbersome. Too many chiefs pushing their weight around, and too many Indians looking to get lost."

"I couldn't agree more," Fable said. "We'll work together, coordinate over landline. You and me are a couple of old hairbags who ain't goin' nowhere in the Job. There shouldn't be any ego problems with us."

"You're right. I'll send you copies of my Fives and you send me yours. If anything heavy goes down, I'll get on the horn to you."

"And I'll do the same."

Deputy Chief McKenzie arrived on the scene a little after 0800 hours. He went directly to the edge of the roof and stared down into the Zimmermans' bedroom window. After a few minutes he turned, scanned the crowd, and called out to Scanlon.

Scanlon heard him and came over to him.

McKenzie was solemn. "Thank God we're off the hook with Gallagher." He wiped the back of his neck with his handkerchief. "It's obvious that Gallagher was just a poor slob who happened to be in the wrong place at the wrong time."

"That's not so obvious to me."

"Whaddaya wanna make problems for, Scanlon? Let it go, for Chrissake."

Scanlon's voice was full of barely controlled anger. "We got four DOAs. One of whom was a police lieutenant. We have a little girl who has been orphaned. And you got the balls to tell me to let go of it?"

"Scanlon, the Nineteenth caught this one. The solution to both cases is across the street in that bedroom. Be reasonable, bang out a Five, and transfer your Sixty-one to the Nineteenth. They'll combine both cases. We'll be off the hook and you'll be able to take an exceptional clearance on your case."

"The answer is no. I'm one of those old-fashioned detectives who still believes in clearing homicides by arrests, not by statistical flimflam." He stormed off.

McKenzie went after him. "I've been approved by the promotion board. This Gallagher thing is a Roman spear that can turn on all of us. Drop it!"

"No."

"You're an obstinate wop, you know that, Scanlon?"

With his right forefinger and middle finger pressed into his thumb, Scanlon shook his hand in McKenzie's face in an Italian gesture of contempt and said, "Va'ffa'n'culo."

"Whaddaya say?"

"I said that I'd love some capicola. That's an Italian cold cut that's made out of salami and mortadella. You people usually eat it on white bread with mayonnaise." He walked away leaving the deputy chief pounding fists against the sides of his legs.

Chief of Detectives Alfred Goldberg appeared, half an hour after MacAdoo McKenzie, accompanied by his usual retinue of Palace Guard flunkies.

Fable and the rest of the Manhattan South brass rushed up to the CofD to fill him in on the preliminary investigation.

Scanlon motioned to his detectives to make themselves scarce.

Nine-three Squad detectives began to drift toward the stairwell. Scanlon noticed Colon lean into Higgins and whisper something. Higgins's elbow smashed into Colon's ribs.

MacAdoo McKenzie ambled over to Scanlon. "Why don't you make yourself scarce before Goldberg spots you? He's bound to ask you questions about Gallagher. Questions that the PC don't want you to answer."

"What a way to run a police department," Scanlon said, moving off toward the stairwell.

"Hey, Scanlon, I wanna talk to you," Goldberg shouted from inside a circle of detectives.

Scanlon sighed and started to go to the CofD.

"Wait there. I'll come to you," Goldberg yelled, dismissing the others with a mere flick of his finger.

Scanlon rested his fake leg on the rim of a skylight and waited.

Goldberg stopped several times to ask questions of forensics technicians. Scanlon noticed that the CofD talked out of the side of his mouth. The CofD worked hard trying to enhance his public image as a tough guy. But within the Job he was known as a guy with short arms and deep pockets who got his fashionable clothes on the arm from his friends in the garment district.

He was shorter than most of his contemporaries and tried to compensate with platform shoes and by smoking big cigars. He was in his middle fifties and wore his hair stretched across his head like a starched rug. He only patronized the city's best hair stylists, and he always went to great pains to tell the owners of the salons to send their bills to his office at police headquarters. The bills never came, and Goldberg never inquired why.

Goldberg shifted the oversize cigar over his thick, protruding lips. "I don't see your friend Bobby Gomez," he said threateningly to MacAdoo McKenzie.

"I guess the PC got stuck someplace else," McKenzie said. "There's a triple homicide in the Bronx—he's probably there."

"Bullsheeit. He's probably in El Barrio sucking on some cuchifrita's cunt," Goldberg said.

"That don't make him a bad person," Scanlon said. "Besides, I'm sure there's a good reason for him not being here."

Goldberg looked at McKenzie. "You're a long way from Brooklyn, Chief."

"Command and Control notified me what went down here. I thought I might be able to help," McKenzie said, wiping his brow.

"That shows a high degree of professionalism, Chief. But I really don't think we're going to be needing your expertise on this one. But thanks anyway."

"Right," McKenzie said and left.

Scanlon took a deep breath of the cool morning air, looked up to the soft blue sky, and thought of Jane Stomer. He wondered if she ever thought about him, and hoped that she had not been with another man. He wondered, not for the first time, what life must be like for men with normal jobs and families. He suddenly felt terribly sad and very old. He came back to the present and saw Goldberg looking at him strangely.

"McKenzie thinks this double homicide washes out yours. But we know better, don't we?"

"Do we?"

Goldberg pulled the cigar from his mouth and pointed the wet end at Scanlon. "You, McKenzie, and Bobby Boy are trying to keep the lid on the Gallagher case. Bobby Boy's escapades are beginning to leak into print. He can't afford any more scandals. A little shove and El Spico is out."

Scanlon made a noncommittal shrug. "I don't know where you get your information from, but—"

"Cut the shit, Scanlon. Gallagher's rep for broads was well known in the Job. He used to score pussy on city time." He pumped the cigar back into his mouth. "I'd like you to tell me exactly what you've come up with on Gallagher."

Scanlon made a gesture of helplessness. He was trapped in a private war between the PC and the CofD. It was not because the PC had told him not to tell Goldberg the details of the case that Scanlon decided not to say anything. It was because he did not want to drop the match that would start a wildfire of rumor about Joe Gallagher. Gallagher was no straight arrow, but he was a cop, and he was the cop who was responsible for Scanlon's being able to stay in the Job after he lost his leg. He owed Gallagher. And Italians don't forget. It's all a matter of honor. "It's all in my Fives, Chief."

A nasty smile was his reward. "I've read every Five you've sent in on the Gallagher/Zimmerman case." His voice stretched thin in anger. "They all read like *Alice in Wonderland.* I've spent most of my life reading Fives. All I have to do is glance at one to know if a score has been made on a case, or whether some sharp-ass detective or squad commander is not putting everything he knows down on paper." He moved in close, said, "Why dontcha tell me about Gallagher?"

"Because there's nothing to tell."

Goldberg pointed his stubby finger at Scanlon's chest. "I'm going to be the next PC. So be advised that I've got a long fucking memory." He turned away and stamped off.

Scanlon stepped out into the street and immediately picked up on Lew Brodie's warning look. Brodie's stare led to a group of reporters trying to talk their way past the police line. Scanlon spotted Daniel J. Buckman, an investigative reporter from the *New York Times*, standing apart from his peers. Buckman, an avowed cop hater, was described by most of the cops in the Job as the Cocksucker with Lockjaw.

Scanlon and Buckman's eyes met.

Scanlon made for the double-parked department car. Higgins was behind the wheel and Colon was in the passenger seat, pressing his knee against hers. Biafra Baby was squeezed in next to Colon. Christopher sat in the rear, eating sunflower seeds and carefully placing the shells in the door's ashtray. Lew Brodie was standing in the roadway, holding open the door.

Scanlon was just about to reach into the car when Buckman rushed over to him. "Don't you have a good word to say to the press, Lieutenant?"

"Long live the First Amendment."

Undaunted, Buckman said, "A little bird told me that there is a cover-up in the Gallagher case."

"Did your little bird happen to be wearing platform shoes and was he smoking a big cigar?"

"He might be your next PC."

Scanlon wrinkled his face. "PCs come, PCs go." He went to get into the car.

Buckman stopped him. "I'm not a bad guy, Scanlon. And I could help you in the Job. Might even arrange a transfer back into Midtown."

"From your lips to God's ears, Sweet Lips."

"The public has the right to know about its public officials, Scanlon."

"Do they now?" Scanlon said, leading the reporter away from the car. "In that case, I'll give you the inside scope. Gallagher died in the performance of duty, trying to prevent a holdup. Period. End of case."

"I've been in this business too long not to know where there is smoke there is fire. Your own CofD has been shut out of the case. No one in the Detective Division with the exception of you and McKenzie knows anything about the case. That tells me that there is something afoot. And now Dr. Zimmerman, son of one of the victims, and his wife have been murdered. No. There's a story here, Lieutenant, and you're trying to sit on it."

"I have no idea why the doctor and his wife were murdered. The only thing I can tell you for sure is that Joe Gallagher's death was LOD."

"Line of duty?" the reporter scoffed. "That's bullshit and you know it. I'm going to keep digging, and while I do, I'm going to show you just how much pressure I can bring to bear to get at the truth."

"You do that, Buckman. I'm a strong believer in freedom of the press and all the rest of that shit." He slid into the car and slammed the door.

Higgins looked at him in the rearview mirror. "Where to?"

"Doctors Hospital."

The unmarked department auto drove into the emergency cul-de-sac and parked.

"Wait here," Scanlon said, pushing open the door. He moved past the two receptionists and scanned the crowded benches in the waiting room of the emergency room. No Linda Zimmerman. He spotted a square-badge standing next to a corn plant in the corner. He went up to him and identified himself, and inquired about Andrea Zimmerman.

The square-badge was in his late sixties and had thin gray hair. "I retired from the Job in '66. Used to work out of the old Fourteenth."

"Who was the captain when you were there?" Scanlon asked, trying to humor the old-timer.

"Fitzpatrick."

"Ol' Blood and Guts Fitz. I worked with him during the Harlem riots."

A forlorn expression came over the older man's face. "I guess the Job's changed a lot since my days."

"The Job never changes, only the cast of characters changes."

"Yeah, I guess you're right," the square-badge said. "Wait here, I'll check on those two names for you."

Scanlon watched him go over to the reception desk and shuffle through forms. He yanked one from the pile, read it, and motioned Scanlon to follow him.

They passed through two large doors that were edged in thick rubber and entered a tiled passage lined on both sides with examining cubicles. "Room nine, around the corner, to your right," the square-badge said, shaking Scanlon's hand.

"Thanks," Scanlon said, watching the retired cop walk away and wondering what it must be like to be out of the Job.

Linda Zimmerman was slouched against the wall outside examining room nine, her composure and elegance gone. Her clothes did not match and her hair was in disarray. She appeared to be in a state of disbelieving shock.

"How is Andrea?" he asked gently, his concern genuine.

Her tone was feeble, her gaze fixed downward on the gleaming tile floor. "My niece is in shock."

"I wish there was something I could say to lessen your pain. I'm so very, very sorry."

She started to rock back and forth on her heels, tapping her head against the wall. "First my mother, then my brother and Rachel. My entire family is gone. I'm alone with a little girl to raise." She stared at him with anguished eyes. "You were supposed to protect us. Why didn't you do your job? Why?" she screamed, and began to slam the back of her head repeatedly against the wall.

"Linda!" He grabbed her.

She fought to free herself from him, screaming, continuing to fling her head back. "Why? Why?"

He pulled her to him, trying to calm her. The back of her head was bloody.

"You murdered my family!" she cried, pounding him with her fists. "Murderer! Murderer!" She collapsed into his arms.

He caught her.

Several nurses rushed over to them. One of them pulled up a gurney. He lifted her onto the medical trolley.

"Are you the husband?" asked one of the nurses.

"A friend."

"Please wait outside in the waiting room."

Scanlon sat in the pew with the other anxious people. An hour passed. The square-badge offered him the privacy of the doctors' lounge. He declined; he wanted to wait with the others. He kept telling himself over and over that logically there was nothing he could have done to prevent what had happened to the doctor and his wife. But that nagging kernel of doubt would not leave his mind.

"Zimmerman?" the intern said, pushing through the double doors.

"How are they?" Scanlon asked, going up to the intern.

"Both sedated."

"Are they going to be all right?"

The doctor looked into his concerned face. "When the girl comes around we'll have a child psychiatrist take a look at her. As for the aunt, we're going to keep her here a little while to check her out. She did a number on her head. We want to make sure there's no fracture." He took a deep breath. "I knew Stanley Zimmerman by reputation. He did good work. It's a real loss."

11

The detectives filed into the Nine-three station house and went upstairs to the squad room to telephone their families that they would not be home until late Sunday night, if then. Scanlon moved behind the Desk and took the key to the property room out of the key drawer. He walked into the room and switched on the lights. He saw the animal lasso and the bolt cutters leaning against the side of the money safe. Two vandalized parking meters were next to them. Property envelopes with their vouchers stapled to the front of them were scattered about the shelves. A stack of old license plates, each wrapped in its letter of transmittal ready for their weekly delivery to the Motor Vehicle Bureau, was piled on the bottom shelf. There was a bicycle with one wheel.

The file that he was looking for was on top of the narcotics safe, a one-drawer metal card file with a notice stenciled in orange on the top: CONFIDENTIAL—UF 10, FORCE RECORD FILE.

He slid out the file and fingered the tabs to the Gs. He pulled out Officer Horace Goodman's Ten Card and left the room. Standing behind the Desk, Scanlon checked the home telephone number as he dialed. He turned to the cop on telephone switchboard duty and asked him what the other cops called Goodman.

"Hank," the TS cop said, turning the centerfold upside down.

Policemen do not answer their home telephones. Their wives and children have been trained to do that for them. My husband is upstate hunting, or my dad is fishing, and thus unavailable. Unavailable, until his next scheduled tour.

A cheerful female voice answered. "Hello?"

An equally cheerful voice replied. "Hi. Is Hank around? This is Tony."

"Hank," she sang out, "it's for you. Tony."

A pleasant male voice. "Hello, Tony."

"Hank, this is Lieutenant Scanlon from the Squad."

Goodman had been snared. Scanlon visualized the lead clerical man making ugly faces at his wife. "Yeah, Lou?"

"We have to get into the old record room, and the keys aren't at the Desk."

"Can't it wait until the morning? This is Sunday."

"No, it can't wait until the morning," Scanlon said, annoyed. "And if the keys aren't here soon I'm going to give the order to kick in the door. And in that case I'll have to make a blotter entry. And someone from the borough is going to want to know why the keys weren't at the Desk as the *Patrol Guide* prescribes they should be. And then it'll be somebody's ass."

"I'll drop them off in a few minutes."

The detectives sat around Scanlon's desk studying the old records.

The original complaint report was dated August 5, 1978. The Sixty-one detailed how at 1957 hours Walter Ticornelli went to get his car, which was parked on the S/E corner of Engert Avenue between Diamond and Newel streets, and discovered that the left rear tire was flat.

Ticornelli was in the process of jacking up his car when several shots rang out. The reluctant complainant stated that he fell to the ground and rolled under the car that was parked behind his.

The investigating officer, Detective Jack Weinberg, reported under details of the case on the original complainant report that the preliminary canvass failed to produce any witnesses to the shooting including the anonymous neighbors who had phoned in the report of shots fired. A search of the immediate vicinity by the patrol sergeant revealed four bullet holes in the complainant's car. Emergency Service responded and conducted a search of the surrounding area for victims of stray bullets. NR. An examination of the flattened tire revealed four punctures, each in close proximity to the others.

When questioned, the complainant could offer no explanation for the attempt on his life other than to state that it was probably the result of some kids fooling around. The attached Fives reported on the result of additional canvasses and on the result of checking the recovered slugs against the Ballistics File. Both proved negative.

Scanlon let the heavy report fall from his hands and looked up at his detectives. He had divided six years' worth of Sixty sheets among them and told them to check the chronological record of cases by complainants and crimes: Walter Ticornelli—Attempted Murder or Assault 1.

It took the detectives a little over one hour to complete this task. NR.

"Looks as though there was only one attempt on Ticornelli's life," Higgins said.

"If there were other attempts," Christopher said, "they probably went unreported, or went down somewhere else."

"Or there were no other attempts," Scanlon said. "This thing between Ticornelli and Eddie Hamill might be nothing more than neighborhood gossip." He looked at Lew Brodie. "What have you come up with on Hamill?"

Brodie consulted his steno pad. "I called the Identification Section and had them read me Hamill's sheet over the phone. His B number is 435897–2. A male, white, forty-three. His yellow sheet starts out in '60. Grand Larceny, Auto. He was adjudicated a youthful offender on that one." Brodie went on to enumerate Hamill's eleven other arrests. "Our boy Eddie has been naughty," Brodie said.

"This is true," Scanlon said. "Lew, I'd like you to go to the big building and pull Hamill's yellow sheet and copy it. Then take out each Nineteen, note the accomplices on each arrest, and—"

"I got the idea, Lou," Brodie said, slowly getting out of his chair.

"And Lew, we're in a hurry, so no stopping off," Scanlon said.

"Ten-four, Lou," Brodie said, leaving.

Scanlon turned his attention to Higgins. "What have you done about our missing witness, Valerie Clarkson?"

"She works as a waitress in the Santorini Diner on Linden Boulevard in Brooklyn. I spoke with her boss, Kostos Kalyviotis. He told me that she's worked for him for ten years, she's always on time, and is seldom out sick. She called in last Friday and told him that she needed a few days' vacation because of a personal problem."

Scanlon leaned back in his seat and put his legs up on the desk. "What else?"

"I got a list of her toll calls from the telephone company. There were two numbers that showed up consistently. Both in Suffolk County. One was in Deer Park, and the other in Huntington. I—"

"Goddamnit!" Hector Colon shrieked, leaping up off his seat and scampering around the office after a cockroach. He caught up with the creature near the corner steam pipe and crushed it with his foot. "I hate them! The son of a bitch tried to crawl up my leg."

"Is macho man afraid of a tiny cockarochee?" Higgins said, aping baby talk.

"Knock it off," Scanlon said.

Smiling at Colon, Higgins continued her report. "I ran Clarkson's name through the precinct computer. She owns a '78 Volvo, which, according to one of her neighbors, is suffering from terminal dents. I had the Suffolk PD check both addresses. Her car is parked in the driveway of her sister's house in Deer Park. Do you want me to take a drive out there and see if she's there?"

"Get me the *Patrol Guide*," Scanlon said to Higgins.

She reached out and took the thick blue book from the library cabinet and handed it to him.

Scanlon checked the rear index, then flipped pages until he came to procedure 116–18, Leaving the City on Police Business. He read the pages, then put the thick book down. "This has to be done right. A request to leave the city requires a Forty-nine through channels to the borough commander, and that takes time."

"Lou," Higgins said, "I'll take a drive out to Suffolk County on my own. No big deal."

"No good, Maggie. If you got into a fender-bender with a department auto there'd be hell to pay. And if you used your own car and had an accident, and your insurance company ever found out that you were on police business, they'd cancel your policy."

"Why not have the Suffolk PD pick Clarkson up as a material witness?" Biafra Baby asked.

"That takes too long. I want her in here today."

"But, *Teniente*, Señora Clarkson don't know that, does she? We can lure her back into the city," Colon suggested.

Scanlon looked at Higgins. "Maggie, contact Suffolk and ask them to lay a phony material witness collar on Clarkson. Have them tell her that she can avoid the collar by making a phone call to us."

Scanlon telephoned the Nineteenth's temporary headquarters. When Jack Fable came on the line he asked him if anything had developed on his double homicide.

"Nothing," Fable said, adding that the CofD had hung around the scene for two hours, breaking everyone's balls.

Scanlon hung up and dialed Doctors Hospital. Linda and Andrea Zimmerman were in stable condition.

"Lou, what was Hamill's B number?" Colon asked, checking over his notes.

Scanlon told him.

"You ever wonder where the term 'B number' comes from?" Colon said, jotting down the number in his notes.

Scanlon leaned forward to massage his stump. "It comes from Alphonse Bertillon. He was a Frenchman who originated the method of classifying perps by their body measurements." He pulled up his trouser leg and leaned back. "Years ago it was known in the Job as the Bertillon number. But like everything else it was shortened, to B number." He took off his prosthesis and stood it on top of his desk.

"Lou? That's fucking disgusting," Colon said queasily.

"What is, Hector?" Scanlon said, feigning innocence.

Colon pointed to the prosthesis. "That is."

"It's only a leg," Scanlon said, pulling off his stump sock and balling it up and tossing it into the bottom drawer. He took out a clean one and stretched it over his stump. "Ahhh. That feels much better."

Colon left the office shaking his head.

An air of casual expectation had taken over the squad room. Christopher had flipped channels until he found *Back Street* on eleven. Maggie Higgins had gotten her period. She quietly left the squad room and went to the female locker room and got what she needed, and knowing that the precinct CO was on his RDO, she went downstairs to avail herself of the privacy of the captain's bathroom.

Scanlon had finished the Sunday papers. On impulse he snatched up the phone and dialed Jane Stomer's home number. He felt like an adolescent as he sat listening to her recorded voice. He hung up before the beep. Then he dialed his mother and spoke to her in Italian, telling her that he would be unable to come for dinner and that he loved her. When, to his surprise, Sally De Nesto answered her phone, he said, "I'm sorry I had to rush out on you last night."

"I understand."

He was aware of a sudden hollowness in the pit of his stomach. "What about tonight?"

She hummed a few bars of "Never on Sunday." "A working girl needs one day of rest."

His hands were wet. He forced an edge of confidence into his voice. "Dinner. Nothing else."

She hesitated, making up her mind. "Dinner, nothing else?"

"Right."

"Pick me up at eight."

He checked his watch. "Make it nine."

After he had hung up he thought, Why the anxiety attack? Certainly he couldn't be falling for a hooker. Every cop who ever did that ended up swallowing his own gun. Crazy thoughts. It's just that he didn't want to be alone tonight, that was all there was to it. He was better off with the Sally De Nestos of the world. He picked up his prosthesis, leaned back in his chair, lifted up his stump, and fitted the beveled end into the socket.

The lazy quiet was broken ten minutes later when Biafra Baby answered the telephone. "It's for Higgins. Where is she?"

"Probably taking a piss," Colon said.

Higgins strolled back into the squad room. Biafra Baby held out the receiver. "Valerie Clarkson on three."

"Lou," Higgins called out, "our missing witness is on three."

"Now," Scanlon said, and he and Higgins pushed down the blinking buttons.

"Hi, Valerie, this is Maggie Higgins."

A scared voice. "I'm no material witness."

"Valerie, we have reason to believe that you are in possession of information that is vital to our investigation. You were given the opportunity to come in and talk to us, but you elected to run instead."

"I've never been involved with the police. I was scared."

"I can understand that, Valerie. You're no criminal. You're a working woman, like me. Look, why don't you come in of your own volition? That way there would be no publicity, no one would ever know that you talked to us, and I promise you that whatever you tell us will be held in strict confidence."

Biafra Baby mimed playing a violin. Colon wiggled his tongue at Higgins and undulated in his seat. Higgins turned her back to them.

"My parents mustn't find out about my private life. Dad has had two heart attacks. It would kill him."

"No one will ever know, I promise."

The reluctant witness said, "Okay, I'll come in."

"How long will it take you to get here?"

Lew Brodie walked into the squad room forty minutes later carrying three bulging folders. Moments later a nervous Valerie Clarkson appeared. Higgins went up to the railing, opened the gate, and ushered the witness into Scanlon's office. Scanlon motioned to Brodie to wait, and followed Higgins and the witness into his office, closing the door behind him. Higgins moved behind the Whip's desk and sat down in his department-issue swivel chair.

Valerie Clarkson glanced around at Scanlon, who had positioned himself in front of the door.

"Do you mind if he stays?" Higgins said. "It's regulations."

"I don't mind."

Higgins began by asking the witness how her trip into the city had been. Clarkson told her that there had been hardly any traffic so she had made good time. Higgins leaned across the desk to admire the witness's pearls. "They're beautiful."

"Cultured. I bought them on sale in Fortunoff's."

"I love pearls," Higgins said, fingering the strand. "I have a string of opera-length pearls that I just love."

Within a short time the two women were chatting as though they had been lifelong friends. The witness's brother-in-law had been laid off from his job at Republic, and Valerie had helped her sister to pay the mortgage. Higgins lied and said that she had just gone to contract on a co-op and confided that she was sweating out mortgage approval. She was a little afraid of the new adjustable mortgage rates.

Scanlon edged along the wall in order to get a better look at the witness. She wore her chestnut hair short and had on a white pleated skirt and violet-colored blouse. Her figure was trim, her face pretty, and with the exception of a little mascara she wore no makeup. When the witness was completely at ease, Higgins gently guided the conversation around to the dead lieutenant.

Joe Gallagher had not employed his favorite traffic ploy to meet this witness. Nine months ago, the witness said, Gallagher began showing up at the Santorini Diner around lunchtime. He always took a booth at her station. He was a big tipper, and never told off-color jokes, or came on to her, like most of her male customers did. Higgins nodded her understanding.

The remainder of Valerie Clarkson's story paralleled those of Gallagher's other girlfriends. Higgins let the witness finish her story before asking her first question. "The Santorini Diner is on Linden Boulevard near Conduit Avenue, right?"

"Yes."

"Do you happen to know what he was doing in that neighborhood?"

"No, I never thought to ask him."

"But you knew that he was a police lieutenant."

"Yes, but we never discussed his job."

"When he came to the diner was he alone?"

"Sometimes, and sometimes he came with a friend. And once he met some man there and they ate and then left."

"Who was the man he used to come into the diner with?"

"I don't know. I think he was a cop, but I'm not sure."

"And the third man that he met there, who was he?"

"I don't know."

"Was Luise Bardwell the other woman in the threesome?" Higgins asked casually.

The witness shifted uncomfortably in her chair and glanced around at Scanlon. She moved her head close to Higgins's and whispered, "It's hard for me to discuss that with him here."

Higgins motioned to Scanlon to leave the room. When Scanlon

walked out into the squad room and closed the door, he asked, "Where is the *Coles*?"

"There in the bottom of the supply cabinet," Colon said.

Christopher moved to the cabinet and said, "What borough do you want?"

"Brooklyn," Scanlon said. The *Coles Directory* is a reference source that lists the telephone numbers and the names of subscribers in every building in the city. The directory is cross-referenced by address and telephone exchanges. Christopher put the thick book on a desk. "What's up?"

"For the past nine months Gallagher has been dropping around a diner in Brooklyn," Scanlon said. "That's a long way from where he worked and lived. I want to know what the hell he was doing around there. The name of the diner is the Santorini. I want you to look up the phone number of the diner, and then pull out Gallagher's address book and check to see if there are any telephone listings around the diner for anyone connected to this case."

"You got it, Lieutenant," Christopher said.

Scanlon moved across the squad room to where Lew Brodie had arranged the criminal record into neat stacks.

"Now, what do we have on Mr. Eddie Hamill?" Scanlon asked Brodie.

"He did a stretch in Attica and is on parole until '89," Brodie said.

"And the Nineteens?" Scanlon said, picking up a handful of DD 19s, Prisoner Modus Operandi and Pedigree Forms. He turned them over to the back where the associates on that arrest were listed.

"Hamill was busted with associates on eight of his eleven collars. A dude named Oscar Mela took the fall with him six times. Mela's folder is here, along with the folders of Hamill's other associates," Brodie said.

"Anyone know this Oscar Mela?" Scanlon called out.

"I know him, Lieutenant," Christopher answered, looking up from the *Coles*. "He's an empty suit who hangs out in Astoria. In the pool halls along Steinway Street."

"I guess Mela is our best shot to find Hamill," Scanlon said. "What was his last known address?"

Brodie checked Mela's package. "Thirtieth Avenue, in the One-ten."

"Call the One-ten Squad and ask them to check their Resident Known Criminal File and their Released Prisoner File. Get Mela's current address. And if he has moved out of the One-ten, call that Squad."

"Right," Brodie responded.

Higgins and Valerie Clarkson walked out from the office together, chatting like old friends. Higgins moved ahead of the witness and un-latched the gate. Clarkson stopped and smiled at Higgins.

"Thank you," Clarkson said.

"I'll call you," Higgins said, pushing open the gate.

"Don't forget," Clarkson said, leaving the squad room.

When the witness had gone, Higgins perched on the edge of a desk across from the lieutenant. "The material-witness bit scared her. She was petrified that the newspapers would pick up on her involvement with Gallagher. Especially the threesome. She told me that after the trio finished playing their game together she stopped seeing Gallagher." Higgins took hold of the sides of the desk and leaned forward. "But she continued to see Luise Bardwell."

"Bardwell told me that she isn't seeing Clarkson," Scanlon said.

"She isn't, according to Clarkson. They only saw each other four or five times after the threesome, and then Clarkson stopped seeing Bardwell too."

"Did she say why she stopped seeing Bardwell?" Scanlon asked.

"She didn't want that kind of a relationship, she told me," Higgins said. "She thought she was gay and then realized that she wasn't."

"Lieutenant, what was the name of the woman who came to see us first?" Christopher asked.

"You mean the first of Gallagher's girlfriends?"

"Yes."

"Donna Hunt," Scanlon said.

"What was her husband's name?"

"Harold."

"Want to take a look?" Christopher said, stabbing a line in the directory with his finger.

Scanlon looked over Christopher's shoulder. Harold Hunt, CPA, had offices on Pennsylvania Avenue. His telephone exchange was 739, the same as the Santorini Diner's.

Jack Fable telephoned Scanlon to tell him that he had decided to assign men to guard Linda and Andrea Zimmerman.

Scanlon told him that he thought that was a good move.

"Oscar Mela still resides on Thirtieth Avenue. I have the address," Brodie said, hanging up the receiver.

A telephone rang. Colon answered. "Nine-three Squad, Suckie-luski." He shoved the receiver at Higgins. "For you."

Higgins took the phone, and her voice became strained. She turned her back to the others, arguing in whispers. She slammed down the receiver and stormed into the Whip's office, banging the door closed.

Scanlon said to Brodie, "I want you, Hector, and Christopher to hit Mela's flat. Get him in here *now*. I don't want to waste any time on this Eddie Hamill thing if it's going nowhere." He rummaged through Mela's criminal record and took out several 4 × 4 mug shots of Mela. "Take these with you. It might help if you know what he looks like."

"We have nothing to hold this guy on—want us to flake him?" Brodie said.

"No. Put on a little performance for him."

When the detectives had left, Scanlon slipped into his office and gently closed the door behind him. Higgins was standing by the window, looking down into the street.

"Anything I can do?" he asked.

She dabbed her eyes with a tissue. "Gloria can't get used to me being on the Job. We were supposed to go shopping on the East Side for sheets today. She's pissed off that I had to come into work on a Sunday that was my RDO." She turned and looked at him. "Civilians will never understand this Job."

"That's what makes us special, Maggie."

She blew her nose.

"Why don't you call it a day? We can handle it."

"No way. But thanks anyway."

"In that case, why don't you make yourself useful and take your cute little behind out of my office and go into the prop room and get a baseball bat and a few collapsible chairs and set them up around the squad room in anticipation of the drama that is about to unfold."

She sniffled, kissed him on the cheek, and said, "My backside isn't cute. It's too big."

When she had left his office, Scanlon wrote a note to himself: "Luise Bardwell and Valerie Clarkson?? Donna Hunt's husband, ck."

"Take your motherfucking hands off me!" screamed Oscar Mela as Lew Brodie heaved him over the squad room's railing. Brodie threw open the gate and stormed in after the frightened man.

Colon and Christopher restrained Brodie. "Take it easy," Colon said to the seething detective.

Biafra Baby went to help Oscar Mela up off the floor and onto one of the wooden chairs that Higgins had placed around the room.

Scanlon rushed from his office. "What the hell is going on out here?"

Lew Brodie pointed at Mela. His eyes were wide with frenzy. "While on patrol," he began, "we observed this man drive past a red light on the intersection of Morgan and Nassau avenues."

"You're a fucking liar!" Mela shouted. "I wasn't anywhere near there. You kidnapped me from in front of my house. What's his name? I want his name."

"His name is Detective Suckieluski," Biafra Baby whispered to the suspect.

"You got the balls to call me a liar!" Brodie screamed, breaking free of the detectives and rushing at the suspect.

Biafra Baby stationed himself between Brodie and Mela. Colon and Christopher grabbed Brodie and pulled him away from Mela. Scanlon placed a calming hand on Mela's shoulder. He noticed the thin man's gaunt face and weak mouth. He had on a dirty pair of jeans and a grimy white T-shirt. Tattoos covered both his arms. Scanlon took note of two of them. A dripping dagger piercing a skull . . . Death Before Dishonor. A dagger piercing a heart . . . Mother. "Let the officer tell his side of it, and then you'll get to tell your side. Okay?"

Mela rapidly nodded.

Brodie leaned against the railing, his right hand inches away from the baseball bat that Higgins had strategically placed there. He continued with his complaint. "I observed that the suspect was driving a '79 Bonneville that had the vent window broken on the driver's side—"

"You broke that window with a blackjack," Mela shouted.

"Please, sir," Scanlon said, gently squeezing the suspect's shoulder. "Let Detective Suckieluski finish."

Brodie continued, "Having reasonable cause to believe that the offending vehicle was stolen, we identified ourselves to the driver as police officers and directed him to pull into the curb.

"While Detective McCann was inspecting the suspect's license and registration, I noticed that the vehicle identification number on the dashboard was altered. I observed that the Car Make Serial Symbol and the Body Style Symbol had been changed. 'N' is the symbol for a '79 Bonneville. The VIN number on this car was 'W,' which is the style symbol for a Firebird Trans Am." He inched his fingers closer to the bat. "I advised the suspect that he was under arrest for forgery of a vehicle identification number as an E Felony, and for Offering a False Instrument as an E Felony. I thereupon advised the prisoner of his rights. It was at this point that the prisoner lunged at me and began to beat me about the head and body with his clenched fists. Necessary force was required to subdue the prisoner."

An exasperated Oscar Mela screamed, "You lying cocksucker!" Brodie grabbed the bat and swung it at Mela, striking the rickety chair's left leg, causing it to shatter, and tumbling Mela onto the floor. Screaming for help, Mela scrambled over the floor in a desperate flight to escape the crashing bat. Holding the bat high above his head, Brodie rushed after Mela.

Every detective in the squad room rushed to subdue Brodie. They dragged him screaming into Scanlon's office, where he continued to vent his rage by shouting and hitting the cabinets with his bat.

"I wanna lawyer!" Mela shouted as he scrambled up off the floor.

"Now calm down," Scanlon said, lifting the receiver. "I'll call Legal Aid and ask them to send someone." He dialed his home number and had a brief conversation with his machine. Inside the Whip's office, Brodie, Christopher, and Colon settled down into a fast game of stud poker. Brodie would intermittently halt the game to emit an angry howl and bang the bat against the side of the desk.

Biafra Baby tried to calm Oscar Mela.

Fifteen minutes later Maggie Higgins walked into the squad room and announced, "I'm Linda Wade. I would like to see my client, Oscar Mela."

Biafra Baby motioned to Mela. "He's all yours."

Higgins dragged a chair over to where Mela was sitting and positioned herself in front of the prisoner so that she blocked his face with her body and whispered, "Tell me what happened."

Scanlon left the squad room and hurried downstairs. He crossed the muster room and went behind the Desk. Pete Doyle, an old-time lieutenant with a brogue, was doing desk duty.

"How are you, Anthony?" the desk officer asked, looking up from *U.S. News and World Report.*

"Okay, Pete. Anything doing?"

"It's quiet. It's always quiet when I work. The lads know better than to bring any bullshit into the house when I have the Desk."

"Anticrime working today?"

"I have two units out there."

"They busy?"

"Anthony? In the Nine-three on a Sunday. You can't be serious?"

"Mind if I borrow one of your teams for a while?"

"The lads are yours." He spun around on the swivel chair to face the TS operator. "Give Anticrime a ten-two." The TS operator picked up the radio and transmitted: "Nine-three Anticrime, ten-two."

No response. The operator waited a few minutes and rebroadcast the message. Still no response. The desk officer glanced with paternal annoyance at the squad commander, as the message was broadcast for a third time. There was still no response from the field.

"It's not like the old days, Anthony, when a desk officer told a cop to shit, and the cop asked how much would you like, sir. The new breed is young, most have never been in the service, and only a few of them have heard terms like 'military discipline' and 'military courtesy.' So every now and then I have to put on my tight pants and give the lads a little in-service training." He angrily spun around to the TS operator.

"Get on that radio and let them know that I am good and pissed off at them."

"Right, Lou." The operator transmitted: "Nine-three Crime! Ten-two! Forthwith! Acknowledge! K!"

The response was immediate: "Crime, Zone A, ten-four." "Crime, Zone B, ten-four."

A self-satisfied grin crossed the desk lieutenant's face. "The lads will be right in." He turned serious. "Have you come up with anything on poor Joe Gallagher?"

"Nothing solid. We're working on a few things."

"Any connection with that double homicide in the Nineteenth this morning?"

"We don't think so." Scanlon leaned against the Desk. "How long you been on the Job, Pete?"

"Thirty-two years."

"You thinking of making it a career?"

They laughed.

"Ever think of getting out, living a normal life?" Scanlon asked.

"Himself invented this Job for poor lads like myself. They'll have to drag me kicking and screaming from the Job."

The doors of the station house swung open and four bearded anticrime cops in old clothes came in and lined up in front of the Desk. The desk lieutenant winked at Scanlon, got up out of his seat to lean across the Desk so that he was staring down at the four cops. "Are your radios working, lads?"

"We didn't hear your transmission, Lou," the oldest of the quartet explained. He looked to be about twenty-four.

The desk officer picked up the roll call and studied it. "You didn't hear my transmissions? In other words you remained on patrol with defective radios." He let the roll call drop from his hands. "I have four more tours to do before I swing out. I come back in on late tours. And I see that you four lads are going to be doing late ones with me. I think that I'm going to have to motivate you lads to pay more attention to radio calls. As dear, departed Sergeant Flynn used to say, ten thousand miles I come to be your boss and be your boss I'll be. Now. Frazier and Walsh, you both have a post change. Frazier, you have traffic post six; Walsh, you have traffic post two. Go upstairs and get into the bag and take your posts, and be quick about it. And you had better be out there, because I'm going to send the sergeant around to give you 'sees,' at infrequent intervals, of course."

The two cops who had just received the post change started to protest, but when they looked up into the restrained fury in the desk lieutenant's face, they just shrugged and moved off up the staircase.

The two remaining cops waited apprehensively for their turn. The desk lieutenant said, "Tomorrow you lads will be assigned to a traffic post along with your two friends. But for now, the good detective lieutenant has a little job that he wants you to do for him. And after you're done doing what he wants, I'd like you to do a little something for me. Stop by Tony's and get me a large pizza with extra cheese and sausage. And also pick me up a cold one. Day tours make me thirsty."

Scanlon walked with the two cops out of the muster room and into the sitting room. He handed them the mug shots of Eddie Hamill that he had taken from Hamill's criminal folder. "In a few minutes a weasel with an armful of tattoos is going to come barrel-assing down the stairs. I want you to follow him and let me know where he goes. I'm particularly interested in knowing if he runs to see this man," he said, tapping the photo of Eddie Hamill.

"Do you want us to lean on this guy, Lou?" one of the cops asked.

Scanlon looked into the babyface playing the tough guy and had to struggle to keep a serious countenance. "Just follow and report, nothing else."

When Scanlon walked back into the squad room he found Oscar Mela and his "attorney" waiting for him.

"You have nothing to hold my client on," Higgins protested, straight-faced. "My client informs me that he was accosted by detectives in front of his residence. He wasn't even in his car."

"That's not the story my detectives tell, Counselor."

Higgins went back into conference with her client.

Scanlon said aloud, "We might be able to work something out."

"For instance?" Higgins said.

"It's my understanding that your client comes from around this neighborhood. There are a few people from around here that we're interested in talking to. Perhaps we can play, make a deal."

A sullen Oscar Mela called out, "What are their names?"

Scanlon walked over to him. "Tony Russo, Tommy Edmonds, Eddie Hamill, and Frankie Boy Siracusa."

"Whaddaya want 'em for?" Mela said, openly hostile.

"That's my business," Scanlon said.

"I never heard of any of them guys," Mela said, folding his arms across his chest. "Any more questions you got, ask my lawyer."

Scanlon scowled at Higgins and then turned on Mela. "You're on parole. You might be able to walk away from some of the charges, but I can promise you that enough will stick to put you back inside." He glanced at Higgins, back to Mela. "Go on, get out of here. You're lucky that you caught me in a good mood and that you got a good lawyer. Go, before I change my mind."

Mela looked for approval from his attorney. "It's okay. Go home," Higgins said.

Mela leaped up from the chair and took Higgins's hand. "Thanks, Miss Wade." He rushed out of the squad room.

Higgins looked at Scanlon and smiled. "Want me to make out a Two-fifty?"

"A Stop and Frisk won't cover it. Make out an arrest report and then void the arrest. Under details, put that further investigation revealed that a speck of dust had covered the 'N' of the VIN number causing it to look as though it was a 'W.' Add that the arrest was voided and the prisoner released under Section 140.20 of the CPL."

The anticrime cops didn't report back to Scanlon until 1800 hours. They had followed Mela back to his Thirtieth Avenue tenement and waited down the block. An hour and fifteen minutes had passed before Mela reappeared. He got into his car and drove to Manhattan, into the Seventh Precinct to a six-story walk-up on Chrystie Street. A man was waiting for Mela in front of the building. The two men shook hands and talked for a few minutes, and then Mela got back into his car and drove off. The man whom he had met was Eddie Hamill. After Mela had driven off, Hamill hailed a taxi and left. The anticrime cops decided to check out the building where Mela had met Hamill. A check of doorbells revealed that an Eddie Hamilton lived on the fifth floor. Bad guys feel comfortable with aliases that are similar to their real names. When the anticrime cops telephoned Scanlon and asked what to do, they were told to return to base.

"Do you want to hit his flat now?" Brodie asked Scanlon.

"He's not there now. I want to hit it when we're sure he's going to be there."

12

Vincent's dining room was crowded with loyal patrons. A violinist strolled among the garish banquettes. A waiter rolled a menu blackboard over to Scanlon and Sally De Nesto. She smiled at the waiter and ordered Scampi in Graticola. Scanlon ordered Red Snapper al Ferri. They decided that they would share an appetizer: Crostini. "Shall I order a bottle of wine?"

"I don't drink, remember?"

"I'm sorry, I forgot." He ordered a half carafe of house wine.

As they talked, he noticed how her freckles spread down her nose, and the way her lips parted into a crooked line whenever she smiled. She wore white slacks and a turquoise voile blouse and white sandals and had gold bangle bracelets on her thin wrists and gold studs in her ears.

Taking in her shapely body, he said, "Did you ever think of modeling?"

"I toyed with the idea when I first came to New York."

"What made you give it up?"

"I got fat."

"Fat? There isn't an ounce of flab on your entire body."

She patted her thighs. "Everything that I eat goes right here."

He shook his head and an incredulous smile lit up his face. "Where did you grow up?"

"I was born in Piscataway. That's in New Jersey. I went to school in Piscataway. And my family still lives in Piscataway. Any more questions?"

"Yes. Were you ever married?"

He had touched a sore spot. Her eyes fell to her water glass, her long fingers stroking the rim. "What do you want from me?"

He became uncomfortable. "To be friends."

She studied him, her gaze settling on his lips. "You have never shown anything but a professional interest in me. Now you ask me to dinner, you want to know about my personal life. It makes a girl in my line of work wary when a john tries to get chummy."

"Perhaps I'm falling for you."

Her look turned hostile. "Please don't make fun of me. I do have feelings."

He felt his ears burn from embarrassment. "I'm sorry. I guess the truth is that I just wanted to see you. To be with you. I don't know why." His sudden candor surprised him.

Her tone softened. "I have other handicapped clients. And I can relate to their loneliness, and to their special needs. But you, I can't figure you out. Your problem is not all that terrible." She leaned forward and asked softly, "So why me? Why not a steady girlfriend, or even a wife?"

He looked away from her. "Because I can only perform with hookers." He shook his head. "I can't believe that I just told you that."

She lowered her voice. "You would be surprised at what people tell me." She brought the water glass up to her lips, gazed down the stem. "Do you want to talk about it? I'm a very good listener."

His eyes drifted around the room. Somebody banged down a pot in the kitchen. They could hear the sounds of a party in one of the private dining rooms at the rear of the restaurant. A cork popped. A waiter stood nearby tossing salad in a wooden bowl.

She brushed a strand of hair from her face, waited for him to speak. The waiter came and served them their appetizer, poured wine, and backed away.

The silence between them lingered.

He picked up his fork and speared a piece of butter. "It began when I lost my leg. . . ."

They picked at their food as he talked. His words came easily. When the waiter returned with their entrees, Scanlon was still talking. He stopped and watched the waiter set down the plates and leave.

He sipped wine. "That's it. The whole mess."

"Did you ever see Jane Stomer again?"

"No. A man doesn't continue to see a woman he can't satisfy."

"I am constantly amazed at the depths of men's ignorance about women," she said, cutting her food. "Women want to be loved and to love in return. Sex to women is secondary."

Scanlon nodded and picked up his knife and fork. He cut his fish, hesitated, put the utensils down on the side of his plate, looked at her, and said, "I wonder why I had this need to lay all this on you?"

She reached out and caressed his cheek. "Because I mean nothing to you. Psychiatrists and hookers have one thing in common. There can be no personal involvements, so clients can confide in them. My johns tell me things and do things in bed with me that they would never say or do with another human being."

"Makes sense," he said, picking up his utensils.

"Did you ever realize that you never address me by name? Whenever you telephone and leave a message on my machine, you never say your name. You assume that I will recognize your voice." She looked into his eyes. "And I seldom use your name, Tony. Or do you prefer Anthony?"

"Tony is fine."

She asked earnestly, "Do you know why you are able to get it on with me and not with Jane Stomer?"

He squirmed, shook his head.

"The shallowness of our relationship makes erection possible for you. I expect nothing from you, want nothing. Love is a complicated game, Tony. People expect things from their partners, they make demands. Hookers and shrinks don't. We only want our money."

"Where does a girl from Piscataway pick up on all this insight into people?"

She laughed. "One of my johns is a blind shrink. We talk a lot. And I'm into daytime talk shows. You would be amazed at how much women learn from watching those programs."

"I didn't mean to unload my problems on you. I'm sorry,"

"Don't be. I like to help people when I can. It helps my self-image, which ain't exactly great."

"You're a nice lady, Sally De Nesto."

"Why thank you, kind sir. Are you ready for me to lay a 'Good Morning America' word on you?"

"Go ahead."

"Premorbid personality."

"Which means what?"

"A person who has a tendency to overreact to things. Say a man loses his pinky in a car accident and as a result he can't talk or he becomes paralyzed. His premorbid personality caused him to overreact emotionally to a minor injury."

Scanlon picked up his glass and swirled the wine around. "And what caused him to overreact?"

"Something in his past, his childhood. Talk shows only cover so much ground, Tony." She placed her hand on top of his. "My practice is limited to the bedroom."

The next morning Scanlon awoke fresh and revitalized. He sat on the edge of the bed staring at the rays of morning sun coming through the blinds. He looked around at Sally's sleeping form and smiled. A nice lady. He looked down at his flaccid member. You are most definitely a bothersome son of a bitch.

He saw his underpants on the floor. Last night when they arrived back at her apartment he had asked her if he might spend the night. She said yes and he assumed that she had changed her mind about making love. While she was in the bathroom, he telephoned the Squad to let them know that he was at his Vulva File location and to ascertain if there were any new developments on the case. There weren't, so he hung up, and thought about Eddie Hamill. The whole thing with Hamill didn't make sense to him. He wished that there were some way that he could forget Hamill, but there wasn't. He was going to have to check the lead out.

When Sally came out of the bathroom in a white nightgown, he hurriedly worked off his underpants. To his profound disappointment, she crawled into the bed, kissed him lightly on his head, turned her back to him, and went to sleep.

Watching the golden rays, he began to run over in his mind all the things that needed doing that day. Joe Gallagher was to be buried this morning, and there were still people to be interviewed. It was going to be a long day, and he'd better get started. He stepped off the bed on his missing leg and tumbled onto the floor. "Goddamnit!"

Startled, Sally sprang up in bed, saw him on the floor, threw off the sheet, and rushed over to him. "What happened?" she asked, kneeling down on the floor beside him.

Vexed, he snapped at her, "I stepped off on my missing leg."

"Does that happen often?"

"Sometimes I forget." A sour smile. "Would you say that was the result of my premorbid personality?"

"I'd say that was the result of your being a klutz." She passed her hand over his prostrate body. "Big tough cop flat on his ass dressed in the altogether." She kissed his nose. "You're cute."

His hand slipped inside her nightgown.

She closed her eyes. "Hmm. That feels good." She reached behind and glided her nails over his naked stump. "Are you sensitive here?"

"Very," he said, aware of the tightness in his chest. He felt his member springing to life. His fingers gently kneaded her nipple.

Arching forward, she lifted up her nightgown and sat astride his stump. Moving to and fro, she humped him.

His nerve endings bristled and his stump brimmed with strange, wonderful sensations. Pleasure surged through his body. His breathing became hard, and he made little yelps as his head lolled over the carpet.

She slid down the stump and rubbed the beveled tip hard against her body.

He groaned.

She gagged from the pleasurable torment and cupped her fingers over the head of his turgid member, kneading the swollen rim, sliding her butterfly fingers up and over the throbbing head.

His moans were deeper, louder. He felt like a boiling caldron ready to erupt. Their bodies moved in harmony. She squeezed hard, milking him, increasing his exquisite torture.

She was humping him faster and faster. Beads of sweat dotted her brow. Her mouth was agape, her tongue out. "I want to watch you come. Come!"

His gagged mumblings had become a loud yell, and then he came, and she continued to hump his stump. She took hold of it with both her hands and pressed it hard into her body, rubbing it against her clitoris. Suddenly, she went into a spasm of humping. She let out a long wail and then collapsed on top of him.

13

A gentle wind blew from the southeast. The sky was clear.

Three police helicopters overflew the crowd gathered outside St. Mary's Church on Provost Street in Greenpoint. Rows of grim-faced policemen stood at attention, tendering the final salute. A bugler sounded taps. Police pallbearers paused with the flag-draped casket at the top of the stone steps. Bystanders bowed their heads. Tearful women leaned out windows, watching the unfurling panoply of an inspector's funeral.

Taps ended. The coffin was carried down the steps to the waiting hearse. The grieving widow, dressed in black and supported on one side by Sgt. George Harris and the other by the Catholic chaplain, followed behind the coffin.

Tony Scanlon stood on the sidelines a block and a half away, lighting a De Nobili. He saw the widow's knees sag, and he was overwhelmed by the pathos of the moment. A lump rose in his throat, and a burning stung his eyes. He swallowed, champed down on his cigar. He thought of the two worlds in which he lived. His cop world of ambiguous loyalties and oversized egos that bore lifetime grudges. He thought of the world of the rookie cop, a pristine place where everything was reduced to its simplest terms: the good guys against the bad guys. Innocents in blue, they were quickly hardened and made cynical by the realities of the Job. He thought about his private life, his days of uncertainty and loneliness, of hookers, and stump-sock maintenance. How easy it had become for him to step between the parts of his life. This morning he had put forty dollars on Sally De Nesto's night table, said goodbye, and stepped into his police world.

The cortege crept away from the curb.

Scanlon said a silent farewell to Joe Gallagher, the man who had helped him stay a cop.

"They gave him some sendoff."

Walter Ticornelli's black ringlets looked as though they had been soaked overnight in a vat of grease. The shylock's reeking aftershave caused Scanlon's nose to wrinkle.

"Do you take a bath in that stuff?" Scanlon said, moving downwind.

"Whaddaya mean? That's Musk for Men by Le Claude."

"It smells like panther piss for schmucks."

"Whadda cops know about fancy things?"

"I guess nothing. But I am glad to see you here, because I want to ask you a few questions."

"About what?"

"Eddie Hamill. I hear stories."

Ticornelli's face darkened with anger. "I hear them too. They're old wives' tales. Don't believe them."

"Someone pegged those shots at you."

Ticornelli made a gesture of frustration. He spoke in Italian.

"Hamill never shot at me. Believe me, there was nothing between Hamill and me, nothing." He shook his finger at Scanlon and his pinky ring sparkled. "Besides, what would that have to do with Gallagher and Yetta?"

Scanlon answered in English. "Mistaken identity. You might have been looking to take Hamill out and the guy you hired to do the job mistook Gallagher for Hamill."

Ticornelli slapped his forehead, said in Italian, "And I suppose that I also had the old lady's son and wife killed?"

"I have to follow up on every lead, every rumor." Scanlon was aware of the unconvincing sound of his response. He was also aware that he did not have the manpower to squander on leads that made no sense, rules or no rules. Still, he probably could put the Hamill thing on the back burner for a while. He knew where Hamill had burrowed. If he wanted him, he could always reach out for him.

Ticornelli glanced around to make sure that no one was within earshot, moved up closer to Scanlon, and confided in Italian, "This Gallagher thing is hurting a lot of good people. Your Irish cop friends got their strawberry noses stuck up everyone's ass. We'd like for things to get back to normal. This is a quiet neighborhood, and we like to help it stay that way." He held up one finger and switched to English. "Whatever you heard about Eddie Hamill and me is nothing but pure, unadulterated bullshit. Forget it. Don't waste your time."

Scanlon grabbed Ticornelli's finger. "And you wouldn't bullshit a cop, would you, old friend?"

The shylock worked his jaw muscles. "Of course I would. But I ain't. And you fucking well know it."

He's telling the truth, Scanlon thought. "Will you work with one of our artists and prepare a composite sketch of the driver of the getaway van?"

Ticornelli was surprised. "Are you going soft in the head? I work the other side of the street, remember? You and me, we talk. Now and then I whisper something to you in Italian. But that's between us. I help you make a sketch, and the world knows."

Scanlon spoke softly in Italian. "A few seconds ago you told me you wanted to help, get things back to the way they were. You help me, no one is ever going to know. I promise."

"A cop's promise is about as good as a barroom promise."

Scanlon's unflinching glare held the shylock's eyes. He said in Italian, "I keep my word, Ticornelli."

A sullen silence came between them and lingered.

Minutes passed. Scanlon said, "I'd owe you one, one that you could call in anytime."

"No one would ever know? They'd be no grand jury, no court, no testimony?"

Scanlon nodded.

"Okay. I'll meet with your artist."

Scanlon left him and moved through the thinning crowd. Rented buses lined up to take out-of-command policemen back to their borough's marshaling points. Several pipers from the Emerald Society band headed for the Dunnygall Bar and Grill. Another group of policemen followed behind the pipers. Scanlon thought, They'll get their loads on, some cop will pull up a piper's kilt, the piper will cold-cock the cop, and the donnybrook will have begun.

Maggie Higgins came out of the church and walked over to Scanlon. "I stayed behind to light a candle for Lieutenant Gallagher."

Scanlon nodded approvingly. "How's everything going at home?"

"It sucks. We never should have moved in together. My car is parked a few blocks from here. I'll meet you back at the Squad."

Watching her shove her way through the crowd, he thought, We all got our problems.

Biafra Baby, Colon, and Lew Brodie were standing beside the department auto, talking. Christopher was leaning against the car reading a book on nutrition. Scanlon walked over to them and told Biafra Baby and Christopher that he wanted them to check out Harold Hunt, the accountant husband of Donna Hunt. As they talked, Scanlon noticed the shopping bag filled with boxes that Hector Colon held in his hand. "What's with them?"

Colon reached into the bag, took out one of the black boxes, and held it up. "Roach motels," he announced proudly. "The *cucarachas* crawl inside and get stuck in the glue. They die a slow, miserable death. I'm going to put them around the squad room."

The long entrance hall of the Gallagher apartment had rooms on both sides. Green linoleum covered the floor. People were arriving bearing platters and trays covered with aluminum foil.

Scanlon made his way around a group of beer-drinking policemen who were standing just outside the entrance and moved into the apartment. He turned to his left and entered the first room. Cigarette smoke tainted the air, and intermittent bursts of laughter punctuated the hum of conversation. A long table had been set up against one of the walls. It was covered with food: bowls of potato salad, macaroni salad, tuna casseroles, platters of American and Swiss cheeses, and baloney, liverwurst, and ham. There were bowls of baked beans and beets. A dozen or so bags of potato chips and pretzels were piled along the back of the table, and there were long loaves of white bread, and large jars of mayonnaise and pickles. A second, smaller table contained a large electric coffee urn, stacks of white cups, and homemade pies and cakes. A third table was covered with bottles of booze and mixes. Two cops acted as bartenders for the thirsty crowd.

Scanlon looked around and pushed his way out of the room. The parlor was down the hall on his right. It had a Colonial-style sofa with a wooden frame. On the wall above the sofa was a painting of Galway Bay. A cross made of palm fronds was stuck into the right-hand corner of the frame. A large color television and stereo were on a portable stand. A St. Patrick's Day hat was perched on top of the television set.

Scanlon moved through the parlor. When he did not see George Harris or the widow, he left the room. The kitchen was at the end of the passage; it too was mobbed with people. Scanlon glanced in and noticed the old-fashioned gas stove with the heavy doors and black legs, and was reminded of his Italian grandmother and of all the wonderful meals she had cooked for him on a similar stove.

He moved through the apartment. A drunken woman pushed her way past him, babbling, "Where's Mary? Mary Gallagher, you poor soul, where are you?"

Scanlon came to a closed door in the middle of the hallway and paused to listen. He heard voices inside, so he knocked and went in. Mary Ann Gallagher was sitting up on a queen-size bed that had a blue chenille bedspread. Her head was back, resting against a headboard covered with tufted burgundy fabric. A dressing table in the room had mirrors on its sides and top. It was covered with jars and tubes. There was a large television, and a dark blue rug, and two overstuffed chairs.

Mary Ann Gallagher was holding a cup and saucer on her lap. Three other women were in the room along with a tired George Harris, who had a mourning band stretched over his shield and a spitshine on his black cowboy boots.

Harris moved to greet Scanlon. "Glad you could make it, Lou." He placed his hand flat on Scanlon's back and guided him over to the bed. "Mary, this is Lieutenant Scanlon. You met him at Joe's wake."

She offered a limp hand, and Scanlon took hold of it. "I'm so very sorry, Mrs. Gallagher."

"You were at the wake," she said.

"Yes, I was."

"Wasn't it grand? Did you see all the flowers? They certainly did Gallagher proud."

"Yes, they did," Scanlon said, looking at Harris and whispering, "I want to be alone with her."

"Can't it wait? She just got back from the cemetery," Harris whispered back.

"No, it can't," Scanlon said.

Shaking his head in disbelief, Harris motioned the other women to leave the room. One of them, a skinny thing with a flat backside and a head of blond hair that was black at the roots, came over and kissed Mary Gallagher on the head. "We'll be right outside the door if you should need us, Mary dear," she said, in a squeaky voice as she cast a hostile look at the Italian interloper.

You frigid, shanty-Irish bitch, Scanlon thought, watching Harris usher the women from the bedroom. When they had all gone, Scanlon dragged over one of the chairs and sat down beside the bed. "We have to talk, Mrs. Gallagher."

"About Gallagher?"

"Yes."

Her striking blue eyes moved slowly over his face, taking his measure. The dark circles that he had seen at the wake were no longer there. And her skin was no longer pallid and sickly. Color had returned to her cheeks, and she wore a light shade of lipstick.

Scanlon saw something in those eyes, deep down. It wasn't sadness. It was a wariness and a hint of her determination to have her way. He wished he had brought Maggie with him. Women are better at questioning other women. They speak the same language, understand the unspoken questions.

"Mrs. Gallagher," he began, "there are certain questions concerning your married life with Joe that I—"

"Why?" she snapped. "Why is it necessary for you to pry into my married life?" She turned and stared at the wall. "Our life together is nobody's business."

He watched her sip tea. Maggie should be here, he thought. She'd probably have started by complimenting her on her nails or something.

Mary Ann Gallagher had long, graceful hands with nails that were beautifully cared for and painted a deep red. They were pampered nails, out of place in Greenpoint, Brooklyn, and out of character for a new widow. He found himself looking at her and thinking that she didn't seem quite right in the part she was playing. Her black chemise dress draped her body, outlining an attractive figure. Her ears were pierced, but she wore no earrings.

"Gallagher died a hero. I really don't have to answer any of your questions, Lieutenant."

His left ankle itched. He tilted down to scratch it, and when he felt the fiberglass he cursed himself for forgetting. He did not want to waste time with the widow. "Mrs. Gallagher, your husband isn't a hero until I say he's a hero."

She looked at him, her thoughts blazoned across her face: You guinea bastard. "What do you mean by that?"

"My Squad caught your husband's case. And I make the final determination on how he died."

"But it was in the line of duty," she protested.

"Not until I say it was." He toyed with the tightly knit balls of the chenille bedspread. "What was your married life like?"

She raised the cup to her lips. Sipping tea, she contemplated the gray hexagon design of the wallpaper. She lowered the cup into the saucer. "My married life with my husband was unsatisfactory."

"In what way?"

She looked into the cup, straining to read tea leaves. "When we were first married, Gallagher wanted me to do certain unnatural acts, things that I could never bring myself to do. I really never enjoyed that part of married life. In time Joe came to understand that and we got along fine. We grew to respect each other."

"How often did he . . ." Damn, he thought. "How often did he make love with you?"

"Once every six months or so," she said casually.

Scanlon felt as though he were one of those creepy, nose-picking detectives with stained ties who get off on asking female complainants for unnecessary details of sex-related crimes. How did you react when the perp came, my dear?

He watched her finish her tea and lean over the side of the bed to put the cup and saucer on the floor. As she moved, her dress clung to her body, outlining bikini underpants.

Scanlon decided that Mary Ann Gallagher was indeed an incongruous woman: pampered nails, sexy underpants, a magnificent ass, and an avowed distaste for sex. "How did Joe spend most of his off-duty time?"

"Gallagher expended most of his time and energy on being a police department celebrity. He belonged to over a half-dozen police-related organizations. And he was active in every one of them."

"Then it's safe to say that he was out most nights of the week."

"He was always at one meeting or another."

"Do you think that there might have been other women in his life?"

Her lips narrowed and tightened. "There was never another woman in Gallagher's life. My husband was a Catholic! A Fourth-Degree Knight."

His thoughtful expression gave way to a question. "Is George Harris a good friend?"

Her slanting eyebrows arched in the center, an involuntary expression of distress. "Yes he is, a dear friend. I don't know what I would have done these past days without him."

"Did you and your husband socialize with Harris and his wife?"

"Occasionally we would attend department functions together. Once we went to the Lieutenants' Benevolent Association's Winter Carnival at the Nevele Country Club."

"Did you or your husband have any contact with Stanley Zimmerman or his wife, Rachel?"

"No we didn't. Really, you certainly don't think that their deaths were in any way connected to Gallagher's? It was nothing more than a horrible coincidence."

"Maybe. Do you work, Mrs. Gallagher."

"No."

"How did you and Joe manage financially?"

"Just fine. Everything is so expensive today, but we managed. We don't owe a soul."

"Did Joe ever gamble?"

"Of course not."

"Did he moonlight or have any other business dealings outside the Job?"

"The department was Gallagher's life; he gave it his all."

Scanlon's mind raced, trying to find new questions. He noticed that she had mentioned going out with Harris and his wife, but not that Harris was divorced. He wondered if she knew, and decided not to ask.

Never put your cards on the table, any cop worth his salt will tell you that. An image of a scared little girl in Mary Janes with the wide, lolling tongue of a Down's syndrome victim and the uncomfortable face of a twelve-year-old boy came to mind. "How are the children taking all of this?"

"The poor darlings really don't understand. They only know that their daddy is gone, and that they will never see him again." She choked up, began to sniffle. Reaching into the Kleenex box on the night table, she pulled out one and dabbed her eyes. "I have to give the darlings back now."

"Give them back? I don't understand."

"They are foster children. We've had them for four years. And now that I'll have to go to work, I'll be unable to care for them."

"I thought they were adopted."

"No, they're not adopted. We couldn't have any of our own so Joe decided to take in some foster children."

When Scanlon left the bedroom he noticed clusters of people standing around in the hallway. He found George Harris standing outside the kitchen, drinking a can of beer. "How'd it go?" Harris asked.

"Okay," Scanlon said, watching a woman inside the kitchen drain a can of beer. He saw her bend the can in half, arch it into a plastic garbage bag, reach down into a metal garbage can that was filled with ice, and pull out another can. She was talking to a man in a bus driver's uniform.

"What did you think of Mary Ann?" Harris asked.

"There was something about her that made me uncomfortable." The muscles on the right side of Harris's face made a lopsided smile. "She's a good woman, Lou," he said, shaking out one of his clipped butts.

"I'm sure that's true, George."

Gales of laughter came from the beer-drinking woman in the kitchen. "Let's get out of here," Scanlon said, and led the way through the crowd.

The fresh air felt good. Scanlon leaned back against the wrought-iron gate and glanced up. He began to admire the Greek Revival houses on the block. He liked the three-sided projecting bay windows. There were two Italianate brownstones in the middle of the block with delicate ironwork and detailing over the doors and windows. A stream of people bearing food threaded their way up the steps of the Gallagher house.

"Have you come up with anything on the case?" Harris asked.

"A lot of stone walls. What happened in the Nineteenth really threw us for a loop," Scanlon said. "I don't know which end is up anymore. Who the hell would want to murder the Zimmermans?"

"Beats the hell out of me, Lou. But you know, both sets of homicides don't necessarily have to be related."

"That's what I keep telling myself. Have you found out anything?"

"I spoke to every cop in our unit and to most of the cops in the One-fourteen. Not one of them knew a thing about Joe's love life or about his gambling."

"That's bullshit. Cops were with him when he stopped women for phony traffic violations. I'm going to have to speak to them myself."

"Lou, they'd speak to me a lot faster than they would to you."

Scanlon looked at Harris. "Do you think Joe could have been getting it off with one of the policewomen in your unit?"

"Anything is possible, but I don't think so. Joe liked the conquest. If he ever made it with a subordinate, he'd never know if he'd scored because he was her boss or because he turned her on."

Higgins was drafting the supplementary Unusual on the double homicide in the Nineteenth when Scanlon walked back into the squad room. "If you had a couple of foster kids, would you be able to just up and give them back?" he asked Higgins.

She looked up from the typewriter. "No way. I love children." She looked down at the keys. "That's my one big regret, not having children."

Scanlon went into his office and telephoned the Nineteenth. Jack Fable had nothing to report. Patient Information at Doctors Hospital informed him that Linda Zimmerman and Andrea Zimmerman had been discharged. He took out the card that Linda Zimmerman had given him and dialed her home. There was no answer. There was also no answer at the Stanley Zimmerman residence. He plucked a pencil out of the coffee can on his desk and jotted in block letters on the pad in front of the can: "WHY? WHERE THE HELL IS THE DAMN MOTIVE?" Staring out into the squad room, he thought, There has to be a connection between Gallagher and the Zimmermans, someplace. He wondered what Jane Stomer would say if he called her. Knock it off, he thought with disgust. You have a homicide on your hands.

Brodie stuck his head into the office. "Lou, we got shots fired on Kent and Franklin streets."

Scanlon broke out of his trance and rushed out into the squad room. The detectives had all gathered around the radio set, heads bowed in concentration. Tension was high. Scanlon lowered himself to the edge of the desk, folded his arms across his chest, and listened to the transmissions.

"We have numerous reports of shots fired at Kent and Franklin. Subject a male, white, heavyset, wearing maroon slacks with a white belt, white loafers, and a long-sleeved brown shirt. Units responding use caution."

"Nine-three sergeant to Central. Advise units, no sirens."

"Ten-four, Sarge. Units responding to Kent and Franklin, do not use your sirens. Authority, Nine-three sergeant."

An excited voice burst over the wavelength. "George Henry, Central. We have 'im in view, walking east on Kent."

The radio fell silent.

Radio cars on patrol in Brooklyn North pulled into curbs, double-parked, their crews refraining from giving back the dispositions on jobs, anxiously awaiting the next transmission. Inside station houses clerical men hurried from offices and gathered around precinct radio sets. The Nine-three detectives fidgeted uneasily and glanced impatiently at one another. The absence of traffic on the radio was ominous.

"Nine-three units on the scene Kent and Franklin advise Central of the condition at that location, K."

No response from the field.

"Nine-three sergeant advise Central of the condition Kent and Franklin. Is further assistance required? Acknowledge, K."

A nonchalant, self-assured voice crackled over the wavelength. "Er, Central, this is the Nine-three sergeant. No further, Central. Call it off."

"What is the condition, Sarge?"

"We're investigating at this time, Central. Will advise by landline."

"Ten-four, Sarge."

Scanlon kicked the side of the desk in anger. "Sheee-it! Just what we need." He hopped off the desk and stormed back into his office. That last transmission from the patrol sergeant had told it all: they'd be dragging trouble in off the street. He figured that he had about ten minutes before it arrived. He made another quick call to Linda Zimmerman, with negative results. He dialed Sally De Nesto's number, and reminding himself to use her name and to mention his, he told her machine that he would like to see its mistress that evening, and hung up. Staring at the phone, he thought, We've become a society of automatons. Machines dial and talk to each other, machines add and subtract for us, pay bills for us. Someday soon we'll be able to stick our dicks into the mouthpiece of telephones and get blow jobs. I'd better hurry out and buy some telephone stock.

Nine minutes later he heard the expected commotion outside in the squad room. Loud, gruff voices, and shuffling, stumbling feet. A boisterous drunken voice shouted, "Get your hands off me. I'm on the fucking Job."

Scanlon pushed himself up out of the chair and calmly walked out into the squad room. A sergeant and five cops were tugging and pulling a drunk through the gate. Scanlon leaned against the doorframe, watching the all-too-familiar sight. The detectives had all found something to do; nary a head was not bent over a typewriter. What you don't see, you don't know, and can't be expected to testify to.

Sergeant McNamara had a ruddy complexion and thinning gray hair. He left the drunk and came over to Scanlon. He shrugged helplessly. "His name is McMahon, Lou. He works in the Four-nine. He went to Lieutenant Gallagher's funeral and afterward him and his buddies stopped in the Dunnygall for a taste." The sergeant moved in close and whispered, "His uncle is Chief McMahon, the Bronx borough commander."

Scanlon eyed the thrashing drunk attempting to straddle a chair. "How many did he let go?"

The sergeant scratched the back of his ear. "Six." He shrugged one shoulder. "Can we say it was a car backfiring?"

"Backfire? Have you canvassed the area to see if his *backfire* resulted in any dead or injured?"

"Emergency Service is on the scene now. They're checking."

Scanlon nodded toward the drunk. "Keep him quiet." He walked back into his office and found Higgins waiting with a smile on her face.

"Seeing you in action reminds me of Baryshnikov making great leaps across the stage, graceful, smooth, always in command."

"And what is that supposed to mean, Detective Higgins?"

"That means, Lieutenant Scanlon, sir, that before you are finished with that caper outside, you are going to be holding a lot of IOUs."

"Why, Maggie chile, whatever do you mean?"

Sergeant McNamara stuck his head in. "Chief McMahon is on the line for you."

"My, the word do travel fast in the Job," Scanlon said, pushing down the blinking button. "Hello, Chief."

The authoritarian voice on the other end was full of concern. "I understand you're holding my nephew."

"He's here."

"What's the story?"

"He might have to take a fall for Reckless Endangerment. He got his load on and let six go." As he talked, Scanlon reached into the top drawer of his desk and took out the Department Directory. He quickly flipped the pages to the M's. Assistant Chief Joseph McMahon was born February 11, 1927, and came on the Job June 1, 1946. That would make him fifty-nine. With the mandatory retirement age set at sixty-three, Scanlon would have four years to call in any markers. Plenty of time.

"Can anything be done?" Chief McMahon said. There was that familiar undercurrent, that slight modulation of tone.

"I'm not sure. Depends on whether or not he hit anyone. If he did, then nothing can be done, and he'll have to take a collar. If not . . ." He did not finish the sentence. The next move was McMahon's.

"I'd be very grateful for anything you could do, Lou."

"I'll get back to you, Chief."

The next call came from Frankie Lungo, the PBA's borough trustee. He too wanted to know if anything could be done, and he too would be grateful. The third call came from the duty captain. He was anxious to dance away from the entire matter, and asked Scanlon to call him with the results of his investigation.

Scanlon got on the horn to the desk officer in the Four-nine. He asked the desk lieutenant one of the Job's most-asked questions: What kind of guy is this McMahon?

"When he's sober, a gentleman. When he's got his load on, he's trouble."

It was almost one hour before the sergeant in charge of the Emergency Service truck telephoned Scanlon and told him that the canvass failed to reveal any casualties or property damage from PO McMahon's unauthorized discharge of six rounds. Scanlon thanked the sergeant and went out into the squad room. The off-duty cop was slumped in a chair, still babbling, "I'm on the fucking Job."

Scanlon went over to him and stared into his blurry eyes.

"Whatharfuck you looking at?" McMahon said truculently.

"I'm looking at you. I've never seen an asshole up close before."

"I know who you are," babbled the drunk. "You're that pegleg lieutenant, ol' shit on a stick himself."

Scanlon kicked the chair out from under the drunk. With arms thrashing upward, McMahon tumbled backward onto the floor.

"I'm the pegleg lieutenant who is going to hand you a collar for Reckless Endangerment."

McMahon sat up, shook his head trying to clear the drunkenness away. "I didn't do nothing. I wanna PBA lawyer," he demanded.

Bending, cupping his palms over his kneecaps, Scanlon said into the drunk's face, "You didn't do anything, huh? I'll tell you exactly what you did. You fired six rounds from your off-duty under circumstances evincing a depraved indifference to human life thereby recklessly engaging in conduct that created a grave risk to human life. And that, asshole, is a D Felony."

McMahon tottered up onto his feet. His cheeks were crimson and his nose a patchwork of broken capillaries. Bracing himself on the edge of the desk, he shook his head, trying to clear the craziness from his mind. He was suddenly scared. "I've got fourteen years on the Job. I've got a family."

"You should have thought of that when you drew your gun." Scanlon looked over at Lew Brodie. "Read him his rights and book him." Scanlon went back into his office and slammed the door.

Higgins was sitting down, applying polish to her nails. "Beautiful, Lou," she said, carefully gliding the brush over a nail. "I just love your lighthearted leaps, your angular foldings and unfoldings."

The door burst open. McMahon teetered over to the desk, gripping it for support. Higgins got up from the chair and with her fingers fanned limply out in front of her moved out into the squad room.

"Please, Lou," McMahon pleaded, trying to hold his swaying body upright. "I'll do anything. My family. Please."

Scanlon glared at him. How many tragedies involving cops had he seen? Too many to remember. Scanlon always thought of the wife and children. How they are made to suffer punishment too. He wondered how many times his drunken father had gotten jammed up and had been cut loose. "You're a police officer. You're supposed to protect lives, not endanger them."

"I can't stop once I start. I lose control. I . . ." He hung his head and cried.

"I'm going to let you slide," Scanlon said, "but I'm dropping the net over you. You're going into the Program."

"Oh, God, thank you, Lou, thank you."

"It means going away to the Farm to dry out and then attending the AA meetings. One slip, and it's your job. Understand?"

McMahon nodded.

Scanlon dialed the Counseling Unit of the Health Service Bureau and told the cop who answered that he had a live one for him.

A harried desk officer was fending off a barrage of reporters' questions. He grabbed the telephone, dialed the Whip's extension, and when Scanlon answered, turned his back to the reporters and said, "I've got a million fucking reporters down here breaking my balls about the Gallagher/Zimmerman connection. Better come down and speak to them."

When Scanlon appeared on the staircase, someone shouted, "There's Scanlon," and the herd turned and stampeded over to the staircase.

"What's the connection between Gallagher and the Zimmermans?"

"Why were the doctor and his wife murdered?"

"What leads have been developed?"

"Do you have any suspects?"

Scanlon moved down to the bottom step and held out the palms of his hands, signaling to the reporters to quiet down. "Gentlemen, our investigations have failed to reveal any connection between the homicides that occurred within this command and the ones in the Nineteenth. At this point in the investigation, we believe it was nothing more than a sad coincidence."

This only triggered a new burst of questions. The desk officer shook his head, signed out in the blotter on a personal, and stepped into the lieutenants' locker room to the right of the Desk.

Scanlon shook his head in frustration.

"Look, guys. I'd be more than happy to give you whatever I had. But the simple truth is, I have nothing for you that you don't already know."

A disbelieving murmur came from the crowd.

"Look. The Nineteenth caught the Dr. Zimmerman case. Maybe they have something to give you."

"That's the same bullshit that Fable fed us," a reporter shouted up at Scanlon.

"Are you and your superiors convinced that Lieutenant Gallagher was killed while preventing a holdup?" a woman reporter shouted.

"Absolutely."

Her raven-black hair was pulled back into a bun, and she wore oversize, tinted aviator glasses. "Would you not agree, Lieutenant, that there is always the remote possibility that you and your superiors are wrong, and that Gallagher was murdered, and that there is, in fact, a direct connection with the homicide in the Nineteenth?"

Scanlon looked directly down at her. "I'm sorry. Would you mind repeating the question?"

She scowled, took a few seconds to gather her thoughts, and then repeated the question in a different form.

"No, I don't see any connection," Scanlon answered, and immediately answered another question. "Ladies and gentlemen, I'm really not conversant with what happened in the Nineteenth. Captain Suckieluski of Press Information has been designated to act as press coordinator for both cases. He's the man you should be talking to, not me."

"And where do we find this Captain Suckieluski?"

"I believe he has an office at One Police Plaza. Room 1010, I think."

The reporters wheeled and headed for the station-house door. Daniel J. Buckman, an investigative reporter from the *Times*, aka the

Cocksucker with Lockjaw, was leaning against the Desk's brass railing, smiling broadly and clapping his hands slowly in mocking applause.

Scanlon walked over to him.

"Suckieluski shows originality. Most cops are only capable of a Mc-Cann or a Smith, but Suckieluski, I like it." He sucked air through his uneven teeth. "And I do believe that Room 1010 is the Pension Bureau."

"What's on your mind, Buckman?"

The reporter looked around at the cop on the switchboard and moved away from the railing, going over to the staircase.

Scanlon went with him.

"Your cover-up on Gallagher's death and the link with the double homicide in the Nineteenth is on my mind. I can't help but wonder what the connection is and what Gallagher was into that caused everyone to get gray hair."

"You're playing with yourself, you know that?"

"I can smell it." He put one foot on the bottom step and gripped the banister. "You know, my job is a lot like yours. I make a pest of myself asking questions, suborning, making promises that I know won't be kept. I keep at it until I find that one person who will talk to me. Tell the truth."

"If you want to waste your time, that's your business." He started to go back upstairs.

"Wait."

Scanlon stopped.

"The public does have a right to know the truth."

"What the public has is the right to expect its public officials who are charged with the enforcement of criminal law to do everything possible to protect the integrity of their investigations. And that is done, Mr. Buckman, by not revealing information that will end up as blaring headlines. So you see, what we have is a conflict of rights."

"They need not be mutually exclusive."

"That is true. But, sadly, they are."

"I've always admired you, Scanlon. Losing your leg, electing to remain a cop. I'm sure that it wasn't easy for you."

"See ya around," Scanlon said, lifting his fake leg up onto the first step.

"A deal?"

Scanlon froze. "I'm listening."

"I'll lay off. I'll even suggest to my colleagues that there is no cover-up, no connection."

"And the bottom line?"

"When it's all over you sit down with me and give it to me chapter and verse."

"You're a whore, you know that?"

"Even a whore has to make a living."

Deputy Chief MacAdoo McKenzie's white shirt had sweat stains around the collar. Pacing Scanlon's office, he growled, "I've just come from the PC. He's a little more than just concerned. The fucking press has been all over him regarding this Dr. Zimmerman case. Even the mayor is taking heat."

"Chief, it's just another homicide."

"That's bullshit. Anytime the rich and famous get blown away it ain't just another fucking homicide. All we need now is for Gallagher's love life to leak out." He wiped his palms with his handkerchief. "What about this Eddie Hamill thing? Anything to it?"

"Hamill's not involved," Scanlon said. "I talked with Walter Ticornelli at the funeral this morning and he assured me that the vendetta story is nonsense."

McKenzie threw up his hands. "And you believe him?"

"Yes, I do."

"Do you think you should at least go and have a talk with Hamill?"

"Probably. But I haven't had the time. As soon as I do I'll go and have a sit-down with Hamill."

Higgins came into the office, nodded to the Chief, and said to Scanlon, "Sigrid Thorsen, our witness with the baby in the park, called. She's agreed to be hypnotized. I've arranged an appointment for her on Wednesday. A policewoman from the Six-oh will be assigned to baby-sit."

"Anything else?" Scanlon asked.

"The spectrographic report from the lab on those peanut shells Christopher sent in was in the morning mail. The shells contained traces of mineral oil, water, propylene glycol, glyceryl stearate, lanolin oil, and other assorted goodies."

"Which all adds up to what?" Scanlon said.

"A hand cream or some kind of skin moisturizer," she said, perplexed. "A woman, you think?"

"Too many people say a man. Besides, men use hand creams. Especially older men with dry skin."

"I suppose so," Higgins said.

When Deputy Chief McKenzie left the Squad thirty minutes later, Scanlon got on the horn to Jack Fable at the Nineteenth Squad and told him about the deal he had made with Buckman. Fable told him that his detectives had come up with a witness, a man who had had a fight with his lover and could not sleep. They lived two houses down from the Zimmerman residence. The witness was looking out the window and saw a man enter and then leave the Kingsley Arms around the time of occurrence. The man was carrying an attaché case and had a mustache. The witness stated that the man appeared to be in his late thirties. The witness was working with the department artist. Fable would send Scanlon a copy of the Five.

The afternoon department mail arrived late.

Scanlon opened the multi-use envelope addressed to CO 93 Sqd. It contained a mimeographed letter from the Lieutenants' Benevolent Association authorizing precinct delegates to solicit donations for the Joseph P. Gallagher Memorial Fund. There were similar mimeographed letters from the Patrolmen's Benevolent Association, the Sergeants' Benevolent Association, and the Detectives' Endowment Association. They were all signed Fraternally Yours.

Scanlon took the letters out into the squad room and pinned them on the bulletin board. "Hector, did you put in a request for the exterminator?" Scanlon asked, seeing Colon looking into a roach motel.

"Sí, Teniente, I sent a Telephone Message to Building Maintenance. One'll be here on Monday." Peering into the motel, he added, "Look at all them son of a bitches squirm." He put the motel back on the floor and resumed typing.

Detective Christopher telephoned and told Scanlon that he and Biafra Baby had located the accountant husband of Donna Hunt. They had tailed the husband from his Pennsylvania Avenue office. Taking turns, the detectives had entered buildings with the accountant as he visited clients. The detectives had noted the names and addresses of several of the clients. Hunt was back in his office now, Christopher reported. Did the lieutenant want them to stay on the accountant?

Scanlon checked the time. 1905 hours. "Call it a day."

"Biafra Baby and I swing out tonight. We're not scheduled back till Wednesday. Do you want us to take our swing or be on deck in the ayem?"

"Come in, I'll owe you the time."

"You got it, Lieutenant," Christopher said.

At nine o'clock that Monday night Scanlon was at his desk with his prosthesis standing in the wastebasket. He felt tired and grubby. He had reread all the reports, looking for something, and found nothing. He had signed a stack of Fives and had made three different attempts to contact Linda Zimmerman, with negative results. He had touched base with Jack Fable twice more and on the last occasion had asked him if he knew the whereabouts of Linda Zimmerman. Fable told him that he didn't. He went on to inform Scanlon that she had adamantly refused his offer of police protection.

Scanlon rubbed his tired eyelids. He took the talc out of the drawer and rolled up his left trouser leg. He powdered his stump, dumped some into the socket, and took out a clean stump sock. He rolled it up over his stump, picked up the prosthesis, leaned back, and slid his stump into the socket.

Taking the bag of dirty socks out of the bottom drawer, he got up, went out into the squad room, and signed out in the Log: "Lieutenant Scanlon left, end of tour."

14

The sky was overcast. The humidity was rising.

The approach to the Williamsburg Bridge was clogged with Tuesday-morning traffic. Scanlon slowed his car to a stop. A swarm of derelicts ran out from the curb, threading their way among the cars, cleaning windows. He waved two of them off. He had spent a lousy night and was not in a charitable mood. Last night when he arrived home he found Sally De Nesto's message on his answering machine changing their date from Monday night to Tuesday night. At loose ends and not feeling much like being alone, he had gone to Roseland and had danced alone among the swirling shadows. Later in the night he had stopped for a drink at Du Soir, Columbus Avenue's latest in spot. He had stood among the crush, sipping his drink, trying to summon the courage to speak to one of the many attractive women in the bar. His problem would not go away. What does he say, when does he say it, and how does he say, I'm an amputee?

A woman in her late thirties pushed her way through the crowd and stood next to him, cuddling her glass in a napkin as her eyes slowly roamed over the crowd. She was tall, thin, and a trendy dresser. She had short two-tone hair, the bottom blond, the top brown. Her look fell on Scanlon. He smiled. She smiled back. Her name was Sid. They began to talk to each other and it was wonderful. He was relaxed, almost confident. Their conversation veered back and forth across many subjects. He searched for an opening to tell her that he was an amputee. Perhaps the terror was behind him, perhaps he had conquered the fear. At one point she reached into her bag to get her cigarettes when another woman bumped into her, causing Sid to stumble. Her keys tumbled from her pocketbook to the floor, and she made a grab for them. In so doing her hand collided with his prosthesis. "What's that you got there?" she asked, straightening, a questioning look spreading across her face.

His heart sank. Trying to force a confident edge into his voice, he said, "I'm an amputee."

"Oh?" She smiled at him. "I really don't think I could handle that." She excused herself, and was quickly swallowed up in the crowd. Scanlon gulped down his drink. He shoved his way out of Du Soir and drove directly to Gretta Polchinski's place.

When Scanlon arrived at the Nine-three on Tuesday morning he parked in the space reserved for the squad CO and went to the corner candy store to buy his daily ration of De Nobilis. Leaving the store, he paused to look at the skyline across the river, glad to be back on his own turf.

He went into the station house and followed his usual routine of going through the latest orders and reports. Two arrests had been made last night by the patrol force. The Gallagher/Zimmerman Unusual was the last one in the folder.

Nearing the top of the staircase he was cheered by the smell of freshly made coffee.

"Anything doing?" he asked, unlatching the gate.

Lew Brodie was sitting with his legs up on a desk, sipping coffee. "Eric Crawford went sick. I put him out in the Sick Log and notified the borough."

Scanlon pulled the handle on the spigot back, filling his mug. He walked over to the row of clipboards hooked onto the wall and took down the weekly roll call. Studying the official form, he said, "Nagel and Lucas are scheduled to do the evening duty with Crawford. They can cover two-handed." He returned the clipboard to its place. "Did Crawford say what was wrong with him?"

"The flu," Brodie answered.

Higgins looked up from the *Times* crossword. "I hope Fatso keeps his tiny weenie warm."

Detectives smiled, remembering Crawford's macho act with Higgins, and her dare to Crawford to break it out.

Grinning, Scanlon went into his office. He had just settled in behind his desk and had begun to look through his messages when someone out in the squad room barked, "Attention!"

The *Patrol Guide* mandates that attention be called whenever a member of the force above the rank of captain enters a room. This procedure is routinely complied with in the Patrol Force. But not in the Detective Division. There are two exceptions: the PC and the CofD.

Scanlon had almost made it to the door when Police Commissioner Robert Gomez propelled himself into the office and slammed a newspaper down on the Whip's desk. "We made the front page of every goddamn paper in this city. Chrissake, we're even nationwide."

"Coffee?"

"Black, no sugar," Gomez said, picking up the newspaper, looking at the front page.

Scanlon returned in a few minutes and closed the door. He put the PC's cup down in front of him.

"Did you see this?" Gomez said, stabbing a finger on a story in the paper. "See? A radio car killed a man crossing the street and the driver of the car fled the scene. In my day whenever you got your load on you went out and got laid. No more! The new breed wants to play at being Attila the Hun." He closed his eyes and rubbed his hands hard into his temples. He inhaled deeply through his mouth and let the air out slowly.

"They're coming at me from all sides, Scanlon. The Job seems to be falling to pieces. I need time so that these scandals can die from natural causes. Gallagher is the only hero that the Job has at the moment. And now with what has happened in the Nineteenth it appears that even Gallagher might end up going down the tubes." He gulped coffee. "I've been the PC for fifty-five months. Five more months and I'm entitled to a PC's pension. I need time, time to get the press off my ass, off our ass."

Scanlon told him about his deal with Buckman.

"There are a dozen other reporters to take his place. What I need is an arrest in the Gallagher caper. That way the press would believe that there was no connection with the Zimmerman homicides in Manhattan." He looked sternly at the Whip. "There is a connection, isn't there?"

"Yes, I believe that there is."

"Is Lieutenant Fable of the same opinion?"

"Yes, he is."

"Have you come up with anything in Gallagher's background that connects him to the Zimmermans?"

"No. Nor have I come up with any *official* improprieties on Gallagher's part that could hurt the Job."

"His personal life is enough to wreak havoc with the department." He thought a moment, staring into his mug. "Lou, I don't want to be boxed into making stupid moves by all this negative publicity." He slammed his fist on the desk. "But I want you to buy us some time so that we can get on with the investigation without the pressures of the press and television cameras."

"Jack Fable has come up with a witness who might have seen the perp enter and leave the Kingsley Arms."

"Eyewitnesses are about as useful as tits on a bull," Gomez said, swirling the contents of his cup. He put the mug down, got up, and moved to the grated window, where, looking into the dirty glass, he straightened his tie.

Always the fashion plate, Scanlon thought.

"If I didn't know better I'd think that that psychopathic midget I inherited as my CofD killed the doctor and his wife just to get my job." He turned. "Let's you and me go over the whole thing from the top."

For the next thirty minutes Scanlon walked the PC through the details of the Gallagher/Zimmerman homicide. Gomez listened without comment. When Scanlon finished, the PC's expression was grave. "Tell me about this Eddie Hamill again."

Scanlon did.

"You've found out where Hamill lives?"

"Yes."

"I think we should pick Mr. Hamill up, go through the motions of an arrest. It would relieve some pressure, give us breathing time. An arrest is the best way to make the press lose interest in a case."

Scanlon sighed. "Commissioner, Eddie Hamill is not the type of guy to come the easy way." He rubbed the side of his face. "Anyway, if we should pick him up, what do we charge him with, barratry?"

"Mopery, impersonating a human being, whatever you want. As long as you buy me some breathing room."

"Commissioner, you just got done telling me that you didn't want to be forced into making a dumb move. Going after Hamill, in my judgment, would be a dumb move."

"Maybe. But it's straw-grabbing time, Lieutenant." He pointed a finger at the Whip's prosthesis. "You owe the Job. It did the right thing for you, now it expects you to do the right thing for it. And besides, you could be wrong about Hamill. Haven't you ever made a wrong move on an investigation? Your friend Walter Ticornelli could be lying to you. There could be a hundred answers. Hamill just might be your hit man."

"I still think it's a bad move."

"Make the PC happy, Lieutenant. Bring Hamill in for questioning. Who knows, you might hit the jackpot."

Scanlon was about to utter another mild protest when the door burst open and a sweating MacAdoo McKenzie plunged into the room. "Commissioner," he said, nodding.

The PC looked at Scanlon and smiled. The Job's unofficial communication system had acted with its usual efficiency. As soon as the PC had climbed the staircase out of sight, the Nine-three desk officer had telephoned upstairs to warn the Squad. Hector Colon had dashed out into the hallway, seen the PC trudging the steps, and run back into the squad room and called attention. Meanwhile, the desk officer had gotten on the horn to Brooklyn North. The sergeant manning the operations desk received the notification, and he immediately got on the horn to Brooklyn North Uniform Command and Brooklyn North Detective Command. Within ten minutes every patrol precinct and detective command within the city of New York knew that Bobby Gomez was out of the big building and in the Nine-three Squad.

"Chief," Gomez said, his smile lighting up his handsome Latin face. The PC had Scanlon fill McKenzie in on the Hamill matter. When Scanlon had finished, Gomez asked McKenzie what he thought of Hamill as a suspect in the Gallagher/Zimmerman caper. "I'm inclined to go along with the lieutenant. I don't think that Hamill is involved."

Scanlon was surprised at McKenzie's support.

Gomez pulled his lips together. "You two might be right. Then again, you might be wrong. I let the chief of operations talk me into letting the cops wear those stupid-looking baseball caps. That was a bad mistake on my part. They look like goddamn truck drivers instead of police officers. Anyway, my gut reaction tells me to pick up Hamill."

Twelve minutes later MacAdoo McKenzie accompanied the PC down the staircase into the muster room of the station house. The PC's female chauffeur was standing at the side of the desk talking to the cop on the switchboard. When she heard the PC coming down the steps she ended the conversation and rushed over to open the door for the PC.

Gomez went behind the desk and signed himself out in the blotter. As he walked out from behind the Desk, his chauffeur called out, "Where to, Commissioner?"

"Let's take a drive over to the Two-four. I'm in the mood to visit a few houses. I don't get out in the field enough," he said in an equally loud voice.

As the PC was walking out of the station house, the desk officer's hand slid over the Desk toward the red department telephone.

The detectives cautiously climbed the tenement's staircase. Music blared from some apartments; canned TV laughter came from behind multilocked doors.

Scanlon had made the proper notifications: Communications had been notified that Nine-three Squad detectives were going into the Seventh to hit a flat; the Seventh's desk officer and the Seventh Squad had also been apprised. The Seventh's desk officer had assigned a marked RMP with two uniform cops to assist the Nine-three detectives —and avert the tragedy of uniform cops shooting at unfamiliar detectives.

The tenement had a weathered brick facade with white trim and black fire escapes winding down the front of the building. Many windows showed chartreuse, electric-blue, and bright orange shades and curtains. Where do they get them? Scanlon thought, studying the tenement's front.

Hamill's fifth-floor apartment was the first one off the staircase, to the right. When the detectives reached the second landing, Scanlon motioned to Brodie to turn off the radio so that Hamill wouldn't be tipped off by the police transmissions. The detectives stopped at the top of the fifth landing. Scanlon and Brodie dashed to the other side of Hamill's door, flattening themselves against the wall.

Higgins and Colon lay back on the staircase. A baby wailed. The detectives drew revolvers.

Scanlon had a nagging feeling in his gut that told him to get the hell out of there. Against his better judgment, he nodded to Higgins.

She stretched out her gun hand and rapped the barrel lightly against the door. The music inside the apartment suddenly ceased. Higgins rapped again. Muffled footfalls came up to the door.

"Yeah?" The voice was gruff, mean.

"Maggie Suckieluski," she said softly. "Oscar Mela sent me. He thought you might be in the mood for a little relaxation."

"Good ol' Oscar."

The detectives heard the loud clicking of tumblers and the rattle of safety chains. Colon nudged Higgins to get behind him. She stuck her tongue out at him. The door jerked open. Displaying her shield, Higgins stepped in front of the door. "Hi, Eddie," she said. Scanlon and Colon stepped into view, their shields held high. Hamill's eyes widened with anger. His left hand was concealed behind the door, gripping the steel bar of a Fox lock.

"We want to talk to you, Eddie," Higgins said, pushing her way into the apartment.

"What do you have in your hand, Eddie?" Scanlon said, noticing the floor plate that the bar wedged into.

"Nothing," Hamill said, pivoting and smashing the bar across Higgins's chest.

She doubled over and crumpled to the floor. Scanlon and Colon jumped over her body and went after him. Hamill made a springing leap toward a room on the left side of the apartment. As he did this, he thrust his hand under his polo shirt and came out with a .38 Colt.

"He's got a piece!" Scanlon warned.

Scanlon and Colon dove for cover behind the furniture. Lew Brodie wheeled and threw himself over Higgins's prostrate body. Hamill ran with a slight limp into the other room and slammed the door.

Lew Brodie dragged Higgins out of the apartment. Colon knelt behind a chair with his revolver trained on the door.

Scanlon rushed outside to see how Higgins was. She was clutching her chest, gagging for breath. Brodie unbuttoned her jacket and the top of her blouse. He and Scanlon propped her up against the wall. Inside the apartment Hector Colon called to Hamill to come out of the room with his hands over his head. Two shots rang out. The bullets smashed through the door and impacted into the wall behind Colon.

Hector Colon did not return the fire.

Scanlon ran back into the room and knelt beside Colon. "You all right?" Scanlon asked.

"Yeah," Colon said.

"Eddie, don't get stupid," Scanlon called out. "Toss out your gun and come out."

Another shot smashed through the door.

Scanlon dashed back out into the hallway and took the radio from Brodie and switched it on. Before he could say anything, the transmission he heard caused him to curse: "All units in the Seventh. We have a confirmed report of detectives engaged in a gun fight. A ten-thirteen at 132 Chrystie Street. Use caution. Units responding acknowledge, K." A spate of hurried acknowledgments flooded the airwaves.

Detectives prefer to operate by stealth, away from the harmful glare of the limelight. In and out quickly, quietly. Scanlon knew that at that very moment mobile press crews had picked up the police transmissions on their car radios and were speeding toward Chrystie Street. He pressed the transmit button. "Nine-three lieutenant to Central, K."

"Go, Lou. What's the condition? Do you require heavy weapons on the scene?"

"Negative, Central. Call it off. Everything is under control. There's no thirteen."

"Were shots fired at that location, K?"

"Negative, Central. Some kids must have set off firecrackers."

"Ten-four, Lou. All units responding to the thirteen on Chrystie Street resume patrol. Authority, Nine-three lieutenant on the scene. Mark that run ten-ninety Y, Unnecessary Call."

Scanlon looked up and down the hallway. The doors were closed, the apartments silent. He checked Higgins once more and rushed back inside, cursing the PC.

The furniture was cheap leatherette and veneer. A velvet painting of the Brooklyn Bridge hung on the wall. The bridge's towers and cables were illuminated with little yellow lights. Scanlon moved the radio to his mouth. "Biafra?"

Biafra Baby and Christopher had been assigned by Scanlon to stay with the two uniform cops from the Ninth and watch the front of the house, the side with the fire escapes.

Biafra Baby's voice came over the airway. "Yeah, Lou?"

"Three."

"Right."

Scanlon switched the wavelength to the third setting, the seldom-used detective channel licensed by the FCC for person-to-person communication.

"Anyone hurt?" Biafra Baby asked.

"Maggie had the wind knocked out of her," Scanlon said. "Who put over that thirteen?"

"The boys in blue," Biafra Baby radioed. "They did it before we could stop them."

"Can you make out the apartment?"

"Yeah. Do you want us to give it a shot?"

"Yeah. He's holed up in what I think is the bedroom. The fire escape cuts across both rooms," Scanlon said. "And for Chrissake, be careful."

In the hallway, Lew Brodie hovered over Higgins. Color had returned to her face and her gasping had stopped.

"You gonna be okay?"

She looked up into his massive face and smiled. "You threw your body over mine to protect me. Thanks, Lew."

He squirmed. "Hey, anything for a free feel. You know how horny us cops get."

"Yeah, I know. Get inside, you big lummox. I'll be all right."

Brodie kissed her on the top of her head. "You're an okay kid, Higgins. I'm goin' inside and get a chunk of that guy's ass for you."

A snarling, avenging bull rushed into the apartment. Before Scanlon could react, Brodie had hurled his massive hulk against the closed door and let out a blood-curdling yell.

The sound of splintering wood filled the dingy apartment. The door flew off its hinges.

Scanlon and Colon rushed into the bedroom behind Brodie. Eddie Hamill had been hastily unscrewing the window lock when the door caved in. He wheeled with his gun pointing at Brodie. Scanlon and

Colon spread out, stalking Hamill. Colon was low, in a combat stance, his revolver pointed at Hamill's chest. Scanlon's revolver was aimed at the belly.

Hamill's nervous eyes darted from detective to detective as they spread out.

"I'm getting out of here," Hamill said. "I'll blast anyone who tries to stop me."

Brodie stopped a few feet from Hamill. He aimed his weapon at Hamill's face and cocked the hammer. "You're gonna die, mother-fucker."

Hamill's gun hand trembled as the fear spread across his face.

Biafra Baby and Christopher appeared on the fire escape.

"I'm counting to five," Brodie announced, "and if that piece ain't on the floor, and your hands reaching for sky, I'm gonna send you to hell. One . . . two . . . three . . ."

Biafra Baby smashed the window with his revolver.

Instinctively, Eddie Hamill whirled to the sound of the breaking glass. Brodie and Colon leaped on Hamill. Colon's hand gripped the cylinder of Hamill's gun, preventing its discharge. Lew Brodie grabbed Hamill by the balls. Hamill screamed and his knees sagged. Keeping a relentless grip on the cylinder, Colon forced the gun upward, exerting pressure against Hamill's wrist.

Brodie twisted Hamill's testicles, crushing them together. Hamill squealed and his body bent in half. Retching, Hamill toppled to the floor. Colon, with his hand still around the gun, knelt beside the downed man and prized the weapon from the resisting hand. Brodie raised his foot to stomp Hamill's face.

Scanlon grabbed Brodie's shoulder. "Enough. We have the gun." Scanlon yanked Hamill up off the floor and slammed him against the wall, pulling his hands behind his back, handcuffing him.

Colon opened the cylinder of Hamill's gun. "He let three go at us."

"Check them out," Scanlon ordered Colon.

Biafra Baby and Christopher opened the window and climbed inside.

Eddie Hamill cringed up against the wall. "Ahhhh, my balls. My balls. Why'd ya have to grab my balls?"

Scanlon turned the prisoner around and rammed his elbow across Hamill's throat, pinioning him to the wall. "This ain't Sesame Street, pal. We get annoyed when people peg shots at us."

"I thought you were burglars," Hamill grunted.

"With police shields stuck into your ugly face?" Scanlon said. "Save your bullshit for Legal Aid."

"Whaddaya want with me?" Hamill said. "I didn't do nothing."

Eddie Hamill had a cloud in his right iris that spread outward into the pupil. Scanlon recalled the description of Hamill that Colon had given him in McJackoo's Bar and Grill. He remembered the clumsy way Hamill had run into the bedroom. "You're missing three toes off your left foot, right?" Scanlon asked.

"Yeah," Hamill snarled.

Hamill was a muscular man with bushy eyebrows and a crooked nose that looked as though it had been broken on several occasions. There were large gaps between his front teeth.

Colon came up behind Scanlon and whispered that the slugs had lodged in the wall without causing injuries.

"Good," Scanlon said.

"Take a look," Biafra Baby called out, holding up a plastic bag containing white powder and the silencer that he had found on top of the battered chest of drawers.

"You can't introduce any of that shit in court," Hamill shouted. "You got no fucking search warrant."

Biafra Baby came over to Hamill, dangling the evidence. "It's gonna be used, m'man. It's gonna be used because we were legally present inside your stinking dom-i-cile, and because the discovery was inadvertent, and because the incriminating nature of the objects were immediately apparent to us police-type professionals." Biafra Baby did a fast shuffle. "And that, m'man, bees known as the Plain View Doctrine, cha, cha, cha."

Scanlon looked at Christopher. "Get him out of here."

Christopher and Biafra Baby hustled the prisoner from the apartment. Hector Colon went outside in the hallway to see how Higgins was, and to help her downstairs.

Brodie was on his knees rummaging through the bottom of the closet. Scanlon glanced around the room, made sure that they were alone, and went over to him. "Lew?"

"Yeah?" Brodie said, looking up at the Whip's angry face.

"Don't ever pull a stunt like that again."

Brodie raised his palms in a gesture of surrender. "That hump pegged shots at us and dumped on Maggie."

"Your Charge of the Light Brigade could have gotten yourself and us dead. You had no way of knowing what kind of artillery was on the other side of that door."

"Aw. You're right. It won't happen again."

"And don't ever cock your hammer unless you damn well intend to shoot."

"Not to worry on that score, boss. I'm one of those cops who leave the first chamber empty. I've seen too many accidental discharges in my day."

"Did you find anything in the closet?"

"Nothing."

"Then let's get the hell out of here."

15

The Seventh Precinct is located on Pitt Street, a dilapidated block of boarded-up buildings and ruined foundations amid weed-filled lots in Manhattan's Lower East Side.

Scanlon had used the direct line to notify the PC of what had happened at the Chrystie Street address. How did the PC want him to proceed? Scanlon had asked.

"Make your notifications, Lieutenant."

Scanlon notified Manhattan South Detective Command and Brooklyn North Detective Command of the arrest of Eddie Hamill. Both commands in turn notified the chief of detectives. CofD Goldberg upon hearing of the arrest got on the horn to the press.

News briefs interrupted regular programs to announce that the NYPD was questioning a suspect in the Gallagher/Zimmerman homicides. The Seventh was soon besieged by reporters.

Scanlon would have preferred to question Hamill back at the Nine-three, but department regulations required that prisoners be processed at the precinct of arrest, in this case the Seventh. Hamill was closeted in the Seventh Squad's interview room, a cell-like place of cinder-block walls and two-way mirrors.

Scanlon felt the tug of frustration gnawing at his gut. He knew damn well that Hamill was a dead end and that valuable time was being squandered, the case's momentum lost. He walked into the interview room and sat across the table from Hamill. Shaking his head from side to side, he looked into the subject's face.

A faint smile came to Hamill's lips. "You ain't got shit and you know it."

Scanlon leaned forward. "Eddie, I'm going to be a nice guy and tell you exactly what we got. For openers, Assault Two on Detective Higgins. And the silencer that we found on your dresser, criminal possession of a weapon, a D Felony. The junk was felony-weight and carries with it a presumption of intent to sell, a C Felony. And then there is that matter of your gun and the shots you fired at us. Attempted Murder of Police Officers, a B Felony."

Hamill folded his arms across his chest and leaned back onto two legs. "Bullshit, and you fucking-A well know it."

"Eddie, I've been lying guys like you behind the wall for years."

Hamill nervously stretched his neck.

"It's time to play 'Let's Make a Deal,' " Scanlon said.

"Fuck off."

"A wise man would at least listen."

Hamill's gaze wandered, stopping at the two-way mirror set into the gray cinder block. "I'm listening."

"I want to know what went down between you and Walter Ticornelli. I also want to know your whereabouts when Lieutenant Gallagher and Yetta Zimmerman were taken out."

Hamill's expression brightened. "That's what this is all about?"

"That's what it's about, Eddie."

"And suppose I tell you, then what?"

"Then I'll be a nice guy and see to it that when the complaint is drawn up no mention is made of Clear View. The evidence will have been discovered in a closet in your apartment. You'll be held for the grand jury and they'll indict. But at the first Huntley hearing to suppress the evidence your Legal Aid lawyer will be able to get the evidence suppressed and the case will go bye-bye."

"And the gun and the shots I took at you?"

"What shots?"

Hamill grinned. "I'm on parole. I owe eight on a seven and a half to fifteen for burglary. I'd have to go back inside."

"I'll square things with your parole officer. You won't have to go back inside, I promise," Scanlon lied.

"In that case . . ." Hamill flipped his palms. "I was into Walter and couldn't make the payments. We had a sort of falling out."

"All of it, Eddie."

As Hamill told it, when he missed two vig payments, Ticornelli dispatched three of his Mulberry Street gorillas to have a talk with him. The Greenpoint burglar took a bad beating and was forced to redouble his efforts to steal enough money to get Ticornelli off his back. It took him three weeks to raise the money.

"I had the hospital records checked, Eddie. You were confined to St. John's with gunshot wounds. Was that Ticornelli's handiwork?"

"He had nothing to do with that," Hamill said, annoyed. "That's them Greenpoint biddies and their rumors. It just so happened that about the same time I was having a problem with Ticornelli I was also seeing this Cuban chick. Her old man found out about us and sent some of his relatives around to see me. I almost didn't get away that time. I'll tell ya, them damn Cubans still live in the stone age. I hadda go out and rob more money to lay on the head spic in order to square myself with them. Tell ya, that was one expensive pussy."

"Someone tried to take Ticornelli out about the same time. Was that you?"

Hamill placed his elbows on the table and held out his hands, palms out. "Look at my sheet, man. I'm a burglar and a lover. Not a strong-arm guy. I never tried to hit Ticornelli or anyone else." He held up a finger. "If you'd bothered to check back you'd have seen that the paisanos were having one of their pizza wars at the time Ticornelli got shot at. It was his own people who tried to take him out."

"Where were you when Lieutenant Gallagher and the old lady were hit?"

Hamill suppressed a smile. "I got the best alibi in the world. I was with Mr. Greenspan, my parole officer. Check it out."

"Your stomping grounds are Greenpoint, Eddie. Why are you living in Manhattan under an alias?"

"Guys in my line of work don't advertise, Lieutenant."

Scanlon scraped his chair back and got up.

"We got a deal, ain't we?"

"Yeah, Eddie, we got a deal."

The Seventh's squad room was a very busy place. Detectives manned telephones, answering the queries of overhead commands who wanted the who, what, when, where, why, and how of the Eddie Hamill arrest. The Seventh's Second Whip was out in the muster room keeping the reporters at bay. Nine-three Squad detectives were at typewriters banging out the considerable paperwork connected with Hamill's arrest.

Scanlon was anxious to leave the Seventh and get on with the investigation. He knew that they'd all be stuck in the Seventh until all the paper was done and all the notifications made. Tradition dictated that detectives who made out-of-command arrests process their own prisoners.

Scanlon went into the Whip's office and telephoned the PC. He told him of his interview with Eddie Hamill and restated his belief that

Hamill was nothing but a waste of time and effort. The PC agreed, but still wanted Scanlon to buy him some time.

Scanlon walked out into the squad room. He went up to Higgins, who was sitting at a desk scratching out the property voucher. "How do you feel?"

"All right, Lou."

"I want you to do an LOD request."

She let the pencil fall from her hand and looked up at him. "I really don't want to go through the hassle of a line-of-duty-injury request, Lou. I'd have to have the guys prepare witness statements, go to the hospital and get a doctor's diagnosis, wait around to be interviewed by the duty captain, call the sick desk and get a serial number. All that paperwork, and I feel fine."

Leaning forward, Scanlon placed a hand on the back of her chair and another flat on the typewriter. "Maggie, if you start to hemorrhage tonight at home, it'll be too late to put in for LOD, so do me a favor, and do it now."

"But Lou . . ."

"Now, Maggie," he whispered into her ear.

Covering the mouthpiece of the phone with his hand, Colon hollered, "Lou, you got a call. Some broad."

"What's her name?" Lew Brodie hollered back.

"Not you, the lieutenant," Colon said.

Linda Zimmerman's voice was strained and very low. "A news bulletin just announced that you have taken a suspect into custody in the Seventh Precinct. Is that true?"

"I can't discuss that over the telephone. Where are you?"

A maid led Scanlon into the sitting room of the Sutton Place apartment. The furniture was wicker and the room overlooked the river and the East Side Highway.

Linda Zimmerman was slumped in a sofa with her left arm hanging limply over the woven arm. Her hair was carelessly pinned up and her face was without makeup, save for some caked-on mascara on her long eyelashes. She was dressed in jeans, an oversize cotton shirt, and Docksiders. Her grim stare followed Scanlon as he crossed the sun-drenched room.

"Are you okay?" he asked, lowering himself down next to her.

"The man that you have in custody, is he the one who slaughtered my family?"

"No, Linda, he isn't. We're holding him on another matter. The press somehow got hold of it and got their wires crossed."

She clutched her arms and shivered. Her body began to shake.

Scanlon was saddened by the sight. "Please believe that we are doing everything possible to catch them."

"Sure you are," she said with a heavy dose of sarcasm.

"I've been trying to contact you. Whose apartment is this?"

"My Aunt Rae's. She's my father's sister, and you can't interview her because she is not here. She's out making the arrangements for the cremation of my brother and his wife."

Scanlon caught a faint whiff of her evergreen-and-orange fragrance. He recalled their first meeting in the drawing room of her brother's home. Then she had been wearing a wide-brimmed hat and black crocheted gloves, and sat on a fragile Queen Anne chair with her long legs crossed at the knees. It seemed as though it was an eon ago, in some far-off place. "How is your niece?"

"Oh, Andrea is just wonderful. Would you like to see her?" She got up, held out a hand to him. "Come, I'll bring you to her."

The exuberance of her tone put him on his guard. She led him through the luxury duplex to a curving white staircase. There was a large window in the wall that overlooked the East River. She hurried up the stairs ahead of him and opened a door at the head of the staircase. Pointing into the room, she said, "Here is my niece, Lieutenant. Andrea, dear, this nice policeman would like to ask you a few questions. When . . ." She wheeled and placed her forehead against the doorjamb and cried.

Scanlon came up behind her and looked into the room.

Andrea Zimmerman, the birthday girl with the shy smile and inquisitive eyes, lay in a big bed expressionless, her blank eyes fixed on some black hole in time. Scanlon clenched his fists, digging his nails into the skin of his palms. His eyes began to fill and his chin quivered. He leaned quietly into the room and pulled the door closed. He put his arm around the crying woman and led her downstairs.

Throwing herself onto the sofa, she said, "I didn't think that I had any tears left."

"What do the doctors say?" he asked softly, sitting down next to her.

"Their glowing prognosis is that time will tell. The truth is, they just don't know. They hedge and say that she'll probably come out of it. She has periods when she focuses her eyes and seems to recognize me."

"Have you made any plans?"

"I've taken a leave of absence from the bank. Andrea and I are going to live here for a while. If Andrea should come around I want her to have a sense of family."

"Will you allow me to look through your mother's and your brother's personal papers?"

"Lieutenant Fable asked me the same question. I'll tell you what I told him. No. I have had enough policemen in my life these last few days to last me a lifetime. I don't want policemen poking around my family's history. And I especially do not want police protection."

Stone walls everywhere. "Now that you have had time to think, can you recall any connection that Gallagher might have had to your family?"

"No, I can't. Your lieutenant was getting Andrea's birthday cake as a favor to Mother."

"Nothing else?"

"Gallagher was not one of Mother's priorities." She glowered at him. "What will happen to them if you catch them? Will they die in the electric chair?"

"No, Linda, they won't. This state does not have the death penalty. If they are convicted, and if they don't plea-bargain, the most that they could get is twenty-five to life on each homicide." He grimaced. "And the sentences more than likely would be made to run concurrent instead of consecutive, which means twelve, fifteen years inside and then parole."

"Parole!" she shouted at him. "And you call that justice?"

"I don't call it anything, Linda. I don't make the law, I enforce it."

On the seat of an armchair in front of the sofa where she sat was a massive glass ashtray overflowing with cigarettes from which, in most cases, only a few puffs had been taken before they'd been stubbed out. There was a box of cigarettes and a Zippo lighter on the chair next to the ashtray. She picked up the lighter and toyed with the cover, clicking it open and closed. She lit a cigarette.

"I wish you would consider allowing us to look through those papers."

She took successive drags on the cigarette and crushed it out in the ashtray. "No."

"Don't you want to help us find the killer?"

She glared at him. "I've already helped your investigation. I've supplied the bodies. People I loved." Crying, she added, "It just isn't fair. Parole after a few years. No. No. That isn't fair." She toppled over and lay on the sofa, crying.

"Let it out, Linda. Let it come," he said, soothing the side of her head with his hand.

Her sobs subsided after several minutes. He continued to soothe her, murmuring calming words.

She abruptly pushed his hand away and sat on the sofa. "I guess you're my only hope of getting justice."

Scanlon made a plea for her total cooperation and said, "You can't hold anything back, because you don't know what is important and I do."

Again she picked up her lighter and clicked the Zippo's top open and closed, then she lit another cigarette, took several nervous drags, and crushed it out in the ashtray.

"I've given Mother's clothes and furniture to the Salvation Army. Her papers are in the dining room. If you want to, go ahead and look."

"When did you gather up your mother's belongings?"

"The day after she was murdered. There were personal things that I wanted to get out of there before the neighborhood burglars had a picnic at my family's expense."

"The day after she died?" he said. "You were composed enough to go to her apartment and clean it out?"

"I told you, there were personal things that I wanted."

"What sort of things?"

"Lieutenant, I'm not one of your suspects. So don't press me to tell you very personal things that I don't want to tell you."

"I'm sorry. Sometimes I can be a little overzealous."

She got up and led him into a formal room with a long mahogany table and a brass chandelier. Three cartons were on the table. She stood by his side, watching, as he sifted through the first of the cartons. He moved slowly, carefully, removing the contents an item at a time, examining them, searching for a reason for murder.

Scrutinized, each item was laid down on the table beside the carton it came out of. He found old letters bound together with rubber bands. There was an old pocket-size address book with odd telephone exchanges: Buckminster, Esplanade, Ingersoll. There was a music box that did not chime, some old photographs, an antique ring, and some long-paid bills.

He put the items back into the carton and went on to the next one.

In the last carton he found a novel: *Rebecca and the Jewess* by Mrs. Madeline Leslie. The copyright date was 1879. He turned the brittle pages.

"A friend of Mother's gave that to me when I was nine years old. I'd forgotten all about it."

He nodded thoughtfully and put the book down.

She reached into the carton and pulled out a slender leather-bound book. "My God. My yearbook from junior high. Mother must have saved it," she said, looking through the book.

Scanlon reached into the last carton and scoured through the debris of a life. To his disappointment, he found nothing significant.

"My brother used his basement as his office. His secretary is there now. I'll telephone her to tell her to expect you."

She walked with him out into the entrance foyer, where he rang for the elevator and turned to face her. "Why did you change your mind about permitting me to look through her papers?"

She looked away from him. "Because you're all I've got. And, God knows why—I trust you."

1853 hours. Scanlon arrived back at the Nine-three Squad. He had wasted five hours sifting through Stanley Zimmerman's personal and medical records. It had been a hot, muggy day and the city's grime clung to his skin.

Scanlon unlatched the squad-room gate and went into his office. He threw himself into his chair, pulled up his trouser leg, removed the prosthesis, and stood it in the wastebasket. He yanked off the smelly stump sock and threw it into the bottom drawer of his desk. He took out the talc, sprinkled it over the stump, and sighed, relishing the soothing effect of the white powder and his massaging hands.

One by one the detectives filtered in and hovered around, watching the Whip tend to his stump. Lew Brodie was the first to speak. He told the Whip that Eddie Hamill had been processed and was lodged in Central Booking for the night. The prisoner was scheduled for arraignment in the morning in Part 1A of Manhattan Criminal Court. The PC had telephoned to say that he wanted Scanlon to attend the arraignment.

Christopher stopped eating his yogurt to tell Scanlon that after he and Biafra Baby had finished in the Seventh they drove to Brooklyn and continued their surveillance of Harold Hunt, the accountant. They tailed Hunt from his office to the Santorini Diner. The accountant had a hamburger and a cup of tea and left. Valerie Clarkson waited on him. The detectives followed him from the diner to a factory on Dumont Avenue. They discovered that it was one of those urban slave plantations that employ Haitian and Hispanic illegals for below the minimum wage.

Christopher paused, watching the Whip kneading his stump, checking the edema. "Are you ready for this one, Lieutenant?" Christopher asked.

"I'm ready," Scanlon said, pulling on a clean stump sock.

"The name of the company was the Luv-Joy Manufacturing Company. Harold Hunt, Donna Hunt's husband, is the accountant for the company that made all those things that you found in Gallagher's splash pad."

Scanlon looked up at Christopher. "Harold Hunt?"

"You got it," Biafra Baby said. "I took off my coat and tie and moseyed into the factory and applied for a job. As I was filling out the application I looked into the adjoining room and saw Harold poring over ledgers."

"Do you think he made you?" Scanlon asked.

"Naw. He has no idea that we've been on him," Biafra Baby said.

"What about Valerie Clarkson—did she see you in the restaurant?" Scanlon asked.

"We didn't go inside," Christopher said. "Biafra Baby waited in the car and I sat in the diner's vestibule watching Harold eat."

"Did Harold and Valerie Clarkson seem to know each other? Were they friendly?"

"Not really," Christopher said. "They seemed to have a casual acquaintance, nothing more than that."

"Find out who owns that company," Scanlon said to Christopher and Biafra Baby.

Higgins said, "Lieutenant Fable telephoned a couple of times. Nothing important, just touching base with you. He said to tell you that he sent you some stuff in the department mail."

Scanlon rummaged through the pile of reports cluttering his desk. He found two multi-use envelopes from the Nineteenth. There was also an envelope from the department artist addressed to CO 93 Sqd. *Personal.*

He pulled the three envelopes from the pile.

"*Teniente*, did you get a chance to read the latest department bulletin?"

"Not yet," Scanlon said, leaning back and affixing his prosthesis.

"Listen to this shit," Colon said, reading. " 'The Gay Officers Action League will hold its annual Stonewall memorial service and breakfast on June 29, 1986, at 0830 hours. Upon completion of the breakfast, members of GOAL will assemble at GOAL Hall in preparation for the Christopher Street Liberation Day March and Rally of 1986. Uniformed and civilian members of the service who are members of GOAL and wish to participate in these functions . . .' " He looked up from the bulletin, troubled. "You know the rest, they throw in a Twenty-eight and take the tour off. You know, *Teniente*, when I came in the Job the precinct whore was always a female and a civilian. And now?" He wafted the green bulletin down onto the desk. "This job has really gone down the tubes."

Higgins glared at Colon, the rebuke on her lips. Instead, she shook her head with disgust and walked from the office without saying anything.

Scanlon checked the time: 1910 hours. "Go home," he told the detectives. "I'll see you on deck in the ayem."

"Sure you ain't going to need us?" Colon asked.

"I'm sure," Scanlon said, scanning a Five, signing it.

"Anyone wanna stop for a taste?" Lew Brodie asked.

"Sounds good to me," Biafra Baby said. "I'm in no rush to get home. My wife took the kids to the Monet exhibit."

Hector Colon stopped at the water cooler for a drink. He gulped the water. From the corner of his eye he saw a cockroach flow into his mouth. He dropped the cup and gagged. He clutched his throat, retching.

Higgins rushed over to him. "Hector, what's the matter?"

His handsome Latin face was pale gray. "I swallowed a cockaroach," he gasped.

"Is that all?" Higgins said, walking away. "There is absolutely nothing to worry about, Hector. Roaches are extremely clean creatures."

Clutching his throat in horror, Colon gasped. "You sure?"

"Of course I'm sure." She turned and hurled a concerned look at him.

"What? Tell me!" Colon said.

"Well, it's nothing. But I just realized that the roach that you ingested might be a female cockroach, a pregnant female cockroach." She let her words hang.

Shrinking away from her, Colon asked feebly, "So?"

Higgins grimaced. "Well, cockroaches lay seven, eight hundred eggs at a time. And your stomach is a dark, wet, warm place. It would be a perfect nesting place for baby roaches. It is conceivable that you could end up with thousands of cockroaches nesting in your stomach lining, a whole darn colony of them. I mean, you could actually have dozens of them crawling in and out of your penis."

"Aaaaaaaahhhhhhhhh!" Colon ran screaming from the squad room.

"I guess he's rushing to the Stonewall Parade," Higgins said, taking a lipstick from her pocketbook. Scanlon sat at his desk, listening, suppressing a grin. Higgins strolled deadpan into the office. "I guess Hector doesn't like roaches."

"Guess not," Scanlon said, unable to keep from smiling. "You heading home?"

"I want to work on my term paper," she answered. "I'll hang around here and do it. Somehow I work better in the squad room."

The first envelope Scanlon opened contained the composite sketch of a man with a walrus mustache and an accompanying Five of the interview of the witness who had seen the mustached man enter and leave the Kingsley Arms apartment building.

He read the Five. He leaned the composite up against the gray department desk lamp, scrutinizing the face. There was something about that face that was familiar. He tried to imagine the face without the mustache. But who was it? Scanlon opened the Gallagher/Zimmerman case folder. He searched through the folder for the composite of the perp the two female witnesses had seen. An old man running from a candy store. He found it near the bottom of the pile. He leaned it against the lamp with the other composite. The pigeon feeder's face was old, while the composite of the mustached man depicted a young man, a man in his late thirties or early forties.

The envelope from the department artist contained the composite of the driver of the getaway van that he had talked Walter Ticornelli into working on with the artist. The sketch showed the side view of a young face with sunglasses and a hat pulled down over the brow. Scanlon recalled that the shylock had only caught the driver's profile.

With the three composites arrayed in front of him, he compared one to the other. He reached out and picked up the sketch of the pigeon feeder. The more he studied the remaining two, the more convinced he was that the man with the walrus mustache and the man in the sunglasses were the same man. He leaned back and rubbed his tired eyes. The phone rang. He snapped it up.

"Lieutenant Scanlon."

"Lou, this is Sergeant Vitali. You know me from the Columbians."

"How are you, Vic?" Vic Vitali had run for recording secretary of the Italian-American police organization two years ago and lost by twelve votes.

"Lou, I just responded to a call from the emergency room of St. John's. They're holding one of your detectives under restraints. He's ranting about colonies of cockroaches nesting in his stomach and crawling in and out of his cock. We had to take his gun for safekeeping."

A broad grin spread across Scanlon's face. I wonder where he got that idea? he thought, looking out into the squad room at Higgins talking on the telephone.

"What do you want me to do about this guy?" Vitali asked.

"It's fate getting back at him for being a wise-ass with one of his partners. He had a practical joke played on him. Where is he now?"

"Strapped onto a trolley outside the examining room."

"Keep him there for a while. I'm sending one of my detectives over to get him. Her name is Higgins."

"I'll take care of it, Lou. See ya at the next meeting."

Scanlon went out into the squad room and told Higgins what had happened to Colon and asked her if she would go to the hospital and get him released.

"It would be a pleasure, Lieutenant," she said, taking her pocketbook and getting up.

Scanlon went back into his office and opened the remaining multiuse envelope. It contained the copies of the forensics reports on the Stanley and Rachel Zimmerman homicides. Included with the reports were photographs of the striations on the roof door of the Kingsley Arms. Each individual characteristic was noted and numbered. There were also photographs of rusty screws that showed fresh screwdriver marks on the heads, and photographic enlargements of screws with small pieces of wood wedged between their threads. The perp lost his patience and tore off the hasp with a crowbar, he thought, examining the photographs. The last batch of photographs in the envelope were of the plaster casts made of the footprints found on the roof of the Kingsley Arms.

Etched sharply into the tarred roof were the deep impressions of a heel. Black lines and numbers noted each characteristic: nail marks, chips in the rubber, wear striations, an imbedded pebble. It was a narrow heel. Scanlon looked down at his own heel. His was much wider. The photographs of the toe showed a triangular impression with a narrow convex tip.

Scanlon read the accompanying Five. The perp's walking picture put him at five-eleven and approximately 185 pounds. The Five detailed each characteristic that made up the walking picture. He had read down to the last paragraph of the report when a phrase leaped up at him: "The sum of these configurations leads the undersigned to conclude that the perpetrator in this case wore cowboy boots."

Scanlon's eyes darted to the array of composite sketches, back to the phrase on the bottom of the Five, back to the composites. He heaved himself up out of the chair and rushed from the squad room.

A string of firecrackers exploded as Scanlon drove into the Onefourteen's walled-in parking area. It was 2110. He rushed up the echoing iron staircase and entered the offices of the Seventeenth Narcotics District. Undercovers and their backups were going over the strategy for the night's buys. Everything seemed to be back to normal at the Seventeenth District. Scanlon moved to a bearded round-faced man who was logging a telephone message. "Is Inspector Schmidt around?"

The bearded man lined off the message and looked up. "He's gone for the day. I'm Sergeant Quigley. Can I help you?"

Scanlon identified himself to the sergeant. "There are a few matters concerning Joe Gallagher that need tidying up. I'd like to take a look at your personnel files."

Quigley looked down at the message he had just logged. "Gallagher's replacement has just been assigned. Frank Devine from the Eleventh District. Know him?"

"I know Frank from around the Job. What about those records?"

Quigley showed Scanlon into the Whip's office. "Yell if you need anything," the sergeant said, backing out the door.

The files were alphabetical, by rank. Scanlon fingered the tabs to the sergeants' section of the file. His fingertips danced over the folders until he came to Harris, George.

Sitting with the folder on his lap, Scanlon stared at the pin maps on the wall, silently admonishing himself. Harris wasn't the only man in this town who wore cowboy boots. So what if there was a resemblance between Harris and two of the composites? That didn't mean that Harris was the perp. Still, Harris was the only person connected with the case who did wear that damn kind of footwear. But Harris involved in Gallagher's death? That couldn't be. He opened the folder.

Harris had submitted two Chief Clerk 30s, Change of Residence or Social Condition. One had notified the department of a change of residence: Long Island to Staten Island. The other form informed the Job of a change in social status: married to separated.

Both forms were dated February 5, 1984.

Scanlon read through years of evaluation reports that attested to Harris's above-average performance. He read letters of commendation from satisfied citizens, and he read requests for departmental recognition that certified to Harris's exemplary performance of duty, his bravery. He came across an old Ten Card, and noted that Harris was forty-two years old.

The off-duty employment requests were pinned together, in chronological order. Permission had been given for Harris to engage in off-duty employment at the Stevens Manufacturing Company. In the space on the form captioned "Describe specific duties and responsibilities," Harris had written, "Administrative." The first request was dated March 10, 1980. It was pinned to four annual renewal applications, each one dated ten days prior to the expiration of the current approved request, as required by Section 120-14 of the *Patrol Guide*.

Scanlon pinned the off-duty employment applications back together and flicked past them through the remainder of the file. Finding nothing else of interest, he began to shape the uneven edges back into a neat pile. Something nudged his memory. He shuffled back through the stack of forms to the off-duty requests. The Stevens Manufacturing

Company and the Luv-Joy Manufacturing Company were both on Dumont Avenue, Brooklyn.

All the shadows had triangular shapes.

Scanlon lay in Sally De Nesto's bed staring up at them, vaguely
aware of her efforts to make him erect, his thoughts filled with Harris
and those damn cowboy boots. He raced mentally over the recent
police scandals, and wondered if they presaged a new breed of cop, a
breed unable to distinguish between the good guys and the bad guys, a
breed that considered themselves a law unto themselves, a breed willing to go to any length to see that their concept of justice prevailed.
What if his growing suspicion was correct? What if Harris was the
perp? What would that scandal do to the Job? But it couldn't be. Why
would Harris be involved in Gallagher's death? For what motive? And
what about the doctor and his wife? There was no connection between
Gallagher and Harris. It was all wrong.

"I'm tired," Sally De Nesto said, resting her face on his groin.

He pressed her head to his body. "I've got things on my mind."

She crawled up the bed and lay next to him, staring up at the
ceiling. "You're not upset, are you?"

"There's a lot on my mind. I'm just not in the mood."

"Would you be upset if I were Jane Stomer?"

He found himself openly measuring her. "Of course I'd be upset,"
he said tersely.

"Then I think that you should ask yourself why."

"Because I can relax with you and not have to worry about satisfying
you."

"That should tell you something about your problem."

"It tells me that I can't relax with a straight woman, especially if I
care for her."

She turned on her side, facing him. "But why?"

"Because I'm afraid of failure," he blurted.

A satisfied smile spread across her face.

He pulled her to him. "What am I, your psychological profile of the
month?"

She shook her head. "I've discussed your problem with my shrink
friend."

"What shrink?"

"My blind psychiatrist trick. I've mentioned him to you."

"Yeah, I remember."

"He said that your problem was more than likely the result of a
premorbid disposition caused by some childhood relationship. A fear
of being unable to satisfy someone you loved."

In a brief flash of recall he saw his drunken Irish father standing in the shadows, laughing at him. "If you keep up with the psychoanalysis I just might not need you anymore."

"I know," she said, flopping off her side onto her back and turning her face from him.

"I'm really drained. May I stay the night?"

"You can, but it will cost you extra."

"What the hell is it with you? One minute you're soft and caring, and the next you're all business."

"I *am* in business, Tony. And I can't let myself forget that I am." She reached out and turned off the soft light on her night table.

Staring into the darkness, Scanlon thought about his parents and Jane Stomer, unaware of Sally De Nesto's silent tears.

16

The pews in the Manhattan Criminal Court complaint room were filled with dozing policemen waiting to be interviewed by an ADA. Coffee containers and blackened cigarette butts littered the floor. Scattered sheets of newspaper added to the mess. Morning rays fought a losing battle to penetrate the filthy windows.

Five court clerks were assigned to the complaint room to assist arresting officers in drawing up the complaints against prisoners, listing the specific crimes charged, detailing the elements of each crime, spelling out a *prima facie* case against each prisoner. The law required that a legally sufficient case be established at the prisoner's arraignment; bail would then be set.

It was 1015 hours and one of the clerks still had not arrived for work. The four who had showed up were sitting behind a long counter that was covered with legal forms and about a dozen manual typewriters. One of the clerks was discussing his margin account over the telephone, one was reading yesterday's *New York Post* and sucking jelly from a sugared doughnut, and the two remaining clerks were typing affidavits by the court's renowned hunt-and-peck method.

A line of waiting policemen stretched out into the hallway.

Scanlon and Brodie entered the courthouse and went directly into the police sign-in room. After they signed in, they went to the complaint room. When the Whip saw the line he told Brodie to draw up the complaint against Hamill. He was going down to the lobby and make some telephone calls, and he would meet Brodie in the courtroom. Scanlon was anxious to put the Hamill caper behind them.

Scanlon crossed the cavernous lobby, taking in the ornate construction, rich in marble. It had been some time since he had been in Manhattan Criminal Court. Jane had been an important part of his life then; now she was nothing but an aching memory. He saw many familiar faces, lawyers holding morning court, doing what they do best, fleecing the unwary, the uninitiated. He spotted Sammy Gold, the court's resident bookmaker, taking down the day's action. His footsteps echoed off the marble floor. Nothing much ever changes around here, he thought, stopping at the building's newsstand to take in the morning headlines.

The NYPD had finally made it off the front page. The PC had been right—there was nothing like an arrest to end public interest in a case. He wondered if Buckman, the Cocksucker with Lockjaw, had anything to do with the sudden loss of interest.

He went over to the telephone bank and slid into a booth. He telephoned the Squad, and when Detective Suckieluski answered, he told Biafra Baby that he wanted him and Christopher to find out if the Luv-Joy Manufacturing Company on Dumont Avenue had once been named the Stevens Manufacturing Company. And if the owners of both companies were the same people.

When Scanlon left the phone booth he spotted Higgins and Colon in the lobby. He called to them. Approaching the two, he noticed a shamefaced Hector Colon looking up at the rococo molding.

"How you feeling today, Hector?" Scanlon asked.

"I don't know what to say, Lou. I mean, thanks for what you did for me. I mean, I guess them fucking cockaroaches just got to me. Where's Brodie?" he asked, obviously anxious to change the subject and get away from Higgins.

"He's in the complaint room," Scanlon said. "Why don't you go and help him draw up the complaint."

"Right, Lou," Colon said, and hurried off.

"What happened last night at the hospital?" Scanlon asked Higgins.

She gave vent to a partly suppressed laugh. "Macho man was tied to a hospital gurney. He'd calmed down, but he'd had the starch taken out of his sails."

Scanlon and Higgins pushed through the padded doors into the courtroom. He gazed at the burnished wood paneling. They never scrimp, he thought, sliding into a rear bench. Higgins slid in next to him.

Policemen lounged around the courtroom, waiting for court to be called into session. A lone court clerk sat in front of the bench arranging the day's arraignment calendar. Lawyers ambled into the courtroom. Some went up to the court clerk; a whispered conversation would ensue, after which a fast handshake would take place, after which the court clerk would move an affidavit from the bottom of the pile to the top of the pile.

The criminal justice system in action, Scanlon thought, slapping another fold into his newspaper. Time passed. Scanlon worked the crossword. Higgins read a Harlequin Romance. A man in a seersucker suit and conservative tie carrying a stack of folders under his arm entered the courtroom and called out Scanlon's name.

"Over here, Counselor," Scanlon said.

"I'm ADA Rabinowitz," he said, sliding into the pew next to Higgins. "I've been assigned the Hamill arraignment." He opened one of the folders on his lap and read off the details of the arrest. "Is there anything else I should be aware of?"

Scanlon looked at Higgins. They both concentrated on the ADA's question, and shrugged. "You got it all, Counselor," Scanlon said.

"As I read this case, Hamill is not a suspect in the Gallagher/Zimmerman homicides," said ADA Rabinowitz.

"Not at this time," Scanlon said. "The investigation is continuing."

"What the hell does that mean, Lieutenant?" the ADA said.

"That means, Counselor," Scanlon said, "that the investigation is continuing."

"You brought me a red herring, didn't you?" Rabinowitz said.

"We're just doing our job, sir," Higgins said.

"I'll go see if I can rush this thing along," the ADA said. "I want to get rid of this case as fast as I can."

At 1120 hours, Scanlon, the ADA, Eddie Hamill, and a Legal Aid lawyer all stood before the bench listening to the court clerk read the complaint.

The prisoner's head was bowed.

The clerk intoned, ". . . all the physical evidence in the case be admitted into evidence under the Clear View Doctrine."

Hamill's head shot up. He looked at Scanlon with a stunned expression.

Scanlon shrugged innocently and whispered, "So I lied a little."

The judge set bail at two hundred thousand dollars. The sullen prisoner was led away by two court officers.

The detectives walked out of the courtroom. Colon and Higgins were waiting. Scanlon noticed Colon sneaking glances at him. Higgins was smiling.

"Hello, Scanlon."

He heard her voice and froze, excitement ripping at his chest. "I'll catch up with you guys later," he told the detectives, watching them cross the lobby.

Jane Stomer was standing to the right of the courtroom's padded doors. She was wearing a paisley skirt and a matching paisley blouse and white shoes. She had a deep tan and her lips sparkled. She wore no hose and her legs were smooth; he recalled how she used to open her legs to him, and he felt the beating of his own heart.

"Hello, Jane," he said feebly.

A wistful smile was on her lips. "You look fit, Scanlon."

"So do you."

"I heard all about your big arrest," she said. "The word is that it's a throw-out."

"How have you been?"

She looked at him strangely, as though checking to see if he was the same man. "I've been good. How is your mother?"

"Very good, thanks. And your parents?"

"The same."

"I've missed you a lot."

"Obviously not enough to call."

He looked down at the floor. "I've still got that problem."

"That *problem* could have been worked out. And I suppose you still haven't sought professional help."

He sighed. "Not yet."

A forlorn look came over her face. "It was good to see you again, Scanlon." She nodded at him and walked away.

A terrible sense of loss possessed him as he watched her thread her way through the swelling crowd. Suddenly he heard his voice calling out her name, and he saw her stop. He rushed through the crowd, shouldering people from his path. He grabbed her by the wrist and led her away, searching for some place where they might be alone. Finding no privacy, he led her out of the building by the Baxter Street exit.

"I have to be in court in five minutes," she protested, tugging her wrist free.

"One minute, please."

The compact street was clogged with double-parked police cars. Department of Correction vans were queued up outside the massive steel doors of the court's detention facility, waiting their turn to discharge their cargo. Scanlon looked up and down the street. Gripping her by the hand, he pulled her along, angling around cars and between bumpers, and led her to a bench inside small Baxter Street Park.

Camera-laden Japanese tourists were milling around the park taking photographs of Chinatown.

"Well?" she demanded, sitting next to him.

Unrehearsed words spilled from his lips. Knowing that he was fighting the clock, he talked fast and convincingly.

Her stern countenance and her unrelenting stare did not deter him; he plodded on. He told her that he realized how badly he had handled his dysfunction. He told her that he had been unable to cope with losing his leg and his manhood at the same time. He told her of the nightmare that he had had in the hospital: naked, she would go to straddle his legs, see that one was missing, and back away, laughing. He told her how much he had missed her in his life, how empty his life had been without her. "I know that I made a mess of things," he said, taking her hand in his.

"Yes, you certainly did." She pulled her hand free and checked the time. "What is the purpose of this exercise, Scanlon?"

"I'm in love with you, Jane, and I want you back in my life."

She sighed. Her voice softened. "I can't, Tony. There is another man in my life now." She got up. "Goodbye."

The Mohawk hairstyle accentuated her high cheekbones. Detective Alice Guerrero was a shapely woman in her middle thirties. She had clever catlike eyes and a narrow chin. She stood in front of Sigrid Thorsen with her forefinger held parallel to the witness's eyebrows. "Sigrid, I'd like you to keep your eyes on my finger and lower your lids, but be sure to keep your eyes fixed on my finger."

Detective Guerrero moved away when she was finished and sat alongside the desk in the soundproof interview room of the Scientific Research Unit on the eleventh floor of the big building.

"What was that for?" Sigrid Thorsen asked, brushing a tendril of blond hair from her shoulder.

"That was a test that helps me to determine if you are a good subject for hypnosis."

"And am I?"

"Yes."

"How can you tell?"

"You were able to keep your eyes fixed on my finger while you lowered your lids. A bad subject is not able to keep his eyes up." She crossed her legs and leaned forward, facing the witness. "Sigrid, we use the relaxation technique of hypnosis. I'm going to relax you, and help you bring down your conscious and bring up your subconscious. Then I am going to take you back in time to that Thursday afternoon in McGoldrick Park. But before we start, I want you to tell me everything you can remember about what you saw in the park that afternoon."

Sigrid Thorsen told her tale to the department hypnotist. When the witness finished her story, the detective said, "I want you to know that when you are under hypnosis you will not say or do anything that you do not want to. We all have skeletons that we want to remain in the

17

It was late afternoon when Scanlon returned from the Scientific Research Section. He immediately set about reading the Fives on each of the women connected to the case. If the pigeon feeder had in fact been a woman, then there was a good chance she was one of these witnesses.

The walking picture of the perp who took out Dr. Zimmerman and his wife showed that their killer was about five-eleven and weighed around 185 pounds. None of the women involved in the case was that tall or weighed that much. There must have been two killers, Scanlon reasoned. And in that case, how could the cases be connected? It was beginning to look as though there were no link between the two double homicides.

Scanlon set aside the interview reports of the two women who had been on their way to the A&P supermarket when the perp fled the candy store and ran to the van. He was sure that they were in no way involved in the murder.

Donna Hunt's report was next. It bothered Scanlon that Donna Hunt had not asked him to return the nude photograph of herself that Gallagher had taken. Could this demure Queens housewife be involved in murder? He glanced over the notes that he had stapled to the Five: "Witness nervous, cried, went to john with Maggie. Colon gave her glass of water."

The next report was of his interview with Mary Ann Gallagher, the dead lieutenant's widow. He read it, pondered its contents, decided that the widow was a dead end, and pushed the report aside along with the statements of the two shoppers.

He had begun reading the next interview report when Lew Brodie ambled in and announced, "It just came over the radio, someone planted a bomb in the PBA's office."

"Anyone hurt?" Scanlon asked, concerned.

"Not so far. The reports are still coming in."

"Fun City," Scanlon said, and went back to reading.

Rena Bedford, the college girl who drove a Porsche and was experimenting with life, and who had come to the Squad with her shyster uncle, was next. He recalled staring into her virginal face and listening to her boldly describe her sexual encounters. He wondered if such a woman would have the nerve to do murder.

Mary Posner, the knock-around lady who had married Sy Posner, the factor, and who had refused to participate in any of Gallagher's parlor games, came next. Sy Posner had been her last shot, she had told Scanlon. What if Gallagher had tried to extort money from her? Greenbacks in return for the nude photograph of herself. Gallagher needed money to pay off Walter Ticornelli. Twenty-one hundred and fifty dollars. And that exact amount had been discovered hidden in the wheel well of Gallagher's car. Had Gallagher become a threat to her?

The Zimmermans. He always returned to them. Although it did appear that two separate killers were involved, he always came back to the Zimmermans. He knew down deep that there *was* a connection. It was there someplace. He knew it, he just knew it. He thought about Linda Zimmerman, the banker who had had her life shattered by the murder of her family. The banker who managed investment portfolios for some of the wealthiest people in the country. Maybe she was involved in some hanky-panky at the bank. Needed money bad enough to kill her family. She had the presence of mind to go and clean out her mother's apartment the day after the woman was murdered. She had wanted to get something from the apartment, she had told Scanlon, something personal. If Scanlon's mother was murdered he wouldn't think of getting property, he'd only think of getting even. He realized that he had never checked out the investment bank where Linda Zimmerman worked. Indecorous or not, he was going to have to check out the bank. Then he caught himself thinking about what he would do if his mother had been murdered, and realized that he hadn't spoken to her in days. He picked up the telephone and called her. When she answered he spoke in Italian and told her that he loved her. Would he come to dinner this Sunday? "I'll try, Mom."

Valerie Clarkson, the waitress who worked in the Santorini Diner, and who had chestnut hair, and who wore pearls, was the next interview report he read. Had he overlooked some connection between her and Gallagher?

Luise Bardwell's Five was the last. Luise Bardwell, Sgt. George Harris's girlfriend. Luise Bardwell, the married bisexual who had been the third participant with Gallagher and Donna Hunt and Gallagher and Valerie Clarkson and Gallagher and Rena Bedford. Luise Bardwell, who bragged to Scanlon that she had brought Valerie Clarkson out of the closet. Why couldn't this have been a simple mob hit where the facts are known, but unproven, and nobody, but nobody, gives a shit? Detectives don't like real mysteries, they give you gas.

He pushed the Fives aside and reached for the pad that was at the top of the heap in the out basket. He wrote "Sgt. George Harris" in the left margin and underneath wrote: "Face similar to composite sketch of driver of van and similar to composite of mustached man seen running from Kingsley Arms. Mustache = makeup. Pigeon feeder a woman = makeup. Impression cowboy boots found on roof. Harris/cowboy boots."

To the right of Harris's name he wrote: "Physical evidence—Sweet Sixteen shotgun, tools used to force roof door, rifle used to kill Zimmermans. Makeup, where purchased?"

He listed the female witnesses on the right side of the page. He boldly underlined Luise Bardwell's name. She was the woman who was connected to more of the people involved in the case than anyone else.

Luise Bardwell offered him a drink, and when he declined, she lowered herself down next to him on the thick, soft cushions of the sofa. She was wearing a loose wine-colored top and tight white slacks. She smiled. "It's nice to see you again, Lieutenant."

"Nice to see you too," he said, watching her arm slide over the back of the sofa.

She leaned in close to him. "I could never refuse to talk to a handsome man."

"That's good to know."

"What are the few questions that you wanted to ask me?"

"How did you first meet George Harris?"

"Two years ago, during the summer. I was driving downtown to go shopping. I stopped for a red light. My car's air conditioner was on the fritz, so I had the window open. Some boys ran up to my car and snatched my pocketbook off the front seat. I dialed nine-one-one. A police car came and escorted me into the station house so the detectives could interview me. And that's how I met George."

"Did he come on to you?"

"No, actually he was very professional. But he was interested, I could tell."

"How could you tell?"

"By the way he kept looking at me and by the questions he asked. He wanted to know if I was married and what my husband did for a living. I mean, it was only a purse snatch and George was making it into a major crime spree."

It was SOP for uniform officers to bring attractive female complainants into the detective squad to be interviewed.

"When did he make a move on you?"

"He telephoned me the next day."

"And you went out with him?"

"I found his arrogance exciting. I thought he might be a man worth getting to know."

"And was he?"

She leaned forward and winked at him. "No," she whispered. "Your sergeant was a passive lover."

"George must have been transferred into narcotics shortly after he met you," he said, remembering Herman the German telling him that Harris had been transferred into the junk squad two years ago.

"Yes, that's right. And George was really annoyed by the transfer. It seems that Joe Gallagher had him transferred without consulting him."

"How did you know that?"

"I was with George one night shortly after his transfer. He bitched most of the night about how he was sick and tired of baby-sitting for Gallagher and having to pull his fat out of the fire while Gallagher spent all his time playing the police department's fair-haired boy."

"What else did he tell you about his relationship with Gallagher?"

"Nothing much, except that he would get very upset every time Gallagher countermanded one of his orders."

"Tell me again how you became involved in Gallagher's parlor games."

She rubbed her breasts against his arm. "Are you sure you wouldn't like to take a break?"

"Later," he said, moving back.

She made an annoyed *tut* sound with her tongue. "I'd become bored with George and thought that it might be exciting if George and one of my lady friends got together. When I suggested it to George he said that he didn't go in for that sort of thing, and he suggested Gallagher."

"And who provided the women?"

"Joe Gallagher."

"I thought you said that you wanted to use your lady friends."

"Originally I did. But when Gallagher said he'd supply the women I saw an opportunity to broaden my horizons."

"Was Linda Zimmerman ever a friend of yours?"

"No, she wasn't," she snapped. "I never met the lady. This is beginning to sound like an interrogation."

"It is."

"Are you serious?" she asked, open-mouthed.

"Your name keeps popping up at every stage of the investigation."

"What investigation?" she demanded. "Gallagher and Yetta Zimmerman were killed in a holdup. You don't seriously think that I took part in a robbery?"

"When the doctor and his wife were murdered we were forced to take a closer look at Joe Gallagher's death. And do you know what we found?"

She scowled and slapped her hands onto her knees. "No, tell me."

"We found you." He held up his hand and ticked off fingers. "You knew Gallagher, Harris, Donna Hunt, Rena Bedford, Valerie Clarkson. Almost everyone connected to this case is known by you."

"You really think I could kill those people?" she said with genuine concern in her voice.

"I think it's possible that you conspired with someone else to have it done."

She got up and moved across the room to the glass wall of her Battery Park penthouse and gazed out at the river. He went and stood alongside her. Yellow fingers of light shimmered across the water.

"Why would I do such a thing?" she asked, her eyes following the wake of a sightseeing boat.

"Love? Jealousy? Revenge? Greed? Take your pick."

"When was Gallagher killed?"

"June 19, 1986. A Thursday, about two-fifteen in the afternoon."

"I think that the time has come for me to put you out of your misery, Lieutenant. From June 8 to June 19, my husband and I were attending a convention in San Francisco. We stayed at the Palm Hotel. I paid the bill with my American Express Card, and I can give you the names and addresses of at least a dozen people who can attest to our being there. We flew home on the red-eye." She turned from the glass wall and left the room.

Scanlon remained staring at the distant shoreline. When she returned she went over to the sofa and sat down. He abandoned the view and sat next to her.

"Here are the names and phone numbers of people we were with in San Francisco," she said, handing him a slip of paper.

"Why didn't you mention this to me the last time?"

"Because the last time you didn't tell me that I was a suspect."

He picked up her wrist and admired her watch. It had a gold link bracelet. "Nice watch."

"Thank you. It's kind of exciting being a murder suspect," she said, leaning in close.

"Really?" he said, checking the time.

She kissed him, plunging her tongue into his mouth and sliding her hand up his leg.

He pushed her away. "I have to get back to the office."

"Don't I excite you?" she said softly, rubbing his groin.

"I couldn't relax. Your husband might come home."

"Then we could have a threesome," she said, starting to work down his zipper.

He lifted her hand away from him.

"Would you like me to suck you?" she said, brushing her lips over his.

"I'd love it," he said, "but I just couldn't relax. Another time."

"Would you like to go down on me?"

"I'm on duty. I can't."

She pushed back. "You're what?"

"On duty. It's a violation of the *Patrol Guide* to do that while you're working."

"Cops! They're all duds."

The door was ajar. Scanlon pushed it open with his foot and stepped inside. A thin coat of dust was collecting on the furniture. He sensed another presence, heard the steady beat of a slight sharp noise. He moved down the foyer to the patients' waiting room on his right.

Linda Zimmerman was slumped on a leather couch, clinking the top of her Zippo lighter open and shut, open and shut. She looked gaunt and tired. Her hair was unkempt, tangled, and there were black rings under her eyes. She was wearing a loose brown dress, the folds of which were draped between her legs. An antique lapel watch was pinned over her left breast. He saw the anguish in her eyes and went and knelt down beside her. "Are you all right?"

"I have a sense of devastation that I can't shake. My body is numb. Why did you want to meet me in my brother's office?"

"There are some questions. And I wanted to have another look through his records. I might have missed something the last time."

"Andrea opened her eyes yesterday and recognized me. The doctors say that's a good sign."

"I'm glad."

She looked at him. "Why are you wasting so much of your time prying into my family's past?"

He met her stare. "Why, Linda? Because it's my job."

A resigned smile came to her lips. "Do you want to check his records first?"

"That'll be fine. We can talk as I go through them." He pointed his finger at her lapel watch. "Do you always wear that? Don't you have a wristwatch?"

"I can't stand anything on my wrist," she said, and got up and led him into her brother's office. The record room door was open, the telephone console silent. She reached into the room and switched on the lights. Fluorescent fixtures fluttered to life.

"There are a lot of folders to go through," she said, motioning to the rotating file racks on both sides of the room.

"Did your brother have a safe in his office?"

She squeezed past him into the room. The plastered walls were painted pink. The center wall between the file racks had an oil painting of a ballerina with her foot on a stool tying on her ballet slipper. She took the painting off the wall and leaned it against the rack. A combination safe was built into the wall. She reached into the file tray and read off the numbers that were written on the wall behind a file of folders. She twirled the black-faced dial several times and pulled the door open. She reached into the safe, removed the contents, and passed them to Scanlon.

There were some business records, stock certificates in a company that Scanlon had never heard of, ten one-hundred-dollar bills, and a packet of love letters that had been written by Stanley Zimmerman's future wife, Rachel.

He looked through the material and passed it back to her. "Nothing of importance here," he said.

She took the contents from him and put them back into the safe, all but the letters. She read one letter. "Oh, Rachel," she said, putting the letter back into the envelope and clutching the packet to her chest.

Scanlon spent the better part of the next two hours going through the files. She stood in the doorway watching him, leaving once to call her aunt to inquire about Andrea. Scanlon finally turned off the light and left the record room. Was there anything he'd missed the last time he was here, he wondered, looking around the doctor's modern office.

"What happened to your brother's secretary?"

"I let her go. The practice is on the market. I have no need for a secretary."

He realized that he had not looked inside the closet the last time he was there. He opened the door and jumped back as a cluster of African spears fell out of the crowded space and came crashing out onto the floor.

She knelt down beside him and helped gather them up.

"Stanley did work in Africa for the UN. They were always giving him these things as presents."

A short time later she stood inside the bedroom and watched him search her brother's dresser. The blood-soaked bed had been removed; in its place was an unfaded square of carpet.

"Do you have any idea what you're looking for?" she said, leaning against the bedroom wall.

"Not really." When he finished his search he went and leaned against the wall next to her. "Do you know a woman named Luise Bardwell?"

"No, I don't believe I do."

"Donna Hunt?"

"No."

"Rena Bedford?"

"No."

"Valerie Clarkson?"

"No."

"Mary Posner?"

"No! Why are you asking me about these people?"

"They are people I interviewed in connection with the case, and I just wondered if you knew any of them."

"Well, I don't. Why all these questions?"

"Just fishing around for some answers." He pushed away from the wall. "What about George Harris? Do you know him?"

"No, I don't," she said, losing patience.

"Did your brother happen to own any rifles or shotguns?"

She waved him off. "No more questions. I have to get back to my niece."

Scanlon drove Linda Zimmerman back to her aunt's Sutton Place apartment and returned to the Squad.

He entered the squad room and went directly into his office, where he took out the Fives on Linda Zimmerman and sat studying them. Why did she rush to her mother's apartment to clean it out? he thought. What was there that she wanted so badly that she couldn't wait? He called Lew Brodie in. "I want you to sit on Linda Zimmerman." He wrote the aunt's address on a slip of paper and handed it to the detective. "You know what she looks like?"

"Yeah, I know," Brodie said. "You want her covered day and night?"

"We don't have the manpower for that. Sit on her till eighteen hundred each day."

"We got nothing on that broad, Lou," Brodie said, putting the slip of paper in his shirt pocket.

"I know that. Sit on her anyway."

"You're the boss."

Scanlon went out into the squad room and called to Higgins. "Grab your pocketbook, Maggie. We're going for a ride."

Donna Hunt was framed in the doorway of her Bayside, Queens, home, staring with wide-eyed dismay at the photograph Scanlon held up in front of her. It was the same one that Joe Gallagher had taken of her in his Jackson Heights splash pad. She was naked on a bed with her legs apart and a dildo in her hand.

Her frightened eyes swiveled to Higgins, who was standing at Scanlon's side, and then to the gray sedan that was parked at the curb. Without a word, she stepped back into her home and watched the policemen enter.

Donna Hunt lived in an attached brick bungalow that had dormered windows and a tiny lawn. She was dressed in jeans and a blue work shirt with the tails hanging out. A feather duster was clutched in her hand.

Higgins smiled at her as she slipped past. The witness managed a weak smile in return.

Scanlon looked around the house. Traditional furniture swathed in plastic, a gold rug, a room divider that contained a collection of Hummels.

"I didn't expect to see you again," the witness stammered. "Is there anything wrong?"

The diminutive woman's face was chalk-white and her lower lip was quivering. Scanlon felt sorry for her. She was a woman on the edge, in danger of losing everything. Yet she was also a murder suspect, and he had come to tighten the mental thumbscrews. He did not like that part of the job.

"Mrs. Hunt," he began, "something has come up that we think you might be able to help us with." He moved to the breakfront and looked over the collection of Hummel figurines.

"I collect them," Donna Hunt said, glancing at Higgins for understanding, perhaps salvation.

Scanlon carefully picked up one of the figurines: a rosy-cheeked girl dressed in the traditional dirndl, with a yellow kerchief around her blond hair. She was drawing water from a white brick well. Scanlon studied the figurine and then returned it to its place on the shelf. As he did, he took in the family photographs on top of the shoulder-high divider.

"What do you want?" the witness pleaded.

Scanlon looked at Higgins. She was dressed in a black cotton dress and a print oversize vest. She always dresses to the nines, he thought, no bib overalls for her. He looked at Donna Hunt. "Why didn't you ask me to return this photograph to you when you were in my office?"

An uneasy laugh. "I was afraid to." Her stare fixed on the photograph in his hands. "Please put that disgusting thing away. Please!"

He slid it into his breast pocket. "Would you like me to return it to you?"

"God, yes. If Harold ever found out, or my children . . ." She began to cry softly.

Tough cop, browbeating a frightened housewife who never as much as received a traffic summons. Sometimes the Job really sucks, he thought, saying, "You can have the photograph, but in return, I want something from you."

She grew wary. "What?"

"Your husband is the accountant for the Luv-Joy Manufacturing Company. I need to know who owns that company, and I don't want your husband to know that I know."

Donna Hunt clutched her chest. "My Harold isn't involved in any of this, is he?"

"No," Scanlon reassured her, "he's a bystander, nothing more."

Relieved, the witness said, "Harold never discusses his work with me. I have no way of knowing who owns that company. And if I asked Harold, he'd want to know how I even knew the name of the firm and I'd have to explain the sudden interest in his practice."

"Does your husband keep any business records at home?" Higgins asked.

"He has an office in the basement that he uses around tax time," Donna Hunt said, "but I don't know what he has there."

The office turned out to be a green file cabinet and a painted desk that were set between a damp cinder-block wall and a flight of squeaky wooden steps. A washer and dryer were next to the file cabinet, and on the floor was a plastic basket full of clothes. Donna Hunt sat on the cellar steps looking down as the two detectives searched through her husband's business records.

Scanlon had taken the file cabinet, Higgins the desk. They were professional scavengers, working methodically, going quickly through each record, ever mindful of the detective maxim: Do it fast and quiet and get the hell out. The tops of the desk and the file cabinet were soon both covered with old records: accordion folders stuffed with out-of-date balance sheets and old bank statements, outdated tax returns, and long-paid bills.

After a half hour, Scanlon complained, "Nothing here."

"Zilch here too," Higgins said.

Scanlon looked up at the cellar steps. Donna Hunt had green eyes and wore a Timex watch with a pink band. "Are there any more records?" he asked the witness.

Donna Hunt lifted her small shoulders. "Not that I know of. Everything that Harold keeps at home from his business is there. Look, please, it's almost six. Harold's going to be home any second."

The policemen took several minutes to tidy up. Leave it exactly the way you found it, another maxim born from cop lore. With the witness in the lead, they climbed the staircase into the house's spotless kitchen. The witness moved across the tiled floor and leaned against the dishwasher, looking apprehensively at Scanlon.

Higgins glanced at him, her brow knitted with curiosity.

Scanlon took in both their expressions, read their questioning eyes: Would he give back the photo as he'd said he would? The photograph was evidence in a homicide case, evidence he had intentionally failed to voucher, evidence that at some point might prove crucial to the case.

Looking into Donna Hunt's brimming eyes, he thought, She's no killer, and she's paid a high enough price for her romp in the hay with Joe Gallagher. He went to her and took hold of her hand. He slid the photograph out of his breast pocket and slapped it down into the palm of her hand. "Goodbye, Mrs. Hunt."

The band played "Moonlight Serenade."

Scanlon sat in a chair behind the brass railing watching the dancers glide around Roseland's dance floor. The disco program would be starting shortly. That was when he would slip out onto the floor and lose himself among the swirling people. He wanted to put some distance between himself and the case, to relax and be with civilians in a noisy place. He looked around at the women and wondered if he was destined to spend the rest of his life going with hookers. He began to run over in his mind all the things that Sally De Nesto and he had talked about concerning his dysfunction. How wonderful it would be to be a normal man again, to be close to Jane Stomer, to live his life out of the sexual underground.

The disco beat boomed. He got up and moved toward the dance floor. A woman in her late thirties who had uneven teeth was standing a few feet in front of him. She looked in his direction. He smiled at her. She looked away. He slipped past her and edged his way out onto the dance floor.

Jane Stomer stood naked before him, caressing her breasts. He was sitting on a strange bed, in a strange room, his manhood in full bloom. There was a soft smile on her face and a tinge in her cheeks. He went to lunge up at her, but she shot out a restraining palm. "Stay there, Scanlon. I'll come to you." It was so wonderful to hear her say his name again, to be with her, to see her body, to gaze with desire at her triangle of tightly knit ringlets. But wait. Where were they? When did they get back together? He couldn't remember them getting back together. All of a sudden they were in a bedroom together. Was he dreaming? No, that was not possible. Everything was too real. She came toward him, sliding her hands around his neck, straddling his legs, lowering herself onto him.

"Jane, I've missed you so. I love you. I love you."

"Yes, Scanlon. Yes. Now. I want it to happen together. Now."

He did not want the exquisite moment to end. He wanted to hold back, to relish the pleasure, but he could not. As his love burst forth he saw his father standing in the shadows laughing at him.

Scanlon sprang up in his bed. A dream? It had been so real. He would have sworn that it was happening. He felt the discomfort and yanked off the sheet. "Son of a bitch!" he shouted across the empty loft. He rolled off the bed, balled up the sheets, and angrily threw them out into his loft, and hopped on one leg into the shower.

18

Scanlon paced the Nine-three squad room, his hands thrust deep into his pockets, aware of the brooding silence around him. He glanced up at the clock: 0346 hours. The new day was two hundred and twenty-six minutes old. The sounds of the night filtered in through open windows: firecrackers exploded, tires screeched off in the distance, and somewhere a woman screamed at someone. The night team was sacked out in the dormitory, catching forty winks. A telephone rang and a lazy arm reached out of a bunk and snatched up the extension. Muted words came from behind the dormitory's frosted-glass door. Scanlon lit a De Nobili as he paced the floor of his office. He had gone back to bed after his shower and tried to sleep. But he had not been able to. A wet dream at forty-three. It sounded like a song title. He was upset and disgusted with his private life, so he got dressed and retreated into the Job.

His brain felt leaden and dull. The list of people that Luise Bardwell had given him to prove her alibi had checked out. They had substantiated her presence in San Francisco with her husband when Gallagher had been killed. Donna Hunt was probably too small to be the pigeon feeder. He reminded himself to check out Linda Zimmerman's place of employment. George Harris? Could he somehow be involved? Where was the damn motive? He paced. The De Nobili had gone out. It was cold and soggy and had a foul taste. He grabbed it from his mouth and plunged it into a nearby wastebasket. From the corner of his eye he caught sight of the announcement-crammed bulletin board. He stopped, took some tentative steps toward the board, his stare locked on the LBA flyer authorizing the solicitation of funds for the Joseph P. Gallagher Memorial Fund. I wonder, he thought. I just wonder.

At 0900 hours that same morning, Tony Scanlon hurried into the ornate lobby of 250 Broadway in lower Manhattan. Stepping off the elevator on the twenty-first floor, he immediately saw the bomb damage: the scorched walls, a boarded-up elevator bank, bent fire doors hanging from hinges. He walked down the wide corridor toward the uniformed guard on duty outside the offices of the Patrolmen's Benevolent Association of the City of New York, Inc.

"ID," said the thickset guard.

Scanlon produced his credentials. The guard compared the official photograph on the laminated card with the face of the man standing in front of him. Handing the leather shield case back, the guard said, "Sign into the Visitors Log, Lou."

The reception area was small and sparsely furnished with a few leatherette chairs and two drooping plants. A gum-chewing receptionist with oversize pink-tinged eyeglasses slid open one side of the alcove's glass partition and said in Brooklynese, "Can I be of some help to you, sir?"

"I'm Lieutenant Scanlon. Louie Pots and Pans is expecting me."

The receptionist typist buzzed open the door leading into the PBA's executive offices.

Patrolman Louie Mastri, the PBA trustee for Patrol Borough Brooklyn South, had been a tough street cop, and a vociferous defender of the Police Officer's Bill of Rights. But Louie Mastri's reputation in the Job had no relationship to his union activities or his arrest record. His reputation had been built upon his lifelong avocation, cooking. Wherever he had been assigned in the Job his reputation as a cook soon caught up with him, causing him to spend most of his patrol time in the basement of station houses cooking for the platoon.

Louie Mastri had been out of the Academy for about two years when an old salt of an Irish desk officer in the Six-two Precinct turned to the cop on the switchboard during a four-to-twelve tour and said, "Call that kid, what's his name, Louie Pots and Pans, in off post. I'm in the mood for that spaghetti he cooks." Henceforth, in the eternal lore of the Job, Louie Mastri would forever be known as Louie Pots and Pans.

"Lou, how the hell are you?" barked Louie Pots and Pans, from across his large corner office. The trustee was standing over three gas barbecue grills that had been set up in front of the window air conditioner. He was wearing a blue apron with the word "Chef" emblazoned across the front.

"I'm fine, Louie. How's the family?" Scanlon asked, taking in the police memorabilia scattered around the office.

"Everything is great. Louie Junior is a sophomore at Albany State, and Maria is a freshman at St. John's. And the little lady is as beautiful as ever."

"Time marches on," Scanlon said, moving over to the grills.

"I'm preparing the sauces for lunch. You gonna stay and eat with us. I'm making Scampi alla Romana."

"I'd love to, but I can't. I've got a lot of things on the agenda today." He moved across the room to the display of police hats on the windowsill and picked up one from London. He put the helmet on his head. "How do I look?"

Louie Pots and Pans glanced over his shoulder. "You look fuckin' adorable." He returned his attention to his sauces. "Can you imagine us wearing a hat like that on patrol in this city? The fucking mutts would use it for target practice."

"You're right," Scanlon agreed, taking off the hat and replacing it. He picked up another, examined the white embossed emblem on the front. "Where's this one from?" he asked, holding it up.

Louie Pots and Pans turned to look. "That's from the Tokyo PD." He adjusted the flame on the grills and went over to his desk and sat.

Scanlon returned the hat to the windowsill, walked up to a chair in front of the trustee's desk, and looked sternly at the trustee. "I love the ambience of your hallway."

"That's known as Ghetto Blight. Some mutt sashayed into the ladies' room and planted a bomb inside one of the commodes. We were lucky no one was inside when it blew."

Scanlon studied the face in front of him, the gray eyes, the dark hair with a silver tinge. "I'm here to pick your brains, Louie."

"Go ahead, pick." Louie Pots and Pans snapped his fingers and scuttled out from behind his desk over to the barbecue grills. He picked up a jar and shook something into the simmering sauces. "I almost forgot to add the oregano," he said, going back to his desk.

"I want our conversation to remain between us, Louie."

Louie Pots and Pans turned wary. "I haven't seen you at the last couple of Columbian meetings."

Scanlon answered in Italian: "*Ho avuto un cacco di problemi personali.*"

"We all got personal problems," Louie said, his stern eyes holding the lieutenant's. "This thing that you want to remain just between us, could it be used in any way to hurt cops?"

Scanlon put on a pained expression. "Louie!"

"What do you wanna know, paisan?"

"You sit on the Board of Trustees for the Police Pension Fund, right?"

"Don't tell me you're looking to get out with three-quarters?"

"No, Louie, I could have had that when I lost my leg. I'm in the Job for the full count." He leaned forward, looking directly into the trustee's eyes. "You must be conversant with line-of-duty death benefits."

"Yeah, I am. Why?"

"A lieutenant, twenty-two years on the Job, age forty-four, LOD death, how much?"

Louie Pots and Pans closed his eyes and groaned. "I heard whispers that there might be a problem."

"How much, Louie?"

The trustee said in Italian, "Tony, you can't be thinking what I think you're thinking?"

"I'm not thinking anything. How much, paisan?"

Louie Pots and Pans picked up a pencil from his desk and began to jot numbers onto a police department scratch pad. "I happen to know that your *fictionalized* lieutenant was a member of both the PBA and the LBA and therefore entitled to both organizations' group life insurance. The PBA pays seventy-five thousand and the LBA pays a hundred. In addition, on all LOD deaths the city contributes one year salary to the family—that would be, roughly, another fifty thousand. So for openers, we got two hundred and twenty-five."

The two men looked solemnly at each other.

Louie Pots and Pans got up to check on his sauces. He added more seasoning to one of the pots and returned to his seat. "The widow would have the option of taking an LOD pension or taking the death gamble. In almost every case we strongly recommend that they take the death gamble."

"Why?"

"Because LOD pensions are paid out in monthly installments over the course of the widow's lifetime and would stop when she dies or if she should remarry. Whereas the death gamble is paid up front, in one lump sum."

"What about taxes?"

"Hardly any. A few grand in state and local taxes, that's all."

"Like most guys in the Job, I know the death gamble exists, but I'm ignorant of its provisions. Explain it to me, will you?"

"The death-gamble bill was passed several years ago by the state legislature to protect the pension rights of guys who die in the Job after putting in their twenty. Under it, your lieutenant would have been deemed to have retired the day before his death. With his time in the Job, he'd have been entitled to an annual pension of about twenty-seven thousand.

"The Pension Bureau woulda looked at their actuarial tables and seen that he had a life expectancy of about sixteen years. Then they'd multiply his annual pension by his life expectancy." Louie Pots and Pans did the arithmetic on the scratch pad. "Four hundred and thirty-two thousand dollars. That would be in addition to the group life insurance policies and the city's contribution of a year's salary. The total would be six hundred and fifty-seven thousand. And then you'd have to throw in any private insurance he might have had."

Scanlon sank down into his seat and slapped his forehead. "LOD widows are wealthy ladies."

"That money don't give them their husbands back. And if they got young kids to raise and see through college, all that money don't go too far."

Scanlon's mind raced ahead. "What about the donations that are made within and without the Job?"

"They can add up to a nice piece of change. If the case gets a lot of publicity it can mean a lot of public sympathy. Especially if there're children involved, and especially if one of the kids got Down's syndrome and the other was slightly retarded. Sometimes those donations can run into six figures."

"Thanks, Louie," Scanlon said, pushing himself up from the chair and going over to the grills. He picked up a wooden stirring spoon, scooped up some sauce, sipped it, and said, "Not bad, Louie, not bad. But it could use just a touch more garlic."

Police Commissioner Roberto Gomez's drawn face reflected his deepening concern as he listened to Scanlon recount the latest developments in the Gallagher/Zimmerman homicide.

Also present in the fourteenth-floor office were Scanlon's immediate boss, Deputy Chief McKenzie, and Inspector Herman the German Schmidt.

"Goddamnit, Scanlon," the PC shouted, angrily slamming his palm down on the desk. "You don't have one ounce of evidence to support this new theory of yours. Nothing that will stand up in court. And you know as well as I do that evidence obtained under hypnosis is inadmissible."

"Commissioner," Scanlon countered, "the death-gamble motive is a lead worth following. It might come to something and it might not. And as far as the hypnosis is concerned, the courts have ruled that it can be used as an investigative tool. That is how we used it, as a tool to find out that the perp was a woman."

"But suppose the perp wasn't a woman?" McKenzie said. "Then what? The entire thrust of your investigation will have been misdirected."

"I'm following up on every lead that we developed. Even if they end in a dead end, like Eddie Hamill."

"Let me understand this new hypothesis of yours," the PC said to Scanlon. "You think that there is a possibility that Gallagher was murdered for his death-gamble money, and that Sgt. George Harris and Mrs. Gallagher conspired to kill her husband. Is that the basic plot?"

"Yes."

"Then tell me, Lieutenant," the PC said, "who killed Dr. Zimmerman and his wife, and why were they killed?"

"I don't know," Scanlon said tightly.

"Assuming for a moment that I buy your new theory, which, I hasten to add, I don't, how would you proceed with the investigation?" Gomez said.

"If the perp who took out Gallagher and Yetta Zimmerman was in fact a woman, and if that woman was Mrs. Gallagher, and if George Harris was her accomplice, then we know who has the evidence that we need to obtain a conviction."

"That's a lot of ifs," Gomez said.

"And would you please tell me what evidence you're talking about?" MacAdoo McKenzie said to Scanlon.

"The shotgun that was used to kill Gallagher and Yetta Zimmerman, the cowboy boots that were worn on the roof of the Kingsley Arms, the rifle that took out the doctor and his wife, and the makeup that was used to turn a woman into a man," Scanlon said.

"Good God, man, do you think that they'd still have that evidence in their possession? They'd have gotten rid of it immediately after the killings," McKenzie said.

"I don't think they had the time to dispose of it, at least not all of it," Scanlon countered. "They've both been in the spotlight from the beginning of this case so I don't think that they would have taken a chance of being seen dumping the stuff. Besides, Harris is cocky, the type of guy who thinks he's smarter than everyone else. People like him can't conceive of getting caught. They're too smart."

Unconvinced, the PC said, "Would someone go to such lengths as to wear a disguise and then forget to remove a wristwatch that could blow her cover?"

"Absolutely," Scanlon said with conviction. "It happens all the time. No matter how clever they are, or how much they plan, there is always some minor point that they manage to overlook. Mrs. Gallagher wore long sleeves, and she probably forgot all about her watch."

"Why kill Yetta Zimmerman?" MacAdoo McKenzie said.

"To make it look as though it were a holdup and to throw us off the scent," Scanlon said. "Gallagher had his time in the Job, so Mrs. Gallagher would have collected on the death gamble in any event. But it's hard to fake an accidental death. The best way to murder a cop is to make it look as though he died in the line of duty. This way you would also collect money through donations. But more important, anything that resembled an LOD death would throw us off, make us look for phantom perps."

Silence fell over the four men as they sat contemplating the monstrous implications of Scanlon's words. For a police sergeant to have engaged in the premeditated murder of a brother officer, for profit, was to their minds the ultimate act of betrayal.

Herman the German shifted in his chair. "I keep coming back to the doctor and his wife. Why them?"

"As I said before, I just don't know," Scanlon responded. "But off the top of my head, I can think of two possibilities."

"I'm listening," PC Gomez said.

"First off, there is a chance that Harris and Mrs. Gallagher might not have had their facts straight regarding the death gamble. They might have thought that in order to collect under it, Gallagher's death had to be designated LOD. And when they saw that it might not be, they decided to ensure that it was by killing the doctor and his wife."

"How the hell would that ensure an LOD designation for Gallagher?" a skeptical MacAdoo McKenzie asked.

"Their deaths gave credence to Yetta Zimmerman being the intended victim of the original hit, thereby setting up the scenario whereby Gallagher died protecting Yetta, guaranteeing an LOD designation."

"And the second reason?" demanded the PC.

"To keep us off balance until nature took its course and the case died a natural death," Scanlon said.

McKenzie stamped his foot. "Do you realize what the hell you are saying? Really realize?"

"Yes, I do," Scanlon said.

Disheartened, the PC got up and walked over to the window. He pushed aside the white vertical blinds and looked out. "Old Steve Kennedy was the PC when I came on the Job. I remember his terminating a rookie in my class because the investigating unit missed three speeding tickets on the original character investigation. And look at the Job today," he lamented. "We're forced to appoint functional illiterates, female dwarfs, and people with criminal records." He kicked the wall. "No wonder the Job is in the state it's in." He went back and flung himself into his chair. "You intend to follow up on this new lead of yours, I gather," Gomez said to Scanlon.

"I think that I should, yes," Scanlon said.

"Then you listen to me, Lieutenant. I don't want you to go near Harris or Mrs. Gallagher until you come up with some corroborating evidence besides hypnosis, composite sketches, and footprints left on a roof. I want something to hang our hats on, something we can go into court with. Mrs. Gallagher is the widow of a dead hero, and Harris is a decorated member of the force. Do I make myself clear, perfectly clear?"

"Yes," Scanlon said.

"In that case, tell me what your next move is," PC Gomez said to Scanlon.

"I've made a list from the Yellow Pages of every theatrical makeup store in the city. I have two detectives checking them out now. I saw to it that they brought along photographs of Harris and Mrs. Gallagher to show the store owners."

"Where did you get their photographs?" PC Gomez asked.

"Harris's is from the department's Force Record File and Mrs. Gallagher's is from a newspaper clipping."

"Why theatrical makeup?" McKenzie asked.

"Because if our perp was a woman, the stuff she used to look like a man sure as hell wasn't bought in the five-and-ten."

Leaning his head back against his headrest, the PC closed his eyes and massaged his forehead. "What else have you done?"

"I have people out checking on the owners of the Luv-Joy Manufacturing Company."

"Why?" the PC asked, rubbing the bridge of his nose.

"We have Gallagher visiting the Santorini Diner on a regular basis for a couple of weeks. The diner is located near the Luv-Joy plant. Gallagher visited the diner during his tour of duty. He had access to a lot of the company's products. There is a connection, and I want to find out what it is. It might prove to be nothing, and then again, it could be important," Scanlon said.

"What else?" the PC asked, his eyes still closed, the deceptive calmness of his voice causing a knowing glance to pass between Scanlon and Herman the German.

"I took it upon myself to ask Inspector Schmidt to come here today because Harris is assigned to his command. I'd like Inspector Schmidt to keep Harris busy, fly him on details. I'm going to start snooping, and I'd prefer it if he wasn't around."

"Do you think that Harris and Mrs. Gallagher were making it together?" the PC asked.

"I don't know," Scanlon said, "but if they were, and she didn't know about his thing with Luise Bardwell, then we just might have a wedge to drive between them."

"Before you use any wedges, you come to me with some solid evidence linking them to the crime," Gomez said.

"Are you thinking of using wires?" McKenzie asked.

"I've decided against using them," Scanlon said.

Surprised, the PC asked, "Why?"

"Because of Section 700.50 of the Criminal Procedure Law," Scanlon explained. "After the eavesdropping warrant expires, you're required to notify the subscriber that you had a wire on his telephone. This case could run longer than sixty days, and I don't want them to know that we're on to them."

"You're going to need extra men on this one," the PC said. "I'm going to assign some people from the Internal Affairs Division to help you out."

"If you don't mind, Commissioner, I'd rather not use anyone from IAD. I believe their involvement in this case would be counterproductive."

Bewildered, the PC asked, "Why?"

Scanlon said, "Because the people in IAD are all mealy-mouthed scumbags who consider street cops to be the enemy. And because all of my detectives are fallen angels, and none of them would be able to work with anyone from IAD."

Scowling, the PC appeared on the edge of rebuking him when Herman the German jumped into the fray: "Commissioner, it might not be prudent to bring IAD into this case, at the present time."

"And why the hell not?" the PC asked.

"Because if we are able to bring this case to a successful conclusion, you will be able to take the credit for personally directing the internal investigation that resulted in arrests, thereby blunting the harmful publicity that the case is bound to generate. And that can only be done if you maintain control of the case."

In an annoyed tone, the PC said, "The CO of IAD reports directly to me."

"I realize that, sir," the inspector said, "but I also know that the special prosecutor has his own spies in IAD who report directly to *him*. And under the special prosecutor's mandate from the governor, he has the legal authority to take over the Gallagher/Zimmerman matter once there is any hint of police corruption." A glint came into his deep-set eyes. "So why let him know? If he ever got wind of this case he'd snap it up in a second. It's tailor-made for his journey to the Governor's Mansion. And then we'd be on the outside, unable to see what the hell was happening on the inside, and more important, unable to protect our own asses."

"You can always notify the special prosecutor later," Scanlon added with a crafty smile. "Especially if the case goes nowhere. Just pass him the ball and step back."

The PC stared down at the black onyx desk set that was embossed with miniature replicas of police shields from patrolman to police commissioner. The set had been presented to him at the Hispanic Association's Man of the Year Award dinner in 1983.

Scanlon noticed the PC's forlorn stare and guessed what he was thinking. It had been a long, hard haul from walking a foot post to sitting behind Teddy Roosevelt's desk on the fourteenth floor of One Police Plaza. He had stayed on the Job too long, a common mistake. He wanted to get out, but he wanted to leave with his three-quarter PC's pension intact. Another major scandal and the mayor might be forced to ask for his resignation. Only five months to go before he was eligible for that pension, five long, precarious months.

Gomez looked up at Scanlon, held his eyes, sensing that he had read his thoughts. "Where would you get the extra men that you need, Lieutenant?"

"I would use some of Lieutenant Fable's detectives from the Nineteenth Squad. It'd be a joint investigation directed and coordinated personally by the PC," Scanlon said.

A perverse smile lit on the PC's handsome face. "You got some line of shit, Lou."

"It's hard surviving in the real world, boss," Scanlon said.

"Tell me about it," Gomez countered. "And while you're at it, someone tell me how we're going to keep this from the CofD."

"I don't see how you can, now," Scanlon said.

"Goldberg is going to have to be brought in on the case," the PC said, "but that's my problem."

Scanlon and Herman the German walked out into the bright sunlight and moved along the tree-lined arcade that connected police headquarters with the open square of Police Plaza.

Scanlon veered off to the right and sat down on one of the concrete cubes. Herman the German followed and sat next to him. "Wonder why the PC wanted McKenzie to remain behind?" the inspector said.

"My guess is that he wanted to discuss how to gracefully bring the CofD into the case," Scanlon said.

"Ain't no graceful way, not now. Too much time has gone by."

"Bobby Boy will think of something. He always does." Scanlon looked upward at the budding maple tree.

Herman the German glanced at him. "Thanks for bringing me into the case the way you did. You've probably saved my career."

"When you allowed me to remove Gallagher's records I told you I'd do the right thing if I could."

The inspector smiled bitterly and said, "A lot of people in this Job threaten to do the right thing, but they seldom do."

They sat in silence, watching the passing crowd; policemen hurrying in and out of police headquarters, civilian employees on extended coffee breaks. Music wafted through the air from a string quartet playing in Police Plaza. Both of them saw familiar faces from the Job and acknowledged faces with mouthed how-are-yous and quick handwaves. The inspector leaned forward, his beefy hands clasped between his legs. "McKenzie was right, you know—you just might be wrong on this one. All you have is motive, and the similarities of a few composite sketches, some peanut shells, and some inadmissible evidence garnered under hypnosis."

"I'm painfully aware of all that, Inspector," Scanlon said, waving at a familiar face. He took out a De Nobili and lit it. "But it's a lead that deserves to be followed up, I think."

"You're probably right."

"Harris told me that he had interviewed everyone in Gallagher's unit. I'm going to have to speak to each of them myself, now."

"You start talking to those cops and Harris is bound to find out."

"I know that. But I can't think of any other way."

"Maybe you don't have to speak to them all. Maybe there are one or two guys in the unit that Gallagher was close to besides Harris. Maybe . . ." He snapped his fingers. "His chauffeur!"

"Damn. Why didn't I think of him? Of course. Gallagher used to go to the Santorini Diner with the same man most of the time. That was probably his driver."

Bosses in the NYPD are assigned cops to drive them during their regular tours of duty. In practice every boss selects his own driver. There are two qualifications to be a boss's driver: a short memory and a zippered mouth.

"Gallagher always used Bert Nocarski as his driver," Herman the German said. "If Gallagher was into anything, Nocarski would certainly know about it."

"What tour is Nocarski working?" Scanlon asked, admiring the backsides of passing policewomen.

"He's working days. I've assigned him to drive Gallagher's replacement until the lieutenant gets to know his people and selects his own driver."

"I'd like to talk to him as soon as possible."

"This is Thursday. The Queens Narcotics Squad's social club holds its monthly meeting tonight. Nocarski is working days, so he's sure to be there."

"Does Harris usually attend the meeting?"

"I'll arrange it so he's too busy to attend."

"Will I have any problem getting in?"

"Naw. You'll be with me. Past and present members and their guests are welcome." He looked at Scanlon. "You know, they usually have *entertainment* at these meetings."

Scanlon drew on his cigar. "That don't bother me."

Lt. Jack Fable's pelican neck was crimson with anger as he listened to Scanlon reveal his suspicions concerning Harris and Mrs. Gallagher. The Whip of the Nineteenth Detective Squad sat shaking his head from side to side. "What the fuck has happened to this Job? Even with a scorecard, you can't tell the players."

"I'm afraid you're right, Jack," Scanlon said, adding, "I've just come from the PC. He wants it to be a joint investigation from now on."

Fable threw up his arms, exasperated. "That's fucking wonderful. I've got some goddamn necrophile using the Nineteenth as his playpen. This weirdo goes to posh hotels with his ax and makes himself dead sex partners. He did one last night in the Hotel Astor. I've been up most of the night." He leaned back and rubbed his tired eyes. "My problem with a joint investigation is that I don't have any warm bodies to assign. I've got five men off the chart on the ax murders, and one off the chart on the Zimmermans. With days off, and court appearances, I don't have enough people to cover the chart."

"Why not ask the borough for some extra bodies?"

"A waste of time, you know that. Every squad in Manhattan North is knee-deep in homicides. And we can't treat them like aided and accident cases like you guys in Brooklyn do."

Scanlon was used to the refrain. There were never enough men and never enough time to do it all. He wondered many times if that was the way the Job always had been. Maybe that was why the first twenty flew by you. You're too busy playing cop to notice the years melting away. He pondered his own manpower problem. "I'll get by using my own people, Jack. If I get stuck, I'll give a holler. And if and when a collar goes down, I'll call you so that you can be in on it."

"I appreciate that, Tony. I really do."

* * *

The obligatory phone call had been made. How is your nephew, Chief? Scanlon had asked Assistant Chief Joseph McMahon, the CO of Patrol Borough Bronx. The chief told Scanlon that his nephew was still in detox in St. Vincent's and that he should be leaving for the Farm in a few days. Scanlon was going to be in the Bronx later in the day and would like to drop in and say hello, if that would be convenient.

Driving through the endless rows of shells of buildings that formed the urban devastation that was the South Bronx, Scanlon thought about how the Job really ran; it was the favors that greased the wheels of justice and made them turn.

Scanlon parked in front of the Four-eight station house on Bathgate Avenue. He identified himself to the two uniform cops assigned to station house security and entered the house. Assistant Chief McMahon rose up from his chair to greet Scanlon. The two men sat in the office exchanging gossip about the Job. No mention was made of the favor that Scanlon had done the Chief in not arresting his nephew for discharging his off-duty when he had his load on. That would have been . . . unseemly. Both men knew the drill, the protocol. During a lull in the conversation, Scanlon looked searchingly at McMahon and said, "Chief, I need a favor. . . ."

When Scanlon left Patrol Borough Bronx twenty-five minutes later he had the names of four Bronx anticrime cops that he had been given by the Chief on a one-week steal.

The four-to-twelve platoon was filing out of the station house when Biafra Baby and Christopher returned.

"Nothing, Lou," Biafra Baby complained, slumping into a chair in the Whip's office. "We checked the tax records and came up with no owner of the Luv-Joy Company. One goddamn corporation blends into another. You can't tell who owns what. And we checked out every theatrical makeup store in Manhattan and Brooklyn and came up dry."

"What about the other boroughs? That makeup had to have been bought somewhere," Scanlon said.

Munching on a carrot stick, Christopher said, "We're going to hit the other boroughs now, Lieutenant."

"Then why are you here?" Scanlon said, looking disapprovingly at the two detectives.

"We came in for gas," Christopher said.

It was an old detective ploy to kill a few hours in the house by coming in off the street for gas. Scanlon felt his anger rise. "The Nine-three isn't the only gas-dispensing precinct in the city. Get your gas and get back out. I want to know where that makeup was purchased."

"Right, Lieutenant," Christopher said.

"Detective Jones, Mrs. Jones is on three," Lew Brodie sang out from the squad room.

Scanlon looked at the two detectives, momentarily forgetting that Biafra Baby's real name was Simon Jones. Biafra Baby snatched up the phone on the Whip's desk. Listening, then nodding his head, he said, "Yes, right. I won't. Right. A half gallon of low-fat milk and whole-grain bread, right." Hanging up the receiver, he arched his brow and said to Scanlon, "That woman is *always* on my case."

Using a department scratch pad, Scanlon began to make a list of the physical evidence that he hoped was still in the possession of Harris or Mary Ann Gallagher. No one does murder and walks away without the fear of getting caught. That raw edge of fear was what he was going to use to break the case. He fumbled around in the case folder until he found Gallagher's Ten Card. He noted the telephone number and dialed.

The dead lieutenant's wife came on the line. "Hello? Hello?" Silence. His hand clamped the mouthpiece. He imagined her standing by the phone straining to hear who was on the other end of the open line. He replaced the receiver and sat back. So it begins, he thought.

Twenty minutes later Higgins and a subdued Hector Colon entered the squad room and went into the Whip's office.

"How did you make out?" Scanlon asked.

"We didn't find any cockroaches, Lou," Higgins said gleefully.

Colon squirmed, embarrassed. "*Teniente,*" he said, trying to ignore Higgins, going on to tell Scanlon that they had canvassed the area where Harris lived on Staten Island, and had discovered that the sergeant's official residence was a frame dwelling at the end of a rutted dirt road. Discreet inquiries by Higgins had revealed that Harris did own the house, but was seldom there. Colon went on to say that the Ocean Avenue splash pad of Harris, the one Luise Bardwell had told them about, was in an eight-story building that was in the process of going co-op.

Scanlon was about to ask Colon a question when they heard Lew Brodie's tense, anxious voice call: "Attention!"

Chief of Detectives Alfred Goldberg bounded into the office followed close behind by a tense deputy chief, MacAdoo McKenzie.

The CofD paused just inside the office and coldly regarded Higgins. He rolled his cigar to the other side of his mouth, looked at Colon, and said, "Excuse us, will ya, Hector?"

Hector Colon and Higgins left the office.

CofD Goldberg closed the door, looked at Scanlon. "The PC filled me in on the Gallagher case."

Scanlon's right hand brushed at his hair as his gaze shifted to Mac-Adoo McKenzie.

The deputy chief nodded confirmation.

"Whatsamatta, Lou? Don't you trust me?"

"Of course I trust you, Chief," Scanlon said.

Goldberg braced his hands on the desk and leaned across. "You ain't supposed to keep things from the chief of detectives." His dour expression broadened into a smile. "But under the circumstances I forgive you. I happen to be a very forgiving man. Ain't that so, Chief?" he said, looking at MacAdoo McKenzie.

"Absolutely, boss. Very forgiving," McKenzie said, rubbing his palms down his trousers.

"We gotta see to it that the PC is protected on this one," Goldberg said, pointing the chewed-up end of his cigar at the lieutenant's face. "We also gotta see to it that if Harris and the widow are the perps, it's us who make the collars and hand out the press releases—very carefully worded press releases." Shoving the cigar back into his mouth, he asked, "How do you intend to proceed?"

Scanlon told him that his main concern was that Harris and Mrs. Gallagher not be given the opportunity to dispose of any of the evidence that he believed was still in the possession of one of them. When Goldberg asked him why he thought that, Scanlon repeated what he had told the PC. "That evidence is someplace. All we have to do is find it," Scanlon finished.

"Maybe," Goldberg said. An expression of doubt clouded his face. He flicked a thick chunk of ash onto the floor. "You got enough manpower to do the job?"

"Jack Fable is sending a few of his detectives over to help, and I've scrounged up a few anticrime cops for a week," Scanlon said.

"Howzat? Fable is up to his ass in homicides and he's sending you men?" There was humor in Goldberg's questioning stare.

Scanlon shrugged off his doubtful look. "We all have to pull together on this one, boss."

Goldberg gave Scanlon a friendly punch on the shoulder. "It really gratifies me to see two of my squad commanders exemplifying such leadership. That's what command is all about. Right, Lou?"

"Right, Chief," Scanlon agreed.

"You know, of course, that I know that you're full of shit. But that's between you and Fable. Just make sure to keep me informed this time around. Got that? The PC and I are operating on the same wavelength on this one." He turned to McKenzie. "Let's go."

MacAdoo McKenzie moved ahead and opened the door for the

CofD. Scanlon scuttled out from behind his desk and hurried over to McKenzie. "What brought about *that* change?" he whispered.

McKenzie looked at the CofD's retreating back, whispered, "The PC told him that he was getting out in five months, and if Goldberg played ball with him on the Gallagher thing, the PC would recommend Goldberg as his successor. Goldberg figures that with Bobby Boy's endorsement he'll be a shoo-in for the job."

"That's if the PC really throws his papers in."

"McKenzie?" Goldberg shouted over his shoulder.

"Right behind you, boss," McKenzie shouted back.

Scanlon looked anxiously into the stern face of Herman the German. They were parked on Carroll Street, in the Park Slope section of Brooklyn. The Carroll Street Bridge, a tiny span that arches over a black stream of polluted water, was down the block from where they were parked. A trucking company was on their right. It was a street of one- and two-story frame houses. Men in undershirts lounged around the sidewalk on lawn chairs. Boys sped by on skateboards. It was 1915 hours. They had been parked there for over fifteen minutes watching off-duty policemen double-park their cars and hurry into the Vito Longoni Hall of the Veterans of Foreign Wars. The hall was across the street, to their left, set back off the street. It was a long one-story frame building that had two wooden steps with a blue-and-white portico.

A Seven-eight Precinct radio car cruised by, slowing to check on the policemen's private cars, to make sure they remained unmolested. The Seven-eight roll call man had received a call earlier in the day from the club's sergeant-at-arms informing him that a meeting was scheduled for that evening. The cops who were assigned to the sector where the hall was located, and the patrol sergeant, had been notified to give the hall "special attention." Cops take care of their own.

Scanlon watched three laughing cops bound up the steps into the hall. He nudged the inspector. "You ready?"

"As ready as I'll ever be," Herman the German said, opening the car door.

Three cops sat around a bridge table just inside the entrance checking membership cards. The recording secretary, a chunky man with a small head, stood up when the inspector walked into the hall.

"Glad you could make it, Inspector," he said, extending his hand across the bridge table.

Motioning at Scanlon, the inspector said, "I brought a friend along."

"No problem, boss," the recording secretary said, nodding to Scanlon.

· Scanlon made his way into the hall. It consisted of one enormous room with a large open kitchen in the rear that was set off from the rest of the hall by a long counter. Swirling blue clouds were painted across the ceiling. Three kegs of beer were set up in front of the counter; many bottles of liquor were on top of the counter along with gallon jugs of wine. A cop was standing over the big pots on top of the gas range. An aluminum folding table had been set up across one side of the room to act as the dais, and there were five rows of metal folding chairs arranged in front of it. An American flag stood behind the aluminum table. Six card tables were scattered about the hall, each one filled with cardplayers. Each table had two pitchers of beer on it.

"Do you see Nocarski?" Scanlon asked Herman the German.

"No," the inspector said, making his way over to the large dice game that was in progress in one corner of the hall. Scanlon moved along behind him. They watched the dice game for a few minutes, the inspector taking in the faces of the players. Herman the German shook his head. "He's not here." They made their way through to the staircase that led downstairs to the cloakroom.

The horseshoe basement bar was mobbed with policemen. There were round tables with flickering candles inside white lanterns. A crap game was in progress in the middle of the room. Herman the German examined each face in turn. Narcs came over to say hello to their boss. Scanlon had never noticed before just how many different kinds of faces made up today's Job. There were oriental faces, and Latin faces, and Mediterranean faces, and black faces, and bearded faces. There were cops in shabby clothes and Italian-cut suits. Cops dressed as Hell's Angels. There were women dressed to look like housewives and business executives. They all had a common denominator, their shields, NYPD Queens Narcotics.

Herman the German moved about greeting his men, listening to their jokes, roaring with laughter, enduring their slurred conversations. Watching the inspector maneuvering among his men, Scanlon thought, A lot of things go into being a boss in the Job. You really have got to know your people, their strengths, their weaknesses. You have got to get them to produce for you, yet, you have to remain aloof from them, not become part of the car pool.

"Nocarski isn't here," Herman the German said. "Let's go back upstairs."

The dice game up in the hall was in full swing. A female undercover was on her ·knees talking to the dice. "Come a seven, come eleven. Baby, talk to your mama!" She rolled the dice.

"Eight's her point," a male voice said. "Twenty says she don't six or eight in two."

Music blared from a tape deck under the long counter.

The cook shouted, "Chow down!"

Policemen began to drift up to the counter.

"Let's eat," Herman the German said.

Holding a paper plate overflowing with frankfurters, sauerkraut, baked beans, salad, and white bread, Scanlon eased himself down onto one of the metal folding chairs and gingerly balanced the plate on his knees. Using a flimsy plastic knife and a fork, he began to cut into the steaming frankfurter. "It takes a certain kind of dexterity to eat at one of these meetings."

Champing on a mouthful of food, Herman the German grunted something that Scanlon took for agreement. They finished eating. Nocarski still had not arrived. The policemen inside the hall had divided themselves into three groups. The boozers congregated around the bar, slopping down drinks; the cardplayers and the crapshooters were intent on their games; the rookies had collected around the dais, exchanging youthful war stories.

"Yoho, m'man," came a harsh voice from the middle of the dice game. "You don't gate in this motherfuckin' game. This ain't no motherfuckin' schoolyard."

Deep lines creased the inspector's brow. "It might be a good time to get out of here."

Scanlon's stump ached. "A little while longer. I gotta speak with Gallagher's driver."

A bearded black man wearing cut-off jeans, sandals, and a T-shirt walked up behind the dais and began rapping a blackjack on the aluminum table, calling the meeting to order. "All stand for the Pledge," he ordered.

Activity stopped as everyone in the hall stood and faced the flag. After the Pledge of Allegiance was over the club's president asked for a moment of silent prayer for the deceased members of the force. All bowed their heads. Prayer over, all activities resumed in muffled tones as the president announced the calendar of coming events: a boat ride in July leaving from the Captree Boat Basin; a family picnic in August; the annual promotion and retirement dinner dance in September.

Scanlon saw two cops moving about the hall, tacking green garbage bags over all the windows. "Looks like the *entertainment* is about to start," he said to the inspector.

The club's treasurer read the financial report.

The club's president rose from his seat. "I'll take a motion to ajoin."

The motion to adjourn was shouted up from the floor and seconded. The din grew. Willie Nelson sang "Till I Gain Control Again." A loud pounding came at the door. The sergeant-at-arms moved up to the door and peeked out from the side of the refuse bag. Nodding in recognition, he unlocked the door.

A stocky blond man with short hair ambled into the hall. Two women followed him inside. One of the women had jet-black hair that was teased up into the shape of a beehive. Her thin body was squeezed into iridescent pink toreador pants. She had on a black pullover with a wide patent-leather belt with a large white buckle. A heavy dose of black eyeshadow gave her small face a chalky hue.

The other woman had a long, angular black face. Her head had been shaven save for a clump of hair on the top that had been styled into a large pompom. She wore a green pullover and Kelly-green toreador pants with a white belt.

Both of the women had on four-inch spike heels.

Scanlon and the inspector had been watching one of the poker games when the women sauntered into the hall. "The guy with them is Bert Nocarski, Gallagher's driver. He must have gone to pick up the hookers," Herman the German told Scanlon.

"Shit, now we're stuck here," Scanlon said.

The cardplayers and the crapshooters ignored the new arrivals. With hoots and howls the rookies rushed to greet the hookers, quickly surrounding them. The two women strutted their wares among the circle, cooing sexual promises, laughingly tickling scrotums. Most of the policewomen who had been in the hall when the hookers entered made their way downstairs to the basement bar. Three remained, trying to ignore the hookers, but every now and then casting side glances at them.

Bert Nocarski shoved his way through the crowd up to the bar and poured himself a shot of whiskey. He held up the tumbler, studying it for a long moment, before he downed the drink in one quick gulp. He poured another and turned to the cop next to him, and Scanlon heard him say, "Did you hear about the fag who walked into the bar with a parrot on his shoulder . . ."

Scanlon made a move to go up to the bar. Herman the German stopped him. "Wait."

Nocarski drank, poured another. Herman knows his men, Scanlon thought, turning his attention back to the poker game. The music was loud. The card and crap games continued unabated. The hookers had taken off all their clothes, except for the spike heels, and were dancing around the hall, swirling and swaying to the beat of the music. Three rookies rushed out onto the floor and began to dance with the hookers.

The white hooker with the teased hair shimmied her body over to one of the card tables and began to hump on one of the player's arms. The annoyed player shoved her away. She danced off. The recording secretary opened the front door for the Seven-eight patrol sergeant and his driver. The hookers danced over to the two uniformed policemen, circling them, rubbing their bodies against them. The hookers began to jostle the sergeant's boyish driver. The black hooker threw her arms around his neck and kissed him, grinding her body against him. The white hooker began to work the zipper of his fly down. The sergeant laughed and walked back toward the bar.

The three remaining policewomen made their way through the crowd to the staircase and hurried downstairs. The sergeant's driver struggled to escape from the hookers' amorous clutches.

Several rookies rushed out from the sidelines to restrain the driver. The white hooker had worked down the driver's fly and was fishing out his penis. To the delight of the rookies, the black hooker went down on her knees and began to suck the driver. The sergeant's driver was turned on. He stood with his head all the way back, his eyes closed, his hands guiding the hooker's head.

The cardplayers anted.

The club's president made six straight passes.

Scanlon threw a quick glance at the raucous policemen and thought, This scene would make one helluva recruitment poster. The white hooker danced her way over to the card game that Scanlon and Herman the German were watching. She dragged a chair from the sidelines and sat with her legs spread up in the air. She smiled at Scanlon. "Wanna taste, handsome?"

Scanlon looked down at her. "No thanks, honey. I'm on a fat-free diet."

One of the rookies rushed over to the white hooker, fell to his knees, and buried his face in her muff. Rookies ran over and circled the kneeling policeman, shouting encouraging advice.

A paper plate sailed through the air. Someone shouted that the Martians were coming. The dice game and the card games continued, undaunted by the ear-piercing din. A fight broke out at one of the card tables. "Let's get this over with and get the hell out of here," Scanlon said to the inspector.

They began to shove their way over to the bar. The sergeant's driver pushed past them, zipping up his fly. The black hooker was spread-eagled on the dais with the sergeant-at-arm's face buried between her legs. Cops were three-deep around the counter. Scanlon shoved his way up to Nocarski. He waited for the inspector, who had been stopped by a drunken cop. Herman the German had just made his way over to Scanlon when silence descended over the big hall. The dice stopped rolling. No pots were anted. No glasses were hoisted. The rookies fell silent.

Scanlon knew what that meant and winced. He turned to look. The hookers were out in the middle of the floor, grinding their bodies into each other, their flailing tongues touching, their hands probing the other body, caressing. The black hooker slithered down onto her back. Her partner knelt down alongside her, kissing her body, her tongue slowly working its way downward.

Scanlon took in the cops' wide-eyed expression, their unconscious gnawing of lips, their heaving chests and flared nostrils and crimson ears. Nothing, but nothing, turns a man on like watching women getting it off together, Scanlon thought, tapping Bert Nocarski on the shoulder.

They went downstairs and sat at a table in the bar, the flickering candle throwing fingers of light onto their faces. Bert Nocarski was fidgety. He looked with suspicion at Scanlon. "Ain't you the Whip of the Nine-three Squad?"

Before Scanlon could answer, Herman the German said, "Bert, I'd like you to continue driving the new lieutenant until he gets his feet wet."

"Whatever you want, boss," Nocarski said, relaxing.

"Bert, how long did you chauffeur Lieutenant Gallagher around?" Scanlon asked, picking at the netting around the lantern.

Nocarski looked at Herman the German.

"Bert, this is a friend of mine," the inspector said, not mentioning Scanlon by name. "He's here to do me a favor, and we need your help."

"Around eleven months," Nocarski said.

Herman the German leaned across the table to confide, "Someone dropped a letter on Joe Gallagher. One of the allegations is that Joe had a girlfriend that he used to visit on city time."

"That's bullshit," Nocarski said. "The boss was a happily married man who never fucked around."

"Hey, everybody knows that, Bert," Scanlon said.

"Anyway, what difference does that make now? He's dead," Nocarski said.

"It makes a big difference to his family and to his reputation on the Job," Herman the German said. "Those humps in IAD would love to be able to smear the reputation of a solid street cop like Joe Gallagher."

"They'd get their rocks off all right," Scanlon said.

"Fucking-A right," Nocarski said, angrily scraping back his chair and walking over to the bar. "Anyone wanna taste?"

Scanlon and Herman the German declined.

Lowering himself back onto the bentwood chair, Nocarski said, "The letter writers in this Job should have their balls cut off."

Assuming a conspiratorial air, Scanlon hunched forward and said, "We know that Joe used to visit the Santorini Diner from time to time."

"He was entitled to a meal period," Nocarski protested.

"Absolutely," Scanlon agreed.

"We want to reach out to whoever Joe used to meet in that diner and tell them that if anyone from IAD comes snooping around asking questions about Joe, they never heard of him," Herman the German said. Stiffening his back in drunken pride, Nocarski said, "I'll take care of it, boss."

"No," Herman the German said. "I don't want you involved. My friend here will take care of that. There is no way anyone can tie him into Gallagher."

"But I am involved," Nocarski insisted. "I was with him every time that he went to that diner, and I even met his pal a coupla times."

"You're not involved," Scanlon countered. "Department regulations prevent supervisors' drivers from being used as witnesses against their bosses for violations of department rules and regulations. You more or less have department immunity. But if you go to that diner now and attempt to head off anyone from talking to IAD, then you'd be sticking your head into a noose."

"I never thought of that," Nocarski said.

He was a small man with a pitted complexion. He sat behind a rather large desk, in a rather big chair, adjusting his rather fluffy orange bow tie. His name was Milton Tablin, and he was a factor, an old competitor of Sy Posner—and an "intimate" friend of Posner's adventurous wife, Mary, who had enjoyed herself with Tablin before Gallagher came into her life. And thus Joe Gallagher knew *all* about Tablin and his work. Tablin was an entrepreneur who lent money to other entrepreneurs, and he was the man Scanlon had rushed to see early the morning after Nocarski gave him the name.

A shapely brunette led Scanlon into the eleventh-floor office at 1380 Broadway, in the teeming heart of the garment district. Walking into the comfortable office, Scanlon took in the photographs and plaques that covered the walls of the rather large office.

Milton Tablin was in every one of the photographs, outfitted in the uniform of a ranking police officer and posing with other uniformed men, most of whom Scanlon recognized as bosses in the Job. The plaques were from different police line organizations, given in grateful recognition to a financial benefactor, Milton Tablin, a cop's friend.

Scanlon was quick to conclude that the factor whom he had come to see was a dyed-in-the-wool cop buff.

"What can I do for you, Lieutenant?" Tablin asked, centering his tie as he watched his secretary's retreating rump.

"I'd like to speak to you about your lunchtime meetings with Joe Gallagher."

On guard, Tablin asked, "Who told you about them?"

"Joe's driver, Bert Nocarski."

"Joe asked me never to mention those meetings to anyone." The factor cast a thoughtful glance at Scanlon. "Where do you work, Lieutenant?"

Scanlon made a quick decision to charm the cop buff by using cop language. "I'm the Whip of the Nine-three Squad."

Milton Tablin grabbed over the telephone console that was on his desk and made a call. "Who got the Nine-three Squad?" he asked into the mouthpiece, his questioning eyes fixed on his visitor. He listened. Thrusting his chin at Scanlon, he said, "You got an artificial leg?"

Scanlon lifted up his prosthesis, rapped knuckles on fiberglass.

"Thanks," Tablin said, hanging up. "That was a friend of mine in the CofD's office. I had to make sure that you weren't one of those snooping humps from Internal Affairs."

A silent smile, a gesture of understanding. Cop buffs think, talk, and try to act like the genuine article.

"Joe is dead," Tablin said. "Why the interest in our meetings?"

"My Squad caught the squeal on Joe's death," Scanlon said. "A few things popped up during the course of the investigation."

"Anything heavy?"

"Minor stuff, but it has got to be answered out."

"Coffee and . . . ?" Tablin asked with a friendly smile.

"Love it. Haven't had my first cup yet."

Tablin pushed a button on the intercom and asked his secretary to get them some coffee and danish. He settled back in his seat and with great delight began to tell Scanlon about all his friends in the Job. Scanlon did not want to alienate Tablin, so he listened attentively, his brow knotted with interest.

Milton Tablin was a captain in the Auxiliary Police. Scanlon was forced to endure an insufferable litany of Auxiliary Police complaints: regular cops consider the auxiliaries psychos and labor scabs; auxiliaries are not permitted to make arrests or carry firearms; the auxiliaries' only function is to give a police presence and to report suspected violations of law. Scanlon swallowed a yawn, smiled, and listened with all the sympathy and understanding he could force himself to muster.

Tablin, with great glee, went on to tell Scanlon the latest scuttlebutt in the Job: who was scheduled for promotion, who was being greased for the slide downward, and who was sleeping with whom. Suddenly Tablin was on his feet, throwing back his suit jacket to reveal his Smith and Wesson automatic pistol in a quick-draw holster secured on his hip. "It's a double-action nine millimeter," he said, caressing the automatic. "I had battle sights put on."

Another psycho heard from, Scanlon thought, saying, "How many rounds does it hold?"

"Ten in the clip," Tablin said smugly, letting his jacket fall back over the weapon and sitting down. Dejectedly, he said, "I'm a captain in the Auxiliary Police and I had to get a carry permit to have a concealed weapon. I mean, I ask you, Lou, is that right? How do they expect us to uphold the law without being armed?"

"I think that sucks, Milton. You guys are an integral part of the Job," Scanlon said, relieved when a soft knock came and Tablin's secretary entered. While Tablin was taking the goodies from the bag, Scanlon said, "Why don't you tell me about Joe Gallagher?"

Handing him a container of hot coffee, Tablin began to talk about the dead police lieutenant. When Tablin had first joined the auxiliaries in '71, Gallagher had been a sergeant assigned to the Auxiliary Forces Section. Gallagher used to lecture Tablin's class on the Penal Law and the Law of Arrest. Tablin liked Gallagher immediately. Gallagher seemed to go out of his way to be nice to the auxiliaries. The both of them hit it off together, almost an instant friendship. One evening after Gallagher had finished giving his lecture he came up to Tablin and asked him if he would like to go to a precinct club meeting. "I think you might enjoy yourself, Milton," Gallagher had said with a mischievous twinkle.

"That was really something," Tablin said, fondly recalling his first witnessing of an act of public sodomy as he bit into his prune danish.

Sipping coffee, Scanlon thought about how the wheelers and dealers on the Job were always on the lookout for businessmen to ingratiate themselves with. One of the best ways of doing that was to invite the entrepreneur to a precinct racket or a precinct club meeting that was going to have *entertainment*. A small segment of the cop world was thus revealed, causing the civilian to feel as though he were now one of the boys, as though he were on the Job, almost.

Scanlon was sure that Tablin's name had been added to Gallagher's list of people who were good—people to whom he could go for a favor. He was just as sure that his own name had been on Gallagher's list. "I've taken care of it, luv. You owe me one," Gallagher had said to Scanlon that long-ago day in Riccardo's restaurant, alluding to the contract that Gallagher had put in with the first deputy commissioner that allowed Scanlon to remain on the Job after he had lost his leg. Scanlon never imagined that the payback would be to a dead Irishman.

"Did you and Joe remain friends after your training ended?" he asked.

"We'd have lunch every couple of months." And Gallagher never once picked up a tab, Scanlon thought. "And we'd run into each other at rackets," Tablin said.

The smart ones always maintain, the friendship, Scanlon thought, asking, "Why were you meeting Joe at the Santorini Diner?"

Looking down his coffee container, Tablin said, "Joe made me promise that I would never tell anyone about that. Joe's gone now, but a promise to a buddy is a promise kept."

Scanlon nibbled on his danish, thinking about what to say next. Tell no one, extract the promise, a cop's way. He looked up at Tablin. "I wouldn't ask you to tell me if it weren't important, really important. We really need your help on this one, Cap," Scanlon said, using the diminutive of captain.

Milton Tablin's face glowed. "Well, I don't know, Lou."

"Cap, I assure you, one cop to another, that if Joe was in this room with us now, he would tell you to tell me. In fact, he'd insist."

Tablin relented. "Well, since we're both on the Job, I guess it'd be okay." He took a gulp of coffee. "Do you know what a factor does?"

"He lends money to businessmen," Scanlon said, breaking off a piece of danish.

"It's more complicated than that," said the factor. "We lend money to our clients on the strength of their commercial paper for ten over prime." The factor saw the puzzled expression on Scanlon's countenance and explained, "Ten over prime means that we take a commission of ten percent over the prime rate. And commercial paper is those instruments that are used in business in place of money." He was no longer the police buff; he had made the transition back into his other world; he was now Milton Tablin, factor. Waving a hand for emphasis, he explained, "Commercial paper can be almost anything—short-term notes, checks, acceptances, bills of lading, orders for the delivery of merchandise."

Unconsciously scratching his left knee, Scanlon asked, "How does it work?"

"Take the rag business, which by the way is where ninety-eight percent of my business comes from. It's a business with a desperate need for ready cash. Manufacturers need money to buy materials for the next season. They don't want to have to wait thirty or sixty days to get their money from a department store. So they come to me with their invoice and I buy it from them, less ten percent. They assign the invoice to me and the department store pays the money to me. This way a dress manufacturer can have cash in his hand in one day and not have to wait a month or two to get paid."

"Joe wanted you to lend him money?"

"No, a friend of his who had this cockamamie company that made dildos and other dreck. His friend wanted to expand the business but didn't have the capital."

"Did you lend the money?"

"No. That wasn't the kind of company that I could get involved with. That business was basically a mail-order house. They had some orders from retail outlets, but not enough for us to get involved. I told Joe this, and I offered some suggestions on how his friend might raise the money."

An anxious feeling welled up in Scanlon's chest. "Who was Joe's friend?"

19

The blinds were drawn in Tony Scanlon's apartment. His dark hair flopped about his head as his body moved in fluid movements to the beat of aerobics music. His support hose felt tight in the crotch, and his body glistened with sweat. He had been at it now for almost one hour, and the gamy smell of his body told him it was almost time to quit.

One, two, three, four, scissor your legs and clap your hands, one, two, three, four. Yesterday he had thought that there was a good chance he had figured the whole thing out. But his morning visit to Milton Tablin had showed him that he hadn't. One, two, three, four, stretch your arms over your head.

With hands on hips and head bowed slightly, he stood catching his breath, aware of the trickle under his armpits. Peeling off his support hose and casting them aside, he moved into the bathroom. He opened the shower door, picked up the slatted folding chair he kept inside, slapped it open, and set it down inside the stall. He took off his prosthesis and placed it over the toilet seat, hopped into the shower, and sat down on the chair. He adjusted the faucets, quickly turning on more cold because he had almost scalded himself with too much hot.

He turned his face upward so that he might better enjoy the stinging spray of water. He had made a ten P.M. date to see Sally De Nesto. Her sex and therapy sessions had begun to intrigue him. In some strange way, everything she had told him about himself made sense to him. The last time they were together he had told her about his childhood, and how his drunken father used to beat up on his mother.

When he saw her eyes grow wide and a knowing glimmer lit up her face, he had demanded, "What?"

"You really don't see it, do you, Tony?" she had said, firming herself up on pillows.

Three fingertips touching in an Italian gesture, he shook his hand at her face. "See what?"

"It's so clear," she insisted. "Your drunken father abuses your mother, and you do nothing to stop it, and then you feel lousy about yourself for doing nothing to protect your mother, for not rushing to her aid. Then years later you meet Jane Stomer, and just like your mom, she gave you her love. And then when you lost your leg and had your problem, you saw yourself as unable to return her love, to protect her, just as if you had let your mother down. So what did you do? You began to seethe inside yourself, and to punish yourself by only being able to get off with people like me."

"Where did you pick up on all that psychological shit?" he had ranted. "I know. I know. From your trick, the blind shrink."

He turned his lathered face up to rinse off. Why the hell did Sally spend so much time trying to help him solve his problems? She must have a mound of her own stashed somewhere.

It was after seven P.M. when Scanlon walked from his apartment by the front entrance. He wasn't much in the mood to climb down the fire escape. The flow of people had spilled over into the roadway. Traffic crept along; swarms of people dodged between cars. The sidewalk cafés and the coffeehouses were jammed with people. Greenwich Village was alive, vibrant.

Thirty-six minutes later when Scanlon drove his car through the sleepy Greenpoint streets he saw a lone woman walking her collie.

He plunged his car up onto the curb cut and honked his car's horn. Rheumy eyes peered out the peephole, and in a matter of seconds the door leading into Gretta Polchinski's garage was churning open. He saw Walter Ticornelli's Ford parked in the first row of cars. Scanlon got out of his car, handed the attendant a two-dollar tip, and moved quickly along the cinder-block passage that led into Gretta Polchinski's brothel.

Men milled about the knotty-pine bar, talking to heavily made-up women in revealing clothes. The jukebox blared. Couples shuffled around the dance floor. Scanlon moved through the crowd, taking his time, checking out faces. One of the bartenders, a short man with big spaces between his teeth, spied Scanlon and mouthed, "Do ya wanna drink, Lieutenant?"

Scanlon shook his head and mouthed back, "Where's Gretta?"

The bartender's thumb jerked in the direction of the dance floor.

She was sitting alone in a shadow, studying the dancers, a teacup in her hands and a silver tea egg on the table next to the saucer.

Uninvited, Scanlon went over to her and sat across from her. She looked at him, lowered her cup into the circle, and asked, "You here for pleasure or for business?"

"I saw Walter's car in the garage," he said, motioning away the waitress.

"He's upstairs comforting his lover. You want to see him?"

"Actually, it's you I've come to see."

Toying with her necklaces, she said, "Don't tell me you've decided you want to throw a hump into me." Overlapping rows of gold chains glistened around her withered neck.

Scanlon grew stern. "I'm here to discuss the Luv-Joy Manufacturing Company with you, since you're the sole stockholder."

"My business interests are none of your goddamn business." She made a move to get up and leave.

He anchored her wrist to the table. "Be advised that I'm not in the mood for any of your parlor games."

"Fuck you!" she yelled, attempting to tug her hand free.

Several of the dancers turned to look in the direction of the disturbance. He continued to pin her hand to the table. "You talk, I listen. If you don't, I not only close down this place, I also sic the IRS on your ass. Think of all those secret business interests of yours, all that undeclared cash stashed in safe deposit boxes. The IRS boys would have a field day with you." He released her wrist.

"Why you pissing on my parade, Scanlon? I didn't kill anyone. You should spend your time busting murderers and dope dealers, not breaking my chops."

"You cause me a lot of extra work, lady. You should have told me about your connection with Gallagher."

"You're making something out of nothing. I needed money for capital improvements. Joe tried to help me arrange financing with a guy. It didn't work out. I gave Joe one large for his troubles. That's it, end of story."

"Not quite. You also lent him an extra fifteen hundred so that he could get Walter Ticornelli off his back. That was your money that we found in the trunk of Gallagher's car."

"And what the hell makes you so sure it was me who lent him money?"

"Street smarts. You're the only one around with a lot of extra cash who would lend a cop money without a vig."

She reached out and patted his face. "You know that I've always been a sucker for a cop."

"What connection did Gallagher have with your company?"

"None. He'd come around every now and then to grab some dildos and things. You know how much cops love to grab things that they get for nothing."

"Does George Harris still work for you?"

"No, he doesn't," she snapped. "He used to work for old man Stevens, the guy I bought the company from. When I took over I decided to reduce my overhead. I put in my own man as manager and got rid of all the moonlighting cops and firemen. I wanted people working for me who were dependent on me for their living, not people with a city paycheck coming in every week."

"Did you ever raise the money you were looking for?"

"After Milton Tablin turned me down, I decided to forget expanding until I had the money."

"Why not try the banks?"

"And use what for collateral—hookers? Banks don't lend money to madams. Them chauvinistic bastards only launder money for drug dealers."

"What about Walter? His vig is probably the same as the banks'."

"Any businessman who borrows money from them ends up with them not only owning his *kishkas,* but also his soul."

"Do you know Mrs. Gallagher?"

"Never met the lady. All I know about her is that she used to work as a teachers' aide in one of the local junior high schools. That was how she met Gallagher. He went there one day to address the school assembly on the evils of narcotics."

"You must have known Gallagher and Harris pretty well."

"What civilian really knows a cop? Gallagher would drop by every now and then. Sometimes he'd take a fancy to one of the girls." She scowled. "He didn't pay either. Harris? He only came in with Gallagher, never by himself. He was a quiet guy, he always seemed preoccupied. Whenever they were here, Gallagher did all the talking. Once I asked Harris if he had a tongue. Gallagher chimed in that he did the talking for both of them. 'But not the thinking,' Harris barked back. Gallagher got real pissed off at Harris over that remark. And I'll tell you something else—Harris was a cheap bastard. The few times he was in here with Gallagher they'd have drinks at the bar. Once Harris actually paid for their drinks and he consulted a tipping chart to see how much of a tip to leave."

"How come Harold Hunt is your accountant?"

"You know about Harold?" she said, surprised. "I'll tell ya, Joe Gallagher recommended him. Said he owed him a favor, and that he was a right guy and a good accountant. And he was right, Harold is a good accountant. I let him come by every now and then for a free screw. I'll tell you, Scanlon, with all this goodwill I pass out, I don't know how I'm able to make a living."

Scanlon heaved a weary sigh. He had wasted a lot of time and manpower on following Eddie Hamill and Luv-Joy leads. That was one of the painful realities of the Job. You can never tell where an investigative lead is going to take you. Most of them end up dead ends. And then there are those that will break a case wide open. The time had come for him to make amends with Gretta. Hookers are one of a cop's best sources of information. No cop wants to lose that source. A warm smile, a flash of teeth. "Can I buy you a drink?"

She shook her fist at his face. "Sometimes you make me so mad that I want to ram this down that beautiful throat of yours."

He guffawed. "Like I told you before, I have that effect on some people."

"What about the money you found in Gallagher's car? My money?"

"I'll see to it that you get it back."

"And you're going to buy me a drink? Here and now?"

"It'll be my pleasure."

"This I gotta see. A cop putting his hands into his own pockets for a change." She motioned wildly for the black waitress. "Siobbhan, a bottle of champagne. And give the bill to my friend here."

Yorkville had changed. The Von Westernvogen Brau Hall no longer existed. The slinking German spies of the forties had been relegated to the pages of pulp fiction. It was a little before ten P.M. when Scanlon drove his car into East Eighty-sixth Street. Human hulks slept on cardboard mattresses along the building sides and in doorways. Pimps lurked in the shadows, watching their women prowl their curbside turfs. A drunk·was urinating between parked cars. Café Geiger and Kleine Konditorei were open, well-dressed people inside, savoring German beer and other delicacies.

Sally De Nesto lived in a building with small terraces, a condominium on Eighty-sixth between First and East End Avenue. Scanlon parked on Eighty-sixth Street, off First. He looked at the traffic sign. No Stopping No Standing No Parking 8 A.M. to 6 P.M. No Standing No Stopping 7 P.M. to Midnight. Towaway Zone.

He spent several moments deciphering the sign and decided that it was all right to park. He switched on the car's alarm system, bolted the steering wheel in place, clicked out the radio and tape deck and stashed them under the passenger seat.

A junkie sat in a shoe store's doorway smiling at his precautions. Scanlon saw him and pantomimed a pistol with his fingers and pegged three harmless shots at him. The junkie shrugged his hands slowly and nodded off. Scanlon felt like Charles Bronson. Death Wish One, Two, and Three. Whadda town!

Sally De Nesto greeted him at the door with cheerful enthusiasm, throwing her arms around him, bending her legs up off the floor.

"What got into you?" he exclaimed, bearing her into the apartment, kicking the door shut.

"I'm in a wonderful, upbeat mood, and I'm glad to see you. I like a quiet Saturday night. But not *too* quiet." She slid her hands from around his neck. "May I get you something to drink?"

"No thank you."

"Then in that case, let's you and me get right down to business." She untied the blue terry-cloth robe she was wearing.

A yelping siren pierced the night. The soft hum of an air conditioner added a sense of permanence to the darkened room. They lay on rumpled sheets, she with her head on pillows, her ankles crossed. Both of them were naked, both spent and relaxed, both coming down from a lovemaking high.

"Have you given any thoughts to what we discussed the last time?" she asked softly.

"Jane Stomer and me?"

"Yes."

"Sally, I told you, it's over. There is someone else in her life now."

"Like the man said, Tony, it's not over until it's over."

He glanced sideways at her. "And exactly what the hell does that mean?"

"It means that sometimes scorned women say untruths that they know will hurt, that are intended to hurt."

He flushed. "Jane Stomer isn't that kind of woman."

The darkness hid her smile.

He twisted his torso toward her. "Now I have a question for you."

"What?" she said, measuring the ceiling.

"Why the interest in my personal problems?"

"I'm interested in all my clients," she said defensively.

"But why? Tell me why, Sally."

She turned her head away from him, lapsed into a thoughtful silence. At length, she asked, "Have you ever wondered why I never drink?"

"I never really gave it any thought."

"I'm not allowed to drink because I take phenobarbital. I have epilepsy."

"Oh?" he said, at a loss.

"And did you know that I was once engaged to be married?"

"No, I didn't," he said, sensing a delicate moment.

"I was twenty-two and in love. His name was Carlo. We were going to live in Parsippany and have four children. Two boys and two girls. It was to have been a June wedding. Carlo had his best man deliver his Dear John letter to me three days before the wedding. I still have it. I read it over every now and then. It serves to remind me what the real world is like, if I'm ever tempted to forget."

Scanlon pulled her into his arms. "I'm sorry."

"I had my first seizure three months later. And one year after that I found myself living in Manhattan, alone and very lonely. I knew that with my illness my prospect of finding a husband was practically nil. And having those four children, well, that was just out of the question, wasn't it?

"Anyhow, one night I went to a singles bar. It was there that I met my blind shrink friend. He looked so helpless and alone standing at the bar by himself, shifting his weight from one foot to the other, fiddling around with his clothes, his head sort of lolling to one side, his eyes hidden behind dark glasses. I took one look at him and my heart broke for him. To live alone and in total blackness must be the ultimate loneliness, I thought. So I went up to him and introduced myself. I took him home with me." A wan smile came to her face. "He was the second man that I had gone to bed with. I was practically a virgin."

He pressed her head to his chest.

"In the morning he gave me money and I took it. He'd always paid for it and he didn't think there could be any other way for him. I felt strangely loved and needed. From then on I just sort of wandered into the business. He would send his handicapped patients to me and I would supply them with the therapy they so badly needed." She broke free of his embrace and pushed herself up in the bed, covering herself with a sheet. "My clients love me, Tony. And I love them. We need each other. They've become my extended family, and in a crazy way they have given purpose to my life."

"I guess we all have to play with the hole card that life deals us."

"That's my point, Tony. You don't. You can rid yourself of your handicap. You don't have to spend the rest of your life in the sexual underground."

"You make it sound so damn easy," he said lamely.

"It is, for you. All you have to do is to understand that we're all the products of our upbringing and then look inside yourself and see how your parents and your childhood experiences helped mold your adult life."

"You still haven't told me why the special interest in me."

She picked up his hand. "Because I love you enough to want to see you end your dependency on me. Don't you know that in order to receive love you first have to learn how to give it? When you share your life with someone you share it all, the good and the bad. You can't separate it, Tony. Your refusal to let Jane share your problem shut her out of your life. You isolated yourself from the rest of the world. And then you punished yourself by only being able to get it up with hookers. There is nothing physically wrong with you. If you can do it with me, you can do it with any woman." She screwed a finger into her temple. "It's all up there, kiddo. All you have to do is figure it out."

20

0840 hours. Monday. Eleven days had elapsed since the Gallagher/Zimmerman hit. Scanlon was sitting in the squad room, a scone and a mug of coffee on a brown paper towel atop the desk's slide-out board. Hector Colon was sweeping out the Whip's office with a long-handled broom. It was his turn to do the morning housekeeping chores. Lew Brodie had taken the call from Christopher and Biafra Baby. They had reported on duty from the field. Brodie had made a Telephone Message and was now making a Log entry: "0800—Dets. Jones and Christopher reported on duty from the field. Re: canvass theatrical makeup stores—UF 61 # 6794."

Three prisoners from the late tour were asleep on the floor of the detention cage. Their arresting officer, a cop with an altar boy's face, dozed in a chair awaiting the van that would transport them to Central Booking.

Maggie Higgins stood by the window, looking out at the sky.

Scanlon glanced over at her and noticed her forlorn look. He picked up his mug, got up, and ambled over to the urn. Bending to work the spigot, he said, "How's everything?"

When she turned to look at him he saw her red-rimmed eyes. "Gloria and I are not going to make it living together." Her voice cracked. "The Job gets in the way."

He nodded and went back to the desk.

"*Teniente*, you got a call on four," Colon shouted from the Whip's office.

Herman the German sounded as though he were champing on a mouthful of Wiener Schnitzel. "I flew Harris on another detail."

"Thanks, Inspector," Scanlon said. "I'll keep you advised." He plunged down the disconnect button with his finger and made another hang-up call to Mrs. Gallagher. Lew Brodie came up to him and wanted to know if he still wanted him to plant on Linda Zimmerman. Scanlon told him he did. Brodie signed himself out in the Log: "0910 —Det. Brodie to surveillance, Sutton Place area re: UF 61 # 6794." The van came to transport the prisoners and the arresting officer to Central Booking.

Realizing that they were at a dead end until he heard from Christopher and Biafra Baby, Scanlon telephoned his mother and promised he would try to make it to her house for Sunday dinner.

"I'll make lasagna," she promised.

Higgins began work on another term paper: "The Weaknesses of Line Inspection."

Hector Colon telephoned his girlfriend.

Scanlon remained in his office wrapped in his own thoughts. Flying Harris should unnerve him. Narcotics supervisors were seldom forced to put on the bag and flown out of their commands on uniform details. It shouldn't take Harris long to realize he was on somebody's shit list. And if he was guilty, he'd start to wonder where he made a mistake. And that was when he would become careless and do something dumb, Scanlon hoped.

Hanging up the phone, Hector Colon glanced around the squad room in search of mischief. He grabbed up the telephone and dialed Patrol Borough Brooklyn North, Uniform Force. "This is Inspector Suckieluski from the chief of patrol's office," he barked. "The chief wants the name and shield number of your borough AIDS coordinator." Pause. A mischievous grin came over his face. "Whaddaya mean you don't know? Don't you people in Brooklyn read the orders?" Pause.

Higgins turned in her seat and tossed a handful of paper clips at Colon.

Colon covered the mouthpiece and mouthed "screw you" to her. "Interim Order 8, current series, requires every borough commander to designate a borough AIDS coordinator. Well, you better. Have that Forty-nine on my desk by fifteen hundred today." He hung up the phone.

Higgins turned around in her seat, one arm hooked over the back of her chair. "Don't you think you're the funny one. Don't you know that cockroaches spread AIDS?"

Colon raised himself up out of his seat and lifted and shook his testes at her. "Wanna get into a dwarf-growing experiment with me?"

"Don't look now, Hector, but there's a nest in your brain."

*   *   *

The telephone message had read: "On Monday 6/29/86 at 0750 hours report to Captain Kuhn in front of the Soviet Mission to the United Nations on East 67th Street between Lexington and Third avenues in connection with demonstration to free Soviet Jewry. Uniform of the day, helmets and batons."

St. George Harris felt uncomfortable in the bag. He hated having to work in uniform. He was standing in front of the Soviet Mission along with the ten men who had been assigned to him, filling in their names, their shield numbers, their commands, and their present assignments on the UF 30, Detail Roster Assignment Sheet.

Completing the form, he thought briefly about how the Job had divided department forms according to the various branches of the Job. UF forms were for the Uniform Force. DD forms were for the Detective Division. He was a DD man. So what the hell was he doing in the bag, standing in front of this damn Commie mission, looking into the faces of ten asshole cops who were all trying to estimate just how much they would be able to get away with, and looking to get lost on him the minute he turned his back. He had flown two of his last three tours. Someone had a hard-on for him. Who? And more important, why? Herman the German? He didn't think so. He had seen the inspector this morning when he stopped by the One-fourteen to pick up his uniform and equipment. The inspector had smiled and waved at him. Scanlon? Maybe that pegleg guinea had gotten wise? Naw. He dismissed that thought. Don't get stupid because of a few details, he warned himself.

Harris became conscious of the noise made by the demonstrators. A circle of jeering people, most of whom were carrying anti-Soviet placards, were marching behind police barricades on the east side of Lexington Avenue. Mounted policemen faced the demonstrators, the horses reined in tight.

His eyes slid over the faces of the ten cops lined up in front of him. Might as well let them know up front who the boss is, he thought. "Our post is the second line of barricades in the middle of the intersection on Lexington Avenue. No one gets past us, understand. I'm gonna be around, so make damn sure you're all out. I don't intend to go looking for anyone. If you're not out, I'll stick one up your ass. Any questions?"

A hairbag with tomato sauce on his shirt said, "You didn't assign us meals, Sarge."

"I'll do that later. Now take your posts."

Harris turned the Detail Roster in to the clerical man inside the mobile headquarters van that was parked across the street from the Soviet Mission. He wished he could get rid of the tremor of uneasiness in the pit of his stomach. I have to stay calm, he told himself, going to join his men on the barricade.

"*Abb-sah-loo-tah-mehn-teh nada,*" Biafra Baby complained, slumping into a chair in the Whip's office. "It took us three days to canvass every damn makeup store in the city and we came up dry."

"Sorry, Lieutenant," Christopher said. "We gave it our best shot."

Taking in the brass buttons on Christopher's sky-blue jacket, trying to hide his disappointment, Scanlon said, "I know you did."

"Where do we go from here?" Higgins asked Scanlon.

Scanlon checked the time: 1640 hours. "We call it a day, Maggie."

The detectives slowly left for home, except Hector Colon, who lingered behind in the squad room. When Scanlon had finished signing a Five Colon walked into his office and said, "Lou, I got a problem."

"Let's hear it," Scanlon said.

"It's my girlfriend. I promised her a couple of months ago that I'd take her to an engagement party. It's tomorrow night. I put in a Twenty-eight a few weeks ago and you signed it."

Scanlon reached into one of the side drawers and took out the Squad's Diary. He flipped the pages to tomorrow's date and saw that Colon had taken three hours off at the end of his tour. "You got the time. What's the problem?"

"Well, with this Gallagher thing going down you might need me. I don't wanna leave you short-handed, so if you want, I'll pull the Twenty-eight."

Scanlon returned the Diary to the drawer. "Go to the party, Hector. We'll hold it down. Wouldn't want you to disappoint your lady love." Scanlon's expression did not betray his thoughts. A detective should know where his loyalty lay; if he didn't, then he would have to learn the hard way.

It was after 1900 when Lew Brodie ambled back into the squad room, slightly tipsy. "I might have somethin', Lou."

Scanlon was powdering his stump. "What?" he said, wondering what bar the detective had spent the past hour in.

"Around thirteen-thirty today Linda Zimmerman comes out of her aunt's apartment house and walks west on Fifty-first Street. I followed on foot. I trailed her to the Chemical Bank on Five-one and Third. She was inside for a long time, so I moseyed in for a look-see. I didn't see her, so I figured she was downstairs in the safety deposit boxes. Sure enough, after about ten minutes more she comes trudging up the stairs like an old lady and leaves the bank. I let her go, then hauled ass downstairs. Turns out that the guy who runs the vault room is retired from the Job. He let me sneak a look at her card. She rented the box on June 20 of this year, one day after her mother was killed. And, I'm willing to bet you, right after she cleaned out her mother's apartment. The vault guy told me that she comes there a lot and that she stays in the room with her box for long periods of time. Once she was inside for so long that he thought something had happened to her, so he went over to the door and listened. He could hear her talking to someone, like she was making a tape or something."

Scanlon rolled on his stump sock, leaned back in his seat, and slid his stump into the socket of his prosthesis. "I'd love to get a look inside that safety deposit box," he said, pushing his pants leg down.

"Yeah, but how? We'd need a search warrant, and we don't have any grounds to apply for one."

"Stay with her, Lew. Let me know the next time she goes there."

"You got it," Brodie said, leaving for the local watering hole.

It was a little past 2000 hours when Scanlon looked up from the report he was writing and saw George Harris standing in the doorway, watching him. The sergeant's head was cocked to the side, and he wore jeans, a blue work shirt, and cowboy boots.

I smoked the bastard out, Scanlon thought. "Long time no see, Sarge."

"I thought I'd catch you in," Harris said, moving to a chair in front of the desk. "You busy?"

"I'm plagiarizing the parameters of my semiannual Management by Objectives report from last year's plagiarized parameters." He leaned back, studying his visitor. "I reached the conclusion a long time ago that the Job is one big word blender. We keep throwing in the same words, mixing them up until they're a mix of polysyllabic bullshit."

"Ain't that the truth," Harris agreed, planting one boot firmly up against the front of the desk and leaning his chair back onto its hind legs.

Picking up the dictionary on his desk, Scanlon said, "A little game that I play with the pencil pushers in the big building. I always include a highfalutin word in the reports that I send downtown and then sit back and wait to see how long it takes some pencil pusher to steal it. Last year's word was 'tableau.' It took them exactly three weeks to put 'tableau' in a department bulletin."

"What's the new word?" Harris asked, examining the tip of his boot.

" 'Affranchise,' " Scanlon said. "Every member of the force has an obligation to affranchise the department from the evil influences of greed and corruption."

Harris's face remained blank. "Do the pencil pushers always steal your fancy words?"

"Yeah. Some people you can count on to always act the same way. Don't you agree?"

Harris's right eye twitched. "Maybe, I don't know. How's the case coming?"

"It ain't. I've got the feeling that it's going to end up collecting dust in the old record room."

"You've come up with nothing?"

"Not a helluva lot, I'm afraid."

"Did you make any tie-in with the Zimmerman hits?"

"The Nineteenth came up with a witness who saw the perp fleeing the scene."

Harris flopped his foot off the desk. "They got a good description?"

"Good enough to have a composite made." Scanlon leaned forward and took his time rummaging in the case folder. "Here it is." He pulled out the glossy black-and-white sketch. He examined the composite and then glanced from the sketch to Harris. He flattened his palm across the mouth of the man in the sketch, looked at Harris again, and said, "You know, Sarge, take off this guy's mustache and he'd be a dead ringer for you."

"Lemme see," Harris said, reaching across the desk. After scrutinizing the composite for several minutes, he tossed it back. "I guess you could say that he looks a little bit like me."

Scanlon took note of the twitch in Harris's eyes. "Tell me, Sarge, do you know anyone who owns a Browning automatic shotgun, Sweet Sixteen model?"

Harris rubbed his chin in concentration. "No, I can't say that I do. Why?"

"The ballistics boys think that was the weapon that was used to take Gallagher out."

"Are you checking the dealers?"

"There are too many of them. Besides, all anyone needs to buy a rifle or a shotgun is a forged or stolen driver's license. And the weapons were more than likely purchased out of state."

"Weapons?"

"The way I figure it, the same people took out Gallagher and the Zimmermans. A 5.56mm was used on the doctor and his wife. An assassin's rifle, capable of being broken down and assembled in a matter of a few minutes."

"What makes you so sure that the rifle was capable of being broken down?"

"Because the witness who saw the perp fleeing the Kingsley Arms stated that he was carrying an attaché case. What do you think the perp had in that case, gefilte fish?" He measured Harris. "How's Mrs. Gallagher?"

"All right, Lou. It takes time, but she's going to be fine."

"Did she return the children?"

"Yeah, she did. That was tough on her. But she decided that it was the best thing for them."

"Sounds like a strong-willed woman to me."

"She is that."

Scanlon placed his elbows on the desk and held his palms skyward. "Any chance she was stepping out on her husband?"

"No way. You asked me that once before—what made you ask again?"

Scanlon shrugged. "There is something about the lady that makes my stump itch."

"I hate to say it, Lou, but maybe you need a bath."

"You just might be right, Sarge," Scanlon said, getting up and going out into the squad room to sign out.

Harris accompanied him downstairs. Scanlon waved to the desk officer and he and Harris left the station house. A distant clap of thunder caught their attention. A radio car jerked to a stop at the curb, and both the driver and the recorder leaped out, slamming their respective doors. These were two pissed-off cops, Scanlon thought, watching the driver pull open the rear curb-side door to reveal a handcuffed man sprawled over the seat. The driver leaned into the car to take hold of the prisoner. The trussed-up man kicked out at the cop. The officer leaped back, out of the way of the thrashing feet.

The recorder of the radio car, a heavyset black cop with short gray hair, pushed his white partner aside, yanked the blackjack from its pocket in his trousers, and proceeded to beat the prisoner on the soles of his shoes. "You wanna kick a cop, haw, scumbag?"

"No more! No more!" begged the prisoner, pulling his feet away from the blackjack.

The cops dragged the man out of the car and stood him upright on the sidewalk. They took turns pushing and shoving the prisoner toward the station house. Scanlon stepped ahead of the prisoner and opened the station-house door. The black cop gave a final shove and the prisoner toppled onto the vestibule floor.

"These fucking polacks can't hold their firewater," the black cop groused, walking past the lieutenant.

"How're you getting along with Gallagher's replacement?" Scanlon asked, walking with Harris.

"I hardly see him. I came back off emergency leave and I've flown two out of my last three tours."

"There are a lot of details this time of the year—what with vacations and military leaves, there's always a shortage of bosses during the summer."

"I know that, Lou. But bosses in the junk squad never fly. Well, almost never."

Scanlon unlocked his car door and slid inside. "Maybe someone is mad at you?"

"I can't figure out why."

"If anything develops, I'll get in touch with you."

Harris nudged the car door closed and watched Scanlon bend forward to insert the key into the ignition.

Mary Ann Gallagher wore a widow's dress with black cloth buttons down the front. Around her neck hung a crucifix on a thin gold chain. She had no makeup on. On her left wrist she wore a watch with a gold link bracelet. She stood in the doorway of her Anthony Street apartment on the western edge of Maspeth Creek in Greenpoint, her anxious eyes sweeping the hallway over George Harris's shoulder. "Hello, George."

"How do you feel, Mary Ann?" Harris asked, stepping inside.

"Thank God, I'm coming along," she said, closing the door and resting her back against the portal.

Harris moved a short distance into the apartment and turned. "Are we alone?"

"The last of the biddies left a few minutes ago. But they could be back anytime."

He held out his arms, and she moved easily into his embrace, biting his shoulder right through his shirt, pressing into his body.

"I need to be inside you," he said.

"And I want you there. But first we have to talk." Taking hold of his hand, she pulled him into the bedroom and over to the bed, where they sat facing each other. "What's going on, George? I have this awful feeling that everything is about to fall apart."

"They have a witness who saw me running from the Kingsley Arms. They've made up a composite."

Her blue eyes blazed with anger, and she froze. "Does it look like you?"

"Without the mustache, yes. But the composite by itself doesn't mean a thing."

"Do you think that they're on to us?"

"No. None of them are smart enough to put it all together." He took out his pack of cigarettes, shook out a clipper, and lit it.

She fought to keep an expression of annoyance off her face. His cheapness, with cigarettes and everything else, disgusted her. He was really another version of Gallagher; like any cop he took everything he could get for free, and his idea of a present was some lousy blender that he had pried out of some merchant or a bottle of perfume that some bookmaker had given him. She fleetingly thought of the single airline ticket hidden in her hat box. Concorde to London. That was the way she was going to live. "Did you get rid of the guns and the rest of the stuff?"

"There hasn't been enough time to do it right. But don't worry. They're in a safe place where nobody is going to find them."

"Safe place, bullshit, George! I told you to get rid of them a week ago."

"I love you, Mary Ann, and I don't like it when you yell at me."

"You'll like it less if Scanlon gets wise to us."

"That dumb guinea can only think in guinea. He's no threat."

"Your dumb guinea didn't strike me as being so dumb. What about those assignments you've been getting?"

"Mary Ann, if they thought for one minute that I was responsible they'd be all over me, and I can assure you, they'd do a lot more than fly me on a few details." He stretched out over the bed and rested his head on her lap. She began to rub his forehead.

"You realize that you almost blew the whole thing by calling out 'Hey you,' " he said.

She bent down and kissed his nose. "I'm sorry, darling. I just couldn't control myself. I wanted him to look into my eyes and see who was sending him to hell. That man kept me like a fucking slave for years. I hated him and I'm glad he's dead, that miserable son of a bitch."

"You should have done what you came to do and left without saying a word, like we planned. It was supposed to look like an attempted robbery."

"I know," she snapped. "Just don't keep harping on it. I said I was sorry."

"But because of that one mistake Scanlon realized that it was a hit and not a robbery attempt. And it would only have been a matter of time until someone thought of the money you were entitled to as Joe's widow. And that's a powerful motive. So because of you I had to run out and do the Zimmermans to throw them off the track, keep them confused. I didn't exactly enjoy doing that, Mary Ann."

"But you did it."

"Yes, I did it. I did it because I love you, because I want to have a wonderful life with you, free of any money troubles."

"I know you love me, George. And I love you too." She stopped massaging his head. "I haven't been laid in days."

"I'm really not in the mood anymore. Let me relax a little bit, first."

"I want it now, George," she said, reaching under her dress and pulling off her underpants and stuffing them under the pillow. "Here, let me get you in the mood." She reached down and, opening the top of his jeans, pushed his pants down, exposing him. She went down on him and ravenously sucked him hard. She flung herself across the bed, tossed up her dress, and gasped as he entered her body.

When she had slaked her thirst for him, she rested her head on a pillow and said, "I haven't been that horny in ages. I can relax now."

He lay next to her. "I love you very much, Mary Ann."

"And I love you, George."

"It's funny how Gallagher threw us together." Harris scowled. "It was a mutual hate society."

"If only they'd known what holy Joe was like at home."

"He used to love to put me down in front of the men. He'd countermand my orders just to make me look like a nincompoop."

"I know, darling, I know," she said, leaning over to kiss his cheek. "Let's not talk about him anymore." In a burst of gaiety, she said, "I got a check from the Lieutenants' Benevolent Association for five thousand dollars."

"That's only the beginning, my love."

"Tell me again how much."

"Close to a million dollars, practically tax-free."

"A million dollars? I can't even begin to think in those sums."

"Well, you'd better get used to thinking in those sums, because we're going to be rich."

She glanced at his contented face, a disingenuous smile pinching her mouth. "Yes, darling, we are going to be rich." She sat up on the bed, and her fingers rubbed his forehead soothingly. "Do you think anyone suspects that we're more than friends?"

"Naw, no one thinks of us in those terms. You're a God-fearing grieving Irish widow who thinks sex is unholy, and I'm your husband's friend. Besides, I got a girlfriend. Luise Bardwell. It's perfect."

"But you're not seeing her anymore?"

"Shit no. She served her purpose. The main thing was for Scanlon and the rest of those assholes not to connect us."

"Do you know when I first felt close to you?"

"No. But I do remember that we used to talk for hours while Joe was out doing his thing."

"It was when you first confided to me that you had never . . . you know, gone down on a woman."

He reached up and brushed the back of his hand across her warm cheek. "I remember that night."

Her voice dropped. "Did you ever do that to Luise Bardwell?"

"No, Mary Ann, I didn't. You're the only woman I've ever done that with."

"Do you enjoy doing that with me?"

A throatiness came into his voice. "I love it."

"Would you like to do it to me now?" she cooed, bending and kissing his neck. "I have all your love inside me and I'm all warm and juicy."

He pressed her face to him. "Yes."

She pushed back from him, letting his head slide off her lap. She lifted up her dress and, inching forward, straddled his face.

The prosthesis stood on the floor beside Sally De Nesto's bed. He had been watching it for the better part of one hour, once again going over his past. If he had not lost his leg, would he still have developed erectile dysfunction somewhere down the line? Why was sex so damn complicated? It had more wrinkles than the Job.

"Can't you sleep?"

He looked down at her curled-up form. "Just thinking."

"Would you like to make love?"

"I'm really not in the mood."

She sat up, hoisting the sheet across her chest. "What's the matter, Tony?"

"I'm not my own man anymore. I'm dependent on that hunk of fiberglass for mobility and on you for sex."

"Am I so terrible?"

"Terrible? You're far from terrible. You're a kind, considerate woman."

"But?"

"I need more. I need someone to love, share my life with, grow old with."

She looked down at her knees, just shapes under a sheet. "We all want to be loved, Tony. But we have to settle for what we can get. Some people get their love from pets. I've found mine with handicapped people who need me." She leaned her head against his shoulder. "If I were you, I'd go after Jane Stomer. Pretend like you've just met her. Women like to be pursued. Take my word for it. Send her flowers. Every woman loves flowers."

"I had an erotic dream about Jane. It was so real that I can remember asking myself if I was dreaming or awake. And I can remember deciding that it was real, that it was actually happening. I soiled the sheets."

"Perhaps that's a good sign. You might be getting a handle on your problem."

"Then why do I feel so lousy?"

"You gotta feel lousy before you feel better. I don't know why things are that way, but they are."

"I've also come to realize just how dependent I've become on you. It's as though I need you to give me a fix that will restore my self-confidence as a man, and enable me to get through the day."

"Everyone needs a friend now and then." She slid her hand across his chest, hugging him.

"It's time for me to start standing on my own two feet without any help. I have to try and get my act together. Can you understand that, Sally?"

"Yes I can. And I want you to know that I'll always be here for you if you need me." She hugged him. "I want to make love to you, Tony."

"I'm really not in the mood."

She worked her hand down under the sheet. "Let me see what I can do about that."

21

A warm, pleasant breeze laced with summer scents flowed through the open windows of the Nine-three Squad. The detectives went about their morning routines, checking their pigeonholes for department mail, notifications, subpoenas, love letters. Lew Brodie had called in from the field. He was on his way to plant on Linda Zimmerman's aunt's house on Sutton Place South.

Higgins had swept out the squad room this Tuesday morning and was leaning on a broom handle, staring thoughtfully at the row of file cabinets. She leaned the broom against the side of a desk and moved up to the Vulva File. She took out a Twenty-eight and filled in the pedigree information at the top of the Request for Leave of Absence form, leaving the space for the date and time of absence blank. She signed the form and took out the Vulva File, a number two department ledger. She flipped it open and wrote Valerie Clarkson's name, address, and telephone number on the next unused line. She placed the Twenty-eight between the pages along with the rest of the unused forms and closed the book.

Turning away from the file, she saw Scanlon watching her. "There are eight million stories in the naked city, Lou."

"Ain't that the truth," Scanlon said, tossing his report into the basket for the department mail.

Howard Christopher sat off in the corner watching "The Morning Show" on television, a mug of cinnamon tea resting on his knee. Scanlon noticed that Biafra Baby was among the missing. He asked Christopher if he had heard from him. "He's on the way in, Lieutenant. He called a few minutes ago to say that he'd be late. He had to drive his daughter to her ballet lesson."

Scanlon received several telephone calls. The first was from Herman the German, who wanted to know if Scanlon wanted him to continue flying Harris. Scanlon told him that he did. The CofD wanted to know if there had been any new developments. Scanlon told him that there hadn't been, and the CofD reminded him of the PC's warning not to move on Harris or Mrs. Gallagher without some physical evidence to substantiate the allegations. MacAdoo McKenzie called next and wanted to know if anything new had been developed. The last call was from Jack Fable. When Scanlon told him that there was nothing new to report, Fable told him that his detectives had developed several leads on the necrophiliac who had been using the Nineteenth as his playpen.

"An arrest is imminent," Fable said mockingly.

Scanlon hung up. He thought of Sally De Nesto's advice to court Jane Stomer and send her flowers. He picked up the telephone and dialed Frank Randazzo, a florist at the north end of the precinct. He took care of the precinct's floral needs. When Randazzo came onto the line, Scanlon said, "*Ciao, Frank, sono Tony Scanlon del novantatreesimo squadrone; come stai? E la famiglia, tutti bene? Per favore, Frank, mada una dozzina di rose rosse alla Signorina Jane Stomer all'ufficio del Procuratore Generale a 100 Center Street al palazzo del Tribunale, firma il biglietto 'Con Amore, Scanlon,' e mandami il conto qua al mio ufficio. Grazie, Frank, a Ciao.*"

Scanlon hung up and saw Biafra Baby standing in the doorway watching him. The detective strutted up to the desk. "I think that I might have something."

"Let's hear it."

"My wife is a big believer in all that family togetherness bullshit and likes to keep a running dialogue going around the dinner table. Last night as I was scooping up some mashed potatoes and telling them about how me and Christopher canvassed all them makeup stores with negative results, my wife stops cutting her lamb chop, looks me in the eye, and says as calm as shit, 'Try Bob Brown on West Forty-ninth Street.'"

"Who is Bob Brown?"

"He runs a theatrical mail-order house that sells makeup and rents stage props to theaters and schools."

"Wasn't he on the list of makeup stores that I gave you?"

"Negative. Brown isn't listed in the Yellow Pages under Theatrical Makeup. He's listed under Cosmetics and Wigs."

Scanlon slapped the side of his head.

Biafra Baby continued, "My wife is a schoolteacher. That's how she knew about Brown. Her school gets their stage props from Brown." He patted down his hair. "Then I remembered that you had told me that Gretta Polchinski had told you that Mrs. Gallagher had once been a teacher's aide. So after I dropped my daughter off at her ballet lesson, I telephoned Brown."

"And?"

"He be's waiting for us."

Scanlon lurched out from behind his desk. The phone on his desk rang. He looked at it, hesitated, and snapped it up.

"This is Thomas Tibbs, the man who saw the killer running from the candy store."

You're also the married banker from Scarsdale who is making it with Sigrid Thorsen, Scanlon thought. "I know who you are, Mr. Tibbs."

"Lieutenant, do you remember when I told you that there was something strange about the way the killer ran to the van? And I couldn't put my finger on exactly what it was."

"I remember."

"I now know what it was that bothered me. On last night's eleven-o'clock news they had a clip on the cross-county marathon in West-chester County. It came to me as I watched the runners."

"What came to you, Mr. Tibbs?" Scanlon said, motioning to Biafra Baby to take the keys for the Squad's car off the hook.

"I realized that women run differently than men. They keep their arms tucked into their sides, and their torsos have a distinctive sway when they run. The person I saw running from that candy store might have looked like a man, but he ran like a woman."

Scanlon thanked the witness for taking the time to call. He pulled over the case folder, wrote the time and date on the inside flap, and added, "Thomas Tibbs called to state that perp who he observed run-ning from scene ran with a female gait." He slapped the folder closed and left the squad room with Biafra Baby.

The glass sign on the door read: Bob Brown Wigs and Cosmetics.

The detectives stepped into a long narrow corridor. The wall on their left was covered with autographed photos of show-business per-sonalities wearing makeup. To their right was a counter that looked out into a work area where several women sat weaving wigs. In the rear of the work area were portable storage racks with rows of wigs set on head mannequins.

Bob Brown was a gaunt man with a flat nose and a receding hairline. "You the police detective who called?" Brown said, coming up to the counter.

Biafra Baby flashed his shield. "I called you. This is Lieutenant Scanlon."

Brown leaned out over the counter and pointed to a door about six feet away. "I'll buzz you in."

The three men sat among the wigmakers. "What can I do for you?" Brown asked.

Scanlon was fascinated by the dexterity of the wigmakers' hands. "We'd like to ask you a few questions concerning your business."

"What sort of questions?" Brown asked, taking up a wig and pushing a long hooked needle through it.

"How do you get your customers?" Scanlon inquired.

"We're well known in theatrical and educational circles. Most of our business is done by mail."

"Do you get many walk-ins?" Scanlon asked.

"A few," Brown said, pushing the needle through the skin. "But most of our customers order from our catalog."

"Then you must maintain a file on your customers," Scanlon said.

"Of course," Brown said. "That's how we know who to send our catalog to."

"Could someone call you up and ask you to mail them makeup?" Scanlon asked.

"Sure," Brown answered, "but they'd have to know what they wanted, and they'd have to send payment before we'd send out the merchandise, unless they were a regular customer."

"Don't you bill most of your customers?" Biafra Baby asked.

"Only the schools, theaters, and individuals with whom we've dealt with before." Brown stopped working and looked at the policemen. "Look, gentlemen, I've got a lot to do, so why not tell me what you want?"

Scanlon said, "We'd like to take a look at your orders for the past few years."

"Why?" Brown asked, picking up the needle and threading it with hair.

"It has to do with a case we're working on," Biafra Baby said.

"I would not want my company to become mixed up in a civil suit because I gave information to the police."

"Mr. Brown," Scanlon said, putting on his serious face, "we're working on a case of child molestation where the perpetrator dons makeup to change his appearance and then forces children to commit unnatural acts. We'd really appreciate your help."

"How disgusting," Brown said, putting down the wig and needle. "Of course I'll help."

They followed Brown through a labyrinth of storage racks containing cartons of makeup. Scanlon noticed some of the labels: Crepe Wool. Rubber Mask Grease. Creme Highlight. Shadow Colors.

Brown led the detectives across the concrete floor to his office, which consisted of two old desks fitted side by side into an alcove in the wall. He opened the bottom drawer of one of the desks and took out five bulging manila folders. He plopped them down. "Help yourself," Brown said. "These are the individual orders for the past two years. If you don't find what you want there, I'll show you the institutional orders." He left the detectives and returned to his wigmaking.

The detectives set about separating the order forms in each folder into stacks. Slowly, meticulously, they went about scrutinizing each form. They had been at it for about thirty minutes when Biafra Baby snatched a form up from one of his stacks, studying it. "Lou, does 34-16 Astoria Boulevard sound familiar to you?"

Scanlon repeated the address aloud. The detectives looked at each other. "The One-fourteen," Scanlon blurted.

The order form had been typed. A Mr. Raymond Gilligan had ordered crepe wool, medium-gray beard stubble, adhesive stick, hair whiteners, latex, cosmetic pencils, nose putty, rubber mask grease, molding putty, and spirit gum. He had also ordered a man's wig and a walrus mustache.

Scanlon hastily signaled for Brown to join them.

"What can you tell me about this order?" Scanlon asked Brown.

The makeup man took the order form and looked it over. "Mr. Gilligan obviously wanted to make himself appear older," Brown said, handing Scanlon back the form.

"Do you have any recollection of filling this order?" Scanlon asked.

"None whatever," Brown said. "We fill hundreds of orders a month."

"What is crepe wool?" Biafra Baby said.

Brown went up to one of the storage cartons and took out a package of crepe wool. It looked like sticks of licorice. He removed the wool from its cellophane wrapping and began unraveling the fibers, spreading them apart. The wool began to curl and resemble beard hair. "It's used to make beards and mustaches." He strung the fiber over his clean-shaven face. "See, now I have a beard. It's applied with spirit gum."

"How would a person not in the business find out what to order and how to apply makeup?" Scanlon asked.

"There are a lot of books on the subject," Brown said. "In fact, I've written a few myself."

Biafra Baby pointed to the order form in Scanlon's hand. "All that makeup is used to make a person look older?"

"Most of it." Brown spread his hands. "I mean, some of that stuff has several uses."

"May we borrow this form, Mr. Brown?" Scanlon said. "It might aid us in our search for this pervert."

"Take it with you. I'm glad to help."

Scanlon went up to the packing table and tore a sheet of wrapping paper from the roller and wrapped the order form in paper. He turned to Brown. "One more favor. May I use your phone?"

The clerical man at the One-fourteen remembered Ray Gilligan. He had worked sector Henry Ida for sixteen years until he developed the Big C four years ago, the clerical man told Scanlon. "Ray went out of the picture three years ago."

Every patrol precinct in the city maintains mailboxes for its cops. Pigeonholes with three or four letters of the alphabet stapled under each hole. It would have been an easy matter for Harris to have sent the order form in the name of Raymond Gilligan and then to check the G mail slot daily for the package, Scanlon knew. He turned to the makeup man. "Can you tell me how this order was paid for?"

Brown removed an accounting ledger from the desk and flipped clumps of pages until he came to the page he wanted. He moved his finger down a column of names, came to Gilligan, slid his finger over to the numbered column, and said, "A bank money order. And there is no way I can tell you the name of the bank."

The Latent Section of the NYPD is located in Room 506 of the big building. Before going there Scanlon and Biafra Baby stopped off on the thirteenth floor to see the CofD. Scanlon asked Chief Goldberg to make a personal call to the CO of the Identification Section, of which the Latent Section was a part, and request the CO of Identification to render all possible assistance to Scanlon and Biafra Baby, who were conducting a confidential investigation under the personal control and supervision of the CofD.

Chief of Detectives Goldberg chewed on his cigar, grabbed up the phone, and, when he got connected, barked, "Harry, I'm sending two of my people around to see you. Do whatever the fuck they ask you to do, and keep your mouth shut about it, or I'll personally stick one up your ass."

Riding down in the elevator, Biafra Baby nudged Scanlon. "Goldberg's a class act."

"He's certainly a hard one to follow," Scanlon said.

The CO of the ID Section was waiting for them when they stepped off the elevator. He led them into the Latent Section, assigned a man to help them, and excused himself because he had a lot of work waiting for him. The fingerprint man who had been assigned to them had green eyes and appeared nervous.

"This is a confidential investigation," Scanlon said. "If word leaks out, the PC and the CofD are both going to be highly pissed off at you."

"Don't worry, Lou. I don't feature being flopped back into the bag. I like working days with weekends off."

"Then we understand each other," Scanlon said.

Scanlon had the fingerprint man check the name index for George Harris's fingerprint formula. Armed with the filing code, the fingerprint man was able to pull Harris's fingerprint chart from the million-plus on file. Scanlon signed the card out of file with a confidential index number. Next the fingerprint man checked the criminal and civilian name file for Mary Ann Gallagher. The dead lieutenant's widow had no record with the NYPD.

When they reached Room 506 the fingerprint man unwrapped the package that Scanlon had handed him and removed the order form with tweezers. "You're interested in knowing if Harris's prints are on this form, right?" asked the fingerprint man.

"Correct." Scanlon turned to Biafra Baby. "Better call the Squad and let them know where we are."

Biafra Baby nodded and moved off.

The fingerprint man went up to a dollhouselike contraption with an open front that sat on top of one of the workbenches. He fastened one end of the order form to one of the three clothespins that hung from the house's ceiling. He attached the other two pins to the order form. He took a tiny dish that resembled a Chinese duck-sauce bowl and dumped crystalline iodine into it. He put the dish inside the house, directly under the hanging order form. "The iodine fumes will bring out any latents," the fingerprint man said. Scanlon watched as the orange outlines began to appear: loops, arches, central pocket loops, whorls.

"All the lines are busy," Biafra Baby called over to Scanlon.

"Keep trying," Scanlon called back.

The fingerprint man unfastened the order form and placed it down on a glass plate that lay on the workbench next to the dollhouse. He picked up a second glass plate and covered the first, then sealed the edges with rubber-tipped clips.

"Why the glass plates?" Scanlon asked.

"It preserves the latents. We can also photograph them, and if we have to, at some later date, we can present them in court." He looked at Scanlon, a smug smile on his lips. "The Best Evidence Rule, Lou. Remember? Present the original trace evidence before the court."

Leaning over the plates, the fingerprint man glided his magnifying glass on a stand over the glass, examining the impressions through the eyepiece.

"I told Higgins where we are," Biafra Baby said, returning.

"Got a lot of prints here, Lou," the fingerprint man said. "And from the diversity of pattern types I'd say that many different people have handled this piece of paper."

"For now, I'm only interested in Harris," Scanlon said. "By the way, who maintains the Typewriter File these days?"

The NYPD files sample type of every typewriter that is used in the department. Each letter and character has individual characteristics that can be positively identified as belonging to a specific typewriter.

Without looking up from the linen tester, the fingerprint man said, "We maintain it."

"I'd like the type on that order form checked against the Typewriter File," Scanlon said.

"No problem, Lou," replied the fingerprint man.

A voice called out, "Is there a Lieutenant Scanlon here?"

The bank was nestled on the ground floor of a high-rise apartment building.

Lew Brodie was waiting in the corridor outside the vault room. "She's been inside for almost a half hour," Brodie said to the approaching lieutenant.

"I left Biafra Baby at the Latent Section and got here as fast as I could," Scanlon said. He looked through the security glass into the vault room. "How many people are in there?"

"We got lucky," Brodie said. "Zimmerman and the vault man. Some old guy just left."

"Let's get in there now," Scanlon said. "I want to see what she has in that box."

"Lou," Brodie said, taking the Whip by the arm, "you sure you wanna go in after her? We don't have a search warrant, and she ain't no bimbo."

"We don't have one shred of evidence, not against Harris, not against Mrs. Gallagher, not against anyone. We have a suspicion that Harris and Gallagher might be the perps, but I could be wrong about them. And then where do we go? Linda Zimmerman cleaned out her mother's apartment the day after she was killed. She rented a safety deposit box the same day. She could very well be involved in the murders."

Lew Brodie motioned for the vault man to open the door. The

retired cop, a big man with a sagging neck and a pallid complexion, opened the door. "I don't want any trouble," he said to Brodie.

Placing a calming hand on the vault man's shoulder, Brodie said, "Ain't gonna be no trouble."

Scanlon looked around the vault room, his gaze coming to rest on the huge stainless-steel door. "What room is she in?" he asked the vault man.

"Number four," answered the retired cop. "No trouble, right? I'm a little nervous. I'd forgotten what it's like to be in the Job."

Scanlon motioned to Brodie and the vault man to remain where they were, and padded over to cubicle four. He listened at the door. He heard muffled sounds, and strained in vain to make out the intelligible words. Should he barge in on her, or should he wait for her to leave? He never felt any hesitation when he had to lean on a wise guy or anyone who lived on the fringe of the law. They were fair game and they knew how the game was played. Linda Zimmerman was different. Or was she? Was she a victim or was she a guileful woman involved in murder? He had to satisfy himself which it was.

A rustling came from inside the room. Scanlon turned quickly and shooed Brodie and the vault man from sight.

Linda Zimmerman gasped when she opened the door and saw Scanlon. She darted back inside, pulled the door behind her. He threw his weight against the door and pushed it open before she could lock it.

It was a cramped space with a desk built into the wall and a straight-back chair padded in green leather. She cowered against the wall, the thin green box clutched to her chest, her face furrowed with confusion. "Please leave me alone."

"Linda, I need to know what you have in that box. Knowing might help me get the people responsible for taking your family away from you."

"It's personal," she said, frantically looking around the room for an escape hatch.

"Linda, please allow me to look inside that box."

"No! I want to call my attorney. How dare you invade my privacy?" She tried to push past him but he blocked her path. She pulled back from him. As she did, he reached out and yanked the box from her grip. She leaped at him, beating him on the head and shoulders, screaming at him to give her back her property. He pushed her away from him. Holding her at arm's length with one hand, he put the box down on the desk and with his free hand flicked the hasp off the staple.

"Don't!" she beseeched him.

He flipped open the lid. The box contained four Ziploc plastic bags filled with gray ash. She pulled away from his grip and slumped down into the chair, defeated. He prodded the bags with his fingers. He could feel bits of calcareous material. In one horrible moment of recognition his heart sank with guilt.

She was crying, talking to the bags of ash. "Daddy, they won't leave us alone."

Scanlon slapped the lid closed. "Linda, please forgive me. In my zeal . . . I . . ." For the first time in his life he was sorry that he was a cop. For the first time in his life he hated the Job. He pressed her head to him, consoling her.

"I wanted them to be safe. They were all that I had. I came here to talk to them, the way I did when I was a girl. I wanted them to be together, always."

Scanlon slid his hand behind him, reaching for the doorknob. He turned it and left the room, leaving her with her head atop the box, crying softly. He stormed out of the vault room.

"Whaddya find out?" Brodie said, hurrying beside him down the corridor.

"Nothing. Let's get the hell out of here."

"But Lou," Brodie persisted, "she must have been doing something in there."

"Goddamnit! I said *nothing*. Now let's go. Biafra Baby is waiting for us in the Latent Section."

The fingerprint man used a Pentel sign pen to rule off the points of comparison. "These characteristics match up with the ring, middle, and forefinger of Harris's right hand," the fingerprint man told Scanlon.

"We hit pay dirt, Lou," Brodie said.

"Maybe," Scanlon said, bending to examine the latent fingerprints. He noted the different points of comparison that had been ruled off on the glass. An abrupt ending ridge. A dot. A short ridge. A meeting of two ridges. The core. The delta.

Looking up from the glass, Scanlon asked, "What about the type?"

The fingerprint man said, "I enlarged and measured the writing. It was one of those check-off order forms, so it didn't present much of a standard to work with. So I had to make do with the name and address. 'Raymond Gilligan' and the Astoria address contained four A's, three L's, three I's, two O's, and two D's. I compared the characteristics of those letters against the writings in our files and came up with a match. An Underwood, assigned to the Seventeenth Narcotics District. Serial number 38J93873."

*   *   *

Chief of Detectives Goldberg trudged six paces ahead of Scanlon into the PC's office.

The police commissioner was standing in his sun-drenched office reading a legal brief. Not looking up from the page, he motioned the two men into chairs. "Tell me what you have, Lou," Gomez said, tossing the brief onto his desk.

Scanlon began: "I've just come from the Latent Section . . ." When he finished, he added, "I know that it's circumstantial, but I believe that we now have enough to move on Harris."

"I'm not so sure," the PC said. "You have no evidence linking Harris to Mrs. Gallagher. In fact, you don't have anything against Mrs. Gallagher. As for the fingerprints, Harris's weren't the only ones on that form. And anyone assigned to the Seventeenth District could have typed out that makeup order. Including Joe Gallagher."

"I'm aware of all that, Commissioner," Scanlon said. "But I'm still convinced that evidence exists that does link Harris and Mrs. Gallagher to the murders. And I want to throw a scare into them that will make them run to destroy that evidence."

"And just suppose that they don't scare, Lieutenant?" Gomez said. "And suppose that they have already destroyed the evidence? Suppose that the evidence never existed in the first place? And I want you to further suppose that we make a move on a lieutenant's widow, the widow of a decorated police lieutenant, and it backfires on us, and we all end up at the other end of a civil suit. Then, what, Lieutenant?"

"Then we'd be up the creek without a paddle," Scanlon said.

"Precisely my point." The PC looked at the CofD. "What do you think of all this, Chief?"

The CofD cupped his kneecaps and leaned forward. "I think that we should go with what we got. Circumstantial evidence can convict, if you have enough of it."

"If I give the green light, how would you proceed?" Gomez asked Scanlon.

Scanlon told him, adding, "I'd like Sergeant Harris to be flown on a detail tomorrow that ends around fifteen hundred hours, someplace where Mrs. Gallagher can't telephone him directly."

"Orchard Beach," CofD Goldberg said.

22

It drizzled that Wednesday morning, and was unseasonably cool. Scanlon darted into the Nine-three station house and turned to watch the rain make tiny dimples in the puddles. Shaking drops from his jacket, he looked up at the heavy clouds. Damn rain had better stop, he thought. All he needed now was for the rain to continue and the Orchard Beach detail to be canceled because of rain. It was 0747 hours. The First Platoon was on duty until 0800. Day-tour cops lolled around the sitting room drinking coffee, consulting scratch sheets, the sports pages.

The late-tour desk officer ruled off his final entry. The cop on switchboard duty yawned and stretched. The one-twenty-four man stuffed the night's mail into the mailbag. The desk officer stood and arched his back. Glancing behind him, the DO saw Scanlon reading the orders. "What are you doing in so early?"

"Couldn't sleep," Scanlon said, returning the clipboard to its hook.

"Must be an insomnia epidemic. All your people are in early. Anything up?"

"Nothing. Detectives love the Job. We can't get enough of it."

"Bullshit."

Going into his office, Scanlon rolled the blackboard away from the wall and pinned the maps that he had ordered from the Cartography Unit to its wooden frame. Yetta Zimmerman's candy store was circled in black, along with the location where the van had been found. The Gallagher residence was circled in green. Harris's official residence on Staten Island and his splash pad on Ocean Avenue were circled in brown.

Leaning against his desk, studying the maps, he ran it over in his head, how he thought the crime had gone down. Somewhere along the line, Gallagher must have mentioned to Harris or to his wife that he was delivering Andrea Zimmerman's birthday cake to her grandmother. They saw this as their opportunity to kill Gallagher. Mrs. Gallagher must have applied the makeup in the van or at home. Probably in the van on the way to the candy store. She would not have wanted to take the chance of anyone seeing her leaving her apartment in a disguise. Harris lets her off near the park and goes and sits on the candy store. When he sees Gallagher carrying the cake box, he leaves and gives her some prearranged signal.

The more he ran it before his mind's eye the more he realized that it had the right feel. And smart cops heed the feel, those moments of intuitive insight born of experience. Many times the feel for a case will go against logic and common sense. Common sense would dictate that Harris would have deep-sixed the evidence. But Scanlon knew that any chintzy bastard who clipped and saved cigarette butts and who used a tipping chart for a lousy bar tab was not about to toss expensive weapons into the drink. Besides, the cocky son of a bitch probably thought he was too smart to get caught.

Herman the German telephoned at 0820 to tell Scanlon that Harris had been flown on the Orchard Beach detail. Hundreds of thousands of people flock to the city's beaches and parks every summer. The NYPD assigns hundreds of policemen from around the city to the beaches and parks for crowd and traffic control.

Scanlon glanced out the window. "We're lucky it stopped raining— otherwise the detail might have been canceled." He asked the inspector if he had spoken to Harris.

"Just as you asked me to. I caught up with him as he was on his way up to the locker room. I told him I had no choice but to fly him out. I told him that while he was out on emergency leave connected with Joe Gallagher's death the other sergeants in the unit had all become embroiled in heavy investigations and that I didn't want to pull them off to fill summer details. So it was his turn in the barrel, I told him."

"Did he buy it?"

"He seemed to."

"Good. We'll put him at ease and then yank the rug out from under him."

"Are you sure you want me to visit Mrs. Gallagher? I was thinking that it might be better if you saw her."

"It'll be more natural coming from you," Scanlon said into the mouthpiece. "I hope she'll know how to get in touch with Harris."

"She was married to a cop long enough. She'll know."

After Scanlon hung up he played with the dial, trying to decide whether or not to call Linda Zimmerman and apologize for intruding upon her privacy yesterday at the bank. His hand slid from the dial. It was better to let time heal whatever wounds he had reopened. He wondered if Jane Stomer had received his flowers, and if she would call him to thank him. He telephoned his mother to see if she was all right and to tell her that he loved her, and to explain why he would not be able to come for dinner this Sunday. He telephoned Jack Fable at the Nineteenth Squad and went over the arrangements they had made late last night.

Three hours passed.

Higgins swept out the squad room. Christopher watched television. Biafra Baby took a shopping list from his wife over the phone, and then swept out the squad room. Brodie came up to Biafra Baby and asked him to give him a piss call at 1345, and then Brodie slipped into the dormitory to sack out.

Hector Colon telephoned his wife and told her it looked as though he were going to have to work late into the night on the Gallagher homicide and he probably would sleep in the dormitory. His wife asked him to call her in the morning to let her know that he was all right. He hung up, then telephoned his girlfriend at her cashier job at Macy's and told her he would pick her up at five o'clock. Higgins swept out the squad room again. Like everyone else she was nervous and trying to keep occupied.

At 1400, Scanlon stepped out of his office and beckoned the detectives inside.

"Let's go over it one more time," Scanlon said, tacking a map of Orchard Beach up on the blackboard. Higgins and Biafra Baby were to plant on the Gallagher residence. Christopher and Lew Brodie were to take in Harris's splash pad on Ocean Avenue. Jack Fable and two of his Nineteenth Squad detectives were to plant on Harris's Staten Island residence. Fable had received photos of Harris in the department mail.

The four anticrime cops that Scanlon had gotten on a steal from Chief McMahon, the Bronx borough commander, had been given photographs of Harris and Mrs. Gallagher and assigned to various locations in and around Orchard Beach. There were only four avenues off the beach that led to the major parkways. Scanlon had one anticrime man assigned to each of those avenues. One cop was going to follow Harris out of the parking field. As Harris drove past the exits leading onto the parkways the cop assigned to the exit would leave and join in with the other mobile unit.

Although trailing a car was difficult to coordinate, Scanlon knew from experience that it usually got the best results. That was because the bad guy was on guard, but scared. Harris would be on the watch for a tail, but he really did not want to spot one, so he wouldn't, Scanlon hoped. The cops assigned to Orchard Beach had been assigned two department taxis, one mail truck, and a tan Buick for the surveillance.

"If everything goes according to plan, and Mrs. Gallagher takes the bait, then Harris is going to try and bolt the beach detail early," Scanlon said. "And when he does, the tail men are going to be waiting."

"I sure hope these tail guys know their stuff," Brodie said.

"Chief McMahon assured me that they were the best tail men he had," Scanlon said.

"They had better be," Biafra Baby said. "Harris ain't no pussycat."

"I want you all to sign out radios. Make sure the batteries are charged," Scanlon said. "We're going to be using one of the closed channels. Number three. Our call letters will be Renegade." He thought a second and added, "I like Renegade—it seems appropriate for this caper." He assigned them call numbers.

"What about the men from the Bronx and the Nineteenth Squad?" Biafra Baby asked.

"Herman the German met with them last night. He assigned them their radios and their call letters," Scanlon said.

"Where are you going to be, Lou?" Higgins asked.

"Right here coordinating everything. Hector is going to be with me. But he has to take a few hours off at the end of his tour, a personal problem."

"I bet," Biafra Baby said, making an obscene plunging gesture with his fist.

A beguiling smile lit up Scanlon's face. "Any questions?" His eyes slid from face to face. There were no questions. "Then let's do it."

After the detectives left, the squad room became unnaturally quiet. Colon took the occasional call and jotted down messages. Scanlon sat at his desk listening to the static coming from the walkie-talkie standing in the middle of his desk. It was too early for anything to be happening, but he listened anyway. He powdered his stump and rolled on a fresh stump sock.

Hector Colon drifted into his office. "Lou, I was just thinking that we'd be in one helluva fix if a heavy case went down."

Scanlon snatched the roll call off the clip. Three detectives were scheduled to do the evening duty, a 1600 to 0100. He checked the time: 1450. A helluva lot could happen in an hour and ten minutes. He telephoned the adjoining detective squad, the Nine-seven. When the Whip came on the line, Scanlon asked him to have his detectives cover the Nine-three for the next hour and ten minutes. "I've got a heavy one going down and I'm working short-handed."

"You got it, Tony," Lt. Roy Benson said. "I'd just love to take my girlfriend to Monte's one night."

"Any night you want, as my guest, of course."

"Gee, Tony. You're a real swell guy."

"Fuck you, Roy. And thanks."

Herman the German rang the bell and stepped back.

Mary Ann Gallagher answered the door dressed in black, a rosary dangling from her right hand.

"I hope I'm not disturbing you, Mrs. Gallagher. But as I told you on the phone, I want to get this money to you as soon as possible."

"I appreciate that, Inspector." She turned and led him down the hall and into the parlor. They sat facing each other. He watched her finger the beads as he slid the white department envelope from his jacket pocket. "Mrs. Gallagher, this money was collected from the men and women in Queens Narcotics. There's thirty-six hundred dollars here. I know that it won't bring Joe back, but it will help you make a new life for yourself."

She leaned up out of her seat and kissed him on his cheek. "May God bless and protect you and your men," she said, taking the envelope from his hand, easing back into her seat. "Gallagher was such a good man. I miss him very much." She looked away.

He stood. "I must be getting back."

"Won't you stay and have some tea with me?"

"I really can't. I have an appointment to see Lieutenant Scanlon. It seems that the lieutenant has developed some leads on the killings."

"What?" she asked, standing up in her excitement.

"I don't have all the details, so I'd rather not say just yet. I'm sure Scanlon will contact you at the appropriate time."

"Please tell me whatever you know. I have a right to know. Any ray of hope that those people will be caught will make my day easier to face."

"I guess you got the right," he said, lowering himself back down into the chair. "It appears that the lieutenant has developed a lead to a theatrical makeup store. And he's come up with some fingerprints on some order form. He's leaning toward the theory that it might not have been just a robbery attempt."

"What? Tell me."

"That's all I know. I'll know more after I see Scanlon."

"That's wonderful news. I pray that they catch them," she said, clutching the arm of her chair.

Mary Ann Gallagher walked with the inspector to the door and waited until she heard the downstairs vestibule door open and close. She threw the rosary on the floor and ran for the telephone.

Herman the German drove to the Nine-three Squad and told Scanlon what had happened with Mrs. Gallagher. The inspector used Scanlon's desk phone to telephone the Seventeenth Narcotics District. The operations sergeant told the inspector that a woman had just called looking for Sergeant Harris. As instructed, the sergeant had told the woman that Harris had been assigned to the crowd-control detail at Orchard Beach and had given her the number of temporary headquarters.

A woman had telephoned the headquarters van at Orchard Beach wanting to speak with Sergeant Harris of the Seventeenth Narcotics District. When she was told that the sergeant was out on patrol, she left an urgent message for the sergeant to call Mary Ann, at home.

Herman the German's face clouded. "Now?"

"Now!" Scanlon said. "Tell them to deliver the message to Harris." Scanlon went and stood by the window. The sun was out, the street below dry.

Twenty-six minutes passed before the call they were waiting for came. "Harris just threw in a Twenty-eight and took the rest of his tour off, a family emergency," the inspector said, gently replacing the receiver back in its cradle.

Scanlon picked up the walkie-talkie. "Renegade base to all units. Stand by. It's going down."

On the map in the squad room, Scanlon could see where a lagoon separated the Pelham Split Rock Golf Course from Orchard Beach. A parking area was sandwiched between the picnic grove and the picnic play area. The beach itself was a crescent of sand on the eastern end of the peninsula. Park Road wound its way across the peninsula connecting the parkway area and the picnic areas. The NYPD headquarters van was parked on the southern tip of the parking field. A number of spaces around the van had been reserved for the policemen who were assigned to the beach detail. Six rows away from the last reserved space a taxi idled, the driver slouched down behind the wheel, a portable radio on his lap.

Scanlon fingered the map of Orchard Beach. Had he covered all the exits? City Island Road leads off the beach. Pelham Bridge Road runs parallel to City Island Road. Both roads flow into the Hutchinson River Parkway, or the Hutch as it was commonly called. Renegades Two through Four were stationed at the entrances to the parkways. Renegade One was assigned to the parking field. It was One's job to tail Harris from the field onto whatever parkway the subject was going to take. As Harris and his tail passed the various entrances the unit at that particular entrance would leave and join the mobile surveillance.

Scanlon thought of something and grabbed up the radio. "Base to Renegade Two, what's the traffic like?"

"Two to Base, weekday summer traffic, Lou. Not too heavy, not too light."

"Ten-four."

George Harris appeared in the doorway of the headquarters van, uniform and equipment slung over his shoulders. Beach-weary people trudged back to their cars. Newcomers unloaded car trunks, gathering up blankets and coolers, preparing for their trek to the sand.

Harris made a rush for his Jeep.

The taxi driver parked in the parking field radioed, "Renegade One to base. Subject leaving in Jeep Comanche."

The driver of the tan Buick parked near the Pelham Bridge Road exit radioed: "Renegade Two, ten-four. No sign of subject."

Another taxi was parked on the shoulder near the entrance to the Hutch, the driver searching for a mechanical problem under the hood. He spoke into the radio that lay across the car's battery. "Renegade Three, standing by."

A mail truck was waiting behind an arbor of evergreens near the entrance of the Bruckner Expressway. "Renegade Four, standing by."

Scanlon radioed: "Base to Renegade Five, radio check, how do you read this unit?"

"We read you five by five," Higgins radioed.

"Renegade Six, how do you read this unit?"

"Five by five," Christopher transmitted.

"Renegade Seven, how do you read base?"

"We read you five by five," Fable transmitted.

Scanlon fingered the map of Orchard Beach. Damn, what was taking them so long?

"Renegade One to base. Subject passing Pelham Parkway."

"Renegade Two is leaving to join up with Renegade One."

"Renegade Three to base. I've got subject turning south onto the Hutch."

"Base to all units. Make frequent changes of close-contact car." Scanlon paced the squad room, his radio held in front of his mouth.

Herman the German stood at parade rest in the middle of the squad room, looking down at the floor, waiting for the next transmission. Hector Colon kept looking up at the clock. He would have to leave soon. He had an engagement party to go to.

"Subject heading onto Bronx Whitestone Bridge."

"I've got 'im."

The units in the field were beginning to transmit without identifying themselves. That happens when cops have worked together a long time. They move and think as one, each recognizing the others' voices, moving as one well-trained unit.

Scanlon inspected the map. "He's going to take either the Cross Island or the Whitestone Expressway."

The tension grew. Colon slipped from the squad room and went to the locker room to change his clothes.

"He's going onto the Whitestone."

"Jack, you fall back, I'll pick him up."

"Ten-four."

"That guy is really pouring on the gas."

"He's turning south on the Van Wyck."

Hector Colon walked back into the squad room dressed in white slacks and a blue sport jacket with orange saddle stitching. He had on shiny white loafers and a maroon shirt and white tie. He sheepishly went up to Scanlon. "Lou, I don't have to go to this party. I can stay if you really need me."

"We'll manage, Hector. Go and enjoy."

After Colon had left the squad room, Herman the German looked at Scanlon and said, "I hope you remember that act of loyalty next time evaluations come around."

"Payback is always a bitch, Inspector."

The radio came to life. "He's turning west on the Long Island Expressway."

"He's making for the Gallagher house," Scanlon said. "He wants to make her rehash her conversation with you. Then he'll go for the guns." Scanlon transmitted: "Base to Renegade Five, subject is heading your way. Stay out of sight."

"Ten-four," Higgins radioed.

A short time later Renegade Five radioed that the subject was parking his Jeep on Anthony Street. "He's out of the Jeep," Higgins radioed. "Looking around, taking his time, being careful. He's moving up the steps, standing there. Now he's coming back down. Walking back over to his Jeep, taking his time, being real careful there's no tail. Now! He's running up the steps. He's in the house."

"Base to Renegades One through Four. Stay out of sight. Renegade Three and Four cover the rear of 32 Anthony Street."

Scanlon imagined the scene inside the Gallagher house. Mrs. Gallagher frantically relating her conversation with Herman the German. Harris picking up on her every word. He'd latch on to the inspector's comment about the makeup and fingerprints. There would be acrimony; heated words would be exchanged. Eventually, Scanlon hoped, Harris would be spooked and make a run to recover the guns.

"Subject is leaving," Higgins radioed. A short time later another transmission came over the wavelength. "Subject is eastbound on the BQE."

Time passed, contact positions changed.

Harris left the BQE at Queens Boulevard. When the transmission came into the base, Scanlon rushed up to the map. Examining the location where Harris exited the parkway, Scanlon cursed in Italian. Harris could not have picked a better location to shake a tail.

Queens Boulevard is a major artery that runs east and west across the Borough of Queens. The east- and westbound lanes are separated by various kinds of road dividers along the length of the boulevard. It is not possible for a driver to turn north or south at every intersection. Sometimes he must drive three-quarters of a mile before reaching a north or south turn lane. Many of the peripheral streets along the boulevard curve into other streets and avenues or dead-end into parkways or residential cul-de-sacs.

"Base to Renegades, what is subject doing?"

"Subject is double-parked on Queens and Five-eight Street. He's sitting in the Jeep watching through his sideview mirror."

"Base to Renegades One and Two, proceed to first eastbound exit and station yourself on the boulevard facing east. Renegades Three and Four, box him in."

"Renegade Five to base. Do you want us to leave this location and join up other units?" Higgins radioed.

"Negative. Stay with our lady friend in case she takes off on us. Harris could be a decoy."

"Ten-four, Lou," Higgins radioed.

"He's out of the Jeep standing on the curb, watching everything and everybody around him," one of the mobile units radioed.

"He's running across the boulevard," someone shouted over the air. "He's jumped the divider and hailed a taxi."

"Get the plate number," Scanlon radioed, a rising urgency in his voice.

"Subject got in yellow cab, license T276598. Heading north on Five-eight Street."

"Base to Renegades One and Two. Are you eastbound yet?"

"Negative. We haven't even reached a turn lane yet."

"Can any unit follow subject?" Scanlon radioed.

"That's a negative. We're all facing the wrong direction and are unable to make U-turns because of the divider." Herman the German was frantic. "We're going to lose him."

"Like hell we are. He's going for the guns and the tools. They have to be stashed someplace nearby. Someplace where he can get at them quickly. Someplace he has access to." Scanlon looked at the inspector. "We need a helicopter to search for that taxi. It takes an MOF above the rank of captain to order a chopper up."

Herman the German rushed over to the nearest desk and seized the telephone. Dialing, he said, "I hope Colon is enjoying his goddamn party. He certainly got dolled up for it."

As the inspector was telling the operations officer at the Aviation Unit what he wanted, Scanlon bolted from the squad room.

"Where are you going?"

Scanlon hollered over his shoulder, "Harris has a splash locker at the One-fourteen."

Scanlon ran from the station house and over to the radio car that had just slid into the curb. He jerked open the rear door and said to the startled crew, "Take me to the One-fourteen. Tell Central you'll be out of service—ten-sixty-one."

The driver of the radio car, a short man with the torso of a body builder, turned to look at the lieutenant. "You want the scenic route or are you in a hurry?"

"I want you to shag ass," Scanlon snapped.

"You got it, Lou," said the driver. "We'll take Manhattan Avenue up to Vernon Boulevard and Vernon all the way up into Astoria. Have you there in no time."

The car's recorder, a willowy man in his early twenties, switched on the turret lights and snatched the radio out of its cradle. "Nine-three Adam to Central, K."

"Go, Adam."

"Nine-three Adam will be ten-sixty-one to the One-fourteen on a precinct assignment, K."

"Ten-four, Adam. Advise Central when you're ninety-eight."

As Nine-three Adam pulled away from the curb, Scanlon caught sight of Herman the German running from the station house. The squealing police car sped under the massive span of the Queensboro Bridge, passed the drab towers of the Queensbridge Housing Project, and raced past the Con Ed generating plant on Vernon Boulevard.

Scanlon felt the bitter tug of frustration in his chest. He should have thought of a splash locker long before he thought about Colon's leaving the squad room to change into his partying clothes. Most cops have extra lockers in the precinct where they stash clothes and things from their secret lives. He blamed himself again and again for not seeing the possibility that Harris might have an extra locker in the One-fourteen. What safer place could there be to hide evidence of a murder than in a station-house locker that had another man's name and shield number on it, a member of the force long since retired or transferred? A perfect hiding place, a place open seven days a week, twenty-four hours a day. It had the right feel.

Scanlon asked the recorder to pass him the radio handset. The cop stretched the black spiraled cord into the rear seat.

"Switch your set to channel three," Scanlon ordered.

When the recorder complied, Scanlon radioed, "Renegade base to Renegades One, Two, Three, and Four. Base has reason to believe subject heading for the One-fourteen. Ten-eighty-five this unit at that location, forthwith."

A spate of hurried acknowledgments came over the channel.

The One-fourteen Precinct was a block away. A taxi was double-parked in front of the building. A swarm of cars gridlocked Astoria Boulevard, blocking the police car. "Turn off your lights and siren," Scanlon ordered. "Go around them."

"Lou, what's going on?" the driver asked, concern seeping into his young voice.

The radio car sped up onto the sidewalk, scattering pedestrians, and bounced back into the roadway.

Harris came running from the station house clutching a brown duffel bag.

The police car came to an abrupt stop behind the taxi. Scanlon leaped out into the roadway. "Harris!"

The sergeant was bending to get into the taxi when Scanlon's voice stopped him. He backed slowly out and stood looking at the man standing in the roadway. The two men remained motionless, as though frozen in time, glaring at each other. The crew of Nine-three Adam got out of their radio car and stood by the open doors watching the confusing scene unfold. Harris glanced down at the duffel bag. He moved around the front of the taxi and stood in the roadway facing Scanlon. He bolted for the Triboro Plaza underpass.

Scanlon yelled for him to stop and took off at a run.

Harris ran up the embankment and tossed the duffel bag over the wall. He wheeled away from the embankment and ran toward Steinway Street. Scanlon rushed up to the embankment wall and peered down onto the highway. A blue car ran over the duffel bag, and then another and another, tossing the cloth satchel across the highway.

Jabbing a finger down at the traffic feeding off the Triboro Bridge, Scanlon called out to the cops who had driven him, "Shut off the traffic." He took off after Harris.

Policemen stood on the steps of the station house scratching their heads and other parts of their anatomies and asking each other what the fuck was going on. Harris dodged his way along the teeming sidewalk. He bumped into a boy on a bicycle and stumbled. The boy and bike fell to the sidewalk. Regaining his footing, Harris ran to Forty-first Street and darted around the corner.

Scanlon careened around the corner in pursuit and came to a stop when he saw Harris leaning against the building wall, lighting up a clipper.

"Whaddaya doin' in this neck of the woods, Lou?"

Scanlon grabbed him by the shoulders and turned him to the wall. "You're under arrest, Sergeant. You have the right to remain silent . . ." He informed the prisoner of his constitutional rights as he frisked him and removed his police credentials and revolver.

The One-fourteen's interrogation room was a stale cubicle, the walls of which were covered by acoustical tiles and a one-way mirror.

Scanlon and Harris faced each other across a small table. Herman the German and Jack Fable watched and listened in the viewing room, a narrow space that also contained the One-fourteen Squad's refrigerator. Harris's cowboy boots had been taken from him and invoiced as evidence. The prisoner was wearing cloth hospital slippers.

"Was it worth it, George?" Scanlon asked, toying with a De Nobili box.

"I want my boots back."

"In time. First tell me about Gallagher and the Zimmermans."

"I don't know what the fuck you're talking about. I got nothing to say to you or the other assholes on the other side of that mirror. I want a lawyer and I want to see my SBA delegate."

"You'll feel better if you tell me about it, George."

Harris laughed in his face. "You really got the balls to try one of those Mickey Mouse interrogative techniques on me? I'll feel better, shit."

"Mrs. Gallagher is talking to us," Scanlon lied. "She's giving the whole thing up. She's agreed to testify against you."

"That's nice. I hope you two have a long talk. Now get me my lawyer."

"About a dozen people saw you throw the duffel bag over the embankment. And we've recovered its contents."

Harris's eyes narrowed to slits. "What duffel bag?"

Herman the German stuck his head into the room. "May I see you a moment, Lieutenant?"

Scanlon pushed his chair back and went outside. Brodie and Christopher were waiting in the viewing room.

"The rifle and shotgun weren't in the duffel bag," Brodie said.

"We've recovered the makeup, including the walrus mustache, and the tools, a crowbar, screwdriver, and a blacksmith's hammer."

Scanlon cursed in Italian.

"We had the southbound traffic shut off," Christopher said. "The men from the Bronx had already done that before we arrived. There were also two highway units on the scene. All the traffic was funneled through the chokepoint and every motorist questioned. We came up with four witnesses who saw the driver of a dark green Chevrolet swerve to avoid hitting the duffel bag. The driver stopped his car, got out, and, according to the witnesses, ran over to the bag and removed an attaché case and what appeared to be some sort of a firearm that had been broken down. He jumped back into his car and took off for parts unknown."

"He must have gotten through the chokepoint before the traffic was shut off," Brodie said.

Scanlon kicked the wall in anger. "Did anyone get a description of the car and its driver?" Scanlon asked, idly opening the refrigerator door and looking into the freezer. It was a solid block of ice.

"A thin male Hispanic with a pencil mustache, wearing a gold earring in his right ear. He had effeminate mannerisms and drove a Chevrolet that had chartreuse venetian blinds across the rear window and a pink animal with a bobbing head," Christopher said.

"No one thought to get the plate number?" Scanlon asked.

"No," Christopher said mournfully.

"Where are Higgins and Biafra Baby?" Scanlon asked.

Herman the German said, "They're still sitting on Mrs. Gallagher's apartment. I told them to remain there on the off chance that she has some evidence stashed in her apartment and might try to get rid of it. I also took the statements of the anticrime men you got on a steal and sent them back to the Bronx. I asked them to drop off the cowboy boots at the lab on their way back."

"What about your detectives, Jack?" Scanlon asked the CO of the Nineteenth Detective Squad.

"Back to command, no meal," Fable said. "No sense cluttering things up around here."

Scanlon nodded.

"Tom McCormick, the president of the Sergeants' Benevolent Association, and one of the SBA attorneys are waiting in the administrative lieutenant's office to see Harris," the inspector said.

"Where are the two cops I commandeered to drive me here?" Scanlon asked.

"They're waiting downstairs in the captain's office with their PBA delegate and one of the PBA attorneys," Herman the German said.

Scanlon looked at the inspector. "We made the lawyers' day for them. Were the PC and the CofD notified?"

"Both of them were," Fable said. "And they're both not responding to the scene. The borough commander and the duty captain were also notified. The duty captain will be here later. He's tied up in the One-oh-three on a shooting."

Scanlon said bitterly, "They're all distancing themselves from the arrest, waiting to see which way it's going to go. Which means, of course, that they think we messed it up." He opened the door to the interrogation room and motioned Harris outside.

The administrative lieutenant's office was on the same floor as the detectives' interrogation room but at the other end of the building. Walking down the corridor, with Harris in the center of the group, they passed cops who either looked away or cast their eyes downward. Policemen do not like to see one of their own under arrest.

The SBA attorney's name was Berke. He had a scabrous complexion, a red beard, and hard, cunning eyes. He was waiting in the corridor with Tom McCormick, the SBA president. Harris went into the administrative lieutenant's office with his representation. Herman the German and Jack Fable stood guard outside the door while Scanlon rushed downstairs to the captain's office.

Disgruntled policemen loitered in the muster room. The grapevine had it that the Whip of the Nine-three Squad had arrested a sergeant from Queens Narcotics. It had something to do with Lieutenant Gallagher's wife, so the word was. Hurrying down the staircase, Scanlon saw the faces of the cops looking up at him. Many of them glared their contempt up at him; some turned their backs to him and shuffled off into the sitting room.

The PBA delegate's name was Frank Fortunado. He was waiting for Scanlon outside the captain's office. "Looks like you grabbed yourself a wolverine by the balls, Lou," Fortunado said.

"Where are the two cops?" Scanlon said, noticing the delegate's iron-gray hair.

Fortunado motioned to the door. "Inside with our lawyer. Their names are Rod and Eichhorn, and they both most definitely do not want to get involved in the arrest of a member of the force."

"Your MOF is a cop killer."

"That's what you say, Lou. But we both know that that ain't gospel until a jury says it's so too, and until the Court of Appeals says it's so."

"Is the captain in his office?"

"He's on his RDO. His next scheduled tour is eight to four, tomorrow," the delegate said, chucking open the door and following Scanlon inside.

Scanlon recognized Police Officer Rod as the driver of the radio car. Eichhorn had been the recorder. The lawyer's name was Eble. Medium-tall, with wavy black hair, and an obvious penchant for expensive clothes.

The lawyer was sitting behind the captain's regulation flat-top desk. The two cops were sitting next to each other on the captain's green regulation leather couch. They appeared nervous and self-conscious.

"I have to take their statements, Counselor," Scanlon said.

"I have no problem with that, Lieutenant," the lawyer said. "Officers Rod and Eichhorn will be more than happy to answer any question put to them that is specifically directed and narrowly related to their performance of duty."

Scanlon bridled at the lawyer's use of the restrictive phrase used in the *Patrol Guide*'s procedure concerning the interrogation of members of the service.

"Counselor, your clients are not the subjects of an official investigation. So spare me that specifically directed and narrowly related bullshit. I commandeered them to drive me here. All I need from them now is a statement as to what they saw and heard when we got here."

"My clients saw and heard nothing, Lieutenant."

Scanlon hurled a withering look at the two cops, who shifted uneasily on the couch. "You didn't see Sergeant Harris run up to the embankment and toss a duffel bag over the wall?"

"I didn't see nothing, Lou," Rod said.

"Me either," followed Eichhorn.

"I suppose the other cops who were standing on the precinct steps didn't see or hear anything either," Scanlon said.

"That would be my guess," the lawyer said.

Rancor showing clearly on his face, Scanlon whirled and left the office. Policemen were still milling about the muster room. Ignoring their searching stares, Scanlon made for the staircase. He heard a rushing footfall behind him and turned. Police Officer Rod was shamefaced. "Lou, I'm sorry for what happened inside. But I had no other way to go."

"I'd like to hear why," Scanlon said.

"I've got fourteen more years to do in the Job," Rod said. "Six months from now the Gallagher case is going to be yesterday's news. But I'd be the cop who helped convict a police sergeant. No one would remember that the sergeant was tried for murder, they'd only remember that I was the scumbag who testified against him."

"Look, kid, it don't have to be that way."

"Bullshit, Lou," Rod said, sweeping his hand at the policemen in the muster room. "Look at the way they're looking at you. They don't even know why Harris was arrested. And they could care less. What matters to them is that a street cop arrested another street cop. Not some bastard from IAD whose job it is to arrest cops, but one of their own, from the trenches. No, Lou. That's a head trip I don't need. I just ain't that dedicated."

Scanlon stood by the staircase and watched Rod walk back into the captain's office. That was one of the major differences between guys who worked in the bag and guys who worked in soft clothes, Scanlon reflected. Detectives and plainclothesmen see many different sides to life. They have to understand a person's motivation and try to figure out what makes that person tick, act the way he or she does. Detectives learn early that there are no black-and-white issues in life, only different shades of gray.

Scanlon glared back at the cops, turned, and hurried back upstairs. Harris was still closeted in the administrative lieutenant's office with his lawyer and the SBA president. Herman the German and Jack Fable were still on guard duty outside the door.

"What did the two cops have to say?" Fable asked Scanlon.

"They said that they saw nothing, heard nothing, smelled nothing, and sensed nothing," Scanlon said. "There are going to be some unpleasant reverberations over this arrest. And I don't see any reason for you two to be hit by any of the shrapnel. So why don't you both sort of disappear into the woodwork?"

Jack Fable made an ugly face. "Tony, my man, I've been a detective squad commander for the better part of fifteen years. And during that time I've developed my own philosophy for dealing with these delicate situations. Simply put, I fuck 'em where they breathe."

Scanlon smiled. Fable was from the old, old school. There weren't many of his kind left in the Job. The new breed of squad commander wore a somber suit and carried an attaché case to work that contained two apples, one banana, and a Thermos of decaffeinated tea. And they wore big college rings, but still said "between you and I," and they loved to go on about how the quality of evidence was determined by the statistical concept of probability.

Herman the German bit his lips. "Gallagher was no bargain, but he was my bargain."

"We're three aging dinosaurs hanging around for that meteor to come hurling down from space and make us extinct," Scanlon said.

"I fuck 'em where they breathe," Fable said again.

Brodie and Christopher rushed up to them. "The lab boys just called," Brodie said. "Harris's boots match up with the impressions found on the roof of the Kingsley Arms. It's a positive match, Lou.

And the tools found in the duffel bag were the same tools that were used to force open the roof door."

The door behind them opened, and Harris's attorney stepped out into the corridor.

"Gentlemen, I have just spoken to my clients at some length. And at this time I am officially advising you that under no circumstances are my clients to be questioned by any member of the police department."

"Clients, Counselor?" Scanlon said.

"I have just gotten off the phone with Mary Ann Gallagher. She has asked me to represent her."

Kings County Criminal Court is located on Schermerhorn Street in Brooklyn's once-fashionable downtown shopping district, which has been urbanized into a seedy neighborhood of hawking street peddlers, shuttered shops, and caged-in stores where customers had to be buzzed inside.

The court's arraignment part was on the first floor of the Baroque-style building. All conversation stopped when Scanlon walked into the police sign-in room. The monster had arrived. A notification tucked into the sign-in log was waiting for Scanlon: "Lt. Scanlon. After you draw up complaint see ADA Goldfarb in Rm 617."

ADA Goldfarb was a short man in his late twenties who had gone prematurely bald. He was dressed in a dark business suit and wore an orange tie. "Let's go into the conference room, Lieutenant."

Scanlon noticed that the assistant district attorney favored built-up heels. He followed the ADA into the glass cubicle.

"I'm handling the arraignment part this morning, Lieutenant. I've read over your complaint and your attending affidavits. And, I have to tell you, your case against Sergeant Harris is flimsy, at best. You are going to have to come up with a lot more hard evidence if you expect the People to win on this one." He sat down wearily in one of the two battered chairs.

"We have evidence that ties Harris directly to the scene of the Zimmerman homicide in Manhattan County," Scanlon said in mild protest.

"Ah, yes, the famous cowboy boots. But can you state with any degree of probability when those impressions were made? A week before the doctor and his wife were killed? A month? The same night?" The ADA quickly lit a cigarette. "And you have absolutely no evidence linking Harris to the murders of Lieutenant Gallagher and Yetta Zimmerman. Your fingerprint evidence is dubious—there were other prints on that form. As for the typewriter, anyone assigned to that unit could have typed out that order. In fact, I'm only going to allow you to charge Harris on the Zimmerman homicide, not on Gallagher's. The court would throw it out on the ground of insufficient evidence. I think you might just have enough evidence to hold Harris on the doctor and his wife. But nowhere near enough to get a conviction."

"Are you forgetting that I saw Harris toss that duffel bag over the embankment, and that that duffel bag contained the tools that were used to pry open the roof door of the Kingsley Arms, the same roof from where the shots were fired that killed the doctor and his wife?"

The ADA got up and started pacing the floor. "What you saw, Lieutenant, was Harris throw what appeared to be a duffel bag over the embankment and onto the highway. You are in no position to testify as to the contents of that duffel bag. Nor can you state beyond a reasonable doubt that the duffel bag that your people recovered from the highway was the same duffel bag that you say you saw Harris throw over the embankment."

Scanlon got up and felt rage growing inside him. "Are you telling me that the tools and the makeup are not admissible as evidence?"

"I'm telling you that I would not be surprised if the court sustained a defense motion to suppress them as evidence." The ADA stabbed out his cigarette. "Were Harris's fingerprints found anywhere on the duffel bag or on any of the tools or makeup?"

Scanlon sighed deeply. "No." He shook his head with disgust. "Tell me what I need for a conviction."

"A lot more than you have. Look, Lieutenant. I only handle the arraignments. I suggest you have a talk with one of our trial ADAs. One of them will be able to put you on the right track."

"Do you think we have enough to indict Harris on the Zimmerman murders?"

"Oh, sure. We can indict the Statue of Liberty. The problems come afterward."

Deputy Chief MacAdoo McKenzie stood in the center of the court's lobby, watching the ornate brass doors of the bank of elevators.

"Over here," he said, waving to Scanlon as the lieutenant stepped off the elevator.

"This Harris arrest has got the Palace Guard jumping," McKenzie said. "We're going to end up in the middle of a million-dollar lawsuit. Harris is going to walk. You and your people fucked it up, Lieutenant. Harris beat you to the punch when you allowed him to get rid of that duffel bag."

"Be advised, Chief, that I didn't let Harris do anything. And be further advised that we're going to convict both Harris and his girlfriend."

"How? You didn't even have enough evidence against Harris to arrest him for killing Joe Gallagher. And you can't even go near Mrs. Gallagher to question her. You don't have one drop of evidence against her." He wiped his neck. "The PC has directed me to tell you to stay away from Mrs. Gallagher. Don't try to question her, don't go near her. Her lawyer telephoned the PC and threatened to sue him personally if anything is said or done by any member of the department to besmirch her unblemished reputation. So from now on, as far as this department is concerned, Mrs. Gallagher is no longer a suspect."

Scanlon sneered. "Ol' Bobby Boy is a real stand-up PC."

"He's a politician looking out for his own ass, just like you would be if you were in his place."

Herman the German, Jack Fable, and the Nine-three Squad detectives were gathered in a circle outside the padded courtroom doors of Part 1A. The circle parted for Scanlon. Hector Colon said, *"Teniente,* I've contacted Jose Rodriguez from the Hispanic Association. He's going to reach out to our members and ask them to have a look-see around El Barrio for the car with the venetian blinds."

Scanlon's eyes locked on Colon's. "Did you enjoy your party?"

The detective shifted uncomfortably, looked away. "It was all right, Lou."

"I've been in touch with the uptown brothers," Biafra Baby said. "They're going to be hitting some of the juice joints and number parlors."

Higgins added, "From the description of the driver there is a good chance that he's gay. I've gotten in touch with Sergeant Rogers, the head of GOAL. He's going to have some of our people hit the baths and gay bars."

"I want you all to go back to the Squad and pull out everything we've got on the case. When the arraignment is over I'll come back and we'll put our collective heads together and see if there's anything we've missed," Scanlon ordered.

"I'll have my people do the same thing," Fable said.

"Please, Jack. Speak to the detectives in your Squad who worked on the Zimmerman case. Maybe one of them scratched something on the back of a matchbook, then forgot to put it on a Five." Scanlon turned to his detectives. "And that goes for all of you. Check your notes, every scrap of paper, every matchbook, see if there's anything you've overlooked."

The echo of the detectives walking away resounded off the marble floor. Scanlon looked at Herman the German. "You going inside to watch the arraignment?"

"Wouldn't miss it for the world. I'm into legal flagellation."

An atmosphere of anxious expectation filled the courtroom. All the seats were filled. Scanlon spotted Mary Ann Gallagher, dressed in mourning black, sitting on the aisle in the middle of the room. She was whispering to the man next to her. Scanlon inched his way around the paneled wall to see if he could recognize the man she was talking to. He did. Ben Cohen, one of the criminal justice system's better-known bail bondsmen.

Scanlon was taken aback when he spotted Linda Zimmerman sitting across the room. He moved along the wall until he reached her and squeezed in next to her. "You all right?" he whispered.

Her stare was fixed on the ornate bench that dominated the courtroom. "Yes, I'm all right."

"I'm sorry for what happened in the bank."

She made no reply.

The court clerk stood in front of the bench and barked: "All rise. This court is now in session. The Honorable Florence Meyers presiding." A rustle swept through the courtroom as the assemblage rose to its feet, and then at the court clerk's signal, sat.

The first case on the arraignment calendar was called. The People against George Harris. Scanlon pinned on his shield and went up and stood before the bench. Two court officers escorted the prisoner into the courtroom from the holding pens behind the room. Harris needed a shave. Berke, the defense attorney, held an impromptu conference with his client.

The court clerk said to Scanlon, "Officer, raise your right hand. Do you swear or affirm to the truth of your affidavit?"

"I do."

"George Harris," the court clerk intoned, "you have been charged with violation of section 125.25 of the Penal Law in that on—"

Defense attorney: "Your honor, if it pleases the court, the defense waives the reading of the charges."

Judge Meyers: "So ordered."

Defense attorney: "Your honor, the defense moves for an immediate hearing on this matter, and respectfully requests that the court release the defendant on his personal recognizance."

ADA: "May I remind the court that this is a homicide case. The People have in my judgment presented a *prima facie* case and request bail be set at two hundred and fifty thousand dollars."

The judge flipped through the legal papers, scanning. "Your *prima facie* case appears to be a bit weak, Counselor."

Defense attorney: "Your honor, my client is a ranking member of the police department. He has an unblemished professional and personal record. He has a family, a home. He has roots in the community. He's not going to run. And I say now, in open court, that I fully expect my client to be exonerated of these trumped-up charges."

ADA: "Your honor—"

Judge: "Save it for the hearing, Counselor. Bail is set at twenty-five thousand dollars. This case is bound over to the grand jury. Next case."

Mary Ann Gallagher, and Cohen, the bail bondsman, got up from their pew. Scanlon left the courtroom, unpinning his shield. Linda Zimmerman followed him outside into the lobby. She caught up with him and seizing him by the arm demanded, "What the hell is going on?"

He led her around one of the marble columns, out of sight of the people leaving the courtroom. "Linda, there is a lot more to the case than you've heard on the radio or read in the papers. And I guess you have the right to know it all."

He went on to tell her about his suspicions concerning Harris and Mrs. Gallagher. As he explained to her the restrictions that had been placed on him, he could see a mounting sense of outrage in her face. He had almost finished when a sudden commotion caused them to step out from behind the column. Mary Ann Gallagher, Harris, Cohen, and the defense lawyer, Berke, were leaving the courtroom. A group of newspaper reporters surrounded them. The defense lawyer said that his client would have nothing to say at this time. Two women pushed their way through the crowd and embraced Mrs. Gallagher.

"Pat? Joan? How nice of you to come," Mrs. Gallagher said, glancing over at Scanlon and Linda Zimmerman. Harris walked away with Mrs. Gallagher. He kept looking over his shoulder at Scanlon, a smile of victory fixed on his lips.

"You," Linda Zimmerman hissed at Scanlon. "You call this justice? Harris is allowed to leave the courtroom on the arm of his whore. And you can't even arrest her."

"Linda, this is only the first round."

"You go to hell," she screamed into his face and stormed off.

* * *

Scanlon stood at the top of the steps of the Manhattan Criminal Court building watching the lunchtime flow of people entering and leaving. When he saw Jane Stomer push her way outside he was instantly aware of the perfection of her body and the lustrous beauty of her lips. He also became acutely conscious of how lonely his life had been without her.

She stopped and swept the sunglasses from her face. She glared at him briefly, then turned and pushed her way back into the building.

He ran after her, catching up with her halfway across the marble lobby. "I need your professional advice," he said, snagging her arm.

She turned. "I half expected you to show up here. The word that I hear is that you really missed the boat on Harris."

"I need your help. Let me buy you lunch, please."

"If you keep it on a professional plane, okay. Otherwise, let's just forget the whole thing."

They left the building by the rear exit. He went up to the frankfurter cart and ordered two with sauerkraut and onions, and two diet sodas. Reaching out to pluck napkins from the holder, he caught sight of her watching him.

They walked across the street and sat on a park bench. Gripping her bun with both hands, she bit into the frank's protruding end and waited for him to begin.

He spoke in an unhurried manner, telling her of his feel for the case; he spoke of how the evidence against Harris had been developed; he told her how the arrest had been made; at length he spoke of the ban against his questioning Mrs. Gallagher.

She listened, occasionally sucking soda through a straw. He noticed how her lipstick branded the tip. When he finished talking, he took a bite of his hot dog, waiting for her response. She carefully wiped mustard off her fingers. "The Brooklyn ADA was correct. The case is a throw-out. You have no corroborative evidence linking Harris or Mrs. Gallagher to any of the homicides. And you have no evidence that proves intent. The 'death-gamble' benefits aren't evidence, although they do create a strong presumption. What you have to do is prove an overt act in furtherance of the conspiracy. If you had arrested Harris with the weapons in his possession along with the tools and the makeup, you would have had a conviction. But you still would not have had a case against Mrs. Gallagher." She drank the rest of her soda. "The only way you are going to make a case against her is to turn Harris. If you can make him roll over, he'll spit her up to save his own hide. But that means a plea bargain, and Harris doing less than life."

"Any suggestions?"

"I'd go for the guns. If you can recover them, you just might be able to trace them back to Harris. Then, with the fingerprint evidence, and the typewriter, and the boots, you just might be able to make a case against him. And if the case is strong enough, he might want to make a deal."

"There are a lot of ifs and mights," Scanlon said. "What about getting the guns admitted into evidence, if I should be able to recover them?"

"If the serial numbers are still on them, and you can trace them back to their original purchaser, and that purchaser is proved to be Harris, then you might have a shot at getting them introduced."

"Anything else?"

"Canvass the banks in the area of where they live and work. That bank money order for the makeup was purchased someplace, and whoever got it had to fill out a request form. I'd also check out the libraries to see if one of them took out a book on how to apply makeup." She balled her napkin and pressed it through the hole in the soda can. "Is it worth it all, Scanlon? The frustration, the aggravation, trying to circumvent a system that just doesn't seem to care, or want to care?"

"I think it is," he said, taking the soda can from her hand and getting up. He pushed the garbage down in the wire refuse basket and came back.

She smiled and said, "Thank you for the flowers. They were lovely. But I wish you hadn't sent them."

"I read somewhere that flowers were the quickest way to a woman's heart." He raised his shoulders, let them fall. "I wanted you to know how I felt about you."

"Please, Scanlon. Don't make it any harder than it already is."

"It ain't easy being a pining middle-aged detective."

"Pining, Scanlon? You?"

"Yes, pining. To have a continuing fruitless desire."

"And that is what you have for me, a fruitless desire?"

He placed his hand on hers. "I screwed us up and now I'm trying to put us back together again. And everything I say or do seems to be wrong."

She pulled her hand away from his. "Sending flowers was the right thing."

"Then I'll send more."

"Please don't. I told you the last time, I'm involved with someone."

"You're not being fair to Mr. Whateverhisnameis."

"Who?"

"The guy you're seeing." He started to make finger circles on the back of her hand. "I believe that you're only seeing him to get over me.

I think that you're still in love with me. And that isn't being upfront with Mr. Whateverhisnameis."

"And where, may I ask, did you acquire your sudden insight into how women think and act?"

"From my shrink, Dr. De Nesto."

"You finally went to see a psychiatrist?"

"Yes, I did. I wanted to learn why I acted the way I did when I lost my leg. To help me understand why I couldn't let you share it with me."

"Was Dr. De Nesto able to help you understand?"

"Yes, Jane. I've learned a lot about myself and what makes me tick."

"I'm proud of you, Tony," she said, placing her hand on his. "It took a lot for a man like you to bare your soul to someone."

He looked down at her hands, said shyly, "I had the right motivation. I realized after I had lost you just how much you meant to me. And, well, I hoped that by understanding why I acted the way I did, I might be able to win you back."

She avoided his eyes. "Was the doctor able to help you with your dysfunction problem?"

"Yes, I was helped, I think." He shifted in his seat. "I haven't been with another woman yet, so I can't be sure."

"In all this time?"

"I just couldn't bring myself to do it. The anxiety is still too much for me to cope with. I never know when or how to tell a woman that I'm an amputee. The fear of rejection can be a horror. You just can't imagine."

She ran her fingers over his cheek. "I guess I never really appreciated how difficult it must have been for you."

"There's another reason why I haven't been with another woman. It . . . it would be like severing the bond that I feel exists between us. I just couldn't bring myself to do that." He looked away, wishing he could muster a single tear to run down his cheek. He faced her, leaned forward, and kissed her on the lips. Without saying a word, he got up and walked alone down the winding path.

There should be fog, he thought. When he saw Robert Taylor play that scene, the actor walked away and disappeared into fog. The only mist he had for his dramatic walkaway was the debris from the stinking maw of a passing garbage truck. He didn't know what had made him come on that way with her. It must have been his cop instincts telling him to play on her sympathy, to use her maternal nature for his benefit. What the hell, he thought, all's fair in love, war, and the Job.

24

Mary Ann Gallagher was dressed in a white nightgown. She was sitting on her bed doing her toenails. The sharp smell of nail polish remover filled the air around her. Her bedside radio played soft music. The last of the biddies had left an hour ago, and she was happy and content to be alone to pamper herself and to think of Harris and everything that had happened these past days. She had known all along that Harris had underestimated Scanlon. From her first meeting with him she knew that Scanlon was a man to be wary of. She had seen that keen sense of determination in those dark eyes of his. She had warned Harris to get rid of those damn guns, but no, he had to have it his way. She could never understand men's fascination with firearms. The lawyer had told her that they had no case against Harris, and she believed him. But no matter what happened with Harris, she was in the clear. There was no way Scanlon or anyone else could ever connect her with any of it. Damn! I smudged the polish, she thought. She took a cotton ball and wiped off the polish and started over.

She had been married to Gallagher long enough to have learned that even if Harris tried to save himself by giving her up, she was safe because there was no corroboration. They'd need some evidence tending to connect her with the commission of the crime. And that evidence did not exist. She had seen to that. It was Harris who had bought everything they needed. It was he who had stolen the van and had gotten the makeup. The more she ran the whole thing over in her head the more secure she felt.

Soon she would be receiving the money from Gallagher's death gamble. And then it would be off to Europe and the good life. All those sexy European men with their heart-throb accents and trim bodies. She was glad in a way that Harris had been arrested. It would be easier now for her to dump him. She would just make up some excuse to go away by herself and disappear.

She wanted men in her life who would satisfy her needs and desires. There would be no more cops in her life, that was for sure. She was sick to death of cops and their infantile desires.

The doorbell. Oh, hell. Don't those biddies ever give up and go to bed? She screwed the brush into the polish bottle and got up from the bed, sliding her pink bathrobe off the chair. The bell rang again.

Putting the bathrobe on, she moved down the hall toward the door, calling out, "Yes, who is it?"

"It's me, dear. Pat."

Cursing under her breath, Mary Ann Gallagher unlatched the door.

A figure loomed on the other side, its hands gripping a weapon, primed to strike the moment the victim came into view. A glossy Botticelli shopping bag that had been used to transport the weapon was on the floor. The hallway was deserted. No sounds came from the other apartments. It was as though the building were deserted.

The door swung open and Mary Ann Gallagher came into view. She gasped and her mouth fell open. Before the scream could reach her lips the blade struck her neck. A horrible gurgle burst from her throat the moment the blow was struck. Smothering the wound with her hands, Mary Ann Gallagher whirled and ran down the hallway as though seeking out safety in the depths of her home. She tottered into the bedroom.

The killer put the weapon into its carrying bag, took hold of the white handles, stepped into the apartment, and kicked the door closed. The victim lay writhing on the bedroom floor, making ghastly noises. The killer moved across the room and stood by the side of the bed, watching the death throes. A cigarette was lit and the lighter carefully put down on the bed next to the Botticelli shopping bag.

Mary Ann Gallagher trembled with violent spasms; her extremities thrashed about the floor. Her body stiffened in a final convulsion and fell still.

The killer reached out and crushed the cigarette into the ashtray on top of the radio. Glancing at the body, the killer noticed that there were no underpants. A woman should be modest even in death. The corpse's nightclothes were pulled down.

The doorbell rang. The killer grabbed the shopping bag and ran from the room. Tiptoeing down the hall, the killer stood by the door, listening to the conversation on the other side.

"Mary Ann, it's us, Pat and Joan. We've come back to keep you company."

Silence.

"I wonder where she can be?"

"Maybe the poor dear went to sleep early? It has been a trying day for her, what with what happened to that nice Sergeant Harris and all."

"Why don't we come back in the morning?"

"Footsteps moved away from the door, down the staircase.

The killer cracked the door and looked out, saw no one, and slipped from the apartment, moving quickly over to the stairs leading to the upper floors.

The killer climbed to the middle of the stairs and pressed against the wall, listening to the conversation that was taking place in the vestibule, two floors below. Maybe Mary Ann was in the bathroom or washing her hair in the sink and didn't hear us. Do you think we should try once more? Yes.

Padding footsteps coming back upstairs. A hard knock at the door. The sound of a doorknob being tried, followed by the squeak of a door being slowly opened. A gasp. "Is that blood all over? Mary Ann! Are you all right?"

Peering over the banister, the killer saw the door ajar and no one standing there.

Rushing down the stairs and out into the night, the killer heard a series of piercing screams.

25

They had done everything they could do. Now came the waiting. Waiting while banks searched their microfilm; waiting for libraries to search through old charge-out cards; waiting to hear from detective squads throughout the city. Scanlon had personally telephoned the Whips of every squad and asked them to have their people canvass their precincts for an effeminate Hispanic who drove a Chevrolet with chartreuse blinds and a stuffed animal with a bobbing head.

It was 2013 hours and they were tired and hungry.

Scanlon suggested that they go to Monte's to eat. He turned to Hector Colon. "Hector, you hold it down, will you? We'll bring you back a sandwich."

"Right, Lou," Colon said, switching on the television set.

The detectives sat at one of the large tables in the rear of the restaurant. They ate in silence for the most part. No one was in the mood for conversation. They were finishing dessert when Scanlon looked across the table at Higgins and said, "Better give Hector a call and see if anything is doing."

She returned in a few minutes with a saucy smile on her face. Rounding the table to her seat, she bent by Scanlon and whispered, "Jane Stomer called and left a message for you to call her at home."

"Jane?"

"Hi." A silence, followed by the sound of her exhaling. "You were right, Scanlon. I am still in love with you. And I want you to know that there is no Mr. Whateverhisnameis. I made him up to hurt you."

"I'm glad you told me," he said, thinking, Thank you, Dr. De Nesto.

"Look, Scanlon, I really don't know if we can make it together. I really don't. But if you're willing to give it another try, then so am I."

"I am willing, Jane."

"I want to start off slowly, get to know you again."

"Whatever you say. I'll play by your rules. Dinner, tomorrow?"

"That sounds nice. Say eight o'clock."

"I'll pick you up." Pause. "I love you, Jane."

"Me too, Tony."

Leaving the phone booth, Scanlon felt wonderful. Better than he had in years. He felt as though he were on his way to being a complete person again. He was going to have to call Sally De Nesto and thank her, to say goodbye. He just didn't have any idea of what he would say. He went up to the bar and motioned for the waiter to give him the bill. He paid the tab and went back to the table. "We ready?" he said to the detectives.

"Let's get the tab," Brodie said.

"It's taken care of," Scanlon said.

"Lou?" Brodie said. "You don't gotta go around picking up our tabs."

"Let's get back," Scanlon said.

They left the restaurant and piled into the unmarked car.

Higgins drove. Scanlon sat in the passenger seat. The three detectives squeezed into the back. Higgins switched on the ignition. Scanlon turned on the radio.

"In the Nine-three precinct a ten-ten. Female calls for help. 32 Anthony Street. Units going, K?"

"That's Gallagher's house," Scanlon exclaimed, grabbing the handset. "Nine-three Squad on the way."

"George Henry going, Central."

"Ten-four Squad, ten-four George Henry."

Mary Ann Gallagher's two girlfriends were standing outside the bedroom screaming incoherent things at the detectives when they arrived. Scanlon rushed into the bedroom, followed by his team. He took in the body of Mary Ann Gallagher on the floor and quickly scanned the bedroom. His eyes latched on to the lighter laying atop the chenille bedspread, and then immediately switched to the crushed cigarette in the ashtray that was on the top of the bedside radio. He moved over to the bed, picked up the lighter, and put it into his pocket. Removing a tissue from the box on top of the nightstand, he snatched the cigarette butt out of the ashtray, wrapped it in the tissue, and put the evidence into his pocket.

The crew of sector George Henry plunged into the bedroom. Scanlon told the two cops to wait out in the hall and try to calm down the two women. He went back to the body and squatted on his heels. The detectives gathered around the remains. They were alone.

"There goes our case," Christopher said.

Each detective withdrew into his own thoughts.

Scanlon thought of Joe Gallagher and Yetta Zimmerman and how they had been slaughtered. He thought of Dr. Zimmerman and his wife murdered in their bed as they slept. He thought of the city's crime victims and the countless unsolved crimes and all the misery they had caused. His frustration turned to anger. Different rules have to apply to cops who turn bad. Renegade cops who murder their own. No! Harris was not going to walk away from this. No matter what he had to do, Harris was not going to walk. He looked up at his silent detectives. His face was solemn. "I'm going to take a dying declaration from her before she dies."

He waited for their response.

Brodie hunkered down next to the body. "That's a good idea, Lou."

Scanlon looked at Higgins.

"You'd better hurry before she goes out of the picture," Higgins said.

Biafra Baby grabbed Christopher by the arm. "Hurry, let's call an ambulance." He and Christopher ran excitedly from the bedroom. "Officer," Biafra Baby shouted at the cops. "One of you wait downstairs for the ambulance and direct the attendant up here. The other get in your car and go get a priest and bring him here. Hurry!"

The uniform men ran off.

"She's alive?" Pat shouted at the detectives.

"Yes," Christopher said. "She's trying to give the lieutenant a statement."

"Praise be to God," Joan said, blessing herself.

Brodie came up and stood in the doorway, hampering the view into the bedroom. Biafra Baby and Christopher stood on either side of Brodie. The terrified women stood away from the door, not wanting to look inside.

"Can you hear me, Mrs. Gallagher?" Scanlon said to the corpse. "Please try and talk louder. I can't hear you."

Higgins stuck her tongue into her cheek and made gurgling sounds.

"Mrs. Gallagher, I must ask you your name," Scanlon said.

Pressing her tongue into her cheek again, Higgins mumbled weakly, "Mary Ann Gallagher."

"Where do you live?" Scanlon asked, brushing his hand across the corpse's eyes, closing the lids.

"32 Anthony Street," Higgins mumbled.

"Do you know that you are about to die?" Scanlon asked.

"God . . . forgive . . . me . . . yes . . . I know."

"Can you ladies hear?" Biafra Baby asked the two women.

"Yes," Joan answered for both of them.

Christopher had his steno pad out, making a transcript of Mary Ann Gallagher's dying declaration.

"Mrs. Gallagher, do you have any hope of recovery?" Scanlon asked, watching the blood seep from the wound in the corpse.

"No hope . . . none . . . a priest . . . please . . . priest," Higgins mumbled, tongue in cheek.

"One is on his way," Scanlon said. "Mrs. Gallagher, will you tell me who did this to you?" He looked at Higgins, who had squatted next to him with her back to the door. "Who did this to you?" he repeated, looking at Higgins.

She took a deep breath, jabbed her tongue against her cheek, and mumbled, "George did it . . . George Harris murdered me. . . . Afraid . . . I . . . would . . . tell . . . about . . . Gallagher . . . and . . . the . . . others. . . . We . . . did . . . it . . . together. . . . I . . . God . . . mercy . . ." She gasped. Hissed out air. Silence.

"Sweet Jesus, did you hear that?" Joan said.

Pat made the sign of the cross. "Mother of God."

Scanlon and Higgins exchanged a silent look of understanding. They stood and left the room.

"Did you get it all?" Scanlon asked Christopher.

"Yes, Lieutenant. Word for word," Christopher said. Scanlon was somber. He took the steno pad from Christopher, read what was written, passed the book to Pat, and said, "Will you ladies please read the transcript and sign it as witnesses?" He waited for them to read and sign the page, and then passed the book to his detectives, requiring each of them to sign the transcript.

One of the radio car crew rushed into the apartment with a priest, who hurried into the bedroom. Scanlon noted the time and date on the top of the transcript. The other part of the George Henry crew ran into the apartment with the ambulance attendants.

"She just expired," Scanlon told the attendants. The older of the two attendants, a heavyset man with wild brown hair, looked into the bedroom and saw the priest standing over the body making the sign of the cross. He noted the time on his watch, and began to fill in his worksheet.

Scanlon exchanged satisfied nods with his detectives. He motioned Biafra Baby aside and whispered, "Get on the horn to the One-two-three in Staten Island. Tell them to send some radio cars to cover

Harris's house. And tell them to put a rush on it. I wouldn't want anyone killing him, not now."

Cassiopeia's Chair twinkled in the northern sky; crickets clicked. Sequine Avenue. Amboy Road. Outerbridge Crossing. Strange names for a strange place. An island within a metropolis. The towers of Manhattan merely a vista, not a place to live in, to raise children in. Staten Island. A frame house stood at the end of Amboy Road facing the Outerbridge Crossing. It was a dilapidated house with an untended yard; in it, a car, tireless, sat propped on concrete blocks. Harris's Jeep Comanche was parked next to it.

George Harris was sprawled over the sofa in his dingy living room, a can of beer resting on his stomach. He was staring up at the ceiling, lost in his own thoughts. He did not hear the three radio cars that glided to a stop twenty or so yards from his house. He was thinking of the duffel bag and how lucky he had been to think of tossing it over the embankment. Now the contents of the bag could not be introduced into evidence against him. He wished that he would stop having to go to the bathroom. His lawyer told him that it was a sure bet that he'd walk away from the whole thing. But he was scared.

It had all seemed so simple in the beginning. Foolproof. When it was over he was going to throw in his papers and retire. He and Mary Ann would sail off into the sunset with a ton of money. He wished she was there now to relax him. Damn, he had to go to the bathroom again.

Walking from the bathroom several minutes later, buckling his belt, he was startled when a hard knocking came at the door.

"Yeah, who is it?"

"Lieutenant Scanlon."

Harris opened the door. He looked at the detectives standing behind the lieutenant. There was real fear in his voice. "What are you doing here, Scanlon?"

"I'm here to arrest you," Scanlon said.

Harris walked back into his house, leaving the door open. Scanlon and the detectives followed him inside. Harris went over to the telephone that was on the table next to the couch and began dialing. "I'm calling my lawyer," Harris said.

"It's kind of late at night," Scanlon said.

Dialing, Harris said, "And what are the trumped-up charges this time?"

"I'm placing you under arrest for the murder of Mary Ann Gallagher."

The phone fell from Harris's hand. He gazed with shock at the lieutenant, his mouth open, his face contorting with fear, disbelief. "Mary Ann?"

"She gave us a dying declaration. In it she named you as her killer."

"You're crazy! I loved her!"

"We have two civilian witnesses to her statement," Scanlon said, motioning to Brodie and Christopher to take him.

"You set me up, you bastard," Harris shrieked, lunging for Scanlon's neck.

Scanlon sidestepped the lunge. Brodie grabbed Harris and tossed him to the floor. Christopher slapped handcuffs on Harris's wrists.

Harris struggled to get up off the floor. Brodie and Christopher hefted him up onto his feet. "You son of a bitch. You rotten son of a bitch. You set me up. I'm going to kill you. I'll kill you."

"Your killing days are over," Scanlon said.

The detectives dragged their screaming prisoner out of the house and over to the unmarked department auto. Cops from the One-two-three who had responded to cover Harris's house watched in silence. Scanlon stood in the doorway of the house, looking around the living room. He noticed the photograph of the two smiling children on the mantel. Harris's, he thought. He felt sorry for them. He closed the door and walked up to the gaping cops from the One-two-three. "You guys can resume patrol," he said.

"What's going down, Lou?" one of the cops asked.

"Somebody forgot which side he was on."

At 0900 the next morning, Tony Scanlon parked his car on the corner of Third Avenue and Fifty-second Street. He tossed his vehicle identification plate on the dashboard and got out. He stood on the corner watching four city buses gridlock the avenue. People rushed past him on their way to work. Delivery boys hustled past carrying cartons filled with coffee containers and goodies bundled in waxed paper.

Ten minutes passed before he saw her crossing Third Avenue; she was just one in a flock of scurrying people. She seemed lost, as though she were being carried along by the momentum of the flock.

Coming up to the bank, Linda Zimmerman saw him and stopped. "Leave me alone, Lieutenant."

"I had a feeling you might be coming here today," he said, moving up to her. "Mrs. Gallagher was murdered last night."

"That's wonderful. I hope with all my heart that she burns in hell," she said, pushing past him.

He blocked her. "The ME hasn't figured out yet what the murder weapon was. My money is on a spear, one of those short-handled stabbing kinds that I saw on the wall in your brother's house, or one that fell out of the closet in his office."

"Please excuse me now. I have things I want to do."

He continued blocking her path. "We arrested George Harris for her murder."

"What?"

"Yes. Before she died, Mrs. Gallagher told us that Harris had killed her. She told us in front of two witnesses."

"But I don't understand. I'm—"

"There is no need to understand, Linda. Just know that one way or the other, Harris is going to pay. The statement that Mrs. Gallagher gave us is going to put him behind bars for the rest of his life."

"There is no question of him not spending his life in jail?"

"None. I have a lead on the man who took the guns from the highway, and I fully expect to get my hands on those weapons soon."

"Those two animals didn't have a millimeter of pity between them. I'm glad they both got exactly what they deserved."

Scanlon slid the lighter he had found in Mary Ann Gallagher's bedroom from his pocket and held it up to her. "A Zippo. You don't get to see many of them these days." He opened the clasp of her shoulder bag and dropped the lighter inside, closing the bag. "Goodbye, Linda. I hope everything works out for you and Andrea."

She stood open-mouthed, looking down at her pocketbook. People rushed past them. A jumble of car horns echoed off building walls. She called to his back. "Why, Lieutenant?"

"Say hello to your parents for me," he said, making for his car.

ONE
POLICE
PLAZA

For my daughters
BETH ANN *and* TAFFY

ACKNOWLEDGMENTS

I wish to thank the following people for their editorial help and patience. Without them *One Police Plaza* would have remained an unfulfilled dream. Knox Burger and Kitty Sprague, Marion Wheeler, Martin Cruz Smith, Martin Sanders, Zena IntzeKostos, Carol Kushner, Bridgette Faul, James O'Shea Wade, Laura Knight, Dr. Patricia Simpson, William E. Farrell.

I acknowledge a special debt to Tony Godwin, who pointed me in the right direction, and to the men and women of New York's finest, who gave these pages life.

1

His body sprawled over the rumpled sheets, legs sticking over the end of the bed. He opened his eyes, attempting to focus them on the telephone.

"Lieutenant, we got a little problem. Can you come in to the Squad?"

"I'm on the way." Malone grunted, fumbling the receiver back, and sitting up. He glanced down at the vacant pillow next to him and remembered that she had not wanted to stay the night. The shrunken blood vessels inside his head were throbbing from last night's retirement party. He looked over at the digital clock on the wicker night table. It clicked over to nine-sixteen. Only the Job would get a man with a hangover out of bed on his day off. "A little problem," he muttered and got out of bed.

Dan Malone made the turn into Elizabeth Street twenty minutes later. Every time he came on the Job he expected to find something changed. But the usual Chinese women in their black pajamas and straw sandals were still shuffling along, accompanied by their daughters in designer jeans. Eternally bored men leaned against doorways, cigarettes hanging from their mouths. Nat Hymowitz's clothing store on the corner of Elizabeth and Hester was open for the early-morning hondling.

Malone loved the smells of Chinatown best: the confection of fresh ginger and Chinese cabbage and onions never failed to give him a high; each season of the year had its own distinct mixture. It was June and the smells swept gently over the neighborhood. He parked at the fire hydrant in front of the Sun Hong Wu restaurant, grabbed the vehicle identification plate from behind the visor, and tossed it onto the dashboard. Across the street was the hundred-year-old yellow cream stationhouse with the black fire escapes arranged down the center of its four-story façade. Nineteen Elizabeth Street: the Fifth Precinct, the only damn building in New York City with DC current. Radio cars lined the curb, three-wheeled police scooters were parked on the sidewalk, and barriers and A-frames were stockpiled on the side of the stationhouse. The precinct's flag was twisted around the pole, and the green globes by the door burned dimly in the clear morning light.

Malone waved to the desk lieutenant as he entered the stationhouse, walked through the muster room, and went up the stairs; a narrow, winding passage of carved, Neo-Gothic wood; its majestic banister old and weak; its metal steps worn shiny by the feet of thousands of cops.

Dan Malone was a tall, solidly built man with a long, thin nose and a head of sandy hair that was splotched with gray. His clothes were casual: beige trousers, blue blazer, and a white shirt, open. He was proud that he'd never been "made" as a cop.

The detective squad room was standard issue. New green metal desks with antiquated typewriters were placed around the room. The door of the lieutenant's office concealed a two-way mirror. The detention cage, crammed in a corner, contained a huge stuffed teddy bear perched on a stool. Someone had pinned a six-pointed sheriff's badge to its chest and tucked an empty can of Rheingold and a toy machine gun into its folded paws. Steel mesh covered all the windows. Cardboard waste barrels were scattered about, the overflowing garbage topped with empty beer cans and pizza boxes.

Det. Gus Heinemann sat typing reports with two fingers, his three hundred pounds squeezed up to the desk, his small eyes almost lost beneath a heavy, overhanging brow. Gus was known throughout the Job for his insatiable appetite and his addiction to playing dice. He was a familiar figure at precinct club meetings and police conventions, always in the center of the largest game looking to roll his point. Det. Patrick O'Shaughnessy, outfitted in his usual ensemble of polyester gaudiness, stood at the cabinets filing away his case folders.

Heinemann looked up. "Ah, the lieutenant is in bright and early this morning."

"What's so important to drag me in on my day off?" Malone asked, reaching over the carved gate, releasing the catch on the other side.

"Sergeant Brady telephoned from One-four-one Chrystie Street. He said that they had a DOA that could be a problem. He wants you on the scene," Heinemann said.

"Did he say what they had?"

"He only said that a problem had developed," Heinemann said. Malone gave a knowing nod. "Who's catching?"

"I am," Stern said.

Jake Stern was a balding weightlifter who was always squeezing a hand grip. He had a large nose that had been shattered while he was doing bench presses at the Y. On the day in question, Jake had pressed two hundred pounds for the fifth time and was struggling to make the sixth. He was straining his arms upward when a fag ambled over and tickled his balls. The barbell and weights crashed down, tumbling Jake, bloodied and dazed, onto the floor. The other guy never knew what trouble was until that day.

As Stern turned the unmarked police car into Canal Street, the lieutenant asked him if anything heavy had come in while he was on his RDO. Regular day off.

Keeping his eyes fixed on the traffic inching its way toward the Holland Tunnel, Jake answered, "It's been quiet. We caught a few grounders, but nothing heavy. Ya know, Lou, I'm getting tired of catching nothin' but easy ones." He addressed him as Lou, the diminutive of lieutenant that was routinely used in the NYPD.

One of the two policemen standing in front of 141 Chrystie Street waved to the approaching detectives. "It's on the third floor, Lou," he said as they came up to him.

The floor of the studio apartment was covered by grungy chipped linoleum that had been there at least fifty years. A kitchenette ran the length of the room. Next to the open window was a brass bed and a chest of drawers with a homemade paint job. The body of a nude white man stretched flat on his stomach lay on the sagging mattress of the bed. His face was at right angles, with the eyes open. Body fluid seeped from the nose and mouth into a puddle of phlegm next to the jaw. Blood had drained to the lower part of the body, causing dark blue discoloration of the lower torso. The neck and jaw had stiffened from the downward contractions of rigor mortis.

Slumped into one of the chairs, her hand half obscuring her face, sat a woman in a wine-colored bathrobe pulled tightly around her waist. Her clear skin was streaked with mascara. She looked about twenty-four or -five. Stern eyed her as they entered. "Nice tits," he whispered to the lieutenant.

Sergeant Brady was standing over her, a wet, unlit cigar jutting out the side of his mouth. His face was deeply seamed and pitted by the acne of thirty years ago. "Good t' see ya, Lou," Brady said, a visible expression of relief crossing his face. He moved away from the woman to meet the detectives, stepping between the lieutenant and Stern. In a low, apologetic voice he said, "This caper ain't exactly yours, but we weren't sure how to handle it." Brady scratched his head, looked over at the body, and announced, "A certain amount of finesse is needed on this one. . . ."

"What's the wrinkle, Sarge?" Malone said, glancing at the corpse.

"He's a priest," Brady whispered.

Malone moved over to the body, placing his palm down on the clammy skin. "How long?"

The woman flicked her eyes to the lieutenant. "About two hours."

Malone grabbed a chair, dragged it to where she was sitting, and sat down facing her. "What's your name?"

"Mary Collins. He was a Monday-morning regular. He arrived around seven each week. . . ."

As she talked he studied her face. High cheekbones that looked chiseled, smooth skin without any trace of hair. His initial suspicion hardened into certainty. Without speaking, he reached out and felt probingly under her chin. The surgeon's thin line was there. He noticed her Adam's apple and then looked down at her hands. They were large and not proportioned to her thin, female body. He slid his hand inside the bathrobe and pushed it aside. The breasts were firm and had perfectly round aureoles that looked as though they had been press-stamped from a sheet of brown rubber and pasted on. He felt one. It was much too firm.

"What was the name you were born with, Mary?"

"Harold."

"Did you have your plumbing fixed?"

She was insulted. "No."

Mary/Harold Collins stood up and bent forward, pulling a limp penis from between her legs. She then tugged the robe closed and sat back down, the perfect lady.

"Did he know that you were a transvestite?"

"Naturally."

"Tell me what happened?"

"He arrived like usual and we went right to bed." She shook her hair back and smoothed it with her hand. "He went down on me. Then he stopped and rolled me over on my stomach. He went into my behind and we were pumping each other when all of a sudden he screams 'Jesus, forgive me,' and collapsed. I thought he came. But I didn't feel his chest heaving . . . hear the breathing." She plastered her hands to her face, rocking from side to side. She was crying.

"What a feeling to have someone die inside of you. God forgive me. I don't know. I don't know . . ."

"Do you live here?"

"No. I use this place for my tricks. My apartment is in Chelsea."

"Get dressed. I want you to leave with us." Malone looked over at the sergeant. "How many people know about this?"

"Nobody outside this room knows anything."

"Let's make damn sure that it stays that way," Malone said flatly. "Has he been I.D.'d?"

Brady waved a brown leather wallet in front of his face. "The Reverend James Gavin of St. Anselm's in Brooklyn."

Malone got up and moved over to the bed. He stared down at the cadaver for a second, then bent downward and picked up the end of the sheet that trailed off the bed. He tossed it over the body and walked back to Mary Collins, who once more had her face hidden. His tone was low, consoling. "Mary? Believe me when I tell you we're just as anxious as you are to resolve this problem as expeditiously and discreetly as possible. Will you do whatever I say is necessary?"

Mary Collins's hands fell to her lap. She looked at the lieutenant. "I'm not going to take a fall. I have no intention of going inside and having to fight for my life. They keep us locked up with the general population."

Malone's lips pursed with satisfaction. He nodded to the others. "You won't have to," he said.

Malone telephoned the medical examiner's office and arranged to have the on-duty M.E. standing by at the morgue to certify the death. Then he put through a call to the archdiocese, confident that the man on the other end would give him no problems. A product of the slums of Philadelphia, an expert on canon law and the head of the ecclesiastical shoofly unit that takes care of problems with rogue priests, Msgr. Terrance McInerney was used to receiving "important" telephone calls from the police. As the personal secretary to His Eminence, it was McInerney's job to handle those unpleasant secular matters that always seemed to crop up.

Malone picked up on the monsignor's calm authority. "What can we do for you, Lieutenant?"

"I am sorry to have to inform you, Monsignor, of the passing of Father James Gavin of St. Anselm's in Brooklyn."

There was a pause on the line. Then, "May God have mercy on his soul. Can you tell me the circumstances of Father's passing? Why are the police involved?"

"Well, Monsignor, it appears that Father was walking down Chrystie Street this morning when he suffered a heart attack. Passers-by carried him into one of the nearby buildings. A young woman was kind enough to let them bring Father into her apartment to await the ambulance. Unfortunately he expired before help arrived. The people who carried him into her apartment left, leaving the poor woman alone with the body. When the police arrived she was hysterical."

"I can well understand the lady's apprehension," McInerney said smoothly.

"I've contacted the medical examiner. Dr. Solomon Epstein is going to perform an immediate autopsy. You'll be able to pick up the remains within a few hours."

The monsignor sighed. "I know Epstein. He's all right. What floor did you say the lady lived on?"

"The third."

"I see. Was Father Gavin wearing his clerical collar?"

"No."

"How was identity ascertained?"

"From the I.D. in his wallet."

"I see. Is there any problem with the press?"

Malone thought he detected the first slight note of tension in the monsignor's voice.

"We've made sure that the incident was not put on the teletype or transmitted over the radio. Only a few people know what happened."

"And how is the young lady holding up?"

"Fine. Although it happened at a particularly difficult time for her."

"Oh? Why is that?"

"She wants to leave New York City. She had been promised a job as a cocktail waitress in a Las Vegas hotel, but it fell through at the last moment. Then this unpleasantness . . ."

"Perhaps we can repay her kindness. What's her name?"

"Harold."

A gasp, followed by stunned silence. Malone waited to let what he had said sink in. "He's a transvestite who goes by the name of Mary Collins."

Deep breaths of anger were coming from the other end. "I am going to make arrangements with Sheehan's Funeral Home to pick up Father's body. I am also sending a representative from my staff to get Father Gavin's personal effects. I want to thank you for your consideration in this delicate matter."

"I was happy to help, Monsignor."

"Will the official report have to mention anything about the *lady*?" Malone could feel the tension on the other end now.

Malone paused a moment before he answered. He wanted the Powerhouse to know that they owed him one. "The lady? What lady,

Monsignor? Father Gavin expired on the street from natural causes. He was alone."

It was after one and Epstein hadn't called. Malone was at his desk trying to reduce the perpetual mound of paper when a thought crossed his mind: What if Gavin's death was not natural? Would his ass be in a sling! He yanked up the phone and dialed.

Epstein answered. "Don't worry. It was natural. A nice, clean coronary occlusion."

"Thanks, Sol."

"Any time. Can't talk now. I'm in the middle of dissecting a spleen." Epstein hung up.

Malone had one more call to make. He dialed Erica Sommers. When her cheerful voice came on the line he smiled and said, "Thanks for last night. You were wonderful."

"It was nice, wasn't it? I'm sorry I couldn't stay. I just had too much work to do today, and I knew you wouldn't let me escape until the afternoon."

He laughed. "Complaints?"

"On the contrary."

"What about tonight?"

"I'm sorry but I'm busy tonight."

"What are you doing?"

There was a pause. Then . . . "Daniel? I don't question you and I don't expect you to question me. They're your rules."

"I'll call you in a day or two."

"That'll be nice."

Malone returned to his paper. The case folder in front of him read, "Anthony Sardillo M/W/33. Homicide by shotgun . . . February 12, 1938." A department photograph of Sardillo lying on a rain-soaked driveway minus most of his head was stapled to the inside cover. Malone got a kick out of examining old photographs of crime scenes. The detectives in them all looked like Mr. Magoo with straw hats and cheap cigars.

The semiannual "five"—DD5 Supplementary Complaint Report, the workhorse form of the Detective Division used to report all additional phases of an investigation—was stapled on top of the forty-odd-year accumulation of fives. Unsolved homicides were never closed; department regulations required that the assigned detective submit at least two fives a year on each of his open homicide cases. The detective assigned to the Sardillo case had nothing to report, as usual.

Malone knew the Sardillo case by heart; he knew all the open cases.

He glanced over the five, signed it, and then tossed the bulging folder into the wire file basket.

Stern and O'Shaughnessy had gone out to pick up lunch, hot heroes, two six-packs, and a pizza for Gus. The detectives were sitting around the squad room eating while Malone was in his office nibbling a strand of melted mozzarella off his eggplant parmigiana hero and reading another case folder.

Stern had his feet up on the desk. He leaned forward and took a can of beer and peeled the top, tossing the tab over his shoulder. He gulped some and looked over at O'Shaughnessy who was sitting across from him.

"You still seeing Foam?" Stern asked O'Shaughnessy.

"Of course. You don't give up a deal like that. Free bed and board and a screw whenever I want," O'Shaughnessy said.

"What's it like to hump a broad who uses foam? Ain't it messy?" Heinemann said.

"No, it ain't messy," O'Shaughnessy snarled.

Stern winked at Heinemann. "Hey, Pat. Does the foam come in different flavors?"

"Yeah, Pat. How does the foam taste?" Heinemann asked.

"How the fuck should I know?" O'Shaughnessy yelled. "You know that I don't go down on women."

"Pity. You really should try it," Stern said.

The telephone rang and Heinemann answered it. He listened for a while, then said, "Right," and hung up. Holding two slices of pizza pressed together, he got up and walked over to Malone's office. He stuck his head inside and announced, "The inspector is on his way over."

Fifteen minutes later Insp. Nicholas Zambrano walked into the Fifth Squad. He was a gravel-voiced, ponderous man with thirty-three years in the department. His body was huge, but still hard and firm, except for his large belly. He had a swarthy face and enormous brown eyes and a warm Mediterranean smile that gave a clue to his inner warmth. But when he had to, Nicholas Zambrano could be a first-class prick.

He walked into Malone's office and plopped his six-foot frame down. "How goes it, Dan?"

"No problems. Want some coffee?"

"Make mine strong," Zambrano said with a sly wink.

Malone got up and walked into the squad room. He returned with two half-filled coffee mugs. He opened the bottom drawer of his desk, removed a bottle of Jack Daniel's, and scowled when he saw that what had been a virgin bottle two days ago was now a third full. He poured a healthy shot into both mugs and slid one over to the inspector.

Zambrano slumped in his seat and held the mug under his nose, sniffing appreciatively. "I was surprised to catch you in. According to your chart, today is your RDO," Zambrano said, his brown eyes moving to meet the lieutenant's.

"Something came up that required my attention. I figured I'd hang around and get rid of some of this paper."

Zambrano frowned mild disapproval. "Don't make the mistake of making the Job your wife. If you do, some day you're going to wake up and discover that you married a whore. Get married, have a family."

"I was married, remember. It sucks."

"Bullshit! They don't all end up on the rocks."

"In this job most of them do."

Resigned, Zambrano sighed and asked, "How many men you got assigned?"

"On paper, twenty-four. I have two men on a steal to the Major Case Squad, one assigned to the borough president's office and one on extended sick, heart attack. That leaves me with twenty men to cover the chart."

Zambrano hesitated. "Dan . . . the mayor wants to borrow one of your guys for a week or so. He has a friend he wants driven around town."

"Inspector! We were stuck the last time driving his girlfriend. Why the hell doesn't he use one of the detectives assigned to guard him?"

"First off, he likes to bounce in Little Italy. He has a lot of friends there. And your squad is the closest. Second, if one of the detectives assigned to Gracie Mansion was spotted in Bloomingdale's carrying packages for some lady, the entire world would know that Handsome Harry has a new girlfriend, that's why. The word is he's stuck on this one. Might even make her a commissioner," Zambrano said.

"Cozy. His wife can swear her in."

Zambrano grinned. He drained his mug, then slid it across the desk. "Skip the coffee this time."

Malone poured a respectable shot and handed the mug back.

Zambrano sat for a moment studying the dark, shimmering liquid and then looked up. "Do you know Inspector Bowen?"

"The one in Community Relations?"

"That's the one. He might be stopping by to examine your community-relations parameters."

"My what?"

"It's the latest brainchild of the paper assholes at headquarters. They've convinced the PC that every unit in the department, including precinct detective squads, should become involved in community relations. You're supposed to get in touch with the various community groups operating within the precinct and find out what their needs are and work out a program for your detectives to respond to those needs. It's called Operation Participation. Bowen's been designated to act as liaison between the DCCR and the Detective Division."

"And what do I put on paper? My detectives try to make every halfway decent-looking female complainant who walks into the squad."

"Just throw the usual bullshit on a forty-nine and have it ready to show Bowen when he pops in."

"Look at that basket of paper on my desk. And they're adding more?"

Zambrano shrugged. "I'll drop you an outline of what they're looking for in the department mail. All you'll have to do is embellish it." Zambrano gulped his drink. "Thanks for the hospitality," he said, getting up. He started to leave, then turned to face the lieutenant. "By the way, the man with the red yarmulke called the PC to say thanks."

2

WEDNESDAY, JUNE 10

At 7:40 A.M. the following morning Sgt. George Brady stepped behind the Fifth Precinct's massive desk and flipped the pages of the sergeants' clipboard. He glanced down at the desk lieutenant who was making his beginning-of-tour blotter entries and then looked up at the clock. Brady took the cigar from his mouth and laid it in the ashtray. It was time to turnout the Second Platoon.

Looking down at the desk lieutenant, Brady asked, "Got anything for the boys, Lou?"

The lieutenant looked up. "Tell 'em not to bring in any Puerto Rican mysteries. I'm not in the mood for that bullshit today. And George, tell sector Charlie I want some roast pork lo mein for lunch."

"You got it, Lou."

Brady tucked the clipboard under his arm and stepped out from behind the desk.

"All right, fall in," Brady shouted, walking into the sitting room.

The members of the Second Platoon reluctantly abandoned their coffee and cigarettes and shambled into two uneven ranks.

Brady faced the platoon. "Attention to roll call."

He called the roll, assigning each police officer to his post, sector, calling off their meal hour; he read off post conditions. "Summonses are down for the month. We need movers. Pay attention to your Accident Prone Locations. Sector Adam, watch out for payroll robberies; Sector David, tag the double parkers around the court. The judges are complaining that they can't get into their assigned spaces. The Seventh Squad is looking for a 'seventy-nine green Olds in connection with a homicide. The right front fender is smashed in. The car has Jersey plates and a broken vent window on the driver's side. If found, safeguard for prints. Sector Charlie, the lieutenant wants roast pork lo mein for lunch. You might as well bring him a flute too—he'll be a little parched by then." He was referring to a soda bottle filled with whiskey. "You all understand your assignments?"

Two files of policemen stood in indifferent silence, their eyes staring blankly ahead.

"Okay. Open ranks for inspection," Brady growled.

Sgt. George Brady had forty years in the Job. Next year he'd have to throw in his papers. Just as well. It was getting harder and harder for Brady to accept the new breed of cops. He missed the spit and polish of the old days. As he moved down the first file, he glanced with dismay at the short, dumpy female officers with asses as broad as billboards, their flabby waists hanging over their gun belts. The blacks with their damn Afros, uniform caps perched on top of a beehive of kinky black hair. Puerto Ricans with their goddamn peach fur on their goddamn wheat-colored chins and their goddamn greasy sideburns. Even the Irish cops had succumbed to the age of permissiveness with their long hair lacquered down with hair spray and their goddamn handlebar mustaches. The locker room smelled like a goddamn French whorehouse. There was only one white cop in the entire precinct with close-cropped hair, spit-shined shoes, tailored uniform that hugged the body, and he was a goddamn fag. Yeah. It was time for George Brady to get out.

The sergeant stopped in front of a female officer who had the contours of a fire hydrant.

"Where's your flashlight?"

"In my locker, Sarge," she replied sheepishly.

"In your locker? And what will you do if you have to chase a holdup man into a dark basement? Call time out and run back to your locker? Go upstairs and get your flashlight!"

Brady walked in front of the platoon. "Take your posts."

Blue-and-white radio cars were parked all along Elizabeth Street. Police officers slumped in their cars, waiting. Pairs of policemen loitered near the precinct steps, talking over the night's activities. When the first police officer emerged from the precinct, the cops of the late tour abandoned their radio cars and hurried toward the stationhouse.

Police Off. Joe Velch and his partner, Carmine Rossi, headed for their radio car. Velch moved around to the driver's side. They jabbed their nightsticks between the rear seat, tossed their memo books into the back, dropped their flashlights onto the front seat, and threw their summons pouches onto the dashboard. Velch started to gather up the early-bird edition of the *Daily News* that was scattered over the seat. Rossi stretched his arm under the front seat and scooped out the beer containers and brown bags that had been squirreled away during the late tour.

Velch looked up at the gas gauge. "Ya suppose to gas up on the late tour, you donkey cocksucker!" he shouted after his hastily departing relief.

They drove over to the Sixth Precinct to get gas and then drove to Moshe's on the corner of Canal and Baxter where two containers of regular, one extra sweet, and two bagels with cream cheese were waiting in a bag next to the cash register. The radio car slid to a stop in front of the luncheonette. Velch raised himself out of the car and ambled into the crowded store.

Moshe was busy behind the counter. The store owner saw the policeman enter and started to work his way down the counter to the cash register.

"So how goes it today, Joe? Catch any criminals?" Moshe asked.

"Not yet, Moshe," Velch said, struggling to pull out his wallet.

Velch took a dollar bill out and placed it in Moshe's palm. The store owner handed the policeman the bag, rang up the sale, and gave Velch his four quarters change.

They parked the radio car under the Brooklyn Bridge. Rossi opened the glove compartment and rested the bag on top of the door. He took out a container and a bagel and passed them to his partner. They pried off the tops of the containers and laid them on the dashboard; cops never throw away the tops of containers. They might have to leave fast.

The view was relaxing—a tugboat was shepherding two garbage scows, its stubby bow pushing aside greenish water. The river's day was just starting when a scratchy mutter on the radio broke the silence.

"Five Boy, K."

"Aw shit!" Rossi said, snatching up the radio.

"Five Boy, K," he answered.

"Five Boy, respond to Chatham Towers, One-seven-zero Park Row. See complainant regarding a foul odor."

"Five Boy, ten-four." Rossi put the mike back into its cradle and turned to his partner. "We'll finish our coffee and then take a slow ride over. It's probably nothing."

The Chatham Towers, a twenty-four-story housing complex of naked concrete blocks and jutting terraces, stood in Lower Manhattan in the shadow of the Manhattan Bridge and Columbus Park. Crescent-shaped driveways angled upward to the building. Isolated tiny playgrounds with modular cubes instead of seesaws made the apartment-house setting seem somewhat bizarre in the surrounding area of old buildings.

Tenants were milling in front of the entrance as the radio car rounded the driveway. The policemen got out and walked down the steps leading into the complex. A porter was waiting for them in the vestibule. "The third floor, officers."

When the elevator was between the second and third floor they got their first whiff of the familiar, awful odor. Velch looked at his partner. "It's ripe."

The elevator stopped on three and they stepped out. Velch made a sudden grab for his handkerchief. The coffee, bagel, and cream cheese exploded from his mouth, splattering his uniform and spewing across the hall. The stench was suffocating. They gagged and their mouths filled with saliva. With every gasp they fought not to swallow their tongues.

"You okay?" Rossi said, pressing his handkerchief over his mouth and nose.

"I'm all right," he choked. "My uniform is shot to hell."

"Chrissake . . . this is one ripe son-of-a-bitch," Rossi said. They reluctantly paused in front of each door in the hall until they got to Apartment 3c.

"Get some ammonia!" Rossi gagged, before he, too, vomited.

Joe Velch ran back along the corridor, banging on doors.

"Police! Open up. We need ammonia."

A door in the middle of the floor finally cracked open and a hand appeared holding a gray plastic bottle.

Velch grabbed the bottle. The door slammed. He ran to Apartment 3c and started to pour ammonia in front of the door. "Carmine, you stay here. I'll call the sergeant and the Squad," Velch said, shaking out the last drippings.

"Tell 'em to bring some crystals with them. We're going to need them!" Rossi shouted after his partner.

Gus Heinemann stuck his massive head in the door of the lieutenant's office. "Lou, they think they've got a DOA in the Chatham Towers. They're calling for the Squad."

"They think?" Malone said.

"They haven't entered the apartment. They're waiting for us to get there," Heinemann said.

"Who's catching?" Malone asked.

"Pat."

"Both of you run over and have a look. If it's a mystery get on the horn and call me. If it's just a grounder, clean it up and forget it."

When the detectives arrived they found Sergeant Brady standing among a cluster of anxious tenants. When Brady saw the detectives getting out of their car, he walked away from the people and went to meet them.

"Whaddaya got, Sarge?" O'Shaughnessy asked, walking up to Brady.

Brady answered, "We were waiting for you guys to get here. We poured some DB 45 crystals around the outside of the door. It was pretty bad up there."

"Anything on who lives there?" O'Shaughnessy asked.

"A female, white, by the name of Sara Eisinger. She's about thirty-four or -five and lives alone. We questioned some of the neighbors, but none of them know anything about her. According to the building's management, she's lived here for five years," Brady answered.

"The first thing we've got to do is find out *que pasa* inside of that apartment," Heinemann said.

An Emergency Service van careened around the driveway, squealing to a stop behind the unmarked detective car.

"Figured we might need gas masks if the crystals don't work," the sergeant said, looking at the van.

Heinemann looked at his partner. "Think we should call the boss?"

"Naw. All we have so far is a case of bad breath. Let's see what we find," O'Shaughnessy said.

A group of detectives and uniformed officers hovered in the hallway, waiting for the disinfecting crystals to work and turn the stink into a bearable smell faintly like violets.

Heinemann turned to the sergeant. "Sarge, will you start a log? If we got a mystery we'll want a record of everyone on the scene."

"You got it," Brady answered.

The detectives put on gas masks. O'Shaughnessy took the bottle of crystals from the sergeant.

"Here goes," said Heinemann, lifting up his right foot and smashing it into the door, splintering it open.

An unspeakable odor gushed out; all the cops started to gag and choke. Two policemen ran retching down the hallway, while O'Shaughnessy stood in the doorway scattering crystals inside the apartment. There was a large kitchen to the right of the entrance. A black wrought-iron table was on its side, its glass top shattered. The cabinets were open, their contents strewn over the floor. O'Shaughnessy stepped inside and turned to the uniformed cops. "Wait out here."

The detectives entered; O'Shaughnessy spread around more of the crystals. A half-open convertible couch was lying on its side, the cushions slashed and shredded. Tables and lamps were broken. There was no sign of a body. "Nothing," Heinemann said, moving through the living room. "It's got to be someplace."

The masks muffled their voices, giving them a hollow resonance.

Heinemann moved to the window and turned on the air conditioner. He glanced down at the street. His eyes wandered to the duplex pagoda roof of the Manhattan Savings Bank on the corner of Chatham Square and Catherine Street. He liked the way the eaves curled under. A queue of tourist buses were starting to unload their passengers. It was a beautiful day to be looking for death.

The living room led into a small foyer. There were two closets on either side. The floor was littered with linens. A closed door at one end apparently led to the bathroom. Pat looked at Gus. "It's gotta be in there," Pat said, moving to open the door. "Dear Mother of God!"

The bathroom was done in blue. Ceramic tiles covered the floor, blue fluffy scatter rugs on top. The tub was filled to its brim with a dark red liquid. Lying face down was the swollen, nude body of a woman. Her long blond hair fanned out on the surface of the loathsome, hardened mixture of blood and other things. Writhing maggots covered the back of the head, sodden wormlike creatures feasting on human decay. Her hands were handcuffed behind her body, intertwined fingers pointing helplessly upward.

"I ain't never seen nothin' like this," O'Shaughnessy said, his mouth gaping. "Better call the boss and tell him to get his ass here forthwith. We got a homicide on our hands."

They were waiting outside in the hall when the lieutenant and the rest of the squad arrived. Walking up to the gathering, Malone asked, "Who's been inside?"

Heinemann answered, "Only Pat and me."

"Let's keep it that way," Malone said. "I don't want anyone inside unless they've got a specific reason for being there. Has Forensic been notified?"

"They're on the way," O'Shaughnessy answered.

Malone turned to Sergeant Brady. "Sarge, you take care of it out here. If any of the chiefs from headquarters come by, keep them the hell out of the crime scene. I don't want them screwing things up. The last one we had, some chief from Planning held up the murder weapon for the newspaper boys. He got his picture in the centerfold and the perp walked."

Brady asked, "And if some muck-a-muck insists?"

"You call me—I'll handle it," Malone said.

"Ten-four," Brady replied.

"Let's take a look," Malone said, moving to the doorway.

Pat O'Shaughnessy was at the lieutenant's side, a steno pad ready in his hands.

The lieutenant stared into the apartment. "What a shambles."

"Looks like somebody put up a helluva fight," O'Shaughnessy said.

"Or someone was searching for something," Malone said.

Malone started to enter the apartment when Brady called him. The lieutenant turned and the sergeant handed him plastic gloves.

"Thanks," Malone said, putting the gloves on. "I almost forgot them. Make sure that no one enters the scene without them."

Malone stood looking down at the tub, shaking his head in disbelief. He knelt down and, with his forefinger, he carefully wiped the slime off the handcuffs. "Smith and Wesson," he observed, twisting his head, trying to read the serial numbers. "We might be able to trace them."

"How long do you figure?" O'Shaughnessy asked.

"It's hard to tell," Malone said, glancing from the body up to the partially opened window. "From the degree of decomposition and the maggot castings . . . I'd say about a week." Malone stood up and faced his detectives. "I want this apartment field stripped. Overlook nothing. Gather up her telephone book, her checkbook, savings book. I want to know her medical history. Who her friends were. Her enemies. I want to know who she was making it with. If she was a switch hitter. Gay. Where did she work? When Forensic arrives, tell them I want the crime scene sketch done in the coordinate method."

"The Forensic boys ain't going to like that. It's a lot of work," Heinemann said.

"I don't give a fiddler's fuck what the Forensic boys like. I want an imaginary line drawn through every room in this apartment and every piece of broken glass, paper, wood, anything, connected to the line by distances."

"Do you want to call in some extra detectives?" O'Shaughnessy asked.

"When I notify the Borough, I'll ask for a few to help with the initial canvasses. I don't like too many men working on a case. They fall over each other." Malone's face hardened. "Let me reemphasize what I said before. I don't want to see *anyone* inside this apartment unless they've got a reason to be here. No cops using the telephone to call their girlfriends or picking up souvenirs."

"We got the message," O'Shaughnessy said.

"Okay, call in the rest of the Squad and let's get to work. We're going to take this one nice and easy. One step at a time, just like they say you do it at the Academy: Who? What? When? Where? How? and Why?" Malone said, elbowing past the detectives on his way to call Inspector Zambrano.

When Malone returned five minutes later he found a photographer snapping pictures of every room from every angle and a detective measuring distances from the imaginary line and calling them off to his partner, who entered them on the crime scene sketch. Fingerprint technicians were spreading powder and dusting with plumed brushes. Detectives were sticking their noses into every nook and cranny of the apartment, searching for physical evidence. Anything that was considered of value was tagged and placed into plastic evidence bags.

Brady had stationed himself outside the apartment. A rope barrier had been erected in front of the door. There were signs prohibiting entrance into the crime scene area. As detectives arrived from the Borough, the sergeant entered their names and times of arrival into the crime scene log. Malone dispatched teams of detectives to canvass the Chatham Tower complex for witnesses, friends of the victim, anyone who might know something. Additional teams were sent to interview storekeepers, garage attendants, people who worked in the housing complex, bus drivers who had nearby routes.

Bo Davis and Gus Heinemann canvassed the parked cars within a five-block radius of the scene. Every license plate was written down. Later they'd be run through the National Crime Information Center. Perhaps the killer had panicked and run from the scene, leaving his car. The building's underground garage was canvassed for unauthorized vehicles.

Jake Stern was on his knees in the apartment searching the bottom of the linen closet. Malone looked down at him. "Anything?"

Stern crooked his body, straining to look under the bottom shelf. He reached his hand under and ran it along the shelf.

"Nothing?"

"Lou, the meat wagon is here," an anonymous voice announced.

"Send them in," Malone said, without turning to look.

Two attendants walked into the apartment lugging a body bag, its wide straps dragging on the floor.

With impersonal detachment the morgue attendants laid the bag alongside the tub and went about their job.

Detectives stopped working and gathered around to watch. Policemen are no different from civilians and firemen when it comes to death. The same thoughts cross their minds: She's dead. I'm alive. Someday I'll be dead. I wonder how long I've got to live. What will it be like, nothingness?

Without hesitation the attendants plunged their bare hands into the red muck. They lifted the body. Slime sloughed off. Maggots rained to the floor. The crust was broken. A new abomination rose from the tub.

The lower part of Sara Eisinger's jaw dangled from one socket. Her battered body was halfway between the tub and body bag when the jaw clattered to the floor.

The body was placed into the canvas bag. One of the attendants bent to scoop up the jaw. He nonchalantly tossed it into the bag.

"Don't close it up," Malone said, kneeling to examine the front of the body. He spread his hands under her neck and slowly ran them down over the body feeling for entrance wounds, something taped to the body. He felt under her deflated breasts. Her armpits. He pushed her legs apart. "Jesus Christ. Look at this."

Protruding from Sara Eisinger's vagina was the curved end of a curtain rod.

Malone sat in his office that evening reviewing the fives on the Eisinger homicide. Outside in the squad room a detective was interviewing a female complainant who insisted she had been raped by her common-law husband. As he flipped the pale blue pages of the Supplementary Complaint Reports he was struck, not for the first time, by the impersonal tone of the narratives: time and place of occurrence; physical description of the crime scene; victim's name and pedigree; name and addresses of persons interviewed; name, shield number and command of MOFs on the scene, and notifications made. Malone wondered if there was anyone who would miss Sara Eisinger.

Malone tossed the case folder into the active basket, then arched his back and stretched. He reached down and slid out the bottom drawer and took out the quart bottle of Jack Daniel's and a glass. He blew the glass clean; the booze would sterilize it. Drink in hand, he got up and walked over to the window. He grinned when he saw the black man on the corner of Canal Street hustling tourists in a three-card monte game. Shmucks. They'll never learn.

Malone's office was a sterile cubicle with dirty green-and-gray cinderblock walls, a locker, two filing cabinets, and a glass cabinet-type bookcase that contained the *Patrol Guide, Penal Law, Criminal Procedure Law,* and stacks of unread department orders. His desk was green metal with a gray Formica top and a glass covering—standard PD issue. Taped to the wall behind the desk was a large piece of cardboard with important telephone numbers.

He moved back to his desk and went to kick in the open bottom drawer when he noticed the ormolu picture frame sticking out from beneath the Manhattan Yellow Pages. It had been a long time since he had stared at her photograph and remembered. He lowered himself into the chair and reached back into the drawer to pull the frame out from under the thick book and set it up on the desk in front of him. He poured more bourbon into his glass and toasted the photograph, staring into her large black eyes. He could still remember the exact date he had snapped it. Sunday, May 4, 1960: over twenty-two years ago. He had caught her preening in front of the seal pit in the Prospect Park zoo, a cheerful nymph with short, coal-black hair and a pixie nose.

She was eighteen. He was twenty.

Dan Malone and Helen Frazer fell in love. Their heads were full of dreams about their future. He was going to earn his B.A. in history from Brooklyn College and become a policeman and go on to become the chief of detectives of the largest police department in the world. Helen Frazer was going to earn her Ph.D. in psychology and become a child psychologist. They were going to marry and live happily ever after.

A marriage that started in bliss and ended in shit, he thought, as he drank. Their union lasted eight years, nine months, and twenty-four days. In the beginning they shared a lot. Each day ended with long, full reports on the day's experiences. By the end of their first year together they had both earned their degrees. She was doing graduate work at Hunter College and was active in both the Literary and Psychology Clubs. In January of their second year of marriage he was appointed to the police department. The metamorphosis from civilian to cop began immediately. His first class at the Academy was a "Don't" class: Don't get involved off duty; Don't discuss the job with civilians; Don't look to be a hero; Don't be a boss fighter; Don't ever trust newspapermen, lawyers, junkies, or hookers.

He enjoyed the structured curriculum at the Academy, learning the law, police procedures, traditions. Twice a week, in the afternoons, policemen from some of the city's busy houses would come to the Academy to conduct informal sessions with the recruits. It was those sessions that would absorb his mind. He would sit wide-eyed and attentive, listening to the experiences of street cops, learning his tradecraft: Never stand in front of a closed door, the person on the other side might fire through it and kill you; When responding to a 10:30 be mindful that the stickup team might have a backup lurking nearby; Remember that a woman or child can kill you just as dead as a man; A woman in a nun's habit is no guarantee that she's a nun; In a crowd stay with your partner, don't get separated; Pull your holster around your front in order to protect your groin and to prevent anyone from coming up from behind and ripping your gun from your holster.

After school, outfitted in recruit grays, he would ride the Lexington Avenue subway uptown to their one-bedroom Yorkville apartment on East Seventy-ninth Street. Usually they would make love and then go out to eat. Luciano's was on Madison Avenue. They both liked Italian food and were too young to worry about calories.

Upon graduation from the Academy he was assigned to the Seven-nine on patrol. The Seven-nine was one of the five precincts that made up the old Thirteenth Division: the Seven-three, Seven-seven, Eight-oh, and Eight-eight. The occupying force of Bed-Stuy, a ghetto ripe with decay and violence. It was during those fledgling years in the Seven-nine that the marriage soured.

There were many cops who were content to do their eight hours and go home. Then there were the active ones, the cops to whom time meant nothing, who doggedly searched out crime and the criminals. Malone was such a cop. As his arrest record soared so did the time he had to spend in court. They were spending less and less time together, the inevitable outcome of a cop's giving more to the Job than to a marriage.

The Seven-nine's watering hole was Leroy's Lounge on Gates Avenue. A smoke-filled room of glittering glass globes, pulsating lights, and soul music. After a four-to-twelve tour, the cops would go to Leroy's to unwind. The session lasted until four in the morning. Policemen's wives have dubbed those tours the "four-to-fours." They despise them. During the four-to-fours Malone was further indoctrinated into the folklore of the department. The rookies went to listen to angry, cynical men recite the epic tales and legends of the Job. Sipping a flat beer, he would listen as ex-detectives told why they had been flopped back into uniform. Someone else was always at fault. Many claimed that a girlfriend or ex-wife in whom he had confided things dropped a dime or wrote an anonymous letter. He heard vice cops tell how girlfriends, the horses, and booze had eaten up all their ill-gotten money. For the first time he heard of the high suicide rate, the divorce rate, even the arrest rate. "I never thought of getting locked up until I came on this fucking job," an old-timer had confided during a four-to-four.

Another old-timer: "Kid, this is the only job in the world where you can go to work hungry, horny, broke, and sober and have all those needs taken care of by the end of your tour."

Helen was alone most of the time now. She kept herself busy with schoolwork and school activities. She told herself that it was the newness of the job that enthralled him. It would wear off in time and they would settle into the normal routine of living. But one morning after a late tour he received a telephone notification at home. He had been transferred into the Detective Division. The sudden promotion was not the result of a blazing gun battle or a spectacular arrest but came about because of the intercession of his Uncle Pat with the then chief of detectives. His uncle and the chief had been radio car partners. That was how men became detectives—contacts.

As a detective third grade he was seldom home. Lovingly prepared dinners went uneaten. Concerts went unheard, shows unseen. He was always busy with investigations or extraditions. Not to mention tails, plants, and testimony before the grand jury and the court. And the paper, the ubiquitous triplicates and quadruplicates. He accepted the long hours and the frustrations. He reveled in it; she came to revile it.

One night after a fifteen-hour tour he came home and undressed quietly. He was bone-weary. He slipped into bed, close to her, caressed her breasts and prodded her warm body with his. She grunted annoyance, slapped him with her hip, and turned away, tugging and tucking the blanket under.

When they awoke in the morning they were silent and tense. She was angry because she was always alone, losing her husband to the damn police department. He was pouting because she had denied him loving. They had their morning coffee and remained in bed reading the Sunday papers, each scrupulously keeping to their own side of the bed.

The awkward silence was broken by the occasional turning of a page. Finally she said, "I see Westenberg is doing the St. Matthew Passion at the cathedral in April. Want to go?" Her face was hidden behind the Arts and Leisure section of the New York Times. He was relieved, the first conciliatory move had been made. "Who is the mezzo-soprano?" He put down the Week in Review section and reached across the separating space to push the paper away from her face. He saw that she was crying.

"I love you," he said.

"What's happening to us, Dan? We've become strangers. What is it about that job that consumes you? Tell me; I want to try to understand."

"It's the nature of the Job. Each tour I go to work intending to catch up on my paper, but I can't. The cases keep coming in. Our squad catches five-handed. Every tour each one of us catches an average of twenty-three cases apiece. Some of them we can shitcan. The burglaries and robberies get a fast phone call to jerk off the complainant and then they're filed. But you can't can a homicide or a felonious assault or a rape or a shooting. There are people walking the street that I don't have the time to go out and arrest. I telephone them and try to lure them into the Squad. It's like shoveling shit against the tide. Unending."

Dismayed, she grabbed his shoulders and shook. "But you love it!" He acknowledged her accusation with a nod. She threw herself into his arms. "Resign and go to law school. Teach. Drive a taxi. Anything so that we can live a normal life. I need my husband."

"It's in my blood. I can't quit."

"Will you promise that you will at least try to work fewer hours, be home more?"

"I'll try," he said doubtfully, reaching into her cleavage, playing with her semihard nipple.

The years passed. He had been promoted to sergeant and was the second whip of the Tenth Squad. Dr. Helen Malone was teaching child psychology at St. John's and had a budding practice with the Jewish Family Service. They had become friendly bed partners who had discursive conversations and who engaged in passionless acts of sex. Helen Malone had learned to fake it.

He returned home one summer evening to find his wife sitting dejectedly on their bed, suitcases at her feet. He went and sat next to her, afraid to speak. He knew what she was going to say. She began to cry softly. "Dan, I don't like what's happening to us. I can't live with it anymore. I'm leaving, for my own sanity." He wanted to plead. She stopped him by placing a finger to his lips. "Please don't make it harder. I've made my decision." She took his face in her hands and tenderly kissed his cheek. "I want you to know that I've never been unfaithful to you."

His eyes brimmed. "Neither have I."

Tears were stinging her lids. "I know."

He still remembered it clearly, but the pain was less. He poured one more drink, returned the ormolu frame to its place beneath the Manhattan Yellow Pages, and pushed the drawer closed.

"Lieutenant, you got a call on two," a detective in the squad room shouted.

Malone looked over at the blinking plastic button. He gulped his drink and yanked up the receiver.

"This is Captain Madvick from the chief of detectives' office." It was a pleasant enough voice.

"What can I do for you, Captain?" he asked, lowering himself onto the edge of the desk.

"The chief asked me to call. He wants to know if there is anything unusual about the Eisinger case."

Malone stood up. Why was the chief of detectives interested in a run-of-the-mill homicide that was probably going nowhere?

"Nothing," he answered, tucking the receiver under his chin and reaching for the case folder.

"Did you come up with any physical evidence or . . . er . . . property that was unusual?"

Malone pressed the earphone close. "What did you say your name was, Captain?"

"M-A-D-V-I-C-K." He sounded annoyed.

"From the chief of detectives' office?"

"You got it, Lieutenant."

"And you're calling from the office now?"

"Of course."

"I'll call you right back." Malone hung up and looked up at the directory. He picked up the receiver and dialed.

"Chief of detectives."

"Captain Madvick please."

"Ain't no Captain Madvick assigned her, pal."

"This is Walter Farrell from the *New York Times*," Malone lied. "I'm trying to get in touch with Captain Madvick. He used to be assigned there. I'm doing a story on the Rosenberg homicide. He was in charge of that case."

"I don't think there is anyone with that name assigned to the Detective Division. Wait a minute and I'll check the ten cards."

There was no active member of the Detective Division with the surname Madvick, he was told by the duty officer. Malone thanked him, hung up, and then dialed Operations. Using the same newspaperman ploy he asked the sergeant on duty to check the uniform force's ten cards and see where Captain Madvick was assigned.

There was no active member of the department with the name Madvick. "Maybe he retired," the sergeant said.

"Yeah, I guess that's it."

Malone sat on his desk idly waving the Eisinger folder. Whoever made that telephone call was on the Job; it was one cop talking to another cop. He opened the case folder and thumbed through to the property vouchers. Physical evidence or property that was unusual, the phony Captain Madvick had asked. He scrutinized the vouchers: a personal checkbook; some keys; a telephone book; thirty-two dollars and sixty-seven cents; a makeup kit; a pocketbook; nail file; emery board; and a lipstick. On a separate voucher—a set of handcuffs and a curtain rod.

*　　*　　*

Malone could not easily open the door to Sara Eisinger's apartment as it was carefully sealed with an official department seal on which was quoted the pertinent provision of the law prohibiting entry for all those not on official business. He took out his police identity card and sliced down through the seal, and then removed a set of house keys from the plastic evidence bag. As he did he noticed a gold-plated key in the bag. He wondered what it was for. The super had repaired the kicked-in door panel. There were three locks and all the cylinders were protected by steel plates. After struggling through several keys he got the locks open and entered the apartment.

He didn't know why he was surprised to find the place still a shambles, but he was. After all, there was no one to clean it up. The air conditioner was still humming. Fingerprint powder was scattered over the furniture and walls and cigarette butts were crushed into the carpet and floors.

Malone didn't know what he was looking for, but whatever it was, it was making someone in the Job very nervous. He decided to start in the bathroom with its horrifying crusted tub. First he opened jars of creams and lotions inside the medicine cabinet. He poked a finger inside the creams and emptied the lotions down the sink, carefully straining the creamy liquids through his fingers. Finding nothing, he went to the foyer outside the bathroom. He reexamined the closets, getting on his knees in order to run his hands underneath the shelves.

Forty minutes later he was standing in front of the refrigerator searching the freezer. He remembered an old Hitchcock television program where the wife used a frozen leg of lamb to bludgeon her husband to death, but there was nothing there but half of a jar of coffee and a stick of butter. He next searched the cabinets and under the sink and then leaned against the wall trying to think of any place he might have missed. He glanced down at the tiny stove and saw a Pyrex coffee pot on the far burner. His eyes swept the apartment. What had he missed? Perhaps nothing. Maybe he had found whatever it was and didn't know it. That gold-plated key? As he thought, he absentmindedly picked up the coffee pot and examined it. There was a metal strap around the middle. A screw was fastened through the handle securing both ends of the strap to the pot. He noticed that the screw was loose. He inserted the nail of his forefinger into the screw head and attempted to tighten it. Then he saw it. A strip of negative 16mm film that appeared to be about three inches long was fitted between the handle and the neck of the pot. Hidden under the metal collar. He looked down at the knife. Eisinger must have unscrewed the handle with the knife, slid the film under the strap and been attempting to tighten it when her killer or killers interrupted her.

Juggling the strip of film up under the light, he attempted to make out what was on it and couldn't. He counted sixteen frames. He put the film into his shirt pocket and went to turn off the air conditioner.

It was a little before nine the following morning when Malone walked into the squad room. O'Shaughnessy was on the telephone promising fidelity to Foam. According to Heinemann, Pat enjoyed walking the tightrope of infidelity with a bottle of nitro stuck up his ass.

Det. Bo Davis, an expatriate from Dixie, lived in East Meadow, Long Island, with his wife and two children. He loved his family, the Job, his ranch-style home with the cyclone fence all around it, and going to bed with women other than his wife. His motto was: Never get involved. And, during sixteen unfaithful years, he hadn't.

Davis was slumped in a swivel chair with his feet stretched up over the desk, admiring his new cowboy boots. He was wearing a white sports jacket with wide blue stripes, white waffle-weave trousers flared at the cuffs, and a blue shirt with a white tie and gold tie clasp with a miniature detective shield emblazoned in the center.

"Getting ready for Halloween?" Malone said, walking past Davis on his way into his office.

"I got a date with a three-way broad with her own mattress," Davis said, leaning forward to buff the point of his boot.

Malone called the detectives into his office. A person who was murdered the way Eisinger was should not end up a faded case folded with years of nothing-to-report fives stapled to it.

"What have we got on the Eisinger thing?" Malone said, glancing down at the sixty sheet, looking over the list of cases that had come in during the night. He was relieved to see that there was nothing heavy. At least he had a clear track for today.

Gus Heinemann spoke first. He had gone through Eisinger's telephone book and found the address of her parents in New Jersey. In line with department procedure he had sent a next-of-kin teletype message to the New Brunswick Police Department requesting them to make the notification. The rest of her book was surprisingly uninformative, except for two numbers, with no names next to them. One had a 703 area code and the other a 212 code. The phone company reported that they had no record of such numbers, so Heinemann contacted the Wagon Board, the department unit that allocated all the department's patrol wagons and as a sideline knew more about telephones than Ma Bell. He had also gone through her scanty collection of personal papers, found her Social Security card, and expected word momentarily from the feds about where she was employed.

Bo Davis was leaning against a file cabinet admiring his manicure and listening to Heinemann's report.

"What about the canvasses?" Malone asked Davis.

"They all came up dry," Davis answered. "We couldn't come up with anyone who knew her. Several of the neighbors said that they'd see her in the elevator or hallway, smile and exchange a few pleasantries, but that was it."

"Did you interview all the people in her building?"

Davis checked the interview sheets. "We missed about a dozen. The apartment numbers are listed on the sheets."

Malone said, "What about the other buildings in the complex?"

"Same thing. The broad was a phantom," Davis answered.

"What about Forensic?"

O'Shaughnessy answered. "They came up with a few partial prints. About twelve or fifteen points. More than enough for a positive I.D. if we can come up with a suspect."

"Were the prints compared with Eisinger's?" Malone asked.

"Yeah. They cut the skin of her fingers off and rolled them at the morgue. They weren't her prints," O'Shaughnessy answered.

"I went back to the scene last night and found this," Malone said, taking out the strip of film and omitting any mention of the phony Captain Madvick's telephone call. "Let's take a look," Malone said, walking out from behind his desk.

O'Shaughnessy went over to the equipment locker and took out the viewing machine. He set it up and then went around the squad room shutting off the lights and pulling down the shades.

Jake Stern slowly maneuvered the film under the machine's glaring light. A conical beam threw a blurred picture onto the wall. Stern reached in front, turning the lens, adjusting the focus. Even in the eerie reversal of the negative, it was clear that the subject matter was a man and a woman in bed, making love.

"That dude can really breathe through his ears," joked O'Shaughnessy.

"I hope he comes up for air so we can get a look at his face," Malone said, watching with interest.

The male star surfaced two frames later.

"Jake, send that film to the lab. Have them blow up each frame and make us some stills," Malone said.

"Ten-four," Stern said, switching off the machine and removing the film.

Malone walked over to the large desk next to the wall. The property that had been removed from the Eisinger apartment was neatly lined up over the desk, each item in plastic evidence bags, tagged with property clerk's evidence tags. Malone picked up the bag containing the keys. "Anything on this?" he asked, holding up the gold-plated key.

"It don't fit any of the locks in her apartment," Stern said.

Malone examined the key. An ordinary house key that had been gold plated. A locksmith's six-digit registration number was stamped across its head. He tossed it to Heinemann. "Check the registration number with Consumer Affairs. Find out who made it and for whom. Anything on the cuffs?"

"Not yet. We're waiting to hear from Smith and Wesson," Stern answered.

Malone walked to the portable blackboard in the corner and wheeled it into the center of the room. He picked up a piece of chalk and started to outline the Eisinger case.

The detectives gathered around.

Across the top of the blackboard Malone blocked out the heading: Eisinger Homicide. Next to it he listed the case's serial numbers: UF 61# 6739; UF 60# 4278; UF 6# 9846; Forensic # 1298-80; Property Vouchers A 456798-812.

The date, time, and place of occurrence were listed below the heading. A diagram of each room was sketched in broken lines, the bathroom done in a larger scale. On the right side of the board each piece of inventoried evidence was listed along with its invoice number. WITNESSES was blocked out on the bottom left side. The space under it was blank.

Malone stepped back, folding his arms, frowning. "Not very much, is it?"

He studied it for a while and then flipped the blackboard to the reverse side.

"Okay! Bo, I want you and Pat to recanvass her apartment building. Get the ones that were missed yesterday. There had to be someone who knew her. Also check with the local storekeepers. She had to eat and brush her teeth. And don't waste time trying to put the make on any women."

Malone listed the assignment on the board. "I want a five on every interview," he added.

The lieutenant turned his attention to Jake Stern.

"Jake, I want you to visit the morgue. Get hold of Epstein. Tell him I want to know when and how."

Malone stared at the blackboard. "The rest of us will hold down the fort. Gus, I want you to stay with the phones and see what you can come up with."

* * *

The flower cart standing against the building with the glazed brick façade on the corner of Thirtieth Street and First Avenue had a red umbrella. Its top was terraced with fresh-cut flowers. Roses, gerbera, carnations, irises, tulips, daffodils, a profusion of color that enhanced a beautiful June morning. Medical students in jeans and white jackets, stethoscopes jutting proudly from pockets, crossed from the Bellevue Hospital Center to their dormitories on First Avenue. A group of student nurses were standing next to the cart eying the students, giggling.

Jake Stern glanced at the cart as he hurried up the wide steps into the building. The flowers reminded him of his wife, Marcia. She loved to work in the garden of their Howard Beach home. Whenever he wanted her for something and could not find her in the house he knew that she'd be outside puttering around her plants and flowers. Now that their only son Jeff was away studying business administration at the State University of Binghamton, she was always in the garden. As he pushed through into the lobby, he reflected on how he had almost lost his family. That was three years ago. He had been having an affair with one of his wife's girlfriends.

One night the girlfriend and her husband paid the Sterns a visit. He had a little too much to drink and got stupid. Marcia caught him playing footsy with the girlfriend under the kitchen table. The next day when he told his wife that he was going to take the car in for a tune-up she followed him. When he and his lady friend left the motel on Crossbay Boulevard two hours later Marcia was leaning up against his car tapping her foot. He would always remember that one excruciating moment when his bowels gave way.

Forty minutes later in the living room of their split-level home Marcia Stern gave her husband a choice: wife or girlfriend. There was to be no compromise. Ashen, he began to look around his home: gold wall-to-wall carpet, French provincial furniture wrapped in plastic to keep it clean, bulbous lamp shades with hanging rhinestones, and, also encased in plastic, heavy dining-room furniture with carved cherubs on the breakfront, and in the basement his weights. He begged; she forgave. He never mentioned the incident to any of the guys in the Squad, nor had he ever cheated again.

Stern's cheerfulness vanished as he walked down the stairway leading into the morgue. In the basement were corridors of stainless-steel boxes, their latched doors shining under overhead fluorescent lights. There were bare concrete floors with evenly spaced drains. Gurneys lined the corridors; bodies under white sheets, protruding legs with slanted feet and identification tags looped over big toes. In the corner of the basement there was a huge freezer. Inside, Stern knew, were baby cadavers, waiting their turns to be cut up by medical students. An omnipresent sweet smell lingered in the cold air, tickling the back of the mouth. Stern had often been a visitor to this timeless place and he hated it. He pushed through the double doors with the black rubber apron and turned right, heading for the cutting room.

Six tables were occupied. Four of the bodies had their chest cavities opened by an incision that ran from the neck, down the center of the chest, to the pubic hair. The rib cages were pried open, exposing the inner organs. There was a scale next to each table. An attendant was cutting off a cranium with a high-speed circular saw.

Sol Epstein was studying the inside of a body, whistling "Zippety Doo Dah" and waving his scalpel in a mime of leading a band. A microphone hung over his head recording words and music.

Stern rolled his eyes as he entered the cutting room. "How's my favorite ghoul?"

"Quick, Jose, my saw. We've got a live one to work on," Epstein said, looking up.

"You look right at home, Sol."

"What brings you into my world?" Epstein asked, reaching inside the cadaver.

"Sara Eisinger."

Epstein lifted the liver out of the cadaver and held it up to the detective. "Hungry? It's yummy with onions and bacon." He turned away and slapped the organ onto the scale.

"Tell me the results of the post so I can get the hell out of here," Stern said, walking over and looking inside the chest cavity.

Epstein looked up and smiled. "Okay. Person or persons unknown did willfully beat the shit out of her and then shoved a curtain rod up her cunt. Sara Eisinger's skull was crushed. The lower jaw was shattered. A twenty-seven-inch curtain rod was jammed into her. Her intestines were ripped to pieces. The abdominal muscle, the vagina, small intestines, colon, stomach, and abdominal aorta were destroyed. Whoever did it poked the rod around inside of her, like he was fishing. It wasn't a painless death. There was massive hemorrhage and shock, either of which was enough to kill her."

"So what finally did the job?" Stern asked, admiring the skill of the doctor's hands as they probed the various organs of the body.

"She drowned. We found water in the lungs. Evidently she was still breathing when they tossed her into the tub."

"How long was she dead?"

"To be positive, we'll have to wait for the laboratory results of her organs. The castings that we found on the body indicated fourth-generation maggots. From that and the degree of decomposition I'd say about a week."

"Malone would appreciate it if you could rush the lab report."

Epstein removed another part of the body and placed it on the scale. He frowned. "Jake, old buddy, your lieutenant is going to have to learn that the man who made time made plenty of it."

Stern shrugged, resigned to waiting. "Did you come up with anything else?"

"We scraped her fingernails and found human flesh. Evidently she put up a fight. The skin was from the face of a male Caucasian with a heavy beard. When I get the lab report I'll send it to you, direct."

"Thanks, Sol." Stern turned to leave.

"Jake?"

"Yeah?"

"I'll walk you out," Epstein said, laying down his scalpel. He stripped off his gloves.

When they were in the corridor outside the cutting room, Epstein draped his arm over Stern's shoulder and shepherded him toward the exit. They stepped aside for an attendant wheeling a loaded gurney.

"I want to thank you and Malone for calling me on the Gavin matter," Epstein said.

"Think nothing of it, Doc."

"Tell Malone that I received a thank-you card from the Powerhouse."

"What was in it? Carving knives?"

"An appointment to the State University of New York Downstate Medical Center in Brooklyn."

"Is that a good deal?"

"The tenderloin, my friend. A dream come true."

"The Powerhouse always does the right thing."

They started on the top floor of Sara Eisinger's apartment building. Today they were lucky. Most of the people were home. But the results were the same: no one knew the victim. After two hours on the recanvass they were only on the sixth floor. One apartment still had to be done, 6B. O'Shaughnessy rang the pushbutton in the center of the brass peephole and stood back as the chime echoed inside the apartment. No answer. He rang again.

"No one at home. We'll have to come back," Davis said, circling the apartment number on the interview sheet.

"May I help you gentlemen?"

The detectives turned and saw an attractive woman in her early thirties stepping off the elevator. She was carrying bundles of groceries.

"I'm Janet Fox and that is my apartment. If you don't tell me who the hell you are and what you want, I'm going to start the loudest scream you've ever heard in your lives."

Davis pulled out his shield and I.D. card and held them up to her. "We're detectives. There was a homicide in this building yesterday and we're investigating it," he said.

"Poor Sara. I just heard about it today. She was such a wonderful human being," she said.

"You knew her?" O'Shaughnessy asked.

"We were friends," she answered.

Janet Fox had a cozy apartment with a terrace overlooking Chinatown. She sat on a cushioned ottoman in front of a recliner. The detectives exchanged glances. Davis arched his brow, indicating that he would do the questioning. O'Shaughnessy picked up the cue, nodded, and moved to the sofa across from where she was sitting.

Janet Fox had first met Eisinger in the building's laundry room. They had become friends; if one of them went on vacation the other would take in the mail and water the plants. Occasionally they had tea together, talked about the latest fashions. Janet Fox wasn't sure where Sara Eisinger had worked. For a travel agency somewhere in Manhattan, she thought. What about her sex life? That was something they never discussed. "Never?" Davis said, not convinced.

The witness stirred uncomfortably. She leaned forward, pulling her knees to her. "I guess there was someone," she said, reluctantly. "But Sara never mentioned him." About a year and a half ago, the witness said, Sara came to her and asked for the name of a gynecologist. "She wanted to get a diaphragm."

"Who were her friends?" Davis asked.

"I don't know."

"What about acquaintances?"

"Sara stayed very much to herself."

"She had no other friends in the building?"

"None that I know of."

Davis said, "You mean to tell me that in the five years that she lived here you never once observed her with anyone?"

"I never thought of it before, but yes. Never," she answered bewildered. "But wait!" she was quick to add. "I did see her with a man. It was about six months ago. It was raining very hard. I had just gotten home from work and was running to get inside when I heard Sara calling to me. She was getting out of a car, opening an umbrella. I ran over to her and we shared her umbrella. A man was driving the car that she was getting out of."

"Did she tell you who he was?" Davis asked, looking at Pat who had his memo pad and pencil ready.

"No, she didn't. I didn't pry and she didn't volunteer any information. I think that's why we got along. Neither of us pried into the other's life."

"Describe the man you saw in the car."

"I was hurrying to get out of the rain. I only caught a glimpse of him."

"Was he white or black?"

"White."

"Was he young or old?"

"Sort of young."

"Was he over twenty?"

"Yes."

"Over thirty?"

"Yes."

"Over forty?"

"Yes."

"Over fifty?"

"I'd say somewhere in his early forties."

"Forty-five?"

"I'm not sure."

"Guess!"

"Forty-three, maybe."

"What about his complexion? Dark? Swarthy? Light? Fair?"

"Fair complexioned."

"What color was his hair?"

"Wiry, blond hair."

"What color were his eyes?"

"I don't know."

She also remembered that he was very handsome. With sculptured eyebrows that seemed tweezed. She couldn't recall how tall he was. After all, he was sitting behind the wheel of the car. About six foot, she guessed. And well built. The car? A little red Japanese one. A Honda, she thought. She told her interrogator that there came a time when she picked up mail for Sara Eisinger. He asked her if there was anything out of the ordinary about the mail that the victim received. Just junk mail and an occasional letter from overseas.

"From what countries?"

"Israel."

"Is there anything that you can think of that might help us?"

"I'm sorry, there isn't. I was surprised that I was able to remember what I did."

"You did real good," Davis said, crossing the room to sit next to his partner.

Janet Fox relaxed. She looked down at her palms. They were wet. She had not been aware of the tension before.

"Janet, there is one more question that I would like to ask," Davis said.

Her stomach tightened. "Yes?"

"You told us that you just heard about the murder today. A homicide in your apartment building, and you just found out about it?"

She looked at the detective and said hesitantly, "I was away for a few days."

"Where?"

The witness shifted. "I was at the Concord with my boss. He's married and his name is Joseph Grossman."

Davis turned to his partner. "Pat, why don't you continue knocking on doors. I'll stay here and ask Janet a few more questions, get the name of the doctor that Eisinger used. It'll save us time."

O'Shaughnessy was on the second floor when his partner caught up with him.

"How'd it go?" O'Shaughnessy asked, making an obscene jabbing gesture with his fist.

"Nothing like that!" Davis said. "She's a very nice lady. We sat and talked, that's all. How'd you make out?"

"Zippo. She paid her rent, didn't cause no trouble, and no one knows shit about her."

"What's with the Curtain Rod Caper?" Inspector Zambrano bellowed, sweeping into Malone's office.

Malone took the Eisinger case folder out of the file basket and handed it to him.

Zambrano sat down, attentively flipping through the fives. He looked up at Malone. "Looks to me like you got a winner on your hands. Need any help?"

"I'll yell if I do."

"Dan, I know that this ain't the right time, but in a few weeks I'm going to do the annual evaluation of your stewardship of the Squad. Try and get your paper in shape and don't forget Operation Participation."

Malone leaned forward, eyebrows raised. "Know something, Inspector. Working here is like pissing in a dark suit. You get that warm feeling, but nobody notices."

"That's a very nice analogy, Dan. But don't forget the fucking paper."

Heinemann came into the office and closed the door behind him.

"Bwana! I just heard from the Wagon Board. Guess where those telephone numbers belong?"

"Cut the bwana bullshit and tell me," Malone said.

Heinemann snapped to attention. "Both of them are confidential listings of Central Intelligence Agency phones."

"Aw shit! Not them bastards," Malone said, slapping the desk.

Heinemann leaned against the door. "The out-of-town number is a direct line to their headquarters in McLean. The other is a restricted line to their New York City field office."

"Did you contact them?" Malone said.

"What for? They're not about to tell us anything over the telephone."

Zambrano turned, on his way out, a sardonic grin on his lips. "Handle this very, very carefully. And I'd watch my ass. They're bigger liars than we are."

It was after three when O'Shaughnessy and Davis returned from their visit to Eisinger's gynecologist.

"The doctor fitted Eisinger with a catcher's mitt," Davis told the lieutenant.

"Did we find a diaphragm in the apartment?" Malone asked, checking the property sheet.

Jake Stern shook his head.

"I wonder where it is?" Malone thought aloud. "That's not something a woman leaves just anywhere."

Malone sat back and laced his hands behind his head, listening to Davis tell him about their interview with Janet Fox.

Heinemann entered the office and perched on Malone's desk. "Those cuffs were shipped to Greenblatts. I just telephoned them," Heinemann said, when Davis finished. "Their records show that they sold them to a Philip Alexander back in December. The name is probably as phony as the address that the guy gave."

"What else have you come up with?" Malone asked.

"My source at Social Security informed me that the Eisinger account showed only two employers. The Eastern Shipping Company in Long Island City and Braxton Tours in Manhattan. I contacted another source at Dun and Bradstreet. They have nothing on Eastern Shipping. Braxton Tours is a big travel agency that's run by a brother and sister, Aldridge and Thea Braxton. They work out high-priced trips for special groups. They specialize in Middle East tours."

"Anything else?" asked Malone, snapping forward and getting up.

"The registration numbers on the gold-plated key were traced to a locksmith on Canal Street. They've been making the keys for a joint on the East Side called the Interlude. I called a buddy of mine in the Nineteenth. He told me the Interlude is one of them posh key clubs that cater to the beautiful people. Anything goes, no questions asked," Heinemann said.

Malone walked into the squad room, checking his watch.

"I'm going to pay a visit to Braxton Tours."

"Want me to tag along?" Heinemann asked, following the lieutenant out of his office.

"Pat caught the case. I'll take him. I want you and Jake to stay on the Interlude. Check with the Hall of Records and find out who owns the building. Then get in touch with the Department of State in Albany. Find out who has the charter for the club. Then check with State Liquor and find out who buys the booze."

Braxton Tours occupied a suite of offices on the sixteenth floor of a huge glass-walled office building on Park. Attractive young women padded their way between glass-partitioned offices. The floors were carpeted; the furniture comfortable, expensive. Thea Braxton was waiting for them. She wore a beautifully tailored white, raw silk Chanel suit. Her shoulder-length hair was ash blond, enhancing the mature beauty of her tanned face. Her expression was coldly composed.

"We've been expecting the police ever since we read of Sara's death in the newspapers," Thea said, dismissing her secretary with a wave.

Malone measured her as he entered the office. He already had guessed just what she would say. Sara had been with the company for a year and a half. She stayed to herself and had no close friends within the company. Thea knew nothing of her personal life. What a pity that such a horrible thing should happen to such a beautiful young girl. Who could be responsible for such an act of barbarism? The newspaper accounts were just ghastly.

Thea moved from behind her desk and motioned to a grouping of canvas director chairs in front of a thermopane wall, through which a huge slice of the city could be seen below.

"What can you tell me about Sara Eisinger?" Malone asked, noticing the sunlight reflecting off her head. Her response was exactly what he had suspected it would be.

"She was a conscientious worker," Thea answered.

"She didn't seem to have many friends. Can you tell us why?"

"By choice, I guess. Sara preferred to stay to herself. Everyone isn't gregarious," Thea said, looking at Malone who was standing directly in front of her.

"Hmm. That's true enough," Malone said, walking over to the far wall, examining the paintings.

"There must be big bucks in the travel business," Malone said, loud enough for her to hear. "What was Eisinger's responsibility with your company?"

"She arranged group tours to the Middle East. Israel in particular."

Thea explained that being an Israeli, Sara Eisinger had access to many Jewish groups. "They love to travel." Eisinger arranged charter tours and received a 5 percent commission on everything over a hundred thousand dollars. When Malone asked her if the travel business was the Braxtons' only business interest. Thea replied that it was their main interest. Lately, they had branched out into social research.

"What's that?" asked Malone, now apparently absorbed by the view of Manhattan.

She explained that before companies do business overseas they want to know all that they can about the country in which they'll do business. A lot of money can be lost if one doesn't know the customs of a host country. What is polite in the United States can be downright insulting in some parts of the world. Malone seemed surprised. "Don't companies have their own research staffs?" he asked.

The large ones do, she told him. But many of the smaller companies that were vying for a piece of the OPEC dollar do not and some of those companies came to Braxton Tours.

"Interesting," Malone said, turning to face her. "Do you know anyone who'd want her dead?"

"Of course not."

"What about her love life?"

Her hands went to her hips. "We do not pry into the personal lives of our employees."

"No office romance?" he asked, sensing her annoyance and deciding to follow it and see where it led him.

"None that I know of."

"Was she straight, gay, or ambidextrous?"

"I don't know what she was. And furthermore I don't care."

"Did she have any close girlfriends?"

"None that I know of."

"How did Eisinger get her job with your company?"

"She answered an ad that we put in the New York Times for someone with language abilities. Sara spoke six languages."

"Really? What were they?"

"German, Polish, English, Hebrew, Spanish, and Ladino," she replied.

"Eisinger was dead for about a week before her body was discovered. How come you didn't report her missing?"

"Sara took a week off. She went to visit her parents in New Jersey. She wasn't due back until yesterday."

"Can you think of anything that might help us?"

"I wish that I could think of something," she said, reaching for a porcelain jar on the table in front of her. She removed a cigarette and lit it.

"I hope that you catch the people responsible," she said, putting the lid back on the jar.

"We will. We'd like to interview your employees. That is, if you have no objections," Malone said.

"Of course not," Thea Braxton said, taking a drag.

The door opened and a thin man in an impeccably tailored beige suit walked into the room.

"Hello. I'm Aldridge Braxton," he said as he moved toward Malone and offered his hand.

Aldridge Braxton's face was starting to wither. Crows' feet furrowed deep around the eyes; dark circles were terraced in various shades of black. He had styled his unruly black hair into a moderate Afro.

"Did you know her well?" Malone asked him after the introductions.

"Not as well as I would have liked to. She was a strange young lady in many ways. She reminded me of a person who was afraid to enjoy life," Aldridge said, moving to the vacant chair next to his sister.

"What can you tell us about her personal life?" Malone asked.

"Nothing, I'm afraid," Aldridge answered.

Malone walked over to Thea's desk. He picked up a figurine that had caught his attention. A gold goddess in a flounced skirt clutching snakes in both outstretched hands. He studied it carefully, then put it back.

"Can either of you think of anything . . . ?" Malone asked them.

The Braxtons looked at each other. They turned in unison and shook their heads.

"In that case, we'd like to interview your employees," Malone said.

Thea Braxton got up, crossed to her desk, and pushed the button on the intercom with her forefinger. Her secretary reappeared. "Arlene, please escort these gentlemen around the office. They're policemen here to interview everyone concerning Sara's death."

As they were walking out of the office, Malone pulled a pad from his pocket and stopped a moment to scratch a note to O'Shaughnessy: *ck. N.Y. Times for Braxton ad seeking employee with language ability. Find out when inserted and withdrawn.* He handed the note to O'Shaughnessy and followed Arlene out of the office.

"That Braxton broad has really got her shit all together," O'Shaughnessy whispered.

Malone shot him a look. "Maybe just a little too together." He then whispered to O'Shaughnessy, "Keep Arlene busy while I talk to the operator." He stepped ahead of the woman and entered the telephone cubicle, closing the door behind him.

O'Shaughnessy moved ahead and blocked the door, preventing Arlene from following inside.

The operator was eager to help. "Sara used to receive calls from a man with an accent," she said. "They always talked in a foreign language."

"What language?"

"I don't know."

"Was it Spanish?"

"Oh, no. It was one of the European languages."

"French?"

"No."

"German?"

"It might have been. I'm really lousy on languages."

"What was the man's name?"

"I don't know. He never gave his name. Just asked for Sara Eisinger."

"How old would you say he was?"

"I don't know. How could I tell his age?"

"By the sound of his voice. Take a guess."

"I'd say late thirties early forties."

"When did this man first start to call her?"

"The very first day she started to work here."

"Are you the only operator?"

"Yes. If I'm sick or on vacation, they get a temporary in."

"Did this man call her often?"

"Every day that she was in the office. Sometimes two and three times."

"And he never once mentioned his name?"

"Never."

"Do all calls come through your board?"

"Yes. Only the Braxtons have direct lines."

"Did she ever receive other personal calls?"

"Hmm. I don't think so."

Malone saw a shadow cross her face.

"What happened to Eisinger could happen to every woman who lives alone. It's important that we know who she talked to. Everything that you tell me will be confidential, I promise."

Malone folded his arms over the top of the switchboard, leaning forward, looking down at her. "Please."

She looked up. The board buzzed. She answered the incoming call and routed it.

"You might save another woman's life," Malone said.

"A woman by the name of Andrea used to call her from time to time," she said.

"What can you tell me about this Andrea?"

"Nothing. They used to talk in different languages."

"What languages?"

"I don't know. Sometimes they'd speak in English."

"What did they talk about?" he asked casually.

"Lieutenant! I don't listen in on conversations!"

"I certainly did not mean to imply that you would intentionally listen in. But everyone knows that sometimes operators accidentally press the wrong button."

"Well, actually I did overhear part of a conversation. They were talking in English, Andrea and Sara. It was the Thursday before she left on vacation. Sara was talking very excitedly about a song. She told Andrea to look at the song."

"Did she mention the name of the song?"

"No. She just told her to look at the song. That she would understand when she did."

"Understand what?"

She raised her shoulders and grimaced. "I don't know."

4

When Malone walked in he saw an old couple sitting on the bench outside the squad room. The woman had drawn her gray hair back into a bun. Her dress was plain and black and too big for her. Her head was lowered, and her thumb stroked the clasp of the plastic pocketbook on her lap. The man slumped and stared at his spotted hands. Malone glanced at them as he passed. He walked into the squad room and went directly over to the coffee urn. As he poured, Malone studied the rolls inside the torn bag next to the urn. He selected one topped with sugar crumbs, bit into it, and stepped back to avoid the shower of powdered sugar. "Who are they?" Malone asked, pointing his head toward the door.

Jake Stern looked up from the typewriter. "The Eisingers. The New Brunswick PD notified them this morning."

"Give me a minute and bring them in," Malone said, taking another bite and heading toward his office.

Malone looked down at the 60 sheet. On the late tour one Rose Jennings, female, black, age 32, got fed up with her married boyfriend's broken promises and urinated into a saucepan. She then went into the kitchen and removed a can of lye from under the sink. She went back to the bathroom and poured the lye into the saucepan. Holding the pan carefully with two hands and shaking the mixture as she walked, Rose Jennings headed for the bedroom. She hovered over the bed, looking down at the sleeping man. "Lying motherfucker," she screamed just before throwing the contents over his face. He'd never be handsome again. Rose Jennings then went to the telephone and called the police, the wife, and an ambulance. Very accommodating lady, thought Malone, sipping from the mug with the word COP stenciled on the front. Another grounder. His luck was still holding.

"Lieutenant, this is Hanna and Jacob Eisinger," Stern said, steering them into the office and gesturing to the uneven cluster of chairs.

"I want to tell you how sorry we are," Malone began. "I want you to know that we're doing everything possible to apprehend the people responsible."

The Eisingers said nothing. They were frozen in shock and grief; they stared fixedly at the cards and telephone numbers stuffed under the glass top. Gently, Malone probed. Who were their daughter's friends? Did they know of anyone who would want to kill her? Was there anything about their daughter's past that the police should know? Malone's questions were met by silence. He looked over to O'Shaughnessy, Davis, and Stern who were lolling against the wall. Davis drew up his shoulders in a hapless gesture.

"Can't you think of anything that might help us?" Malone pleaded. Cold silence. "Don't you want us to catch the people who killed your daughter?"

Hanna Eisinger started to speak. She told a story that Malone had heard before. She had been persecuted but had survived Nazi Germany. She had emigrated to Palestine and started a new life. She told of the birth of their daughter and the joy of watching her grow into a beautiful woman. When Sara was of age she went into the army and met a boy and fell in love for the first time. When the Eisingers decided to come to the United States their Sara said that she would come with them.

"Do you know any of your daughter's friends?" Malone asked.

Jacob Eisinger stiffened. His shoulders reared up in defiance. "Friends?" he said. "We have learned to live without the luxury of friends. Our Sara was the same way."

Malone started to ask random questions, searching for something that might give him a lead.

"What did your daughter do when she was in the army?" Malone asked.

"She was a clerk at a supply base forty kilometers from Jerusalem," Jacob Eisinger said. Hanna Eisinger leaned across the desk and clutched Malone's arm. A supplicant's grasp. "Why won't they let us have our daughter? We have to bury her. It's the law."

Malone swallowed. He looked over at his detectives in time to see Stern push away from the wall and leave the office.

"I'll see that she is released," Malone said gently.

Jacob Eisinger asked if they might leave. "Just a few more questions," Malone said. "How old was your daughter?"

"Thirty-four," the mother answered.

"And how long had she lived in this country?"

"Six years," answered the father.

"Do you have any photographs of your daughter?" Malone asked, remembering that the only one they had was taken at the morgue. Hanna Eisinger looked to her husband. The old man's face quivered as he reluctantly nodded consent. Hanna Eisinger opened the pocketbook and removed a snapshot. It was a small black and white with a coarse grain. Sara Eisinger was standing on a long pier in front of a file of freighters that stretched along a dock, the ships secured by taut mooring lines. Mounds of crates were stacked on the pier. The girl in the photograph was laughing and waving off the unknown photographer.

"Where was this taken?" Malone asked, studying the photo.

"I don't know," the mother answered.

"When was it taken?" Malone asked.

"It was taken on one of Sara's European vacations before she came to live in this country," replied the father.

"Did Sara take many vacations when she lived in Israel?" asked Malone.

"Yes," the mother said.

Malone laid the snapshot down in front of him, tapping it with his middle finger. "You have no idea where this was taken?"

"No," Hanna Eisinger said. "Is it important?"

"Maybe. May I keep it for a while?" He saw their hesitation. "I promise that I'll return it to you."

Jacob Eisinger lowered his head. Malone took his silence for consent.

"Did your daughter ever mention any of the men in her life?" Malone asked.

"No," Hanna Eisinger said flatly.

"What kind of work did Sara do in this country?" Malone asked, watching them closely.

"She worked for a travel agency arranging tours to Israel," the mother said.

"Will that be all?" Jacob Eisinger said, lifting himself up out of the chair and turning to help his wife.

"Thank you for coming by," Malone said, standing and rounding his desk. "I'll have one of my detectives drive you to the station."

"We'll take a taxi," Jacob Eisinger said.

*　　*　　*

The department mail arrived at 1400. The blowups Malone had ordered were in a manila folder. He removed the enlargements, thumbed through them quickly, and then examined them a second time, scrutinizing each one. There was a chair next to the bed on which an army officer's uniform was neatly folded. The blouse was draped over the back of the chair and the insignia on the lapels showed that the owner of the uniform was assigned to the Quartermaster Corps. Malone handed the photographs to Davis.

"He's a major," Bo Davis said, flipping through the photographs. "And I'm willing to bet that the ring he's wearing is from the Point. He also likes to eat hair pie."

"She's a pretty lady," Davis added. "Wonder what her name is?"

It was at that moment that Gus Heinemann shambled into the room and lowered his hulk into a chair. "Have I got some bad news," Heinemann said, struggling to lift his left foot onto the edge of the desk. He had just returned from the Hall of Records. The Interlude was owned by the Agamemnon Entertainment Corporation and the building wherein the club was located was owned by the Menelaus Realty Corporation. After that it was a dead end. Finding the real owners could take weeks. "I hope you gentlemen don't have any pressing personal plans for this evening," Malone said firmly. "We're going to be sitting on the Interlude tonight."

Sitting on a "plant"—what cops on TV call a stakeout—is like looking at a small section of a street under a microscope. Few people ever take the time to examine a mailbox or a street lamp. Detectives do. They spend many hours sitting in parked cars or standing in the shelter of doorways waiting for someone to arrive or leave a location; or just waiting for something to happen.

The Interlude was a four-story brownstone on East Fifty-eighth Street. The streets in this part of town were clean and litter free. Each tree had its own well-tended square of dirt. Doormen strolled along the streets holding onto leashes with expensively groomed little dogs. Joggers navigated the sidewalks. Six stone steps led up to a double door with scrolled grillwork. The windows were dark and blank.

O'Shaughnessy and Davis were in the front seat of a department taxi that was parked on the south side of Fifty-eighth Street. Det. Starling Johnson was slumped in the rear. Johnson was a recently divorced black man with a cherubic face, oversize horn-rimmed glasses, flaring sideburns, and plenty of time to kill. The other detectives were on O.T. from the day tour; Johnson was working a night duty. A green Buick Electra that had been confiscated by the Federal Narcotics Task Force in San Francisco, driven cross country by an automobile transporter with a government contract, and traded to the NYPD for a white Eldorado that had been confiscated in Harlem, was parked on Sutton Place a block from the Interlude. Malone and Stern were in the front seat. Gus Heinemann was stretched across the back seat, stuffing Milky Ways into his mouth and discarding the wrappers on the crushed velour seat. An hour passed. The Interlude was in darkness, save for a single light on the top floor. Heinemann felt the gurgling in his stomach. "I'm starving," he bellowed, patting his large belly.

"Any of you ever work with Hy Rothman?" Jake Stern asked, pressing an exercise hand grip in his left hand.

"Suicide Rothman? I had that pleasure," Malone said. "That son-of-a-bitch tried to turn every homicide he caught into a suicide. I was working a late tour one summer on temporary duty in Central Park. I was only out of the Academy a few months. It was around six in the morning and I'd just come out of the heave to make a ring. I was talking to the sergeant over the call box when I noticed a set of legs sticking out of the bushes. It was a stiff with a hole in his left temple and a thirty-eight clutched in his right hand. I called the sergeant, roped off the crime scene as best I could. . . . I did the whole bit. An hour later Rothman comes strolling up to the scene chewing on a five-cent cigar. He looked down at the body, moved the cigar to the other side of his mouth, and said, 'It's definitely a suicide.' I couldn't believe what I was hearing. I told him he was nuts. The stiff would have had to wrap his arm around his head in order to shoot himself in the left temple. Besides, I told him, there weren't any powder burns. Rothman gave that . . . 'Let me take a look, kid' routine and bent to examine the body. He pried the gun out of the DOA's right hand, lets one go up in the air, rubs the barrel against the left temple and plants the gun back in the left hand. He looks up at me and said, 'As I was saying, kid, it's a suicide.' Could you imagine pulling that shit today?"

"No way," Stern said.

Malone ducked his head down and pulled the mike from the cradle of the concealed radio set under the dashboard. He checked to make sure the frequency dial was on two, the frequency which permitted car-to-car communication. He stayed low to make sure that anyone looking in would not see him using the radio. "Bo?"

"Yeah, Lou?"

"See anything?"

"Nothing."

The detectives waited. No one entered or left the Interlude. Business hours had not yet begun. A light summer rain danced over the cars; uneven rivulets streaked the windshields. Davis and

O'Shaughnessy slumped low in their seats. Starling Johnson cat-napped.

"How's Foam?" Davis asked O'Shaughnessy.

Starling Johnson flicked open his right eye. "You still seein' that woman?"

"Yep. It's four years and I haven't gone for a nickel."

As though a magic button had been pressed, the Interlude sprang to life. The lights blazed on and shortly afterward limousines and taxis began to pull up in front of the club. The beautiful people were gathering.

"On deck," Malone said into the mike.

Each license plate number was recorded. A description of each guest was taken down. Johnson kept a record of the times of arrival of each vehicle. It stopped raining; the night turned quiet, the stillness occasionally broken by muted bursts of noise from the Interlude. Just after one, a limousine slid around the corner of Sutton Place and pulled into the curb in front of the Interlude. The windows of the car were oversized and tinted a smoky black. Aldridge Braxton and two men got out and went up the steps of the club, disappearing into the vestibule.

"What the fuck is he doing here?" Malone said.

The detectives slumped lower. Then a darkened panel truck stopped half a block behind Braxton's limousine. Someone inside the truck lit a cigarette.

"Braxton has a shadow," O'Shaughnessy said over radio.

"Stay low," Malone warned. "We don't want to be made."

More time passed. A stray taxi would occasionally stop in front of the Interlude and discharge its passengers. Davis and Johnson dozed; O'Shaughnessy stood vigil, while Malone kept watching the club and the truck. A cigarette flew out of the truck's window and hit the pavement. Somewhere in the distance a siren wailed. The detectives could tell that it was a radio car on a run; the pitch was right.

Ninety minutes later the door of the Interlude opened and Aldridge Braxton came reeling out followed close behind by his two playmates. There was a woman with them. She was wearing a flowing black-and-white scarf dress and had heavily made-up eyes. Everyone was laughing. One of the men was pulling her by the arm as though playfully forcing her to leave with them. Braxton ran ahead, opening the limousine's door.

"It's now post time," Malone said into the mike.

"Who's the girl?" Heinemann asked Malone.

"Dunno, but she looks vaguely familiar," Malone said.

They piled into the rear and the limousine slid away from the curb.

Malone waited. The truck moved off after the limousine with the clouded windows.

"How do you want this to go down?" O'Shaughnessy asked Malone over the radio.

"We'll leapfrog them. I'll start," Malone said.

The dead hours of the night were over. Delivery trucks cut their way through the new daylight. Taxis cruised the empty streets. A lone jogger made her way unencumbered by traffic, and the detectives swiveled their heads to watch her bouncing breasts as she passed. The Buick took up position behind the truck for a dozen blocks. A taxi took its place. The limousine sped north on York Avenue. At Eighty-second Street the sleek vehicle cut diagonally across the avenue and came to a stop in front of an expensive co-op. Aldridge Braxton pulled open the door and got out. He stood with his arm draped over the open door, leaning into the car, talking and laughing. After several minutes the woman and two men got out and hurried into the building. Braxton got back inside and the limo sped off. The panel truck parked three blocks away on the east side of York Avenue.

Stern turned to the lieutenant. "What now?"

Malone checked his watch: 4:48. He assumed that Braxton was going home. Anyway, he knew where to find Braxton if he wanted him. Right now he wanted the pedigree on the three people who ran into that building and on whoever was inside that truck. He decided not to follow Braxton. He might need all his cars later. "We sit tight," Malone said, snatching up the mike. Staying low, Malone switched the frequency dial to the number that carried the regular police transmissions. He requested Central to dispatch a marked RMP to 10:85 them at their location and identify the panel truck and its occupants. Within a few minutes, a blue and white rolled to a stop behind the truck. Two hatless old-timers with sagging guts and drooping gun belts struggled out of the radio car. They meandered over, each separating and walking along the opposite side of the truck. "Lemme see ya license and registration, pal. Wadaya doin' parked here this time of the morning?" It wasn't necessary for the detectives to hear the monologue, every cop knows it by heart.

As the policemen waited for the driver to pass out the documents they scrutinized the two occupants. The driver was in his middle twenties. He had black curly hair that danced over a low forehead. A small knitted yarmulke was fastened to his pate. The passenger was shorter; a simian-looking fellow who also wore a yarmulke. Both of them wore rumpled khaki shirts.

The documents were passed out to the policeman. The other officer strolled to the rear of the truck. When he rounded the back, he rested his right foot on the bumper, bending as if to tie a shoelace. He tried the rear door and found it unlocked. He put his foot down and opened the door. When he did this the passenger leaped from the truck and ran to the back. He stood toe-to-toe with the cop, his angry face jutting at the policeman.

"You have no right to open that door!" His challenge of the cop's authority was a serious mistake. They began a shouting match and without warning the policeman kicked the man in the groin. As he doubled over, the policeman grabbed his hair, snapping the head upright. A fist smashed into the man's face, sending him staggering backward. The policeman came after him, ramming his fists into the man's shoulders. The force of the blows slammed him against the truck. He slid to the ground, blood trickling down his shirt front. The driver jumped from the truck and ran back to help his fallen friend. "Take your fuckin' buddy and get the hell out of here," the document taker said, throwing the license and registration inside the truck. The driver helped his friend off the ground, leading him back to the safety of the truck. The detectives watched as the truck bucked several times and then lurched forward and sped off down York Avenue.

"Let me see what that was all about," Malone said, yanking open the door. He walked over to the policemen. "Did they give you a hard time?" he asked.

The policeman who had attacked the passenger had grease stains over the front of his summer shirt. Too many pizzas, thought Malone, looking over the team. The attacker's breath was stale and smelled of alcohol. Both needed a shave.

"A search warrant," the attacker grumbled. "Imagine that fuckin' foreigner asking to see my search warrant."

"What were their names?" Malone asked.

The one who accepted the documents read from his memo pad. The driver was Hillel Henkoff and the passenger Isaac Arazi. Both gave an address on Borden Avenue in Long Island City. The truck was registered to the Eastern Shipping Company of the same address.

Malone looked at Heinemann and said thoughtfully: "That is where Sara Eisinger worked before she went to work for the Braxtons." Malone turned to the cop. "Was there anything else inside the truck?"

"A bunch of boxes with funny markings," said the officer who had knocked the passenger around.

"What kind of markings?" Malone said.

"Dunno. But I'll tell you one thing for sure, the inside of that truck stunk from cosmoline."

Malone's left eyebrow arched. "You sure?"

"I spent four years with the First Airborne. I know cosmoline when I smell it. I woulda popped one of them crates open only I didn't figure it a smart move with that guy throwing a shit fit."

"Anything else we can do for you, Lou?" the document taker said. "We're anxious to get back to serving the public."

Bullshit. They probably have a six-pack stashed under the seat of their radio car, Malone thought, but replied, "That's it. Thanks."

As the two uniformed cops sauntered back to their radio car, the document taker half turned and waved over his shoulder.

"What now?" O'Shaughnessy said.

Malone looked over to Gus Heinemann who was leaning against the fender of the Buick, matching the sides of a pair of dice. Seven all around. "You in the mood for one of your performances?" Malone said, lifting his chin toward the building Braxton's friends had entered.

Heinemann nodded, dropped the dice into his shirt pocket, and pushed away from the car. He returned fifteen minutes later, a satisfied smile on his face. "The doorman was a retired cop. He told me that they went to the thirty-first-floor apartment that's owned by Braxton Tours. The corner apartment, facing Eighty-second."

Malone looked up, surveying the canyons of terraced elegance which surrounded them. "That building over there," he said, pointing, "faces the Braxtons' apartment. If we could get onto the roof with a pair of binoculars we just might get a look-see inside that apartment." Malone turned to Davis. "Bo, get the glasses from under the seat. You and I will take a look. The rest of you stand by. If any of them leave before we get back, tail them."

Early-morning haze lingered high above the city streets. Davis looked over the edge, quickly stepping back. His palms were suddenly sweaty. Malone stood with his feet firmly planted on the pebbled roof, trying to get his bearings. Everything looked different so high up. He squandered a minute and took in the view across the river. The red-tipped stacks of the Con Ed plant rose majestically in front of the new sun. He could make out the bubbled tennis courts that dotted the shoreline of Long Island City. The brick-sheathed generator plant of the Midtown Tunnel ascended vertically over the mouth of the tunnel. The gothic crockets of the Queensborough Bridge seemed to be holding up the sky.

Malone looked away and walked over to the edge, staring across at the range of buildings, searching for the target building. He saw acres of glass and silver and steel skyscrapers and medium high-rises and low apartment buildings and terraces and penthouses and duplexes—Manhattan.

He picked out the Braxtons' building and leaned over the edge, starting to count the floors upward from the street. When he reached the thirty-first floor he brought the binoculars up to his eyes and began scanning the floor, adjusting the focus. He moved the glasses right to left. Suddenly he lurched forward, straining, sharpening the focus.

"Wadaya see?" Davis asked.

Malone kept silent. He remained motionless, the glasses fixed to his eyes. After some minutes, he turned abruptly and handed the binoculars to Davis, pointing to the corner apartment on the thirty-first floor.

Davis took the glasses and looked through them, making a slight adjustment on the focus wheel.

"That's one helluva party they're having. It's hard to tell who is doing what to whom," Davis said.

"Recognize the woman?"

"Noooo. But she sure has one beautiful pair of tits."

"You're looking at the female star of the porno film that we found in Eisinger's apartment."

Metal lockers lined one wall of the dormitory, black-faced combination locks hung through the hasps. Four bunk beds were flush against the wall. Large slivers of peeling paint drooped down from the walls and ceilings. Glossy posters of nude women covered the wall next to the beds. Heinemann lay on the bottom bunk, his right leg hanging over the edge. The men snored and the ripe smell of their farts hung in the air. O'Shaughnessy slid off the top bunk and padded to his locker. He pushed it open and took a toilet kit from the shelf. He left the room with his kit under his arm and his right arm thrust into his underpants, scratching his ass.

Starling Johnson was half asleep when O'Shaughnessy returned twenty minutes later, shaved, washed, and smelling like a perfume factory. Johnson shot up. "You mother! Bad enough I've got to listen to all this farting and snoring. I don't need you sashaying in here smelling like a French whore." Johnson leaped off the top bunk, put on his trousers, and walked barefoot out into the squad room. The smell of freshly made coffee filled the air. He walked over to the urn and poured a cup. A lone detective was doing day duty. He was at the far desk with his head buried in the typewriter. He looked up and nodded to Johnson who grunted hello.

Malone was leaning back and resting his shoeless feet on the desk. He had a coffee mug on his knee. He was looking at the blackboard, digesting the growing outline.

"It's beginning to fill out," Johnson said, walking in and draping an arm over the filing cabinet next to the door.

"We've still got a long way to go," Malone said.

Johnson asked, "Are you going to cut them men loose or do we keep going?"

Malone's left hand rose in a gesture of despair. "I hate like hell to lose the momentum, but we can't keep going forever."

One by one the detectives started to file in, sleep-filled eyes glancing at the blackboard. The telephone rang. Without taking his feet down, Malone stretched over and snatched up the receiver. After spending most of the night sitting on the Interlude, he was in no mood for Zambrano's abrasive voice. "Wadaya come up with last night?"

Malone pushed the instrument away from his ear and grimaced. Holding the phone in front of his face, he recounted the night's activities. He told Zambrano that O'Shaughnessy had followed the woman to a row house on Park Place in Brooklyn. The men were tailed to a loft in Soho.

"Did you get a make on them?" Zambrano asked.

"Not yet. O'Brien and Mullens are on the woman. Martinez and Valenti are on the men. They'll I.D. them."

"Why didn't you tail the guys in the truck?"

"Because I didn't have enough vehicles or men and because I wanted to get them the hell out of there so I could find out what was going down inside that apartment."

"How many men you got doing day duty?"

"I've got one detective holding it down. The other two are on the woman. The detectives on the men I pulled off tonight's night duty."

"So you're going to have just one man covering the chart tonight." There was a tinge of annoyed doubt in the inspector's voice.

"That's right."

"And you're holding yesterday's day duty team on O.T."

Malone forced a flat calmness into his voice. "Right again."

"You're stretching it kinda thin."

"Don't you think that I know that."

Zambrano yawned. "Guess it's time for me to get out of bed and get into the salt mine. Seeya later." Zambrano hung up.

Malone stared at his mouthpiece. "Son-of-a-bitch." He looked over at the detectives. Tired men make mistakes. "Go home and get some sleep."

"What are you going to do, Lou?" Starling Johnson asked.

"I'm going to pay a visit to a shipping company in Long Island City."

As Malone was about to leave, O'Shaughnessy called out and told him that he had a telephone call on line three. He went back into the squad room. This time there was no pretense or introduction. The voice that had been attributed to the name Madvick was harsh. "If you know what's good for you, Malone, you'll shitcan this Eisinger thing."

"Go fuck yourself, pal." He slammed down the receiver and left.

A maroon sedan kept a respectable distance behind the taxi as it maneuvered through the morning traffic on Flatbush Avenue. The cab made its way onto the Brooklyn Bridge. At Park Row it exited the bridge and sped east to Chatham Square. At the Bowery it turned north. When the taxi reached the corner of Hester Street it double parked and a woman got out. The chic clothes and fashionable wig of last night were gone. She was dressed quietly, her hair was held tightly in place by a paisley kerchief. She hurried away from the cab, walking up Hester Street. In the middle of the block she ducked into a three-story building. A sign in Hebrew was over the entrance. A plaque in English was bolted to the right of the door: EAST SIDE MIKVAH.

The maroon sedan glided in to the curb in front of a fire hydrant near the corner. "What's a mikvah?" O'Brien asked his partner.

"It's a religious bath that Jewish women go to once a month to get cleansed after their period," Mullens said.

"A hooker like that?"

"It takes all kinds."

Twenty minutes later the woman exited the mikvah and walked north. O'Brien slid out of the car. The woman walked five blocks, occasionally casting a nervous glance over her shoulder. In the middle of the fifth block she entered a restaurant with Hebrew lettering on the window. She went to an empty table next to the window. She was so distraught that she did not notice the man who entered a short time later and sat three tables away.

A stooped waiter with a seamed face shuffled over to O'Brien. "You vant something?"

The woman played with the food the waiter had brought her. She kept looking out the window, casting glances up and down the street, checking her watch. O'Brien had finished his dairy dish and was considering ordering another when a man walked into the restaurant and moved directly to the woman's table.

"Well?" he demanded, lowering himself into the seat across from her. O'Brien could just overhear their conversation.

"It wasn't there," she said.

"Are you sure that was the only mikvah she went to?"

"Yes, I'm sure," she said peevishly.

"We must locate that damned list," the man said.

"What more can I do?"

"I don't know. But I do know that the police are involved." The man leaned across the table, whispering, and O'Brien was unable to hear the rest of the conversation. Suddenly the woman sat back in her chair, agitated. "I don't know where she hid it. She kept mentioning some goddamn song."

5

Van Dam was the last westbound exit on the Long Island Expressway before the Midtown Tunnel. Borden Avenue began on the other side of Van Dam and sliced through the industrial heart of Long Island City. At Borden and Thirtieth the men in hard hats from Tauscher Steel were standing on flatbeds loading shipments of I beams. The sidewalk in front of Alcock and Alcock Box Company was blocked with workmen assembling wooden crates. There was a continuous scampering of hi-lows in front of Capital Provisions as condiments for the city's restaurants and hotels were loaded. Detached trailers were parked everywhere. Railroad sidings crisscrossed the avenue. The normal flow of traffic was constantly blocked by tractor-trailers backing into loading bays. The outdoor vats behind Biddle and Gottesman Pickle and Sauerkraut Company gave the air a sharp, tangy smell.

Starling Johnson had not gone home. He had nothing better to do so he decided to tag along with Malone. He wasn't tired, so why not? Lately he found himself able to get by with less and less sleep.

He had not gotten used to living alone even though he had been divorced for two years and living alone for three. The clock still ticked too loud and the quiet was still too thunderous, and booze was still needed to get to sleep. He hated going into his apartment and turning on the TV or the radio right away. He knew that it was a sign of loneliness; but he just had to hear voices, see people. He had a girlfriend; in fact, he had quite a few girlfriends. He found them boring and found himself counting the minutes until they got up, dressed, and left. He had a standing rule: no women were permitted to stay the night, nor were they allowed to leave any personal things in his apartment. If they left and he found anything of theirs he'd throw it in the garbage. No female was going to stake a claim on him or his apartment.

They had stopped for some eggs and coffee before heading to Queens. After breakfast they drove through the Midtown Tunnel and exited onto Borden Avenue right after the toll booth. It took the toll collector a few extra seconds to copy down the number of their vehicle identification plate before he waved them through the toll. Johnson was annoyed at the delay; perhaps he was tired.

Johnson parked the department auto across the street from the Eastern Shipping Company. After spending thirty minutes watching the place they both decided that there was something definitely off key. The other businesses on Borden Avenue were busy, with trucks pulling in and out of loading bays. The Eastern Shipping Company appeared to be abandoned. The building that they were watching was one and a half stories high and built in the shape of an irregular octagon. There were several banks of loading bays, each bay sealed by a sliding metal door. The windows were high and covered with steel mesh. In the rear of the building there was a railroad siding that was enclosed behind a chain-link fence topped with barbed wire. The filthy water of Newtown Creek flowed past the building's end. Gray crisscross girders of the Long Island Expressway dwarfed the front of the building. All around the outside were high-density lights, as well as TV cameras which surveyed the structure's periphery.

"Somethin' strange going down inside that place," Johnson said, puckering and lifting his eyebrows.

"Why don't we go see what." Malone got out now and led the' way to a door with a sign on it that read NO SALESMEN EXCEPT BY APPOINTMENT. They walked into a tiny drab room paneled in fake pine veneer. Behind a sliding glass panel in the far wall a receptionist who wore astoundingly oversized pink-framed glasses greeted them with total indifference. "May I help you gentlemen?"

"We are here to see the boss," Malone said, reaching into his pocket and pulling out a packet of business cards. He extracted one and glanced at it before handing it to her. "I'm John Grimes of the U.S. Department of Labor and this is my associate Tyrone Washington. We're here on official business."

The woman took the card, swung around in her chair, and pressed a button on the switchboard.

Johnson poked the lieutenant. "Tyrone Washington, man. That be an ethnic name."

Malone winked at him. "Ten-four," he whispered, looking around the reception area. There was only one inner door and it was fitted snugly into the wall. An avocado plant was next to the railing by the entrance. A few leatherette chairs and a coffee-stained table with some out-of-date magazines completed the décor.

A man in his late thirties came out. He had a large, hawklike nose that dominated his dark features. He wore khaki shorts, a sweaty undershirt, and Roman sandals, no socks. His muscular torso strained against his undershirt.

"I am David Ancorie. What can I do for you gentlemen?" he asked, kicking the door closed and leaning against it. He had a smooth British accent. Malone took the card back from the woman and walked over to Ancorie, handing it to him. Ancorie looked at the card and smiled. "So?"

"We have reports that there are violations of Federal Employment Guidelines within the Eastern Shipping Company," Malone lied. "We're here to discuss the matter with your boss."

"I see." A mocking grin lit up Ancorie's face.

Malone had the uncomfortable feeling that he had not fooled Ancorie with the card. But fuck it. He'd go through the motions and see where the game led.

"If that's the case, I'd better let you talk to Anderman himself," Ancorie said, snapping the door open and motioning the detectives through.

Malone went first. He stepped into a narrow passageway of corrugated sheet metal. There were no windows. Ventilation fans hummed overhead. At three-meter intervals push-bar doors led off the corridor. Centered in each door was a combination box lock with twelve numbered buttons.

David Ancorie stopped before a door numbered 6 and punched in the combination. The door clicked open and the detectives were led through it into another narrow hallway with cinderblock walls. Ancorie walked rapidly ahead of them. At the end of the passage he opened a heavy push-bar door and held it as they walked past.

Ancorie introduced Yachov Anderman. His desk was cluttered with shipping invoices and ICC regulations. He was portly and appeared to be in his late fifties. He had hooded eyes that were cold, weary, and decidedly unwelcoming. His hair was thin on top and thick around the sides with many errant strands looping the ears. An occasional twitch squeezed the right side of his face, and he exuded the strong smell of tobacco and cheap aftershave. He was wearing a white short-sleeve shirt that was spread wide at the collar exposing the matted graying hair on his chest. His blue trousers were strikingly fashionable, cut in a flashy Italian style, and seemed out of key with the rumpled rest of

Anderman. He looked balefully at the intruders. "Spare me that non-sense about being from the Department of Labor. You're policemen. So state your business with me and leave," he said harshly.

"What makes you so sure that we're policemen?" Malone said.

"I have lived in many countries during my lifetime. And the one thing that I have discovered is that you and your kind are the same all over the world." Anderman strummed the tip of his nose. "I can smell you."

Malone controlled his rage. He produced his credentials and passed them across the desk to Anderman.

The man behind the desk looked at them and tossed them back to Malone. "So? I'm impressed. Why are you here?"

"Listen, pal! Don't you come on to me with that attitude of yours. We're here on official police business. If you don't want to cooperate here, I'll drag your fat little ass down to the stationhouse and effect an attitudinal change on it. Understand, pal!" Malone said.

David Ancorie made a move toward Malone. Starling Johnson stepped forward, barring Ancorie's path. "Be cool, man, be real cool."

Anderman raised his hand, motioning Ancorie back. He picked up a package of Gauloises, took one out, and lit it. He started to cough. Then he raised his shoulders and smiled. "It has been a difficult week. We all have them, yes. What is it I can do for you?" he asked, dragging on the cigarette.

"We're investigating the murder of Sara Eisinger. She used to work for you," Malone said.

"Yes, I read about her death. But why are you being so devious?"

Malone said, "Because many people are reluctant to speak to police-men. But everyone has time to talk with representatives of Uncle Sam."

"I see," Anderman said, flicking ash into his overflowing ashtray. "I find it difficult to understand why anyone would want to kill Sara. She was such a nice girl." Anderman told him that Eisinger had worked for him for four years. "One day she pranced into the office and an-nounced that she was quitting."

"Did she tell you why she was leaving?"

"Sara had become afflicted by the great American way of life. She told me that she wanted to find herself. Roam the beaches with her tits hanging out, toe the sand, and listen to the cosmic force of the waves breaking over the beach. The usual dribble of the frustrated."

"Why was she frustrated?"

"How should I know?" Anderman said.

"What was her job with you?" Malone asked.

"She maintained running inventories and arranged our shipping schedules. And she was quite good at it," Anderman said, crushing out his cigarette.

"Inventories of what?"

"High-precision industrial machinery."

"I notice that your loading bays are locked. And I don't see any activity in or around the plant. Would you mind telling me why?"

Anderman brought his left elbow up and rested the heel of his hand under his chin, his fingers rubbing the lips, as he decided whether he was going to answer the policeman's question.

"My company is self-insured," Anderman said, deciding it was better to cooperate than fight, at least for now. "I refuse to pay the outrageous premiums that the insurance companies charge. By providing our own security and carefully selecting my own people I am able to eliminate losses due to theft. As a result, our rates are cheaper than our competitors'. Those loading bays are open only when trucks are entering or leaving."

"You don't employ union teamsters?" Malone said, surprised.

Anderman was suddenly annoyed. "I employ whomever I want. Gangsters are not going to run my business." Anderman grinned. "Of course every now and then it becomes necessary to grease a few palms. . . . I employ Israeli students who are studying in this country and American students who come recommended by friends. I will hire no one who is not vouched for."

Malone asked Anderman if he ever heard from Eisinger after she left.

Anderman made a sour face. He told Malone that at first there were a few telephone calls, then nothing.

Malone craned his neck and looked at David Ancorie, who was lolling by the door with his arms folded across his chest. "Do you know Aldridge Braxton?" Malone asked, looking back at Anderman.

"No, I have never heard that name before. Have you, Ancorie?"

Ancorie pushed away from the door and moved across the room, glancing at Johnson. He stood next to Anderman. "No, the name means nothing to me," Ancorie said. "Why?"

"Because Hillel Henkoff and Isaac Arazi, both of whom work for you, were following Mr. Braxton last night in a truck that was registered to this company. Harassment is against the law," Malone said.

"Were you responsible for the beating that was inflicted on Arazi?" Anderman was stern. He had removed another Gauloise and was tapping it end over end, staring at Malone through narrowed eyes.

"Beating? I know nothing of any beating," Malone said, turning to Johnson. "Did you hear of any beatings?"

Starling Johnson shook his head.

"Humph. Of course you didn't. Policemen never know of such things," Anderman said. Sunlight poured through the meshed window high on the wall, patterning the cramped office in uneven strips of light.

"Why were they following Braxton and his two friends?" asked Malone.

"You'll have to ask them that," Anderman said.

"Where are they? I have to interview them," Malone said.

"No problem," Anderman said. "I had to send them to Chicago to pick up some merchandise. As soon as they return I'll have them get in touch with you."

"What can you tell me about them?" Malone asked.

"I can tell you that they're both a pain in the ass," Anderman said. "They are our JDL zealots who try to out-Zionist the Zionists. They're both students who spend most of their time mouthing JDL bullshit instead of working. I've been thinking of getting rid of them. I'm in this business to make money, not fight causes. Those two think that by breaking some Arab's balls they're going to be big heroes on campus. Peer-group bullshit. But they're harmless. Together they couldn't fight their way out of a paper bag."

"When do you expect Henkoff and Arazi to return?" Malone asked.

"A day, maybe two. Don't worry, policeman. They'll get in touch with you. I promise," Anderman said.

"Did you know Sara in Israel?" Malone said.

"I did."

"Have you heard from her parents?" Malone asked casually.

"No," Anderman answered.

Malone saw the small shadow that crossed Anderman's eyes when he lied.

Starling Johnson drove the unmarked car into Ericsson Place and parked behind a Sealand truck. He turned to Malone. "Want me to come with you?"

"I'd better go alone. They're funny people."

Malone cut through a line of traffic that was moving into the Holland Tunnel. He stood on the curb on the south side of Varick Street checking to see if he'd been followed. He turned and entered the gilded lobby of 131 Varick Street. According to the directory, the Funding Development Corporation was on the tenth floor. It was the home base of NYPD's Intelligence Division. Any cop in his right mind stayed well away from it.

Malone stepped off the elevator into an enclosed anteroom that consisted of an old plug-type switchboard and a green metal desk topped with gray Formica, NYPD issue. A well-groomed woman in her late forties looked up.

"I'd like to see Lt. Joe Mannelli," Malone said. "I think he's in Public Relations."

She gave Malone a cold glance, flopped open her palm, and said in a deadpan voice, "Credentials."

Malone handed them to her.

She reached beneath the desk and pulled up a thick file of computer printouts fastened between blue plastic covers. While she was occupied flipping the pages to the M's, Malone's eyes scoured the tiny alcove. Two cameras were bracketed on the walls. Every damn place that he went in connection with this case had cameras.

The woman slapped the identification card down on a line of typed symbols that contained the coded pedigree of Lt. Daniel Malone, NYPD. Her middle finger darted across the line. "What is your tax registry number, sir?"

"Eight three three nine four nine."

"Date of promotion to Sergeant?"

"August, 'sixty-seven."

"Where were you assigned when you left the Academy?"

"Patrol in the Seven-nine."

She handed back his documents and slapped the binder closed. "By the way, sir. What's a forty-nine?"

"Hmm?"

She repeated the question. Her right hand was hidden under the desk. Malone wondered if a .38 was aimed at his stomach.

"A UF forty-nine is the official letterhead of the department."

"A twenty-eight?"

"A UF twenty-eight is a request for time off."

"Thank you, Lou." She grinned.

Malone leaned across the desk. "Did I pass?"

"Sure, lieutenants always pass." She reached under the switchboard and pressed a button. The only door in the alcove sprung open. "Through there, Lou."

Malone stepped through and it closed behind him. There was another door in front of him. When it popped open, Malone saw the smiling face of Joe Mannelli. He hadn't changed much in three years. There was a little more gray around the edges, but the stomach was still flat. One thing that Malone did notice was that the sparkle was gone from his friend's eyes.

They shook hands and Mannelli led him to his office.

"How's the spy business?" Malone asked, easing himself into a chair.

"Full of trenchcoats falling over each other. What brings you here,

Dan?" Mannelli's tone of voice was normal, even casual, but Malone saw wariness around his eyes and mouth.

When Malone finished telling Mannelli about the Eisinger case, Mannelli made a deprecatory shrug. "So? Why come to me?"

Malone uncrossed his legs. "I want to know Eisinger's connections with the CIA. Those two telephone numbers were restricted listings. Which means that she had a direct wire to someone in New York and McLean. I want you to arrange a meet with one of their people. Someone who'll be able to give me some answers."

"Is that all?" Mannelli asked sardonically.

"No. There's more. I also want you to run some names through our intelligence file." Malone took a piece of paper out and slid it across the desk. "Here is a list of everyone connected with this case, including the victim. I'll probably have some more names for you as the case progresses."

Mannelli moved forward, strumming his fingertips on the top of his desk. "Have you any idea what you're asking me to do?"

"According to the department T.O. this unit is still part of the NYPD. Where the hell should I go for help, Nassau County?"

"Danny boy, this department has no, repeat, *no*, connection with the CIA. And we don't, repeat, do not, maintain intelligence files on American citizens. It's against the fucking law, department policy, and the goddamn U.S. Constitution."

Malone's reply was curt and precise. "Bullshit."

Mannelli watched him for a long minute, a cold smile on his lips.

Malone was first to break the uncomfortable silence. "Joe, we've been friends a lot of years. We came on the job together. Were in the same class in the Academy. I've run into something that I think is in your ballpark. I need a favor. I've done a few for you over the years and now it's my turn to ask. Remember Ann Logan?"

Mannelli looked at him. He had not thought of that name in several years. Ten years ago Mannelli was a married sergeant with a pregnant girlfriend. He went to his friend Malone who arranged a visit to a doctor in Jersey City. Abortions weren't legal then.

"Got a cigarette?" Mannelli asked, reaching across the desk. "I gave them up two years ago. Now I only smoke O.P.'s . . . other people's. . . ."

Malone lit the cigarette for his friend. Mannelli leaned forward, clasping Malone's hand, watching him over the flame.

"Have you ever stopped to consider how many idioms we use in our job?" Mannelli said, resting his head back.

"Not really."

"When someone 'wants to buy you a suit' or 'give you a hat' that means that there is a payoff waiting for you if you overlook a violation of law, fail to do your job. And then, Danny boy, there is the biggie, 'he's a standup guy.' That little idiom refers to a man who can be trusted, a man who will deny everything, who will go before the grand jury and commit perjury to protect his friends and the Job. Are you a standup guy, Danny boy?" Mannelli suddenly looked very old. A knot of concern twisted Malone's stomach. He looked at the solemn face in front of him. "I've always been a standup guy."

"Okay, old buddy." Mannelli slapped his palms over the Formica. "After Knapp, things got tough in the Job. But the PC and the rest of the shining assholes left the Intelligence Division alone. They were so paranoid with corruption in the street that they forgot we existed. But along came Watergate and that changed fast. This end of the business got tighter than a clam's ass, and that, in case you didn't know, is waterproof. No one trusted anyone. The CIA got their pricks burned because they trained our people in the late fifties and early sixties. One of the Watergate bagmen came from our job and he didn't stand up. Our covert operations were ordered disbanded. We were ordered to destroy our intelligence file, pull out all wires that were not *ex parte*, and stop playing nasty games with subversive groups. Chrissake, we were damn near out of business."

A skeptical grin appeared on Malone's face. "You closed up shop?"

"Not really," Mannelli said, with a little smile. "We blended our records with the records of the Youth Division and subcontracted our subversive business to private detectives who we can trust. Officially, we went into low gear, concentrating only on the wise guys. And you know how goddamn boring they are."

"And now?"

"Things have changed, pal. We get all kinds of foreign spooks and creeps, plenty of them with diplomatic cover, blowing away anybody they get mad at in every single fucking borough. Today we operate on a strictly need-to-know basis. Everything is compartmentalized, every unit has a little piece of the action. We work pretty close with the feds. What they are prohibited from doing under federal law we sometimes do for them. We also run interference for them when things get sticky . . . like now." Mannelli leaned forward, his face somber. "Danny boy, you could not have picked a worse fucking time to come to me with this little drama of yours."

Malone was forced into a corner. "Why is that, Joe?"

"What I'm going to tell you, I never said. Understand?"

Malone nodded.

"Do you remember reading about the hit on the second secretary of the Cuban Mission to the U.N.? His name was Rodriguez and it happened on May twelve of last year on Fifty-eighth Street and Queens Boulevard."

"I remember."

Mannelli continued. "Well, it turned out that Rodriguez was the head of Cuban Intelligence in this country. Castro went bananas over it. He threatened to blow away every CIA station chief in Latin America. The Agency people were able to convince him that we had nothing to do with the hit. They told him that it was some anti-Castro nuts operating on their own. They promised Castro that we'd do everything possible to I.D. the perps and pass their names on to him so that his people could deal with them. But here comes *el rub-o*. Detectives Caulfield and Williams of the One-oh-eight Squad caught the case. Two sharp pieces of bread. A nine-millimeter Deer gun was used to make the hit; it was found at the scene."

"A Deer gun," Malone said, puzzled.

Mannelli explained that during World War Two the OSS manufactured about a million units of the assassination weapon dubbed the Liberator. It was a small handgun that could be concealed in the palm of the hand and chambered a 45-caliber cartridge. The weapon had a simple twist-and-pull breechblock with extra rounds stored in the hollowed-out handgrip. The Liberator was distributed to the OSS clandestine forces in occupied countries. It had a smooth bore and was an excellent weapon for close killing.

During the Vietnam War the design of the Liberator was brought up to date by the CIA. They developed the 9mm Deer gun for use in Southeast Asia. This weapon had an aluminum butt and a steel barrel that screwed in from the front. "I don't know how the hell Caulfield and Williams did it, but they traced the murder weapon to a consignment purchased by the CIA over eight years ago. They also came up with four witnesses who positively I.D.'d the perp. They not only put him on the scene, they have him walking up to the car, raising the gun and firing."

"So? What's the problem?"

"The problem, ol' buddy, is that the perp and his accomplices are all CIA contract operatives in Omega Seven, the anti-Castro movement. And if that's not bad enough, the weapon used on Rodriguez was also used in six other homicides around the country . . . all Fidel's people."

"Christ! What a can of worms."

"You got it. Caulfield and Williams want arrest warrants issued for homicide and Washington wants the entire case shitcanned."

"What's going to happen?"

"I don't know." He plucked a pencil from a blue mug on his desk and started to doodle, his head lowered in concentration. "The CIA boys aren't going to tell you anything, Danny boy. They're up to their asses in El Salvador and Nicaragua. They'll deny everything. Do yourself a favor and don't get involved in my league. You could get hurt." He looked up, studying his effect. Satisfied, he waited for Malone to reply.

"No way, Joe. I don't shitcan cases."

Mannelli started to doodle again. "Maybe someone'll shitcan *you* if you don't take advice."

Malone appeared calm; he wasn't.

"Oh yeah? Any idea who?"

"Just rumors," Mannelli said, doodling.

Malone snatched the pencil out of his hand, snapped it in two, and threw the pieces over his shoulder. "Tell me about them, Joe."

"Whispers that you're getting involved in something you don't belong in. Something that's not in your league."

"Really? Well you listen to me, pal. I'm not going to close the Eisinger case with no results. I'm going to break the fucking thing wide open. And if I can't do it with help from inside the Job, I'll go to some of my newspaper friends who'd just love to do a little investigative reporting on a homicide that is CIA connected."

Mannelli studied the man sitting in front of him. He crumpled up his artwork into a ball and extended his arm sideways, suspending it in midair. He sprang open his fingers and watched the ball of paper fall into the wastebasket. "Okay, Danny boy. You're over twenty-one. I'll make a phone call for you. But don't come crying back to me when you step on your cock."

Mannelli escorted Malone out to the elevator. They parted without speaking or shaking hands. Mannelli went back to his office, locked the door, and walked slowly across the room, deep in thought. In the corner next to the window was a file cabinet with a metal bar stuck through each handle of the five drawers and secured by a hasp drilled into the top and a thick magnetic lock. He reached behind the cabinet and pried off a magnet. Next he held the magnet over the lock and watched it spring open. The bar was slid out and laid over the cabinet. He pulled out the top drawer and removed a telephone, placing it on top of the cabinet and staring at it for several moments as though deciding whether to use it. He gnawed his lower lip as he picked up the receiver. When it was answered at the other end he simply said, "I need to have a piano tuned."

Ahmad Marku and Iban Yaziji saw the taxi make the right turn off Flatbush Avenue and drive onto Lafayette Avenue. They hurried over to the curb. When the taxi cruised to a stop in front of them, Marku opened the door and both men slid into the rear seat.

The driver checked the oncoming traffic and drove away from the curb. With one eye on the road and the other on the rearview mirror, watching his two passengers, the driver said, "A problem has developed and you two are being detailed to correct it."

The passengers did not answer. They sat, staring into the face in the rearview mirror.

The driver continued. "Andrea St. James was observed having lunch with Yachov Anderman. One of my men happened to be shopping on the Lower East Side. He saw her walking along Hester Street. He also saw two detectives in a department car tailing her. My man decided to tag along. He saw her enter this restaurant. One of the cops followed her inside. A short time later Anderman showed up and entered the restaurant. He sat at her table and they had what appeared to be a heated discussion."

"Damn!" Iban Yaziji exclaimed, slapping the seat next to him.

"It looks like she was working for Anderman all along," said the driver. "Either way, she has become a liability."

"What do you think she knows?" Marku said.

"I don't see how she could know very much. Working around the Interlude and doing those little odd jobs for us, she might have picked up bits and pieces. But we do not intend to take any chances. We want you to have a nice long talk with her."

"And after we are done talking?" Marku asked.

The taxi pulled into the curb in front of the Brooklyn Public Library and stopped. The driver craned his head over his shoulders and looked at his passengers. "We feel that she should be silenced, permanently."

Ahmad Marku handed the driver a dollar bill. "Keep the change."

"Thanks, sport. You can catch the subway across the street. I'd drive you back into Manhattan, but I don't have the time. There are things that I have to do."

"We understand," Yaziji said, shoving open the door.

The taxi driver watched as the passengers crossed Eastern Parkway, making for the subway station. Suddenly the radio under the dashboard blared. "SOD Seven, what is your location, K?"

The driver snatched the hand mike from its hook. As he did this he glanced out at the massive façade of the Brooklyn Public Library. It would not do to give this location, he thought. "SOD Seven to Central. This unit is at Christopher and Ninth, K."

"SOD Seven—ten-one your command, K."

"SOD Seven—ten-four."

The taxi driver returned the mike to its hook and drove off in search of a telephone to call his police command.

When Malone and Johnson returned to the squad room they found Heinemann typing fives and Davis jerking off an outraged citizen who thought that her apartment should have been dusted for fingerprints. After all, they did steal her television and a pair of earrings.

Malone went over to Davis. "I told you guys to go home and get some sleep."

Davis held up a protesting hand. "We figured we'd hang around till you got back, in case you needed us. But don't worry. It's on the arm. We're not going to put in overtime slips. You can make it up to us when this caper is over. It'll give us some splashin' time."

Malone went into his office, glanced over the 60 sheet, and then looked over to O'Brien who was slumped in a chair, waiting. The detective told Malone that the woman they had followed from the Interlude to Braxton's apartment had been I.D.'d as Andrea St. James. Further investigation revealed that St. James was a hooker who worked at the Interlude. O'Brien reported tailing her to the mikvah and he described her conversation in the restaurant with an unidentified man. He and his partner had followed her back to her apartment when she left the restaurant.

"Describe the man she met in the restaurant," Malone said.

O'Brien flipped open his memo pad and read off the description.

"Anderman!" Malone said, going over to the blackboard. He wrote "St. James" on the board and then blew his hands clean. He concluded that Andrea St. James had to be the same Andrea who had telephoned Eisinger in her office.

Malone reluctantly telephoned Joe Mannelli and gave him the latest additions from central casting. Mannelli promised to do what he could. The exchange was cold and very formal.

The detectives filed into Malone's office. "What next, Lou?" Heinemann asked.

Malone looked at their tired faces. "Go home. We'll pick it up in the morning."

O'Shaughnessy pulled out a timetable and made some quick mental calculations. "I could see her and still catch the eight forty-two to Hicksville. That'll give me time to see Foam."

"What about your marriage vows? Do they mean anything to you?" Davis said jokingly.

"I took them fifteen years ago. The statute of limitations expired."

Malone picked up the receiver and tucked it under his chin as he dialed. With his free hand he started to jot down things he needed.

"Inspector, Dan Malone. I'm in the mood to spring for dinner. Interested?"

Gino's was a miraculous little restaurant in the heart of Little Italy, miraculous because it had never been "discovered." Sawdust covered the floor. Antique tables with scrollback chairs were haphazardly scattered about the bar and dining area. A large oil painting hung by the side of the oak bar. It showed Gino surrounded by a group of old Italian men laughing and drinking wine.

"Danny how'r' ya?" Gino said as Malone stepped through the door. Gino's bald egghead seemed as shiny as ever. Only his stomach had changed; it had grown to astonishing proportions. Malone made the introductions. Gino moved the DiNobili to the other side of his mouth. "Pleased to meet you, Inspector. It's good to see one of our own make it in the department."

"We'd like a table in the blue room," Malone said, smiling.

"Why-a sure. Just-a follow me, sir." Gino led them into the dining area, a square room with a miniature balcony running across its length. Several of the neighborhood regulars looked up and made faint signs of recognition and then returned to their pasta. Gino ushered them to a table next to the stairway leading to the overhead balcony. "One minute, sir, while I prepare your table." Gino picked up the grubby ashtray, emptying it on the floor. He snatched off the tablecloth, shaking it clean and reversing it before spreading it back across the table.

Zambrano moved his head next to Malone's. "A class joint," he whispered.

"I always take the boss top drawer," Malone said.

They ordered drinks. Malone told Gino to bring the special of the day.

When their drinks arrived, Zambrano raised his. "Salud, goombah."

They touched glasses.

Gino brought over a bowl of mussels, a platter of pasta shells, a bowl of linguini in white clam sauce, and a large salad. "A feast," he said, putting the food down and turning, walking back into the bar area. He returned with a bottle of Chianti and two water glasses. "All the crystal got broke in the dishwasher," he said, handing each man a glass. Gino leaned across the aisle and took Italian bread from the wall cabinet.

Zambrano broke off the heel of the bread and dunked it into his wine. "What's doing with the Eisinger case?" Zambrano asked, shoving the bread into his mouth.

"If I had some extra men I'd like to plant them on the Eastern Shipping Company and the Interlude." Malone sipped his wine, watching Zambrano over the rim. The next move was Zambrano's.

The inspector dug his fork into the pasta, rolling it onto his spoon. "What else would you do, if you had the men?" Zambrano shoveled the pasta into his mouth. Permission had been given. Malone could continue.

"Tails. On Anderman, the Braxtons, and Andrea St. James," Malone said, rolling his pasta.

"Anything else?" Zambrano asked.

"Wires on all the locations."

"You're talking about a very expensive operation," Zambrano said, reaching for the salad. "I'd be hard put to justify setting up an operation like that for one insignificant homicide that was yesterday's headline. This is June, and we've had over seven hundred and eighty-three homicides. No one gets excited over one more."

"My instinct tells me that this is a heavy case."

Zambrano sipped his drink. "For instance?"

"Little things," Malone said, picking up a spoon and moving shells around in the bowl. "The fact that she had two CIA telephone numbers in her book and they never heard of her. The fact that a certain member of our Intelligence Division knew about the case, and suggested that I forget about it. The fact that I've been getting threatening telephone calls from someone on the Job. I've got a feeling that there are heavyweights involved in this one."

"Wanna tell me about those telephone calls?"

"No. When I know more, you'll be the first to know."

Zambrano gulped the remains of his drink and looked at him. "From what you've told me, you don't have any grounds to go into court and ask for *ex parte* orders."

Malone shoveled some shells onto his plate. "We could employ extrajudicial methods," he said, raising his glass.

"Black-bag stuff? In this day and age? They'd slice your balls into the lasagna if you got caught. Mine too."

They settled in to enjoying their dinner and ate with gusto. Malone waited; first food, then talk—it was a ritual evolved by wise men, one that both men understood and respected.

Zambrano pushed away from the table, reaching down and taking hold of the roll of fat hanging over his waist, shaking it. "I must have put on five pounds." He reached for the wine. "I can let you have some men on a steal for a week," he said, pouring.

"How many?" Malone asked, scraping a piece of bread around the bowl of mussels.

"Six, maybe seven."

"What about conversion cars for the tails?"

"There aren't enough to go around now."

Malone drank. "I'll manage without then. Any chance of getting a surveillance truck?"

Zambrano waved his hand. "No way. Each borough has one assigned. Ours is being used uptown."

"If I should manage to lay my hands on one would you look the other way?"

"As long as no weight comes down from headquarters, yes."

"I'll need a second whip to help me coordinate the operation."

Zambrano sighed. "I'll let you steal Jack Harrigan from the Tenth. He's one of the best and a solid standup guy."

A consensus had been reached. Malone had gotten what he wanted without asking directly; without putting Zambrano in the uncomfortable position of having to say no. Malone ended the ritual with the ordained, "Thank you, Inspector."

Malone motioned to Gino. "Black coffee and Sambucca, with coffee beans."

Zambrano raised his pony glass and stared at the thick white liqueur.

"Dan, you're a good cop." He sipped the Sambucca and smacked his lips. "This Eisinger thing is a bone stuck in your throat. Spit it out before it chokes both of us. Put it on the back burner."

Malone looked down. "No way, Inspector."

"You're telling me that it's personal."

Malone's head shot up. "You're fucking-A right I am."

"Why do you have such a hard-on for this case?"

Malone swirled the liqueur around in his glass. "So far the Job has cost me my marriage, most of my normal friends, and a lot of sleep. But I still like being a cop. It's what I do best. Most of the homicides I catch are grounders; the rest are either drug related or mob hits and who gives a fuck anyway. But every now and then one comes along that cries to be solved; that's the Eisinger homicide. Besides, I don't like to be pressured into not doing my job. Irishmen are like that; we're ornery and thick-headed."

"I know. But you've just used up a lot of credit. I'm going to give you eight days then I'll let you take an exceptional clearance and file the damn thing."

"You're telling me to dump this case."

"No, I'm not. God help me if I ever gave such an order. But there are other priorities."

6

Janet Fox was sitting cross-legged on the bed removing the rollers from her hair when the doorbell rang. She looked at her watch and saw that it was only ten minutes after eight. She got off the bed and went to see who was at her door.

"Detective Davis," the voice said. "I was here the other day with my partner."

She remembered. He was the one with the nice shoulders and cute behind. She looked through the peephole to make sure, told him to wait a minute, and then ran back into the bedroom. She put on a pair of slacks and a plain cotton top and quickly brushed out her hair.

"I had a few more people in the building to interview," Davis said, stepping into the apartment.

"You've already questioned me," she said, closing the door.

He faced her. "Janet, this case is going nowhere fast. So far you're the only person we've come up with who called Eisinger a friend. I came by this morning to ask you if you've thought of anything additional that might help us, no matter how insignificant you might think it is."

She smiled. "I'm useless in the morning without that first cup of coffee. Care to join me?"

It was a small kitchen with a lot of sunlight and a round table next to the window. She put a plate of hot croissants down and sat opposite him.

"I've been racking my brain to see if there was anything that I forgot to tell you," she said, reaching for the butter. "There isn't."

"We find it difficult to believe that Eisinger was so closed about her personal life," he said, breaking off a piece of the croissant, his eyes never leaving her face.

"Why? A lot of people are very private types."

"Hmm. Tell me, what kind of person was she?"

"Sometimes she seemed afraid of the world and then there were times she appeared strong and completely in control." She watched him. "Will you catch the people responsible?"

"We're going to give it our best shot," he said, noticing that her eyes were green.

"She was also a kind and considerate woman. I had recently ended a long relationship and was quite distraught. Sara spent time with me and listened and let me cry on her shoulder. That Friday when I was about to leave for the weekend, Sara came to my apartment and gave me her Bible as a gift. She said that it would bring me peace and help me find the right road."

"You just ended a relationship and were upset over it and then you went away for a weekend with your boss?"

"That was nothing. I had to see if I could be with another man after . . ." She looked down into her cup.

He understood. "Why didn't you tell us about the Bible before?"

She lifted her shoulders in a gesture of indifference. "I didn't think of it. It's just a Bible. Would you like to see it?"

"Yes."

Its edges were frayed and brittle. On the inside cover was a colored lithograph of barefoot Arabs loaded down like beasts of burden, walking along the timeless Bethlehem Road below the Citadel of Zion. One of the Arabs reminded Davis of Malone. He smiled. In the background an old man was leading a donkey. A girl was astride the weary animal. She was laughing and waving at the long-forgotten photographer. Davis felt he had been transported to a day when the earth was barely formed. He felt Sara Eisinger's presence. Her smells clung to the book—perfume . . . lipstick . . . makeup . He haphazardly flipped the pages.

"May I borrow this for a few days?" he asked.

"If you promise to return it."

"Of course. One good turn deserves another," Davis said, picking up his coffee cup. "How about dinner some evening?"

Another one who is married, with a problem, but then, aren't they all, she thought. But she smiled and said, "Why not?"

The squad room was deserted. The rumble of laughter seeped from behind the door of the lieutenant's office. Malone went over and slowly turned the knob. A cluster of detectives were gathered around the blackboard. O'Shaughnessy was standing in the middle. Draped over the board was a poster of a nude woman. She was lying on her back and her legs were spread wide. Jake Stern was standing beside the poster holding a ruler and pointing. Starling Johnson was standing next to Stern.

"This, gentlemen, is the female sex organ. The vagina," Stern instructed. "Our friend and colleague Pat O'Shaughnessy has finally tasted its wondrous fruit."

A polite smattering of applause rose from the group.

"Good show."

"Better late than never."

"Welcome to the club."

"Gentlemen, this slivered erectile structure here that resembles a long boat is the most sensitive part of a woman's body. The clitoris. Kindly observe at the top . . . a small rounded tubercle consisting of spongy erectile tissue. This is the glans clitoris, the most erotic part of this wonderful, sweet-tasting paradise."

"Brilliant dissertation," Heinemann said, clapping from the sideline.

Another burst of applause rose from the detectives.

Stern bowed, acknowledging the acclamation. He held up a quieting hand. "Please observe that the glans clitoris resembles a man standing in a boat. Hence, we receive the nickname . . . the man in the boat. It was here that our friend Pat went astray. Instead of concentrating on the man in the boat he licked the vaginal orifice."

"That's what I did," O'Shaughnessy agreed, crestfallen.

"A common mistake among beginners," Starling Johnson said.

Malone was fuming. He threw the door fully open and stormed in.

"I really hate to interrupt your critique! I went for twenty-five bucks taking Zambrano to dinner . . . telling him how overworked you are . . . how we need help on the Eisinger thing; and what do I find? A bunch of middle-aged whoremasters trying to teach someone how to eat a woman. If he doesn't know now he'll never know!"

"It's never too late to learn," Stern said, ducking out the door.

Malone was unable to suppress a smile.

"How'ya doin', Lou?"

Malone turned. A wiry Irishman was leaning his chair back against the wall cleaning his nails with a silver pocketknife.

"I'm Jack Harrigan. Understand I'm on lend-lease for a couple of weeks. I got six detectives with me." Det. Sergeant Jack Harrigan had graduated summa cum tough from Stickball U. in Greenpoint. Malone felt that he could be trusted.

"What about the men who came with you. Know them?" Malone's forehead furrowed, eyes clouded.

Harrigan saw the doubt, understood the seemingly innocent question; a query steeped in the subtle nuance of the policeman's language.

"I picked each one myself," Harrigan confided. "If the shit hits the fan each one of them will stand like the Rock of Gibraltar."

"Do they know how to install wires and video tape?"

"Do Guineas wear undershirts in the summer?" Harrigan popped the chair forward. "Wadayagot for me, Lou?"

For the next ninety minutes Malone detailed the Eisinger case. When he finished he looked at Harrigan. "I want you to coordinate the operation."

Harrigan cocked his head, tugging at his right earlobe. "A lot of homicides go down each year. Except for a cop killing or when some heavy dude gets his ass blown away, we don't pull out all the stops. So why have so many men been taken off the chart on the Eisinger case?"

Malone steepled his hands over his nose, massaging the bridge with his forefingers. "Because I want this one, Jack."

Harrigan pursed his lips, nodding. "I can dig that. Four years ago I caught a case that became *personal*. Almost came in my pants when the perp was sentenced from zip to life." A puzzled frown crossed Harrigan's face. "For the kind of operation you want, we don't have enough men or wheels. We need conversion vehicles and men. Ain't no way six or seven detectives are going to keep half a dozen under surveillance round the clock."

Malone agreed. He told Harrigan that he wanted the Eastern Shipping Company sat on. Two teams of two men each working twelve hour tours should be able to do. Also the Interlude. Any extra detectives were to tail randomly; jumping from one suspect to the other. ". . . We could get lucky."

"And what do we do for wheels?" Harrigan asked.

"I've arranged things," Malone said. "The telephone company is going to lend us some repair trucks. I got a mail truck from the post office and an ambulance from Gotham Ambulance Service. Con Edison is lending us one of their vans. On Monday I visited a friend in Bed-Stuy. He's letting us use two of his gypsy cabs. I went by the radio shop and signed out eight portables. All set on the same frequency."

"And where do we park this motor pool?" Harrigan asked.

"At the First. You'll use that as headquarters. I've spoken to the C.O. of Narcotics. He is going to let us use a desk and a telephone."

Harrigan grinned. "You've done your homework."

When Bo Davis arrived later that morning he went directly into Malone and told him of his visit to Janet Fox. He handed the lieutenant the Bible and left. Malone hefted the book in his hand, thumbed through a few pages, and dropped it on his desk.

Three hours later Gus Heinemann thrust his head into Malone's office. "Anderman is outside. And he has two beards with him."

"Arazi and Henkoff," Malone said, rounding his desk and hurrying into the squad room.

"See, policeman, I told you I'd bring them around," Anderman said, beaming.

They stood in silent defiance looking up at the ceiling, NEVER AGAIN buttons pinned to their shirts. Both wore patched jeans and had fledgling beards and yarmulkes. Arazi was a skinny kid with bulging china-blue eyes and a large Adam's apple that slid up and down every time he talked. Henkoff was short. He had a barrel chest and rounded shoulders that gave him an appearance of brute strength. A wide bandage ran vertically along the bridge of his nose.

Malone motioned them to sit. They shuffled over, sprawling into the chairs, surveying the walls with do-me-something smirks on their faces.

Malone began. "What were you two doing following Aldridge Braxton and his friends?"

Arazi glared up at the policeman. "We don't have to tell you anything."

Arazi's shrill voice irritated Malone.

"No fascist cop can force us to answer questions," Henkoff said.

Heinemann slipped off the desk and moved between Malone and the two seated men. The heel of his shoe crashed into Arazi's foot—a demolition ball falling down.

Arazi leaped up, dancing on one foot, holding the injured limb. "You did that on purpose," he screamed.

Heinemann's face was wrapped in a blanket of shocked innocence. He clutched at his heart. "Sir. We do not beat people . . . it's unprofessional."

"And counterproductive," Starling Johnson hastened to add.

Anderman moved between the detectives and his employees, his eyes narrowing with displeasure, glaring his warning to behave at Arazi and Henkoff. "Save that undergraduate bullshit for the campus," Anderman said.

"We'll try again," Malone said. "Why were you following Aldridge Braxton?"

Henkoff answered. "We weren't following him. We were interested in his two Arab friends."

"What Arabs?" Malone said.

Arazi looked up at him. "Ahmad Marku and Iban Yaziji—the two men who were with him at the Interlude. Marku is a Saudi and Yaziji is a Libyan. They both belong to the Moslem Brotherhood."

"So what?" Malone said. "That don't give you the right to follow people."

"We belong to the Jewish Defense League at City College. Part of our duties is to follow Arab fanatics and report their movements to our superiors in JDL," Henkoff said.

"Be advised, my young friend, that there are many people who think the JDL is as loony as the Moslem Brotherhood. And be further advised that, according to section 240.25 of the Penal Law, any person who follows another person in or about a public place or places is guilty of harassment. If I find either of you stepping out of line again I promise you a little vacation on Rikers Island. Understand?"

They nodded their heads sullenly.

"Who killed Sara Eisinger?" Malone said.

Arazi shook his head. "I don't know. I heard about Sara's death from Mr. Anderman."

"You said her name like you've said it many times before . . . Sara," Malone said. "Gus, watch the schoolboys. I want a conference with our Mr. Anderman." Malone grabbed Anderman by the elbow and herded him into his office.

Malone held a pencil loosely in his hand, tapping it over the desk, occasionally playing tag with a couple of paper clips. Anderman sat opposite, staring up at the wall.

Malone pushed one paper clip against another. "Mr. Anderman, you and your two schoolboys are full of shit. You don't really expect me to buy that cockamamie story about following Arabs for a JDL fraternity?"

Anderman shrugged. "Policeman, it's the truth."

"You wouldn't know the truth if you fell over it."

"I'm in the importing business—nothing else." Anderman started to get up.

"Plant your ass down there, Anderman. I'm not finished with you yet."

Anderman complied, reluctantly.

"Who killed Eisinger?"

"I . . . don't . . . know!"

"Why was she killed?"

"Same answer, policeman. Those two assholes were only trying to be big men on campus; don't look to make something out of nothing."

"By the way, how was your lunch with Andrea St. James? It's too bad you didn't find the list in the mikvah." Malone leaned back, watching him.

Anderman gasped; his mouth opened, stunned. "How did you know about that?"

"We have our ways. We found the list in her apartment during our initial search," he lied.

"Impossible." Anderman cut the air with a disbelieving hand.

"It was hidden behind the kitchen molding," Malone said, twirling three paper clips around the point of a pencil.

Anderman got up, leaning across the desk. His face was inches from the policeman's. "I want that list."

"Why?"

"If you have it, you know why." Anderman's eyes widened with enlightenment. He knew a good shot at a con job when he saw it. Slowly he retreated back across the desk and sat. "You're good, policeman."

"People do have the habit of underestimating us," Malone said, grinning.

Anderman pushed himself up out of the chair. "Policeman, it has been a pleasure. If you ever want to talk again, just call. I'll be waiting with my lawyer."

"We can do business now, Anderman. Later there will be no deals. Help us and we'll do right by you."

"Shalom, policeman. I have to go and unpack some crates."

After Anderman and the schoolboys had gone, Malone went over to Heinemann and told him to try to scrounge a surveillance truck from somewhere.

"Lou? Those things are worth their weight in gold. It's almost impossible," Heinemann said.

Malone gave him a reassuring pat on the shoulder. "Give it a shot anyway."

Malone went back into his office and picked up the Bible. He flipped through its pages looking for a cutout compartment and found none. Next he rubbed each page to see if they separated. They did not. He held the book up to the light and looked into its spine and saw nothing. He placed it down in front of him and stared at it.

He chucked open the cover with his middle finger and ran his fingertips over the back of the cover. Then he felt it. A thin serration of glue at the bottom. There was something concealed underneath. He pushed back from his desk and opened the top drawer; as he did this he called out to the detectives. "Get in here."

Before he closed the drawer he removed a penknife, opened it, and carefully guided the blade along the bottom of the page. When the incision was complete, he fished his forefinger inside the cut and slid out a sheet of onionskin. Ten addresses typed single space: Trenton, Wilmington, Savannah, San Diego, Eureka, Corpus Christi, Juneau, Texas City, Newark; he recognized the last address. It was on Borden Avenue in Long Island City. He got up and walked over to the filing cabinet. He slid open the bottom drawer and removed a road map of the United States. He then went over to the blackboard and taped the map over the top of the board. Holding the list in front of him, Malone proceeded to circle each of the cities in red pencil. When he finished, he took three steps back and began to study the map.

"Maybe they're cat houses for horny Jews," O'Shaughnessy said.

"Jews don't get horny," Stern said, moving up to the blackboard. He stared at it thoughtfully. "They're all on or near the coast."

Heinemann looked at Malone. "Any ideas?"

"Not really." Malone took out a memo pad and made a copy of the locations. He slid the list into his pocket and handed the original and the Bible to Davis. "Invoice these and put them someplace safe."

"How do you want me to list them on the voucher?" Davis asked.

Malone pondered the question. "A book and one sheet of onionskin."

"Aren't we going to try and find out what's at those locations?" asked Heinemann.

Malone's eyes swept the detectives. "We're going to find out. But not through official channels. They've had a tendency to leak lately. I want none of you to discuss what we've found. No one outside this squad is to know. *Capisce?*"

The detectives nodded.

Starling Johnson meandered over to the blackboard. "That bes a lot of territory to cover. How ya goin' to do it without help?"

Malone winked at him. "It's dues-payin' time, ma man."

It was after lunch when Davis received a telephone call from his friend in Army Intelligence. The male star of the porno film that they had found in Eisinger's apartment had been identified. His name was Maj. James Landsford, and he was stationed at Fort Totten in Queens. "He's waiting to be interviewed," Davis said to Malone.

"Pat and Starling will come with me. The rest of you, hold it down," Malone said.

Fort Totten is squeezed onto a few acres of land that overlooks the western tip of Long Island Sound. The Cross Island Parkway runs past the main gate. Smart-looking M.P.'s with patent-leather holsters and white lanyards are stationed outside the gate's guardhouse. Parked clusters of military trucks with white stars painted on their doors can often be seen from the parkway.

No regular military units were assigned to Fort Totten, as far as Malone knew. Ostensibly it was a place where military dependents waited for transportation overseas. Three barracks with bizarre-shaped antennas that ran hundreds of feet into the sky were located in the center of the fort. An electric fence surrounded the barracks. Dressed in army fatigues, men with automatic weapons strapped across their chests patrolled the perimeter. There was a helicopter pad nearby. There was also a marina where pleasure craft tied up at night—boats with bulkheads crammed with high-frequency radio panels and strange antennas cluttering their masts. But Malone would learn about them in days to come.

A jeep with two armed M.P.'s led the unmarked police car to a Quonset hut where two more M.P.'s waited. The soldiers snapped to attention and saluted. One of them turned smartly and opened the door. A tall, thin man in tailored fatigues and short gray hair was waiting. There was a slight touch of Dixie in his voice. "Welcome, gentlemen. I am Colonel Claymore, the provost marshal of this base."

Claymore's office was functional and strictly government issue. An American flag was on station in the corner; pictures of the president, secretary of the army, the joint chiefs, and a print of Washington crossing the Delaware were on the wall.

"Why do you want to interview Landsford?" Claymore asked, swiveling from side to side in his chair.

"We have reasonable grounds to believe that Landsford is involved in a homicide."

"Well . . . I'm afraid you've arrived a bit too late. He's dead . . . just found a few hours ago. Heart attack."

"I want to see the body," Malone said.

"Want, Lieutenant?" Claymore said, hunching forward.

"Yes, Colonel. Want!"

"I think you're forgetting that this is a military reservation. You have no authority on this land, Lieutenant."

Malone smiled. "That's what I would call a cloudy issue, Colonel. Some people, in fact most, agree with you. But I'll tell you what the NYPD does have. We have access to the little old newspaper and television people. They're our friends. Allies. Why those people in the Fourth Estate would jump on a story about how a Colonel Claymore of the U.S. Army refused to cooperate with the local sheriff in solving the murder of a poor defenseless girl."

Claymore glared and then said, in a deliberate, slow way, "There are matters of national security involved."

"Aren't there always?" Malone said, adding, "Don't worry, we're good Americans."

Resigned to giving ground, Claymore reluctantly replied, "He killed himself."

Malone didn't know why, but he had half expected that answer. He canceled Claymore's questioning look with one of his own. "We think Landsford was being blackmailed."

"He was," Claymore agreed. "Landsford left a suicide note. In it he mentioned the blackmail."

"May I see it?"

"It's classified."

"What were Landsford's duties at Totten?"

"His work was secret . . . sorry."

"What can you tell me about him?"

"Married. Three children. Graduated from the Point. Picked up a couple of Purple Hearts and other decorations in Nam."

"I'd like to see the body . . . just to satisfy my morbid curiosity."

The provost marshal of Fort Totten shook his head in disgust. "Aw shit. Okay. Let's go."

As they were walking to the jeeps that were waiting to take them to the BOQ, Malone turned to Claymore and asked him if Landsford had always been assigned to the Quartermaster Corps.

"He was an infantry man," Claymore said, stepping into the front of the jeep.

There was very little of Maj. James Landsford's face that wasn't bloody. Brain matter splatted the wall. A small entrance wound in the right temple was covered with heavy powder tattooing. The left side of the head was gone. No weapon was in sight; Malone assumed that the army had grabbed it fast, before the NYPD arrived.

Even in death Landsford possessed a strangely military bearing. His chin was tucked in tight against his neck. Legs together. It was as though he had stood at attention the second he pulled the trigger.

Men in tailored fatigues without any insignia or badges of rank were systematically searching the BOQ with grim concentration. They ignored the detectives.

Malone knelt next to the body. He rubbed his forefinger around the entrance wound. Charcoal grains stuck on his fingertip. Malone brought his hand down and slid it inside Landsford's shirt. The skin was cold. He looked up at Claymore who was standing over him, watching.

"Where is the weapon he used?" Malone asked, getting up.

"We have it."

"Any chance of getting a look at the suicide note?"

"As I told you before . . . it's classified."

"Appears to me that everything around this fort is secret or classi-fied. Makes one kind of curious. . . . What the hell kind of place you running, Colonel?"

Claymore looked angry. He moved off, without responding, to a group of army personnel who were huddled in the next room. Malone went after him, catching him by the elbow.

"Where is Landsford's family?"

Claymore shook his arm free. "In Texas. Landsford used to fly home on weekends."

"That's a long and expensive flight to take every weekend," Malone said.

"Takes civilians time to understand us simple army folk," Claymore said.

Lt. Joe Mannelli leaned against a jeep smoking a cigarette. When he saw Malone and the detectives leave the BOQ, Mannelli flipped the cigarette away and waved to them.

"Well, I'll be," Malone said, watching Mannelli approach.

"Just happened to be in the neighborhood. When I saw the car, I said to myself, 'Joe, I bet that unmarked department auto belongs to my old friend Malone.' "

"Bullshit, Lieutenant, sir," Johnson said.

Mannelli grabbed Malone's arm and waltzed him away. "Look at that grass. Wish I could get my lawn to look like that."

"Cut the small talk, Joe. What the hell do you want?"

"I'm the liaison between the fort and the city."

"That includes the Job?"

"It does."

"What's on your mind?"

"I'm here to tell you . . ." He stopped midsentence and looked at Malone. "No. Not to tell you. To suggest, that you forget about this base and everything on it. Including Landsford. That's the way they want it on the fourteenth floor."

Malone looked him in the eye, surprised. "This thing reaches up to the PC?"

"The PC has cognizance of and control over everything that hap-pens in the Job."

"Save that bullshit for the rookies in the Academy. Why this case?"

"Because the fucking powers that be don't want the U.S. Army dragged into your fucking little drama. That's why. In case you've for-gotten, the banks and the U.S. Government are supporting this town. It just wouldn't do to get either of them mad at us."

"You suggesting that I close the case with negative results?"

"Just leave the goddamn army and Landsford out of it." Mannelli hooked his arm around Malone's shoulder, pulling him close. "There are matters of national security involved." Malone pulled away. He was getting tired of hearing about national security.

They strolled in silence down the winding streets, admiring the willows and manicured lawns.

Malone finally looked at the man walking at his side and said, "What the hell is going on here, Joe?"

"Danny boy, I don't know and I don't want to know. I'm only the guy they call whenever a problem arises with the local gendarmes."

"When am I going to hear from your connection at the CIA?"

"Things like that require careful orchestration. They don't happen overnight."

After several moments, Malone turned to him. "Tell the people on the fourteenth floor that I'll do the right thing."

"Never doubted it for a minute," he said, patting Malone's back.

As the detectives were getting back into their car, Malone turned to Starling Johnson. "Remind me to ask Bo to contact his friend in Army Intelligence. I want a copy of Landsford's military record. I can't help but wonder why a decorated infantry man was working in the Quartermaster Corps."

"Right," Johnson said, starting the engine.

The department auto slowed as it approached the guardhouse. An M.P. stepped outside and bent to scrutinize the occupants of the vehicle. He waved them through. O'Shaughnessy was sitting in the back seat. He suddenly lurched forward, shaking Malone by the shoulders. "Lou, look!"

A panel truck turned off the service road from the Cross Island Parkway and sped into the semicircular driveway to the main gate. David Ancorie was driving. An M.P. leaned out of the guardhouse, looked at the approaching vehicle and its driver, and waved it through.

A gypsy cab with LICENSED BY THE PEOPLE stenciled across its rear doors followed the panel truck into the driveway, then made a U-turn and drove out, parking on the service road. The driver of the gypsy cab adjusted his sunglasses as the department auto drove by. Harrigan's man was sticking close.

Malone was turned in his seat, watching the panel truck disappear inside the base.

"What the hell is Ancorie doing on a U.S. Army base?" O'Shaughnessy said.

"I've got a better question. Why did that M.P. wave him on through without even asking him what his name was?" Malone said.

*   *   *

Malone was examining the equipment in a square, gray, windowless van parked in the no-parking zone in front of the Fifth Precinct. Large red reflectors had been set into the corners of the van, peepholes through which detectives could film and watch unsuspecting people. A person walking by the rear of the van who glanced inside would see stacks of cartons piled to the roof, a special optical illusion of which the van's creators at Motor Transport were especially proud. Malone had entered the interior of the van through a sliding metal door with a two-way mirror in its center. Immediately on the left was a chemical toilet. When Malone turned from examining the telephones, electronic and movie equipment, he found Heinemann standing in wonder over the toilet. He was fascinated by its compactness. His ass would smother the bowl, he reckoned.

"How'd you ever manage this coup?" Malone said.

" 'Twas nothing, master," Heinemann said gleefully. "A war veteran I was in the Crimea with, Seventh Hussars, works in Motor Transport. To make a long story longer, the van came in from the Bronx for a tuneup. We got it on the Q.T. for a few days."

"I think the time has come for us to take a look inside the Interlude," Malone said. He turned to Bo Davis. "I'd like you to run over to Abe's Army and Navy store on Whitehall Street. It's next to the old draft induction building. Show Abe your shield, tell him you work with me, and ask him to lend us two army officer's uniforms. Starling and Jake are going to make outstanding officers. We'll use the key we found in Eisinger's apartment and try to bluff our way inside."

"What about Andrea St. James?" Davis said. "After your talk with Anderman she's going to know we're on to her. Want us to pick her up?"

"Let's play her a little longer," Malone said. "Anderman might spook her when he tells her that we know about their lunch together. She just might get careless and lead us somewhere." Malone turned and asked Heinemann if the telephones inside the van were working. Heinemann assured him they were. Malone moved to the battery of telephones and picked one up, dialing.

Jack Harrigan answered. "Lou, I was just about to call you."

"What's the story with Ancorie at Fort Totten?" Malone asked.

Harrigan told the lieutenant that Ancorie had left the Eastern Shipping Company and driven directly to the fort. One of Harrigan's men followed in a gypsy cab. Ancorie stayed at the fort for forty-six minutes and then left, going back to Eastern Shipping.

There was a pause on the line. "Lou, there is something else that I have to tell you. Andrea St. James has given us the slip. She went into the Hotel Granada and my men lost her. We figure that she must have ducked out one of the side entrances."

Pat O'Shaughnessy sprawled over the lumpy sofa and lit a cigarette. There had been four hours to kill before they tried to get into the Interlude, so Pat decided to give his old standby Foam a call. The other detectives went on to do their own things. Heinemann went to the Ninth's club meeting; he knew there'd be a big game; Stern went to the precinct's gym in the basement to work out; Malone and Johnson drove to Second Avenue to get some Indian food.

Pat watched her standing in the cramped kitchen off the living room doing the dishes. He wondered what she would say if she knew the nickname the guys in the Squad had given her. When she first told him that she was going to use contraceptive foam, she'd said, "Now you won't have to use those rubber things anymore," watching his face, waiting for his approval.

It was a primitively furnished apartment that in many ways reminded him of her life—empty and dismal. Whenever he called her she was available. He wondered if she spent her life waiting for his infrequent telephone calls. Did she really believe the lies that he told her? Men have been telling women those same lies since the beginning of time. How could she possibly believe me? Single broads who date married men need those lies to maintain their self-respect, he reasoned. There were times when he felt sorry for her and the legions just like her. They spent a few nights a week with their married boyfriends and the weekends alone, usually in a bottle of gin.

Foam was not the usual Manhattan type who had been knocking around the singles' bars for years. She never went to bars. She was a simple woman who Pat knew loved him very much. And that was the part that bothered him. She gave him everything that she had to give and he gave her nothing but lies. But she was over twenty-one, and whatever she did was her decision. He never forced her. She was with him because she wanted to be with him, he reasoned. And there was no way he was going to give up such a good deal. If she wanted to waste her life on him, that was just fine. He watched her drying the dishes and thought, She's a real boat jumper; brogue and all.

When Pat had telephoned her and told her that he was coming over, Karen Murphy hurried from her second-floor walkup on Sixty-first Street and spent her last fifteen dollars on a roast. It did not matter that she only had change left in her pocketbook. She was going to cook dinner for her Pat.

Karen had been a thirty-one-year-old virgin when they met. Many times before that first meeting she had lain in her bed at night and wondered what it would be like to be with a man. Sometimes she would let her hand roam her body, pretending that she was not alone.

They met at one of those large Manhattan parties where few of the people know one another and everyone appears clutching a green bottle of wine in a paper bag. She was taken back by the forcefulness of his warm personality and his beautiful smile. He had a cleft in his chin that she loved almost immediately. He was everything she ever wanted in a man; there was only one problem—he was married. They spent that first evening together, talking. He was so sincere that it never crossed her mind that he might not be telling her the truth. He spoke of his loneliness and of his quest for someone with whom he might share his life; he told her of his wife's unfaithfulness, her drinking, how she mistreated his children. She saw in him a man in need of a woman's love; a troubled man with great inner conflict. Here was a man who put the needs of his children before his own needs and desires. She could love such a man.

Tonight she was taking her time doing the dishes, trying to muster the courage to ask Pat about his plans for their future. Over the years he had often alluded to a life together, but somehow he always avoided being specific. The years were going by, and she felt that he should make a commitment, one way or the other. When the last dish was dried she cleaned off the sink and folded the towel over the faucet. She walked into the living room and sat on the floor next to him. Resting her face over his groin, she asked him how he had enjoyed dinner.

"Terrific. You are some cook."

"I love you so." She was looking up into his eyes.

He tried to reply in kind but was unable to. He had never been able to say those words. Many times he tried to say them, wanted to say them; but they just would not come. "Me too, Karen."

"Pat, will we ever have a life together?" She was aware that she was holding her breath.

Here comes the bullshit, he thought. What do I do? Get up and leave, or stay and feed her some more lies. He felt a pang of guilt for helping her waste so many years of her life; but her face sure felt good resting over him. He felt himself getting hard. I'd sure hate to have to give her up, he thought. I'll string her along for another year, maybe two, and then . . .

"Karen, I always thought that you knew how I felt about us. As soon as my children get a little older I'll leave my wife. We'll have our life together. I promise."

She was happy. Her Pat had reassured her. She touched the swelling in his pants. "Let's go into the bedroom," she said.

Karen Murphy arched her back and slid off her cotton briefs. She was naked. She watched him undress. His boxer shorts were two sizes too big and his undershirt was gray and stretched out of shape. He flipped off his shoes and came into her bed wearing his socks and undershirt.

Karen loved him for himself, not for his lovemaking. He had a small penis and was conscious of it. He required constant assurance and would always ask her if he satisfied her and if he was big enough for her. She had never really enjoyed sex. As her mother had told her, it was something that women have to do, so it was best to get it over with as quickly as possible. She had learned to fake an orgasm to coincide with his.

She sucked him until he was hard and then lay back. He entered her immediately, without benefit of a kiss or foreplay. Karen undulated wildly. She began to say, "Fuck me. Fuck me." He liked to hear her curse when they were doing it. He pumped her in silence, never emitting a sound. She could tell from his breathing that he was almost ready.

"Now! Come with me." She clamped her legs around his hips and rammed her pelvis up into his body. "I'm coming."

His body sagged on top of her.

She continued to vise him to her. "You're so wonderful. I love making love with you."

He did not answer her. He broke her grip on his body and rolled off her. He was asleep within minutes.

She studied his face as he slept. Sex is so unimportant, she thought. She leaned over and kissed his lips.

That night just before nine a gray van rolled to a stop and parked across the street from the Interlude. The spill of street lamps sliced through the darkness, spreading their even circles over the sidewalk.

Starling Johnson and Jake Stern, both of whom were dressed as army officers, turned the corner of Fifty-seventh Street and started walking in the direction of the club. Johnson peeled away from his partner and walked over to a fire hydrant. It was time to test the Kel set that was strapped under his arm.

"Honk if you read me," Johnson said, putting his foot on the fire hydrant and bending to tie his shoelace.

A horn blared.

Johnson took his foot from the hydrant and tugged at his uniform blouse to make sure that it was even all around and then faced his partner. "Come on, brother, let's you and me earn our daily bread."

A heavy mahogany door with large brass door knockers was at the top of the steps. Johnson lifted the knocker, looked at his partner, and rapped four times.

A tall, strikingly thin man with sculptured black hair, glossy fingernails, and an oversized bow tie that complemented large protruding ears, opened the door and motioned them inside.

"Good evening, gentlemen. My name is Paul. Are you members of the Interlude?"

"I am Captain Jefferson," Johnson lied. "And this is Capt. Jake Stern. A buddy of ours, Major Landsford, is a member of the club. He was transferred and he gave us his key. He told us that there'd be no hassle . . . his dues were paid for three years, he told us."

"May I have the key, please," the maître d' said.

Unruffled, Johnson handed it to him.

"Please wait here, gentlemen." The maître d' turned and walked over to a door that was to the right of the hatcheck cubicle. He opened the door and entered, clicking it closed behind him. He went to the filing cabinet by the window and opened it to the L's. He pulled out Landsford's file. Each member's file had statements relating to the member's sexual preference and personal proclivities, and special instructions on how the member was to be treated. Landsford's file told a story of a fun-loving army officer who enjoyed spending an evening with the ladies. Fortunately, the file also gave instructions that Landsford and any of his army friends were to be given the run of the club and extended every consideration. He closed the file, returned it to its place, and slid the drawer closed.

Paul, the maître d', did not know what was going on at the Interlude, nor did he want to know. He followed his instructions, minded his own business, and made a lot of money. That was all he was interested in—the money. If the owners of the Interlude wanted Landsford and his army friends to be shown special consideration, Paul would see to it that they received it.

"You're both friends of Major Landsford?" the maître d' said, leaving the office and walking over to the two detectives.

"Yes we are," Stern said.

"We haven't seen Major Landsford for a while," the maître d' said.

"He was transferred," Johnson said. "Before he left we had a poker game. Landsford ran out of money and called a raise with a watch and this key. He told us that his membership in the club was transferable. Jake won the pot and the key."

"You must have been close friends of Landsford's," the maître d' said.

"We are very good friends," Stern said firmly.

"In that case, gentlemen, I would like to invite you both to be our guests tonight. For the first round of drinks."

The bar was smoky and crowded; its décor tasteful decadence—there were banquettes of red velvet, etched glass partitions, soft lights, and thick carpet. As the maître d' led them into the long bar he explained that there were private dining rooms on the second and third floors where couples, gay and straight, might enjoy the pleasures of cold wine and clean sheets. Waitresses, showing ample amounts of breasts and asses, threaded their way among the guests carrying trays of drinks and canapes.

Two women were sitting at a corner banquette. One was a Valkyrie, a statuesque woman whose long blond hair was braided. She went by the name of Ursula. The other woman was Vietnamese, and she had long black hair that ran down the length of her back. She answered to the name of Iris Lee. Ursula watched the two soldiers being led up to the bar. She gave Starling Johnson the kind of a look that makes a man check to see if his fly is open.

"Who are they?" Johnson asked, catching the look.

"Hostesses. Would you gentlemen like to meet them?" Paul asked, glancing over at the women.

"I think that might be very pleasant," Stern said, adjusting his khaki tie.

The maître d' ordered a round of drinks for his guests, excused himself, and then pushed his way through the crowd over to where the women were sitting.

"Who are they?" Iris Lee asked the maître d' when he came over to them.

"Friends of Landsford's. They are to be treated as special guests of the house," the maître d' said.

Ursula raised her glass and started to dart her tongue over the rim. "And who is going to pay us?"

"You will both be taken care of," he said.

"The nigger looks like he is hung," Ursula said.

"A little change of luck can't hurt," Paul said, moving away from the women and going back to the bar.

The two women slid out of the booth and followed the maître d'.

"How long have you been in the army?" Iris Lee asked Stern.

"I enlisted when I was sixteen," he said, glancing down at the slit that ran along the front of her dress.

Ursula leaned close to Johnson, examining the three rows of campaign ribbons. "You've seen a lot of combat," she said, running a finger over the ribbons.

"A little," Johnson said, looking at his partner who was now ensconced against the bar with Iris Lee, whispering and smirking like a prepubescent adolescent.

"Violent people get me off," Ursula said, moving even closer, and sliding her knee between his legs.

"Me too, baby," Johnson said.

"I'm getting a hard-on listening to this crap," O'Shaughnessy said, his ear near the receiver inside the surveillance van.

After they had consumed two rounds of drinks Iris Lee suggested that their little party adjourn to one of the private dining rooms on the second floor.

The detectives cheerfully agreed.

"She doesn't buy their story," Heinemann said.

"She's not sure," Malone said. "When they get them alone upstairs, they'll start to play some parlor games with them to see if they'll go all the way. It's the old hooker game. They figure a cop is not going to play it out until the end."

"Those ladies have the wrong two guys," Davis said, grinning.

"What if she feels the Kel on Starling?" Heinemann said.

"Then we make like the cavalry," Malone said.

Ursula and Johnson were sitting on a cane-backed loveseat that complemented the baroqueness of the second-floor dining room. They had been on the second floor for almost fifty minutes. It was time for the girls to get to work. Iris Lee looked at Ursula and nodded slightly. Ursula picked up the cue and slipped out from under Johnson's arms and went to her knees in front of him. She moved close, rubbing her hand in the crook of his thigh.

Iris Lee and Stern kissed. She reached down and forced his legs apart, then slid out of his embrace and knelt on the floor in front of him. "Does it turn you on to have people watch?" she said, reaching for his zipper.

The receiver inside the van went silent. Detectives crowded around, each raptly concentrating on the black piece of mesh in the center of the receiver.

"They better not," Malone said, shaking his head incredulously.

"Lou, I think they're going to," Heinemann said.

Slowly, almost inaudibly at first, sounds of carnal pleasure began to seep from the mesh. Detectives snapped to attention, ears pricked.

"I don't fucking believe it," Malone said, turning to O'Shaughnessy and shouting, "Turn off the goddamn tape."

"Can I go in tomorrow night?" O'Shaughnessy asked, laughing as he flipped off the switch on the recording console.

Gus Heinemann leaned against the wall, his head resting on folded arms, laughing.

The sounds of sexual pleasure reached a violent crescendo, and then avalanched into an elongated sigh. . . .

"Lou, I . . . do believe that the cavalry has come!" Heinemann said, wiping his eyes with a handkerchief.

Iris Lee insisted on ordering dinner for her guests. Tanqueray martinis were served in frosted glasses. After two rounds of drinks the door opened and a waiter with a butchboy haircut wheeled in a serving cart. Iris Lee ordered him to put the dinner on the table in the corner of the room.

When they were finished eating, the waiter put a tray of fruit and cheese down on the table. He then reached under the cart and removed an unopened bottle of Courvoisier. He put it down next to a silver humidor.

Blouses open, the detectives sprawled in their chairs sucking on large and deliciously illegal Havanas. "That sure wasn't anything like army chow," Johnson said, blowing a thick ring of smoke.

"You ladies sure know how to treat a soldier," Stern said, raising the snifter to his nose and inhaling the strong bouquet.

In unison the detectives inside the van harmonized, "You fucking humps."

Iris Lee was coiled on the floor next to Detective Johnson, her head resting on his lap, her arms looped around his leg. She glanced up at him. "Can I get you anything else?"

"Nothing, thank you. Everything was perfect," Johnson said, stroking her hair.

"An experienced soldier like you must have a really important job at Totten," Iris Lee cooed, rubbing the tips of her fingers over the back of his thigh.

"Why the hell would you be interested in that?" Johnson asked.

"I'm a taxpayer. I'd like to know that I'm well protected," she said.

"Don't worry" Stern said. "You'd be surprised if you ever knew the stuff we got there."

Johnson shot a warning look at Stern and started to say something when a piercing scream came from the floor above. Both detectives' heads snapped up.

"What the hell was that?" Stern said, getting to his feet, staring up at the ceiling.

"Relax," Ursula said. "That's the Turk. He likes to do it in the rear. The louder the girl screams the more he pays her."

"I think we're going to enjoy being members of the Interlude," Johnson said, sliding his hand inside Iris Lee's silk blouse.

Another scream! Faint. Subdued.

"Sounds like the Turk has finished playing," Stern said, glancing upward.

Iris Lee reached back and unhooked her bra. Her breasts were large, out of proportion to her thin body. "Play with them," she said.

Johnson fingered her nipples.

This time there could be no doubt, a terrifying scream that begged for mercy. The detectives leaped to their feet and ran for the door.

"It's nothing," Iris Lee said, hooking up her bra and going after them.

The detectives ignored her. They stood outside the room and looked up and down the deserted corridor. Another violent scream forced a decision. The detectives hugged the wall, moving cautiously in the direction of the scream. At the end of the corridor they discovered a darkened staircase partially hidden behind dusty, faded drapes. Stern jumped to the other side of the drapes and pulled them aside. Johnson covered.

The staircase ended in darkness. They stood at the bottom step, straining to see and hear what was going on at the top, where only a faint sliver of light could be discerned. They ascended the steps, one at a time, their backs rubbing the wall, and had almost reached the top when a large, shadowy form stepped out of the darkness and peered down at the two wary cops. "This floor is private," he said in a low, menacing voice.

Johnson moved away from the wall. He braced his right leg behind, slowly moving his left onto the next step, firming his stance. "We're members," Johnson said, sliding his left foot up another step.

The man's hand came out of the blackness gripping a metal bar. He lunged down at the detective. Johnson ducked under the powerful swing. The detective came up hard, slamming his left hand into the man's elbow, at the same time banging down on top of the wrist with his right hand. Johnson pushed in the opposite direction and suddenly the elbow snapped. Then Johnson pivoted, tugging the man forward, tossing him, screaming, down the flight of stairs. The body crashed into the drapes, tearing them off their rod. The man lay whimpering from the agony in his arm.

Johnson and Stern rushed to the top, where they crouched down and let their eyes grow accustomed to the semidarkness. A line of light seeped under a door at the end of the hall. Hearing eerie sounds coming from behind it, they ran toward the door. Johnson moved his mouth to the miniature microphone concealed inside his shirt. "Stay in the van," he shouted. "We'll handle it."

"What should we do?" O'Shaughnessy said, concerned.

"Wait and listen," Malone said. "They know what they're doing, most of the time."

"And if they need help?" Davis asked.

"Then we make like fucking Gang Busters," Malone said.

Stern smashed his foot above the knob. The door splintered and crashed open; the two cops rushed in, crouched defensively to minimize the targets they offered.

The windows were shuttered; street light filtered through the slats. The room was large and bare save for a grotesquely ornate four-poster bed and one heavy wooden armchair. Two swarthy men were standing over a semi-conscious, half-naked woman who was tied in it. Her body was swollen, bloody; both breasts were peppered with festering red blotches. Burnt matches were scattered around the chair.

The tormentors whirled as the detectives crashed into the room. One of them pulled a blackjack from his rear pocket and leaped at the detectives. Stern met the attack and pivoted the threatening hand with his outstretched arm, rammed his knee into the man's groin, and smashed his gun's frame into the man's forehead. He crumpled to the floor, blood spurting from the jagged gash on his head.

"Okay, Abdullah, play time's over," Johnson snarled. "Get against the wall before I give you a second asshole!" Johnson cocked his revolver, assumed a combat stance, and leveled the weapon at the man's face.

Andrea St. James tried to get up. She and the chair tumbled to the floor.

"Help me," she pleaded.

Stern stepped back, covering the two men. Johnson removed his blouse and went to her, kneeling at her side. He untied her and gently placed the blouse over her. "Let's get you out of here," Johnson said. "We'll put these two bastards behind bars for a couple of years."

Andrea St. James clutched at his arm. "No police, please," she said, tears streaming down her swollen cheeks. "Just get me out of here."

"But . . ." Johnson started to protest.

"Please . . . no arrests."

Johnson looked over to Jake Stern who shrugged. "Without a complainant we got nothing," Stern said.

The maître d' and the two hostesses burst into the room.

Stern whipped around. "Against the wall, my lovelies."

"What do you think you're doing?" the maître d' demanded.

"We're leaving and the lady is leaving with us," Johnson announced, cradling Andrea St. James in his arms.

"Who the fuck are you?" Ursula yelled.

"Why, mamma, we're officers and gentlemen," Starling Johnson said, backing out the door.

The emergency room at Bellevue was filled with the night's casualties. Malone peered past the partly drawn curtain at the doctor working over Andrea St. James. It never changes, he thought. She was just another person caught up in mindless carnage; night after night—cuttings, stabbings, shootings. Malone scanned the people patiently waiting their turns to be patched back together. A white man sat pressing a flap of skin from his cheek in place. Malone looked at him. Just your friendly corner knife fight, no doubt, he thought.

A dead-tired intern left the cubicle and shambled over to Malone.

"Are you going to keep her, Doc?" Malone asked.

"Where?" the doctor said. "They're packed in here like sardines. I've patched her up. Her private physician will have to take it from there."

Malone went into a huddle with the detectives. "We need a safe house."

"Do we go the official or unofficial route?" Davis asked.

"Unofficial," Malone said. "We've nothing to hold her on." Malone pondered the situation for a moment. "Bo, call Delamare at the Barton Hotel. He'll give us a room for a few days, no questions asked."

"What about baby-sitters?" O'Shaughnessy asked.

Malone sighed. "We'll have to steal two of Harrigan's men."

The management of the Barton Hotel on Lexington Avenue was glad to cooperate with the NYPD. They knew from experience that small favors reap a large harvest.

Andrea St. James was tucked away in a suite of rooms for which a paying guest would have had to pay three hundred dollars a day. Large windows overlooked the Manhattan landscape. There was a large living room decorated in almost-French Provincial. A rose-pink bedroom and lace-bordered sheets seemed an incongruous setting. She lay in bed, wearing an open-back hospital gown, twisting and turning, her face swathed in bandages.

Malone dragged a chair over to the bed and placed a cassette tape recorder on the marble-topped night stand, thinking of how to question her. He knew only that she was the hooker who had made the porno film with Landsford and that there was a definite connection between her and Anderman. And he assumed that it was she who used to call Eisinger at Braxton Tours, and was the same woman Eisinger told to look at the song.

Frightened, unsure eyes peered up at him from behind an embrasure of gauze. He noticed that her fingernails were broken and chipped. The smooth colored glaze that once covered them had been chewed, leaving atolls of ugly yellowish nail.

Andrea St. James was semiconscious. Her hands worked on the sheets, squeezing and scratching. She let her eyes close. Malone was afraid she would be lost to the sedation they had given her at Bellevue.

His knees pressed into the side of the bed. "You took a bad beating. Feeling any better?"

"Who are you?"

"The police."

"Oh. Thank God. Yachov sent you. You're from the Unit."

"Yes. Yachov sent me," he said, playing her.

She clutched his shoulder. "Tell Yachov it was Westy. I saw Westy with them. . . . He gave it up. . . . Yachov was right . . . tell him . . . should have pulled me out . . . no list . . . couldn't find list . . . Sara . . . poor dear Sara . . ."

She was scratching his shoulders as though she was trying to claw her way back to consciousness. Her tongue was heavy in her mouth; her eyes would open, focus, and then close. She tried to get more words out, but could manage only a low mumble.

Malone took her hand in his, soothing it with gentle strokes. His voice was low, calming. "Andrea. Tell me so that I can tell Yachov."

"Yachov . . . the Unit has been breached . . . warn him. Westy . . . I saw him that first time with Sara . . . in the restaurant with the other two . . . one was wearing that stupid shirt . . . it was a beautiful day . . . Fort Surrender . . . Sara . . . remember . . . he waved at her . . . oh, I hurt so much." Her hand slid from his shoulder.

Malone licked at the film of sweat that had formed above his lip. His eyes were wide, fixed in a disbelieving stare. He began to gnaw at the extremity of his lower lip. Had he heard correctly?

He was suddenly conscious of his throbbing temples. He shuffled closer. He now had his direct link. Cops were involved—somewhere, somehow. He bent closer, not speaking, studying her, trying to unscramble her words.

He moved his lips next to her ear and whispered, "Tell me who killed Sara."

Her consciousness was slipping away. "Westy . . . no . . . don't know . . . yes . . . him . . . Westy . . . warn Yachov . . ."

"Andrea. Tell me about the song."

"Sara tried to warn us . . . she . . . found out . . . about . . . the Unit within a unit . . ."

"The song," he repeated.

"Song of Asaph . . . Sara's way . . ."

He could feel his heart beating faster. "Andrea. Tell me about the Unit."

Her eyes opened wide and she struggled up, bracing herself on her elbows. "You're not from Yachov!" she yelled with surprising energy. Then she collapsed and curled into a fetal position.

Malone reached out and shut off the recorder. As he started to get up he noticed the antique telephone next to the recorder. He picked it up, stretching it as far away from the bed as the cord permitted. Placing it on the floor, he returned for the recorder.

When he was by the door he stopped. Without turning to look at her he said, "You owe it to Sara to help us. Not to mention the fact that a couple of cops risked their lives to save your ungrateful ass."

Andrea St. James lay alone, her eyes closed as she listened to the endless ticking of a clock off somewhere in the distance. *Tick, tick, tick.* It never missed; each tick falling with monotonous regularity. Her head had begun to clear. She wasn't sure if it had been a dream; it was so real. She was being questioned by a man who had said that he came from Yachov. The pain was still there, a terrible ache throughout her body. She lifted her head and looked around the room, ensuring that she was alone. One by one she slid her legs out from under the sheets and touched the floor. The rug felt soft and cold against her feet. Light-headed, she collapsed over the bed, her legs dangling over the side.

She rested, gathering her strength; her chest heaved from shuddering painful breaths. Several minutes passed and she tried again. This time she slid her body over the edge, outstretched hands acting as her guide.

On hands and knees she looked across the room at the telephone. So far away. She crawled over to it, inching painfully over the shaggy surface. When she reached it she stared down at the white circle in the center of the telephone: Barton Hotel, Ext. 345. She knocked the receiver from its cradle and lay on the floor next to it, her face next to the mouthpiece, trying through her blurred eyes to make out the direction over each of the ten circles on the dial. Dial 6 for a local call. A finger moved haltingly toward the sixth circle. She took her time, knowing that she had to get it right the first time. There was no strength left for a second try. The phone on the other end was answered on the first ring. She spoke haltingly in Hebrew.

Andrea St. James felt secure. Friends would be coming for her.

The Golden Kitchen on First Avenue was one of Malone's favorite eating places. He picked his way through the crowd to an unoccupied table by the window. He saw some familiar faces; couples were quietly eating their dinners and sharing a carafe of wine while the singles sat alone reading a book or newspaper and secretly prayed for someone to share their meal. He thought of Father Gavin. Had Monsignor McInerney officiated at the funeral? Was Mary, nee Harold Collins, still turning tricks? Probably. . . . He wondered how many other people in the restaurant were carrying on conversations with themselves. Most, he thought. And then the Eisinger caper swirled into his thoughts. How did they manage to get Andrea St. James into the Interlude without Harrigan's men seeing them? One of the detectives was probably taking a piss someplace and the other was more than likely bullshitting with some broad. And Westy? That was obviously the name of a man. But who? And the Unit within a unit. What was it? Was it part of the Job? Anderman was the key. Who was that son-of-a-bitch anyway? And then there was Fort Surrender. Only a cop would know about that. He had played the tape a dozen times; Andrea St. James did not say it was a T-shirt. But he knew that it was. He had seen them. Did Westy and his two pals come out of Fort Surrender? His thoughts quickly returned to the present when an outrageously attractive woman strode past the restaurant. Her white gauze skirt fell between her long legs, revealing the welt of her bikini underpants. He was suddenly aware of an uncomfortable ache in his balls. His daydreams changed. He was in bed with a woman, her long legs wrapped his body, holding him as he pumped relentlessly. Her head thrashing the pillow; guttural whimpers caught in her throat. Her black hair was disarrayed and beaded with sweat. He could feel her spasms, the sliding of her body against him.

He did not wait for dessert. He got up, paid the bill, and headed for the old-fashioned telephone booth in the rear of the restaurant. He slid open the door and dialed, standing. A self-mocking smile flitted across his face as he tried to remember if he had made the obligatory "it was wonderful" telephone call after the last time.

Erica Sommers chuckled when she heard his voice. "I figured you would be calling soon."

"If you can tear yourself away from your work I'd sure like to see you."

"Where are you, Daniel?"

"Four blocks away." He was aware of a sudden burning sensation in his stomach.

"Give me an hour to finish my work."

"Ten-four," he said, letting the phone fall onto the hook.

Erica Sommers read the page in the typewriter.

Jefferson Stranger watched the silky garment slide over his bride's sensuous body. He moved back, casting a lustful eye.

Christina Stranger stepped out of the nightgown, her arms beckoning. This was to be a new beginning; an escape from her secret past. She prayed that Jefferson would never discover her previous life. As he took her into his arms she thought of David and how much stronger his arms were.

Tapping a pencil over her teeth, Erica Sommers reread the page. She took the pencil and struck out an adjective. Enough is enough, she told herself, glancing at the time. Shit! Malone would be here soon. She hurried into the bathroom, pulling her top off as she went.

Erica Sommers wrote Nightingale Romances—two hundred pages of escape that sold at drugstores and supermarkets.

Erica had showered and was standing naked in the bathroom with one leg on the rim of the tub, trimming her pubic hair. She thought of Malone. They had met two years ago at a performance of *Dancin'*. He had arrived late and was trudging down the aisle when he stepped on her foot. During the intermission he came over to her and apologized. She found herself drawn to him from the first. His body excited her and his smile possessed a warmth that caused her to glow inwardly. But during their first date she concluded it would be a mistake to permit herself to become involved with him. He was the kind of man no woman could really be sure of, she decided. A character straight out of one of her Nightingales. But then, perhaps she was wrong. Maybe they could have something together. She went to bed with him on their fourth date and it was nothing like her fantasies, but something better and totally unexpected. He was physically demanding, direct, and at the same time a gentle, considerate lover. Of all the men she had known, he was the first to excite and fully engage her sexuality. They discovered that they were both capable of multiple orgasms and spent hours in bed reveling in each other's body. At times when she was alone she would find herself thinking of his body and would suddenly be consumed by desire for him.

In many ways she found Malone to be a strange and lonely man. A man capable of giving himself totally in bed, yet unable to share any part of himself out of bed. IT was always there, that monolithic secret society of unwritten laws and unspoken nuances that prevented some men from giving of themselves, the NYPD.

She had reached the point where something had to give in the relationship. A commitment or an ending. She had been divorced for five years and was ready to share her life. She demanded only two things of a man: honesty and sharing. To her mind they were simple things. It perplexed her that men found them so difficult.

Erica Sommers was a strikingly handsome woman with a high forehead and an aristocratic nose. Her eyebrows arched sharply and then flowed downward over her brow. Her brown hair was cut in bangs with the back cascading past her shoulders. Deeply tanned skin accentuated her large amber eyes.

Malone had arrived exactly one hour after he telephoned.

She had made them drinks and they were sitting on her minute terrace staring at the inky river.

Malone said, "You get more beautiful each time I see you."

"Why thank you, Lieutenant. I hope you don't tell that to all your lady friends."

He wanted to tell her that there were no others. Instead he said, "I don't."

She was wearing a white caftan and sandals. Getting comfortable, she tucked her legs under her body and looked at him. She then proceeded to tell him everything that she had done since she last saw him. She had gone shopping for a dress and discovered this wonderful delicatessen off Second Avenue that specialized in Greek delicacies. She had cleaned the apartment and done her laundry. Her latest Nightingale was almost completed: *Christina's Fury.* She was giving some thought to writing a serious novel set in the antebellum South. Finished recounting her days, she sat back and looked at him. "Tell me what's new in your life." She sipped at her drink, watching him. "Any interesting cases?"

There's this Eisinger thing, he wanted to say. And these telephone calls from a Captain Madvick who does not exist; and a guy named Mannelli and another guy named Anderman. This and more he wanted to say. But he couldn't. She wasn't on the Job. Wasn't a part of it. His fingers were bobbing the ends of her hair. "Naw," said he, "there's nothing new. The same old stuff day in and day out."

Her face reflected her disappointment. She sipped her drink slowly, thinking. She was in love with a shadow who had built a wall of silence around him. A protective moat. He was a man with no past, no present, and no future. She wanted him on equal terms and would go out of her way to assert her independence with him. She was not a camp follower. Whenever she would ask him about his divorce or ex-wife, or the damn PD, he'd either snap at her or give her an oblique answer. They had been seeing each other for almost two months before he gave her his home telephone number. There were times when she wondered why she bothered, but, then, when she looked into his face and touched his shoulders, she knew. She always knew. "For a lieutenant of detectives you have a decidedly boring job, Daniel."

He flipped his right hand back and forth. "It's just a job, not a calling."

They sat in silence for a while and then he leaned over and kissed her breast through the soft fabric. She moved her head back and pressed him to her body. His hand glided up her smooth leg. "Not here, Daniel."

They walked into the bedroom holding hands.

It was much later. They had made love twice and were lying in bed silently listening to the not-so-muted noise of the City. She decided to try again. She turned toward him. "Tell me about your marriage, Daniel."

"There's nothing to tell," he snapped.

"Please don't be hard with me. I don't like you when you're like that."

"I was soft a few minutes ago," he said, reaching over and running a hand over her thigh. She lifted his hand from her body and carried it out over the bed where she dropped it with a look of exaggerated disdain. "All men are soft then! When they're hard they're soft and when they're soft they're hard. All women know that, Lieutenant."

He looked at her and smiled.

Holding hands, they fell into a peaceful sleep.

The sun rose at 5:12 A.M. Malone was sitting up in the bed staring down at her naked beauty, marveling at the pleasure they were able to give each other. I know what you're trying to do, he thought. You want me to give you what I can't. Would you believe me if I told you that one human being could kill another with a curtain rod, that a father was capable of sodomizing his daughter, that a person's body could be turned into an unrecognizable black mass, that bands of animals roam our city robbing and killing, that the police are the only ones that stand between you and barbarism? Would you believe those things? A cop would. Shall I tell you that there are only a handful of politicians and judges in the city who give a good fuck what happens to you or the rest of the drones? Do you want to know what it's like to work in a concrete sewer; to walk armed through the night constantly watching the shadows, listening for footsteps behind. Perhaps I should tell you of the pervasive corruption. Do you know what a judge has to pay for his black robe? I do. You want to know why policemen don't share. I'll tell you. It's because they see the city being submerged in a sea of stinking shit and because they don't want the excrement of the savages seeping into their private lives. I wish that I could share more with you.

She opened her eyes and saw him looking at her. For a moment she thought she noticed his eyes glistening. She cupped his face with her hands. "Can't you sleep?"

"I want to tell you about my marriage."

She sat up, wide awake.

Squares of light dotted the facade of the Barton Hotel. Frustrated waiters stood grumbling, waiting for the last patrons to leave the darkened nightclub. There was an empty stillness about the near deserted lobby. A cleaning woman dusted the plants, just starting her night's tasks. An occasional couple walked in from the night and went directly to the elevators. Every now and then a Mr. Brown or Smith exited the hotel's piano bar and went to the desk clerk to register while his "wife" fidgeted with her drink at the bar, waiting for him to return with the key.

A man strode briskly into the lobby and hurried to the elevators.

Andrea St. James slept restlessly, waiting.

Two detectives sprawled over a couch outside her bedroom, sipping the last of a six-pack and watching the "Late Late Show." A hard, deliberate knock made their heads jerk toward the door. They put their beers down and looked at each other, concerned. They slid their revolvers out and went to the door, positioning themselves against the wall. "Yeah?"

The reply was sure and crisp. Andrea St. James's attorney. His card was slid under the door:

HANLEY, GREEN, DAYTON, FORBES
12 Wall Street
New York, New York
G. JUSTIN HANLEY, *Attorney-at-Law*

G. Justin Hanley was the senior partner in an impeccable law firm well known both for its discretion in handling delicate matters and its enormous fees. G. Justin Hanley looked like a G. Justin Hanley of Exeter, Yale, Southampton, and Park Avenue should look. Even at 2 A.M. he looked as fresh as he would at the start of any business day. His dark gray suit was sufficiently unfashionable, and his expression the right mixture of amusement at and distance from the company in which he now found himself.

Hanley was polite, firm, and more than a little condescending. He told the detectives that he was aware that his client was being held. She was not under arrest but was being protected by the police from unknown assailants. For this he and his client were grateful. However, it was incumbent upon him to see that his client received proper medical attention. He was therefore taking his client with him, now. The efforts of the NYPD were greatly appreciated. He hoped that the matter might be settled here, now. He would find it distasteful if he had to go into court and lodge a complaint against the NYPD for unlawful detention. He casually asked if the detectives were familiar with the Civil Rights Act. "Its penalties are quite severe," he assured them.

Limping alongside the lawyer with a bed sheet covering her hospital gown, Andrea St. James left the lobby of the Barton Hotel and was guided toward a waiting limousine.

A solitary figure sat in the rear. The lawyer helped her into the back seat. She threw herself crying onto the man's lap.

Anderman stroked her hair. "Everything will be fine now. You're going home."

7

Yachov Anderman arrived early in order to supervise the loading of the trailer. It was a shipment that required his personal attention. Fork-lifts darted into the belly and dropped their skids; workers inside ensured that the load was secure. When the trailer was full, the doors were closed and sealed. Anderman gave a signal and a button was pressed. The loading-bay door churned upward. The scrunch of wheels jerked Anderman's head toward the street. He saw a car in front of the bay, blocking it. Malone was climbing out of the front. There were other detectives with him. Anderman handed his clipboard to the man standing next to him and jumped from the platform. A glint of victory shone in his eyes. "Still chasing windmills, policeman?"

"Andrea St. James," Malone shot back.

Malone went up to Anderman and looped his arm through the trucker's, turning him and walking him back toward the platform. "That was a very neat operation last night. My compliments."

"I haven't the slightest idea what you're talking about."

They strolled along the side of the tractor-trailer, Malone watching the monstrous wheels. When they reached the cab they turned and headed back toward the door. Stern and Heinemann waited just inside. David Ancorie peered out from the dispatcher's cubicle.

"If they get their hands on her again I might not be around to save her," Malone said.

"Save who?" Anderman was enjoying his moment.

"I have a few more questions that I'd like to ask the lady."

Anderman wrenched away from the policeman. "Wait right where you are. I'll go and telephone my lawyer. You can ask him your questions."

Malone's eyes narrowed. He turned abruptly and headed for the platform, motioning the detectives to follow. A short ladder led up. Malone gripped the top and climbed. When he reached the top he straightened, looking around. He moved to the three men who were loading wooden crates onto skids. He asked their names. Each replied in broken English. Malone produced his shield and demanded to see their Alien Registration Cards. The confused workers looked to Anderman and shrugged in gestures of dismay. Malone ordered the detectives to arrest the men. Stern and Heinemann started to handcuff them together.

"What the hell do you think you're doing?" shrieked Anderman, running for the ladder.

David Ancorie came out of the cubicle.

"Every alien is required by federal law to carry and produce on demand his green card. Failure to do so is presumptive evidence of illegal entry into this country," Malone said.

Anderman reached the top. He was out of breath. He bellied up to Malone. "You're city cops, not federal! Their damn cards are in their homes. Each one of them are here legal."

"Too bad." He pushed Anderman aside and prepared to leave. Ancorie was there, blocking his path; his anger evident. The two men stood toe-to-toe, glaring. "If I were you I'd move," Malone whispered.

The pulse in Ancorie's neck pounded. His cheeks were flushed.

"I mean right now, laddie," Malone said, his tone now harder.

"David?" Anderman called.

Ancorie's stare flashed to Anderman. He moved aside. As Malone was climbing down Anderman shouted to him. "You're persecuting me, policeman."

"Some people might say that," Malone said.

G. Justin Hanley, Andrea St. James's attorney, was waiting impatiently in front of the federal detention center. As the prisoners were being led from the car, the lawyer walked over. "Lieutenant Malone?"

Malone looked at him. "Yes?"

"My card." It was not the plain kind of calling card that he had left at the Barton Hotel. The paper was expensive; the words on it in elegant raised lettering. Lieutenants must rate the expensive ones, Malone thought, handing it back. "Thanks, but I don't need any right now."

Hanley stiffened, his patrician feathers ruffled by the glib reply.

"Those men are not slaves; they're my clients," the lawyer said, pointing to the handcuffed men being led into the detention facility.

Heinemann paused and looked back at Malone. The lieutenant waved him inside. "I told you they're my clients!" Hanley insisted.

"What are their names, Counselor?"

"Their what?"

"Names. Almost everyone has one these days. You should know theirs . . . if they are your clients."

Hanley's face twisted into a grimace. "That makes no difference," he stammered. "I represent those men." '

"Oh, but it do make a difference, Counselor." Malone walked away.

Hanley went after him, grabbing him by the shoulder and turning him.

"I demand their immediate release." The lawyer's voice cracked; his lower lip was quivering.

Malone smiled. "Please get your hand off me, Counselor." It was a thin voice, hardly a whisper. Hanley knew that a second request would not be forthcoming. He removed his hand. How he hated the flotsam of the street. In boardrooms among his peers G. Justin Hanley was a champion; but here, at society's lowest rung, he felt outmatched.

"You're stretching the rubber band too far, Malone. It's going to snap and take your head off."

Malone moved close to him. He noticed the beads of sweat bordering the hairline. He ran his fingernails over Hanley's lapel.

"Threats are very unprofessional, Counselor." Malone walked away, leaving the lawyer clenching his fists. Malone craned his head to him. "When you see Anderman tell him that he should have given you all the facts . . . like the names."

A long corridor led to the holding pens where illegal aliens waited inside to be processed. Orientals huddled together, speaking softly in their native languages. Latins talked rapidly in Spanish, casting nervous glances at the immigration officials taking pedigrees through the bars. Some of the aliens were sitting cross-legged on the floor; old habits quickly return. Heinemann was waiting. "What took you so long?"

"It became necessary to give an eminent member of the bar a lesson in street law."

"That eminent member of the bar will have them sprung within the hour," Stern said.

Malone agreed. "I just couldn't let him get away with last night without breaking some balls. Besides, by the time Anderman gets them out the surveillance van is going to be parked on the south side of Borden Avenue. I want to know what's going down inside that place."

It took Anderman and his lawyer the better part of two hours to obtain releases. Malone had laid a professional courtesy requested on the people at Immigration and they complied; stalling and shuffling Anderman and Hanley from office to office. It was almost 4 P.M. when a blue Ford sedan drove into the loading bay of the Eastern Shipping Company. Anderman and his workers left the car cursing the police in four different languages. Anderman hurried off by himself. During the drive back he had reached a decision. Andrea St. James's presence had become a risk. Too many people were looking for her. When he got back to his office he called El Al. There was a flight out in ninety minutes.

A frankfurter man set up his pushcart in front of Tauscher Steel. The peddler snapped the blue-and-yellow umbrella up over the cart, locking it into place. He flipped open the steam tub and stirred the orange-colored water. A log jam of frankfurters concealed the Bren gun wrapped in a waterproof covering. The man's long hair covered the plastic wire that ran up the side of his neck into the miniature receiver plugged into his ear. A steel hat came over and ordered a frank with all the trimmings. The iron man strolled off, gnashing the strands of sauerkraut and onions hanging out of the roll. The peddler waited until the customer was gone. Then he leaned forward, adjusting the stacks of plastic cups. "The gray van that was outside the Interlude last night is across from the plant," he whispered into the cups.

The reply was immediate. "We wait."

The blue sedan bolted from the loading bay and crossed Borden Avenue. Andrea St. James was sitting in the rear next to Isaac Arazi. Hillel Henkoff was behind the wheel. A flatbed of I beams lumbered out of Thirty-first Street. The frankfurter man leaned forward. "A blue Ford sedan just left. Andrea was in the back."

Inside the surveillance van O'Shaughnessy radioed Malone that Andrea St. James had left. "Stay with her," Malone said. "I'll try and catch up with you."

Bo Davis wiggled the transmission into first gear and released the clutch. The van moved from the curb.

Malone and Heinemann hurried from the precinct.

"We're in a hurry," Malone said, sliding into the car. Heinemann reached to the floor and picked up the portable red light. He reached out of the car and slapped it onto the roof.

"We're on our way," Heinemann said, flipping the siren switch.

The blue sedan entered the Long Island Expressway at Greenpoint Avenue. Traffic was backed up over the hump. Andrea St. James stared at the row of A-frame houses that lined the service road. She had never noticed them before. There was a vest-pocket park that she had never seen; the handball court was covered with graffiti. It was funny the things people never take the time to notice, she thought. She was overcome with a sense of sadness at leaving. A delivery truck nosed past the blue sedan blocking her view; a graffiti was fingered in the dirt: IRAN SUCKS.

O'Shaughnessy maintained radio contact with Malone. The sedan was fifteen cars ahead of them. "Lou, do you want us to pull them over and grab her?" O'Shaughnessy radioed.

"No," Malone said. "I don't want to blow the van. And besides, I want to see where they're going."

Traffic exiting the Brooklyn-Queens Expressway merged into the Long Island Expressway at the bottom of the hump, creating a bottle-neck of inching automobiles and frustrated motorists. O'Shaughnessy was standing by the two-way reflector, looking down into passing cars. A white Cadillac inched parallel with the van. A woman was driving. Her skirt was pulled up over her knees; her legs were apart. O'Shaughnessy gaped down at her but managed to tear his eyes away when he considered what absolute hell he'd catch if something went down while his attention was otherwise engaged.

As the blue sedan made its way on the expressway an unmarked police car screeched into the entrance plaza of the Midtown Tunnel on the Manhattan side. Port Authority police were waiting to guide it through. The left lane of traffic inside the tunnel was stopped, locked bumper to bumper. Motorists felt twinges of excitement at the sight of the speeding police car, its revolving turret light throwing out waves of red. They wondered what was happening. Maybe they would have something new to talk about over dinner, something that broke the monotony of the Long Island Expressway at rush hour.

The blue sedan drove onto the Van Wyck Expressway heading south.

O'Shaughnessy radioed the location. "It looks like they're heading for Kennedy."

Traffic thinned past Liberty Avenue. Motorists pressed down on their accelerators, jerking their vehicles forward, releasing pent-up frus-trations.

Bo Davis shifted up to fourth gear.

Heinemann was driving on the shoulder of the Long Island Express-way. When he reached the Van Wyck, the detective forced the police car in ahead of the line of traffic and sped south.

The surveillance van maintained its distance behind the blue sedan. The detectives inside the van did not notice the Hertz truck bearing down on them. The truck cut to the left of the van and continued past, zigzagging the lanes of traffic. When it overtook the blue sedan it swerved in front of it.

"Pat! That Hertz truck!" Davis rammed the accelerator to the floor.

A hand pushed the canvas backing of the truck aside and two rifle barrels were extended. Long, egg-shaped projectiles protruded from both.

Hillel Henkoff saw the puffs of smoke and the vapor trail. He wrenched the wheel sharply, trying to escape. Andrea St. James threw her hands up to her face and screamed.

The car erupted into a ball of orange and yellow flames. The explosion lifted it twenty feet into the air, bending it in half and sending its twisted parts spiraling downward.

One hour later the southbound lanes of the Van Wyck Expressway were still closed, traffic being detoured at Jamaica Avenue. Ambulances and other emergency service vehicles lined the shoulder of the parkway. A Fire Department pumper was watering the smoldering wreck. The steel-basketed bomb squad truck was parked across the highway, blocking it. Detectives sifted the debris. Parts of bodies were being collected and tagged and then put into body bags.

Malone and his detectives were holding a roadside conference with Queens detectives and their commander, Assistant Chief Walter Untermyer, a particularly offensive scumbag who was known throughout the Job for his deep pockets and short arms. The head of Queens detectives wanted no part of this one. Since the place of occurrence was Queens, technically it was a Queens case. But Malone realized that it was part and parcel of the Eisinger thing—so he agreed that it was his. Besides, he wanted to get the hell out of there. There was work to be done. After the mess was cleaned up and the traffic lanes reopened, Malone made a beeline for the Eastern Shipping Company. It was sealed tight. Accordion doors were drawn over the entrance and locked. The loading bays were closed. Only the wall cameras were moving, their little red lights constantly blinking. He rushed back to the surveillance van. Jake Stern stepped out of it and gave him the message he'd just received from Harrigan: Anderman and the Braxtons had disappeared. The detectives had lost them.

Malone kicked the van's tire and turned, leaning against the side, his foot against the hubcap. He lit a cigarette, dragging deep. High above him the constant whine of spinning tires played off the massive underpinnings of the Long Island Expressway. To the west the Empire State Building rose majestically against a backdrop of deep purple. Malone knew that he was in a war zone. Person or persons unknown were turning his city into a battleground.

When they returned to the Squad twenty minutes later they found Zambrano waiting.

"Nice little war ya got goin', Lieutenant," Zambrano said.

"It's not my doing," Malone said, rounding his desk and taking a virgin bottle of Jack Daniel's from the bottom drawer.

"Oh, I know that. But you see . . . it's the mayor. He's suddenly lost his sense of humor. He gets upset when people are blown away by rifle grenades on the parkways of his city. It's bad for the tourist industry. And he wants answers to certain little questions. Like who did it? And why? And more importantly, will they do it again?"

Malone poured.

"Do you have anything? The commissioner has to tell handsome Harry something," Zambrano said.

"Why don't you tell him to take a flying fuck at a rolling doughnut?" Malone said, handing him his drink. "Untermyer decided that it was our baby. So far all we got are some fragments from the grenades"—he raised the cup at Zambrano and drank—"and a description of the truck."

"You were on the scene when it went down. Didn't you give chase?"

"O'Shaughnessy, Davis, and Stern were behind the van. They had to swerve off the road to avoid the flames. It was a goddamn mess. By the time I reached the scene the truck was long gone."

Zambrano stared down into the shimmering liquor. "What's going on, Dan?"

Malone gulped the drink. "I'm not sure."

"But you've got an idea, haven't you?"

Malone shrugged wearily. "When I know for sure, you'll be the first to be told."

Zambrano stood up and measured him. "Be careful. Remember that it's better to be judged by twelve than carried by six."

Malone poured another drink and hoisted the cup. "That, Inspector, is something I never forget."

As soon as Zambrano was gone, Malone called in the detectives. The blackboard was wheeled from the wall and turned to the unused side. Chalk in hand, Malone paced in front of the board, looking at his tired detectives. He started to free associate. "Anderman and the Braxtons have run for cover. We're back to square one and all we have is a body. We don't even have that; it's been buried." He turned and faced the board. "Eisinger worked for the Braxtons after she quit Anderman."

"Lou?" O'Shaughnessy interjected, slapping his leg. "I forgot to tell you. I checked with the *Times*. There was never an ad put in by Braxton Tours. I even checked with their billing department. And there's another thing. My sources in the travel business tell me that the Braxtons don't specialize just in tours to Israel. They handle a lot of travel to the Arab states. Mecca and things like that."

Malone shook a stern finger at the detectives. He turned to the board. "We have Eisinger going to Janet Fox's apartment and giving her her Bible. That was early Friday evening. Epstein's lab report states that she was murdered sometime Friday night going into Saturday morning. I had an Emergency Service crew remove the lock cylinders of her apartment. None of them were raked or picked. Which indicates to me that she let the killer or killers into her apartment, or they had a key"—the finger was again waved at the detectives—"or, the humps were waiting for her when she returned from Janet Fox." He looked at Bo Davis. "You been dancin' with Janet Fox?"

Grinning faces turned to Bo Davis, waiting.

"No, Lou," Davis said. "I interviewed her. That's it. She's real nice, but I haven't had the time to make a play. Exigencies of the service."

"Well make the time. Take the lady out to dinner and get close to her. I want the answer to one important question."

"And where do I get the bread to wine and dine her?" Davis said.

Malone shook his head disbelievingly. He went to the telephone and called Arthur's Cloud Room on Baxter Street. He spoke to Arthur himself. When he was through he replaced the receiver and said to Davis, "It's arranged. Soup to nuts, all on the arm. We owe Arthur one." Next he turned his attention to Gus Heinemann.

"How have you been making out with the ownership of the Interlude?"

"Zilch," Heinemann said. "I traced the ownership from one corporation to another."

Malone folded his arms across his chest, rocking on his heels. "You're using the wrong track. That neighborhood is zoned residential. In order for that place to operate they need a zoning variance from the City Planning Board. You don't use dummy corporations with them. Check it." He looked down, avoiding their faces. "Now comes the unpleasant part. Someone, somewhere in the Job is involved in this caper. I don't know who; and I don't know how. And I don't think it's a corruption matter. It's a question of being involved in a homicide and of fucking around with me personally. If any of you guys are squeamish about working on cops let me know and I'll make adjustments in your charts so you don't get involved."

"Hey, Lou," Pat O'Shaughnessy shouted. "How come Bo gets to get laid in the line of duty and I don't?"

Malone closed his eyes and smiled. "You have Foam."

* * *

It was late and the detectives had gone home. Malone remained, drinking and staring at the blackboard. Outside in the squad room two detectives from the night watch were watching "Barney Miller." The din of Chinatown mixed with the scratchy cadence of the police radio and the canned laughter coming from the television set. No matter how much he drank he couldn't drown the stench of burned flesh. It was everywhere. He kept seeing the charred parts of bodies scattered over the grass. Unrecognizable lumps of charcoal fused together. What the hell was it about the Job that he loved, needed? He poured another drink. He didn't want to be alone tonight. A cop never has to be alone. There are plenty of watering holes where he can spend the night with other cops drinking and bullshitting about women and the Job. But not tonight. Not for Malone. He wanted the comfort of a woman's body. To be able to smell her softness, to taste her. To awake in the morning with his hand snug between her legs and to feel her soft ass pressing into him. To press back. To purge himself of the smell of death. He picked up the phone and dialed Erica Sommers.

She sensed his weariness. "Come over, Daniel. I'll fix you something to eat and fill a hot tub."

He was halfway out of the squad room when he remembered something and went back to his office. He picked up the pad, thought a moment, and wrote: "The Song of Asaph"?

8

Bo Davis clasped his hands behind his head and sat up, watching as Janet Fox got out of bed. He cast an anxious glance at the telephone and then focused in on her retreating backside. He had decided last night that she had one helluva perfect ass. Smooth and firm, not one shell crater.

When she reached the bedroom door she turned. "I'll go fix us some breakfast." She pointed her chin at the telephone. "Why don't you make your phone call?"

She returned a short time later carrying a tray with a pot of coffee and a plate of cheeses. There were also two glasses of orange juice. She slid the tray onto the end table and looked at him.

"Everything all right at home?"

"Fine. The kids are going to Jones Beach with their mother."

As she was handing him his coffee, he reached out and caressed her breast. "I like you a lot, Janet."

She fixed him with a distant stare and smiled. Inwardly she was screaming. Why do they all think they have to come on with the tenderness routine? He has a wife and kiddies stashed out in Little Leagueville and I'm here in the big city in bed with him. I understand. Why the hell can't he?

She got back into the bed and propped some pillows behind her. Sipping coffee, she said, "Bo, the last married man I went with told me that he was separated. I didn't know at the time that just meant his wife slept in a separate bed. I've had the moonlight-and-roses bit with married men. It hurts too much and I'm tired of waiting for the phone to ring. You've been honest with me. I know that you're married. So let's keep us light and lively. Okay?"

"I was only trying to tell you . . ."

She placed a quieting finger to his lips. "I know. You'd like to convince me that I mean more to you than just a good screw. Don't."

He raised the cup to his lips and shook his head incredulously. "You're something else."

"I've managed to save a few dollars and have decided to go back and get my degree. I always wanted to go to law school and I'm going to try before it's too late." She leaned over and put the cup on the night table. She then popped onto her side and ran her hand over his chest, dallying with the hair. A cooing lilt came into her voice. "What was it that you told me last night in the restaurant about an eighty-five?"

He brushed an elusive forelock from her forehead and smiled. "Code signal ten-eighty-five—meet a police officer at a certain location. When one cop tells another that he has an eighty-five, he means that he has a date. In the slang of the Job, and eighty-five is a girlfriend."

A silly grin came over her face. She plucked a hair from his chest.

"Ouch!" He feigned a chest wound.

"Well Detective Davis, that is exactly what I am interested in. An eighty-five. A happily married man who does all those wonderful things a man is supposed to do to a woman and who is available one or two nights a week." She began to toy with his penis. "Do you happen to know where I might find such a fellow?" She felt him growing hard.

"I might." He reached over the side of the bed and placed his cup on the floor. Turning back he took her into his arms. They kissed, their embrace growing in intensity. She continued to stroke him, guiding the foreskin up and over the head and then down. He pushed down to her breasts, licking and sucking the erect nipples. She reached down with both her hands and pushed at his head. He obeyed, sliding down between her legs. She cried out sharply as he sucked her wet body up into his mouth, thrashing the man in the boat with his tongue. She vised his head to her, lashing him with her body. Her head mauled the bed, unendurable moans choking in her throat, becoming louder and more painful. And then, as a series of violent convulsions racked her body, she screamed.

He continued to suck her. She could stand it no longer. Clawing, pulling, tugging, she moved him up and pushed him onto his back and mounted him. Legs straddling his hips, she leaned forward and took hold of him, guiding him into her body.

Hearts pounding, they lay holding hands, staring blankly up at the artery of cracks that traversed the ceiling.

"I'd love to be your eighty-five," he said.

She smiled. "I'm so glad."

"Would you mind if I asked you a question concerning Sara Eisinger?"

She turned her head and fixed him with a curious stare. "When you telephoned last night and asked me to have dinner I assumed that your intentions were lustful. Was I wrong?"

"You were right. But there is one question that needs answering."

She was toying with his hair. "What is it?"

"Eisinger came to your apartment on the Friday evening you were going away with your boss."

"Ex-boss," she corrected.

"Sara gave you the Bible and left. It now seems certain that she was murdered sometime later that night." He was watching her. "Think back. When you opened that door and saw her standing there holding that book, what was your first impression of her composure?"

"Scared."

"Why?"

She shrugged. "Fright was written across her face. She kept glancing up and down the hall. She thrust the Bible at me with both hands and practically shouted at me to take it. I asked her what was wrong, and she told me that she had just gotten her period and was edgy."

"Thanks, Janet. You've been a big help."

"Anytime, Detective Davis. Is there any other service that your eighty-five can perform before you leave for work?"

He pulled her close. "Yes."

There were no appointments on the monsignor's calendar. The afternoon was to have been spent reviewing diocesan financial reports. He was deep in thought when the intercom buzzed. He glanced with irritation at the offending machine. His immediate inclination when he heard Malone wanted to see him was to tell his secretary to make an appointment for some time next week. Then he associated the name with Father Gavin. A problem might have developed.

McInerney was a big man with a disarming Irish smile and thick black hair. He was wearing a pair of black trousers, a polo shirt, and down-at-heel moccasins. He had the handshake of a miner. "What can we do for you, Lieutenant?" he asked.

"I need a favor."

McInerney relaxed. It was business as usual. A knowing smile creased his lips. "One good turn deserves another. What is it; a change of assignment?"

Malone took out a sheet of paper and handed it to him. "I want to know exactly what is at each of these locations."

McInerney's eyes narrowed appraisingly. "They're all over the bloomin' country."

"I'm aware of that."

McInerney's face was indecipherable. He studied his visitor. "Why the Church, Malone? You have your own sources."

He lifted his palms helplessly. "Because I need this information fast and because I can't use regular police channels and because you owe me."

The priest scowled. "And what the hell makes you think that I have the resources at my disposal to get you this information?"

"Every archdiocese in the country has specially trained priests who handle delicate matters for the Church. They're able to obtain information fast and discreetly; if the right person presses the right button."

"And you assume that I am the right person."

"You got it, Monsignor."

McInerney looked at the sheet of paper. "You of course realize that under no circumstances can the Church become involved in secular intrigues. We have enough of our own to deal with."

"You have my word. Except for my detectives, no one will ever know."

The monsignor escorted him to the door. "Do you have any idea what we'll find at those locations?"

"Warehouses," he said, walking from the office.

On December 2, 1978, at about 12:40 A.M., an old plumber had left the Bobover Synagogue at 1533 Forty-eighth Street in the Boro Park section of Brooklyn. He bent low and pressed the collar of his coat against his ears to protect them from the howling wind. Even the barren tree branches were straining. As he hurried past the house on Forty-seventh Street, three men had stepped from the shadows and demanded his money. "Don't hurt me," he had pleaded. They had taken the plumber's money and left him sprawled over the sidewalk bleeding from multiple stab wounds in the chest and abdomen. The plumber had died.

At noon that same day there had been four police officers on duty inside the Sixty-sixth Precinct. Three RMPs were on patrol. A sergeant was on the desk and another sergeant was in the stationhouse on meal. A cop was manning the switchboard and one detective was on duty in the Squad.

Suddenly there had been a commotion and within seconds the desk sergeant had been confronted with a mass of bearded, pushing humanity dressed in black coats, fedoras, fur caps, knickers, and white socks. Another two thousand Hasidim had surrounded the stationhouse.

They had come to demand greater police protection. They screamed and pushed and threw chairs and typewriters and pulled apart filing cabinets. Hand-to-hand fighting spilled through the stationhouse. The policeman on the switchboard had managed to get one message off before he was fought to the ground: 10:13, the Six-six was under siege. The three RMPs on patrol raced to the aid of their besieged comrades. RMPs from adjoining precincts responded. The Rapid Mobilization Plan had been activated.

They came with their hats and bats—helmets and nightsticks. Within ten minutes of the initial 10:13 one hundred police reinforcements and a dozen ambulances had been on the scene. The battle to retake the stationhouse had lasted thirty minutes. When it was over the ground floor of the building had been heavily damaged and sixty-two policemen and eight civilians were injured.

On orders from the fourteenth floor, the PC's office, no arrests had been made.

At 6:25 A.M. the same day—almost six hours before the assault on the stationhouse—detectives had arrested three men for the murder of the plumber.

As policemen sifted through the debris of the ground floor a black policeman was heard to remark, "Man, if my people ever pulled this shit there'd be black bodies littering the motherfuckin' streets."

Everyone who had heard him knew that he was right.

From that day the Six-six precinct had been known in the folklore of the NYPD as Fort Surrender.

Malone wasn't sure what he was going to find at the Six-six. He didn't even know what he was looking for or how to garner whatever it was that he was looking for. Three men, one of whom was wearing a Fort Surrender T-shirt, Andrea St. James had told Malone in the Barton Hotel.

It was not a promising lead, but it was worth a shot. Malone was aware of the xenophobic personality of policemen. He knew that there was only one way to obtain unrestricted examination of police records.

He was relieved when he entered the stationhouse and saw a sergeant behind the desk. A lieutenant might know him. He walked up to the desk, flashing his shield. "I'm Lieutenant McDermont from IAD," he lied. "I have to check your rosters for the past two years."

The sergeant looked down at him with an icy disdain that policemen reserve for the humps from IAD and without a word pushed away from the desk and got up.

Malone followed him into the clerical office.

"This lieutenant is from IAD," the sergeant announced in a loud voice, warning all that a Judas was among them.

Malone faced down the cold stare of the lead clerical man. He was an old hairbag with horn-rimmed glasses and smooth face that didn't show its age. He must have had it lifted, Malone thought. He was an essential type in the department; he had mastered the administrative secrets of the Job; he knew how to order toilet paper and towels; how to get plumbers and electricians to come and fix things; what forms had to be prepared; he knew that he was an indispensable necessity to the effective and efficient operations of the precinct. Captains come and go, but clerical men stay, year after year after year, building their empires. Malone had met many of them and knew how to deal with them. For he knew their common nightmare—being forced to do patrol.

The NYPD uses a three-platoon system to divide the day. The first platoon works midnight to eight; the second platoon eight to four and the third platoon, four to midnight. A certain number of squads are assigned to work each platoon on a rotating basis.

The *Patrol Guide* mandates that each precinct prepare a new roster listing each officer in his assigned squad on the first of each month. This is done because men are constantly being transferred in and out.

As Malone sat at a desk in the corner of the clerical office poring over the old rosters, he could almost feel the furtive glances of the clerical man, who was standing nearby trying to make out in which names IAD was interested. I wonder what he'd say if he knew I don't know what the hell I'm looking for, Malone thought.

When he had completed his examination of the rosters he paused to think out his next move. He had discovered nothing. Perhaps coming to the Six-six had been a mistake. He had exposed himself. Malone hadn't forgotten those telephone calls from Captain Madvick or Mannelli's threats.

Malone turned and looked at the clerical man who was tying last month's roll calls into bundles for storage in the precinct's old record room. "Let me see your In/Out Book," Malone said, his tone harsh and authoritative.

The In/Out Book was a number-seven ledger that contained the names of each policeman transferred in and out of the command, the date and authority of the transfer and the command to which the man was transferred or from which he came.

The clerical man went over to a file cabinet, got the book, and almost pushed it into Malone's face. I'll fix his ass, Malone thought, snatching the book from him.

Malone turned the pages slowly, running his eye down each column, still not knowing what to look for. He smiled inwardly as he spotted the contracts: Patrolman Richard Coyne transferred to the Six-six from the recruit school on March 12, 1979, and transferred out to the Bureau of Management Analysis on June 10, 1979. Another Irishman buried in the bowels of headquarters.

He flipped the pages, his impatience growing. It was a mistake coming here, he thought in a moment of self-criticism. He began to flex his calves and tighten the muscles in his thighs. And then he saw them. Three names, Kelly, Bramson, Stanislaus, all patrolmen, all transferred on the same day, in the same orders, to the same place—the Police Academy. Such multiple transfers were not only very unusual but would have required a very heavy contract. He studied those three names and knew that he had found what he came for.

There were thirty-four patrolmen listed on that particular page and the clerical man knew every damn one of them. He turned to the clerical man. "Come over here a minute. I need your help with something."

He shambled over. "Yes, Lieu-ten-ant?"

"I have to answer out a communication that concerns an unknown member of this command who was assigned here at some time during the past two years. All that we know about this cop is that he's white and short and very thin. I'm going to go over the transfers that took place within the past few years and I want you to tell me what each of the cops looked like and anything else you can think of about them."

A silly smile came over the clerical man's face. "I got a real bad memory, Lieu-ten-ant. Why, I can't even remember what I had for breakfast this morning."

"Is that so? Listen to me real good, pal. You might be the head honcho around here, but that don't cut no shit with me. If you impede this investigation by refusing to cooperate I'll get on the horn to the chief of Inspectional Services and before this day is out you'll be doing a straight eight on a foot post in Harlem. Comes next Christmas you won't be here to collect all them nickels and dimes and bottles of booze that the cops slip into your desk for doing those little favors throughout the year. You'll be freezing your balls off on a school crossing. Understand, pal?"

The clerical man was ashen. A thick belt of moisture had formed across his upper lip. "Whatever you say, Lou," he said, pulling over a chair and sitting down.

Fear was a wonderful interrogator, Malone thought, turning and pointing to the first name.

*   *   *

Malone walked away from the Umberto's trailer nibbling brown onions from his sausage sandwich. Umberto's was one of many of the city's best and most famous ethnic restaurants that had set up trailers along the sides of the cobbled arcade behind One Police Plaza. They brought with them shiny yellow tables and white umbrellas—an urban picnic area in the shadow of the severe government buildings. Malone was trying to let go of the Eisinger case for just a few minutes. He walked around to the front of Police Plaza by the Rosenthal sculpture, a massive piece of metal made of five disks, one for each of the five boroughs that make up the city. He headed toward a walkway lined by files of trees. The question DONDE ESTA ALFREDO MENDEZ? was stenciled on the walkway wall and signed FALN. Still restless, he crossed to St. Andrew's Church. He bit into his sandwich and moved from the front of the church to the small garden on the side. He stuck his foot between the fence and studied the statue leaning on the St. Andrew's Cross.

"He's the patron saint of Scotland," Zambrano said, walking over to Malone.

"The patron saint of bullshit," Malone said, looking at Zambrano.

"I take it you're a nonbeliever," Zambrano said, with a scowl.

"I stopped believing in that mumbo-jumbo about the same time I started to masturbate."

"Humph." Zambrano walked away. Malone fell in beside him, taking another bite.

"How did you know where to reach me?" Zambrano asked, staring ahead.

"I telephoned your office and was told that you were at a commanders' conference at headquarters."

"What's on your mind?" Zambrano said.

And now for the moment of truth, Malone thought, taking a deep breath before telling Zambrano of the telephone calls from Captain Madvick, his conversations with Mannelli, his interview of Andrea St. James, and everything that had happened since he opened a file on Sara Eisinger. Now he told Zambrano that after he left the Six-six he went back to the Squad and telephoned the Academy, asking to speak to Kelly, Bramson, or Stanislaus. He was told that no one by any of those names was assigned there. He then went through the Personnel Orders for the last two years and discovered thirty-seven similar transfers. Two and three cops transferred in the same orders from the same command and to the same administrative or support unit. He made a list of the transfers and started telephoning. It was the same at each unit. There was no cop by that name assigned there. He then left the Squad and drove to headquarters. His first stop was the Personnel

Bureau. Using the same IAD ploy he had used at the Six-six, he asked to see the personnel folders of each of the forty cops. They were out of file, he was told. Next he went to the Identification Section where he asked an old friend for a favor. The fingerprint cards for each of the forty cops had been pulled and replaced with a chargeout card bearing a confidential file number. Only the chief of Operations knew the significance of the file number, his friend told him.

Malone looked at Zambrano. "Forty cops have been buried in the Job."

Zambrano stopped and faced him. "Dan? How do we put men in deep cover?"

"We transfer them to some administrative or support unit and they disappear. All their records are removed and locked up in a safe in the Identification Section. Their names are expunged from the city record and their salaries are paid by other city agencies or deposited in cash directly into blind checking accounts."

"So?" Zambrano demanded, displaying a growing exasperation.

"What do you mean, so? We're talking about forty bodies. I'll bet you there aren't ten cops in the entire department in deep cover. Those telephone calls from Captain Madvick and those three cops walking into that restaurant with Sara Eisinger form a direct link with my murder and the Job. Someone is using cops for something that's not kosher, someone at the top."

Zambrano walked away from him, staring ahead, his cheeks crimson.

Malone remained in place, watching. The inspector went about ten feet and then turned, motioning him to follow.

They strolled through the plaza, each man a prisoner of his own thoughts. When they reached the archway of the Municipal Building, Zambrano veered to his left and walked over to a small monument that had rusted bars set into it. He bent forward, trying to make out the withered plaque: Prison window of the Sugar House, 1765. Used by the British during the Revolutionary War to detain patriots.

Zambrano straightened. "Did you know that I lost my older brother on Guadalcanal?"

"No, I didn't."

"I always fancied retiring from the Job as a chief." He shrugged. "I guess I'm not going to make it. Tell me how I can help."

"I'm going to need some more time. That means keeping Harrigan and his men longer. In addition, I'll need someone upstairs to nose around and at the same time keep the hounds off my ass."

Zambrano put an arm around his shoulder, turning him and leading him away. "Did I ever tell you about my very first tour on the Job?"

*　　*　　*

Malone walked into his office and called in Davis and O'Shaughnessy. He handed Davis a piece of paper containing the names of the forty cops. "All these guys are on the Job. And they've all been buried somewhere in the department. I want you two to find them."

Davis and O'Shaughnessy looked incredulously at each other.

O'Shaughnessy spoke first. "What's it about?"

Malone lowered himself onto the edge of the desk and told them of the Fort Surrender T-shirt and his visit to the Six-six.

O'Shaughnessy looked over the names on the paper and said, "How are we going to locate these guys?"

"I don't think that the person or persons who buried them also went to the trouble to wipe out their personal lives. My guess is that most of them are married-type people who reside within the City or the nearby suburbs." He popped off the desk and went to the library cabinet where he removed the *Patrol Guide*. After consulting the rear index, he flipped clumps of pages of the massive loose leaf to the front. "Here we are," he said. "Procedure one-oh-four-dash-one; page four of six pages; Residence Requirements. Members of the force will reside within the City of New York or Westchester, Rockland, Orange, Putnam, Nassau, or Suffolk counties."

O'Shaughnessy whistled a sigh. "That's one helluva tall job."

"Not really," Malone said. "I think you should find some of them without too much difficulty. Go over the list and select names that are not common." He took the list from O'Shaughnessy. "Here, Edwin Bramson from the Six-six. Check the telephone directories for each county for that name. You're bound to find some of them. When you do, note the address and then pay a discreet visit to their neighborhood. Ask questions. Once you've established that they're on the Job, it's just a question of sitting on their homes one morning and following them to work. I've got a feeling once you've located one of them, you'll find the rest. Remember one very important thing. They're cops; don't get careless; give them a long leash. I don't want you being made."

Fifteen minutes later the detectives were gathered around a desk in the squad room poring through telephone directories. Jake Stern walked by on his way to the file cabinet to put away a case folder. He bent and whispered to O'Shaughnessy. "How is Foam?"

"Knocked-up," O'Shaughnessy said.

The detectives looked up.

"Oh, that's ducky. Are you and the wife planning a big wedding?" Starling Johnson asked.

"Don't be fucking funny. I got enough problems," O'Shaughnessy snapped.

"What happened?" Davis asked.

"The fucking foam didn't work, that's what happened," O'Shaughnessy said. "She's been calling me for days. I thought that she just needed to be serviced. I went to see her last night. She met me at the door full of love and kisses. I took her into the bedroom, took off her cotton drawers, and threw her a hump. 'Don't leave,' she says after I dropped my load. 'Come out naturally,' she says. I'm on top of her trying to figure what train I got to catch to get home when she starts to ask me if I really meant all them things that I told her"—he waved a hand in front of him—"you know, that bullshit about a lasting relationship in the distant, distant future."

"And?" Jake Stern said.

"And she told me she's late and the rabbit died," O'Shaughnessy said.

"And?" Davis said.

"And I asked her if she was sure," O'Shaughnessy said.

"And?" Johnson said.

"And she said she was," O'Shaughnessy answered.

"And?" Stern asked.

"And? What is it with you guys and this *and*? And nothing. She's having a baby. That's what's and!"

"Wadaya tell her?" Johnson asked.

"I told her that I was married, had a house in Hicksville, a mortgage, and six children. I also told her that I'm a Catholic and don't believe in divorce. Then I told her that I'd pay for the abortion."

"Oh, man; real smooth," Johnson said, slapping his forehead.

"And what did she say?" Stern asked.

"She went nuts and threw me out of her apartment. She screamed at me, calling me a male hypocrite and ranted something about not murdering her baby."

Bo Davis looked up from the directory. "Here's an Edwin Bramson, listed at 21 Woodchuck Pond, Northport."

"Where's that?" O'Shaughnessy asked.

"Suffolk County," Davis said.

9

McInerney's messenger arrived in the morning. He was a large man with black shoes and a black suit that was too small and made him look like a biped mammal with a crew cut. He was one of the monsignor's shooflys and he did not strike Malone as the type of curate who gave absolution too easily. His message was succinct: McInerney wanted to see Malone, now.

Jake Stern parked the squad car on the west side of Madison Avenue, three blocks away. A nun dressed in the traditional habit of her order admitted them into the cardinal's residence and led them down a sparkling hall, her hand fingering her rosary. Malone wondered what it was about rectories and churches that gave them their peculiar scent. Greenbacks and incense, he decided.

McInerney rounded his ornately carved desk to greet them. He stepped past the detectives and held the door for the nun.

"Thank you, sister," he said, watching her leave. When she had gone he kicked the door closed. "They don't make them like that anymore," he lamented. He went to a table by the window and picked up a folder, flipping it open. He took out a sheet of white bond paper and handed it to Malone.

"Here are your locations. You were right, they're warehouses."

Malone scrutinized the paper. "Were any of your people able to get a look inside?"

McInerney scowled. "We're priests, not burglars."

You're not? Malone thought. He held his own counsel and asked, "Were you able to find out anything else?"

"They are all operated by Israelis." McInerney regarded the lieutenant with the look of a maternal uncle.

"What the hell are you up to, Daniel Malone?"

"I'm not sure," he said, folding the paper and sliding it into his pocket.

McInerney checked his watch. He was not the kind of man who wasted time on nonproductive matters. "If there is nothing else, I'll bid you both good day. Holy Mother Church is a hard taskmistress."

"Thank you, Monsignor," Malone said, walking with him to the door. Malone stopped short and looked at the monsignor. "Do you have any connections in Tin Pan Alley?"

McInerney looked puzzled. "We have friends all over. Why?"

"We're trying to locate a copy of a song. 'The Song of Asaph.' Ever heard of it?"

McInerney slapped his chest and arched his back, laughing.

"It is apparent that your religious training is somewhat wanting, Daniel."

Fuck you, Your Holiness, Malone thought. Aloud: "How's that?"

He removed a Bible from the shelf and opened it, thumbing the pages. "Here is your 'Song of Asaph.' The Seventy-third Psalm." The monsignor read aloud: " 'Truly God is good to Israel, even to such as are a clean heart.' " The psalm told of God's displeasure with his people. Of how the rich are not troubled like other men; neither are they plagued like other men. It told of how pride encompassed the rich like a chair; violence covering them like a garment. McInerney's voice was solemn. He read how God saved the people from destruction and led them through the wilderness to safety: " 'And they sinned yet more against Him by provoking the most High in the wilderness. And they tempted God in their hearts by asking meat for their lust. In spite of all He did for them they spoke against God. They said, "Can God furnish a table in the wilderness?" ' "

The detectives listened intently. The rhapsody of horns on Madison Avenue was dispelled by the priest's hypnotic voice. Each man was transported in his thoughts back to the days of Jacob. McInerney read how they lied unto Him with their tongues. For their heart was not right with Him, neither were they steadfast in their covenant. But He, being full of compassion, forgave their iniquity and destroyed them not; yes, many a time turned He His anger away, and did not stir up His wrath. For He remembered that they were but flesh; a wind that passes away, and cometh not again.

McInerney closed the book and walked over to the window where he stared down at the bustling avenue. Opening the book, he repeated,

" 'They were but flesh; a wind that passes away; and cometh not again.' "

Jake Stern was thirteen again. It was Shabbas and his mother was in the kitchen lighting the Sabbath candles. His father was saying Kaddish for the dead. The smell of chicken floated back over the years and filled him with bittersweet nostalgia.

Malone, too, was thirteen. He was standing inside a church with his mother. They were in front of the Seventh Station of the Cross. "Mom, how can God be in every church in the world at the same time?"

McInerney stopped reading and let the Bible drop to his side.

An awkward silence filled the room.

Malone broke it by getting up and going to the telephone. He dialed the Squad. Heinemann answered. Malone told him to get the Eisinger Bible. The metallic clanging of the receiver being dropped resounded in Malone's ears.

Heinemann came back onto the line. "Got it."

"Turn to the Seventy-third Psalm," Malone said.

"Here we are," Heinemann said, " 'Truly God is good to Israel . . .' "

"Never mind reading it. See if anything is stuck between the pages or if there are any underlined passages."

Heinemann flipped pages, babbling as he went. " 'God put His trust' . . . nothing . . . 'They are corrupt' . . . blab . . . blab blab . . . 'put my trust' . . . more bullshit . . . 'O my people' . . . bullshit . . . here it is! The Eighty-third Psalm. The first four are underlined in ink."

Malone hung up and unceremoniously took the Bible from McInerney. He turned to the Eighty-third Psalm.

> Keep not thou silence, O God: hold not thy peace, and be not still, O God.
> For, lo, thine enemies make a tumult: and they that hate thee have lifted up the head.
> They have taken crafty counsel against thy people, and consulted against the hidden one.
> They have said, Come, and let us cut them off from being a nation; that the name of Israel may be no more in remembrance.

Malone had been closeted with Jack Harrigan for forty minutes. He had given the sergeant a "forthwith." Malone wanted to know if he had come up with anything on Anderman or the Braxtons.

"Nothing," Harrigan said.

Malone was standing by the window in his office looking out. "What about David Ancorie?" Malone asked, gawking at the tourists flowing through the street in an unending procession.

"Ancorie and three trucks pulled out of Eastern Shipping shortly before Andrea St. James left. Your men were on the scene in the surveillance van, so my men followed him. They went to Kennedy Airport and picked up a load of sealed containers from France. One of my men questioned the customs people and was told that the containers were filled with automotive parts that were consigned to Eastern Shipping. From the airport they drove to Fort Totten. My men waited and waited. Ancorie and the trucks never left Totten. As far as we know they're still there."

"Any idea what's going on at Totten?" Malone said.

Harrigan shook his head. "We can't get too close. If we do, we'll blow the whole thing."

Malone reached into his pocket and handed him a slip of paper. "Here's a list of forty cops that have been transferred and the precincts they've been transferred from. I want one of your men to visit the watering holes of those precincts and start asking questions about those men. Tell him to play it down. You know. 'I was in the Academy with so-and-so. How's he been?' Stuff like that. I want to know what kind of cops these guys are."

Harrigan took the list and put it into his shirt pocket.

Malone turned and looked him in the eye. "I also want wires on the Eastern Shipping Company and the Braxtons. They might return and get stupid."

Harrigan leaned against the wall, bracing himself with his right foot. "We don't have enough probable cause to go into court and ask for *ex parte* orders."

They exchanged wary looks. "This time we make our own probable cause," Malone said.

Harrigan nodded, pushed himself away from the wall, and left the office. Malone continued to look out the window. The sun was against it now, and because it was dirty he couldn't see past the glass. Cigarette butts, burned matches, and dirt covered the sill. Dead flies were snarled in a cobweb between the mesh and jamb. Damn window probably hadn't been cleaned in years, he thought. He suddenly remembered the Grayson case. It had been years since he recalled that one. Malone was a new detective in those days. Patrolman Joseph Grayson had walked the same beat for twenty-three years. He knew everyone. It was a November four-by-twelve tour when it happened. Grayson strolled into McDade's bar and grill. The unusual occurrence report stated that he entered the license premises for personal necessity. But everyone knew that Grayson liked his ball and beer. Grayson walked into a holdup. Two punks wheeled and put five into the cop's chest. The M.E. said Grayson never knew what hit him. Malone caught the case. It was to be his first murdered cop, not his last. The day after the killing a bird dropped a dime to the Squad. Nicky Giordano, a neighborhood punk, had bragged in a bar that he knew who blew the cop away. Malone could still recall Giordano's swaggering arrogance in front of his friends as Malone dragged him out of the pool hall.

"Lock the door and get his clothes off," the squad commander said, staring at the frightened man as Malone pushed him into the squad room. Giordano was hand-cuffed spread-eagled to the detention cage, Michelangelo's anatomical drawing of a man. The lieutenant handed Malone a Zippo lighter. "Burn the truth out of the fuck," the lieutenant ordered. Malone's hand shook as he approached him. One pass of the lighter under Giordano's balls was enough. "Esposito and Conti," he screamed. Known punks from Navy Street.

"Take 'im down," the squad commander ordered. Malone released him.

"Get over here, scumbag," the lieutenant barked.

Giordano approached hesitatingly, his hands covering his genitals.

"Bend over and spread your cheeks," the squad commander snapped. Giordano hesitated. The lieutenant slapped his back, forcing the torso down. "Spread 'em!"

Giordano reached back and spread the cheeks of his ass. The barrel of the squad commander's revolver was rammed into Giordano's anus. "This ain't no prick you feel in your ass, Guinea. It's my fuckin' gun. You're going to testify in court against your two friends. You're going to get up on that stand and tell the truth. You're also going to tell the court that we treated you like a fucking gentleman. 'Cause if you don't, one dark night I'm going to meet you in an alley and empty this gun into your asshole."

Giordano got the message. He testified and Esposito and Conti went to the electric chair.

And now, years later, Malone was a squad commander. The Grayson case was the type of a caper that he understood, knew how to deal with. But this Eisinger thing? He wondered what the common thread was that tied the whole mess together. He found himself searching the cobweb for the spider. But it was nowhere to be seen.

10

Malone drifted in and out of fitful periods of sleep; his dreams a kaleidoscope of his frustrations. When daylight slid into his bedroom he was propped on pillows staring at dust particles riding the rays of the sun. They reminded him of those damn containers being shipped in and out of those damn warehouses: so visible, yet untouchable. Just for one quick look inside one of them. But how? he asked himself. They'd know how. Of course! He looked at the clock. They'd still be around. He untangled himself from the sheet and sat up, taking the telephone book from inside the night table. Opening it, he slid his finger over the alphabetized tabs until he reached the Z's. Zambrano's number was the only listing on the page.

Zambrano's drugged voice came alive when Malone asked him to meet him right away. "At this time of the morning?" It was a *pro forma* utterance. Inspectors weren't supposed to be called out at five in the morning.

"It's important. I need your help."

"When and where?"

Malone stopped the car for the red light on the corner of the Bowery and Broome Street. He glanced over at the derelicts sleeping in hallways, then directed his stare up to the traffic light. There was no traffic coming so he drove through the light, turning into Broome Street.

He parked on Center Market Place and walked to the corner of Grand Street. He stepped into the opaque doorway of the Dutchman's to wait.

"Hey, Dan," Zambrano shouted, crossing the street.

Malone could see the excitement in his eyes. Zambrano was doing what he loved most in the whole world; playing cop in the streets of New York City. "Whadaya got?" Zambrano asked, stepping into the doorway and taking his place next to him.

"I want you to arrange a meeting with Carlo Fabrizio. I want a favor from him."

Zambrano's face became taut. "And what makes you so sure I can arrange such a meeting?"

"It's an open secret that you have a special relationship with him."

Zambrano spread his hands in front of him and at the same time shrugged an Italian gesture of mercurial agreement. "What do you want from him?"

Malone told him.

Peddlers were setting up their stands along Mulberry Street. Neighborhood women bargained in Italian. Malone noticed one dressed in mourning black bartering with a fish peddler. The man ignored her entreaties and continued to bathe his fish with buckets of ice.

Three-quarters of the way down the block they stepped off the curb and cut across the street. They nudged their way through a crowd and around two stands to four steps leading to a cellar club. The two small windows on the side of the facade were painted black. Brass letters across the door read: NESTOR SOCIAL CLUB, MEMBERS ONLY. They started down the steps. Malone rapped on the door with the hard knocks of a cop demanding entrance. A big man whose muscles were outlined in a dirty T-shirt opened the door. He wore a Byzantine cross on a gold chain around his neck. He raked his fingers through his hair, measuring the strangers. "Wadaya want, cop?"

Malone pushed past him. It was a large room with a padded bar running the length of the far wall. A grossly ornate espresso machine on the end of the bar reminded Malone of an altarpiece. Several card tables were scattered about. In the corner, next to the bar, five men sat playing poker. They looked up at the intruders. The bouncer ran up behind Malone and turned him. "You gotta motherfucking search warrant, cop?"

A distinguished-looking man in a blue business suit lumbered up from his place at the card table and waved the bouncer off. "It's okay, Cheech." His hair was pure white and the nails manicured. Malone noticed that his teeth had been capped and that, despite his smile, his eyes were cold and menacing. He came up to Zambrano and threw his arms around his shoulders. The ritualistic hug and kisses of old friends followed. "How are ya?" Tony Rao asked.

"Good, Tony." Zambrano made the introductions. Rao motioned

them to sit, at the same time holding up three fingers to the bouncer to indicate that he wanted three espressos.

"What brings you here?" Rao asked Zambrano.

"I want to see him," Zambrano said.

Cheech brought the espresso and backed off.

Rao fixed his stare on the thin slice of lemon floating in his cup. He picked up his spoon and aimlessly dunked the skin. "Impossible. He don't see nobody outside the Family. That Abscam thing made him leery of all outsiders"—Rao looked Zambrano in the eye—"even old friends."

Zambrano leaned across the table. "You tell Carlo Fabrizio that Nicholas Zambrano wants to see him."

Rao daintily picked up his cup and drank. "I'll see that he gets your message." Rao wrote a telephone number on the back of a matchbook and handed it to Zambrano. "Call this number at eleven o'clock this morning."

When they walked out of the Nestor Social Club twenty minutes later, Mulberry Street was still crowded with vendors and early-morning shoppers.

Malone turned to Zambrano. "Breakfast at Ratner's?"

"Why not? We got four hours to kill."

Carlo Fabrizio's legs dangled over the side of an immense bed. He was a frail man with sunken eyes and a beaked nose. A smile graced his lips when he heard Zambrano's request. He dismissed Rao and lay back in bed, staring out the open doors at a gently swaying tree. He thought back to his first meeting with Zambrano.

Twenty-nine years had passed since the day he first saw the cop trudging through the snow. When Zambrano passed the Hicks Street Social Club he glanced inside. Carlo Fabrizio and another man were standing by the window watching the shifting snowdrifts. Fabrizio nodded to the patrolman. Zambrano nodded back.

"Carlo, watch!" The man standing next to Fabrizio ran to the door. He went outside and scooped up a handful of snow, pressing it into a ball.

Zambrano had a sudden sense of something behind him and wheeled. His face recoiled from the sting of the snowball; his hat flew into the snow. The man turned and ran back into the club, laughing. "Didya see the look on that dumb cop's face?"

The door was flung open. Patrolman Zambrano stood in the frame, hands tucked deep into his winter overcoat. Water dripped down the side of his face. His eyes scoured the club, darting from man to man.

He spotted his quarry leaning over the bar. Zambrano moved toward him. Fabrizio watched. The cop had balls, he thought.

"Whatsa matter? Can't ya take a little joke?" the attacker bantered at the approaching cop.

Zambrano answered in Italian. "Me? Sure, I can take a joke. What about you?" Zambrano slid his hands out of his pockets. Thongs of a blackjack were tightly wrapped around his right hand; garbage can handles that had been woven with black tape were gripped in his left hand. The attacker's eyes widened and his hands shot up to his face in a fruitless effort to protect himself. The blackjack smashed into the side of his head. A jagged gash appeared and quickly filled with blood. The man started to sink to the floor. The cop pivoted to his left and lashed forward, smashing the metal knuckles into his face. The scrunching of shattering bone caused men to shiver. The man's eyes rolled up into his head as he splayed to the floor, unconscious. Zambrano tucked the blackjack and knuckles back into his overcoat pocket and turned to leave.

Fabrizio blocked his way. "He's one of my people."

"Then you should teach him some manners."

"And why is that, *paisan?*"

"Because your men are a reflection of you. If they're assholes that automatically makes you one."

Fabrizio nodded. "Makes sense." He moved aside.

Zambrano moved past him then stopped, turning to face him.

"That street out there belongs to me. If any of your people ever give me a hard time again, I'll blow their fucking brains out and plant a throw-away on them. I'll be a hero."

"A *capisce.*"

During the succeeding years their paths continued to cross. Whenever Fabrizio saw the brash cop he'd walk away from his entourage and spend a few minutes talking with him. The seeds of a friendship were sown; a friendship that could never come to fruition. Fabrizio would always end their chance meetings by saying he'd better leave. "Someone might see us together. I wouldn't want you to get into trouble."

When Zambrano married there was a coffee table of Italian marble, a gift from Carlo Fabrizio. When Fabrizio's mother died, the Zambranos attended her wake. As Zambrano knelt at the prie-dieu, Carlo Fabrizio came up behind him. "I hope you didn't park around here. They're taking pictures across the street."

The bond between the cop and the mafioso was sealed forever one sweltering August night. Patrolman Zambrano was standing in the lee of a doorway sneaking a smoke as he waited for the sergeant to come by and give him his "see." The crack of gunfire jolted Zambrano into a tingling state of awareness. He dropped his cigarette and stepped from the doorway. There were two more distinct shots. Zambrano drew his revolver and moved cautiously in the direction they came from. A man staggered from an alley holding his side. He stumbled across the sidewalk and sprawled into the street. It was Carlo Fabrizio.

"I think they've cashed in my chips for me," he said to the familiar face kneeling over him.

"Shut up! I'll get you to a doctor."

Zambrano snapped his head toward the sound of the running feet. Three armed men careened the corner. "Kill them both," one shouted. Zambrano threw himself over the wounded man. He gripped his revolver with both hands. The men were firing at him. Zambrano was scared but he recalled the admonitions of his firearms instructor at the Academy. Don't jerk the trigger; cock and squeeze; aim for the body; keep both eyes open. Zambrano fired; one of the advancing men fell with a bullet in his stomach. A fusillade of gunfire erupted and bullets thudded into the asphalt around the cop. One of the men stopped to take careful aim. Zambrano fired two rounds double action. The man lurched forward, his gun went limp in his hand; he looked with disbelief at the cop then fell dead. The third man looked at his fallen comrades and ran.

Fabrizio clutched the policeman's arm. "I'll never forget what you did tonight . . . never."

At precisely eleven o'clock, Zambrano telephoned the number Rao had written on the matchbook.

"La Terazza at three o'clock," an anonymous voice said.

A Ford station wagon and a Mercedes were parked in front of the restaurant. Well-dressed men loitered on the sidewalk in front of La Terazza. "Are they for us?" Malone asked.

"That's his normal retinue."

The trolling men spotted the policemen and separated, taking up positions along the building line and against parked cars, their surly eyes locked on the cops. Tony Rao was sitting by himself in the outdoor café. "Tony?" one of the bodyguards called. Rao looked up, casting an appraising eye in the direction of the policemen.

La Terazza was a tumult of activity. Waiters in white tailored shirts picked their way from table to table. Tourists gawked at the display cases filled with Italian delicacies.

Carlo Fabrizio was in the rear of the restaurant. He was alone, save for one waiter by his side. He sat erect, his hands clasped in front of him.

"He looks like the little old winemaker," Malone whispered.

Fabrizio rose to greet his friend. The head of the largest crime family in New York City hugged Zambrano and kissed his cheeks. He acknowledged Malone's presence with a nod.

"You look well, Carlo," Zambrano said, choosing a cannoli from the tray of pastries on the table.

"I feel good, Nicholas." He smiled. "Remember that night with the snowball?"

"Whatever happened to that guy?"

"He continued to do stupid things until one night he had an unfortunate accident . . . a permanent one."

Malone felt awkward listening to Zambrano and Fabrizio reminisce. He had done business with *them* in the past and would be the first to admit that they can make impossible things possible. But sitting with Fabrizio was like extending diplomatic recognition to organized crime. You do what you gotta do, Malone rationalized.

"What is it you want?" Fabrizio asked, shifting his eyes from Zambrano to Malone.

Zambrano turned to Malone who took the cue. He removed a folded sheet of paper from his pocket and slid it across the table. Fabrizio looked down at it.

Tapping the paper with one finger, Malone said, "This is a list of warehouses that are located in various cities around the country. It's important that we find out what's stored inside of them."

"Is this important to you, Nicholas?"

"Yes it is," Zambrano said.

"Will there be any . . . problems?" Fabrizio asked, sliding the paper into his pocket.

"They're all guarded," Malone said. "But your people, with their special expertise, should have no trouble getting in and out without being spotted."

Fabrizio looked stern. "I hope not, Lieutenant. That could be very unfortunate. For both of us."

At 2 P.M. that day Yachov Anderman, David Ancorie, and the Braxtons suddenly resurfaced and started to go about their daily routines as though nothing had happened. Malone's first instincts were to drag them into the Squad and have a nice long talk with them. But he knew that that would gain him nothing. By this time they had their stories straight and their lawyers waiting. And they could stall any interrogation for some time, time that Malone instinctively knew he didn't have to spare.

At 3 P.M. Thea and Aldridge Braxton entered the subway station at Fifty-ninth Street and Lexington Avenue. The subway was not the

Braxtons' regular method of travel. But today they were forced to tolerate the indignities of public transportation in order to ensure that they
were not being followed.

Afternoon shoppers crowded the subway platform, many carrying
the Bloomingdale's "brown bag." Aldridge Braxton leaned over and
looked into the dark tunnel. He stepped back and checked the time.
"Damn trains," he muttered. A businessman stood a few feet away
from him meticulously turning the pages of the *New York Times* into
another fold. A black man sashayed along the platform. He was wearing jeans and a brightly colored dashiki. His feet were encased in a
worn pair of blue-and-red sneakers. A red portable radio in the shape of
earphones was stretched over his head. There was a bone necklace
hung around his neck and dark sunglasses hid the movements of his
eyes. White people gave him a wide berth. Middle-class blacks
withered him with their looks while the brothers and sisters smiled.
The businessman looked into the tunnel and slapped his newspaper
into another fold.

An RR rolled into the station. Passengers stepped back from the
edge of the platform. Every car was tattooed with graffiti. One of each
double door shuddered open. People lunged out of the train even as
new passengers pushed forward. Arguments started and profanity seasoned them. Thea and her brother elbowed and shouldered their way
aboard. A finger was thrust into Thea Braxton's crotch. "Did you do
that?" she snapped at her brother.

"Do what?"

"Never mind," she muttered.

Every conceivable part of the car was covered with spray paint. People were crushed together and groped for straps that were already
crowded with hands.

"Wachder doors," shrilled a barely discernible Latin accent over the
loudspeaker. "Denext estacion goinbe Blige Plaza." The train jerked
forward, stopped, lurched several times, jerked forward again, then left
the station. Aldridge Braxton surveyed the crush of pressing people. He
moved his head close to his sister. "God! How do they survive this day
after day? They're like fucking cattle."

The businessman stood among the crush, the top part of his paper
dropping into his face. He stared out at the naked lightbulbs as they
whizzed by the graffiti-covered window. He could see the Braxtons in
the glass's reflection.

The black man in the dashiki was in the front of the car, listening to
his music and shuffling to its beat. The people around him tried to
keep their distance, none looking at him for fear of offending. During
his last musical gyration he snapped his head back and adjusted his

sunglasses. He could see the Braxtons clearly. They were the strap-hangers in front of him, to his right.

As the RR train bearing the Braxtons roared through the tunnel approaching the Queensborough Bridge, Ahmad Marku and Iban Yaziji left their Soho loft and hailed a passing taxi. A Con Edison repair crew was at work on the corner. One of the crew slid the manhole cover back while the other member of the crew folded the orange safety stanchion. The taxi bearing Marku and Yaziji turned south onto West Broadway.

Jack Harrigan had just completed the details for the installation of wires on the Braxtons' telephones when the detectives inside the Con Edison truck radioed. They had tailed the two men onto the FDR Drive and were now driving over the Triborough Bridge heading south.

At Bridge Plaza the Braxtons left the train at the elevated station and hurried down the staircase. They stopped in front of the change booth and watched the passengers descend the steps. The business-man had his *Times* neatly folded under his arm when he walked past. Aldridge Braxton went to the exit door that led to the connecting bridge between Bridge Plaza north and south. He pushed through the door and moved to the middle of the bridge. Traffic coming off the lower level of the Queensborough Bridge was heavy. Green Line buses queued the north side of Bridge Plaza. He saw nothing suspicious. They weren't being followed, he was convinced. He motioned to his sister.

The black man with the dashiki danced down the staircase. He hur-ried over to the exit and peered down into the street. He watched the Braxtons get into a taxi. He made a mental note of the license plate number and pushed the antenna on the right side of his earphone down in front of his mouth.

"Special two to Central, K."

At 3:58 P.M. a citywide alarm was transmitted over the police radio network. All units on patrol were instructed to be on the lookout for the taxi carrying the Braxtons. "Do not intercept. Report location and direction of travel," the dispatcher radioed.

Patrolman Frank Murphy got out of his radio car with the majesty of a true motorcycle cop. His black leather puttees were spit-shined. His breeches bloomed smartly; yellow mohair braid on the outside seam was trimmed of lint. He strutted over to the car he had just pulled over. A woman was driving. Murphy knew the routine by heart. He'd tell her that she was speeding and she would play the coquette. When he asked for her license and registration she'd rummage helplessly through her pocketbook. "Officer, I've never received a ticket before," she would say with feigned innocence. Then she would proceed to confide some personal problem that caused her to forget how fast she was driving. Murphy would smile understandingly, take the license and registration and walk back to his radio car where he would write out her summons. He would then slide out of the car and amble back to her car, summons in hand. It was at this point that the lady would snatch the official paper from him, call him a cocksucker, and plunge her automobile off the shoulder into oncoming traffic.

All part of the J-O-B, Murphy thought, walking toward her, summons in hand. It was by sheer chance that he happened to glance at the parkway traffic and spotted the taxi with the man and woman sitting in the rear. He noted the license plate number and broke into a trot, rushing up to the driver and throwing her documents and the summons onto her lap. As he was running back to his own car he heard her yell after him, "Fascist cocksucker."

At 4:14 P.M. a taxi glided to a stop under the portecochere of the International Hotel at Kennedy. The Braxtons inched their way out of the compact cab and hurried into the lobby. A radio car from Highway Two cruised past the hotel and drove onto the shoulder of the Van Wyck. Patrolman Murphy reached under the front seat and removed the portable radar device. He attached the mechanism to the doorpost and then slumped down in his seat to wait.

Thea and Aldridge Braxton walked through the crowded lobby to the bank of elevators. When they stepped from the lift on the sixth floor they walked down a long carpeted hallway, heading for the fire door at the end. Aldridge Braxton looked over his shoulder and, seeing that there were no other guests in the hallway, pushed through the door with his sister following close behind. They hurried down the clanging staircase and exited the stairwell on the third floor.

They stood outside Room 302 listening. Aldridge Braxton held a fist inches above the door and at the same time eyed the second hand of his watch. Exactly fifteen seconds passed and he knocked three times, paused, and then immediately followed with four additional raps.

Ahmad Marku jerked open the door.

They exchanged nods with Marku and entered the room. It looked like any other hotel room: twin beds were covered with a fading gray bedspread; prints of pastoral scenes bolted to the wall; night tables, their edges peppered with black caterpillar-shaped burns.

The drapes were drawn, darkening the room. A file of four chairs had been lined up in front of the window. Iban Yaziji was sitting at the end of the file. He did not acknowledge the Braxtons. Ahmad Marku locked the door and sat next to Yaziji. Aldridge Braxton sat next to Marku, and Thea Braxton next to her brother. Lowering herself slowly into the wooden folding chair, she crossed her legs, revealing the finely shaped topography of her legs, thighs, and hips.

The quartet faced front, watching the shadowy figure standing in front of the drapes, peering out.

Thea Braxton twisted uncomfortably in her seat, tucking the folds of her skirt under her legs.

"Are you all sure that you were not followed?" Police Officer Joseph Stanislaus asked, watching the entrance of the hotel. He noticed a police car parked on the west shoulder of the highway about thirty feet from the entrance. The policeman had just left his patrol car and was approaching a Con Edison truck.

"Yes," the quartet answered in jumbled unison. They were sure they had not been followed.

Westy Stanislaus turned to face them, an automatic held loosely in his hand. He danced it along the file, his eyes studying each face.

Thea Braxton could feel the moisture take hold of her palms. Her brother's mouth was unexpectedly parched. He swallowed the lump in his throat. Ahmad Marku and Iban Yaziji sat perfectly still, their stares fixed on the finger inside the trigger guard.

Stanislaus looked at Marku, his eyes hard and cold, his lips wearing a feigned smile. "I want to congratulate you on the way you handled Andrea St. James. It was a professional job, and a good object lesson for Anderman."

His attention next went to Thea Braxton. He moved close to her, glowering down. "You should have brought in someone from the outside to set up Landsford. It was a mistake using anyone from the Interlude."

"I realize that now," she said.

Stanislaus caressed her cheek with the barrel of his automatic. "Perhaps your taste for women made you call on her services?"

She stared up at him; then, with both her hands, she took hold of his wrist and pushed it away from her face. "St. James was selected because I thought she was the best one to do the job."

Stanislaus stepped back. He tucked the weapon into the small of his back and smiled. He began to pace, deep in thought, and then, suddenly, he whirled to face them, an ugly look on his face, his nostrils flared in anger. "St. James should never have been used! It was a bad mistake." He turned his wrath on the Arabs. "Because of your stupidity she got away and we had to engage in an action that might have exposed all of us."

The four of them waited nervously for his wrath to subside. Thea tasted her tongue.

"No more mistakes will be tolerated. If any of you get stupid again I'll personally see to it that you're made into chopped liver."

There was a fearful silence.

Stanislaus turned from them and moved to the window where he peered out from behind the drapes. "Does Anderman suspect anything?"

"I don't think so," Thea said, running a hand through her hair, trying to appear calm. "After St. James was killed, he sent a messenger to us and told us to go immediately to a safe house in Jersey. We remained there until he sent word to resume our normal activities."

"Did he make any contact while you were in Jersey?" Stanislaus asked, pushing the drape farther aside.

"No. He gave us the name and number of his law firm. We were to call them if the police tried to question us," Thea Braxton said.

"What are we going to do without the list of warehouses? It screws up all our plans," Aldridge Braxton said.

Stanislaus noticed that the highway cop had snared a gypsy cab with its radar device. "There is a new plan," he said, edging himself onto the sill.

The meeting lasted another hour. Business concluded, Stanislaus got up, turned, and looked out the window. A Pan Am 747 was making its final descent. It slid past the cocooned control tower and disappeared. The police car was gone and the Belt Parkway was spilling back. "Aldridge, you and your sister leave first."

The Braxtons were alone in the elevator. Thea was watching the blinking floor indicator. "He was his usual obnoxious self," Aldridge said.

She looked at her brother. Reaching out, she took hold of his hand. "I was just thinking how vulnerable Stanislaus and his friends are. I think, dear brother, that the time has come for us to renegotiate our contract with the police department."

11

All the fives from Harrigan's detectives added up to the same thing: subjects followed to International Hotel. Subjects remained thereat for ninety-six minutes. Subjects left separately. Braxtons first. They went directly back to their office. Marku and Yaziji left together and went back to Soho. They remained in the loft for two hours and then hailed a taxi and went to Atlantic Avenue in Brooklyn, the Arab section. They ate in the Kurdistan restaurant and engaged in conversation with several Middle Eastern types and then left.

Malone sat back, flapping the fives against the edge of the desk and looking up at the chunks of peeling paint. Icicles of decay, he thought. He tried to run through in his mind the reasons the Braxtons and Marku and Yaziji could have for going to the hotel. He snapped forward and moved a spiral-bound pad over to him, tossed it open, and started to list the reasons he could think of for such a meeting: To meet someone? Who? To pick something up? No. It doesn't require four bodies to do that. To have an orgy? Why travel to Queens? To receive instructions? To plan something? He continued jotting down ideas. When he had listed his thoughts, he sat studying them.

Heinemann broke Malone's concentration by shoving his head into the doorway. "Ya gotta call on three."

"Wanna meet me for a cup of espresso?"

Malone hung up slowly; he thought that he had detected a tinge of hostility in Tony Rao's voice.

*　　*　　*

Malone walked down the steps leading to the Nestor Social Club and stopped, deciding if he should knock. Screw it. He pulled open the door and entered. The bouncer was at a table playing a game of five-card stud. He was wearing the same russet shirt. He looked at Malone, scowled, and lowered his eyes.

Tony Rao was standing behind the bar pouring Amaretto into a pony glass. When he saw Malone he put the bottle down and came out from behind the bar.

Rao stood in front of him tapping his lips meditatively with his fingertips. He suddenly looped his arm in his and ushered the policeman outside. They walked along Mulberry Street. Rao would pause occasionally to speak a few words of greeting to some peddler or wave at a Mustache Pete sitting on a milk box, or to pat a child on the head while he cast an appraising eye at the mother. When they reached Grand Street, Rao turned in and walked to the middle of the block. He ducked into a cheese store. Malone followed. Customers turned to look, but quickly turned away when they saw who it was.

The mafioso stood behind the row of long cheeses that hung in the window, casting constant glances up and down the street. "Catch." He tossed a small box to Malone.

A label in Hebrew was glued over the face. A blue cord handle stretched from the corners. Malone ripped open one end and spilled out the contents. Several 9mm bullets tumbled out; their tips were painted red. He turned to Rao. "Tracers? This is military hardware."

"Yeah." Rao turned from the window and left the store.

They crossed Grand Street, turning into Center Street.

"Ya wanna know what's inside them joints?" He bent his head to his cupped hands and lit a cigarette. "Military supplies. One of my boys almost got his ass taken off by some punk kid carrying a small machine gun. Those tracers come from the place in New Jersey. That's all my guy could grab. The security was too tight."

Questions began to whirl through Malone's mind. Rao was still talking . . . "What's with them joints? Anything in them for us?"

Malone glared at him. "Forget them, Tony."

Rao grinned.

"I mean it. You couldn't take the heat."

"Where do I send the bill?"

Malone looked at him. "What bill?"

"Hey? I hadda make a lot of phone calls. Ya got any idea what it costs to use the telephone these days?"

"Take it off your taxes; we're a charitable deduction."

* * *

"I want to see your boss," Malone bawled.

The receptionist stared at him then hurriedly swung around to the switchboard.

Within minutes David Ancorie was leading him through the corrugated security tunnel that snaked into the interior of Eastern Shipping. Ancorie held the door open and Malone sallied into the cramped, smoky office and plopped himself down in a chair next to Anderman's desk.

Anderman smiled confidently. "You just won't give up, will you, policeman?"

"We're a persistent bunch," he said, placing the cassette recorder he had brought with him onto the desk. He looked his adversary in the eye and snapped down the play button. The slow-moving spindles churned out Andrea St. James's disconsolate voice. Anderman's face twisted with anger. He spun in his chair, showing the policeman his back; his head and shoulders sagged. Words that Malone had listened to dozens of times now filled the office.

When the tape played out, Malone pushed the stop button. Anderman remained still for a moment then spun around and started to raise himself up, an angry finger stabbing the space in front of him. His breathing was labored and his eyes leered down at the policeman. "You! Take your tape. Recorder. And get out of this building. And don't ever come back. I am going to sue you. The City. And the police department. You're harassing me! Preventing me from conducting my business." His face was inches from Malone. The breath was hot and coated with garlic and cigarettes. Suddenly he slammed his hands over the desk with such force that Malone thought he surely must have broken his wrists.

Malone looked at him, a sarcastic grin on his face. He was savoring his moment. And now for the square knot. He reached into his pocket and removed the box of 9mms which he casually tossed onto the desk.

Anderman stared at the box. He picked up a letter opened and fished the point into the open end. One by one the bullets tumbled out. Anderman gnawed his lower lip, his head shaking with diminishing belief.

Anderman said, "Where did these come from?"

"A warehouse in New Jersey."

"I've been getting reports of strange occurrences." He slapped his knee in frustration. "I really underestimated you, policeman." He looked at him. "Can we still do a little business?"

"Wise men can always do a *little business.*" He started to gather up the bullets. "I want to know about Eisinger. The Braxtons. Marku.

Yaziji. A cop called Westy. The Unit and a man by the name of Captain Madvick. You can start any place you want."

"How many people know about the warehouses?"

"I know and my detectives. But only me and a friend know what's inside of them." He grinned. "A little life insurance."

"And if I tell you what you want to know, you'll return the list to me personally?"

"I will."

"Where did you find it? We searched everywhere."

"Hidden inside the binding of her Bible."

"Humph." He lit a cigarette. "And if I don't tell you?"

"In that case, your military depots will be page one in the morning editions. And that, Mr. Anderman, is a promise."

"It's difficult for us to trust a *goy*. Especially one who wears a blue uniform."

Malone frowned. "I recall reading about an entire country of *goys* who sewed the Star of David onto their clothing so as to be indistinguishable from the Jews of their country. Denmark? The last war? Perhaps you've heard of it."

Anderman sank into his chair. A long silence passed before he spoke.

"We're a small country without the vast spaces that you have. A surprise attack could deprive us of the spare parts for our machines. So, we store a portion of our spare parts in friendly countries. If we had to, we could airlift them back to Israel within hours. We use Fort Totten as a conduit for our supplies coming into the United States. Someone found out about our operation. They blackmailed Landsford and obtained a copy of the location of the warehouses. Somehow Sara found out about this and recovered the list. She was murdered for her efforts." He leaned back, hands laced behind his head, studying Malone. "That's it. Everything."

"Not quite. I've got a few questions." Malone rested his elbow on the edge of the desk and placed his chin in the palm of his hand. He said, "Tell me about Sara Eisinger. She was one of your people? Right?"

"Yes," he answered reluctantly. "When she was in Israel she helped establish a worldwide computerized inventory of our warehouses. When she came to this country she continued to work for us." He stopped, trying to think of what he was going to say next.

Malone kept up the pressure.

"Tell me what happened," Malone said, watching him.

"She fell in love and went crazy. She started to take days off. Would disappear for long weekends. She became a security risk, so I had to fire her. When she refused to tell us who she was seeing it became intolerable."

"You mean to tell me that you have no idea who she was sleeping with."

"That's exactly what I'm telling you. Sara was a professional. She knew how to avoid being followed. She refused to tell me anything about her personal life. She even accused me of being jealous, of wanting her for myself."

"Was there anything between you?" Malone studied the face.

"No. It was business, nothing more."

"When did she start seeing this person?"

He shrugged. "I'm not sure. Maybe about a year ago."

"Tell me about the Braxtons. How are they connected to this?"

"I don't know. After Sara left me she started to work for them."

"And Marku and Yaziji?"

"They're in the States posing as students. Somehow they're connected with the Braxtons. When we saw that Sara was working for the Braxtons and that there was a connection between the Braxtons and the Interlude and the two Arabs we decided to plant Andrea St. James inside the Interlude."

"Weren't you fearful that Sara would see her in the Interlude?"

"There wasn't much chance of that. Sara never went there and Andrea's *duties* required her presence there at night."

"How did you maintain contact with St. James?"

"We have a safe house on West Seventy-second Street."

"I see. How do you get to use a United States military reservation as a conduit for your spares?"

"With the consent of your government. Some of your people in Washington don't trust us. They think we're erratic. They're fearful that we might hide atomic weapons or some other horrible things within your territory. So as part of the agreement your army gets to inspect everything we bring in."

"And what does Uncle Sam get in return?"

Anderman stabbed a finger upward. "In return, we act as surrogate for your intelligence service in certain"—he pinched the bridge of his nose—"unmentionable parts of the world."

"Why did you go into hiding after St. James was killed?"

"Because I didn't want to get involved and because I wanted time to assess the situation and try to find out what the hell was happening."

"Were the Braxtons with you?"

"Of course not. I know nothing about them."

Malone did not speak right away. He measured his adversary. "You're a very convincing man, Anderman."

"The truth speaks for itself."

"Bullshit. Keep it simple and stick as close to the truth as possible. That's the rule in your business, isn't it?"

"I'm telling you the truth. Everything I know."

"Really? Why would anyone go to the trouble to get the list of warehouses? For what purpose?"

Anderman raised his palms and then let them drop. "I don't know. I guess if their existence in this country became known it could be embarrassing for Washington. The United States is trying to obtain bases in the Middle East for the Rapid Deployment Force; a special relationship has been fostered with Riyadh. Perhaps"—he waved his hand in the air—"there are endless possibilities."

Malone fixed him with a stare as Anderman lit another cigarette. He was ready to ask about cops and Captain Madvick. "Ever hear of a Captain Madvick?"

Anderman exhaled smoke. "No."

"What is the Unit?"

"I don't know, policeman."

"Who is Westy? Is he a cop?"

Anderman was no longer the harried, angry businessman. After a long pause, Anderman said, "Malone. I know nothing of any policemen, any Unit, or Captain Madvick. I have enough problems of my own without getting involved in any of yours." He arched his shoulders back. "I'm telling you the truth. You are relying on the delirium of a semiconscious woman. That is not a clever move, policeman."

He's good, Malone concluded. Lies with the aplomb of a cop or a politician. Looking directly into the face in front of him, Malone thought, You're giving me a handjob, Anderman. An intelligence agent in the Mossad falling for a guy and you can't find out who this guy is? In a pig's prick.

Malone said, "How did you know that Eisinger had stolen back the list?"

"She telephoned. I told her that I'd come right over to her apartment, but she insisted that I come in the morning. I asked her who was behind it and she refused to tell me over the phone. She said that she would explain in the morning. She was murdered that night."

"Did she sound nervous when she talked to you?"

"No. She sounded relaxed. If I had thought she was in any danger I'd have rushed right to her apartment."

Malone remained with him for another hour. It was not easy distinguishing the truth from the lies. But Malone was patient. He was determined to break this one.

As Malone was getting up to leave, Anderman leaned forward and grabbed his wrist. "I'm sure you'll not repeat anything that we just discussed. I'd find it most unpleasant if I had to . . ."

Malone pulled his arm away. "Top of the day to ya, Anderman."

"Shalom, policeman."

When Malone was gone Anderman went over to the wall and pounded it in a paroxysm of anger and frustration. When he had calmed down he picked up the telephone on his desk.

It rang about fifteen times before being answered. Anderman spoke. "This is an emergency. John Harrison Burke in three hours."

The person on the other end clicked off.

Within the three hours Yachov Anderman was standing on the bow of the Circle Line boat watching the panorama of Manhattan Island unfold. He had made the trip to the Statue of Liberty, trudged up the shoulderwide spiral to the crown, circled the narrow platform to ensure no one was following, and was now returning to keep his appointment.

The boat was crowded with Chinese tourists dressed in drab clothes and with Japanese cameras slung over their shoulders; Germans, Latins, English, French, and Americans. When the boat docked he waited until most of the passengers had disembarked and then strolled off the gangplank. He walked on the promenade and stared into the choppy waters. When he reached the red buildings of Marine Company I he stopped and examined the fire boat, still watching to see if he was followed. He abruptly turned and walked through Battery Park until he came to the West Battery where he slowly made his way around the circular fort.

He moved off, walking along a winding path until he came to a crescent-shaped monument site. Two benches were set against an iron fence. Bags, beer cans, aluminum foil, Big Mac boxes were piled up along the bottom of the fence. Clumps of grass and weeds had sprouted up between the chipped plates in the ground. He strolled around the column reading the plaques: Erected in memory of wireless operators lost at sea at the post of duty: David Staier, SS *Mezada*, 3/2/22, North Atlantic; Jack Phillips, SS *Titanic*, 4/5/12, Atlantic. He moved slowly, taking his time, surveying the surrounding area.

Fifty feet away another monument site had been established to commemorate American heroes of both wars who now sleep in the American coastal waters of the Atlantic Ocean. The site had eight massive steles with thousands of names carved in alphabetical order. Four steles were on each side of the site, and in the center, on a pedestal of black, reigned an American bald eagle, its black talons cocked. Anderman spotted the person whom he was to meet standing in front of the first stele, glancing up at the column. He walked up behind the person. "John Harrison Burke, Seaman First Class, U.S.N., Virginia."

Lt. Joe Mannelli glanced over his shoulder. "What the hell is so goddamn important for you to risk this meeting?"

"Malone knows about the warehouses. He also has an inkling about the Unit."

"Balls!" Mannelli said, toeing the monument.

"My sentiments exactly."

Anderman told him of his meeting with Malone.

"Do you think he's onto us?" Mannelli asked.

"I'm not sure. I told him enough to sound convincing, but I don't know how much of it he believed or what else he knows."

Mannelli rubbed his tired eyes. Anderman moved close to him.

"He has to be eliminated," Anderman whispered.

"Whataya mean eliminated? Fa' Chrissake, he's a cop. We don't kill our own."

"That man is a danger."

"We don't kill him! So he found out about the warehouses. No big deal. Everything is deniable. You hear me, deniable. You do nothing. I'll tell my people what happened and get back to you," Mannelli said, turning and walking away.

A bebopper skated past Anderman. He was a black man and he was wearing a dashiki and had a radio headset on. He adjusted his sunglasses as he danced past.

12

What time do ya make it?" O'Shaughnessy asked.

Bo Davis was slumped behind the wheel, his hands limp over the inside post. He stretched, looking at his watch. "Five thirty-four."

"Gettin' up at four in the morning in order to plant on some cop's house sucks."

"It's all part of the J-O-B." Davis closed his eyes.

"Ya hear what happened to Crazy Eyes McCormick?"

Davis squint-eyed. "What?"

"The asshole had his load on and turned Saint Pat's into a shooting gallery. Some Rican pickpocket lifted eight bucks from some broad's bag. McCormick opened up on the guy inside the church. He misses the Rican and ended up blowing away sixty grand worth of statues and stained-glass windows. The Powerhouse wanted his balls sautéed and left on the altar as penance."

Davis grunted. "That guy could fuck up a wet dream."

At 7:46 A.M. a man left 21 Woodchuck Pond Lane and opened the garage door. He was a bruiser who stood six-five and had large hands, big feet, and shoulders that looked like a dam. The detectives were parked a block away.

The man backed the car out of the garage and stopped. He got out and went to close the door. As he bent down to close the door his Hawaiian shirt rode up in back. On his right hip was a holster with a thin leather strap securing the gun in place. Equipment Bureau issue. They had found Edwin Bramson, formerly of the Six-six precinct.

*   *   *

He opened his eyes and sensed unfamiliar surroundings. He lay naked in a bed with fresh sheets. He recognized the jade-green wallpaper. He saw his trousers crumpled over a chair. On the floor were a pair of panties and a bra. He remembered their rush into bed. He poked his hand behind and felt her. He turned over.

Last night he had decided that Erica epitomized the perfect woman: beautiful, intelligent, tantalizing. In his own mind he still was not completely sure what he wanted from her. Lately he found himself wanting to be with her, to share with her. And last night, he had talked about his ex-wife again and had found himself beginning to understand his part in the failure of the marriage. It was a beginning.

He kissed her lightly on the temple and got up. Anderman was coming for the list of warehouses sometime this afternoon, and he wanted to be there when he arrived.

The first thing Erica saw when she opened her eyes was Malone dressed only in briefs, balancing on one leg, and tugging a sock up over his calf.

"Good morning," she purred, stretching.

"I tried not to wake you."

She patted the space next to her. He came over and sat on the edge. She pushed herself up. The sheet clung to her body, large aureoles half-moons over the edge.

She said, "I'm glad you came by last night."

He kissed her on the nose. "So am I."

"I enjoyed the things we did. The way you . . ." She felt the flush come to her cheeks.

"You're blushing."

She blocked his view with her hands. "You're not supposed to look."

The sheet plummeted, revealing firm breasts. He bent forward, taking one into his mouth, sucking it. She lay back and touched his lips. "Quickies count, too."

Edwin Bramson drove a battered Ford with a broken left taillight. The snow tires were still on. A bumper sticker read: GUNS DON'T KILL . . . PEOPLE DO.

Motorists stared blankly ahead as they inched through the heavy traffic. Bramson stayed in the middle lane. Not once did he bother to check the rearview. The sign of an overconfident man.

At the Lakeville Road exit of the Northern State Parkway, Bramson drove off onto the feeder road and cruised to a stop alongside a bank of telephone kiosks. He reached over and pushed open the door. A man trotted over and slid into the passenger seat. He was a big man with a large head and a torso that ballooned from the neck and gathered into a tiny waist. No hair was visible on his body. Although he appeared bulky, the man moved with grace and suppleness.

Overhead the WABC traffic helicopter skirted the parkway.

O'Shaughnessy nudged his partner. "Did you see the shape on that guy?"

"I wouldn't wanna have to lock assholes with either one of them," Davis said.

Bramson left the parkway at the westbound Queens Boulevard exit. He drove north. At Yellowstone Boulevard he made a left turn and continued two blocks, stopping in front of an apartment house—the Hamilton.

A man stepped from the lobby and got into the rear seat. He had a ruggedly handsome face and blond wavy hair. Unlike the other passengers, this man was particularly well groomed, wearing a blue summer suit and a quiet patterned tie.

The Doric Diner was crowded.

The three men decided on an empty booth next to the long counter.

They talked in whispers, leaning across the table. A waitress came over to take their orders. When she left, the man in the suit took out a handful of change and played the small jukebox that was affixed to the side of the booth.

O'Shaughnessy went directly over to the counter and sat on a stool. His jacket and tie were in the car. The right side of his shirt was bloused, concealing the handle of his .38 S & W. When the counterman looked his way he ordered coffee and a toasted corn muffin. Elbows on counter, he leaned forward, staring at the reflections in the display case, straining to pick up snatches of conversation from the booth to his right. Someone roared with laughter. He thought it was the weirdo with the watermelon head. Was a guy with that shape really on the Job? A cowboy blared from the jukebox; he had met a lady in tight-fittin' jeans. Whenever the music would stop the guy in the suit would feed the box. O'Shaughnessy ordered a second cup and asked for the bill. The three men remained twenty-two minutes and then struggled out of the cramped booth.

Bramson left the tip.

O'Shaughnessy left nothing. He'd never see the hump again.

O'Shaughnessy lingered, examining his check and searching his pocket for change. He ambled up to the cashier. They were ahead of him, each paying a third. Watermelon-head paid his share and turned to Bramson, poking him. "We got the range on Wednesday and then we weed out and we're all set to go."

The man in the suit whirled. "Shut the fuck up."

"Hey, Westy? There ain't no one here . . ."

The man in the suit talked through clenched teeth. "I told you to . . ."

Watermelon-head held up his hands. "Okay. Okay. Don't get your balls in an uproar."

The day started officially for Malone when he walked into the squad room and looked up at the clock. That was some quickie, he thought. It was 9:37 A.M. He adjusted his watch as he walked into his office. Davis and O'Shaughnessy were waiting to report the results of their stakeout.

Malone asked, "Are you sure that he called him Westy?"

"Positive," O'Shaughnessy said. "I was standing right behind them."

"What happened after they left the diner?" Malone asked.

Davis looked at his partner who shrugged. Malone caught the exchange. "What happened?"

"We tailed them to the SOD compound in Flushing Meadow," Davis said.

Malone slapped the desk. "Oh Christ!" He leaned back, steepling his fingers.

The silence grew.

The other men watched him, trying to figure out what Malone was thinking. When he finally spoke, his dispirited tone revealed his misgivings. "What about the guy Bramson picked up in Queens?"

O'Shaughnessy said, "After they entered the compound we hightailed it back to Yellowstone Boulevard. He lives in the Hamilton House. His name is Joseph Stanislaus; he's divorced and has lived there for two years."

Malone took out the list of transferred cops. Edwin Bramson, Joseph Stanislaus, Charles Kelly. All from the Six-six; all transferred in the same Personnel Order; friends who went into something big. He assumed the man from Lakeville Road was Charles Kelly. Malone yelled out to Stern to bring him the teletypes for the past twenty-four hours. Stern walked in with the gray posted binder with the thin multiholed pages compressed between the covers. He asked Stern if there were any notifications concerning the range and watched anxiously as the detective slowly turned each page. They at last had three names to work on. But he was bemused because they were cops and concerned because he did not know how or why they were involved.

Stern stabbed a page with his finger. "Here is something. Transmitted 0130 hours yesterday." He read. "The regular outdoor shooting cycle scheduled for this Wednesday is canceled. Members who were scheduled to shoot on that date will be rescheduled by roll call." He looked at the lieutenant. "That's it."

Lacing his hands across his chest, Malone leaned back and recalled Harrigan's earlier visit. The sergeant had been anxious to tell him the results of the canvass of precinct watering holes. O'Brien had spent the better part of a four-to-four drinking with cops from the Six-six and bullshitting about the Job, the lousy contract that the PBA had just negotiated with the City, the injustice of pay parity with firemen, and women.

Fort Surrender's watering hole was Jerry's, a sleazy blue-collar joint that was tucked away under the Brighton line's elevated Utica Avenue station.

O'Brien had latched onto a tipsy Anticrime cop from the Six-six. Every cop in the precinct knew about Stanislaus, Bramson, and Kelly, the Anticrime cop had told O'Brien. "Chrissake, those three guys are legends." He told O'Brien that they were assigned to the precinct's Anticrime Unit. They turned out to be a no-nonsense team who took no shit in the street. Stanislaus was the team's brains. He could con the spots off a leopard. Stanislaus had served in a Special Forces unit in Vietnam that operated behind enemy lines. The others in the unit found out one night when they were drinking that Stanislaus thought General Westmoreland was the greatest thing since Alexander, and tagged him with the nickname Westy. He had been on two sergeants' lists but had never been promoted.

He felt the Supreme Court of the United States, Affirmative Action, and the Department of Personnel were responsible. Blacks, Hispanics, and women who had failed the written test were placed on the lists ahead of Stanislaus because of those damn affirmative-action suits. Both lists ran their normal four-year life and died with his name still on them.

Charles Kelly, the Anticrime cop had told O'Brien, was an ugly brute who enjoyed inflicting pain. He liked to slap nippers around a prisoner's wrist and twist until his victim was groveling in pain. He was also an avid gun collector who was reputed to have a valuable collection of Nazi military small arms.

Bramson was a psycho son-of-a-bitch who drank too much and was ecumenical in his dislikes: he hated just about everything and everybody. When he was in the army, Bramson had been assigned to the military police battalion at Leavenworth. His lumbering walk and chilling brutality sent fear through prisoners and guards alike.

Each of them was morose and brooding. They never mixed with other cops. But when they were together they came alive, each one garnering strength from the other. They drank and carried on outrageously.

They had an incredible arrest record, but it was abnormally full of violence and death. Every cop in Brooklyn South knew of their arrests. Once, two escaping muggers were killed accidentally by falling from a roof. A witness in the adjoining building told the Homicide detectives that she had seen both of the dead men being thrown off. She later denied making that statement. The grapevine had it that Kelly and Bramson had a private little chat with the lady.

During their six years in Anticrime they had been involved in eight shootouts in which nine perps had been blown away. In each case a gun was found next to the body; a weapon which ballistics tests showed had been fired at the pursuing officers. During one of the investigations into these shootings, a witness came forth and stated that he had seen the cops shoot the perp; fire several shots from a gun that one of them had removed from his own pocket, and plant the weapon directly into the dead man's hand. Four days later the witness changed his mind about what he had seen. "Ain't it amazin'!" the cop guffawed, lifting his beer mug at O'Brien. He told O'Brien that the ranking officers who investigated the three men's use of deadly force knew damn well that they were using throw-aways but could never prove it. "You ever hear of a nigger using a Walther PPK? I didn't."

They were being hauled before the Civilian Complaint Review Board on complaints of unnecessary use of force or abuse of authority almost monthly. But they always managed to dance their way out of it. The CCRB could never pin anything on them. Each interrogation was a carefully staged production.

One time, Stanislaus, Bramson, and Kelly wanted to take off one of Frankie the Fish's number banks but did not know the bank's location. They scooped up the head numbers runner and planned to sweat the address out of him. The runner proved most uncooperative. Bramson and Kelly handcuffed him to a chair in the Anticrime office and left the room. Stanislaus remained behind with the prisoner, leaning against the wall, saying nothing, fixing the frightened man with a crazy stare. Ten minutes passed and the door was thrown open. Bramson and Kelly danced naked into the room, whooping Indian war cries. They had on feathered war bonnets, and each one had a long red ribbon tied around his penis. War paint was drawn across their chests and faces and they both were waving cattle prods over their heads as if they were tomahawks.

They danced around the petrified man, whooping.

On a signal from Stanislaus they started to jolt the runner with the cattle prods. Within seconds they had the man scurrying on his back across the floor, desperately trying to escape the war party. A few more jolts and he was begging his tormentors for mercy. He blurted out the address of the numbers bank. Kelly stormed over to him, kicked the chair out of the way, and gave him a final jolt to the testicles.

They then carried him out to the detention cage and locked him in. Stanislaus stayed behind to guard the "prisoner" while Kelly and Bramson went out and held up the numbers bank. When the runner was released he was warned to keep his mouth shut. He didn't. A week later they were given a "forthwith" to report to the CCRB. When they were informed of the charges against them they looked incredulously at each other and then burst out in uproarious laughter. "Naked? Ribbons on our shlongs? Feathers? You guys gotta be off your rockers. Your complainant sounds like an escapee from a fucking loony pen," Stanislaus was reported to have shouted at his inquisitors.

The charges against them were unsubstantiated.

O'Brien listened, rolling his glass between palms, staring ahead at the rows of terraced bottles. O'Brien turned sideways on his stool and looked stolidly at the bearded cop in threadbare clothes. He raised his right hand, rubbing three fingers together. "They were big money men?"

The Anticrime cop from the Six-six cast a furtive glance around the noisy bar. "Very big," he whispered. "They had everyone on: bookmakers, numbers men, dealers, even the pros. Word was that each pimp had to spring for a dime a night for each hooker that he had out. In return they saw to it that no independents worked the stroll."

O'Brien became wary. Drunk or not the guy on the next barstool was a cop with a cop's predatory instinct. He did not want to appear too interested in these three crazies, so he changed the subject to the latest labor contract and that got him an instant harangue. "The fucking garbage men make more money than we do and not one of them fuckers works more than three hours a day. Drive along Fourth Avenue any weekday and you'll see six or seven garbage trucks parked outside McGill's Bar from eleven in the morning till four in the goddamn afternoon."

When the cop paused to call the bartender over, O'Brien said casually, "I guess their home life must have been shot to shit?"

The bearded man glanced at him, not understanding. "Who?"

"Those three cops you've been telling me about."

"Oh, them." He did not know much about their private lives. He did know that Stanislaus was divorced and the word was that he liked the ladies. But he was cool about it and never brought any of them around. Kelly had a family somewhere on the Island but lived alone in a decrepit clapboard house at the end of a dirt road on the outskirts of

Great Neck. Kelly had gotten drunk one night and had to be driven home by one of the precinct cops. The cop who drove him home had confided to a friend that it was a creepy place with a couple of wrecked automobiles parked on the lawn, one of which was up on milk boxes. The word around the precinct was that Kelly had an almost sexual fascination with guns and didn't waste time with women. Whatever went on in that lonely house was probably best left unknown.

The only thing the Anticrime cop from the Six-six knew for sure about Edwin Bramson was that he was married. He had heard rumors about the fear and hatred his family had for him. But he knew nothing of the tirades, the beatings, the awful, silent dinners, or the consuming panic that gripped family members whenever Bramson stalked into a room.

Jack Harrigan came away from the meeting with a clear and disturbing picture of three loners who were over the thin line between normality and psychosis. The three of them shared other characteristics with the rest of the forty transferred cops: all had outstanding arrest records and most of them had seen combat in the infantry.

Malone shifted in his seat, a melancholy expression on his face. His gaze took in the photograph of the flag raising on Mt. Suribachi that was taped to the side of his locker. He had put it there years ago. The edge of the tape was frayed, curled, and yellow. He thought of all the marines who had died to plant that flag. He got up slowly from his chair and reached for the keys to the department auto that were on a hook over the filing cabinet. Those three men were not his kind of cops. There were things that needed doing.

Malone loitered across the street from the Hamilton House. When he saw that the doorman was busy he quickly crossed the street, brushed past the doorman, and entered the glittering lobby. The doorman gave him a cursory glance and then returned his attention to the blonde with the capped teeth. A respectable-looking white man was nothing to get alarmed about. The mailboxes and directory were in an alcove in the rear of the lobby.

Joseph Stanislaus lived in apartment 24 J. He counted A through J. The tenth floor.

There was only one cylinder in the door, a rarity in New York City. He slid a thin black pouch from his breast pocket and checked the hallway. A line of round fluorescent lights extended over the ceiling, casting an unnatural chalklike glow over the flower-patterned carpet. The corridor was deserted, closed doors lined both sides. There was an eerie silence. He checked for trip wires and noticed that the mat was flush with the floor jamb. He cautioned himself to leave it that way.

He shook out a cluster of thin metal bars and selected two. The tension bar was inserted into the cylinder at twelve o'clock. He pressed it forward until he could feel the first tumbler pin. He looked up and down the corridor, making a final check, and then inserted the raking bar. Applying just the right amount of pressure on the tension bar, he began to rake the lock clockwise. As each tumbler pin was raked open, he pressed the tension bar deeper, past the open pins. One by one the tumbler pins fell and the lock snapped open. He entered quickly and quietly, closing the door behind him, and locking it.

Rows of flowering plants were terraced in front of a casement window. The apartment was clean and neat with everything in place. The furniture was expensive and in good taste. A well-stocked bar was in the corner.

Joseph Stanislaus was a meticulous man.

He moved about, taking his time, studying each piece of furniture before moving it. When he completed a search he made sure that the piece was restored to its original position. On a shelf in the bedroom he found two off-duties: a Colt Cobra and an S & W Chief. Padlocks secured the opened cylinders. Stanislaus was a cautious man.

The bathroom had sparkling gray tiles and silver wallpaper. He poked around the shower curtain. The tub was clean; a face cloth hung limp over the faucet. He flipped open the medicine cabinet, looked at the glass shelves, and then pushed the door closed. Next he bent to check the vanity. Packages of toilet paper. A shoe brush. Stacks of soap. A saucepan. A clump of rags. Standing upright, wedged behind the plumbing, was a bathroom scale. He noted its position and then reached inside, working it out. Behind it he saw a shopping bag. He reached for it but at the last moment snatched his hand back. He ripped off a few sheets of toilet paper and spread them between his thumb and forefinger. He reached inside the bag. A diaphragm. A light coat of powder covered the device. Holding it up to the light and turning, he was able to make out some fingerprints. A triumphant grin crossed his face. Eisinger's diaphragm had never been found. He put the compact back and returned the bag. Next he wedged in the scale. He remembered seeing an electric razor in the medicine cabinet. He took the razor out, opened the top, and began shaking the shavings into the toilet paper. He then folded the paper inward on all sides and slid it into his shirt pocket. When he slipped from the apartment fifteen minutes later he made sure that the mat was flush with the jamb.

When Malone returned to the Squad after lunch he found an impatient Yachov Anderman waiting. There were many things that Malone wanted to accomplish and he certainly did not want Anderman around. He promptly reached into his shirt pocket and withdrew the list of warehouses which he silently handed over. When Anderman asked him if he had made a copy he lied and said that he hadn't. Anderman did not bother to hide his disbelief.

Malone walked into the squad room and saw O'Shaughnessy off in a corner talking on the telephone, trying, without success, to placate Foam's wrath.

Bo Davis was on another line with Janet Fox. He was beginning to like being her eighty-five. Sergeant Harrigan alternately drank beer and cleaned his fingernails. Malone had just finished writing Anderman's name alongside the slash that was behind the word *Interlude*. Bramson, Stanislaus, and Kelly, Charles, were already on the blackboard. An asterisk was next to Stanislaus and in parentheses: "diaphragm." The blackboard was no longer kept in the squad room. Malone wanted it in his office, next to his locker and shrouded in a musty sheet. No one outside the Squad was to see it.

He moved away from the board, tapping his lips with a piece of chalk. After studying it for a few minutes he moved close and bracketed the names of the three cops with the acronym SOD. He turned to Harrigan. "Did you install those wires?"

Harrigan rubbed the side of his face. "N.G. on Eastern Shipping. Their wires don't run in from telephone poles. They're underground. And the terminal boxes are inside. We can't get at them. If you want that place bugged we're going to have to use lasers or conic beams." He leaned back and scratched his testicles. "And we don't have that kind of equipment."

Malone frowned. "What about the Braxtons?"

"A piece of cake. The only problem with them is that they don't talk on the telephone. And when they do, it's strictly business. But there is one little thing"—he scratched his testicles again—"there is a telephone booth on the corner of Aldridge Braxton's residence. A few times we've caught him running out and using it, and then running back inside. He thinks he's being cute. I put a wire on the booth."

Malone said, "I want you to start to concentrate on Stanislaus."

Harrigan nodded, lips pursed. "If we do, we're going to have to shitcan someone. Ain't enough guys to go around."

Malone said, "Have the tails on the Arabs been productive?"

"Zilch. Marku and Yaziji are a couple of creeps. They go to school and hang around their friends on Atlantic Avenue. They don't get laid, that's for sure."

"Take the men off them and cover Stanislaus," Malone said.

O'Shaughnessy slammed the receiver down so hard that it bounced off the hook. "Cunt!"

"Whatsa matter?" Harrigan said.

"Broad's givin' me a hard time."

Harrigan spiraled a finger heavenward. "Hell hath no fury, ma man."

The Fifth's watering hole was Bradley's, a singles' bar on Lafayette Street. It was after 6:00 P.M. and a crowd was starting to pack the place. A little before five each weekday a table with hot and cold hors d'oeuvres was set up. Manhattan's rent poor came to eat and mingle.

Malone was sitting at the end of the long bar making rings with his glass, only dimly conscious of the eddy around him. Heinemann had gone out to Queens to sit in on a card game at an Elks Lodge in Astoria. Stern, Davis, Johnson, and O'Shaughnessy were clustered at the bar nearby. It amused them to watch the maneuvering of older men with dyed hair, gold bracelets and chains, who tried to put the make on anything that moved. Novice cheaters and shy singles fumbled for the right words. Single women wanted desperately to meet a "good" man, tried much too hard.

Malone sipped his drink. He was confused. Was she really making it with Stanislaus? The movie *Laura* came to mind. The detective conjured up a picture of Laura in his mind and fell in love with the murder victim. He was pissed off at Eisinger for going to bed with him. She could have done much better. He glanced toward the entrance. His friend should arrive any minute.

Jake Stern tried to fill the silence. "A woman is like a bus. If you miss one all you gotta do is wait at the bus stop. Another one'll be along in no time."

Erica Sommers was no bus, Malone thought, holding up his glass to the bartender.

A brunette was alone at the other end of the bar. She was a big woman with broad shoulders and a pretty face. The detectives watched as a lawyer-type in a vested suit made his play. She rebuffed him. The rejected suitor slunk back, seeking the anonymity of the crowd. O'Shaughnessy sipped scotch on ice, watching with muted admiration as the brunette foiled the amorous advances of another would-be suitor.

O'Shaughnessy said, "I just might be looking at Foam's replacement."

Jake Stern's face clouded. "Man. I'd love to have her sit on my face. Did you catch them tits? They're magnificent."

Starling Johnson slid his glass onto the bar. "Make your move, ma man. All the lady can say is no."

Stern drank, watching her. He banged his glass on the bar. "Why not?"

She sensed the presence elbowing its way toward her. Another shmuck. Suddenly he was next to her, alternately snapping his fingers and pointing. It was a brawler's face that was dominated by a broken nose and low-set cheekbones. The lips were thick and he was almost completely bald. But he did have a cute smile.

"That's it," Stern blared, with a discovering snap of his fingers.

"What is it?" she said, icily.

"Where I know you from. We were in the navy together. Submarines. Don't you remember?"

"Navy?" Her incredulity turned to a smile that showed her straight white teeth. "That *is* a good opening line."

"I gave it my best shot," he said, careful not to move too close. They laughed.

She sipped a Bloody Mary. "You married?"

"Yes. But there's a problem."

She smiled knowingly. "Isn't there always. Do you like cats?"

"Oh. I just love them. They're such adorable creatures."

"I have three."

Your apartment must stink of piss, he thought, motioning to the bartender.

She avoided his eyes. "My name is Helen McGlade."

He saw the red that tinged her earlobe and moved close. "Jake Stern."

Jack Fine was a minor celebrity with a thrice-weekly newspaper column in the *Daily News* and a few beer commercials on television. He was a thin man with a perpetually dour face and a crew cut and always wore a bow tie. His drinking was legendary; his wild parties envied; his tough talk emulated. It was not an unusual occurrence for him to be observed in the wee morning hours pissing on a Third Avenue lamppost.

Fine stood at the entrance. Malone saw him and waved. The newspaperman nodded and started to shoulder the crush, returning the proffered greetings with perfunctory grunts and feeble handshakes. "How'r'ya. Goodtaseeya'gain."

Malone had a very dry martini in his hand. Fine took it and gulped it down in one violent swallow. Malone had another in reserve.

"Got your message. What's up?" Fine said.

Malone leaned close and confided, "I want you to plant something in your next column. 'Usually reliable sources report stuff to the effect that a certain government agency and high-ranking members of the NYPD have colluded to suppress a homicide investigation.' " He sipped his drink, staring at the rows of bottles.

Fine inched close. "You got sunstroke or something. I'd never get a story like that past my editor. He'd want to know my source and I'd damn well have to tell him."

Malone held the glass up to his eyes and looked through it at the distorted face of the newspaperman. "I'm your source."

Fine eyed him warily. "You'd have to come out of the closet."

"Only to you and your editor."

The newspaperman leaned his back against the bar, arms folded tightly into his chest, thinking.

The bartender came over to them. Tony, No Butter, a KG—Known Gambler—wanted to buy them a drink. The bartender put the drinks down and nodded toward Tony, No Butter. They raised their glasses at the gambler. Tony, No Butter acknowledged with a feeble nod of the head. Malone noticed that Stern and the brunette were gone.

Fine said, "This thing has to be big for you to put your head on the chopping block. Want to tell me about it?"

"I'll tell you this much. Play ball and I'll guarantee you an unabridged exclusive. Could get you a Pulitzer."

Fine smacked his lips. He took the olive out of his glass and plopped it into his mouth. "Did I ever tell you about this chick I met in McBain's. She was the best blow job this side of the Mississippi."

They were naked in bed, exploring each other. She was big-boned with strong, firm legs and sagging breasts. Three cats were perched atop a fiberboard wardrobe next to the bed. An Abyssinian, a Rex, and a Havana brown. Tails coiled, the cats stared down with yellow and green snake eyes at the lovers. The apartment was a scuzz affair with old newspapers and bags filled with clothes scattered about. And the place most definitely reeked of cat piss.

Stern wasted no time. After what he considered an appropriate waiting period, he made his play.

Helen McGlade was receptive.

She was breathing in deep heaves, almost grunts. That consuming passion that caused her to do horrible things was coming. To scream, curse. She loved it when her body was wasted by a ferocity that was beyond her control. She pulled from his embrace and started to kiss him, her tongue moving over his flabby body, gnawing at the folds of skin. She lifted his testicles into her mouth, sucking them ravenously. Then she pushed his penis down and embraced the underside with her lips, moving up and down the hardness, flicking the velvet skin with her tongue. And then she took him deep into her mouth, sucking him.

He was lost in the rapture of the moment. There were no thoughts, no problems, only pleasure. From deep within his body he could feel the beginning eruption. He clamped her head to him. She broke his grip by pushing his arms aside. She leaped up, rolling onto her back. Her legs were up in the air, far apart. "I want you inside of me. Hard. Now."

He hopped between her legs and rammed his erectness into her wet body. She went wild. Her body undulated forcefully, pumping him with hard methodical grinds. And then the horror began. Without warning her powerful legs scissored him at the waist, locking at the feet. He was clamped in a vise grip. She squeezed. The air was forced from his lungs. Her fists sprang for the sides of the bed and began pounding his back. Pain blanketed his shoulders and spread downward. He gagged, gasping for air. "You're crushing me." He frantically tried to extricate himself. He was screaming. The pain was awful. She continued to pound his back. He collapsed on top of her. Prostrated. Helpless. She laced her hands together and beat him. She screamed. Her pelvis rammed him. She screamed once more and then went limp, her body spent by the force of orgasm. "Did you come?" she murmured.

He shot up, choking, gasping. "No . . . I . . . didn't . . . come . . . How . . . could . . . I? You . . . were . . . beating . . . the . . . shit . . . out . . . of . . . me."

"I love doing it that way. Passionate. Hard." She started to stroke his wet head. "You're quite a man. I've never known anyone like you."

Her adulation inflated his ego, dissipating the pain. "Well, it's just that I've never known a woman as passionate as you."

"Lie back. I'll make it up to you."

She saw the look of concern. "I'll be gentle. I promise." She pushed him down and started to lick his body. When he was hard she took him into his mouth. The cats watched, purring. Any lingering fears were swept away. He reached down, guiding her head. Her pace quickened, sucking him in rapid, hard jerks. "I love it," she screamed.

Oh, my God. She's getting hot again, he thought, glancing down at her.

She glared up at him, her face contorted. "I want you to come in my mouth." She threw herself against his thigh and bit him. At the same time her hand vised his penis, squeezing. He howled in pain. His hands banged her head.

"You're killing me." He pulled her hair in a desperate attempt to drag her away from him. One hand tugged at her thumb. "My cock! You're breaking my cock!" With great effort he was able to free himself from her painful clutches. His penis was limp and very sore. His leg throbbed pain and there were two red crescent marks where she had bitten him. He was almost off the bed when it flew by. For a split second he did not know what it was. Then the Abyssinian's claws furrowed his groin. His screams ricocheted off the walls. He grabbed the cat by the neck and heaved it across the room. Then he ran from the bedroom gathering his clothes and dashing naked out into the seedy hallway.

Never again, he swore, driving home in agony, trying desperately to conjure up a reasonable excuse to account for the teeth marks, bruises, and scratches that marred his body.

13

Malone watched a group of joggers round the track. The man whom he had come to see led the pack, his proud jaw stabbing the space in front of him. He had a high, smooth forehead and deep-set eyes guarded by bushy black eyebrows. His ears had great black tufts sprouting from them. His gray hair was cut military style.

Malone draped his arms over the fence and watched the runner's legs scissor the track with mechanical precision. Though the leader was older than the others, none was able to pass him. Was that due to lack of stamina or fear? Assistant Chief Whitney Zangline was known as a man of iron discipline. He had spent the last ten years molding the Special Operation Division, SOD, into the tactical strike force of the NYPD.

When Zangline assumed command of SOD there were three units under its umbrella. He methodically absorbed the mobile and tactical units within the department. "We're the Job's Rapid Deployment Force," he once told a newspaperwoman who was doing a piece for a Sunday supplement.

Zangline refused to socialize within the Job and never attended department functions. He had managed to circumvent the department's normal chain of command and report directly to the PC.

The SOD compound, in a desolate part of Flushing Meadow Park, and surrounded by high fences and deep underbrush, was patrolled around the clock. The only entrance was manned by motorcycle men. After Malone left the Hamilton House he telephoned the SOD compound and requested an appointment to see the chief. He made the call from Sol Epstein's third-floor office when he dropped off the shavings he had removed from Stanislaus's apartment. He asked the pathologist to compare them with the scrapings that were found under Eisinger's nails and cautioned Epstein not to mention it to anyone. The scrapings had been obtained by black-bag methods and could not be used in court. If they matched, Malone would have to invent some probable cause and apply for a search warrant.

Zangline put on a sudden burst of speed and trotted over to where he was standing. He snapped a towel from the fence and wiped his neck and face, watching him. "Lieutenant Malone?"

"Yes, Chief."

"Come with me," he said authoritatively.

Radio cars and Emergency Service vans were precision parked in front of the headquarters building. Zangline led Malone directly to his spacious office. Trophies won by various SOD units crammed each shelf. Zangline told him to wait while he showered and changed. Malone stood in front of the cabinets. There were framed photographs of Zangline shaking hands with President Carter, the mayor, and the governor. Even one with the cardinal. He studied the man in the flowing silk robe and wide red sash. Pompous prick, he thought, moving off. Four separate piles of reports were on the desk. He started to rummage through them but resisted his impulse and moved away from the desk. The SOD logo emblazoned one wall. Malone had done his homework before he came. Zangline commanded a small army. All Marine, Mounted, Aviation, Tactical Patrol, Emergency Service, and Anticrime units were under the SOD umbrella. Most of the structural changes that had occurred within the Job in the last three years had a direct bearing on SOD functions. Every Emergency Service truck in the city now carried two thousand rounds of 38-caliber ammunition, shotguns and AR-I5s with scopes with nighttime capabilities, and tear gas and concussion grenades. SOD was the perfect place to hide forty cops.

Zangline came out of the dressing room in the tailored uniform of an assistant chief of the department. Malone focused on the two gilt stars on his shoulders.

"What can we do for you, Lieutenant?" Zangline said, walking to his desk.

Malone felt uneasy. He had heard that voice before. "I'm endeavoring to locate three officers whom I have reason to believe might be assigned to your command."

Zangline was watching him. "Why do you want these men?"

"It has to do with an investigation my squad is conducting."

Zangline started to roll a pencil over the desk. "I take it then that you're not from IAD."

He nodded.

"If you locate these men are you prepared to give them Miranda or GO 15?"

"No I'm not."

Zangline doodled. "Tell me their names."

"Edwin Bramson, Joseph Stanislaus, and Charles Kelly."

Zangline pointed the pencil at him and said, "None of them are assigned to SOD." He threw the pencil down and leaned back, watching him.

"Isn't it possible that you're . . ."

". . . Lieutenant. I know every man assigned to my command."

"But perhaps?" He raised his palms and let them fall.

"There are no perhapses in SOD. But to put your mind to rest . . ."

He snapped forward, yanking out the top drawer of his desk. "Here is an up-to-date roster of all personnel assigned."

Malone flipped the pages, glancing up and down the neatly typed column of names. There was no Bramson, Stanislaus, or Kelly. His mouth went dry. He looked at the chief and placed the roster on the desk.

He knew where he had heard that authoritative voice. He calmly got up and left.

A door opened and Bramson, Westy Stanislaus, and Kelly entered the room.

Zangline stared at them. "You heard?"

"We heard," Stanislaus said, going over to the window and watching Malone walking toward the SOD parking lot.

Bramson rubbed his chin. "Anderman told Mannelli that he thinks we should hit Malone."

Kelly said, "The problem with that is that neither Anderman nor Mannelli knows what is really going down."

Shea Stadium loomed in front of him, a silent colossus with fluttering banners. Malone sped the department auto across the empty parking field, heading for the bank of telephones next to the press gate. He left the motor running and the transmission in park, and got out, fishing in his pocket for a dime.

"Chief Zangline, please," Malone said to the impersonal voice who answered the SOD switchboard.

"The chief is busy on another line."

"I'll hold." The glass panels of the booth were smashed. Names flared in black over the shiny shelf. Empty beer bottles and a used sanitary napkin were on the floor. More urban rococo. He tucked the receiver under his chin and lit a cigarette, his stare wandering the parking field. A few cars were parked next to the press gate. A bumper sticker caught his eye: SAVE A MOUSE, EAT A PUSSY. He laughed.

"I can put you through now."

"This is Chief Zangline."

Malone held the mouthpiece close. "I recognized your voice, *Captain* Madvick." He dropped the receiver onto the hook.

Zangline tore the phone from his ear and stared at it, not wanting to believe what he had just heard. He looked slowly away and stared blankly at Stanislaus. "Do Malone. Use Marku's friends from Atlantic Avenue and make it look like an accident."

"Malone is not the kind of man you catch off guard. He's going to have to be finessed into his grave," Stanislaus said.

"I don't care how you do it. Just do it. And there is something else that needs to be discussed. I got a call from Thea Braxton today. She and her brother think that they're worth more money, a lot more money. She insinuated that we"—he waved his hand at them—"are in a precarious position and should see to it that we don't make enemies, keep our friends."

Stanislaus, Bramson, and Kelly looked at one another and then each broke into smiles. They were going to enjoy the next few days.

14

Malone, Heinemann, Stern, dressed in prison denim, stared out the barred windows of the Department of Corrections bus. The bus threw up a cloud of dust as it lumbered along, and veered to avoid potholes. It jerked to a complete stop inches from the gate of the NYPD's outdoor range, in front of a large red warning sign that read: STOP, POLICE PERSONNEL ONLY, SHOW SHIELD AND I.D. A guardhouse was just inside the gate, and beyond that a parking field that was terraced into three sections by old telephone poles.

A restricted-duty police officer, his face scarred from the ravages of alcoholism, stepped from the guardhouse and ambled over to the gate. Raising himself up on the balls of his feet, he studied the sullen prisoners inside the bus. Shrugging as if to say No one tells me nothing, he unchained the gate and stepped back.

The NYPD's outdoor range was on a secluded tip of Pelham Bay Park. Five ranges built on the water's edge surrounded by high mountains of dirt; barriers to protect boaters in Eastchester Bay from stray shots. Ranges A through D could accommodate fifty shooters at a time; Range E had moving targets and was used for combat and barricade shooting. Alongside E range were the kennels where the department's narcotic- and explosive-sniffing dogs were housed. In the interior of the compound was an explosives range where deadly devices were detonated and a Hollywood-type street where policemen role-played combat situations.

Malone had felt a twinge of guilt lying to his boyhood friend, Tom McCauley. They had grown up together in the old neighborhood, went to the same schools, played on the same teams, screwed the same baby-sitters. McCauley joined Corrections a year after Malone became a cop. McCauley was now the assistant warden of Rikers Island, the city's correctional facility.

Housekeeping duties at the range were done by trusties from Rikers. They arrived each day at 8:00 A.M. and left at 4:00 P.M. This was the one glaring weakness that Malone had discovered when he studied the range's security system. The perimeter was constantly patrolled by men in jeeps. Attack dogs roamed free at night. The bunkers were wired with alarms. Department helicopters flew over at irregular intervals, their powerful searchlights slicing through the night and sweeping the land. But every weekday a busload of prisoners arrived to pick up the garbage and police the brass. With nerve and the right disguise he just might brazen his way inside. He had paid a visit to Tom Mc-Cauley. "Need a favor, ol' buddy. A prison bus and some uniforms. For a tail job," he had told McCauley.

Starling Johnson parked the bus in front of A range. The cramped walkways were made of packed dirt; the gutters, uneven files of painted stones. A few skimpy trees shaded the outdoor eating area which had several seldom-used picnic tables. Most men elected to make the four-minute drive to City Island because alcoholic beverages were not permitted on the range. Someone once said that guns and booze don't mix but most cops don't believe it.

A group of range instructors were standing in front of Classroom 3 discussing the latest model Colt. A combat masterpiece, one of them called it.

The detectives left the bus and separated. Each one was to look around on his own. They pulled their denim hats over their eyes. There was a chance one of them might be recognized.

A group of men were lounging in front of Classroom 2. They were dressed in threadbare clothes and had gunbelts strapped around their waists. Goggles hung from their gun handles. Malone had counted thirty-one men when an instructor appeared in the doorway and motioned the class inside. On his haunches, pretending to realign the stones of the gutter, Malone worked his way toward Classroom 2. He moved slowly, not wanting to call attention to himself. Three prisoners were sitting next to a Quonset hut, killing time and sharing a cigarette. He met their eyes, then let his gaze drift slowly away, just another prisoner minding his own business. He moved to the next stone.

The double doors of the classroom were open. His leg muscles were starting to ache. When he reached the doorway he glanced into the classroom and recoiled, looking quickly away. A range instructor was lecturing the class. His khakis were tailored and a .38 Colt, in a quick-draw holster, hugged his right hip. Two men were sitting on a metal folding table behind him. One was a big, blond man with fair skin and wavy hair. The other man was David Ancorie, Yachov Anderman's trusted associate.

While the instructor lectured on the use of deadly physical force, Ancorie and the other man sat patiently, legs swinging over the side of the table.

Malone turned his back to the open door and moved past on his haunches. Pretending to concentrate on work, he made his way around to the side of the Quonset hut. He slumped to the ground with his back against the corrugated shell. He stretched out his legs in front and lit a cigarette. Just another trusty on another self-imposed break. An open window was inches above his head. He could hear clearly. Heinemann and Stern rounded Classroom 3 and saw him. They moseyed over, pausing at discreet distances to police the area.

They sat on either side of him. "Anything?" Heinemann whispered.

"Shhh. Listen," Malone said.

The instructor was lecturing. "Gentlemen, I am now going to read to you Section Thirty-five-point-thirty, paragraph two, of the *Criminal Procedure Law*: 'The fact that a police officer is justified in using deadly physical force under circumstances prescribed in these paragraphs does not constitute justification for reckless conduct by such police officer amounting to an offense against or with respect to innocent persons whom he is not seeking to arrest or retain in custody.' "

The lawbook was slapped closed.

An echo reverberated through the half-empty classroom.

Malone visualized the instructor scanning the faces of his students, getting ready to drive home his point.

"In other words, gentlemen, if you open up at high noon on Madison and Five-three in an attempt to apprehend a perp who just blew away the Pope and all the saints and in the process kill a junkie who was nodding by"—a long pause for effect—"your ass, gentlemen, would be in a whooooole lot of trouble."

Another pause for effect.

"Are there any questions, gentlemen?"

A range officer made his way along the footpath heading for the latrine. He glanced at the three goofing-off prisoners and continued to his destination.

A voice bellowed from the rear of the classroom. "Hey, Westy, when are we going to get the scoop?"

For the first time Malone heard Stanislaus's voice: "Okay. Okay. I'll tell you what I can." He sounded poised and confident. "After our good friend, Dave, gets done giving you his spiel, you're going to be divided into two groups. The first group will go out to Easy range and fire the Uzi. Group two will remain here and be tested. Then the process will be reversed. 'Course, the questions we ask the first group will not be the same as those asked the second group."

A chorus of boos went up.

Stanislaus continued. "After you're tested you'll be rated and ranked. When there are openings in the Unit you'll be transferred in. In the meantime you're to be transferred back to commands. Each one of you will get to pick your own house."

A chorus of hoots, whistles, and applause.

"Gentlemen, you are to tell no one about the Unit. Secrecy is vital to our mission. Never discuss what you've learned. Not with your wife. Your girlfriend. Your confessor. Not even with your partner. Are there any questions?"

There was a long silence.

The detectives could hear shuffling from inside the classroom. Westy Stanislaus said, "Good. Now I'll turn you over to our good friend, Dave Ancorie."

Ancorie's now familiar voice announced: "This, gentlemen, is a five-inch gray attaché case that is completely lined with ballistic armor. Every member of the Unit will be issued one. This particular case uses a type-C liner that is one-quarter-inch thick and will defeat, at a distance of four inches, the three-fifty-seven- or one-fifty-eight-grain jacketed cartridge. Keep it close to you. It could save your life." He opened the case and removed a Uzi submachine gun. "You are looking at one of the finest weapons in the world. It was developed in Israel by its namesake Maj. Uzi Gal. This weapon has a cyclical rate of fire of six hundred and fifty rounds per minute. A velocity of thirteen hundred and ten feet per second. It fires nine-millimeter parabellum bullets from a detachable staggered-box magazine with three separate load capacities. Fully loaded the Uzi weighs eight-point-eight pounds. This weapon has a slide selector switch which permits single action or fully automatic bursts." The bolt was slid back, cocking the weapon. "This weapon has almost no recoil." The trigger was pulled and the bolt snapped forward with a clanging thud. "The front sight is a truncated cone with protecting ears. The rear sight is L shaped with sight settings for one hundred and two hundred yards." He placed the Uzi under his right arm. "This weapon is easy to conceal on the person." Malone heard what sounded like the weapon being put down on a table. "Now. If you will all gather around me I will show you how to clean and field strip this weapon."

Malone nudged the detectives. "Let's get out of here."

✳ ✳ ✳

Dr. Solomon Epstein used a diluted solution of gelatin when he mounted the hairs. He placed the fibers side by side on the slides so that he could study them at full length.

Leaning into the comparison microscope, he adjusted the focus. His white hospital coat was unbuttoned. He glanced up at Malone. "What do you know about hair?"

"It thins in men past twenty."

Epstein smiled and peered into the lenses. Concentrating on the slides, he lapsed into a forensic litany. Head hair was round and curly. Torso hair was oval and kidney shaped. Beard hair was triangular, with concave sides. Hair was generally divided into three parts: the medulla, cortex, and cuticle. The medulla of human hair was narrow; the medulla of animal hair was medium or thick depending on the kind of animal. By checking a hair fiber against the *Medullary Index* a pathologist can determine if the specimen is human or animal and what part of the body it originated from.

Epstein pushed away from the table. "Take a look."

Malone straddled the white adjustable stool and lowered himself. The doctor looked over his shoulder. "Notice that the air network is a fine grain. The network in animal hair is formed in sacs. You are looking at human hair. The fibers on the left slide were taken from Eisinger's fingernails. Notice how the shaft is broken around the root. If you look close you will be able to see the longitudinal splits around the shaft."

Malone had a wry look on his face. "Which all means?"

"It means that Eisinger tore those hairs from someone's face. Most probably her killer's."

"What else can you tell me?"

"Both slides contain beard hair of a male, Caucasian. A man with a heavy beard and blond wavy hair."

Malone stood. He plunged his hands into his trouser pockets and strolled around the room. He stopped in front of a specimen case. Epstein's reflection was in the paneled glass. He was staring at him, a smug smile on his hawklike face. Glass shelves were filled with jars containing human organs.

A brain had pins sticking out of it. Little tags were attached to the ends. Right and left cerebral hemisphere. Right and left frontal lobe. The infoldings of the gray mass seemed intertwined in an insoluble puzzle.

"Doc, I have the million-dollar question for you," Malone said.

"You want to know if the hairs on both slides are from the same man," Epstein said, moving to the specimen case.

Malone turned to face him. "Are they?"

"The best I can give you is a definite maybe. The hairs do have the same microscopic characteristics and in my opinion could have come from the same individual."

Malone's disappointment was obvious.

Epstein said, "Hair fibers are not positive like fingerprints. They're circumstantial evidence. You go and bring in your killer. I'll testify. Those fibers might be the nails in his coffin." Epstein smiled impishly. "That is, if the shavings you bring in next time are admissible in evidence."

Wednesday night was cheater's night at Bradley's. The bar and lounge were crowded. Soft music floated from speakers. The telephone calls had been made; the wives had been notified that their husbands would not be home for dinner. An unscheduled meeting or an important buyer were the usual lies.

Malone was squeezed in at the end of the bar, sipping Jack Daniel's on ice. Reasonable Cause does sometimes get in the way, but Malone was fond of saying that a good cop can always make his own. The trick was not to get caught. In order to reenter Stanislaus's apartment legally and dust the compact and diaphragm for her prints and obtain more shavings, he would need a search warrant with a "No Knock" clause. And in order to get one he would have to go before a competent court and show reasonable cause, some evidence, even hearsay, linking Police Officer Joseph Stanislaus to the murder of Sara Eisinger.

Drink finished, he pushed his glass onto the bar's runway and motioned to the bartender for a refill.

Malone hefted the glass without drinking. What was Erica doing at this very moment, he wondered. Probably typing or editing her manuscript. He thought of her shaped triangle of downy hair and sighed. What the hell was he doing in this place? He drank and a euphoric glow began to spread through him. People around him were laughing and the music was louder. He was attuned to the charged atmosphere. His feet tapped to the beat of the music. He spun on his stool to watch the dancers. Small tables with flickering candles stuck inside netted red lanterns ringed the cube-size dance floor. The lights were dim. Swaying dancers pressed close to Malone. A "garmento" held a beautiful black woman in his arms. His knee slid between her legs. She pressed him close, pelvis grinding rhythmically, her head resting on his shoulder. Wifey was probably at home in Jericho playing Mah-Jongg with the girls. Go to it, ma man. As he spun back, a nagging thought came to mind. The *Patrol Guide* mandated an immediate notification to IAD whenever there was an indication of an MOF's involvement in a crime. He sipped his drink, scoffing. Dear IAD. Forty cops and an

ONE POLICE PLAZA • 779

assistant chief might be involved in a homicide. Wanna take a case on it? Tell the mothers nothin'. He gulped his drink and ordered another.

Stern, Davis, and Johnson walked in. They hovered around the entrance, looking.

Malone turned and saw them shouldering their way toward him. Business should never be discussed in the presence of civilians, so he looked around and spotted an unoccupied banquette between the service bar and kitchen. He wrapped his glass in the cocktail napkin and motioned to the detectives to follow.

"Heard you had a big day at the range," Starling Johnson said, sliding in next to him.

Malone raised his glass and nodded. "We have to come up with something that links Stanislaus to Eisinger. Any ideas?"

The detectives looked to each other. As their eyes met, they shrugged.

Malone looked at Bo Davis. "You said that Stanislaus was divorced and has been living at the Hamilton House for about two years."

Davis spread his hands expressively and let them drop on the table. "Right."

Malone said, "That is within the time frame that Eisinger started to work for the Braxtons."

Stern wrinkled his brow. "So?"

A waitress came over to take their orders. They stopped talking. Stern leered at her, his eyes taking in her trim body. She wrote down their orders and turned to leave. Stern reached out and snagged her by the hip, turning her. "I'd love to get into your pants."

She glowered at him. "I've got one asshole there now. I don't need a second one." She pulled away from his clutch and left in a huff.

The detectives laughed.

"The broad wants my form," Stern said, watching her swaying backside.

When she was gone, Malone said, "I want to locate Stanislaus's ex."

Davis told him, "Pat and I checked with the phone company."

Malone realized that Pat O'Shaughnessy was among the missing. "Where is Pat?"

"A problem at home," Davis said. "Anyway, according to Ma Bell there are over two hundred Stanislauses in and around the metropolitan area."

The waitress brought their drinks. Stern gave her a big smile. She wrinkled her nose at him and sneered.

Davis said to Malone, "Lou, it'll take a lot of time to check all them subscribers. And the ex coulda moved or remarried, or be living under her maiden name."

Malone toyed with his glass. "Time is one thing we don't have a lot of."

Nobody talked.

Stern watched with growing disbelief as Starling Johnson drank a Galliano with a beer chaser.

Stern grimaced. "How the fuck can you drink that shit?"

Johnson licked his fingers. "Each man to his own poison." Starling Johnson's face harmonized with the darkness, teeth and eyes accentuated by the glow of the flickering candle. "Stanislaus's personnel folder is missing, right?"

"Right," Malone said, wary.

"And we want to find out where he used to live on the assumption that his ex still lives there and might be able to tell us something about hubby and his love life."

Malone held the glass in front of his face and nodded.

Johnson smiled. "This be a very ethnic job. I belong to the Guardians. Limp-dick Stern belongs to the Shomrim. Bo belongs to the St. George. And Stanislaus be a Polish name . . ."

Malone leaned over the table and punched him on the shoulder. "And you be a bloomin' genius."

"Are you sure that you want to use a direct approach?" Johnson said, sipping his cordial.

Malone pondered the question. "No. I don't think I want him to know that we're zeroing in on him. I'm gambling that he's forgotten about those items his girlfriend left in his bathroom." He grabbed a handful of pretzels from the bowl and started to toss them into his mouth one at a time, thinking. He said to Johnson, "Steal a policewoman from the precinct. Locate the ex and have the policewoman hang around some of the beauty parlors and Laundromats. They're hotbeds of local gossip."

15

When Malone walked into the squad room, Heinemann glanced at him and nodded toward the lieutenant's office.

Bo Davis was perched on Malone's desk, trying to console O'Shaughnessy who was slumped in a chair, hands limp between his legs. Dark folds of skin sagged his eyes.

"Lemme 'lone," O'Shaughnessy was saying.

Malone pushed the door closed and looked at Davis.

"His wife left him," Davis said.

"That cunt!" O'Shaughnessy stormed from the chair and kicked the desk.

Malone was concerned. "What happened?"

O'Shaughnessy lit a cigarette. "The minute I walked in last night I knew somethin' was wrong. 'We have a dinner guest, dear,'" he mimicked, sarcastically. "I just knew. I went into the dining room and there she was, sitting at my table, drinking my tea. That Irish whore."

"Oh shit. Foam," Malone said.

Davis said, "How did she find out where you lived?"

"She works for Sears, Roebuck. She ran a credit check on me. Bam! There I was. A computer printout, address and all. 'Hi. I'm Foam. Your husband has been screwing me for years. I'm in a family way and he's the daddy.' 'Oh?' says my wife. 'Do come in dear. Watch the steps. I'll make us some tea and we'll have a nice long talk.'"

"Any chance of patching things up?" Davis said.

"No way. My wife got no sense of humor."

* * *

The tour was almost over. O'Shaughnessy had put in a 28 for the remainder of it and was off apartment hunting. Harrigan had telephoned to tell Malone that one of his detectives had taken photographs of three men who fitted the descriptions of Stanislaus, Bramson, and Kelly. They were snapped leaving the SOD compound. Malone had telephoned Erica to ask if she could have dinner with him.

"I'd love to, Daniel."

Her voice caused a stirring in his stomach. He had been contemplating her willing body when a commotion in the squad room shook him from his reverie. Zambrano plunged into the office waving a newspaper in front of him.

"Good afternoon, Inspector. And how has your day been?"

"How has my day been? My fucking telephone hasn't stopped ringing." He shook the paper at Malone. "You better get your fucking circus in the tent. Have you gone mad, planting a story like this?"

"What story?" His expression was deadpan.

Zambrano had read Fine's column. The last paragraph dealt with a usually reliable source within the police department. Zambrano stabbed the column with his finger. "That story!" His eyes were wide and it seemed that every vein and artery in his neck and face was about to burst.

Malone glanced up at the flaking ceiling. "Who said I planted it?"

"Fine's motherfuckin' byline says you planted it! Everyone in the Job knows you two are asshole buddies."

Malone took out two cups and an unopened bottle of Old Grand Dad. He held one of the cups up to his eye and then blew the inside clean. He cracked the bottle and poured. "I needed some answers. Figured a little fire under some ass might make people a wee bit more cooperative."

Zambrano looked at him sharply. "Or desperate."

Malone shrugged indifference and pushed a cup across to him.

Zambrano picked it up and drank. When he put the cup down, he appeared somewhat mollified. "I've just come from the Chief of Op. He wanted to know about you."

Why would the Chief of Operations, the department's highest-ranking uniform member, be interested in him? Malone wondered. Rolling his cup between palms, he asked, "What did you tell him?"

"I said that you were one hundred percent." He moved close to the desk, tapping a fist against his lips. "The Chief of Op is not the kind of man you play grab-ass with. He's where he is because he was the most ruthless and cunning of the palace guard. I strongly suggest that you start looking over your shoulder."

Malone looked up at him. "What can you tell me about Chief Whitney Zangline?"

Zambrano rolled his eyes upward and whistled. "You got a big one. Know anything about the Red Squad?"

"Rumors mostly."

"At one time the Red Squad was a covert subunit of the Intelligence Division. Their mission was the penetration and disruption of subversive groups. Five years ago they were given another mission"—he pulled out a fugitive nose hair, held it up in front of him, examining it —"terrorism."

Malone rubbed his lips in concentration.

Zambrano continued, "Remember the bombing at the World Trade Center five years ago?"

Malone nodded.

"The Red Squad knew about that before it went down. One of their stools sold them the information. Instead of passing it on, they sat on it until every one in their internal chain of command passed on the information's authenticity. When they finally let it out-of-house, it was too late. Twenty-seven lives could have been saved. When the PC found out he went nuts. The C.O. of the squad was reduced to captain and forced to retire. Everyone in the squad who had their time in was told to throw in their papers. The rest of the squad was transferred back into the bag and told to walk with twenty." Zambrano pushed the empty cup across the desk.

Malone broke his concentration and poured.

"About the same time Whitney Zangline had developed SOD into an antiterrorist strike force. That's SOD's real mission. Chrissake, he has more men under arms than some countries. Zangline went to the PC and complained about a lack of communication between Intelligence and SOD. He thought that Intelligence was too compartmentalized. He convinced the PC that SOD needed its own Intelligence arm. The Red Squad was transferred to SOD. Zangline was able to build from the bottom, with his own hand-picked men."

Malone thought of Ancorie training policemen in the use of the Uzi. "Where does his weight come from?"

Zambrano shook his head. "Dunno. But he is heavy. His budget requests are never trimmed." He toasted him. "And that my brash, young lieutenant, takes powerful connections."

"And who are these connections?"

Zambrano grinned. "Whatya tryna do, make me spread rumors?"

"Yeah!"

"I hear whispers, mind you, not many, or loud, but I hear them all the same. Zangline is supposed to be close with Carter Moorhouse."

"The politician?"

"Yep. When Moorhouse ran for mayor a few years back he asked the PC to let Zangline have charge of his security detail. Since then, they've been spotted having dinner a few times."

"That's not very much."

Zambrano flicked his cup aside with his fingernails. He got up and stretched, his arms reaching for the ceiling. Relaxing, he strolled over to the window. He sat on the sill and leaned forward, hands cupping kneecaps. He realized that his socks did not match. One was black, the other charcoal. "Yesterday I went to the Captain Endowment Association's monthly luncheon. Over the clink of martini glasses, I picked up a few whispers concerning Zangline. Grapevine has it that he's up to his ass in something heavy."

Malone was interested. "Can you find out what?"

"Did you ever stop to think that nothing happens in this job without first passing through some pencil pusher's desk in the Bureau of Audits and Accounts. My brother-in-law is a SPAA there. I've been planning to take him to lunch." Zambrano got up. "What are you doing tomorrow?"

Malone spread his lips and gestured nothing.

"That's good. The Chief of Op wants you in his office at five P.M. He said to be on time."

Photographs of three unsuspecting men walking toward a car were spread over the desk. Malone shuffled them, looking at each one. He recognized Stanislaus from the range. Davis identified Bramson and Kelly. He opened the top drawer of his desk and took out the snapshot of Sara Eisinger that her parents had lent him. He put it with the others and tapped them together into one neat stack. He handed the stack to Jake Stern. "I want you to do a canvass of the joints around the Hamilton House. That part of Queens is a big singles' area. Show these around. See if you can put Eisinger and Stanislaus together."

Jack Harrigan's head was way back, draining a container of beer. He snapped forward and at the same time arched the empty tube into the wastebasket. Malone caught the look that crossed the sergeant's face as he watched Stern walk out. "What's bothering you, Jack?"

Harrigan looked him in the eyes. "Some of my men don't feature working on cops."

Malone gave a worried sigh. "None of us do. I think most of the cops involved are either legit or dupes in a caper they know nothing about. Someone out there is using the department, manipulating it."

"I don't want my men branded IAD scumbags."

"They won't be. We won't be. We're doing the right thing."

Harrigan nodded feebly and left.

Malone knew that he had just about used up all his time.

Washing machines rumbled on concrete platforms. Dryers spun. Local announcements tacked on bulletin boards advertised fifteen-year-old girl, available to babysit; a two-room mother/daughter was for rent at 7 Plumeding Lane, Pearl River, New York; and there was to be a mammoth garage sale this Saturday at 12 Rosehaven Hollow, Pearl River, New York.

Women waited inside the Laundromat for their clothes to dry. Others pulled items from machines and tossed them into plastic baskets.

Jean O'Day had her hair in rollers. A housecoat with a lavender-and-yellow forget-me-not design concealed her shapely body, hiding the waistband holster.

O'Day was a cop from the Fifth.

She stuffed her laundry into the front-load machine and closed the door. She measured the proper amount of detergent and softener, set the wash cycle, and inserted coins. The machine started to spin, a mass of suds formed behind the porthole. When she turned around, she caught three pairs of eyes leaving her. She gathered up her boxes and walked over to the women. "Hi. I'm Jean O'Day."

Detective Starling Johnson parked the department auto so that he might have an unrestricted view of the Laundromat. He slouched behind the wheel, working the *New York Times* crossword puzzle. One eye was glued on the Laundromat. She was standing among a group of women, gabbing.

The day had begun early for Johnson. He had left one of his girl-friends' bed at 4:13 A.M., dressed, and driven to the stationhouse. In order to steal a policewoman for a day he needed the approval of the precinct commander. Patrol precincts are made up of two separate commands: patrol and detective. A captain is usually in command of the uniform force; a lieutenant commands the detectives.

The precinct captain is charged with the responsibility for the plant and its maintenance. Sometimes the lines of communication between the two commands get twisted and there is friction. But not at the Fifth. Captain Bruno Carini was first, last, and always a street cop. The Fifth was his third command and the word was that he was one of the rising stars. The pressure of running an urban police precinct was taking its toll. There was a time when Carini always wore a smile on his face. No more. He looked tired and drawn. He was finishing up a late tour when Johnson knocked on the door.

After studying the eight-by-four roll call, Carini had said, "I'll let you have O'Day for the day. She's about the only female who knows where it's at." As Johnson was leaving he had said, "Tell your boss he owes me another one."

The first thing Johnson noticed about Police Officer O'Day was that she was flat chested. The second thing was her eyes. They reminded him of gray bottle caps. The third was the smile. It burst over her entire face.

A few minutes alone with her in the sitting room told him that she was intelligent, quick, eager, and had a glowing ambition to get a gold detective shield. As they discussed her assignment, Johnson had fantasized about Police Officer O'Day sprawled naked in bed. White skin blended with black. She only had nipples, brown and hard. He gnawed them and she writhed with ecstasy. She stroked his black hardness. When she could no longer stand it, she demanded that he enter her.

"What I would like you to do is go home and change into something that will make you look like a housewife. I'll meet you back here in one hour."

Johnson had located Stanislaus's neighborhood through the Pulaski Association. He had gone to their suite of rooms in a downtown office building. The grandmother type who worked there looked concerned when she saw him standing there. She was nigger scared. He smiled warmly and showed her his shield and I.D. She relaxed immediately. Her late husband, God rest his soul, worked out of old Traffic B. She went on to berate the inadequateness of the Article I pension system. The cost-of-living escalator clause sucks, she told him.

"Yes'm." He listened to the litany of woe with interest and patience. Twenty minutes later when she paused to catch her breath he leaped into the opening. He told her that he was trying to get the home address of someone he had come on the job with. They were planning a class reunion. Joe Stanislaus was a member of the Pulaski and since he was in the neighborhood he thought that he might save himself a trip to headquarters. Four wooden file boxes were on a clerical cart. She swiveled around and slid open the last one.

"Stanislaus, Joseph," she said, nimbly fingering the cards. She flicked one out. There was a recent address change. What was the old address? "24 Pickwicklan Drive Circle, Pearl River, New York," she read.

"That's the one. I remember Joe always complaining about the damn crabgrass in Pearl River."

A covered carriage carried by poles. Nine letters down. He tapped the pencil against his teeth. O'Day was engaged in animated conversation. He caught her glance in his direction and thought he saw a glimmer of lust. Wishful thinking, he thought.

Palanquin. Nine letters. He filled in the boxes.

Detective Johnson and Police Officer O'Day had a pleasant ride back. They got to know each other, a little. When they drove up in front of the Fifth, the Third Platoon was flowing into the street. O'Day was anxious to make her report to the detective commander. The ladies of the Laundromat had been most helpful, she reported. There was not much that went on in Pearl River they did not know about. Especially when it concerned the carryings-on of husbands. A fat woman with a hairy birthmark on the tip of her nose had been eager to talk. She confided that Joe Stanislaus was having a "thing" with one of the policewomen in his precinct. Pranced home one night and told his dear wife that he was leaving. He was in love for the first time in his life, he told his wife, the woman with the birthmark said. She had moved close to the ladies and murmured, "I suppose *she* did all those disgusting things that men like." Jean O'Day had nodded knowingly. It was at that point that she had glanced in Johnson's direction. Did he always wear tight trousers?

Malone gave her his full attention.

When she finished making her report he got up and went to the blackboard. Next to Stanislaus's name he wrote: Policewoman? Eisinger was not on the Job. If she was Stanislaus's girlfriend then someone was mistaken. He moved back, studying the board. Stanislaus might have had two women on the string, one of whom could have been a policewoman. Eisinger found out. They fought. He killed her. Or? If David Ancorie could train policemen in the use and care of the Uzi, why could not Eisinger train them in computers or warehouse maintenance, or something? They could have met at a training session. Lovers have to meet someplace. It would be a natural mistake for the ex to assume she was on the Job. He liked it. It had the right ring.

Detective Johnson leaned close to Police Officer O'Day.

"How about a bite to eat?"

She looked at him and smiled. "Sounds good to me."

In the window of the restaurant on Austin Street a statue of a boy held a pizza in his outstretched hands. Heinemann and Stern had worn down shoe leather in Stanislaus's Queens neighborhood for the past two hours. The owner of Ricco's was a rotund man with a chunky face and a prairie of shiny skin stretched over his cranium. Heinemann showed him the photographs. "They're not in any kind of trouble, are they?" Stern assured him that they weren't. It was an accident case and they had been witnesses. The owner was relieved. They were such a nice couple. The blond man in the one photo and the woman standing on the pier in the other photo used to eat here all the time. He moved close to the detectives. A man ready to share a secret. "They were very much in love. It made my heart good to see them holding hands and kissing. Like young kids." They questioned him closely. When they finished, Heinemann telephoned Malone and told him what they had discovered. They had a pizza that tasted even better because it was on the arm, and then drove to Hamilton House.

The doorman was a patronizing shit who always had his hand out. The detectives sized him up at once. Stern told him that they were private detectives working on a matrimonial. Their client was a doctor who would do the right thing if someone were to come up with some information on his wife.

"What kinda information you lookin' for?" the doorman asked, squaring his hat to the front.

Heinemann told him the doctor had reason to believe his wife was sleeping around with a resident of Hamilton House. He had followed his wife there on more than one occasion. Stern passed the doorman the photographs. He flipped through them, giving each photo a perfunctory glance. Finished, he flopped the stack into Heinemann's hand and hurried to open the door for a lady and her sheepdog. Returning, he asked slyly, "How much?"

Stern spoke out of the corner of his mouth. "A yard."

"I got a piss-poor memory. Make it five hundred," said the doorman.

"Fuck you, pally," Stern said, walking away.

"Three hundred," the doorman said.

"Two," Stern countered.

"Gimme a break," said the doorman.

"Two fifty," Heinemann said.

"Okay. Apartment 24 J. Name's Stanislaus. She had her own key."

Heinemann looked at him sternly. "You sure she had a key?"

The doorman snapped a thumb in his face and raised his voice. "I'm sure."

The detectives looked at each other. "You wait here. I'll go," Stern said.

"Whaddabout my money?" said the doorman.

"I'm going to see about that right now," said Stern.

It took him forty-eight minutes to drive back to the stationhouse. He trudged the steps to the squad room, pausing to catch his breath.

Sara Eisinger's property was stacked in plastic evidence bags with property vouchers wrapped around them. Each key that had been identified had a tag attached to it that noted the lock that it opened. Two keys had no tags. He signed them out on the voucher: name, rank, shield number, and date and time. He returned the rest of the evidence and locked the locker.

"Got my money?" said the doorman, walking up to him.

Stern ignored the question. "Does Stanislaus own a car?"

"Yeah. A red Honda. He keeps it in the garage."

Janet Fox had seen Eisinger get out of a red Honda on a rainy night long ago.

"What kind of rent does he pay here?" Heinemann said.

The doorman pulled on his ear. "Five and a quarter for a one bedroom and another seventy-five for the garage. What about my money?"

Stern grabbed him by the gold-trimmed lapels of his uniform. "Three weeks from today at exactly 2 P.M. a guy is going to walk up to you and hand you an envelope. Your bread'll be in it."

"Three weeks!"

Stern tightened his grip. The doorman's lip quivered.

Stern said, "That's the way things work, pally. We gotta check out your story. In the meantime, you button your mouth." He released one hand and pointed at Heinemann. "If you don't, my large friend here will come back and dance the tarantella on your nuts."

"It's over here," Stern said, standing in front of apartment 24 J. The first key unlocked the door. Supressing an urge to enter, Stern locked the door and dropped Eisinger's key into his pocket.

Waiting for the elevator, Heinemann said, "Wait a minute." He ran back and toed the mat square with the jamb.

Stern held the elevator.

Malone spent the rest of the day reading and signing fives. How does a cop pay alimony and still afford six hundred dollars for an apartment and garage? The answer was simple. He doesn't. Not unless he has an unreported source of income or some old ammo boxes stuffed with greenbacks.

It was almost 4 P.M. when a gruff voice piped in from the squad room. "Lou, you gotta call on three." Malone checked the time. Erica would be waiting and he was anxious. He almost yelled out to tell the caller that he was on patrol but the nagging feeling that it might be important caused him to yank up the receiver and press the blinking button.

"Lou, this is Sergeant Vincent from the Nineteenth Squad. Do you know an Erica Sommers?"

"Yes!" he blurted, jerking forward in the chair, aware of a sudden thumping in his chest.

"You better get over to her apartment. There's been a homicide."

Three East End Avenue was on a bluff overlooking the East River. The building had thirty-five stories of reflective glass topped by a penthouse and a huge lobby filled with paintings and sculpture.

With roof light and siren on constant, Malone sped the unmarked car north along the FDR Drive through the blossoming evening traffic. It took him thirty-six minutes to get to Eightieth Street. East End Avenue between Eightieth and Eighty-first was cordoned with police vehicles. Several unmarked cars had been abandoned in the middle of the avenue. Radio cars were parked on the sidewalk. The Crime Scene Unit's blue-and-white station wagon was blocking the entrance to 3 East End's underground garage.

Malone drove the car around the west side of the Eightieth Street cordon and up onto the sidewalk. Halfway down the block he parked, leaving the roof light flashing red. He ran from the car over to the nearest policeman. "Where is it?"

"In the garage, Lou," the startled cop said, staring at the gold lieutenant's shield that Malone thrust at him.

As he ran down the curving two-lane driveway, he was breathless and conscious of a sharp welt of pain across his forehead. He reached the bottom and found himself in an underground garage full of cars, each one in a stall designated by a little yellow number and enclosed within yellow boundary lines. Save for its silent tenants, it was empty. Off in the distance he could hear the echo of voices. He made for them. Walking rapidly, his footfalls added to the hollow sounds. He could smell gasoline fumes and the heavy odor of motor oil. The voices grew louder. He broke into a trot.

When he reached the eastern extremity of the garage he turned the bend and stopped short. Grim-faced detectives, their shields pinned to their sport coats, were gathered around Erica Sommers's green Oldsmobile Cutlass. A photographer was kneeling on the front seat of the green car flashing pictures of the rear.

He hesitated, afraid of what he was going to see in the rear seat of the Cutlass. And then, with his shield case dangling open in his hand, and the cold knot in his stomach getting tighter, he began pushing past the detectives.

Sprawled over the seat was the body of a man. His hands were tied behind his back and a bloody plastic bag was pulled over his head and garroted around the neck with wire. The cadaver's eyes bulged from their sockets in a wild, dull stare and the tongue protruded limply over the lip.

An overwhelming sense of relief swept over Malone and he felt weak. Sergeant Vincent had told him that she was all right, but he needed to see for himself.

He turned to meet the stares. "Where is she?"

Two policemen were on guard outside Erica's sixteenth-floor apartment. Malone flashed his shield and rushed past them.

She was sitting in a high-backed chair in the sunken living room staring down at the geometric pattern of the carpet. When she heard the sound of the closing door she glanced up and looked disbelievingly at him. She was wearing a pair of white jeans and a blue tunic-top blouse. Before a word could pass between them she sprang up and ran into his waiting arms. He began to say sympathetic things, trying to console her. And then he realized that she was not hysterical. Her face showed no trace of tears. She bore a countenance of resigned bewilderment. "I was going shopping and found that thing in my car. I feel as though I've been personally violated. What kind of animals are there in this world?" For the first time he sensed fear in her voice.

Lt. Jack Weidt, the "whip" or boss of the Nineteenth Squad of detectives, was a trendy dresser. A medium-size man with a throaty voice, he was completely bald and had deep green eyes that had gray spots in both irises. He walked in off the terrace followed close behind by Lt. Joe Mannelli, who looked almost sick with worry. They walked over to the embracing couple and waited for Malone to notice them.

Malone looked at them over her shoulder.

"I saw to it that her name was left out of it, Dan. There'll be no mention of her on any five or to the press hounds," Weidt said.

Malone nodded his thanks.

"Can you give us a few minutes?" Mannelli said in a low voice, motioning toward the terrace.

With a quick movement of his eyes, Malone indicated that they should wait for him out on the terrace and then led Erica into the bedroom and closed the door.

"Lie down and try to get some sleep."

"That was a body, Daniel. In my car. Why? Why me? Does it have something to do with you, with us?"

"Someone probably thought it was a convenient place to dump a body."

"Don't tell me fairy tales, Daniel. I have a right to know what the hell is going on."

"I don't know what's going down. But be assured that you're going to have round-the-clock protection."

"I don't want a bunch of grubby policemen following me every time I go to the bathroom or sit down at the typewriter."

He spent the next thirty minutes soothing her; then he left her to join the anxious men on the terrace of her apartment.

"What the fuck went down in that garage?" Malone said, stepping outside.

Jack Weidt replied, "She discovered the body about three forty-five P.M. A garage attendant heard her screams and came a-runnin'. When we arrived on the scene she dropped your name and we called you. The M.E. hasn't been here yet. He's stuck on a triple homicide in Whitestone. I took a looksee at the body. There's some lividity. Rigor mortis has set in around the head and neck. There are three tightly grouped entrance wounds above the left ear that look as though they were made by twenty-twos. I'd say that he was wasted four to six hours ago, which would make the time of occurrence somewhere between nine and twelve this morning." He paused to light a cigar.

"There were two attendants on duty from eight A.M. The body had to have been planted here during their tour. We've been leaning on them and they know from nothing. And I believe them. We checked both of them out and they're clean. Not so much as a summons for drinking beer in the park." Weidt cast a worried look in Malone's direction. "Somebody went to a lot of trouble to plant that stiff in your girlfriend's car. Any ideas?"

Malone ignored the question. "Had he been I.D.'d?"

Joe Mannelli had been standing with his back to them, watching the river, seemingly oblivious to the conversation behind him. Now he turned abruptly, a look of alarm etched into his face. "He's from my league, Dan—Ismail al Banna."

Malone was astonished. "Banna!"

"You got it. Banna was wanted in half a dozen countries for terrorist acts. Everything from political kidnappings to murder. We recently received word through the French secret service that he was hiding in New York. SDECE's Bureau Five turned someone around in Morocco. The word within the community is that it was Banna who pulled off the New Year's Eve bombings. It was a contract job for the FALN. Ever since the P.R. freedom fighters blew up their bomb factory in Greenwich Village they've lost their stomach for explosives. They hire out their jobs now, and Banna was one of the best."

Mannelli was frantically rubbing his left thumb. "I don't like it. I tell you, I don't like it. Terrorists are a tightly knit fraternity of nut jobs.

They'd only waste one of their own if they thought he had turned. And Banna wasn't—not by us, not by the FBI, and not by the agency."

"Maybe someone in your minor league blew him away," Malone said sarcastically.

"And dumped the body in your girlfriend's car? That ain't how it's done," Mannelli said.

Malone wanted to get back to Erica. "If you don't need me for anything I'm going back into the bedroom."

"I'll clean up in the garage," Weidt said.

The three men walked back into the apartment. Weidt and Mannelli headed for the door, and Malone moved off toward the bedroom. The two lieutenants had climbed the three steps leading into the marble-walled foyer when Mannelli turned suddenly and roared at the back of Malone's head. "Someone is sending you a message in the clear. And it's signed Eisinger."

When they had left the apartment Malone telephoned the Squad and told Stern what had happened. He gave him Erica's telephone number and told him that he was going to stay with her. Then he hung up and went into the bedroom.

Erica was sitting up on the bed with her head resting against the brass-railed headboard and her arms folded tightly across her chest. She was staring unseeingly at a television quiz show. He went over to her and took her hand. Lowering himself he said, "You okay?"

She looked at him wearing a wan smile. "That body had something to do with us. Doesn't it, Daniel?"

He took a deep breath and sighed. "It was a warning. For me. Back off a certain case or . . ."

"They'll kill *me*."

"Nobody is going to kill anybody. I want you to go away for a while. A few days, until I can get to the bottom of this."

She looked away from him. "I think that that might be best." She was crying.

The late tour was coming out of the stationhouse when Malone returned later that night. He walked into the squad room and found one of the desks covered with white containers of Chinese food. He picked up a cold egg roll on his way into his office. Three detectives were present. Two were hunched over typewriters and the third was purring over the telephone to a female who obviously was not his wife. The detective using the telephone saw Malone and clamped his hand over the mouthpiece. "Some guy has been calling you every hour on the hour. Wouldn't give his name."

Not acknowledging the message, Malone walked into his office and slammed the door. He wanted to be alone and think. That body had reinforced his belief that he was dealing with ruthless, brutal men, and he was apprehensive for Erica and himself.

He took out the bottle and poured a stiff drink into a dirty cup. Whoever had done in Banna had done the world a favor, but he knew that that was not the intent behind Ismail al Banna's sudden demise. He was relieved to know that Erica was now safe. He had driven her to her sister's house in Washington Heights and had extracted a promise from her: she would call no one and tell no one where she was.

The liquor had just started to have its relaxing effect when the voice piped from the other side of the door. "That guy is on four."

It was only a frightened whisper. Malone could hear no background noises, but he did pick up on a slight accent.

"I was in the garage. I saw them."

Malone had pad and pencil ready. "How many were there?"

"Three. And I recognized one of them."

"Who was he?"

"Mr. Malone, I'm afraid. I have a family. I live in the same building and know Miss Sommers. She's a lovely lady but I just can't become involved in anything like this. You have to understand."

"How did you know my name and where to contact me?"

"I heard policemen talking in the elevator. They said that her boyfriend was a lieutenant who worked in Chinatown. Malone was his name, they said."

"I can promise you anonymity. No one will ever know we've talked."

A long pause. "If you're willing to meet me I'll tell you what I saw. But you must promise . . ."

"I do. Tell me when and where."

"Tomorrow night at eleven. Drive east on the LIE and get off at Glen Cove Road. I'll be waiting for you on the service road."

"Why so far out of the city?"

"I have a business in Roosevelt Field. We close at nine. By the time I clean up and get ready for the morning it'll be ten. I can't take any chance of us being seen together."

"I'll see you tomorrow night at eleven."

They clicked off.

Across the river in Brooklyn, Achmed Hamed's eyes were fixed on the barrel of dried dates in the rear of his Atlantic Avenue grocery store. He turned slowly away from the wall phone and looked into the face of the man standing next to him, studying the crazed eyes for a signal. "Was it all right?" he asked in an unsure voice.

Stanislaus slapped Hamed's shoulder. "You did real good, my friend. Real good."

On the other side of the street directly in front of the Dime Savings Bank two detectives slouched in the front seat of a taxi. "Wonder what brought him to that place?" a heavy-set detective said to his partner.

"Who the fuck cares," the other detective said, closing his eyes and dozing.

16

It was a black-tie affair.

Crystal chandeliers sparkled over the dining room of the Algonquin Club where judicial dignitaries had gathered to pay honor to retiring Judge Michael X. Brynes. Judge Aristotle Niarxos tapped the sterling-silver bread knife against the linen tablecloth, his stare fixed attentively on the podium, not hearing a word. His mind was consumed with the image of Markell's plump body.

A burst of applause rousted him back.

Judge Brynes was making his way to the speaker's stand. The old man firmed his stance by gripping the edge. He started to speak. Will the senile bastard ever end, Niarxos thought.

Niarxos was a distinguished-looking man in his late fifties. He hated testimonial dinners. Their redeeming feature was that they gave him a solid excuse to get out of the house. The invitation was always left in some convenient place where his wife was sure to see it. Over the years he had learned to employ every weapon at his disposal to further his quest for the perfect woman. His search had ended two years ago when he hired Markell Sphiros as his secretary.

After thirty minutes of dreadfully boring reminiscences, Judge Michael X. Brynes stepped from the podium, tears in his eyes. Niarxos leaped to his feet, applauding. A cue to leave. He backed away from the table and quickly left the room.

"I say, governor, will ya sign a search warrant for an old war veteran?"

Niarxos wrenched, staring at the form looming at him from the shadows.

"Gus? This is one helluva time to ask me to sign a warrant. I'm on my way to see a lady. Catch me in the morning. In my chambers."

Heinemann moved up to him and whispered, "We've always done right by you, your honor. Your name was never mentioned during Knapp. Now we need one."

Niarxos cleared his throat and mimed surrender. He thrust his hand into his tuxedo and removed half glasses.

Heinemann said, "Have all the papers right here. Made them out myself." He proffered the documents with a pleading smile. "How is Markell?"

"She's waiting for me," Niarxos said, scanning the legal papers.

Heinemann said, "She is one helluva woman. Always reminded me of a girl I met when I parachuted into Greece during the big war. OSS. Difficult times."

Niarxos looked at him over his half glasses. "I suppose if my name was Goldberg you would tell me you fought with the Haganah."

Heinemann lifted his shoulders and let them fall slowly.

Niarxos returned to the papers, scanning, picking out main points. The judge's mouth became a straight line. "Have illegal wires been employed in this case?"

Heinemann feigned shock. "Your honor?"

"Your probable cause is weak."

Heinemann did not answer. He knew how to play the game. Always give the man in the black robe an exit.

"Why the request for the 'No Knock'?"

"We have reasonable cause to believe that the suspect has weapons concealed therein."

Niarxos flipped to the last page, turning the others over and under. He took out a ballpoint pen and snapped the button down, holding it over the line requiring his signature. He read the last paragraph and affixed his name to the order. "This warrant will have to be executed within ten days."

"May Allah grant you ten erections this night."

The judge laughed. "I'll settle for one."

17

Morris Dunbar had gotten four feet inside the reception area when he stopped in his tracks. He blanched. The muscles in his stomach and arms tightened and his eyes grew wide with alarm. He reached up and took the cigar from his mouth, swallowed hard, and then, forcing a smile, rushed to greet his unexpected visitor.

The reason for Morris Dunbar's sudden discomfort was sitting in a canvas-backed chair flipping through the latest issue of *Yachting*.

Lt. Dan Malone, NYPD.

Dunbar had met Malone eighteen years before. A chance encounter in Tompkins Park, Brooklyn.

Patrolman Malone was working a four-to-twelve on Patrol Post 4. The post condition card said to give special attention to park lavatories. Prevent the congregation of sexual perverts. Malone checked the bunker-type bathrooms every hour.

It was September and the leaves were beginning to give hint of yellows, oranges, and umbers. Around 6:45, Patrolman Malone strolled into the foul-smelling bathroom. He saw that all the spaces in front of the urinals were empty. The doors to the toilet cubicles were open, except for the last one. Keeping his distance, he bent dog fashion and peeked under the closed door. He saw a pair of feet, crumpled trousers, and a shopping bag between splayed legs. Grinning knowingly, he got up and padded his way into the next-to-last cubicle. He stood up on the seat and peered over the partition.

Morris Dunbar was seated on the throne. Standing before him with his legs hidden inside the shopping bag, and his naked and erect penis in Morris Dunbar's mouth, was a seventeen-year-old black boy.

"Hi guys," Malone said, waving down.

Morris Dunbar took short deep breaths, trying to shake the panicky feeling that suddenly engulfed his confidence. Right hand extended, he went to greet his old friend.

Malone tossed the magazine on the glass table and got up to accept the proffered hand of the president of Dunbar Research Associates.

Malone saw the same weak smile that always appeared whenever he made one of his infrequent visits. No arrests were made that long-ago night in Tompkins Park. Malone's wife, Helen, had been waiting for him to finish his tour. They had planned to make love, and then go to Luciano's for late night pasta and wine, afterward return home and love again. He had had no intention of giving that up for a bullshit collar that he knew would end up with a hundred-dollar fine, and a "don't do it again boys" reprimand from some liberal judge, so he cut the lovers loose with a warning to keep their private lives out of the public domain.

Morris Dunbar had almost collapsed with relief. Hyperventilating at the thought of not being arrested, he had thrust his business card into the patrolman's hand. "Anytime I can ever be of any assistance, please come by and see me."

Morris Dunbar had always regretted that momentary lapse of discretion. Every few years the cop who knew his secret would appear to collect on his noncancelable marker.

"Morris, ol' friend, need a small favor," Malone said, looking into the man's troubled face.

"Dan? Anytime. You know that," said Morris Dunbar, throwing a welcoming arm around the policeman and steering him into his plushly carpeted office with large tinted windows.

Malone looked into the owllike face with the spirals of smoke rising past the nose. "If I were to give you the names of four men, would you be able to give me a financial profile on them?"

Dunbar drew on his cigar. "Got their Social Security numbers?"

Malone looked puzzled. "Are they necessary?"

Morris Dunbar guffawed. "You kiddin'? They're everything. You can't open a checking account, rent a car, buy a house, or have a telephone installed without listing your Social Security number." Morris Dunbar puckered his lips and blew thick smoke rings. "They're our identification papers and the backbone of my business."

"I'm in a hurry, Morris."

"There are other ways. What are the names?"

Malone handed him a folded sheet of paper. Dunbar read aloud.

"Whitney Zangline, Edwin Bramson, Joseph Stanislaus, and Charles Kelly. How do they make their living?"

"They're policemen," breathed Malone.

Morris Dunbar shot him a look and then swiveled his eyes back to the paper. "I think that we will be able to manage without their numbers. They're uncommon names, except for Kelly. Might not have much luck with that one. Our data banks are cross referenced by name, pedigree, occupation, and Social Security number."

Dunbar Research Associates was the seventh largest credit-research company in the country. It occupied the twenty-first, -second, and -third floors of a modern building on Madison Avenue. The twenty-third floor was divided into glass-partitioned spaces that were filled with intricate electronic equipment and tape consoles with constantly spinning and jerking oversized spools.

Morris Dunbar led him into a windowless alcove with four rows of desks with computer consoles mounted on each one. Next to each desk was an electronic printer. Workers were busy typing coded information into data banks.

As they entered the alcove, a thin Oriental man rushed over to them. "Good morning, Mr. Dunbar. May I help you?"

Morris Dunbar shook his head and quickly turned to his visitor. "No thank you, John." He moved to a console and sat down, motioning for Malone to drag a chair over.

Malone looked at the lime-green screen. "How does this thing work?"

Morris Dunbar said, "Each employee who is authorized to extract information has an identification number. The employee types in his I.D. and the computer gives him permission to proceed. When the go-ahead signal is flashed, the employee inputs the access code to the desired data bank. If he is authorized to enter that particular bank the computer will acknowledge his entry by flashing an entry code onto the upper-left-hand corner of the screen. After the access code is displayed, the desired information is then inputted and the input button depressed. And that is all there is to it."

Malone said, "Each data bank has its own access code?"

"That's correct. You must input the right code to enter each bank. Financial, Medical, Sexual, Property, Criminal. Only certain employees are authorized to enter all the banks."

"Do your banks cover the entire country?"

"No. Only the tri-state area. If a client should want information on an individual who at one time lived in California, we have to type in the access code for California. Our computer is then hooked into a

California data bank. It's a subscription service. Like Home Box Office."

A grin came over Malone's face. "Do the civil libertarians know you have these capabilities?"

Dunbar replied in a mocking tone of voice. "Fuck 'em where they breathe." He pushed his chair closer to the console. "I'll need as much pedigree information as you have."

The next fifteen minutes were spent listing every scrap of information that Malone knew about the four policemen. Dunbar listed each trait in a column under the man's name.

"I'll start with Whitney Zangline. I don't think there are too many Zanglines around." Morris Dunbar typed in his I.D. and depressed the input button. The letters RM flashed in the lower-right-hand corner of the screen. He inputted the proper access code. DALL NYSP flashed onto the upper-left-hand corner of the screen. He inputted the pedigree and depressed the PA 1 button. A line of symbols appeared across the top of the screen: RNAM, NYSP, ORI/NY U3U30F1. The PF 3 button was then depressed and a display peeled onto the console, limning the screen with the financial profile of Whitney Zangline, a white male, age 55, assistant chief, NYPD.

Whitney Zangline was a wealthy man.

Morris Dunbar chewed the end of his cigar. Tawny snippets of tobacco splotched his lips and his teeth were coated with a brownish slime. He turned sideways. "Want a copy?"

"Yes," Malone said, thinking that cops will never learn. After the Gross and Knapp investigations into police corruption you'd think that they would hide their money. But they don't. Dishonest men never think that they will be found out.

Morris Dunbar inputted the print code and depressed the PF 3 button. The spoked wheels on the sides of the printer sprang to life, churning out an endless stream of four-ply paper.

Whitney Zangline was a remarkably wealthy man.

Eighteen minutes later Malone was armed with computer printouts on Edwin Bramson and Joseph Stanislaus. They, too, were amazingly well off. The profile on Charles Kelly, patrolman, NYPD, remained a secret. Dunbar said that he needed a DOB or the Social Security number. Nevertheless, Malone assumed that Kelly, too, was a wealthy man.

Tourist buses were disgorging their cargoes on Elizabeth Street when he arrived back at the stationhouse. He paused in front of the steps to watch them. Wide-eyed and country clean they rushed off the buses into the waiting arms of the hawkers. Package tours, the theater, and egg rolls for sixty bucks, he thought, turning and entering the stationhouse.

Malone waved to the desk officer as he made for the stairway. He spotted Starling Johnson in the muster room talking to P.O. O'Day. He smiled and took the stairs two at a time.

Inspector Zambrano was standing by the window with his hands thrust into his pockets, rocking on his heels. He looked troubled. Malone crossed the squad room to him. "What's up?"

"I had lunch yesterday with my brother-in-law, the one in Audits and Accounts."

"And?"

"Whaddaya know about the financial administration of the Job?"

"I get paid every second Friday."

Zambrano turned and gripped the mesh window covering. "That's just about what most cops know." He launched into a long-winded dissertation on police department finances.

Before the end of each fiscal year the PC is required to submit the operating budget for the new year. Most of the lines are mandated expenses like salaries, rents, maintenance of equipment, telephone, electricity, heat, and gasoline. A cash fund is maintained to supply buy money, pay for sting operations, informers, and for travel expenses for members required to leave the city on official business. Whenever cash is needed, proper authorization accompanied with cash vouchers is submitted to Audits and Accounts. No commander is authorized to make purchases on his own. Everything must go through the deputy commissioner in charge of administration.

Malone said, "So? What has that got to do with the Eisinger caper?"

Zambrano faced him. "Zangline is running his own goddamn corporation. My brother-in-law told me that SOD has its own fund which Zangline controls. He is able to buy whatever he wants and he uses the fund to pay. That running track you saw in the SOD compound was built and paid for out of this special fund. He just purchased one hundred Uzi submachine guns and twenty-five silencers."

Malone said, "Where does the money come from?"

"Zangline draws checks on the account of the Simonson Optical Division. A Netherlands Antilles corporation. The checks clear through the Willemsteal Bank of Curaçao."

Malone let out a long, low whistle. "Simonson Optical Division. SOD, the acronym for the Special Operation Division."

"Sounds like that, doesn't it," Zambrano said.

"Any idea where the money comes from?"

"Not an iota."

"If Zangline is into something illegal, why would he have to use the department to make purchases?"

"What better way to hide something. And there is Title Eighteen, the United States Code. Under the Gun Control Act of 1968 corporations and individuals are prohibited from owning machine guns without obtaining federal permits and paying a special tax. Silencers are contraband except for government agencies and the police. And"—he shook a finger at him—"police departments do not pay taxes. A lot of money can be saved by making purchases through the department."

Malone took out the computer printouts and shoved them at him. "Read these."

They told a story of policemen without debts. Of savings accounts far in excess of earnings, of real-estate holdings, private schools, of automobiles without chattel mortgages; policemen with paychecks without any deductions for the Municipal Credit Union. Zambrano handed the printouts back, a scowl of disgust on his face. "What is your next move?"

"I have a command appearance with the chief of Op at five P.M. after which I have to go . . ." His voice trailed off and he moved across the room to where O'Shaughnessy was typing a five.

"Go and what?" Zambrano said, wry.

"Aw, nothing," Malone said lamely, looking over O'Shaughnessy's shoulder.

"Go and what, Lieutenant?"

Malone's eyes narrowed and his face became hard.

Zambrano said, "There ain't no stars in this job, Dan. We're all character actors."

Reluctantly he told him of the telephone call and his 11 P.M. rendezvous at Glen Cove Road.

"And you're going?" Zambrano said.

"Uh-huh."

"Alone?"

"Uh-huh."

"That's real clever. I assume that it just might have crossed your mind that you'll be driving into a setup."

"I thought about it."

"Well to put your mind at ease, I'm going with you."

Malone started to protest. Zambrano shot out a hand in front of him. "Save your breath. That's an order."

Zambrano walked over and looked down at O'Shaughnessy.

The detective wore an angry expression and was typing as though he had a life-long vendetta going with the typewriter. "What got into him?" Zambrano asked Malone.

Malone shrugged his shoulders. "He has a personal problem."

O'Shaughnessy looked up at the inspector. "Did you ever stop to realize that life ain't nothing but a shit sandwich?"

Zambrano folded his arms across his chest and pondered the remark. "Well. I'll tell you somethin' young fellow. You might as well be happy, 'cause no one gives a fuck if you're not."

The tripod of the one-on-one camera straddled the diaphragm on the bathroom floor. O'Shaughnessy peered into the wide lens, centering the crosshairs of the viewfinder on the fingerprint. In the bedroom, Johnson was spreading black powder over the top of a highboy. Knees bent eye level, he carefully spread the adhesive powder with the plumed end of a dusting brush. He could see the powder clinging to the friction ridges, making them visible against the wood background. He returned the brush to its assigned place inside the fingerprint kit and removed three pieces of rubber lifting tape. After he peeled off the celluloid covering from the adhesive side, he carefully placed the tape over the latent fingerprint and pressed it evenly and firmly to the surface, taking care not to shift its position. Snipping one end, he gently peeled the tape away from the surface. Examining the lift, he was able to distinguish three fingers—a forefinger, middle, ring.

He placed the tape inside a plastic envelope and clipped it inside the kit.

A partial palm print and several more fingerprints were lifted off the highboy. After all the lifts were secured in the kit, he reached into the bottom and took out a battery-operated hand vacuum and cleaned all traces of powder from the dresser and floor.

Malone was leaning against the bedroom wall pondering the dimensions of the queen-size bed. He was deeply uncomfortable at the thought of Sara Eisinger making it with Stanislaus on that bed. To his mind, it just did not ring true. A woman reared in the laws of Abraham, a woman who cleansed herself in the prescribed way, would not hop into the feathers with a gentile cop. The more he thought about it, the more it bothered him.

As Malone and his men worked silently inside Stanislaus's apartment, a telephone repair truck was parked outside the SOD compound. Stanislaus, Bramson, and Kelly had been followed into the compound.

If the trio left the compound the detectives inside the repair truck would radio a warning that would be passed over the phone in the apartment to Malone.

The search warrant was in Malone's pocket, officially, unexecuted. He wanted to wait until the fingerprints lifted from the apartment were compared with those lifted from the Eisinger crime scene. If there was a match he would return and execute the warrant officially. The proverbial cat should remain in the bag as long as possible, or nails in the coffin, as Epstein had said.

One Police Plaza is an orange brick mass that resembles a Rubik's cube on stilts. It is a building renowned for its conference rooms. There are small ones with small tables, medium-size ones with medium-size tables, and still larger ones with great tables. There are no executive toilets or dining rooms to differentiate the proletariat and bourgeoisie. There are only the conference rooms.

It was into one of the larger rooms that a female sergeant with a head of thick red hair ushered Malone at five o'clock that afternoon. "The chief will be with you in a minute or two," she said, casting a pitying look at him.

White Formica paneled the walls and red cushioned chairs were arranged around the oval-shaped table. Photographs of former Chiefs of Operations hung on the walls. He moved from frame to frame looking at the dour faces. When he had first come on the Job the Chief of Op was called the Chief Inspector. A lot of changes, a lot of years.

He went over to the window and pushed a vertical blind aside. Far below the evening rush hour was congealing into the usual traffic jam. The FDR Drive was packed bumper-to-bumper, cars spilled off the Brooklyn Bridge blocking Worth Street, and the noise of traffic reached up and penetrated the thermopane. He could see the people rushing into the subway under the archway of the Municipal Building, steeling themselves for the perilous journey home.

The rattle of a doorknob caused him to turn. Joe Mannelli was standing in the doorway, surveying him coldly, his face expressionless, the eyes wide and sullen.

Neither man spoke.

Malone went over to the table and sat down, his gaze riveted on the man in the doorway. Without uttering one word, Mannelli pivoted to the left and slammed the door. So that was how it was to be—a stress interview. Do things to fray his nerves; keep him waiting. Well, two could play at the same game.

At 6:48 P.M. Chief of Operations McQuade entered the room with a manila folder snug under his arm. He glanced at the nodding lieutenant and moved quickly to his place at the head of the table.

Malone opened his eyes, saw him, and eased his back to attention.

The four gilt stars on his shoulders glittered as brightly as the rims of McQuade's gold-rimmed glasses. "So, Lieutenant, we meet at last. I have been hearing your name quite a lot these days."

Malone cleared his throat. "I hope favorably, Chief."

McQuade opened the folder and removed a stack of evaluation reports. He read from them. "Lieutenant Malone is a loyal and competent commander. He is forthright and tenacious in carrying out his responsibilities and is rated above average."

Malone listened with interest.

McQuade read the summaries of eight evaluations. He then tapped them together and returned them to the folder, flipping the cover closed.

McQuade gazed impassively down the length of the table. "It appears that your superiors in the Detective Division consider you a loyal and competent subordinate. Do you agree with their assessment?"

Malone saw the rancor in the tightly pressed lips and was wary. "I've always tried to do my job," he said.

"Have you now? Tell me, Lieutenant. How would you define the adjective *loyal*?"

Malone thought of a response. "Fidelity to the job and its bosses."

McQuade slapped his hands down with such force that his eyeglasses popped off his face. He was on his feet, screaming. "Then why the hell are you trying to destroy this department? Mannelli warned you. Zangline warned you. But no! You persist in blunderbussing through the Job, raking up all kinds of shit. You listen and listen good. Lay off this department or I'll ruin you. I'll flop you out of the Bureau so fast that your eyeballs will dance. You got that, Malone?"

Malone looked him in the eye. "I won't dump the Eisinger case."

McQuade was furious. "Do you really think you're so goddamn perfect? Have you ever made a score? Ate on the arm? Nobody in this job is untouchable. When we want you, your ass is ours." He spilled the contents of the folder and started to shuffle through the pile. He snatched up a sheet of paper and waved it at him. "The statute of limitations for a felony is five years. But we both know that there is no statute in the Trial Room. It's a Kangaroo Court. Everyone on the Job knows that. I have here information that you arranged for an out-of-state abortion ten years ago. You committed a felony."

Mannelli, you dirty son-of-a-bitch, Malone thought.

McQuade continued. "I could serve you with charges and specifications. Conduct unbecoming an officer and prejudicial to the good order and efficiency of the department. And, I can guarantee the outcome. You would be dismissed."

Malone forced a smile. "A stunt like that would never stand under judicial review and you know it."

McQuade leaned forward. "Maybe it would, and maybe it wouldn't. Whenever you go into court it's a crap shoot. And, a legal fight could cost you twenty-five large, out of your own pocket. Line organizations do not pick up the tab for appeals from administrative decisions. Can you afford that kind of money, Lieutenant?"

Malone nodded grimly and got up.

"I will tell you when this meeting is over," McQuade shouted.

Malone continued toward the door, sweat trickling under his armpits. He was reaching for the knob when McQuade's hoarse voice caused him to turn.

"You just won't stop, will you?"

"I can't," he said quietly.

The expression on McQuade's face became benign. He patted the chair next to him. "Come here and sit down."

Malone hesitated, unsure.

"Please."

The careful tread back was filled with reflections. It ain't easy going up against the system. Many have tried it; few have succeeded.

McQuade was wiping his forehead with a handkerchief when Malone lowered himself next to him. "You think that all the life-and-death decisions are made in the street," he said, heaving to one side and tucking the white cotton cloth into his back pocket. "Well, let me tell you that they're not. Don't think for one minute that working in this pressure cooker is any bargain. The right wants us to kill the niggers and spicks and arm the cops with bazookas and flame throwers. The left wants us to countenance anarchy, riot, and murder. The politicians see the size of the police budget and salivate. They want lateral entry for their cronies." His right hand was chopping the air. "No more captains and lieutenants. They want civilian managers in charge of police operations. A pork barrel like the Board of Ed. Just take a look at what's happening in the Job today. We have cops with yellow sheets. Cops who cannot communicate in the English language. We're forced to hire females. Some of them don't weigh a hundred pounds soaking wet; they can't reach the accelerators of radio cars; don't have the physical strength to pull the trigger of their service revolvers. We were forced to lower the height requirement to accommodate women and Hispanics. We're becoming a department of goddamn dwarfs. Juggling interest groups and somehow keeping the department in one piece is no easy task." He picked up his eyeglasses and started to tap them against his teeth, his crafty eyes holding him. "Now I am going to tell you why you must drop the Eisinger case." He moved close and confided, "This department is involved in a covert operation that is so sensitive that its exposure would mean the end of the Job as we know it. And that, Lieutenant, is all that I can tell you. You are going to have to trust me."

Malone was cold. He fought a shiver. "Zangline is running this operation?"

"Yes."

"And what do we do about Eisinger, Andrea St. James, and the two kids who died with her on the Van Wyck. Just forget about them?"

McQuade steepled his hands under his chin. "I give you my personal guarantee that no member of this department had anything to do with those deaths."

Malone covered his face with his hands and rubbed tired pupils. "Exactly what do you want me to do?" he said, dropping knuckles to the table.

"Forget any connection this department has to the Eisinger caper. Don't be a party to the destruction of this great department."

A tired man nodded his assent.

McQuade sighed relief. "Good. You don't have the money, do you?"

Malone knew that this particular piece of police argot referred to the designation of a detective supervisor as a commander of detectives and carried with it a five-thousand-dollar yearly increment.

"No, I don't."

"I'm going to put you in for the money."

A bribe by any other name is still a bribe, Malone thought. Aloud, "Thank you, Chief."

Two things had caught his attention when he examined the fingerprint card. The first was the biting smell of death impregnated in the fibers of the paper itself. The second was the empty pedigree boxes on the top. Blocked across the head of the form was: HOMICIDE, SARA EISINGER.

The digital impressions looked like a worn parchment of loops and whorls with big uneven spaces where the skin was gone. They had cleaned her fingers with xyline but the flesh was rotten and flabby. So they cut off the tips of her fingers and soaked them in a 15 percent solution of formaldehyde to harden the ridges. Then they took them out and inked and rolled them. Poor Sara. Her only legacy was a filing formula deduced by counting her ridges and tracing her whorls:

$$4 \ 0 \ 5ulol \ 12$$
$$I \ 17w100$$

She no longer had a name. Only a formula. Poor dead Sara.

The Identification Section was on the fifth floor. Before he kept his appointment with McQuade, Malone had delivered the latent prints lifted from Stanislaus's apartment to a friend in the I.D. section. "Need a favor, ol' buddy."

That had been at 4:20 P.M.

Now he left the Chief of Op, pushed through the heavy fire-exit door, and entered the stairwell, a spiral of metal steps that wound down through a vast open shaft. He needed to vent his rage. "The mother is going to get me the money," he said angrily, rushing down the steps.

The DOA fingerprint form, the lifts from the crime scene, and the blowups of the fingerprints from Stanislaus's apartment were clamped together on a comparison board back at his office. Black lines indicated the similar points of comparison: a dot, a bifurcation, an abrupt ending ridge, a short ridge, a meeting of two ridges, a core, a delta.

The prints off the plastic case and diaphragm matched Eisinger's left thumb and forefinger. There were eighteen points of comparison. The prints taken off the highboy matched up with those lifted at the crime scene. Fourteen points of comparison.

Malone had just hammered some more nails into a coffin.

18

A hooker pushed away from the building on Crescent Street and walked over to the car. She stopped a few feet away and began to scan the interior. She saw no radio under the dashboard; no official forms scattered over the rear seat; no coffee containers with the lids on. Her streetwise eyes went to the driver. Just another john who dashed out for a pack of cigarettes and a quart of milk, she decided. She ambled over and smiled.

"Hi, sugar. You goin' out?"

"How much for a blow job?"

"Twenty, honey."

"Make it ten."

"Fifteen and I'll give you a real good one."

"Okay."

She pranced around the front of the car to the passenger side. She hesitated and shot a look over the top of the car at another strolling prostitute. Her "sister" saw her signal and nodded. The license plate number and a description of the john had been noted. Street insurance against freaks.

She jerked the door open and slid inside.

Det. Patrick O'Shaughnessy handed her fifteen dollars.

"Go down Crescent and turn into Forty-fourth Street," she directed. "Park in front of a truck and then back your car up against it." She put the fifteen dollars in a large pocketbook and removed a handful of tissues. She placed the bag on the floor and locked it between her ankles. Sliding next to him, she draped her left arm around his shoulder and with her right hand started to circle his groin.

"Hmmm. It's nice and big," she said, working the zipper down.

O'Shaughnessy made a quick check. All the buttons were down. The motor was running and the window on the driver's side was cracked inches from the top.

She cupped the tissues in the palm of her right hand and moved her mouth down to meet his body.

Fifteen minutes later her head was still bobbing, the tissues unused. She stopped and looked up.

"You been drinking, honey?"

"No." He felt disgusted.

"Well, sugar. I can't make you come. If you want me to continue, it's going to cost you another ten. Can't spend all night on one trick."

"I'm not in the mood anyway." He pushed her head away, arched upward, and hoisted his zipper.

"Sure, sugar. I understand," she said, returning the tissues to her pocketbook.

He let her out of the car at Hunter and Twenty-seventh. He felt awful. He felt angry, inadequate, lonely, and disgusted. He pounded the steering wheel.

"I can't even get it off with a nigger hooker," he cried.

The traffic light on Twenty-seventh and Bridge Plaza South turned red. Garishly dressed hookers lolled at the corners, beckoning to motorists. Transvestites swaggered up and down Twenty-seventh Street. Standing in the shadows were the pimps, their hard eyes fixed on the hookers they had on the charge.

"I'm right down on their level," he cried, violently shaking the wheel.

The light changed to green.

Suddenly he couldn't breathe. His hands were clammy and he felt nauseated. He tugged at his shirt. He had driven halfway across Bridge Plaza when a bolt of pain struck. He felt a wave of agony in his left arm. He clutched at his chest and gasped for air.

Startled motorists wrenched their wheels to avoid his car as it veered across Bridge Plaza. O'Shaughnessy's automobile jumped the curb, careened along the sidewalk, and plowed through the glass façade of a luncheonette.

The pain was gone. Everything was black and still.

He and Zambrano had just about finished their lasagna when Gino came up to their table and told Malone he had a phone call. It was Bo Davis. "Pat is in the emergency room of Elmhurst General."

*   *   *

"O'Shaughnessy, Patrick," Malone shouted to the woman inside the reception cubicle.

"Down the hall and to your right," she said, leaning out and pointing.

They rushed along the crowded corridor, threading their way past the miseries of the day. Malone banged through a pair of double doors with a thick rubber apron and plunged into the cardiac emergency ward. A black male nurse with muscles pushing against his white nylon uniform blocked his path. "You are not allowed in here, gentlemen."

Malone dug out his shield. "One of my men was brought in here," he said and gave O'Shaughnessy's name.

"They are in with him now," the nurse said. He pointed to a door with a small window in the center.

The two policemen walked over and looked through the glass. The room was divided into private cubicles by curtains. O'Shaughnessy lay on a gurney, his feet over the edge. Tubes ran from his body up to plastic bags. Wires fed from his arm and chest into a series of pulsating monitors. A group of doctors and nurses hovered over him and fought to save his life. Malone composed himself. For some reason he watched O'Shaughnessy's big toe, expecting it to move. It never did.

"For all his macho bullshit he was a lonely man," Malone said, backing away.

"He shouldn't have lived like he did after hours," Zambrano said.

A voice called to them. "You guys from the Squad?" A hatless police officer had pushed his way inside and was standing behind them. He was in his twenties, with black, curly hair, big bulging brown eyes, and a mouth full of horsy teeth. The three top buttons of his shirt were open. A gold rope chain coiled around his neck and a ball of gold pierced his left ear.

Zambrano showed him his shield. The policeman took hold of the inspector's wrist and pulled him close, examining the shield. "Hey, man. That's cool. I've never seen an inspector's up close before. I really dig the big bird on top."

Malone turned and swallowed a smile. Zambrano snapped back his hand and shook his head with disbelief.

The cop said, "We invoiced his gun and shield in the One-fourteen. We did everything we could for him."

"Thanks," Malone said.

"We were able to get his home telephone number off his ten card. His wife told the desk officer that she didn't give a damn what happened to him."

"They were getting a divorce," Malone said.

"Another one down the tubes," the cop said. "I've been in the batter's box twice."

Zambrano looked at his watch and nudged Malone. "Gotta go. We got an appointment on the LIE."

Malone went back for a final look. A nurse was bending over the gurney adjusting a tube. Her uniform rode up in the back. She had long legs and nice thighs. She was top heavy. Pat would have given her a solid eight.

They sped east on the Long Island Expressway in an unmarked police car. Saplings lined the slopes and grass glistened with dew. A full moon lingered in a star-filled sky.

The next green illuminated sign they saw read DOUGLASTON PARKWAY. Five minutes later they passed another sign: NASSAU COUNTY. The panorama changed. The massive housing complexes of Queens were gone, as well as the constant glow of the city. The night was darker and more ominous.

At Shelter Rock Road there was a stone overpass. A black car hid behind its south base, parked uphill on the sweep of land. Joseph Stanislaus and Edwin Bramson had unwittingly shaken off Harrigan's men by making a precautionary U-turn in the middle of the Queensborough Bridge. They sat in the front seat of the black car and checked each passing automobile with a night-vision handscope. They would recognize a department vehicle, and they both knew Malone. They had seen him at the SOD compound.

Malone glanced sideways. "There was really no need for you to tag along."

"I enjoy playing cop. My time in the Job is almost over and I'd like to get in a few more licks before I leave."

"When do you have to put your papers in?"

"I have three more years," he said.

"You have a lot of friends on the Job. They'll take care of you."

Zambrano roared with laughter. He leaned close to Malone. "When you're in, you're a guest; when you're out, you're a pest. Remember that."

Malone scoffed. "I've heard that one from a lot of old-timers who were getting out."

Zambrano sliced the air with a karate chop. "When your time comes, walk through the door and don't look back. One fast, clean break."

"Any plans?"

"I'll more than likely end up in Florida with the rest of the retirees. Probably spend my days bullshitting about the Job and taking poolside cha-cha lessons in Bermuda shorts, argyle socks, and black-laced shoes."

"With your background and experience? Private industry will scoop you up."

They didn't notice when the black car rolled down from behind the base of the overpass and fell in several lengths behind them.

Stanislaus picked up the walkie-talkie and transmitted a description of the unmarked car and its occupants.

Edwin Bramson was driving. "There is someone in the car with him."

Stanislaus said, "That's his tough luck. Get off at the next exit and head back to the City."

At Willis Avenue an eighteen-wheel tractor-trailer idled on the service road, its chattering diesel emitting a black cloud. Two short, muscled men sat inside the cab. Stanislaus's message had been received. The two men were watchful. Ready.

Zambrano pulled up the headrest and leaned back. "In a way I'm glad to be getting out. The Job is really going downhill fast."

"How so?"

"You saw that cop back in the hospital. Shirt open, no tie, a necklace around his neck, and to top it off a fucking earring stuck through his goddamn ear. Can you imagine that, a New York City cop with an earring. Next thing you know they'll be putting on rouge and eye shadow."

Malone smiled. "Times change. Cops aren't so uptight about being on the Job."

"Come on, Dan. Earrings? Where the hell is the discipline?"

"It's still there. Only it's less formal."

"That is a crock of shit and you know it. Did you hear what happened last week in the One-twelve?"

"No."

Zambrano sat up and shifted his weight onto one side of his rump and leaned toward him. "A late tour. Sunday going into Monday. The sergeant on patrol can't locate sector Ida-Mary. They weren't answering his eighty-fives. The sergeant starts to mosey around the heaves. His RMP cruises into Macy's parking lot on Queens Boulevard. The building is built in the shape of a beehive with circular ramps running top to bottom. Near the roof he spots a turret light sticking up over a ramp. he tells his driver to stop and he gets out and walks over." Zambrano punched the dashboard. "And what do you think the good sergeant found? He found Police Officer Debra Bowden wearing only her open uniform shirt with one leg up on the dashboard and the other hooked over the front seat. And would you like to know where her partner was? Police Officer Frank Watson."

Malone was grinning broadly. "Where, Inspector?"

"With his face in her muff, eating her. On duty. In a police car. And do you know what she had the balls to tell the sergeant?"

"That they were on their meal period," Malone cackled with laughter.

"That's right. Howd'ya know that?"

"Because that's what I would have said."

As the two policemen talked, the tractor-trailer behind them resolutely closed the distance. When it drew parallel with the police car the driver wrenched the wheel and turned the massive cab toward the passenger door. It rammed into the police car and plowed it across the parkway, smashing it into the road divider.

"Watch out!" Zambrano screamed, too late.

As Malone fought the wheel, the unmarked car bounced off the divider, its doors and side panels crumpled inward, and then Malone regained control. The semi continued the pursuit, its bumper homing in on the rear of the automobile.

Zambrano opened his window, thrust his revolver at the approaching beast and fired six rounds double action into the cab. The tractor-trailer backed off. Zambrano opened the cylinder and plunged out the spent rounds. He reloaded from the ammo pouch on his belt.

Every time their pursuers got close enough to ram, Malone had been able to turn the car in the opposite direction and dart to safety. Now it was on them again, a lizard snapping its forked tongue. Malone swerved the car to the right. It was still with them, its mass casting a deadly shadow over the hood of the police car. It plowed into them. The two rear tires of the police car came off and went spinning across the highway. The car spun helplessly, its undercarriage screeching over the concrete, throwing out a fusillade of sparks. Finally it slammed into the road abutment.

"Get out!" Zambrano cried.

The door on the driver's side was crushed, the windows shattered but still in place. Malone kicked out the front window and started to climb out onto the hood. Zambrano lay back across the seat and kicked the door open. He threw himself out and got to his feet in time to face the charging monster. He turned and saw Malone crawling over the hood on all fours. Assuming a combat stance, Zambrano cocked his revolver, aimed, and fired single action at the driver.

At that precise moment in his life Nicholas Zambrano did not think of issues like life or death. His thoughts were of honor. He could hear his father calling to him. "Nicholas, conduct your life with honor. We are Italians. Ours is an honorable and proud heritage."

Malone was almost off the hood when the tractor smashed into Zambrano, propelling his body off into the night. The semi continued its run, smashing into the car and hurling Malone into the air.

The tractor-trailer backed away from the smoldering wreck and stopped. Although the traffic on the expressway had been very light at the start of the battle, it was now backed up in both directions. Motorists gaped in horror, but none got out to help.

The cab's door swung open on the passenger side and Achmed Hamed, the man who had telephoned Malone at Stanislaus's behest, climbed down. He looked across the highway at the smashed body that was once Zambrano and smiled. They had done their work well. He took out a Heckler & Koch P9S pistol from his waistband and ran for the road divider. Looking over, he saw Malone's body splayed out and motionless. His right arm was bent under his chest and his left was alongside the body with palm up. The head lay in a pool of blood.

Achmed Hamed tucked the pistol back in his waistband and started to climb over the steel divider.

He knew that Stanislaus would ask him if he made sure that Malone was dead. He wanted no problems from him.

Achmed Hamed's right foot had just touched the other side of the divider when Malone whipped up, a .38 Detective Special in his right hand. He shoved the revolver at the frozen man and quick-fired three rounds. In that split second Achmed Hamed knew that he was about to die. He stared down with disbelief at the growing crimson stain. He started to claw at his shirt. He saw the three puffy holes in his stomach and slowly, against his will, corkscrewed to his knees.

Malone approached the kneeling man at the ready. He cocked his right leg and kicked the man in the face, toppling Achmed Hamed into eternal darkness.

Malone was only dimly conscious of what happened after that. He vaguely recalled leaning on the divider and firing his revolver at disappearing taillights. He could recall the warm, thick liquid seeping over his trousers and chilling his thighs as he sat cross-legged on the expressway cradling the body of Nicholas Zambrano. The smells of hot metal and blood made him vomit. He did not hear the excited CBers shouting into their sets. A parhelion of rotating lights came toward him. The taste of tears mixed with blood in his mouth. Most of all he could feel an awful sense of irreplaceable loss.

19

Malone opened his eyes and almost cried out, conscious for the first time of pain, first in his neck and shoulder, then in his rib cage. There was an awful throbbing ache inside his head. He moved his hand out from under the sheet and let his fingertips gingerly probe the gauze. He had landed on his head, causing a long gash in the hairline.

"It took sixty-eight stitches to close you up," Gus Heinemann said in a small voice.

Malone's eyes drifted to the two men looking down at him. Heinemann and Bo Davis. He could see the concern in their faces.

"Where am I?" A dry mutter.

"Nassau Hospital," Davis said. "You're going to be all right."

"Zambrano?" Malone asked, without any hope in his voice.

Bleak expressions gave him an answer. He was seized with a consuming rage to kill, to deal out tough street justice. The detectives pretended not to notice when he brushed his arm across his face to rub his eyes dry. He forced himself up into a sitting position and cleared his throat. "Whattaya got?"

Heinemann slapped open his memo pad and began to read in laconic police prose. "Tractor-trailer found abandoned at Guinea Woods Road. Nassau County PD dusted for prints. Negative results. Vehicle reported stolen yesterday from Hunts Point Market, alarm 14061-52. There were tire tracks next to the vehicle which indicate that an escape car was waiting. Nassau County PD made plaster casts of the tracks. A canvass was conducted of the motorists caught in the spillback. The police came up with twenty-eight names and twenty-eight different descriptions. The hump you iced was I.D.'d as Achmed Hamed. He entered the country on a tourist visa from Libya on May twelfth, 1976 and pulled a Mandrake. The duty captain from the One-oh-five responded to the scene. Captain McCormick. He prepared the 'Unusual' and the 'Line of Duty Injury Report.' The 'Assault/Firearm Discharge Report' was made out. McCormick found your use of deadly physical force to be within department guidelines. The PC and the Chief of Op were on the scene." Heinemann looked up from his pad. "That's it."

Malone recalled the five that he had read from one of Harrigan's detectives. Stanislaus had visited a grocery store on Atlantic Avenue. Achmed Hamed's store. "How long have I been out?"

Davis said, "About twelve hours."

Malone groaned as he swung his legs out and over the side of the bed. He sat up, doubling over and hugging himself in a futile effort to relieve the pain. "How's Pat?" he grunted.

Davis flinched at the sight of his pain. "They think he'll make it. But the job is finished. He's gonna be surveyed out."

Malone took in a large breath and slowly and painfully hissed it out. "What else?"

Heinemann said, "You have been page one. We gave the press the usual arrests-are-imminent bullshit. You're stashed here under a phony name." He waved his hand in front of him. "No sense giving them another shot at you."

Bo Davis said, "Jake and Starling managed to get inside Stanislaus's garage and plant a beeper under his car. The Braxtons, Kelly, Bramson, and Stanislaus have been very cautious since you got hurt. They seemed to have arranged a signaling schedule at various telephone booths around the city. One of them must have gone around copying down locations and numbers."

Malone said, "What about the telephone outside Braxton's apartment?"

Heinemann said, "None of them have gone near it."

Malone stared at his feet.

Heinemann said, "Sergeant Harrigan has taken over in your absence. He detailed us to guard you. He has the rest of the team out following suspects. I checked with him a few minutes ago. He told me that some sort of meet is going down. Aldridge Braxton, Kelly, Stanislaus, and Bramson have all hit the bricks. They're scurrying around town, keeping both eyes over their shoulders."

"Jack is a good man," Malone said, easing himself off the bed.

Davis and Heinemann each took an arm and helped him.

"Where are my clothes?" Malone said.

"You ought'na leave," Davis said. "The doctor said . . ."

Malone cut him off. "My clothes."

Davis shrugged, as if to say You're the boss, and went over to the clothes cabinet. "I went to your place and got some things. The clothes that you were wearing were ruined." Davis took out a pair of brown corduroy trousers, a white pullover, and an Irish poplin sport jacket. He bent down and picked up a pair of penny loafers and underwear.

Untying the loose-fitting hospital gown, Malone said, "My gun and shield?"

"Vouchered at the One-oh-five," Heinemann said.

Stepping into his briefs was painful. He pulled them up slowly. "Who made the notification to Zambrano's wife?"

Davis said, "The PC and the Catholic chaplain."

"How'd she take it?" Malone asked.

"I hear real bad," Heinemann said.

Davis got on one knee and helped him on with his socks.

He looked up at Malone's grimacing face. "Erica Sommers has been calling the Squad every hour on the hour. She is really concerned about you. Naturally, we didn't tell her where you were."

Heinemann said, "Want me to dial her number for you?"

Malone looked at the telephone on top of the white hospital stand. "I've got more important things to do right now." There was a soft, menacing lilt to his voice.

A lash of warm air slapped Aldridge Braxton's face as he stood in the middle of York Avenue waiting for a break in the traffic. He was sure that he was not being followed. When the opening presented itself, he made his way to the other side and stood on the curb checking. Even confident men do not take chances.

A stocky middle-aged man came around the corner on the other side of York Avenue. He had on pilot-type sunglasses and was carrying a yellow sun hat in his left hand. He walked in a slow, unhurried gait, like a shopper searching the window displays.

The man with the yellow sun hat came upon a florist who had taken up half the sidewalk with his wares. He bent to examine them more closely. He picked up a gloxinia and held it up in front of him admiring its luscious purple buds. He shifted his gaze to the impeccably dressed man a block away. He held the clay pot with one hand and with the other depressed the transmit button on the walkie-talkie that was concealed inside the sun hat. "He is walking north on York. Just past Sixty-ninth Street."

A blue Sting Ray pulled up to the corner of Seventy-first Street facing York. The driver was in his middle thirties and had eyebrows that ran a straight line. The passenger was older and completely bald. His taut skin gave him a plastic look. The driver scowled with displeasure. "Here he comes," he said into the walkie-talkie.

Jake Stern was driving the gray van while Johnson, in the rear of the van, studied the signal motes as they bounced across the direction grid.

"How far ahead is he?" Harrigan said, as they emerged from the Brooklyn Battery Tunnel.

"About a quarter of a mile," Johnson answered.

Joseph Stanislaus came out of the tunnel on the Brooklyn side and wormed his way out of the exact-change line into a toll collector's lane.

The toll plaza was crowded. Stanislaus kept examining the faces of motorists. He had the uncomfortable sensation of being followed. He wished he had been out there on the LIE that night. Why did it have to be Zambrano and not Malone?

When he reached the toll booth he rolled down his window to show the collector his shield. "I'm on the job. I got into the wrong lane in Manhattan and ended up here. Any chance of turning me around? My wife is waiting for me at the Vista."

The collector leaned out to look at the shield. "No problem." He walked from the booth over to the traffic cones that separated the lanes. He kicked away four cones and then halted the queue entering the tunnel from the Brooklyn side. He turned to Stanislaus and waved him to make a U-turn through the space.

"He's doubling back on us," Starling Johnson shouted, a note of alarm in his voice.

"Stop the van," Harrigan ordered. "If we came out of the tunnel now he is bound to see us. He might recognize the van. We should wait until he is back inside the tunnel."

A sudden cacophony of horns reverberated throughout the white-tiled tunnel as bumpers rear-ended bumpers.

Edwin Bramson drove his car over the George Washington Bridge and onto the Palisades Parkway. Charles Kelly was turned in the passenger seat looking out the rear window for any car that had been with them for too long a period of time.

Bramson said, "Anyone on us?"

"Don't think so," Kelly replied, not taking his eyes from the window. "There was a taxi with us for a while but he turned off at Fort Lee."

Bramson said, "There is a rest area up ahead where we can pull in. We'll take in the view and at the same time watch the road. Then just to make sure we'll drive into Nyack before we turn around. It shouldn't be too hard to spot a tail."

"Them camel humpers really fucked things up. We shoulda handled it ourselves," Kelly said.

"What we shoulda done and what we done are two different things," Bramson said, turning on some music.

A taxi exited the bridge's quickway in Fort Lee. The driver leaned over and opened the glove compartment, pulling out a radio handset. "Bird Two to Nest, K."

Inside the surveillance van Jack Harrigan plucked the microphone from the hook. "Nest. Go ahead, K."

"Subjects drove over the G.W. Bridge into Jersey. They are now proceeding north on the Palisades Parkway. Bird Two continued into Fort Lee. If I had stayed with them much longer they would have made me for sure."

Harrigan toed the metal floor. "Where are Birds One and Two, K?"

"Both waiting on the New York side of the bridge. We figured that whatever was going to go down would go down in New York. It stands to reason that once they feel safe they are going to double back."

"I hope you're right, K." The frequency went quiet. Then Harrigan transmitted. "Bird Two, head back to our side of the bridge and ten-eighty-five Birds One and Three. When you reestablish contact with them I want you to use the leapfrog, but be sure to change the 'close contact car' frequently. I don't want to take any chances on losing these guys, K."

"Ten-four." The detective in the taxi returned the handset and slammed the lid shut.

Harrigan transmitted, "Nest to Birds One and Three. Did you read my last transmission, K?"

From inside the telephone repair truck that was parked on the New York side of the toll plaza came the transmission: "Bird One, ten-four."

Near the entrance of the FDR Drive a gypsy cab was stopped with its hood up. A black man was leaning under checking the carburetor. He picked up the paper bag that was lying on top of the battery and moved it toward his lips, "Bird Two, ten-four."

Starling Johnson did not permit his eyes to stray from the monitor. "Do you really think they'll come back into the City?" he asked Harrigan.

The sergeant's face was grim. With Malone in the hospital and Zambrano dead the whole weight of the case was on his back. The fact that they were going up against other cops was finally beginning to frighten him.

"They'll double back." He tried to sound convinced. Harrigan absent-mindedly depressed the transmit button several times and then snapped the microphone up to his mouth.

"Birds Four and Five, what are your locations, K?"

The detective with the plastic face inside the Sting Ray transmitted. "Bird Four is proceeding north on York. Just passing Seventy-fourth Street. Subject in view."

"Bird Five on foot, going north on York. Subject now turning into Seven-six Street."

An elegantly dressed woman looked with mild curiosity at the pot-bellied man jogging York Avenue and yelling at a yellow sun hat.

"Turn south. West. Lay back. We're too close. The signals are too strong. He is heading over to the East Side."

Starling Johnson sat before the tracking monitors in the van, the bombardier directing the ship, calling out coordinates.

Harrigan shouted out to Jake Stern, "If you can see him, we are too close."

"He's not in view," Stern piped, suddenly filled with a disquieting sense of insecurity at the sight of a bus gridlocking Tenth Avenue and blocking their path.

Harrigan rushed up front. "Why are you stopping?"

"That bus is blocking us," Stern said.

"The signals are getting weak," Johnson warned.

"Go around the cocksucker," Harrigan said.

The van leaped the curb. Stern blared the horn and pedestrians flattened themselves against the building. The van rounded the rear of the bus and plowed back into the roadway.

"Five Detective C.O. to Nest. What is your location, K?"

A momentary silence fell over the radio frequency. Starling Johnson turned away from the monitor and exchanged a quick smile with Harrigan. The sergeant grabbed the microphone.

"Is that you, Lou?"

"Ten-four. What is your location, K?"

"Eight and Five-two, heading east," Harrigan transmitted.

"On the way," Malone radioed without inflection.

"All right!" someone shouted happily over the restricted frequency.

The Pavilion is a luxury apartment complex with massive wood-paneled lobbies and spiring water fountains separated from the East River by the compact John Jay Park. Aldridge Braxton drew parallel with the Volkswagen dealer on Seventy-sixth Street and turned to cross to the other side of the street. A small group of liverymen were standing in front of the Pavilion's garage. Braxton glanced at them as he passed and continued on to his destination.

Braxton walked into the Seventy-sixth Street entrance of John Jay Park, an area of benches and trees that continued through to Seventy-seventh Street. He walked through and exited the park onto Seventy-seventh Street and Cherokee Place. He looked across the street at a building with an unusual façade of white stone and yellow brick. The apartment house had mullioned windows and buff fire escapes. He was interested in the arched ambulatories that led through the building on the corner of Cherokee Place to Seventy-eighth Street. If needed, they could be his escape hatch. He turned and looked around the park. Au pair girls and their wards, chic ladies with their custom jeans and expensive accessories, paddleball players using the handball courts, and a queue outside the bathhouse of people eager to use the Olympic-size pool represented normal activity. The bow of a freighter, its black riveted hull slicing the view, slid past Seventy-seventh Street.

Aldridge Braxton was not a particularly nervous man. But the force of recent events had changed that. He could almost reach out and touch the presence of danger. It was all supposed to have been so easy. Risk free, Stanislaus had told him. He should have known better. Now this meeting and the sudden precautions, the warnings only to use safe telephones. He felt almost physically ill.

Inside the surveillance van Jake Stern turned and glanced into the rear. "Hey, Sarge, will you take the wheel for a minute? I gotta piss so bad I can taste it."

Harrigan made his way out front and exchanged places with him.

Stern steered himself into the back and squeezed himself into the cramped toilet. Urinating into the waterless bowl, he shouted to Johnson. "How you makin' out with P.O. O'Day?"

"We're practically *mispocah*," Johnson said grinning.

Stern stepped out of the cubicle pulling up his zipper. "I'm glad that the boss is all right."

"Me too, ma man."

"Nest and Birds, what are your locations, K?" Malone's voice came over the wires.

"Five-two and Madison, heading east," Harrigan transmitted.

"Birds One, Two, and Three on FDR Drive," the detective in the gypsy cab transmitted.

"Bird Four is parked on the corner of York and Seventy-six. Subject has entered John Jay Park, K."

"Bird Five is on foot at Cherokee Place and Seventy-sixth Street. About to enter park. I am going off the air now."

Malone turned to Heinemann. "Looks like the meet is going down in the park."

Heinemann nodded. Bo Davis was in the rear of the car. He leaned forward and tapped Malone on the shoulder. "Braxton or one of the others might recognize the van."

Malone picked up the handset and transmitted. "Five C.O. to Nest, K."

"Go. Nest, K." Harrigan's voice.

"Nest. Bury the van nearby. They might spot it."

"Nest. Ten-four." Harrigan returned the microphone and reached up to the photographic cabinet above the radio set. He flipped the hasp and reached inside, removing two movie cameras. He placed them carefully on the ledge and then selected the correct telescopic lenses.

The van was buried among the jumble of sanitation trucks on Seventy-third Street and the River. Harrigan and Stern got out and walked over to the cavelike entrance of the sanitation garage to wait for Johnson, who was still inside the van securing the equipment. As they stepped out of the way of a lumbering garbage truck, Harrigan walkie-talkied their location to Malone. When Johnson joined them, the three men trotted to the apartment house on the corner of Seventy-seventh Street and Cherokee Place. They entered through the Seventy-eighth Street ambulatory and rushed up to the roof.

Peering down over the edge, the detectives had an unobstructed view of the park. Johnson used a waist-high vent to steady his camera. Stern gripped his camera against the side of the stairwell housing. They were careful not to go near the edge because a sudden movement could attract attention from below. Bird 5 was stretched out on a park bench, his head tilted back to catch the sun's rays.

They sat on a bench near the wading pool and watched Stanislaus pace back and forth in front of them. Stanislaus appeared to be tendering a lecture to backward students. The cameras could only record lip movements, and only when the actors faced them. Stanislaus looked gloomy. Bramson and Kelly would occasionally interrupt to say something. From time to time Braxton would look up and make a comment.

Harrigan transmitted their location to Malone. He cautioned the C.O. not to 10:85 them thereat. The meeting that was going on in the park might adjourn at any moment. One of the conferees might spot him when he was leaving the park.

The meeting inside John Jay Park lasted for another twenty-two minutes and then broke up. Bramson and Kelly were the first to get to their feet and leave. Braxton was next. Stanislaus lingered behind, watching them depart. When they had all gone, Stanislaus walked over to the edge of the park and stared down the precipice at the fast-moving water.

Bird 5 got to his feet and stretched, his arms a V over his head. He turned to his right and walked slowly out of the park.

Malone, Davis, and Heinemann were parked by the sanitation garage, waiting.

Harrigan, Stern, and Johnson were still on the roof watching Stanislaus watch the river.

Stern was the first one to notice the man walking close to the building line on Cherokee Place. The man crossed Seventy-seventh Street and stopped by the entrance of the park. He turned and let his eyes take in the windows and terraces of the Pavilion. He then turned his attention to the cars and vans that were parked nearby. Apparently satisfied that he was not being watched, the man turned back and made his way over to where Stanislaus was standing.

The man leaning over the fence turned and looked into the stern face of Chief Zangline.

"The piano tuner wants to see us," Zangline said, leaning his back to the fence and examining the park thoroughly.

Stanislaus turned. "When?"

"Now. And we better make damn sure that we're not followed," Zangline said.

The Cloister, an igloo-shaped restaurant with triple lancet windows and a groined ceiling, sits atop the heights of Tudor City. It took Zangline and Stanislaus the better part of three hours to reach the restaurant. Their extended journey took in the Staten Island ferry, a tour of Harlem, and a drink at the long bar of Windows of the World. At 6:20 P.M. Zangline's unmarked car rolled to a stop below the summit of Tudor City. Stanislaus tossed the Vehicle Identification Card on the dashboard and got out. While Stanislaus locked up the car, Zangline read the slogan painted on the stairway wall: HONOR NEW AFRIKAN FREEDOM FIGHTERS!

A Mercedes-Benz limousine was parked in front of the restaurant. A man in a dark suit and wearing a black chauffeur's cap stood nearby. When the man saw Zangline and Stanislaus he waved and walked over to them. There was a round of handshakes. Zangline touched the man on the shoulder and then he and Stanislaus turned and walked into the restaurant.

The surveillance van was parked a block away, its two-way reflectors facing the Cloister.

Malone pressed the transmit button. "Nest to Central, K."

"Go. Nest."

"A ten-fifteen on New York plate Oscar, Union, Charlie, four-eight-six: not holding."

The answer came in seconds. "Oscar, Union, Charlie four-eight-six comes out to a 1949 Mercedes-Benz limousine, color black; Vin number Frank, Oscar, George, eighty-seven David, one, zero, nine, zero, three, zero, Frank. That's a ten-seventeen all around. One minute and I will check NCIC."

Malone waited for Central's computer to check the stolen-vehicle data bank for the United States. His eyes cut to the chauffeur leaning against the fender and lighting a cigarette. The man' had the look of a moonlighting cop or a retiree.

"Central to Nest, K."

"Go. Central."

"NCIC is negative, K."

"Registered Owner, K?"

"Vehicle registered to Moorehouse International, Eighty-one Wall Street, New York City, K."

"Ten-four." Malone turned to Harrigan. "I want our people inside that restaurant."

Harrigan warned, "They'll be made. Zangline and Stanislaus can smell a cop up close."

Malone said, "Those two went to a lot of trouble to make sure they were not followed. I intend to know why." His head still ached and his eyeballs felt swollen. He could still taste the blood. He swallowed hard, forcing down the heave. He still had not telephoned Erica, but he promised himself that he would as soon as he could. One detective might get inside without being recognized. Who? He looked from man to man and his stare settled on Starling Johnson. "If you removed your jacket and tie and went around to the service entrance you would look like just another black dishwasher showing up for the evening rush."

"I'll give it a shot," said Johnson, tugging off his tie.

"Give 'em a little soul strut," Davis said, snapping his fingers and miming a swagger.

Malone said, "When you get inside tell them that the agency sent you. Most restaurants hire their dishwashers on a per diem basis from employment agencies."

"And then what do I do?" Johnson said.

"You're a detective—improvise," Malone said, taking his jacket.

20

Malone awakened with a start, not sure of where he was. He picked up the sound of a music box, and in the distance, the blare of fire engines. His body throbbed with pain and his eyeballs hurt. His tongue was caked dry. He rubbed his stubble and thought how nice it would be to feel Erica's thighs pressing against his face. He made a small smile and told himself that he must be getting better. Those thoughts were returning. He dabbed fingertips over his wound. He had removed the bandage. Someone had once told him that fresh air was the best thing to heal an injury. The sutures looked like long, black-legged creatures.

Malone checked the time: 8:15 P.M. His brow knitted into deep lines. Had he really slept that long? He had only intended to rest his head on the desk for a minute or two. The movie film was being developed and then rushed to the Concord School for the Deaf in the Bronx where students would read the subjects' lips and make transcripts of the conversations. One of the detectives had been dispatched to the telephone booth in front of Aldridge Braxton's house. Returning home directly after the meeting in John Jay Park, Braxton made a fast telephone call from the booth before he hurried into the lobby of his apartment house. The detectives in the Sting Ray had followed him home and seen him make his call.

There had been nothing for Malone to do but wait and think. Sometimes that gets to be the hardest part, waiting, thinking. Police texts discuss the connective-disconnective relationship to the trier of facts. It ain't that way. It's plodding the streets, barrooms, and strolls asking questions, calling in past favors. And then waiting, thinking.

His pupils felt like they were floating on ponds of molten lava. He rested his head in his hands. As he did his gaze went to the notes that he had jotted on the pad.

Carter Moorehouse of Moorehouse International, 81 Wall Street, New York City. He was the man Zangline and Stanislaus met in the restaurant.

Detective Johnson had indeed improvised. The black detective had walked into the kitchen of the restaurant unopposed. The help was too busy to take notice of another nigger who had come to clean dirty dishes for below the minimum wage. He walked through the kitchen and entered the locker room that was next to the meat freezer. He grabbed a service jacket from the hook, shrugged it on, and then pushed his way through the swinging doors into the dining room.

The detective spotted Stanislaus and Zangline sitting at a table within the main dining area. Johnson recognized the third man at the table—Carter Moorehouse. The same Carter Moorehouse who had stood for mayor.

As Malone looked over the notes on Johnson's visit to the restaurant, he became aware of just how much he knew about Moorehouse.

Carter Moorehouse's great grandfather made the family fortune in the China trade. The grandfather doubled it in railroads and the father tripled it in banking. The son, Carter, collected companies and other profitable things.

A Calvinist strain had always stiffened the Moorehouse clan and made them frighteningly rigid and vengeful people. It was said that the present patriarch was no exception.

Carter Moorehouse once made a bid for Gracie Mansion on the Conservative line. His defeat was the first of his lifetime and a humiliating one at that. Calvinism and Conservatism were not the in "isms" in New York City.

But if Moorehouse had not won the hearts of the voters, he had become a popular candidate with New York's Finest. He had pushed a very hard line on crime and made many intelligent suggestions about overhauling the entire criminal justice system. Even the *New York Times* had to grant him points for his long, thoughtful proposals on city financial reorganization. But as the campaign wore on, the crime issue seemed to evoke something deeply buried in Moorehouse, something more frightening and savage than the voters wanted to hear, even if a lot of them had similar private fantasies of revenge. Malone couldn't remember exactly when it happened, but the outspoken *Times* editorial against Moorehouse was brought on by his remarks, delivered off the record, at a meeting of the National Associations of Chiefs of Police in Washington. And from that point it had been downhill. Even the *National Review* had dropped him in embarrassment.

Malone tried to remember the specifics, the later speeches and doomed battles with the media that had characterized the last, desperate days of Moorehouse's campaign. But his recollections were too vague; he needed to find out a great deal more about this man, to study him the way he had been trained to study the motives and behavior patterns of criminals. As he sat in the semidarkness of his office, he was filled with a growing conviction that while the public Carter Moorehouse was made inaccessible to him by layers of money, class, and power, the private animal inside Moorehouse was like a lot of the ones he tried to take off the street and put in cages called prisons.

He thought of Zambrano. The wake would be tomorrow night. He had already decided not to attend. He wanted to avoid those curious, secret looks. Besides, he hated wakes. They were barbaric rituals that only served to enrich undertakers. The Jews had the right idea: plant them right away. He knew exactly what Zambrano's would be like. White-gloved policemen milling about whispering. A large room filled with foul-smelling flowers, stands, overflowing with mass cards, chalices, and vestments. An honor guard formed around the coffin. A priedieu that was never empty, an immediate member of the family hovering nearby to accept condolences. The body, cold and stiff and regaled in full uniform, the lips sewed into a death smile. Having to endure the endless, stupid asides: Doesn't he look wonderful; he looks just like he went to sleep, so natural.

Malone wanted no part of it. He would attend the mass and remember his friend as he was, not as a broken corpse smelling of formaldehyde and undertaker's cosmetics.

He leaned over and took the bottle of bourbon from the bottom drawer. He poured three fingers into a mug and toasted the empty chair. "Gendarme, my friend."

As soon as he gulped the drink his head started to spin and his stomach churn. All at once his mouth was filled with saliva. He clasped his hand across his mouth and stumbled from his office into the bathroom, a one-cubicle, one-urinal cubbyhole with a faded mirror that was splotched with soap and other substances.

He knelt in front of the bowl, one hand supporting his head, and vomited. Yellow green chunks. His eyes teared. The floor was cold. Brown dots caked the bowl. He heaved and heaved until there was nothing left to come up. His stomach was raw. Sore. He gripped the rim and hoisted himself up.

The basin was laced with dried suds and the one piece of soap was smudged black. He put his head under the faucet and turned on the cold water. Zambrano had been right; he was turning into a bum in a flophouse.

When he got back to his office he started to telephone around town trying to locate Jack Fine. He was not at his desk at the *Daily News*. He started to phone Fine's haunts. Vinny at Dangerfield's told him that he had not seen the reporter in a few days. He called P.J.'s, Dewy's, and Mary Ellen's Room, all with negative results. He located Fine at Weston's. Bob Dingle, the saloon's major domo, told him to hold while he dug Fine out of the crowd.

The din coming over the line was most definitely that of a saloon. Live music, clinking glasses, loud voices mixed with sudden gales of laughter—he could visualize the smoke raftering the bar.

Fine's choppy voice. "Dan, I was terribly sorry to hear about Zambrano. He is going to be missed. You all right?" Fine was shouting over the clamor.

"Jack, I need one and I need it fast." He realized that he was shouting. His voice drifted downward. "Can you help me?"

Fine said, "If I can, you got it."

"I want you to arrange for me to get into a television film library. I want to know all there is to know about Carter Moorehouse."

Fine made a sound of exasperation. "Wow. Is Moorehouse involved in the Eisinger caper?"

"Maybe."

"I have a lady-type friend who works at CBS. I will give her a call at home. She starts work at seven A.M. Likes to get a jump on the day before the place turns into Willowbrook East. I'll call you right back. Where are you?"

"In the Squad."

He waited for Fine to call back and confirm the appointment on Monday morning before he made the second call. He studied the telephone a long time before he finally picked it up and dialed.

It was answered on the first ring.

"Hello, Erica," he said softly.

Her voice was strained and distant, as though she wanted to detach herself from him. "How are you, Daniel?"

"I'm all right. I miss you." He held his breath, waiting to hear her tone of voice. Listening for the inflection.

"When were you released from whatever hospital you were in?" A cold and reserved tone, one that said, Keep your distance.

"This morning."

"I see." Icicles in June. "Didn't you know how frantic I would be? I have been crying all day. I must have telephoned your rotten office a thousand times. None of your macho detectives knew anything. They never do. It's one big chauvinistic conspiracy. I've broken every one of my nails and to top it off I look like shit. And you, Daniel Malone, could not spare me one lousy minute of your precious time to let me know that you were alive."

"I'm sorry," he said, haltingly.

"Like hell you are. The only thing that you're sorry about is that there are not seventy-two hours in one day so that you can play at your cops-and-robbers games."

"Erica. A cop was killed. There were many things that needed doing. Believe me, I tried to call you several times but the Job always interfered."

"Your job is just too big for both of us. I'm sorry, Daniel. I really wanted us to make it." She began to cry.

"Let me come over. We'll talk."

"No! I'm not the wham-bam-thank-you-ma'am type. I want more out of a relationship. You make me feel like a whore."

He lowered his eyes and shook his head. He was wrong and he knew it. And now he was sorry. "Erica, please let me . . ."

"How could you have done that to me," she cried. "Not one call. I have to feel secure in a relationship. I . . . I . . . Please don't call me again, ever."

A click.

He sat holding the phone and listening to the sound of the dial tone. "If you want security, marry a rent-a-cop," he shouted at the mouthpiece. "Don't bark up this tree."

He pushed himself up out of the chair and went into the squad room. He was on his way to the coffee machine when he turned and went back into his office. He dialed her number and the line was busy. He sat on his desk and dialed over and over again. It was always busy.

He went back into the squad room and told the detective who was typing up the arrest reports on a feral youth that he was going to sack out in the dorm. "See that I get a piss call at six A.M."

"Hi. I'm Evelyn Norton. Jack Fine told me that you would be coming my way Monday morning."

She was thirtyish, with scalloped black hair and green eyes. A nice smile and a firm handshake. Her blouse was open just enough to make a man curious. Black skirt with side slits, and dark stockings and a man-tailored jacket. A very attractive lady.

She swept her hand toward a chair. A television set displaying a colorful test pattern was on a table next to her desk. Her fragrance reminded him of Erica.

Evelyn Norton said, "What can I do for you?"

He told her that he wanted background information on Carter Moorehouse. She picked up a pencil and leaned forward in her chair. "Can you be a bit more specific?"

"I'd like to see everything that you have on him."

"Let me explain how our indexes work," she said, a pleasant smile on her face. "Our film library employs several systems. We have a Personality File on the famous and infamous. A Shot Listing Index which lists specific scenes of news footage. An example would be"— she paused a second to think—"Sadat's assassins rushing the grandstand. And we have a Line-up Book which lists the stories carried on CBS news in the sequence that they were aired. We also maintain a card index by subject and story. Everything from 'seventy-five to the present is available on CRT computer terminals, everything before 'seventy-five is still on index cards.

"So you see," she concluded, "it would help if you could be more exact."

"I want," he said, "to get a sense of the man."

She folded her arms across her chest. "I see. S'pose I prepare you a pre-obit on Carter Moorehouse."

"That would be fine."

She got up. He followed her out into a row of secretarial cubicles and down the aisle into a large room filled with movable film racks and card drawers. She pointed to a room with video playback machines and large tape spools on the wall. "This is a shot-listing room."

For the next thirty-two minutes they combed the indexes for material on Carter Moorehouse. She searched and called out reference numbers and he copied them down on gray charge-out cards.

When they were finished, she looked over at him, smiled, and said, "Some of this material is in our basement library."

The library was two stories below ground. Stepping off the elevator, they entered a labyrinth of underground passageways with vaulted ceilings and white stone walls. She saw the surprise register on his face. "At one time this building was a slaughterhouse for one of the big milk companies," she said.

She led the way through passageways crowded with maintenance men. At the end of a long serpentine route she turned right and signaled him to follow. They were in a cloistered area with fourteen-foot ceilings. There were files of portable racks that were crowded with film canisters and storage boxes. The yellow labels on the boxes' spines contained reference codes and content annotations.

It was a cold, damp place.

He noticed the oxygen tanks and masks encased in glass.

"What are they for?"

She pointed to a sign on the door—WHEN HELON ALARM SOUNDS LEAVE IMMEDIATELY OR PUT ON OXYGEN MASK.

She said, "We use Helon in our sprinkler system. It removes oxygen from the air and extinguishes fire. That way our film is protected. The difficult part is that anyone trapped in here at the time of a fire would have to put on an oxygen mask or suffocate."

Reference slips in hand, they combed the aisles and removed material. Their quest complete, they retired to a fourth-floor shot-listing room where she spent ten minutes showing him how to work the equipment.

When she was gone he put on the first cassette, sat back, and fixed his attention on the large screen.

Stewart King, the CBS anchorman, appeared in a standup open shot introducing Carter Moorehouse, the candidate. The scene switched to a tracking shot of Moorehouse moving among a cheering constituency. Malone noticed something and depressed the frame-hold button. Although they were much younger, their features lean and hair darker, he recognized Stanislaus and Zangline shouldering a path for the candidate.

It was early in the campaign so the crowds were big and still friendly. Moorehouse had used the occasion, a speech at the old Brooklyn Navy Yard, to present the broad outlines of what came to be known as "Remobilize New York's Industry." As he moved forward in the file tapes, Malone found himself admitting how much sense Moorehouse made when he outlined his program of tax and development incentives for smaller businesses, rebuilding, and restoring the fabric of neighborhoods, creating industrial development zones in dying areas of the city. But then, in a tape made three weeks into the campaign, Moorehouse began discussing rehabilitation of mass-transit services. Business needed workers arriving on time and unharassed by marginal equipment and operations. But they needed, above all, employees who felt they could use subways and buses in reasonable safety. And that took him off on a long tangent about crime. Malone watched with fascination as the tape ran over into outtakes, the unedited footage. Moorehouse left his prepared speech behind; the carefully modulated tones were replaced by the relentless harangue of a religious fanatic. And the crowd loved it, at least for a while. It went on for a long, long time. Moorehouse approved the death penalty and went on to suggest special courts for felony offenders that left no room whatsoever for due process.

In later tapes, Moorehouse's tendency to break into extemporaneous remarks about crime became more pronounced. Toward the end of one such speech a desperate aide had almost pulled Moorehouse away from the podium. The crowds were less and less responsive. There would always be a considerable number of people in each of Moorehouse's different audiences who *would* listen, who seemed locked in a kind of terrible communion with Moorehouse. Malone remembered, now, what the *Times* had said in that damaging editorial: Moorehouse wanted to return to pure retributive justice, the kind of blood-vengeance suited to a savage tribe rather than the measured, constitutional law of a civilized city. As he watched the tapes unroll, Malone saw the animal emerging; it was signaled by the peculiar gleam in Moorehouse's eyes, or the darting of his tongue. Malone also understood the code words. Moorehouse talked about blacks, Hispanics, the welfare poor as the "criminal element," without differentiating them. Malone knew what he meant; and so did the hard knot of true believers in every audience.

Late in the campaign Moorehouse began to address the issue of terrorism. Again, in an outtake that, fortunately, had not aired, Moorehouse gave his thoughts on the subject, even going as far as to warn his somewhat perplexed listeners that New York City would have to look like Beirut before people took the threat seriously. When Moorehouse talked about the horrifying ineffectiveness of our immigration controls, Malone got the clear impression that Moorehouse felt the wrong sort of people had been let in for the last fifty years. That kind of message, in the racial and ethnic stew that constituted the human element of the city, was not likely to be popular. But in the later tapes it was clear that Moorehouse cared little about popularity. He was speaking out of deep conviction and the public be damned.

Malone saw the tapes as a portrait of self-destruction. He was amazed by the kindness of the media to Moorehouse, the same media which Moorehouse perceived as his personal enemies. What had been aired was bad enough; what remained unaired and in the can revealed Moorehouse's pathological disregard of the bare minimum of polite disguise. The code words were there, especially, in his concession speech. When Moorehouse talked about "malign foreign influences" on a free press, he was talking about Jews and Zionists. Perhaps, Malone conceded, Moorehouse had been right in a twisted way. Reporters, producers, and editors had kept many of Carter Moorehouse's less attractive sentiments out of the news, not so much as a means of protecting Moorehouse from himself but to protect a troubled city from the suggestion of remedies that were worse than any disease. The cumulative effect of the footage was overwhelming; Moorehouse was a man who held in contempt much of the law that Malone served. He despised many of the ordinary people who Malone tried to protect.

The grinding political process had stripped Moorehouse of his civil veneer and led him to defeat by a humiliating margin.

Malone watched all the tapes and then switched off the machines. He lit a cigarette and remained in his seat, watching the smoke drift upward. He had gotten what he wanted; a sense of the man. He now knew a great and frightening thing about Carter Moorehouse. He knew that Moorehouse was a man who did not know how to forgive or forget.

In the lobby of the CBS building Malone called the precinct. Bo Davis answered. "Are the transcripts ready?" Malone asked.

"Everything is waiting on you. The film, the transcripts, and the wire. You better get back here fast. This shit is dynamite."

"I'm on the way. Who's on deck?"

"The whole crew is here."

Malone looked at his watch: 9:58 A.M. "I want you and Jake to hit Stanislaus's place and execute the warrant, just for the record. Before you go, check with Harrigan and make sure Stanislaus is at the SOD compound. This way he won't know that we were there until he returns home. It'll give us some extra hours. And, Bo, don't forget to leave a receipt for the property."

Malone hung up and dialed Erica Sommers at her sister's house in Washington Heights. The line was busy. He called the special operator and asked her to check it. When she came back on the line the operator told him that the phone was off the hook.

A man with a moon face was waiting on the stationhouse steps. "Lieutenant Malone, I am Deputy Inspector Obergfoll. You have a Forthwith from the Chief of Op." He was a heavy man somewhere in his fifties. A man who had forgotten how to smile.

"What is it about?" Malone said, searching the blank face for a clue.

"The chief will tell you."

"I'll just be a minute. There are a few things I have to tell my men." Malone started to walk around him.

Obergfoll grabbed his arm. "Forthwith, Lieutenant. Your men are waiting for you at One Police Plaza."

While every crime scene has its own special aura, they are essentially all the same.

Policemen loitered in the corridor. Two officers stood guard outside the door leading into Joe Mannelli's official office at One Police Plaza. They had stretched a rope across the doorway and hung a crime-scene sign on it. Deputy Inspector Obergfoll climbed over the rope and then lifted it up so that Malone could duck under.

The cameras in the outer office had been switched off. The Chief of Op was in a corner talking to the first deputy police commissioner. McQuade caught sight of Obergfoll and Malone and excused himself.

The top echelon of the department had gathered in the outer office and were talking guardedly. Malone spotted his detectives and started for them. Obergfoll grabbed his arm and told him to remain where he was. The inspector then went over to the detectives and told them to follow him. They were to wait for their boss in McQuade's office. As they filed past Malone each one looked the lieutenant in the face and made a deprecatory little shrug. Malone was relieved to see that Davis and Stern were among the missing. The search warrant was being executed, officially.

McQuade came up to him, and without saying one word looped his arm through his and proceeded to shepherd him across the width of the room to a window.

McQuade said, "Things have changed since we last talked."

"How so?"

"Zambrano. And now this," McQuade said.

Malone looked him in the eye, waiting for an explanation.

McQuade rubbed his palms together. A film of sweat covered his lip. "There has been an accident. Mannelli is dead. Suicide."

Malone was stunned. He slapped his hands over his face and began to press his pupils until he could see shimmering tiles rushing through the blackness. Another dead cop. Sara Eisinger, what hath your grounder wrought? He stared out at the City.

"It's your baby," McQuade said.

"Any direction from the fourteenth floor?" he said, looking up at the golden cupola of the Municipal Building, and envisaging the PC sitting behind Teddy Roosevelt's massive desk pondering what to do with the Mannelli caper.

"The place of occurrence is within your zone. Handle it as you would any other suicide."

Malone glared scorn. "Fuck off with that bullshit."

McQuade bit his lips. "Do what ever you have to, Lieutenant."

"What happened?" Malone flared.

"The PC received an envelope with photographs of Mannelli. They were sex pictures of him in bed with a man and woman. The PC called him in and told him that his position in Intelligence had been compromised. He suggested that he vest his pension and get out. Whoever sent the envelope to the PC also sent one to Mannelli's wife. She's a tight-assed Bronx Irish Catholic. She ordered him from their home. I guess something inside him must have snapped." He reached into his pocket and took out a letter. "This is addressed to you."

He took it from McQuade and read it.

Dan. Believe me when I tell you that I did not know what they were doing. They used me. Watch yourself. They are out to kill you. The Braxtons set me up. I'm scared. Stop them before it is too late. I want you to do me one last favor. Please . . .

The letter ended.

Malone folded it and slid it into his pocket. "Where is he?"

"In there," McQuade said, pointing to an inner door.

"Where are my men?" Malone said, with an undercurrent of hostility in his tone.

"Waiting for you in my office."

The apprehension in McQuade's face was apparent. Suicides do not fit the public image. "Let's take a look."

They entered the quiet room. McQuade drew the door closed. The body was slouched in the white plastic chair. The head was back and tilted to the side. The right arm was extended, the weapon clutched in a death grip. His mouth was agape and the eyes half open. A pool of red mud seeped down over the left shoulder.

Malone circled, examining the scene. He placed the back of his hand against Joe's face. The skin was rubbery and cold. Capillarity cast its spidery hue. There was a heavy accumulation of powder grains around the center of the flame zone.

"Goddamn it!" He kicked the desk. "You could have prevented this."

McQuade shrugged helplessness. "How? I had nothing to do with any of this."

"You are the Chief of Operations. You knew damn well what Zangline and his crew were into." He pointed to the body. "No way you can escape responsibility."

"Lieutenant, not now! We can talk later. At this moment there are more pressing considerations that require our attention."

"How many children did he have?"

"Three. One still in grade school."

"At least they will get his pension."

"They get zilch," McQuade said. "Mannelli did not have his time in the Job, and suicides are not classified line-of-duty deaths. His family will get whatever money he contributed to his pension fund and one year's salary."

Grainy black-and-white photographs were strewn over the floor.

Malone bent and harvested them. Mannelli in bed with Aldridge and Thea Braxton. A threesome. Ain't no way, he thought. That was not Mannelli's bag. He remembered Major Landsford and how he died. A suicide by gun with incriminating film as the catalyst. He began to wonder if they *were* suicides.

Malone said, "Is this my investigation?" A purposeful tone.

"Yes."

"Then you better leave. Because I am going to conduct it my way."

McQuade said, "I'll stay. There might come a time when you will need a witness."

They looked into each other's eyes, two policemen understanding a contract. Malone knew what the Chief of Op expected of him.

Standing over the wastebasket that was on the side of the desk, Malone tore up the photographs and rained the pieces into the basket. He shot out a hand. "Gimme a book of matches."

McQuade handed them to him. He squatted and struck a match, turning the contents of the basket ablaze.

He got to his feet and started to rummage the desk. Each drawer was pulled out and searched. Not finding what he wanted, he slowly scoured the room. The coat closet? He went over and jerked the door open. First he checked the floor and then he started to push uniforms aside.

"What the hell are you searching for?" McQuade said.

"Something that every cop keeps nearby," he said, stepping back to check the shelf. Three shoe boxes were stacked one on the other. The corners of the bottom one were stained with oil. "Here it is," he said, sliding out the box.

Mannelli's gun-cleaning kit was placed on the desk. "You don't have to be a party to any of this."

"I am just beginning to appreciate your style, Malone. I will stay. Might learn a thing or two."

Malone assembled the cleaning rod. A patch was removed from the crumpled box and inserted through the rod's eye. The cap was taken off the bottle of cleaning solvent and the patch dipped inside and soaked.

He had to pry the fingers back in order to retrieve the revolver. He opened the chamber and plunged out the rounds, returning the one spent cartridge. He checked the make of the pistol. A Smith & Wesson. The cylinders on S & Ws turn counterclockwise. The cylinder was spun until the spent round fell under the firing pin. It was then closed and the revolver placed on the floor beneath the stiffened hand. He stepped back to check the scene. Realizing that some of the stage props were missing, he then spread the remaining rounds over the desk. He moved away like a director checking the scene before the final shot. Nodding satisfaction, he turned to McQuade. "My investigation leads me to conclude that Lieutenant Mannelli died as the result of an accidental discharge incurred while he was cleaning his service revolver. I shall so testify before the grand jury."

McQuade said, "The *Patrol Guide* requires members to maintain their service revolvers in a clean and serviceable condition. Since his death was the direct result of that provision it would be line-of-duty."

Malone took out the suicide note. He glanced at it briefly and then tossed it into the flickering flame. The center of the paper scorched outward and the ends began to char and curl under. Soon there was nothing left but a smoldering charcoal mass.

McQuade came up to him. "Obergfoll can clean up here. We had better go to my office and talk."

21

Some of the men shuffled about the room as though they had no other place to go while others slouched in chairs; each man shared the patina of gloom. Malone stopped short, surprised at the unexpected gathering in the Chief of Op's office.

Yachov Anderman wore a melancholy expression. "Hello, policeman."

David Ancorie's ears were beet red and his face bore a steady, bland expression.

A movie camera and screen had been set up. A tape recorder and a pile of mimeographed transcripts were next to the camera. McQuade saw Malone looking at them. "When Obergfoll went to get you and your men he found the detectives examining this material. He directed that it all be brought here."

Malone nodded to his detectives and crossed the room to Anderman. As he lowered himself into the chair next to Anderman he said, "So? What's new?"

"What could be new, policeman?"

"Well. For starters, the man you met in Battery Park is dead. Mannelli, perhaps you remember him?"

Anderman's face set in a scowl.

Malone continued, "And now I find the man who never associates with policemen in the office of the Chief of Operations with a rabbinical student who instructs policemen on the use and care of the Uzi submachine gun. Don't you find that interesting, Mr. Anderman?" He spat his words with contempt.

Anderman turned in his seat to say something, then at the last second changed his mind and looked away.

Malone edged close. "You have been pissing on my parade since the beginning. One of these days I am going to shove a cattle prod up your ass and put your balls on trickle."

Anderman got halfway up and leaned across the table, tapping the stack of transcripts. "I suggest that you wait until you read these."

McQuade's face reflected his grave concern. "We are facing a crisis." He looked to Anderman and Malone. "We must work together, past differences forgotten." He waved a hand at Deputy Inspector Obergfoll, who nodded and went around the room closing blinds. McQuade picked up one of the transcripts and then went over to the light switch and flipped it. He cracked the door so that a sliver of light shone in.

Obergfoll turned on the projector. Holding the transcript in the light from the beam, McQuade watched the screen, ready to deliver the dialogue. A bleak, unsteady picture fluttered onto the screen. Stanislaus was pacing before a park bench. The men sitting were watching him.

McQuade said, "Stanislaus speaking: 'We make our move now. Bramson will contact our Arab. . . . We have enough people to destroy. . . . All the equipment is ready. There is enough Plactic C to do the job and . . .'

"Kelly speaking: 'Some cops are bound to get hurt.' "

"Stanislaus speaking: 'That can't be helped. We all knew what we were getting into. . . . Mannelli must go. . . .' "

Malone watched intently, and strained to read their lips.

Aldridge Braxton jumped to his feet.

"Braxton speaking: 'You are all crazy. My sister and I want no part of this. It's madness. We will not go with you. . . .' "

Stanislaus's back was to the camera. A fist was waved at Braxton. Bramson was on his feet pushing Braxton back down. The camera recorded the tremor in Braxton's legs.

McQuade read aloud, "Kelly speaking: 'All right.'

"Bramson speaking: 'I will see to it.'

"Stanislaus speaking: 'Afterward we go about our business as though nothing has happened.' "

One by one they got up and walked from the park. The film quickened. A jumble of white dots flicked past the upper-right-hand corner of the screen. Smoke floated inside the beam. Zangline appeared walking through the park. He went over to Stanislaus. Both men walked away from the river. The camera recorded their lip movements.

McQuade read aloud, "Zangline speaking: 'The piano tuner wants to see us.'

"Stanislaus speaking: 'When.'

"Zangline speaking: 'Right now. And we better make damn sure that we're not followed.' "

Cameras followed their departure from the park. More dots appeared on the screen, and then Stanislaus and Zangline reappeared walking past a small park in Tudor City. They had a brief conversation with a man in a chauffeur's hat and then walked into the restaurant. McQuade nudged the door closed with his knee and switched on the lights. He walked over to the tape recorder. As he did his eyes met Malone's. He made a tentative movement with his head as if to say, How did we ever get into this mess? He depressed the play button. A hollow sound churned forth followed by a click and then Thea Braxton's voice.

"Hello?"

"It's me." His tone a shrill. "They are all out of their minds."

"Are you nuts calling me here!"

"I have to talk to you now. They are all crazy."

"Aldridge. Calm down and tell me exactly what happened."

"They are going to detonate bombs around the city and then all over the country. That Jew's warehouse in Queens is the first place they're planning to hit. And they expect us to go along with them."

"I will leave the office in five minutes. Meet me in my apartment and we will talk. There has to be a way out of this."

"Okay. Do you remember that cop who Stanislaus wanted insurance on?"

"Mannelli. Yes, I remember him. And I also recall that you were particularly wonderful that evening." He ignored her and went on speaking rapidly. "They are going after him. After that cop was killed on the expressway, Mannelli put two and two together and threatened to go to the state prosecutor."

"What are they going to do?"

"I don't know and I don't care. Mannelli is not our concern. What we're going to do is what concerns me."

"And that, brother dear, is what makes life so damnably exciting."

The machine clicked off. Obergfoll went around the room opening the blinds. Malone stood, his fists clenched tightly at his side. "Who is going to tell me how this abortion got started and how the hell this department got itself involved?"

Anderman shot McQuade a look of frustrated helplessness. "Tell him."

McQuade started to pace around the table. He punched his palm, stared upward, and said, "I guess it all started several years ago when an oil executive was kidnapped in Latin America and held for a multi-million-dollar ransom. And then on April third, 1977, the FALN blew up the Mobil Oil building in New York City. One person was killed and seven wounded. After the Mobil thing, we started to get a lot of heat from the top management of major corporations with headquarters in New York City. It got worse when Moorehouse formed a 'citizen's committee' to study the protection that the various law-enforcement agencies afforded to companies with their executive headquarters in the city. To make matters more difficult, Moorehouse brought in Washington. Everyone was seeing terrorists under their beds. Up to that point we had no kind of intelligence picture on Arabs, good or bad. We told that to the Agency people and they admitted that Arab nationals can move in and out of New York just as easy as they do in France. Or fucking Algiers or anywhere. The Agency tells us, Why not try a little quiet infiltration?"

The Chief of Op glared at Anderman. "I tell them that we haven't got an awful lot of cops who fit the part of Lawrence of Arabia. So they suggest that maybe we can make a deal with people who have a lot of resources in that area. And that was how we got involved with Anderman and his crowd. And I mean *crowd*. You would not believe how many 'assets' the Mossad has got sitting in New York, not to mention God knows how many elsewhere."

Anderman interrupted angrily. "We have no more people on the ground here than does any other first-class intelligence operation. From friendly countries. You should be worried about the unfriendly ones. Did you ever take a close look at the Cuban Mission? What do you think such a small island needs with such a big building? You think they store sugarcane there, maybe."

McQuade continued as if Anderman was not even in the room. "We believed what the Agency people told us: The Israelis are good at getting their people inside the structure of all the Arab fronts. Trouble is, once we got into bed with Anderman then the whole arms-storage deal was the price tag."

McQuade turned and looked pleadingly at Malone. "Look, Lieutenant. This started out being no big deal. We agreed to beef up the department's surveillance capability. Period. But you know, it gets to be like elephants fucking. There's a lot of noise, a small earthquake, and it all goes on at a very high level. The order came down from the PC. We gotta have a counterstrike capability. So I agreed, hell, how could I say no? But it was to be a small unit. Its primary mission was to take out suspected terrorists before they struck. They were to employ extra-judicial methods. Zangline could release the Unit only with the explicit authorization of the PC. Fine. Just fine. Until it snowballed and types like these Braxton people got mixed up in it."

Anderman stood up, his face flushed with anger. "The Braxtons were misused by your people, just please remember that. Besides, they were small change. The Libyans used them for minor errands, moving their own assets around, occasionally blackmail. We decided to turn them, and then, the minute we started, Zangline stepped in and insisted that he be allowed to use them for infiltration. It was senseless. They had access to nothing. He wouldn't trust my people. And what your chief failed to tell you was that it was thoroughly agreed that all the policemen in the Unit were to be psychologically screened. We work with professionals, no *meshugas* like Stanislaus and the other two."

Chief of Op McQuade took an immaculate handkerchief out of his pocket, removed his glasses, and began to polish the lenses thoughtfully. "Zangline. Goddamn him. I backed him one hundred percent. Until you started making waves, Malone. Well, your fitness reports were right on. I figured you were just what they said, a good cop. A commander of men. So, after I failed to buy you off"—he smiled bitterly at Malone, replaced his glasses, and took a sheet of paper from the drawer of his desk—"I called up Jack Breen, Zangline's exec. It was like Jack was waiting for my call. You know that loyalty comes first on this job, it's got to. We have to trust each other, particularly when we are running this kind of a crazy show. I ordered Jack to tell me what was really going on, and he did, enough to scare the shit out of me. You see, Anderman is right. The three cops in the middle of this didn't belong in the Unit. I think that they should have been thrown off the Job a long time ago. Jack Breen told me they'd all failed to pass the psychological profile screening. But fucking Zangline kept them on. He told Jack they'd be used only for training. Said they had the right kind of killer instincts." The chief shook his head as if he could not believe what he was saying. "Well, at least Zangline was right about that."

Malone walked over to Anderman and stood implacably in front of him. Anderman was staring down at his shoes. Malone waited a long time and then in an ominously quiet voice asked: "Where does Carter Moorehouse fit in all this?"

Anderman continued to stare down. "I don't know, but I can give you a lot of guesses. Zangline had many connections with Moorehouse, because Moorehouse was on the liaison committee of VIPs who formed the Unit's oversight board. We were supposed to coordinate our efforts with the private security forces of many companies in the city." His head shot up and he gave Malone a baffled look. "It's madness, you know. You can't mix outside people up in a clandestine operation like this one." He stopped, thought, and said, "Policeman, I can give you my guess. And I think Joe Mannelli's guess too. We think Moorehouse was . . . is funding something private. A unit inside the Unit."

Malone shook his head in disbelief. "A hit squad for the elite buried in the department."

"What choice did we have? The banks and oil companies hold the first mortgage on this city. They can foreclose any damn time they want," McQuade said.

"And this other unit? Who gave the order for its formation, and what is its mission?" Malone asked.

"I wish that I knew," McQuade said.

"Zangline ordered the formation of the official hit squad," Malone said.

"It was a deniable undertaking. Top secret. Only handpicked men were brought into it," McQuade said.

Malone glowered at the chief. "It's no longer deniable, is it. There are too many bodies." He walked over to McQuade. "Who picked up the tab?"

McQuade said, "A slush fund of several million dollars was established. Each corporation contributed. They picked one of their own to act as overseer of the money. He was to be the liaison between the department and the business community."

"Carter Moorehouse. The piano tuner," Malone said.

"Yes," McQuade said lamely.

"Very nice," Malone said. "They set up the Simonson Optical Division in the Netherlands Antilles to launder the money and pay the bills. And I bet there's another one like it that we don't know about. And presto, Zangline, Stanislaus, Kelly, and Bramson have their own wishing well full of greenbacks. All they had to do was to get Moorehouse to look the other way while they helped themselves."

Malone thought. Why should Moorehouse look the other way? Certainly not for money. And why the bombs? Why risk exposure? Why? Where is the motive? Malone turned and addressed Anderman. "What went wrong? Why was she killed?"

Anderman took out a cigarette and started to tap it end over end. All of a sudden he broke it in half and threw the ends on the floor. "You want it all, policeman? All right, you can have it all. Sara was training your men in the use of simple codes when she met Stanislaus. They started to see each other. When I discovered their relationship I ordered her to stop. I told her that fraternization with policemen would make her position with us untenable. She told me that her life was hers to lead as she saw fit. We fought. She quit and went with

Stanislaus. He got her a job with the Braxtons. I tried to get her to come to her senses, but it was no use. She started to socialize with Stanislaus and his friends, and saw that they had unlimited funds to spend. She became suspicious and telephoned me. She started to ask me questions about the Unit's financing. I asked her what was wrong and she told me. By this time she had become bored with Stanislaus and wanted to come back. I told her to stay with him and try to find out what they were doing. It was at this point that I was able to plant Andrea St. James in the Interlude. Sara was told never to contact me directly. She was to communicate through Andrea. They telephoned each other every day. Sara was onto something.

"She started to mention her Bible and the song. She could never say too much on the phone. One of the Braxtons or the cops were always around. When Andrea informed me about Landsford I never made the connection with the fort. Some army officer, she said."

Anderman got up and walked over to a filing cabinet. He opened the top drawer, pulled some folders to the front, and then slammed the drawer shut and walked away, aimlessly pacing the room. He appeared to be a man lost within himself, searching for the right turnoff. The City's flag was in the corner. He unfurled it, studying the emblem. He let it drop and returned to his seat. He looked into each man's face and then lowered himself into the chair, ready to continue his narrative.

"The Thursday before she was killed, Sara spent the night in his apartment. She was in the bathroom getting ready for him. She discovered the list and the film hidden under some rags inside the vanity. She recognized the locations on the list. She took them and hid them in her pocketbook and then went into his bed. In the morning he asked her to marry him. She was caught off guard and laughed. She saw the look that crossed his face and quickly regained her composure. She told him that she liked the relationship the way it was. Her parents would never consent to such a marriage." He looked up at Malone. "You see, policeman, in many ways Sara was a troubled woman. She was only able to have intense relationships with gentile men. One short affair after the other. When the man would get serious with her she would end it. A tormentor of gentiles. Unfortunately, the children of the Holocaust did not escape unscathed.

"Stanislaus became enraged. He had left his family for her. He was in love with her. Sara realized that she was in danger and asked him for time. Perhaps she could work out something with her parents, she told him. She left his apartment and rushed home. She phoned me immediately and told me what had happened. I told her to leave and come to me. She was petrified that she might meet him in the street. She was afraid that he could have discovered the list and film missing and might be on his way to her apartment. Of course, she should have come to me instead of going home. But she panicked. I tried to calm her but it was no use. So, I did the next best thing. I told her to lock all her doors and let no one in. I was on my way to her. I should have been there within the hour." He cupped his hands over his face and started to shake his head. "Ancorie and I rushed out. We took the BQE to the Williamsburgh Bridge. A three-car accident happened up ahead of us and we were stuck in the middle of the bridge for over forty minutes." He took his hands away. "When we arrived at her apartment we found the door ajar. Sara was dead in the bathtub. He must have discovered the things missing from his bathroom and rushed over to her apartment. From the look of the place he had help."

Malone unconsciously felt the wound on his head. "And then you locked the door behind you and left."

"What else could we do?" said David Ancorie.

"Was it Stanislaus who used to call Sara at the office?"

"Yes," said Anderman, "he was always calling her. It was his way of checking on her. Making sure she was where she was supposed to be. He would talk to her in Polish and German."

"Who picked Zangline to run the Unit?" Malone asked McQuade.

"The mayor. But I know Moorehouse engineered it. They knew each other from Moorehouse's political days," McQuade said.

Malone rushed over to the telephone on McQuade's desk.

"What are you doing?" McQuade asked.

"I'm going to try to stop this thing before it's too late," Malone said, dialing.

Det. Sergeant Jack Harrigan answered the telephone inside the surveillance van.

"Jack, where are the suspects?" Malone said, an anxious edge to his voice.

"I have been trying to get in touch with you," Harrigan shouted. "Marku and Yaziji showed up at the Braxtons' apartment and took them for a ride in a rented car. They are on the FDR Drive. Stanislaus, Kelly, and Bramson are in another car behind them."

"What is their location?" Malone said.

"Hold on." Malone could hear the Nest communicating with its Birds. Static replies brayed in the background. Then the sergeant's hurried voice. "The drive and Seventy-first Street, heading north."

"Scoop them all up," Malone ordered.

"Ten-four."

Malone said, "I am going to keep this line open. Stay with me and let me know when you have them in custody. I have to call the Squad, but I will get right back to you."

"Okay."

Malone pressed the hold button and then took an outside line.

"We couldn't figure out where everyone went," Bo Davis said.

Malone said, "Never mind that now. Did you execute the warrant?"

"No problem. We got everything we came for and we left a receipt."

"Hang loose in the Squad. I will get back to you," Malone said.

He depressed the open-line button. "Jack, what is happening?"

A high-pitched voice. "We lost them in traffic."

"Get on the air! Have the drive blocked," Malone ordered. All eyes were on the lieutenant. Malone could hear the urgent transmissions. Radio cars would be speeding toward the drive. Would they be in time? Where was Stanislaus going? The frustration of not being there tore at him. Things would be different if he were on the scene. He should have been there. Harrigan was yelling orders, giving directions. "Harrigan, what the hell is going on?" he shouted. He could hear a great commotion. A short time later Harrigan came on the line.

"We lost them. They sped into the East Side Heliport. Our people were crashing through the gate as their chopper was lifting off the pad."

"Call Aviation and the Coast Guard. I want choppers in the air and . . ."

"No need. I talked to the heliport manager. They had a helicopter waiting to take them to Rabbits Island. A four-minute flight. I have cars from the One-fourteen and One-oh-eight converging on the island."

"I'll hold," Malone said, his gaze darting from face to face. Anderman looked glum, deeply worried. Heinemann and Johnson were anxious to get into the fray, waiting for the word to go. McQuade rubbed the side of his nose, examining contingencies, searching for some way to make it all deniable again. The wait seemed endless. Eight minutes later Harrigan came back onto the line. "They're gone. A car was waiting to pick them up. I've transmitted a description over the citywide band."

Malone said, "Stay on it." He slammed down the phone and quickly redialed. The operator at SOD informed him that Chief Zangline was on vacation for a week.

Anderman said, "What are we going to do?"

"Stop them," Malone said, motioning his detectives to follow as he hurried from the room.

"Where are you going?" McQuade yelled after him.

"To the source," Malone shot back.

22

The Stuyvesant Club was on Park Avenue in the Sixties, one of the last of the great old mansions. It was a quiet, conservative place filled with somber rooms and heavy furniture that glowed from years of polish and care. The first four floors had the clean, slightly sweet and musty smell of old books and older money.

Malone had left One Police Plaza and rushed to the executive offices of Moorehouse International at 81 Wall Street. He presented himself to Moorehouse's secretary and told the blue-haired spinster that it was urgent that he see Moorehouse immediately. He was in possession of confidential information that an attempt was going to be made on Moorehouse's life. The secretary had gasped and clutched her meager breast. He was at his club—the Stuyvesant.

The club's hall porter was an old man who had spent his life serving the rich and powerful. When Malone told him about the threat to Carter Moorehouse he immediately told the policeman that the man he had come to see was in the sauna. He led Malone down to the basement and into the locker room, a place that was full of the faint sourness of sweat and the sharper, more pleasant odor of wintergreen.

The porter left him in the empty locker room. Malone undressed and put his clothes in an empty locker. He took a towel from the pile on the wooden table next to the shower and wrapped it around his waist. He removed another one from the stack and slid his gun inside the fold and carried it with him into the sauna.

A single light glowed down from through the swirling gray mist. He was struck by the tangy aroma of dry, hot wood. He made out the outline of a shadowy figure sitting alone on the top row. "Moore-house?"

"Who is it?"

Carter Moorehouse appeared to be in his late forties, but he was actually closer to three score. He had an interesting face and a muscular body. His lips were thin and he had a cleft chin. His eyes were black and cold and he used them to intimidate others. The hair was silver gray and formed thick ringlets. He seemed smaller than the man Malone had seen on the TV tapes.

"Police," he said, climbing up onto the first rung.

When Malone reached the uppermost row he sat down next to Moorehouse, who growled, "What do you want?"

Malone looked sideways and made out the eyes peering at him through the steam, searching out his eyes. "I want you to tell me where to locate Zangline, Stanislaus, Kelly, and Bramson."

"I am afraid that I do not know who you are talking about. What made you think that I did?"

"Look, scummer!"—a knifelike tone that caused Moorehouse's face to fill with malice—"I'm telling you right from the giddyap that we know all about your hit team for the rich and the 'Simonson Optical Division of Curaçao.'" He ended his dismal narrative by paraphrasing the transcript of Braxton's telephone call to his sister. Water hissed over hot stones in the claustrophobic wood-lined room. "We traced the ownership of the Interlude."

Moorehouse raised his brow in a look of wary resignation.

"It was clever the way you set up that one. A cop would never have known how to do it."

Moorehouse ignored him, leaning forward, his elbows resting on his knees.

"The property was bought by an attorney for a dummy corporation in Delaware and then the shares in the corporation were transferred to another corporation in Delaware. When you applied for the zoning variance you had to produce the principal owner of the property and the attorney of record. So, you just transferred some stock to Aldridge Braxton, making him the principal owner, and you had him sign un-dated stocks in blank transferring the corporation back to one of your dummy entities. Aldridge Braxton, the perfect stand-in. All you needed was an attorney whom you could trust. And who was that? Preston Welwyn Moorehouse, your nephew and the legal representative in the United States for the Simonson Optical Division. A little nepotism can sometimes screw things up, can't it?"

Moorehouse threw his head back, brushing his hands over his fore-head and through his hair as though he were completely at ease. "That is an interesting story. Have you ever considered writing fiction? You have a truly vivid imagination. Too bad that is all you have. There is not one shred of evidence to support that hogwash."

Malone watched him closely. "The department and Anderman are no longer team players. It's down the tubes for you and your friends." Malone brushed the sweat from his chest. "Help us avert disaster and I'll see to it that you are left out of it. Otherwise you'll take the fall with the rest of them."

Moorehouse was unconcerned. "You are serious, aren't you?"

Malone began to wipe his face with the corner of his towel. "Deadly serious."

Moorehouse looked at him and laughed a mocking laugh. "When was the last time you heard of a man of my stature being arrested, tried, and convicted? Not to mention that you would also have to arrest some of the most powerful men in this country." He stretched out over the bench, luxuriating in the heat.

Malone measured him with baffled fury. "Do you really expect people like Zangline and Stanislaus to stand up? Policemen do not like the thought of prison. They are not treated well by the rest of the population. And the Braxtons—they'd turn each other in to stay out of jail."

Moorehouse raised his head. "Didn't you tell me that the Braxtons were brother and sister? Isn't blood thicker than water?"

"So is shit."

Malone realized that he was wasting time. He got up and left the sauna.

Moorehouse glanced at him as he left. He made no comment, but remained on his back, staring upward.

Malone quickly showered and dressed. He was sitting on a bench in front of his locker putting on his socks when Moorehouse came out of the sauna, wrapping a towel tight around his waist. He came up to Malone, who looked up at Moorehouse's wet body and flattened hair.

Moorehouse said, "I confess a mild academic interest in your hypothesis. I assume that you realize that there is a major flaw in your conspiracy theory?"

Malone slipped into his loafers and stood, stamping his feet. His face was inches away from the quarry. "And what would that be?"

"Motive. Why would I permit myself to be a party to such acts?"

Malone became taut. "For the oldest motives of them all. Greed and revenge."

Moorehouse took a step backward. "You must be joking."

"Your election defeat was a little too much for the great Carter Moorehouse to handle. Your first and only rejection in life. You skulked back into your own world and started to brood. Before long all you could think of was getting revenge on the people who had spurned you, the blue-collar slobs who saw through your racist bullshit. And then there was the liberal press, or should I say the Jewish press, who helped sow the seeds of your defeat. You hated them all."

Moorehouse's eyes widened with anger.

"When you were asked to oversee the money for the Unit you saw your opportunity. Anarchy in the streets, you had warned. You intended to make your prophecy a reality. You knew Zangline and Stanislaus from your election campaign. It was easy for you to have the Unit placed under SOD. Then you made your pact with Zangline and company. They could help themselves to the money, not all of it, but enough to make some middle-class cops happy. All they had to do was gather some Arab types around them and plant a few bombs around the city. The Israeli warehouses were high on your list of things to do. What better way to get even with the Jews than to expose their existence and to force them to remove their arms depots. Violence in the streets. Everything was going according to plan until Stanislaus and Eisinger got the hots for each other."

"All right! That is quite enough." Moorehouse wrapped his towel more firmly around his hips and started to walk away from Malone. "I am going to place a call to the commissioner. Perhaps he can handle this in a compassionate way. You are a sick man, Lieutenant."

Malone lunged at Moorehouse and threw him against the locker, bloodying his nose.

Moorehouse whipped around, staring with disbelief at the blood on his hands. He became enraged. "I'll see you dead for this, Malone. You hear me! Dead!"

"You will? Let me tell you something wise-ass. The kind of justice that you and your friends are fond of dishing out knows no distinction between rich and poor. It's a fucking two-way street, pally."

Malone started to leave, hesitated, and spun around, throwing a right cross to Carter Moorehouse's jaw. Arms thrashing at his side, Moorehouse plunged backward into the locker and then slid to the ground.

23

Westy Stanislaus had rented a garage on West Eighty-ninth Street under the name of Frank McMahon as a safe house. From there they would begin the next and crucial move. In the neighborhood surrounding, Latin music blared from tenement windows. The flower boxes on each sill were empty save for soda bottles and cans. On the sidewalk men in T-shirts sat on crates playing checkers while a fire hydrant sprigged a steady stream for children to run through. A patrol car turned in off Columbus Avenue and cruised down West Eighty-ninth Street. One of the players looked up from the board. "*Maricon*," he muttered, glancing back down.

Inside the garage there were two flatbed trucks stacked high with scrapped automobiles, lashed to the beds by steel cables and secured on the sides by long metal slats fitted into the steel edges of the beds. Each of the scrapped cars was full of plastic explosives and the gas tanks had been topped off with gasoline. A pyromaniac's delight. An Econoline van with tinted Plexiglas was parked behind the trucks.

Under a line of bare lightbulbs that hung from grimy S-chains, Ahmad Marku and Iban Yaziji were sitting cross-legged on a blanket that had been spread out over the floor. Five other Arabs surrounded them. They were cleaning Uzi submachine guns and talking in low tones, oblivious to the large black flies buzzing around them.

Zangline, Stanislaus, Kelly, and Bramson were sitting around a folding table playing seven-card stud. Aldridge Braxton and his sister were sitting on an army cot between the two groups watching television. Aldridge was busy swatting the flying pests with a folded magazine while Thea reached up to adjust the rabbit ears.

Chief Zangline had the deal. He shuffled the cards meticulously, his pitiless eyes peering through the veil of smoke, studying the face of each of his colleagues. Stanislaus, Kelly, and Bramson reveled in watching the light dim in other men's eyes. Zangline had conducted his own private investigation into their use of deadly physical force when they were assigned to the Six-six's Anticrime Unit. He had located three witnesses who had seen the cops throw the two fleeing muggers off the roof. He was also successful in tracing three of the throw-aways that they had used. All of them had been removed from prisoners at the time of their arrests and never vouchered. The prisoners never complained; it was one less charge. Zangline had decided that if any problems should develop because of the Unit's excesses or because of today's forthcoming action, Stanislaus and his pals were going to take the fall. Whitney Zangline was a survivor.

Each of the players was dealt two hole cards and one facing up. Kelly was high with an ace showing. Zangline anted and began playing by rote, as he contemplated the day's work which lay ahead of them, searching for a flaw in his carefully conceived plan.

They were to leave the garage at four-thirty in the morning and drive by a prearranged route to Anderman's warehouse in Queens. Detonators primed, six of the wrecked autos would be quickly off-loaded by means of the hoist in the rear of each flatbed and placed up against the walls of the arms depot. After a seven-minute time lapse, the explosion and mushrooming fireball would turn the warehouse into a smoldering hole in the ground. They would then leave Queens and drive into Harlem and El Barrio where the rest of the junk would be randomly detonated, precipitating riots. Thing about those people, he thought, was that they can always be counted on to burn and pillage; all you have to do is give them a little incentive. The arms depots would then be exposed and the Israelis would be forced by an outraged public to leave the country. Moorehouse had even suggested to Zangline that one or perhaps two dead Arabs left at the scene of one of the explosions would add authenticity and also lay a false trail of responsibility. Zangline thought that that was an excellent idea. The Moslem Brotherhood and Black September made perfect scapegoats.

The prophecies of Carter Moorehouse's failed campaign were about to come to pass. And, in a certain way, Zangline, too, was about to have his revenge on those who had stymied his drive to become PC. He saw an irony in it all. He was the catalyst for Moorehouse's revenge. And as the commanding officer of SOD he would be called upon to squelch the riots that he was about to start.

Moorehouse had promised each of them a payday of two hundred thousand dollars for today's action. A cop's dream—the big score. He had heard about this small country in Europe—Liechtenstein—where they had numbered accounts and, unlike the Swiss, asked no questions and kept their mouths shut.

The plan called for Bramson and two of the Arabs to ride in one truck, and Kelly and two other Arabs to ride in the other. Zangline, Stanislaus, and the remainder would ride shotgun in the van, ready to take out any interference. He could see no flaws in the plan. But just in case, he had made escape contingencies. Whitney Zangline was indeed a cautious man.

Tossing each player their last card down, Zangline's eyes darted over to the Braxtons and then flashed back to meet Stanislaus's waiting stare. "Now is a good time," Zangline said in a low voice, picking up his hole cards, studying them.

Stanislaus acknowledged his direction with a fitful flicker of his eyes and an evil little smile. He gathered up his hand and tossed it into the center of the pot. "I'm out."

Westy Stanislaus pushed away from the table and got up. Walking over to the van, he slouched against it and lit a cigarette. He had not been home and therefore was not aware that his apartment had been the subject of a search warrant. After leaving the SOD compound the three policemen had driven to Manhattan and waited while Marku and Yaziji gathered up the Braxtons. During the ride to the heliport he kept checking for a tail. He had that feeling that people were onto them. But the traffic was too damn heavy and he could never be sure.

One of Marku's men had been waiting for them on Rabbits Island. He wondered suddenly why the hell it was called an Island. There was no water. Just a large tract of land that was shaped into a pair of rabbit's ears by the railroad tracks of the L.I.R.R. yards in the valley between Skillman Avenue and Northern Boulevard and connected to the outside world by the Honeywell Viaduct in Long Island City.

He thought of Sara and became angry at himself for still missing her. He had never known a woman like Sara. He had been used to the bimbos that he picked up in the singles' bars. Sara was different, so different. She always smelled nice, and her face was always made up to look natural, like she wasn't wearing anything on it. And there was that special way that she had of looking at him, that gleam that told him that she wanted him, that he was her special man. He could never fathom what an elegant lady like her saw in him. One day when they were alone in his apartment he asked her. "Because you're so cute. You're my own big goy," she had teased.

They had been together only three times when she had asked him playfully if he enjoyed doing certain things to women. "No real man does that," he had said. She pushed her naked body close, running her tongue over his lips and a hand through his hair. "I would love if you did it to me," she said, taking his head into her hands and guiding it down her body. "I'll teach you how."

He had given up everything for her and she had betrayed him. He began to vent his sudden rage by heeling the van's tire. She had used him. She had stolen the list, never really left Anderman, and laughed when he asked her to marry him. How could he have been so fucking stupid? He was glad that she was dead, glad that he had done it. It had given him pleasure. He would always remember the horrified look in her eyes, her painful moans as Bramson and Kelly held her and he slowly, methodically pushed the curtain rod into her battered body. And she still didn't talk, he thought, with grudging admiration.

Looking up from the oil-stained floor, Stanislaus noticed the Braxtons sitting on the cot with their heads together, whispering. He pushed away from the van and moved around to the rear where he opened the door and climbed inside. He bent to make his way into the tool chest and flipped open the lid. He reached inside, moved some canvas about, and took out one Ingraham submachine gun. He opened the tubular stock and then reached back into the chest and took out one fully loaded magazine and a stubby, bulbous silencer. He inserted the magazine into the weapon's housing and attached the silencer to the end of the barrel. He then put the gun into a paper bag and climbed out of the van the same way he had entered.

"Just look at those slobs playing cards as though they haven't a care in the world," Aldridge Braxton said to his sister. "And those foul-smelling Semites, picking their noses, impervious to all these goddamn flies."

His sister whispered, "When we leave this place they are going to be too busy to keep constant watch over us. At some point they are going to be distracted, and that is when we will get away from these madmen."

"Thea, I am getting bad vibrations from these people. I wish to hell . . ." He froze as he saw his sister's head explode into gore. Before he was able to utter a sound his body was thrust up off the cot with his outstretched arms flapping through space. For the brief part of a second Aldridge Braxton had the sensation of being spun through a dappling light, and then there was nothing.

24

The locker room in Midtown Precinct North smelled of moldy old sweat. Long benches lined the rows of lockers and old newspapers overflowed from the tops. Empty garment bags hung from hangers that were stuck into the air slots. Bleary-eyed policemen were busy exchanging their street clothes for the bag. Some of them donned their bulletproof vests, most did not; it was too hot to wrap your body in a furnace of Kevlar. The policemen reached into their lockers and took out their gun belts. When fastened around their waists, the hickory batons that were hooked around their revolvers swung freely, striking metal and wood and occasionally a kneecap. It was the same scene in every patrol precinct in the city: policemen suiting-up for another cursed late tour.

Tuesday was about to begin.

At fifteen minutes before the hour the First Platoon was formed into ranks in the muster room of Midtown Precinct North to receive their instructions and assignments for the tour.

The sergeant had called half the roll when the carriage of the teletype machine sprang to life, shattering his monotonous drone.

The urgent-message bell clanged, demanding immediate attention. The lieutenant strode from behind his raised desk to read the orders that were being ejected. He perused them, then tore them off the machine and started to assemble them in consecutive order. He then walked into the muster room to address the platoon. "Gimmeya attention. We got some special orders for this tour."

The lieutenant's gaze slid over the platoon. Fidgeting stopped. He held the teletype sheets out in front and started to read. "Until further orders, routine calls for service are to be canned. We're directed to respond only to emergency calls involving life-threatening situations or to reported crimes in progress. Every member of the patrol force is directed to give continual and sustained attention to the search for the following individuals."

Descriptions were read. They were not read names, nor were they told that the people they were to look for were cops. There was a chance, they were told, that the people they were searching for might be accompanied by three or more Arab extremists. These people were wanted in connection with a breach of national security and were to be considered armed and extremely dangerous. Confidential information revealed that they would be heading toward Queens. Members were therefore directed to give special attention to bridges and tunnels leading into Queens, paying particular attention to two or more vehicles that give the appearance of traveling together. Under no circumstances were any efforts to be made to apprehend these individuals. If observed, their location and direction of travel were to be reported. Aviation would have helicopters standing by to follow them. Borough Task Forces had been mobilized and were standing by. Detective and plainclothes units were patrolling in unmarked cars.

"Look. I don't know what this is all about, but it has got to be a heavy. So protect your ass and follow instructions. If you spot these humps, lay back and report. Do nothing else."

He started to pace the length of the platoon and grinned lightly. "There is one more minor point that I want to cover. We expect sixty minutes to the hour on this one. No eighty-fives with the girlfriends." His eyes moved from face to face.

"Anyone got any questions?"

There were none.

"Take your posts."

Patrolmen Andy Jenkins and Juan Rivera walked out of the stationhouse with the rest of the First Platoon.

"Wonder what it's about?" Andy Jenkins said.

Juan Rivera raised his shoulders. "Who the fuck knows?"

They walked over to RMP 2356. Rivera went around to the passenger side and opened the door. He stabbed his nightstick between the seat and started to clean out some of the garbage. Andy Jenkins tossed his summons pouch and memo book on the dashboard and then slid in behind the wheel. "Ya'ever see any Arab extremists?"

"Naw. I useta screw an Arab chick from Fourth Avenue when I worked in the Seven-eight."

"She any good?"

"Her armpits smelled like an asshole."

It was ten minutes past the hour when RMP 2356 pulled away from in front of the stationhouse. Their first stop was Rocco's on Amsterdam Avenue where pizza and a six-pack were waiting for them.

The ramparts were manned. Men were stationed on the roof, at exits and windows. Anderman had fought this kind of war before and knew how to prepare. His office had been converted into the message center for the coming battle. Radios bristled with messages in English and Hebrew. Maps of the city were spread over tables and chairs, every conceivable route to the warehouse outlined in red. Crash cars had been dispatched to prowl the streets with instructions to intercept. He had combined forces with the police force he had been fighting.

Anderman moved about, shouting orders, making sure that his people had taken up their positions in and around the warehouse.

Det. Gus Heinemann was manning one of the radios, logging every transmission, and between messages munching on Milky Ways. His Israeli counterpart was next to him, monitoring the Hebrew transmissions.

Detectives Davis, Johnson, and Stern were busy studying maps, ensuring that no routes had been overlooked.

Malone, McQuade, and Jack Harrigan were standing around Anderman's desk discussing the disposition of their forces.

"Has Harbor been notified?" Malone said.

"Why Harbor?" McQuade asked. "It would seem to me that we need men, not launches."

Malone held up a map and pointed. "Here is Manhattan Island. To the east, the East River; to the north, the Harlem River; south, the Upper and Lower Bays; the west, the Hudson. We know that their destination is here in Long Island City. Here at Newspoint, Brooklyn and Queens kiss each other. Zangline could load his circus onto a boat or barge in Manhattan and cut across to Brooklyn or Queens.

"Brooklyn is a borough of creeks and canals. The Spring Creek is a few blocks from here. And here is the Maspeth and the Gowanus." He held the map at his side and looked at McQuade. "I really think that we should notify Harbor and the Coast Guard."

McQuade acquiesced. He went over to the radio and made the necessary notifications. Anderman came over to Malone and laid a hand on his shoulder. "I have one of my helicopters standing by at Fort Totten."

"We have our own," Malone said, fixing his gaze on the map.

Anderman grinned, patted him on the shoulder, and walked away shouting something in Hebrew.

"What other precautions have been taken?" Malone asked McQuade when he walked back.

The Chief of Op told him that sniper teams had been posted around the depot. The bomb squad had a detail hidden in a building one block away. Temporary headquarters had been established inside the warehouse. The fire department had been notified and a hook-and-ladder company was on alert. St. Johns, Elmhurst, and Doctors Hospital were notified to have their disaster units standing by.

"Looks like everything has been covered," Malone said.

"Do you think there is a chance Moorehouse will call it off? Your visit might have put the fear of God into him," Jack Harrigan said.

Malone flared. "Wishful thinking. Moorehouse is a psycho who really believes that he is above the law. He thinks that he is leading a crusade against the infidels who caused his election defeat. Besides, I doubt that he could stop it even if he wanted to. These things have the habit of taking on their own form, building up their own momentum until there is only one way to stop them—by force."

Time passed and they waited, tensing with each transmission, straining to hear every word. Empty Styrofoam cups littered desks and radio panels, and a thick cloud of smoke wafted over the converted message center.

Malone was weary. It was three-thirty in the morning and the new day gave promise of being even longer than the last one. On an impulse, he picked up the phone and dialed Erica's number. It rang a long time before he heard her sleep-filled voice answer. He hung up.

RMP 2356 was parked in the shadows on Pier 90. Jenkins and Rivera were working on their second six-pack. They had spent most of their tour patrolling their sectors. Rivera had suggested that they pick up some more beer and go into the heave for a little R and R. Jenkins thought that was a good idea. It was going to be a long tour.

Rivera popped open the top and passed the can to his partner. "I wonder what those guys did to generate so much heat? I can't ever remember the radio being so dead. It's eerie. Central must be shitcanning everything."

Jenkins gulped beer and belched. "Maybe they stole some secrets or something."

"Who gives a shit?" Rivera said, hefting his can.

"Didya hear what them humps in Congress did? They voted a special tax bill for themselves so that they don't have to pay any more taxes."

"So what else is new? Everyone knows that they're a bunch of crooks. Yet they keep gettin' elected. The people of this country are gettin' just what they ask for. A Congress full of pompous, low-life, theftin', scumbag, fag motherfuckers."

"Yeah!" Jenkins bent his can in half and tossed it out the window. "Hey? Didya hear why God gave women pussies?"

"No. Tell me."

"So men would talk to them."

Jenkins laughed. His eyes teared and he started to cough. "I like that . . . so we would talk to them . . . that's good." He was reaching for another beer when he noticed the two flatbed trucks speed past. "Hey? Didya see that?"

"What?"

"Them two trucks. One of them guys had on one of them head scarfs you always see them PLO dudes wearing on television."

"No shit? Let's have a look-see." Rivera gulped the dregs and tossed out the can.

RMP 2356 drove off Pier 90 and fell in behind the trucks, quickly closing the gap.

The radio car crept alongside of the trucks, the policemen feigning early morning doldrums.

Iban Yaziji was driving the last vehicle. Bramson was next to him and Marku was by the window. At the first sight of the police car, Marku tightened his grip around the Uzi which was on his lap. Bramson saw him tense and placed a calming hand over his. "They're just cops on patrol. No problem."

RMP 2356 inched past the trucks and made a right-hand turn into Pier 84. "Get on the horn. It's them."

Everyone in the converted message center was either sleeping, dozing, nodding, or staring at the walls. Malone had been staring for the past hour. He was tormented by the thought of another man possessing Erica. He lived in a world of men; he needed more—he needed her. And he lost her over one lousy phone call that he failed to make. He felt rotten.

He was just starting to nod when the sudden commotion caused him to snap his head up. His countenance was that of a man unsure of where he was, and of what was happening. He saw the men scurrying for the radio sets and plunged up off the floor and made for the map table.

"They've been spotted," Heinemann shouted.

"Where?"

"West Four-four and One-two Avenue, heading south. They're in two flatbed trucks that are loaded down with junked cars and it appears that they are being led by someone driving an Econoline van."

"Have all surveillance teams in the area close in. But tell them to lay back and do nothing," Malone said.

Men gathered around the map table. His gaze went to each one. He could see their excitement blossoming.

Malone bent over, fingering the map. After scrutinizing it for several minutes he began. "As I see it, there are three ways in which they can come at us. First, they take the West Side Highway to the FDR and over the Triborough Bridge and onto the LIE. They go west and exit at Van Dam. They'd be two blocks from here. Two: the West Side Highway to the FDR and then through the Midtown Tunnel," he traced the route. "They exit immediately after the toll and turn onto Borden Avenue and make a left. They'd be here in less than a minute. Three, the West Side Highway to the FDR and over the Brooklyn Bridge and onto the BQE. They'd exit at McGuinness Boulevard in Brooklyn and take McGuinness over the Pulaski Bridge and into our backyard."

"Before we make any moves against them we'd better make damn sure that they're isolated within a frozen zone," McQuade said.

"But where?" Malone said, studying the map.

"Aviation has them spotted," Heinemann piped. "Still proceeding south, just passing Three-four Street."

Starling Johnson poked the lieutenant. "We're getting real short on time."

Malone glared at him with a look that said, I know, and then returned his attention to the map. "Isolate inside a frozen zone—some area where they'd be boxed," he said as his finger prowled the map.

He jerked his head up and faced the Chief of Op. "We're going to have to have details at three locations. The Midtown Tunnel on both sides. If they come that way, we'll wait until they're inside and then spring both ends closed. The expressway. If they come that route, we wait until they pass the Greenpoint Avenue exit and then spring a blockade across the expressway between Greenpoint and Van Dam. The Pulaski Bridge. If they come through Brooklyn we wait until they're on the bridge and then choke off both ends."

"How many men do you think they have with them?" Anderman said.

"The radio car team that spotted them reported seeing three men in each of the two trucks. If they brought along four or five of Marku's friends plus the Braxtons, that would give them around fifteen people," Malone said.

"Five and fifty at each choke point?" McQuade said.

"Should do it," Malone said.

"I have to talk to the PC," McQuade said, as he walked over to the telephone on the desk and dialed. He cupped his hand around the receiver as he talked. It was a short conversation. When he was finished, he went over to the radio and picked up the handset. "This is the Chief of Operations."

"Go, Chief."

"Signal ten-seventy-seven. Five and fifty at each of the following locations." When he finished his message to Central, McQuade telephoned Deputy Inspector Obergfoll and issued him specific instructions. A captain or above was to be assigned to command each choke point. Personnel to be concealed at least one block on either side of each choke point. When the suspects' route was definitely ascertained the point concerned would be notified. Personnel assigned at other locations were to remain thereat. The suspects might have divided their forces and could be coming at them from different directions. TPU and Borough Task Force Units were to take up positions around the warehouse.

The whirlybirds were now the department's eyes and ears; their assignment, to track the caravan without being spotted and report its direction of travel.

The surveillance vehicles on the ground began to close the gap between the air and ground. Throughout the city policemen responded to the Rapid Mobilization Plan. Vacant patrol sectors were added onto other sectors to provide maximum coverage with a depleted force; desk officers made the necessary adjustments on roll calls.

Inside temporary headquarters, Detective Heinemann manned the radio, calling out the coordinance.

The helicopter pilot's voice was loud and clear despite the static and engine noises: "Passing West Houston . . ." A short time later: "Chambers Street . . . Broad Street. . . . They're turning onto the Battery."

"We'll know soon enough," Jake Stern told the silent men.

Anderman tugged at the lieutenant's arm. He grabbed him by the elbow and walked him across the room to a corner. "Policeman. Listen to what I'm going to tell you. You are not going to be able to talk those men out of what they plan to do. They are fanatics. Greed might have been the catalyst for this whole thing, but the thrill of killing has become the reason. I have seen many such men. You are going to need my help. Police weaponry is no match for military ordinance. Uzi submachine guns can cut your police line to shreds. And who knows what other weapons they might have with them? Your people are going to die without reason unless you let me help."

"We have shotguns and automatic rifles." A weak retort.

Anderman clutched his arms. "Don't be a fool! Let me call in my men. A precaution, nothing more."

Malone knew that there was no time to argue. He also knew that Anderman was right. He went over to McQuade and pulled him from a huddle. When he finished whispering to the Chief he looked over to Anderman and shoved his thumb upward.

Anderman went over to the radio operator and spoke a few words of Hebrew. The operator wrote something on a sheet of paper and began to send the message.

Five minutes after Anderman's message was transmitted a twin-engine helicopter lifted off the pad in the center of Fort Totten. This craft had camouflaged markings and showed no identification numbers. Twin lights blinked from the rear. It rose slowly at first but then gathered momentum. When it had risen to a point parallel with the middle span of the Whitestone Bridge, it hovered a short time, and then set off on a compass heading of southwest.

There are many spans in New York City that jut across anonymous creeks and canals. The Pulaski is one. It arches across the Newtown Creek, binding Long Island City to the Greenpoint section of Brooklyn, and to McGuinness Boulevard, an artery that leads to the industrial heartland of the Borough of Kings. The most noteworthy thing about this bridge is its incredible view of the Manhattan skyline. This morning the outline was sharply defined against a backdrop of a purple sky.

The Econoline van drove off the exit ramp and stopped for the red light on the corner of McGuinness Boulevard and Humboldt Street.

The transmission from the department helicopter that was following the caravan was received simultaneously at Communications and temporary headquarters. "Subjects exiting the BQE at McGuinness Boulevard."

Inside the temporary headquarters, McQuade grabbed the handset. "Close off the Pulaski Bridge on the Queens side."

In Long Island City a line of police cars drove out of the schoolyard on Forty-ninth Avenue and went one block to Jackson Avenue where they snaked into position across the foot of the Pulaski Bridge. When the blockade was established there were three files of radio cars that were backed up by four Emergency Service vans.

On the Brooklyn side of the Pulaski Bridge everything appeared to be normal. Trucks were making early-morning deliveries; bundles of newspapers were stacked on curbs; bags of bread and rolls waited in grocery doorways; rattling milk cases could be heard off in the distance, morning sounds of a city not yet awake.

On cramped streets with names like Clay and Box and Commercial, radio cars idled, their crews lolling about and shooting the breeze, asking one question—What's it all about?

Westy Stanislaus looked into the rearview and saw the trucks struggling with the grade. "Come on. I wanna get this thing over with."

Zangline was in the jump seat. "Patience. We're almost there."

Stanislaus looked back at his passengers and saw that they were wearing kaffiyehs and cradling Uzis. Without headgear and guns they'd look like college kids in patched jeans and worn sneakers, he thought.

As the Econoline van peaked the brow of the bridge, Stanislaus's eyes widened with incredulity. He jammed on the brakes and lurched forward, gripping the wheel, leering at the barricade. Suddenly he threw open the door and leaped out, running back to the trucks.

Marku leaned out the window. "What's the trouble?"

"Police! We've been had," he shouted, pointing toward the crest.

The caravan had stopped.

Marku climbed down and ran up to the crest. He stood, defiant, shaking his fist down at the police. He turned back in time to see the police line draw across the Brooklyn side, choking off escape. Suddenly the retiring night was filled with the chilling cry to Jihad—war.

They held an emergency conference behind the Econoline van. Scared men, unsure of what had gone wrong, searching for a way out.

Kelly looked at Stanislaus. "Waddawe do now?"

Stanislaus flashed his eyes to Zangline. "It's up to you, Chief. We're with you all the way."

Zangline was shaken, his face drained. An adage came to mind: If you can't do the time, don't do the crime. He was too old to start over. There were no more chances, no more roads. If he could get himself out of this trap there might be a way out for him. There was no direct evidence linking him to any crime. He was working undercover, trying to ferret out bad cops, protect the security of the country. He had money, enough to last him the rest of his days. He looked at the men around him. "This is the big one. I say we go for broke."

Stanislaus reached out and opened the rear door of the van and climbed inside. He motioned to someone for help. Marku climbed in, and together they dragged up five cases to the edge. Stanislaus opened one and took out an olive-green tube that was about three feet long and cupped on both ends. "These babies are going to get us out of here."

"What are they?" Marku said.

"M-72-A disposable antitank rockets that'll take the treads off a Russian tank at fifty meters. Each one comes loaded with a sixty-six-millimeter shell."

Stanislaus squatted on the edge and held out the tube. He took less than a minute to show them how to use the weapon and then said, "There are six rockets in each case. Each vehicle will take one case with them. I'll lead in the van. I'll blast a hole through their line and we'll plow right through them. The warehouse is near. We'll detonate all the cars up against the depot and make a run for it in the van. We'll stick to the original plan, only now we will use the rockets instead of the cars. It'll have the same effect."

There was a moment when they stood in silence, each man contemplating his own future, and then, they clasped their hands together in the center of the group, and broke, each running to his vehicle, shouldering his weapon. For one fleeting second Edwin Bramson felt the urge to run the other way; to surrender. But he couldn't, not in front of his friends.

Capt. Jeffrey Sefton walked out from behind the police barricade, a megaphone in his right hand. He was a big man with impressive shoulders and a head of untamed hair. He wore no hat; he never did when he thought there was a chance that television cameras might record his heroic deeds for posterity and the promotion board. Peeved that his forthcoming act of bravery was not to be immortalized on film, the captain started his famous strut up the Pulaski Bridge.

"He sure eats this shit up," Police Officer Edmonds said.

"One of these days he's going to get his prick shot off," Police Officer Neale said.

They were slouched up against the side of their Emergency Service van watching the captain. Their shotguns were resting on their hips and their caps were pulled down to their brows. Rows of decoration bars were stacked up over their shields, symbols of their male pride.

Other policemen were gathered around their vehicles, not really caring about what was happening on the bridge. Scuttlebutt had it that this caper was nothing to get excited about. Just another talk-down; some asshole with an ax to grind.

Neale nudged his partner. "I sure hope they get this bullshit over with so I can get home on time. I wanna rap the old lady before the kids get up."

"Boy, do I know that feelin'. Sometimes after a late tour I'm so horny even the crack of dawn ain't safe," Edmonds said, lifting his cap and patting down his pompadour.

They watched as the three vehicles rolled over the crest of the bridge in a wedge formation. The van was on the point, the embrasures were down, the weapons thrust out, cross-hairs zeroed in on the center of the barricade.

"Here. Comes. The. Bullshit," Edmonds said, reaching down the front of his pants and scratching his scrotum.

Captain Sefton raised the megaphone to his lips. "I am Captain Sefton of the Hostage Nego-"

The burst of automatic fire lifted the captain up off the ground and spun him completely around. He was dead before he reached the ground.

"Holy shit!" Neale shrilled, diving behind his van.

Two ear-shattering explosions sent policemen running for cover. Submachine-gun fire raked the police line. A radio car blew apart, and then another and another. The van carrying all the automatic rifles exploded. The center of the barricade had turned into an orange fireball. Policemen fled the conflagration. Veterans of the Bulge, Inchon, Tet, remembered their forgotten trades. They popped up from behind their cover to fire at the enemy and then ducked back down. Some fired and rolled away to a new position.

Edmonds and Neale were crouched behind their van.

"Ready?" Neale said.

"Let's do it."

They stepped out from behind their cover, pump-fired two rounds apiece, and ran back. The shotguns had little effect; the distance was too great. A few feet away from them, Sgt. Sam Nelson was crawling on his stomach over to a radio car. He reached up and opened the door and then bellied inside. He glanced up at the radio panel and thought how strange it looked upside down. He pulled down the handset and then tried to figure out which was the right switch. Praying that it was the right one, he pulled one out. "Aim for their tires!" he shouted over the loudspeaker. Bullets riddled the radio car, disgorging chunks of steel and slivers of glass; the fragments tumbled down on him. "Fucking humps can't take a joke," he mumbled, crawling back out.

On the bridge the approaching formation maintained its unrelenting field of fire. It crept down, moving closer and closer. The barricade had been turned into a flaming shambles. Cowering behind their van, Edmonds and Neale reloaded their shotguns. Edmonds pointed to the wire trash barrel on the bridge's walkway. "The garbage cans!"

"What about it?"

"Bottles."

They sprinted from their cover, running low, zig-zagging. Slugs slammed into the ground around them. They made a headlong dive, rolling into the can and toppling it, littering the ground with all sorts of disagreeable debris. Lying prone, they rummaged through the garbage. Edmonds found an empty pack of Coke bottles still in its carrying case. They popped up off the ground and made for the van. A radio car behind them exploded in a violent blue flame. A wave of intense heat struck their backs as they ran, scorching their hair. They dived behind the van and fell to their knees, breathless. Edmonds unclipped a knife from his belt and pushed himself under the van. He opened the blade and started to dig it into the gas tank. He punctured the tank and it dripped gasoline. He increased the pressure on the blade, and increased the circumference of his wrist movement, enlarging the hole until the drip was a steady flow. Neale passed him the bottles and he quickly filled them. "Let's get the fuck away from here," Edmonds said, pushing himself out from under the van. As they ran for the radio car about twenty feet away, the van blew apart. Neale tripped over a body, regained his footing, and continued to run. They ran behind the car and Neale immediately ripped off his shirt and started to tear it into strips. He handed them to his partner who stuffed them into the neck of the bottles.

The van and two trucks had stopped in the middle of the downgrade and were spraying the barricade with automatic fire, preparing for the final assault. There was a large hole in the center of the police line. Stanislaus had waited until the flames had died down. Now he gave the signal to move out and the vehicles started the slow, inexorable advance, making for the hole in the barricade.

The police opened fire. Their bullets began to find their mark; miraculously none hit a gas tank. The front tires on the Econoline van blew up and the radiator billowed a thick cloud of steam. The van careeed on its rims, thumping to the right and plowing into the side of the bridge, finally tearing out a section of railing.

Neale and Edmonds made their way around to the bridge cutoff on Forty-ninth Avenue. They sprang up from behind the stone balustrade, their arms cocked and the fuses burning. "Now!" Edmonds shouted. They hurled two Molotov cocktails, and, then, in quick succession, tossed two more.

An avalanche of flaming gasoline and dense black smoke rolled across the bridge, engulfing the disabled van. The doors flew open and coughing men jumped out and began to run back to the trucks. Marku, Kelly, and Bramson saw them and leaped down from their trucks. They formed a line across the bridge, firing through the smoke to cover their retreat.

Charles Kelly was down on one knee putting a new clip into his weapon when a spray of slugs tore into his body. His Uzi clammered to the ground. The last thing he saw before he slumped over was his right eye dangling out of its socket, held by a twisted white cord.

Two more Molotov cocktails exploded.

"Everyone onto the trucks!" Stanislaus shouted. "When the flames die we'll smash through them!"

They threw their weapons on first and then climbed up onto the bed; the first aboard turning and helping the next, extending a hand to a comrade. They squirmed between the flattened heaps of rusting junk, taking up firing positions, in their excitement forgetting the explosive nature of their cargo.

Westy Stanislaus looked out at the body of Charles Kelly and muttered an obscenity.

Edwin Bramson leaned around the skeletonized frame of a '77 Buick and launched a missile.

On the Brooklyn side of the bridge, Capt. George Macklin could not see what was happening in Queens, as the battle was out of sight, beyond the brow. But he could see the smoke, hear the explosions and gunfire. The radio bristled with urgent appeals for help from the Queens choke point.

"I wanna move my men out," Macklin walkie-talkied temporary headquarters.

"You will hold your assigned position, Captain." McQuade's transmission left no room for doubt or maneuver.

"Ten-fucking-four!" Macklin slammed the radio down over the hood of a radio car, venting his frustration. He dented the hood. He looked over his position and saw his men, their weapons at the ready, aimed at the bridge, tensing to go. He wanted to lead them in a valiant charge; to relieve the beleaguered choke point. Should he disobey a direct order from the Chief of Op and give the word to go? He could be a hero. His picture would be on the PBA calendar. But what if he disobeyed and screwed everything up. After all, he did not know the whole picture. No! The smart move was to follow orders. He and his men would have to wait. There was nothing else for him to do but to listen to the din of battle and stare at the flames and smoke and smell the acrid stink of cordite that laced the air—and pray.

The fire on the bridge raged and both sides waited.

"My job is here, coordinating this fiasco," McQuade said to Malone inside the message center.

"And my job is out there," Malone said, leading his men from the room.

Anderman ran up to him. "Policeman, a helicopter is landing in the parking lot. Follow me."

"We don't need a chopper to go a few blocks," he said, tugging away.

"Listen to me, you thickheaded *goy*! Didn't you hear those radio messages? Your side is losing. When those flames die they are going to come at you with everything they have. And! They won't be isolated on any bridge. They'll be in the streets of Queens where there are houses with people in them, women, children, old people. It will be a bloodbath. Do you want that on your conscience?"

A strained silence followed.

Malone was haggard, the shadows on his face were dark, the lines deep. He knew that there was no more time for discussing. It was decision-making time. And that was what it was all about, the rank, the extra pay, department courtesies. To make decisions. Assume responsibility. He knew that Anderman was right. "Let's go."

Anderman led them through the darkened depot, past high mounds of crates and down aisles lined on both sides by phalanxes of oil drums. Anderman ran ahead of the group and rushed up to a metal door that had no knob or hinges. He punched in the combination on the box in the center of the door and it sprang open.

The helicopter had already landed; its propellers were revving down, sending up funnels of dust and papers off the Tarmac. The aircraft's hydraulic system was grinding the nose open.

Malone was aghast when he saw inside the belly of the craft. Five jeeps were lined up single file, each one mounting a GE Minigun M 134 multiple barrel Gatling-type machine gun. Antennas protruded over the rear of the jeeps; each one bore a blue and white pennant with the Star of David. Anderman's students were behind the wheels, manning the guns. A nameless man with an ugly scar was standing in the lead jeep, gripping the vehicle mount. He looked so at home, a warrior readying himself for battle.

"Anderman, you crazy son-of-a-bitch. Someone will have my balls over this!"

"So, we'll lie a little. We'll say that we were on a UJA fund-raising mission and got lost."

"Let's go!" Malone shouted.

They ran up the ramp and into the belly of the helicopter, spreading out and climbing into the jeeps. Anderman straddled into the last one. Malone waited until his detectives were safely aboard the pug-nosed vehicles and then climbed in next to Anderman.

Engines were started. The dull clang of rounds being rammed into chambers reverberated throughout the craft.

The nameless man with the ugly scar craned his head over his shoulder, making sure all hands were aboard the jeeps. When he saw that they were, he made a wide sweep of his arm, motioning the column forward.

The lead vehicle jerked forward and wrenched. The brakes squealed and echoed in the helicopter and then the first jeep surged forward and sped out, followed close behind by the others.

The column drove from the parking lot, turned left, and after fifty feet made a sharp right turn onto Borden Avenue, their proud pennants fluttering.

The Queens choke point was in a starfish-shaped plaza; five streets and avenues fed into a central disk—the bridge. A tall triangle-shaped building, a garage and a box-shaped building with orange letters on its side spelling: J&D BRAUNER—THE BUTCHER BLOCK, overlooked the bridge. The Hunters Point Long Island Railroad station was nearby, as was the Bloomingdale's warehouse.

Disaster units were arriving and people rousted from sleep by the explosions and gunfire peered from their windows and ran to safer parts of their homes. The braver residents of the neighborhood appeared on rooftops for a grandstand view of a battle.

Across the width of Jackson Avenue policemen ducked behind anything that would protect them. They tensed for the final onslaught.

Police Officer Edmonds was prone behind a steel chassis that had been blown off a car. His head rested on the stock of his shotgun. His stomach was snarled with cramps and flashes of cold sweat racked his body. His partner, Neale, lay six yards away, his intestines a seeping mass oozing from his stomach. In front of his position lay the body of Sgt. Sam Nelson, his legs still inside the burning radio car.

He thought of his wife and Kenny and Billy and Mary Ann and little Artie and wondered what they would do without him. He had made an Act of Contrition and was now asking God to let him survive. Without warning a warm mass exploded from his body, running between his legs and over his genitals.

A sudden whine filled the air. Two dull thuds were followed by loud explosions. He buried his head in his arms. The rockets hit the center of the police line. Shrapnel splintered in the air. A radio car disintegrated in flames while another one leaped up in the air and tumbled down. A body cartwheeled through space. Heavy automatic fire raked the barricade. The carnage had begun again.

Edmonds forced himself to look. The two trucks were rolling down off the bridge, looming through the smoke and shimmering waves of heat. They reminded him of dune buggies from another planet with their flattened pieces of junk stacked one on top of the other. Flames burst from hidden guns; slugs whined incessantly. The men inside might prevent him from seeing his family again; these men had killed his partner. He pushed himself up off the ground into a standing position, his weapon firmly pressed to his shoulder. He leaned forward and pump-fired double action at the advancing enemy.

The trucks were halfway down the bridge. Westy's team was crouched behind piles of junk, firing their weapons at the police. Zangline was in the front seat of one of the trucks. He had smashed out the windshield and was firing his Uzi at the barricade. Not once did he give pause to think that they were policemen he was trying to kill. Ahead lay the enemy. He threw his Uzi down and picked up a rocket launcher. He assembled it and fired at the center of the line.

The men manning the barricade were no match for the combined firepower of the Uzi and the rockets. They started to back away from the barricade, firing as they went. Some ran, to put as much distance between themselves and the trucks as possible. People on the rooftops cheered and cat-called. The first train of the morning pulled into the Hunters Point station from Port Jefferson. The platform was crowded with bewildered passengers, none of them willing to climb the steps up into the street.

Jeeps appeared from nowhere. They were first seen speeding up Jackson Avenue. Men were at the guns, and others knelt beside the weapons and fingered belts of ammunition. Some people on the roof started to cheer. Others booed.

The column sped across the rear of the barricade and made a sharp right-hand turn into Hunters Point Avenue and then pushed its way around the left flank of the police line to take up a position in front of the barricade.

Ahmad Marku and Iban Yaziji were the first to see the fluttering pennants. "Jews!" Marku yelled.

The GE Miniguns laid down a withering field of fire. Tracers found their marks. The tires on both trucks exploded. They were stopped dead in their tracks. A fender flew off one of them and tumbled through the air. A hood was ripped from its chassis and tumbled down. Both radiators exploded. A smoke screen of steam covered the bridge. A loud hissing sound came from the trucks.

Whitney Zangline leaped down and knelt at the side of his truck. He wanted to run, to get away. But how? Where would he go? Perhaps if he could reach the barricade he could find some way to convince them that he was really on their side? Working undercover. A body toppled from the truck and splayed next to him. Run! Get away! Before he was like that lifeless mass with blank eyes. The creek! Dive in

and swim away. He leaped up and ran for the railing. He gripped the
top and started to push himself over when a hail of bullets cut his
body in half. The top part toppled over into the water; the bottom
crumpled onto the bridge.

Stanislaus and Edwin Bramson were together, hunched down behind a rusting '69 Ford. Bullets chunked around them. Stanislaus
passed his friend a tube. He could see the fear on his face. "We're
going to get out of this!" he shouted.

Bramson forced a smile as he readied his launcher.

When their weapons were assembled they looked at each other.
Stanislaus nodded and they leaped from their positions and fired.

The jeep bearing the nameless man with the ugly scar blew outward
and then collapsed in a fireball. Gus Heinemann was in the next vehicle, kneeling beside the gun mount, feeding the ammo belt up into the
action body. The missile hit underneath the jeep causing it to bound
up into the air and tumble backward into the barricade. Heinemann
was thrown out. His body slammed down over the hood of a radio car
and bounced off. Two policemen ran up and dragged him to safety.

The gunner in Starling Johnson's jeep lurched forward, clutching his
throat. He knocked into the gun and toppled backward onto the
ground. Johnson jumped up and took his place. Another jeep exploded. Missiles were exploding around them. Two jeeps were left.
Policemen were running back to the barricade, joining the fight. Jake
Stern and Harrigan were fighting on foot from behind a disabled jeep,
firing their .38s and cursing at the enemy.

"You better send us help," Malone shouted into the radio. "We're
catching hell from those rockets."

"I'll release the Brooklyn choke point," McQuade radioed.

"No! We'd be caught in a crossfire. Our own people would be firing
down on us." As he talked, he was watching Anderman feed the ammo
belt. He heard his name screamed and turned in time to see Starling
Johnson spin in a swirl of blood and fall. He threw down the handset
and bounded from the jeep. Slugs chewed up the ground as he ran. He
leaped into Johnson's jeep and grabbed the machine gun. "You moth-
erless cocksuckers!" he screamed, firing. Bo Davis was suddenly by his
side feeding up the belt. He fired again and again, longer and longer
bursts. The Gatling rotated on cue, the ejector spewing out a colony of
casings. He sprayed the enemy with a devastating fire. The steel cables
that had lashed the junked automobiles to the truck beds were
snapped by bullets. No more fire came from the trucks. Clusters of
slugs continued to chew up the junk as Malone maintained a relentless
field of fire. The cargo started to shift. Then totter. One by one the
stacks caved in. And then an enormous explosion shook the earth.

Malone was pitched out of the jeep and slapped to the ground. Bo Davis was flung into the front of the jeep, his body smashing into the gear stick. Both Jake Stern and Harrigan were thrown onto their backs. Anderman landed on his shoulders and rolled about four feet.

A fireball shot hundreds of feet into the air. And then a gush of water frothed down over the bridge, with a waterfall of muddy water that rushed down at the police.

It was quiet. Men began to stir. Màlone looked up, slowly pushing himself up off the ground and feeling his body. He was covered with slime and mud and soaked with putrid water. He wiped his palms over his face and body. There was no blood, no holes. He was alive. He looked up at the bridge where the trucks had been. They were gone. In their place was a gaping hole. Girders twisted in the churned-up waters of Newtown Creek.

"It's over, policeman."

The voice came from the rear. He turned his head and saw Anderman lying on his back, looking at him.

"Over? It's far from over. We have our dead and wounded to care for. Notifications to make. And we had better concoct some plausible story to explain this madness. And then there is the matter of Mr. Carter Moorehouse. His ass belongs to me."

25

The first news team arrived at the One-oh-eight, the precinct of occurrence, about twelve minutes after the bridge blew up. By 5:02 A.M. the front of the stationhouse was jammed with camera trucks and police vehicles. Inside, the muster room swarmed with shouting, pushing newspeople demanding information. The desk lieutenant was besieged by cameras, microphones, and screaming reporters. Tell us what happened. Who was involved? Is it true that it was the FALN? What is your name, Lieutenant? Why are you withholding information?

"I wasn't there so I don't know what happened. You're going to have to wait for the official release from the PC." He had his orders. Direct from the Chief of Op. "Keep your mouth shut until I tell you what to say," McQuade had told him when he rushed into the stationhouse.

Policemen stood across the stairway leading to the upper floors, and the stairs were crowded with more. Their orders were to prevent unauthorized personnel from gaining access to the upper stories—newsmen in particular.

In the second-floor detective squad the mayor, PC, first deputy police commissioner, the chief of detectives and several State Department types were closeted with Malone and McQuade and Anderman. They searched for a way out. It was no longer possible to deny; they needed a cover story. They argued and cajoled each other, while each man attempted to protect his vested interest. The Israelis had to be left out of it, one of the men from State said. National interest demands it. The City must be protected from lawsuits, the mayor told them, kicking a chair and glaring at his police commissioner. Every telephone in the squad room was ringing. "Shut off those goddamn phones!" shouted the PC.

A detective scurried to take the receivers off their hooks.

"Our story has to be believable, plausible, and verifiable," McQuade said, looking over at Malone, who sat on the floor with his back against the wall, not paying attention or caring.

Malone was bone tired and his teeth felt numb and cold. His clothes were still wet and he smelled of smoke and cordite. He yearned for a bed, clean sheets, and to awake from this nightmare. But he knew that was impossible. He kept seeing the ambulances pulling up to the bridge; then the doctors and nurses working on the wounded and finally the neatly arranged rows of body bags. He would never be able to find peace until he got Moorehouse. He dwelled on it, searching for a way. He caught himself staring at the tiles, green tiles splotched with gray. Why did every stationhouse have the same ugly tiles and cinderblock walls? Why not oak floors and wallpapered walls? A little class to jazz up the shithouses. Maybe he would kill Moorehouse. Stalk him, learn his routine, and then waylay him. Four in the head with a .22 throw-away. It would mean twenty-five to life if he got caught, and a cop does hard, hard time. Was it worth the chance? He thought so today, but how would he feel tomorrow, or next week, or next year? He could hide in the shadows with a baseball bat. Savor the exhilaration of feeling his skull shatter; watch the blood spurt from his ears and flow from his eyes. Turn him into a living vegetable. Or he could employ all of his investigative skills and gather enough evidence to convict. I could investigate until hell freezes and still come up with zip that would stand in any court, he told himself. He would think of a way. He needed sleep and a clear head. Then the answer would come to him.

Yachov Anderman was sitting on the floor next to him, his knees pulled up into his chest, his chin resting on kneecaps.

"I'm going to miss Ancorie, policeman." A sad tone.

Malone looked sideways. "I'm going to be missing people, too."

The other men in the room were shouting. The PC and McQuade and the mayor wanted to cover up Zangline, Stanislaus, Kelly, and Bramson's complicity. If it were to become known the department would be destroyed, the PC reasoned, and the mayor and McQuade concurred. "But they committed serious crimes," a man from State said.

"So what?" the mayor said.

"I don't believe you people!" Malone shouted. "You want to make heroes out of those humps? Besmirch everything this job stands for?

I'd vomit every time I'd walk into headquarters and saw their names up on those scrolls."

"And what choice do we have?" the PC shouted back.

"The truth is available," Malone said.

"Are you for real, Malone?" said the mayor.

"The department would be finished for all time. We would end up with civilians running the show. Every precinct, division, and borough command would have a fucking civilian politician running it. Everyone connected with this case would end up with his head on the chopping block. Including you," McQuade said.

"No way would I make martyrs out of them," Malone said.

"You're overruled, Malone," said the mayor.

"Why don't you fuck off," Malone said, turning and looking at Anderman.

"Shmucks," Anderman muttered.

"What will happen to you?" Malone said.

Anderman twitched his thumbs. "I'm a survivor. I'll be okay. We'll more than likely move the warehouses to different locations."

A detective walked into the room and looked around. He saw Malone and went over to him. He bent down and whispered to him. Malone leaped up from the floor and ran from the office. He threaded his way through the gauntlet of policemen on the staircase and plunged into the throng of reporters at the bottom, parrying the microphones with his hands and ignoring their questions.

He saw her standing in the 124 room. She looked beautiful and nervous as she stroked the edge of a desk. "Erica!"

She looked up and waved to him. They ran into each other's arms and began kissing each other with a mixture of affection and relief. The newshounds set upon them, shoving their damnable microphones into their faces and shouldering them with their endless goddamn questions.

He took her by the hand and led her through the crowd, searching for someplace where they might be alone—and talk.

The stationhouse broom—a thirty-year hairbag who in addition to keeping the stationhouse clean was the precinct's gofer—saw his plight and shouted to him. "Lou! Over here!"

Malone heard the unfamiliar voice calling him and looked over the heads of the crowd. He spied the broom standing in front of the door which led into the detention cells.

He pulled Erica through the throng of reporters, slapping their microphones aside, forcing himself to remain calm. He was not going to do what they wanted him to do. Lose his cool before the cameras. Explode at them. Tell them what he thought of them.

When he neared the empty jail cells, the broom pulled the steel cover open and let them slide past him, blocking the reporters with his body and slamming the door closed.

They were alone in a cold, gray hall of empty jail cells. Bare lightbulbs caged in their own tiny cells ran the length of the corridor. Steam pipes were high up on the walls.

For a moment they just stood there, a foot apart, staring at each other, and then, as though on cue, they rushed into an embrace and kissed.

He was holding her again! He felt her press to him. He smelled her scent and felt her hair on his face, caught between their lips. Her tongue caressed his in that special, wonderful way.

He slid a hand over her back, satisfying himself that she was really there, that it was not a dream.

"Erica. I love you. I've been miserable. I know that I was wrong about not telephoning. Forgive me?"

"I've been a shit, Daniel. I'm sorry. I've been unable to sleep. I was sitting up in bed at five this morning watching TV when the news flashed on. My heart stopped. I just knew that you were involved. I prayed that you were alive."

She kissed him lightly on the lips. "I realized then just how much I love you."

He looked around for a place where they might sit down and talk. He took her by the hand and led her into the nearest cell.

The walls, the floor, the ceiling, the bars, the plank that hung down taut from the steel wall and served as the bed; everything was shiny battleship gray—everything except the stainless-steel toilet with a rounded lip and without a flush or a seat. Holding hands they lowered themselves onto the plank. His eyes were on her face, not daring to leave, afraid that he would wake and find her gone. He became conscious of the tumult beyond the door, a muffled din. He told her about the Eisinger caper, all of it, omitting nothing. Except Carter Moorehouse.

They sat in the cell for a time, he talking; she listening, gazing into his eyes, caressing his hands, occasionally bending to kiss them.

"I telephoned you this morning. When you answered, I hung up."

She reached up and touched his cheek. "I. Love. You. Daniel. Malone. You are my Lou."

He kissed her and began caressing her breast. She forced his hand away. She wore a faint smile, one that said, Men! She turned and swept her hand around the cell. "This place is hardly what I would call conducive to lovemaking. Where do you suggest that we do it? On the cold floor? Or shall I lie down on this wonderful slab of wood?"

They looked at each other and burst into laughter.

"Your place or mine, handsome?"

"Yours is closer." He held her face and kissed her. He then broke away and went to the door and cracked it, peering out.

It was 7:50 A.M.

The mayor was standing on the first landing. The PC, McQuade, the Chief of Detectives, the First Deputy Police Commissioner, and the men from State were at his side. Reporters and TV crews pressed against the cordon of police at the foot of the staircase. All cameras and microphones pointed upward. Despite the size of the crowd, there was an unbelievable hush; the only sounds were colliding microphones and shuffling feet.

The mayor put on his glasses and held the prepared text out in front of him. The cover story was ready. The mayor had spoken but five words when Malone was able to imagine the banner headlines around the world—LIBYAN HIT SQUAD FIGHTS TO DEATH ON PULASKI BRIDGE. The mayor told the assemblage that the United States Government had previously announced that it was in possession of irrefutable intelligence that Libya's Muammar al-Qaddafi had dispatched teams of assassins to this country to assassinate the president and other top leaders. He told them how upon receipt of this information the Intelligence Division of the NYPD had launched a massive search for these individuals. Deputy Chief Whitney Zangline had headed up the investigation.

Zangline and an elite unit of SOD trapped the suspects on the Pulaski Bridge as they were on their way with a cache of explosives to blow up the Con Edison generating plant on Vernon Boulevard in Long Island City. This attack was to have been a diversion for the assassination of the United States Ambassador to the United Nations.

Malone knew that the newspapers would graphically detail the battle and tell how the beleaguered police had to call for help and how a special army unit stationed at Fort Totten was airlifted to their aid. Chief Zangline and three of his bravest men were killed in the final assault. The centerfolds would have photographs of the battle scene and picture spreads of the dead and wounded. Good ole Muammar al-Qaddafi. What would the Job have done without him? He was the perfect fall guy.

He had heard enough. Let them do whatever they think that they have to do. He had a life to live and he wanted to get on with it. He turned and motioned Erica forward. He pushed the door open, and holding hands, they slipped out unnoticed.

They made their way through the army of cars parked on the sidewalk to the Associated Food Store around the corner on Vernon Boulevard. Her car was double parked. She handed him the keys. "You drive. This way your hands will be busy and off of me." She chucked his chin and smiled.

"You don't trust me?"

"I know you, Daniel. You think it's always the right place and the right time."

"A little traffic foreplay can't hurt." He shrugged philosophically and opened the door for her.

"That's what you think," she said, sliding into the car.

He started the engine and was about to slide the transmission into drive when he suddenly remembered to check the time. He looked over at her.

"We don't have much time. There is something that I have to do this morning."

She could feel her stomach begin to knot, and all of a sudden she was scared.

She folded her arms across her breasts, cupping her elbows with her hands. "Oh? At this moment in our lives I thought there was nothing more important than us being together."

"Zambrano is being buried today. I want to be there. That means going to my place and showering and changing clothes. I'd like you to be there, too. He was a special man. A cop's cop."

She felt guilty for her anger and relieved that he had told her. She sighed. Leaning across the seat, she kissed him. "How much time do we have?"

"A couple of hours. It's at eleven forty-five mass."

"We can do a lot of lovin' in a couple of hours." She folded her legs under her and then took his hand from the steering wheel and guided it under her dress.

"I thought you were the one who said no traffic foreplay."

"Did I say that?" She pulled his hand out and slapped it back onto the wheel. "Let's go home, Lou."

26

The rows of policemen standing at parade rest in front of St. Anthony's Church seemed to stretch into infinity. They had come from as far as Texas to tender the final salute to Nicholas Zambrano.

A thick-set drum major led the cortege. His baton a dead-slow gait. Behind him marched the Pipers, their black-plumed bonnets bobbing above the heads of the onlookers. And behind them crept the hearse, locked between a wedge of motorcycles whose handlebars were aflame with flashing red lights. The limousines bearing the mourning family followed.

A dirge of bagpipes and the timbre of a single drum pealed over the unremarkable Park Slope neighborhood.

As the hearse slid into the curb in front of the church an anonymous voice barked the assemblage to attention. "Present! Arms!" Thousands of white-gloved hands snapped the salute while a lone bugler, standing on the church steps, blew Taps.

The flag-draped coffin was lifted from the hearse and hefted onto the pallbearers' shoulders.

Malone was at attention behind the mayor and other dignitaries. He swallowed hard, but the lump would not stay down. His cheek quivered, and he could feel the sting of tears as his gaze followed the coffin up the steps and into the church. He began to sum up the Eisinger caper. Starling Johnson dead. Gus Heinemann in the hospital with burns and multiple fractures. The Braxtons. Their bodies had been discovered around 8 A.M. when a neighborly wino broke into the garage searching for money to buy his morning bottle of Thunderbird. The nameless man with the ugly scar and David Ancorie both dead. And the others. Twelve policemen, not counting Zangline and his humps. There were going to be a lot of inspector's funerals during the next week.

The Eisinger case had proven to be a deadly little grounder.

When the coffin had disappeared inside the church the voice barked, "Order! Arms!"

The family was the first to start up the steps, assisted by policemen who had been assigned to aid them. After the family came the police brass, followed close behind by the men who had worked with Zambrano.

The little church filled quickly. Most of the mourners remained outside, with no chance but to hear the mass over loudspeakers.

The cardinal and Monsignor McInerney were waiting on the altar, police chaplains at their sides, their hands clasped in prayer.

A Mass of the Resurrection began. Mourners knelt in prayer. Malone remained seated, staring at the coffin, and recalled the moments that he had shared with Zambrano. But still he dwelled on how he was going to get Carter Moorehouse.

High in the choir loft, above the organist and the tenor, an old man sat alone, leaning over the pew. His eyes bored through the coffin. Carlo Fabrizio remembered a summer night long past. He could still feel the policeman's strong body covering his, protecting and saving him. "I don't forget, Nicholas. Your family will be taken care of; your death avenged," he prayed.

The cardinal walked down off the altar and circled the bier, sprinkling it with holy water. He intoned, "Eternal rest grant to him, O Lord." To which the mourners chanted, "And may perpetual light shine upon him."

Malone was leaning forward, his arms folded over the top of the next pew, his forehead resting on top of his arms. But he was not in prayer or mournful contemplation. He had finally thought of a way to get Moorehouse and was thinking out the best way to set his plan in motion.

Mass over, the ranks reassembled.

The pallbearers halted at the top of the church steps and the honor guard presented arms, while the bugler played the final Taps.

Malone was at attention, tendering a breast salute. His eyes fell on the faces of the onlookers—most of them strangers who happened to be passing by, the curious who always come to police funerals. They were neighborhood people who had never seen such a spectacle and most of them had tears in their eyes. It was a sight that they would never forget.

When Taps finished, the coffin was carried down and slid into the hearse. The cortege pulled away from the curb. When it had driven a block away from the church, the anonymous voice barked its last command. "Company! Dismissed!"

The ranks broke.

Policemen looked around at each other and renewed acquaintances. Many of them headed for the local gin mills where they would spend the rest of the day and most of the night drinking and talking about the Job and broads.

Malone moved among the thinning crowd looking for Erica. He had caught a glimpse of her in church, but then was unable to locate her when he was filing out into the street. He saw many faces that he recognized; nameless men who had crossed his path somewhere in the Job; some of them required a nod, some a meaningless How'r'ya, and some were to be ignored. He saw her standing in front of the church talking with Bo Davis and Janet Fox. The detective and his girlfriend were holding hands. He wondered if they were coming out of the closet. Sometimes 85s have a way of becoming more. He started to make his way over to them when he spied the man he was looking for. The man who was going to be his agent for revenge.

Carlo Fabrizio was being ushered toward his limousine by a phalanx of bodyguards. Up until that moment Malone was not sure how he was going to handle things when he saw Fabrizio, but as he watched his people make a path through the crowd, he knew exactly what he was going to do and say. He made his way over to the bodyguards and intercepted them in front of the open door of the limousine. Tony Rao nodded to him. He made a move to enter into the phalanx but was blocked by four mean-looking men, one of whom he recognized as the bouncer from the Nestor Social Club. Fabrizio grunted to let him pass.

"I want to talk."

"About what?"

"Our dead friend."

Fabrizio made a guttural sound which Malone took to mean assent. They walked away from his men and strolled along the curb, Tony Rao and three of the bodyguards close behind. Fabrizio clasped his hands behind him and looked downward at the street. "What's on your mind?"

"Carter Moorehouse had Zambrano killed and he is going to walk."

"You telling me the truth?"

"I wouldn't bullshit you about something like that."

"Why is he going to walk?"

Malone raised his shoulders and arms in a gesture of helpless frustration. "Because he is rich and because the people who might have testified against him are dead."

"Why you telling me your problem?"

"Because the grapevine has it that you owed Zambrano."

"That was a long time ago."

"Some debts can never be canceled."

Fabrizio made a jeering hiss through the nose. "You're beginning to sound Sicilian."

"Moorehouse entered our world uninvited. Your world and mine, a world where we got our own set of rules. Rules that civilians could never understand; but rules that you and I understand. They keep us from becoming complete animals. He came and killed our friends, yours and mine, and now he thinks he is going to prance back into the good life unharmed. It shouldn't be allowed to happen."

Fabrizio regarded him slowly. "You asking me to have Moorehouse whacked?"

"Don Carlo? I'm a cop! I would never ask anyone to take a human life. You should know that. It would be a violation of the *Patrol Guide*."

"Of course you wouldn't."

Malone started to walk back toward the church.

"Seeya 'round, Don Carlo."

Carlo Fabrizio's lips came together in a thin line. "*Ciao*, Malone."

Malone and Erica stood in front of the church watching the last mourners leave. He felt an obligation to be the last. Bo Davis and Janet Fox had left some fifteen minutes earlier. They had gone back to her apartment to spend some time together before he left to catch the 5:18 to East Meadow.

"Who was that man I saw you talking to?"

"Just an old friend of Zambrano's. I hadn't seen him in a long time and wanted to say hello."

The crowd was gone, and the Brooklyn street had retreated back into its normal state of oblivion. A sanitation sweeper was roaming the gutters for litter. He saw an ice-cream parlor on the other side of the street, a block away. "May I buy you an ice-cream soda?"

Her eyes were wide. "Oh yes! A black-and-white with loads of whipped cream and sprinkles and a cherry. And then I want to take you home and work off all those wonderful calories."

They wrapped their arms around each other's waist and started to